# Falling
## with
# Folded
## Wings

BOOK 3

# FALLING WITH FOLDED WINGS

BOOK 3

## Plum Parrot

Podium

*To my sisters*
*Thank you for believing in me, even when I didn't*

All rights reserved. No part of this publication may be reproduced, stored in a retrieval system, or transmitted in any form or by any means electronic, mechanical, photocopying, recording, or otherwise without prior written permission from Podium Publishing.

This is a work of fiction. Names, characters, places, and incidents are either products of the author's imagination or used fictitiously. Any resemblance to actual events, locales, or persons, living, dead, or undead, is entirely coincidental.

Copyright © 2023 by Miles C. Gallup

Cover design by Podium Publishing

ISBN: 978-1-0394-2767-9

Published in 2023 by Podium Publishing, ULC
www.podiumaudio.com

# FALLING
### WITH
# FOLDED
# WINGS

BOOK 3

# OLIVIA

Olivia stood at the mouth of the tunnel, looking out over the strange, frozen landscape. After seeing the change from the top, the three of them had made their way back out of the structure, encountering no other living soul during their trek. Now, they stood staring into the icy plains, cold wind blowing frigid, and damp air already starting to form icicles around the various eaves and ledges of the ziggurat. Olivia heard Bronwyn's teeth chatter as she took a deep breath, feeling grateful for her Elemental Resistance.

"The entire fucking thing teleported," Morgan said, bewilderment making his voice rise at the end of his statement.

"Yeah, and this place is even worse than the hot one; at least in my opinion," Bronwyn added, crossing her arms and rubbing her hands over her biceps to create friction. "It's still a System world, though; we wouldn't have gotten the Energy from those kills if the System didn't gather it for us."

"That's interesting." Olivia looked at Bronwyn. "What makes you say that?"

"The person who gave me information about Morgan explained that things like levels happened before the System, but you had to know how to make them happen. Like, you had to actually gather Energy and create classes and skills on your own."

"Gave you information about me?" Morgan turned from gazing out at the white expanse with a raised eyebrow.

"Yeah, she's sort of like a mentor, or maybe *patron* is the right word. She's the one who gave me the portal stone which allowed us to come help you."

"Huh." Morgan's face indicated he had more questions but was thinking things over. "You know," he started after a moment, "I have an item that lets me teleport to First Landing once a month. If you're planning a way home for us, keep that in mind."

"Oh," Olivia said, frowning. "You want to go?"

"No! Hell no, I won't leave you two stranded; I was just thinking, if there's someone who can help us back on Fanwath, that's an option."

"You mean my patron? Maybe, but I don't know if you'd be able to get in touch with her. I'm not even sure I know how; she kind of gets in touch with me, if you know what I mean." Bronwyn sighed.

"Guys, do you think you could explore this ziggurat? If it teleported us here, maybe there's a way to use it to get back home. I'm not trying to be lazy, but I hit level twenty, and I think it would be smart to look at my advancement options—they might present new opportunities."

"And you don't want to listen to our banter while you contemplate your future?" Morgan chuckled.

"Sort of." Olivia smiled. "I'll be right out there." She pointed to the long row of steps leading down to the plains.

"Aren't you cold?" Bronwyn shivered again, stepping back toward the tunnel leading into the ziggurat.

"No—part of my elemental heritage. I know, I know," she said, seeing their faces. "I need to explain all I've been through. Let's have a sit-down and share some food after we gather back here in an hour or so."

"Sounds good," Morgan replied, turning to Bronwyn. "C'mon, Bron."

She grinned and started back into the tunnel, ambling so Morgan could catch up. Olivia heard their animated chatter fade away before she walked down the steps about halfway and sat down on the cool stone.

Something stopped her from opening her status screen and accessing her class refinement right away. Instead, she just stared out at the sea of white. From this distance, she could see the brown-yellow grass under the snow, indicating it wasn't very deep, but the air was cold, and the clear, pale blue sky made her think of Montana or Wyoming. The looming, sharp purple peaks in the extreme distance added to that illusion. If it weren't for the dual suns, she might have imagined they'd somehow found their way back to Earth.

She hoped Morgan and Bronwyn would find something in the alien ziggurat, but she wasn't expecting much. It had been evident that the gargoyles had used the life force or Energy of captives to power their strange technology, and there wasn't any way that Morgan, Bronwyn, or herself would allow something like that. Maybe they could find a way to power the process without sacrifices, but it didn't seem likely. She sighed heavily, realizing she was procrastinating; for some reason, she was worried about her class selection. "Maybe it's because I don't have Alyss here to guide me."

Olivia wondered what her friends from the academy were doing. They were all still on vacation and had no idea what had transpired for her. "Alright, enough of that! Quit stalling!" she scolded herself, then she opened her status screen and selected the Class Refinement option that had appeared upon her leveling.

**\*\*\*Class refinement option 1: Energy Weaver—Advanced. Energy and its peculiarities are second nature to you. Weaving new spells, manipulating**

natural forces, and dominating the will of lesser Weavers are your hallmarks. Class attributes: Intelligence and Will.\*\*\*

\*\*\*Class refinement option 2: Surge Caster—Epic. Prerequisites: Tempered Pathways, Superior Energy Affinity. With raw, overwhelming power, you remove obstacles and reduce enemies to their constituent parts. Class attributes: Will, Intelligence, and Vitality.\*\*\*

\*\*\*Class refinement option 3: Elemental Paragon—Legendary. Prerequisites: Four or more elemental affinities. You've entwined your spirit with a being born of the elements and furthered your connection through arduous mutual strife. Elemental Energies are your lifeblood, part of your being as much as your mortal flesh. Continue to nurture this side of yourself, building your elemental abilities to suit your design. Class attributes: Intelligence, Will, and Unbound.\*\*\*

\*\*\*Class refinement option 4: No Refinement—You are pleased with the path on which you find yourself and choose to continue until your next refinement option.\*\*\*

"Well, now I know what comes after epic." Could there be any question about her choice? Olivia tried to argue with herself, taking the role of devil's advocate. Maybe Energy Weaver would allow her to find a way to cast a teleportation spell more easily. Perhaps Surge Caster would lead to her having a new refinement that would overshadow her Elemental Archon option. "Yeah, right."

The only genuine concern that gave her pause was the very real worry that she'd lose more of herself with the Elemental Paragon route. "I could just stay with my Archon class." She realized she was probably right to worry when she thought of those two options and considered those descriptive words. An Archon was a ruler—she ruled the elements. A Paragon was an exemplar, a perfect example. Would she become more like an elemental, a creature of the elements? "But it's legendary!" she hissed at herself, and that little flame in her heart leaped and a wild grin spread on her face and she touched the button to select her new class.

\*\*\*Congratulations! You have refined your class: Elemental Paragon. Class skill gained: Elemental Form—Advanced.\*\*\*

\*\*\*Elemental Form—Advanced: You are able to take on many of the physical attributes of specific primal elemental beings. Energy cost: 1000. Cooldown: Medium.\*\*\*

"Wow! Straight to advanced?" Olivia was thrilled with the new spell; the Elemental Form had been her number one ace during her time in the Proving Grounds. It would cost more, but the cooldown was shorter, and she could only imagine how much more powerful her forms would be. She was thinking about trying out the spell when a chilling thought occurred to her—she hadn't gotten any sort of notification about being the "world-first" to acquire her new class.

Before letting her mind spiral with that revelation, Olivia decided to apply her eight extra attribute points to vitality. Being durable hadn't done her wrong so far, and it seemed like this world might have a lot of dangerous mysteries in store.

On a whim, Olivia decided to run through her cultivation drill. When she got to the part where she started to draw on ambient Energy, she was startled by its richness. She figured that either the area they were in was rich in Energy or the world itself sat in a deeper part of the Energy stream. "Or ocean or whatever analogy you want to paint," she said, finishing her thoughts aloud.

"Hey! Talking to yourself?" Bronwyn called from a short way up the stairs.

"Yes." Olivia stood up and climbed toward her friend who was shivering against the wind, rubbing her pale arms with her red hair blowing in the breeze. She was beautiful. Olivia wanted to talk to Bronwyn—and Morgan, for that matter—about everything that had transpired for them all. Bronwyn was different; she seemed lighter, happier, surer of her actions, and wasn't dwelling on mistakes. Olivia knew she was jumping to a lot of conclusions after just a short amount of time with her friend, but she felt like she knew her well enough to see the changes. "I just noticed how rich the Energy is here. It feels very different from back on Fanwath; at least from the areas I've visited."

"Well, that's one bit of good news," Morgan spoke, stepping out of the shadows of the tunnel. "We couldn't find anything working in this place, and nothing is alive. Either we killed all the gargoyles or the ones who lived got out while that alarm was going on."

"Rakeyda," Bronwyn said.

"What?"

"The gargoyles—when I track them, I can see what they are."

"Huh, well, I'm afraid I'm pretty much stuck thinking of them as gargoyles after all this time." Morgan shrugged.

"Let's sit down in there and make a plan," Olivia suggested, gesturing inside. They all walked a short way into the dried mud tunnel, where clumps of the stuff had fallen when the ziggurat shook. Pale green stone blocks had been exposed in the mud's absence. "This ziggurat isn't made of mud," she said, pointing.

"Hmm, those gargoyles stole it, maybe? Coated it with mud to make it more like their preferred environment?" Morgan postulated as he sat down with his back against the tunnel wall. They were far enough inside that the wind didn't reach them anymore, and the ambient temperature was tolerable for Morgan and Bronwyn. Olivia sat across from him, folding her legs underneath her, and Bronwyn sat next to Morgan, kicking her feet out.

"I'll start," Olivia said. "First of all, I know I look different, and I'm more capable with Energy than I was before, but I'm still me. I've just gained a lot of racial advancements, and my class connects me more viscerally with the elements."

"Come on! Give us more detail than that! Tell us about the academy a little," Bronwyn prompted, producing a leaf-wrapped package and slowly peeling it open. The most wondrous odor emanated from the little loaf of bread she revealed, and Olivia's mouth started to water.

"Um, yeah, tell us more, Olivia," Morgan said. "Hey, Bronwyn, can I have a piece of that?"

"Sure. Here, I'll split it into thirds." Bronwyn held out a hand. "Got a knife?"

He produced a small dagger and handed it to Bronwyn. As Olivia watched his long arm stretch forth with the blade, she could only marvel at his lanky form.

"You advanced your race more, didn't you, Morgan?"

"Yeah, but you're telling your story right now," he replied, eyes still on Bronwyn's loaf of bread.

"Alright," Olivia said, and then she went into a brief overview of the main events of her time at the academy, culminating with her triumph in the Proving Grounds and her reward allowing her to visit home. While she spoke, they shared the bread Bronwyn passed out, and Olivia savored every nutty, flavor-filled morsel. She'd never felt so satisfied and full before, even after a huge meal.

"Okay, Bronwyn, your turn! Start with where you got that magical bread!"

"Hold on, not yet," Bronwyn said. "First, I want to see you cast something that makes your eyes light up with fire!"

"Oh, all right!" Olivia concentrated briefly and conjured an orb of hissing, roiling blue plasma.

"Holy shit," Morgan exclaimed, leaning in close, staring at her face. Bronwyn, too, seemed enthralled with something behind her eyes. Olivia started to blush and canceled her spell.

"Enough of that, now. What's the deal, Bron?"

"Okay, well, long story short, fairies are real, and I met with the Summer Queen. I kind of work for her now." She paused, seeing the concerned looks on her friends' faces. "It's not exactly how it sounds; she saw something in me, you guys. Or she brought something in me out is maybe a better way of saying it. She wants humanity to thrive on Fanwath, and she needs people to help her. There's another fairy faction that doesn't have our best interests in mind, and with her help, we should be able to fight against their agents."

"You took all that on face value?" Olivia couldn't stop herself from asking.

"Hold on, Olivia. You weren't there! I felt her honesty, and I felt her love for me. She sees us as her children. Did you know the fae were on Earth for real? That the reason Earth lost the Energy was because of the Winter Court?" Bronwyn started to scowl, seeing the question marks on her friends' faces.

"She told you this?" Morgan asked.

"Yes, she did, but she can't lie directly; none of the fae can."

"According to whom? Her?" Olivia scoffed, then instantly regretted it.

"She fucking gave us the stone to get to Morgan, didn't she? I fought one of the Winter Court's agents, and I can tell you for sure that he was pure evil. As I said, you guys weren't there!"

"Alright, alright. I'll take your word for it, Bronwyn, but don't get mad at us for being skeptical; like you said, we weren't there. Imagine yourself in our shoes too, okay?" Morgan placated smoothly.

"Right, I'm sorry, Bronwyn."

"Whatever. Anyway, I have a different class and different abilities now. I was feeling a lot better about myself too." She looked down, a sulky look on her face.

"I'll be honest, Bronwyn, I was just thinking about how much happier you seemed. I'm happy that you're feeling good about things, okay?" Olivia reached out and squeezed Bronwyn's hand. It was warm and full of life, and she couldn't help the genuine smile that lit up her face.

Bronwyn looked at her, and her frown dissipated.

"Alright, well, that's about it. What about you, Morgan?" Bronwyn sat up straight and turned her gaze toward the tall, darkly clad man.

"I'll give you the short version, okay? I'm feeling stressed about getting back, and I want to get to the next phase of this conversation—our plan. So anyway, I did some adventuring with Issa, and my arm got cut off. We traveled to Tarn's Crossing, figured out a way to advance my race which healed my arm, then we learned of these gargoyle invaders. Issa and I led some Ardeni into a place called the Deep Down and found their portal. As I fought their leader, the portal started to close, and I got sucked through. You know the rest of the story."

"Holy shit. There's a lot I want to unpack in there," Bronwyn said.

"Yeah, what do you mean advancing your race healed your arm?"

"Ugh, alright, listen: your body undergoes a metamorphosis when you advance to a new tier—old injuries sort of get erased. We can talk more about it as we travel. We've got to find a way out of this place because I'm desperately worried about Issa. Do you guys get me?"

"Travel where, though?" Olivia asked.

"The only place we can see from the top of this ziggurat: the mountains."

"What makes you think we'll find anything there?" Bronwyn looked out toward the mouth of the tunnel.

"I don't know. A feeling, maybe. It's better than sitting here doing nothing, though."

"There's one more thing you guys should know about," Olivia spoke. "I gained a new class—a rare, legendary one. On Fanwath, the lower tier of the same class gave me a 'world-first' title. Here, I didn't get one."

"What does that mean?" Bronwyn asked.

"It means that there are probably powerful Energy users here, and lots more of them, unless it's just a crazy coincidence that someone had this class before me."

"Are you saying it's rare because of its 'legendary' status?" Morgan asked.

"Partially, but also because I was offered the lower-tier class because of my bonding with a shard of a primal elemental's soul. I don't think that's something that happens commonly."

"Gotcha." Morgan scratched the stubble on his chin.

"Well, let's get going," Bronwyn prompted after a moment. "The suns are still high in the sky, and I have a tent and supplies for camping. Olivia can make fire easily enough."

"True!" Olivia said, standing up. The three of them moved back to the mouth of the tunnel, facing into the cold wind, toward the distant mountains, and then they began their long trek.

## ◈ MORGAN ◈

I have a book I got as a reward from the Proving Grounds. I think it's got something to do with teleportation magic. It's called *Tuzrenstil's Basic Primer for the Efficient Use of Energy to Manipulate Spatial Connections*. I'm going to study it as we travel; you never know—maybe I can find a way to teleport us back home," Olivia spoke between bites of trail mix that Morgan had shared out. They were camping for the second night out on the frosty plains, sitting around the large globe of fire Olivia had created.

"You think I could read that, too? I already have a short-range teleportation spell," Morgan said.

"You what?" Bronwyn stared at Morgan.

"Yeah, when I advanced my class at level thirty, I learned a spell which lets me step through space to a spot I can see."

"This is very promising news, Morgan! You know, you can study the spell pattern and learn a lot from it. I wonder if you could draw it?" Olivia leaned forward excitedly.

"Hmm, maybe. My mentor mentioned something like that. I guess people used to make their own spells before the System came along."

"See! That's what the Summer Queen told me!" Bronwyn looked between Olivia and Morgan as if daring them to question her trust in the mysterious fae. "And why are you guys just mentioning these things now?"

"Well, I was exhausted yesterday and fell asleep right away, and it just now occurred to me!" Olivia produced a small, densely packed book. It reminded Morgan of a bible with its thin, innumerable pages filled with tiny words and runes.

"Damn, that looks dense," he said, giving voice to his thoughts.

"Yeah, isn't it great?" Olivia's tone was soft and full of wonder. Morgan watched her study the first few pages, and he chuckled.

"Sure, I like a good, dense book too."

"Not me," Bronwyn spoke. "I'd take my VR gear any day over a book."

"Olivia," Morgan said. "Before you get too far into that, do you mind talking to me a bit about spell patterns? I have a feeling you learned more about them in your classes than I did talking to my mentor for five minutes. I'd like to help you figure out teleporting, but I'm not sure how to begin drawing the pattern for my spell."

Olivia closed her book and looked at Morgan, an enthusiastic grin spreading on her face.

"Of course! Let's start with you studying the pattern and trying to describe it to me, at least its overall shape. Just turn your attention to your Core and start concentrating on the spell. Watch the pattern start to form in your pathways, but clamp down on your Energy with your will; don't let the spell pull it, or else the pattern will go away, and you'll teleport!" She laughed like the idea of Morgan teleporting without intending to was funny to her.

Morgan did as she said. He was already familiar with looking at a pattern and altering the spell by changing the Energy going into it, but he'd never really studied the pattern itself before. As he turned his mind inward and studied the maelstrom of his Core, he took a few calming breaths. Then, he primed his Void Step spell while focusing on keeping his Energy clamped down. It was harder than he thought it would be—the spell pattern was hungry, and his void-attuned Energy was eager to go to it, but he managed to contain it, and while the pattern pulsed in his pathways, he tried to describe it.

"The overall shape is like a big *S*, with hundreds of whorls and twists."

"Great, Morgan! Is it hard to hold it steady?"

"No, not too hard. I can feel it trying to complete, and I can feel my Energy trying to surge into it, but I have it locked down now."

"Alright, I'll give you a notebook and a pencil. It's hard to draw when you can't see what you're doing but just go by feel. I have a feeling, with your advanced attributes, you'll be better at it than you might think."

"Yeah, I was actually pretty good at drafting and diagramming before I came here; I'm a bit rusty, but, like you said, my intelligence and dexterity are much higher now." He felt Olivia press a notebook into his hand and a pencil into his other, and he started trying to draw what he was staring at in his mind's eye.

While Morgan worked on the pattern for his Void Step spell and Olivia pored over her thick little book, Bronwyn sat back, enjoying the warmth of the fire, and watched the endless expanse of stars. After a long period of silence punctuated by the occasional turning of a page or Morgan's scratching pencil, she started to feel her eyes growing heavy.

She glanced at the tent. It was a large, canvas affair that Morgan had set up. While he'd been putting the stakes into the hard, frozen soil, he'd grumbled again about missing Issa. Bronwyn felt sorry for him and worried about Issa, too. She hoped they'd find a way back to Fanwath soon.

"This whole thing is crazy," Bronwyn spoke suddenly. Olivia looked up at her with a question on her face. "I mean, think about it. This is the third planet we've visited since leaving Earth. Now we're trying to figure out how to get back to the first one, and spaceships aren't even part of the equation."

"Yeah, a lot has certainly changed," Olivia mused.

"Anyway, I'm beat; I'm going to sleep. Some of us don't have a ton of racial enhancements." Bronwyn stood, brushed off her butt, and walked to the tent.

"No problem," Morgan said. "I really don't sleep much anymore."

"Yeah, I'm going to study this book for a few more hours." Olivia glanced at Bronwyn and added, "Everything alright, Bron?"

"Aside from being stranded? Yeah, I'm good; at least I'm with you guys." She slipped into the tent, and Olivia turned back to her book. Morgan hadn't yet opened his eyes, still carefully sketching, having already filled a few pages of Olivia's notebook.

Time passed like that for a while, perhaps a couple of hours, before a sound split through the silence of the wintery night. A shriek tore through the air and over their campsite with such volume and ferocity that Olivia's fireball sputtered and nearly went out as she jerked her eyes away from her book in surprise. Morgan slammed his notebook closed and stood up, drawing Bloodfang from the metal ring at his belt and activating Void Vision.

He saw Bronwyn dart out of the tent, her fists ablaze with light, and he scanned past her. Panning his vision, he tried to spot the source of the shrieking cry. He couldn't see anything standing out on the frozen plain, absolutely nothing moved or stood out on the flat expanse as far as the horizon. Then, a flicker of movement caught his eye, and he looked up to see a massive shadow gliding away toward the mountains. It had a long tail and enormous wings, and the Energy within its long, serpentine form pulsed in his Void Vision like a miniature sun.

"We need to start keeping a lower profile," Morgan said.

"What is it?" Bronwyn's voice came from a short distance away, where she crouched, ready for a fight.

"I'm not sure, but it looks like what I'd imagine a dragon to look like. It's flying toward the mountains."

"Oh God," Olivia murmured softly, her mind drifting back to her time in the Proving Grounds.

"What?" Morgan asked.

"I met a dragon in that dungeon I told you guys about. I wasn't meant to fight it—I'm pretty sure it was there as a lesson in humility. If what you just saw is a dragon, we really need to make sure it doesn't spot us." The night became suddenly darker as Bronwyn canceled the spell making her fists light up like flares. Olivia turned to her and nodded. "Best to put our lights out for now." She dismissed her own orb of fire.

"Yeah. You guys go ahead and try to get some rest," Morgan said. "I'll keep watch; it's like broad daylight for me out here with my vision spell."

"Alright," Bronwyn agreed. "I'm happy to get out of this cold air." She ducked back into the tent, and Olivia followed after her.

Morgan looked out toward the towering mountains, suddenly wishing he'd spent more time talking to Tiladia about her people. Why hadn't he? Looking back, he felt he'd taken her for granted and wasted a chance to learn a lot about elder races, Energy, different worlds, and even his tower and the wizard who'd created it.

"That's not fair," he muttered, shaking his head. He'd always been on the go, with one thing after another taking his attention. In the back of his mind, he'd always meant to talk to her; he'd always meant to do a million things, including working on his Core. "It'd be nice to catch a break once in a while." He looked at the notebook and pencil he'd dropped. He picked them up, putting them into his ring.

Suddenly, he sat down and turned his mind inward. He determined to stop making excuses and start working on what he had control over, and at that moment, it meant cultivating and working on his Core.

Issa watched over the prow of the merchant vessel she'd managed to flag down as it passed through the Deep Down. She'd spent more than a day sneaking around in the deep tunnels, hoping for some sign of Morgan or a gargoyle that could give her information about where he'd gone. After killing several more of the large, stupid creatures and failing to find any of the more intelligent leader types, she'd finally decided that the Deep Down was a dead end, and she'd need to seek answers elsewhere.

With no other leads, she had two thoughts which gave her comfort: one, Morgan had a token which he might use to recall to First Landing, and two, he could sense where she was, and she knew he'd find her if at all possible.

With those thoughts in mind, she'd flagged a passing vessel and begun the long journey back to First Landing herself.

"Maybe he'll be waiting for me," she said softly. The sailor handling the mooring lines gave her a funny look. "Never mind," she snapped. She frowned, instantly regretting her short temper. "I'm sorry; I have a lot on my mind."

"Nothing to worry about, miss. My captain says I stare too much."

Issa chuckled at his words and watched, tapping the rail impatiently, while the dockhands pulled the lines the sailor threw and secured the vessel to the pier. Not wanting to get caught up in another conversation, Issa looked at the portly old captain, and when their eyes met, she gave him a wave and jumped off the boat. She'd already paid the man handsomely for her passage and didn't feel bad for not spending more time chatting.

Storm clouds in her eyes and purpose in her steps, Issa made her way through town to the stables where she and Morgan had left their mounts. She saw several people she knew, including one of the soldiers who had been part of their rescue party. She wanted to avoid talking to anyone but felt like she should at least let someone know she was alive, so she called the soldier over. "Hey, Rissa!"

The woman's head jerked around, her bright pink ponytail whipping behind her.

"Issa! We thought you died!"

"No, I'm alive. Morgan is missing; he got pulled through the invaders' portal as it closed. Please spread the word that I'm okay and that I'm going to First Landing to see if he finds a way back."

"Don't you want to rest? Shouldn't you speak to the mayor or the captain?"

"Maybe I should, but I'm not going to. I'm getting our mounts and heading out. Sorry to dump this on you, Rissa, but I appreciate it." She clasped the woman's shoulder and squeezed it while looking into her mauve eyes. When the soldier nodded, Issa smiled and hurried on her way.

She had a lot of miles to cover before dark.

# OLIVIA

Olivia studied the pages of drawings Morgan had created the night before, simply amazed at their precision and complexity. "All seven pages are the same spell?"

"Yeah, I couldn't write small enough to put all the details on one page. I'm sorry."

"Don't be. Do you think I want to strain to read microscopic print?" She laughed.

Olivia and Morgan were resting for lunch, and Bronwyn had run ahead to scout out the foothills they were fast approaching. She'd proven to be able to run nearly twice as fast as Morgan and maybe three times as quickly as Olivia when she went all out. At first, Morgan had been bewildered, trying to figure it out; he was taller than Bronwyn, and his agility score was tremendous in comparison, but then Bronwyn had told them about her Blessing of the Herd, and he'd let it drop.

"Does it mean anything to you?"

"Surprisingly, yes. I'm able to make out what different parts of the pattern do. Like here, where this weave starts, I can see that it's specifying your attuned Energy—void, right?"

"Yeah, that's right."

"I think this branch on the third page is indicating your sight line. You know what would help? Could you try to draw the pattern for your vision spell?"

"Alright, I'll work on that when we camp tonight."

He stood and stretched, and Olivia went back to studying the pattern he'd drawn. Its complexity was on par with her Elemental Form spell, and parts of it were utterly foreign to her, but she thought she recognized some portions of the pattern from what she'd read in her text. She pulled out the thick little book, thumbed through some of the example diagrams, and was pleased to find a match.

"Morgan, this pattern tree on the second page indicates a spatial fold!"

"Oh? You really are good at that stuff. How far have you read into that little dictionary?"

"I'm still reading the primer on terms and concepts. I'm hoping to get into the novice applications tonight."

"You think my spell patterns will help you understand?"

"Definitely! With any luck, I can help you modify your spell, too. Testing it might be a bit risky, but we'll cross that bridge when we come to it."

"Hah, right."

Morgan looked at the sky, scanning in all directions, and Olivia also felt compelled to look around. So far, they hadn't seen any other signs of the dragon or whatever it had been, but they were ever watchful.

"Man, I hope that thing wasn't a dragon, but its Core was flaring like a supernova in my Void Vision. I can see your Core, and it's very bright, brighter than Bronwyn's, but it's like a candle next to a five-alarm fire compared to whatever was flying through the sky last night."

"That sounds about right. When I met that dragon in the dungeon, I felt like a flea being regarded by a lion."

"Huh."

"What?"

"I just feel like an idiot for not spending more time talking to Tiladia. Imagine! She was one of those things! I had an elder being's spirit acting like my butler, and I never really spent much time getting to know her or about her kind."

"Well, be a little reasonable. How many nights total would you say you've spent in your tower?"

"I don't know. Ten? A dozen?"

"Right, and all those times, you've had plenty to worry about. It's not like you spent months sipping brandy in your library and ignoring Tiladia." Olivia smiled while Morgan chuckled over her words.

"Thanks, Olivia." He stood up and pointed. "Here she comes." A few moments later, Bronwyn came charging over the grass, her cheeks flushed with exertion and a big smile on her face.

"There's a city up there!" she announced, gesturing behind her.

"Up where? In the mountains?" Olivia asked, looking at the tall, snow-covered jagged peaks.

"Yeah, like, literally in the mountains. I saw buildings all over one of the bigger peaks; you'll see them when we get over these hills and turn up into a canyon. The mountain's base has a huge wall around it, and I could see a road leading into an enormous cavern."

"What about people?" Morgan asked.

"Nothing. Nothing was moving on the road, nothing on the wall, no smoke, no noise. Nothing." Bronwyn shrugged.

"Alright, I don't think it takes a genius to see the writing on the wall here," Morgan spoke. "We see a dragon flying toward the mountains; Bronwyn sees an abandoned city in said mountains. You see what I'm getting at?"

"Yeah, it seems like too big of a coincidence. Did the dragon kill them all? Did they flee? Did the dragon just move into an abandoned city? Is the dragon not there and was just passing by? We won't know until we do some more exploring." Olivia started walking as she spoke; she didn't want to spend another night out on the plains.

"Well, we haven't seen another living thing since we got here, so yeah, I'd say that's a little ominous," Bronwyn added, walking along with Olivia.

"Mm-hmm, so keep your eyes peeled," Morgan warned, his long legs carrying him past the two of them. He had a naked sword in his hand—the bright, silvery one with the wolves heads carved into the guards he usually kept hooked to his belt.

Olivia glanced at Bronwyn, who grinned, shrugging. Leave it to the man to try to be all serious, her wink said.

They progressed quickly through the foothills, entering the canyon that Bronwyn had scouted. There, laid out before them, was the massive mountain with its strange, silent city adorning its hills and slopes like a stony infestation of walls, roads, soaring towers, and squat buildings. On both sides of the canyon, sheer cliff walls guided the travelers toward the city, and Olivia saw the remnants of a cobbled road beneath the snow and overgrown scrub and grass.

"No one's lived here for a long time," she pointed out, gesturing to the old road.

"Yeah, I was thinking the same," Morgan said over his shoulder. "Looks like this old road led right up the slope to that wall." He stared for a moment, and Olivia felt a surge of Energy emanate from him. "There's a huge iron gate in that wall. It's closed."

"You can see that from here? It's gotta be ten miles!" Bronwyn sounded more impressed than disbelieving. Morgan tapped his temple just behind his eye and winked at her.

"Tricks of the trade. Speaking of which, any tracks?"

"Nope. I'd say something if I saw some tracks, knucklehead."

"Hah! Nice to hear an old phrase from Earth. Don't get me wrong, I love Issa to death, but her vocabulary is so serious!"

"Well, you should be teaching her some colorful vocabulary—that's on you!" Olivia said.

"Yeah, yeah, I'm working on it." He strode forward, and the two women followed, content to let him take the lead, at least for the moment.

They advanced rapidly, soon closing the distance with the tall, gray wall enough so that Olivia could make out the black gate at the center. They'd just crested a gentle rise and were on a very slight downward slope when a cracking, rumbling sound brought them to a halt.

"Where's it coming from?" Morgan asked, whirling around, his sword at the ready.

"There!" Bronwyn yelled, pointing to a spot on the canyon wall to their right where a wide fissure had begun to form.

Chunks of rock and dirt fell in a shower of dust as the fissure opened, and the three adventurers backed away, watching it warily. As soon as the rumbling started, it stopped. Then, a long, black limb with a massive, hooked claw extended from the crack in the canyon wall. The hook scrabbled on the rocky ground then seemed to pull forth a long, segmented body composed of hooked arms, gnashing mandibles, and razored spines.

The creature had to be twenty feet long, and if someone asked Olivia to describe it, she'd say it was something like a mix between a centipede, an ant, and a scorpion. The thing had a nest of beady black eyes mounted above its largest mandibles, and when they zeroed in on the trio, the mandibles spread wide, and a loud, hissing trumpet of a cry burst forth. Then, it launched itself at them faster than it seemed possible for something so enormous to move.

Suddenly, a black rift in space erupted around Morgan—a terrible antisound accompanying it—and with a shudder of reality, he was gone, only to reappear beside the charging creature, his sword hacking madly at its passing limbs. It shrieked and tried to turn on him, but its size and momentum kept it from nimbly confronting him. Meanwhile, Morgan racked up a dozen more blows at its limbs and side. Olivia, stunned into inaction at first, snapped out of it and pointed her hand at the creature's rear as it finally made the turn toward Morgan. She strode forward, closing the distance, and fired off an Arcfrost Cascade.

She knew insects rarely thrived in the cold, but if that didn't work, she knew the electric charge in the spell would have a powerful effect. Her assumptions proved correct. As the wave of frosty, electrically charged air showered the back end of the monstrosity, it writhed and trumpeted again, falling flat for a moment. Morgan, taking advantage of the stunned creature, leapt forward with a lightning thrust of his sword toward the area beneath the massive head and mandibles.

Olivia could barely track his movement, he moved so fast, but the sword, his gleaming, beautiful sword, skidded along the thick plating of the creature's neck. Morgan seemed surprised, taking an extra step closer. That's when the monstrosity proved to be quite resilient to Olivia's stun attempt, and it snapped its huge, sharp mandibles around Morgan's right arm. He screamed and thrashed for a moment, caught by surprise.

She began to ready another spell, but then, a beam of brilliant light ten feet wide, erupted out of the ground beneath the creature, dissolving its carapace and causing the softer innards to smoke and combust. The monster screeched again, opening its mandibles, before Morgan disappeared as a globe of nothing, of utter nonexistence, billowed out of him.

Olivia heard something like the end of the world as the wave of annihilating force rolled out, capturing half of the writhing, screeching giant insect in its grasp. As it thrashed in one last mighty convulsion, the bubble of what Olivia assumed was void Energy winked out, and Morgan stood there, hands on knees, panting. His arm was still in one piece but bloody.

Bronwyn jumped down from the boulder she'd climbed at some point, a strange, smoking hammer in her hand, and yelled, "Morgan! Is your arm alright?"

"Yeah, thanks. I guess my bones are a hell of a lot tougher since I upgraded my race." He stood up, and a stream of golden Energy motes began to flow out of the corpse toward the three of them. As the Energy surged into her, Olivia noticed a faint purple tinge to the motes, and she wondered what that meant.

"Holy shit! I just hit level twenty!" Bronwyn crowed.

"Yeah, I'd say you got most of the credit for that kill. That sun spell is amazing!"

"Thanks, but I can only do it once in a while, and it takes most of my Energy."

"Let's get moving; I should find a place to put on my armor. Damn, that thing's bite hurt!" Morgan rubbed his arm and started walking.

Olivia took a step to follow, but then cracking, rumbling sounds echoed up and down the canyon. She looked to the left and right and saw dozens more fissures opening up on the rocky walls.

"Run!" Bronwyn yelled. "Get to that wall!"

## BRONWYN

"Hurry, Olivia!" Bronwyn yelled, pausing to look back. Olivia was quite a ways behind Morgan, who was a good two dozen steps behind Bronwyn. Olivia paused and waved for Bronwyn to keep running, then her robe became translucent, her skin and hair became cloudy and animated, and she streaked forward, seemingly blowing on a breeze. Morgan caught up to Bronwyn and kept running, and Bronwyn glanced back at the rifts on the cliffside.

A dozen giant insects had begun to crawl out of the fissures, and more cracks were erupting along the canyon walls every minute. Soon, there might be hundreds of those things chasing them down. She turned and sprinted for the wall and the massive iron gate, happy that her Blessing of the Herd still considered this flat area between the peaks as plains. She raced up behind Morgan, overtaking him, and within a minute, she was sliding to a stop in front of the towering rust-covered metal gates.

She could see the top of the wall, some thirty or forty feet up, but there wasn't a gap big enough for even a hair to pass through the gates. Bronwyn couldn't even see a place to grab on to if she wanted to try to pull them open. Olivia reached her at the same time as Morgan, and when Bronwyn looked back down the road, she saw the writhing, stampeding mass of insects tearing toward them, just seconds or maybe a minute away.

"We're screwed," she said, pointing at the gate.

"Not yet. You have a rope?" Morgan asked. "I have one, but it might not be long enough," he added.

"Yeah, here." Bronwyn pulled the rope she'd carried for months out of her storage bag. "I got it from the Contribution Store ages ago." She handed it to Morgan, and he stepped a couple of paces to the right, looking up at the top of the wall. Suddenly, a rip in the universe swallowed him with a terrible, strange absence of light and sound, and Bronwyn stumbled back. She'd never been that close to him when he teleported, and it was disorienting as hell.

"Just a minute!" Morgan yelled from the top of the wall.

"I'll go help him. Don't worry, Bron, we won't leave you." A gust of wind blew up around Olivia's shimmering, cloudy form, and she floated up the side of the wall like a feather blown by a child's breath.

"Oh, great," Bronwyn murmured, looking down the road toward the incoming horde of clacking, clicking mandibles and spikes. She glanced up just in time to see the rope falling toward her, and she jumped to grab it, trusting that Morgan had either secured it or was strong enough to hold her weight. It held, and she started rapidly climbing, walking her feet up the side of the wall. The climb was easy, and she once again wondered at how her physical aptitude eclipsed her old Earth self. Morgan was waiting with an extended hand, and she grabbed it, allowing him to hoist her through a crenellation in the battlement.

Up close, it was clear the wall was ancient and in disrepair, the mortar crumbling here and there, and windblown debris piled against the ramparts. Bronwyn spun and looked out over the approaching horde of giant insects, only to see that they'd uniformly stopped about fifty paces from the wall. They writhed and clicked and jittered, but none took a step further.

"What are they waiting for?" Morgan asked. "Those things are built for climbing."

"Are they afraid of this place?" Olivia looked around. Her usual physical aspect had returned, the strange, cloudy, windblown form having faded or been dismissed. "Or maybe it's warded against them."

"Warded?" Morgan repeated. "As in spells to keep them away?"

"Yeah. If they're not new to this area, I imagine the city builders would have taken precautions." Olivia shrugged.

"Makes sense." Bronwyn turned to the other side of the wall, some ten paces across, and walked toward it. "You guys look on the other side yet?"

"Nah, bit busy saving your ass," Morgan quipped, turning from the horde of giant insects to follow her.

"Oh, shush, Morgan." Olivia also crossed the parapet to stand next to Bronwyn.

"Wow," Bronwyn said, taking in the scope of the city crawling up the side of the mountain and inside the giant tunnel. "I don't see any corpses or bones. Of course, I've got no idea how long it would take them to decay or be scavenged."

"Could take decades for bones to decompose in this weather. If storms come through here or snow collects, it wouldn't take as long," Olivia said. "There might be remains inside the buildings, but a lot of the roofs are gone."

Bronwyn looked out over the buildings and saw she was right. Most of the stone walls were intact, but whatever the common roofing material had been, it hadn't lasted as well. "This place could have been abandoned for a thousand years for all we know."

"Yeah, true. There're some steps over there. Let's get down to ground level and see what we can root out." Morgan started walking without waiting for an answer, and Bronwyn felt a twinge of irritation. He was a good guy, but he seemed to have decided he was the leader of their group. He might be a higher level, but in her opinion, Olivia knew more and was at least as capable as he was. She looked at Olivia to gauge her mood, but as usual, she seemed perfectly fine with everything. She strode along behind Morgan, a neutral—even pleasant—expression on her face.

Bronwyn sighed heavily and followed after. She'd been in such a good mood the last week or so that she'd almost forgotten how irritated she used to feel all the time. She thought about when she'd started feeling agitated again, and she supposed it was when Morgan and Olivia had acted like she was being stupid for trusting the Summer Queen so much. While she'd argued with them, she respected them both, and their opinions had sunk into the back of her mind, causing her to doubt herself again. "Which makes me irritated," she let out with another huff.

"What?" Olivia looked back at her.

"Nothing," Bronwyn said, hopping down one of the flights of steps to get ahead of Morgan. He grunted in surprise but didn't say anything. "I say we find a building with all the walls intact and set up a base to explore from." Bronwyn grinned. If she didn't like Morgan acting bossy, maybe she should out-boss him.

The street below the ramparts and in front of the enormous gate was deserted save for the piles of old leaves, dried-up weeds, and the ancient cobbles with dry yellow grass growing between them here and there. The main road leading from the gate ran in a straight shot up the slope of the mountain and into the yawning cavern. Streets branched in every direction, and at ground level, they couldn't see far beyond the buildings lining the main road.

"How thoroughly do you guys want to explore?" Olivia asked suddenly.

"Why?" Bronwyn looked at her with a raised eyebrow. What did she have in mind?

"Well, I have tons of art supplies. We could put $X$s on the doors of buildings we've checked out. Who knows what kinds of goodies we might find in an ancient, abandoned city!"

"Also, what kinds of monsters and traps and, oh, I don't know, dragons!" Bronwyn laughed. Morgan laughed too, and as their voices echoed back to them from the abandoned streets, they all got quiet.

"Yeah, let's try to be a bit stealthier; if that dragon is living in that cavern, I'd rather we didn't get its attention," Morgan said softly.

"Agreed." Bronwyn nodded and moved out of the middle of the street over to a low, stone building. "Let's keep our profiles a bit more discreet, like maybe don't stand in the middle of the street," she told her friends after they didn't move right away.

"Right, let's not split up right away. Let's explore for a while together, and if nothing comes up, we can talk about maybe splitting up to make things faster. Agreed?" Olivia asked.

"Agreed," Morgan and Bronwyn replied at the same time.

"Jinx!" Morgan laughed.

"Oh man, don't get me thinking about soft drinks," Bronwyn said, staring into space wistfully.

Arthur stood at the head of the council's meeting table, waiting for the others to take a seat before he did. Rene Bisset and Maria Rios were already in their places, talking animatedly about something. Alec Green was standing by the door with Tanya Delgado and Dr. Kerns, apparently oblivious to the time. Finally tired of waiting, Arthur cleared his throat and said, "Can we get this meeting started?"

The three council members and friends looked up from their conversation and walked over to the table.

"Sorry about that," Alec said, taking his usual seat two down from Arthur. The others sat as well, and Arthur smiled, sitting down.

"No problem, Alec. I know we all have a lot to talk about. Let's go over the status reports, please, and then I have a few topics we tabled to bring up today." Arthur had been filling the unofficial role of secretary and often led the council discussions based on his notes. "Maria? Do you mind starting? We can go around the table."

"Sure. The biggest news I have is that Boris Saltzki and his team have perfected their method for storing Energy and using it as a power source, at least in simple machines. They're working to combine the system with rifled barrels and projectiles to make far more reliable, clean, and powerful weapons. They're also working to make transport vehicles. We think these innovations are going to make us popular with the people of Tarn's Crossing and, eventually, the wider world. Captain Gella has promised us new trade contacts before winter."

Murmurs broke out around the table as people speculated on the uses for Saltzki's new tech. Arthur cleared his throat and asked, "Anything else, Maria?"

"Yes, there's been another purchase of a commercial lot from the Stone. Our Town Credits are at their highest level; we might want to discuss purchasing another structure from the System."

"Excellent. I'll add it to the new business agenda. Okay, how about you, Alec? Anything to report?"

"Nothing really to report. General morale seems good, and business is booming; the refugees really seem to like beer, especially the frog people."

"The Grugell," Dr. Kerns corrected.

"Right, the Grugell. Um, I don't have a lot to add. Maybe you should go next, Dr. Kerns. What's up with all the refugees?" Alec sat back and fiddled with the pipe he had taken to smoking these days.

"Oh, well, things are progressing quite well! Our linguists have worked out a basic alphabet for both of the major races—the Grugell and the Krystree. The, uh, you know, bird people. We've begun talks about their permanent settlement here, and many of them are learning English. It won't help them with the other races of Fanwath, but it will certainly make their lives easier here."

"The Krystree are amazing hunters," Maria chimed in.

"Mm-hmm, mm-hmm," Arthur said. "Anything else, Dr. Kerns?"

"The hospital is taking shape nicely. The Artificers have built us refrigerated cabinets, and we're starting to build quite a store of antibiotics and medicines that we've engineered from the local flora."

"Aren't those a bit out of style?" Rene Bisset asked, his French accent notable, which made Arthur wonder just how in the blazes the System's Language Integration actually worked.

"Not necessarily. Sure, we have citizens learning to use Energy for healing, but they won't always be available, especially as our population grows," Dr. Kerns responded defensively.

"Alright, alright. Anything else, Dr. Kerns?" Arthur knew that if he let them, Bisset and Kerns would speculate about the effective use of Energy versus traditional medicine for an hour.

"Not that I can think of."

"Tanya? Anything to add?"

"Just that construction is going gangbusters. The sewage system is in place, and the roads are making good progress, including the trade route to Tarn's."

"Excellent! Imagine us driving a convoy of new vehicles over those plains and into Tarn's! That'll boost our reputation!" Alec laughed, slapping the table.

"Hmm, very good. I don't mean to rush everyone's update, but we have a lot of new business to discuss, and I've promised that Captain Gella fellow a tour of our game processing facility. Maria, can you give us more details about Saltzki's innovations?"

"Yes, he's learned to fabricate those crystals that can be used to store Energy," Maria began. Arthur settled back in his chair, ready to listen to the inevitable debate about how best to use the tech and the follow-up about what sorts of weapons were ethically permissible to introduce to a new world.

# MORGAN

Morgan looked around yet another empty, dusty building with no roof. He and the others had spent two days searching through the outskirts of the ancient city, and they'd come away with nothing but some old silverware and bits of petrified wood that might have once been furniture.

The day after their arrival to the city, they'd looked out over the wall to find the giant insects gone and their burrows filled in with loose dirt. Perhaps they were waiting for the next creatures or people to wander down the ancient road. They'd also started to notice birds in the sky and more and more rodents and small animals scuttling through the ruins. Olivia had hypothesized that all the wildlife had gone into hiding as the dragon Morgan had seen passed by; they'd convinced themselves it wasn't lurking in the ruins somewhere.

Morgan was starting to feel like the search of the city was a waste of time; they could be making progress through the mountain range and trying to find a city or even a village with some actual people in it. Sighing heavily, he decided to make his way back to their camp. Olivia and Bronwyn had gone in a different direction today—the three of them had decided that, having seen nothing larger than a fat rat in three days, they should speed things up by splitting up.

Feeling frustrated, Morgan determined to tell Olivia and Bronwyn that he wanted to move on from the old city. Olivia was making good progress with her book, and Bronwyn seemed content to explore, but Morgan couldn't do much other than worry about Issa and feel guilty about leaving her in the Deep Down. Logically, he knew it wasn't his fault, but still, that nagging voice in the back of his mind kept saying he should have been more careful.

When he got back to the building they'd set up as their home base—a two-story structure with marble floors on the second level that still served as a solid roof for the first floor—he stirred the coals in their little cook fire and added some wood from the stack Bronwyn had set out; she said she'd recently collected a ton of it while she was out in the mountains.

Morgan sat in front of the coals and pulled out the fragments of his first good weapon—his Umbral Razor. He'd collected all the pieces he could find before leaving the ziggurat, but he had a feeling the only salvageable part was the smokey black gemstone that had given the weapon its infrequent precognitive abilities.

Still, he remembered how he'd felt when Roald had made it for him—his very own magical sword. He shook his head in dismay; Roald was dead, and worse than that, there hadn't been anything left of him after those gargoyles had used him in their vats. Morgan knew he hadn't seen Roald being put into one of those green tanks, but the other prisoners had seen him taken to the ziggurat, and there'd been no trace of him. How could he explain all that to Issa? Maybe he should just tell her that Roald had died fighting.

Morgan wrapped the pieces of his sword into the leather cloth he'd used to gather them and put them back into his ring.

"Still moping about that sword?" Bronwyn asked, causing him to jump.

"Jesus! You startled me!"

"I wasn't even trying to be sneaky; you should be more alert in a place like this!" Bronwyn tutted.

"Yeah, logically, I know you're right, but I'm bored to tears here, and I feel like we're wasting time."

"What else can we do? Olivia's studying that book more than is probably good for her brain, trying to figure out portals and teleportation magic. I don't know another way to teleport. Do you?"

"We could be moving on, finding some people."

"Or finding a dragon and getting eaten. It's not like we're being lazy; we've all leveled up our Cores since making camp here."

"Yeah, I know. But what if time is different here? What if every day in this world is a fucking year on Fanwath?"

"Why would that be? Are you just trying to find things to worry about?"

"I don't know. Yeah, maybe I am. This shit is killing me. What if Issa is being held captive down in those tunnels?"

"God, Morgan! We've been over this a dozen times. One: Issa isn't helpless. Two: it's already been days; there's nothing you can do about it at this point. Three: you know the Rakeyda fled Fanwath, and the Urghat were dead or captured. Issa's fine."

"Yeah, I know I'm annoying with this stuff, but it makes me feel better when you say those things, so thanks."

"You're welcome, but that's the last time I'm doing it for, oh, at least two days." Bronwyn chuckled, but then her face grew more serious, and she continued, "Hey, I've been wanting to talk to you about something, but I didn't want to call you out in front of Olivia."

"Call me out?"

"Yeah. Um, the . . . uh, Summer Queen told me something about you that's got me kind of wondering."

"Go on," Morgan prompted, sitting back against the wall, kicking his legs out, and crossing them at the ankles.

"She said you had some kind of title that gave you a pretty big advantage. She said it was transferable and that you might not be the right person to hold it. Any of that make sense?"

"I," Morgan started to answer, but he trailed off. He hadn't thought about his Human Champion title in a long while. Even so, it was kind of weird that he'd never told anyone about it. Why hadn't he? He realized his silence was growing awkward, so he decided to explore his thoughts aloud. "I do have a title: Human Champion. I think the System gave it to me because I was the only one awake when we arrived in the *Pilgrim 9*. I honestly don't know why I never mentioned it. I think I'm kind of embarrassed by it, to be honest. I'm not much a champion for humanity, am I?"

"Oh, I wouldn't go that far. You've done a lot for the people on Fanwath. I mean, I'm not a hundred percent sure anyone else could have killed the Overclaw. Not to mention you brought Issa and her people to our aid."

"Nothing anyone else wouldn't have done in my shoes."

"Bullshit! Plenty of people would have laid low or just tried to benefit themselves. I'm not saying you did anything super special, but you at least aren't, like, a villain." Bronwyn laughed.

"Oh! Such accolades!" Morgan chuckled. "Seriously, though, I don't know how to transfer this title, but I bet we can figure it out. If you or others think I should pass it on or that we should have some sort of trial or election to see who gets it, I'm fine with that too."

Morgan thought about what he'd just said. Was he really fine with it? Would he just roll over and give up the title?

The truth was, he wasn't the kind of person who would want to hold on to something meant for the benefit of his entire species if they didn't think he should have it. The other truth was that he felt there was a damn good chance the council and the people of First Landing would vote for him to keep it anyway if it came to that.

"Sounds like you've thought about it a little. I hadn't gotten that far in my speculation." Bronwyn sat across from him and began pulling out some cooking supplies. "Sounds fair, though. Let's maybe get more people to weigh in on the matter when we get home."

"Sure. You see where Olivia went?"

"She was finishing up exploring along the western wall, going through those alleys and narrow buildings you can see from the top of the gate."

"And I didn't find anything worthwhile," Olivia spoke, stepping through the doorway.

"Blegh," Bronwyn said, pushing hunks of raw meat onto a skewer. "Shish kabobs alright with you guys?"

"Yeah, sounds good!" Morgan leaned toward the fire and adjusted a log, letting air underneath so the flames shot up. Olivia walked over and sat with a loud huff, pulling out her book and thumbing through the pages.

"I'm almost ready for you to try a new spell, Morgan. Or more precisely, to alter your existing spell. If you're successful, I might be able to develop a similar spell that uses pure Energy."

"Well, that's some progress, at least! I hadn't wanted to bug you for an update because I know it's complicated." Morgan couldn't keep his excitement out of his voice. He felt starved for any development whatsoever. "I think we should start exploring up the road—see what's in that cavern. The road might continue out the other side, too."

"Yeah, I can't argue. We could spend months going through all these buildings, and we might never see any payoff for our efforts. What about you, Bronwyn? Any arguments?"

"No, I guess not. Let's head up in the morning."

They spent the evening around the fire, eating their meal, cultivating their Cores, and watching Olivia pore over her textbook. They'd agreed on a watch schedule that saw Bronwyn sleeping nearly eight hours and Morgan catching an hour or two before dawn, which was about all he needed. Olivia spent a lot of the night awake but so engrossed in her research that she wasn't really reliable when it came to watching for trouble.

After a cold breakfast, the trio started up the long, sloping road that led from the gates into the yawning cavern on the side of the mountain. Every so often, they'd pass an ancient building that looked promisingly whole and give it a quick inspection, only to find more dust, cobwebs, windblown debris, and rodent droppings.

"I guess if this place has been empty for centuries, we aren't the only people who've come poking around," Morgan noted as they resumed their hike for the third time.

"Yeah, I guess. Still, it would be nice to find something. Maybe an old rocking chair or a magically preserved library," Olivia said wistfully.

"Pretty big contrast!" Bronwyn laughed. "Rocking chair or magical library, hmm?"

Morgan was about to make a quip about Olivia and books when he saw a flicker of color in his peripheral vision coming from the darkness of the cave. When he tried to spot what it had been, all he saw were the shadowy buildings within and the road winding toward them.

"Did you guys see that?" Morgan asked suddenly, pointing with his gleaming sword toward the big cave.

"What?" Bronwyn asked.

"I thought I saw something moving by the cave out of the corner of my eye."

"Well, let's quiet down," Olivia urged.

"Right," Bronwyn replied in a hushed voice. Then she glanced at Morgan again and said softly, "Hey, do you have an extra weapon? In case we fight something I'd rather not punch?"

"I have a couple of decent spears and lots of knives. I only have one backup sword, or I'd offer you that."

"Let me borrow a spear for now?"

"Alright." Morgan's free hand moved to touch his ring, then it was suddenly holding a long, black spear with a wicked eight or ten-inch blade. Bronwyn had seen it before.

"That's the one you left in the Yovashi cave."

"Not by choice, but yeah." He held it out to her, and she took it.

"Thanks."

Morgan nodded, and the three of them continued walking. When they made the last bend in the road, and the wide cavern entrance was directly in front of them, the source of the flash of color Morgan had seen became apparent. The road continued through the mountain, winding upward and exiting through a small daylit opening in the distance, but much closer, amid the ruined, fallen buildings that had once stood in the cavern, a vast, swirling disc hung suspended a few feet above the surface of the road.

The disc was yellow at its center, then darkened to gradients of green, which darkened to gradients of blue at the edges. Morgan knew a portal when he saw one, but this one was easily twice as large as the huge red one he'd taken to the gargoyle stronghold. He could imagine a commercial airliner comfortably soaring through it.

"A portal," he said.

"A damn big one," Bronwyn added.

"Look at all the ruined buildings in there," Olivia continued.

"Well, let's stay frosty—never know what might come out of it while we're poking around."

"Forget what might come out; we need to talk about if we're going into that thing," Bronwyn said.

Olivia didn't respond, staring at the portal with a pensive look on her face. They continued into the cavern, and as they entered the shadowed enclosure, it looked even more vibrant. Its spinning, vibrating pattern of shifting colors was almost mesmerizing.

"I think we should investigate," Olivia finally spoke. "If this portal is responsible for this city becoming deserted, I'd like to know how it's been here for so long. Portals require a lot of Energy to open, let alone keep that way for centuries or more."

"We don't know that it's responsible. For all we know, this city was built because of this portal," Bronwyn said.

"Even more reason to investigate." Still holding his naked sword, Morgan walked forward, scanning the darkness with his Void Vision.

# OLIVIA

The enormous portal hummed ever so slightly, and the colors seemed to pulse from the center, shifting in tone just enough to catch the eye. Looking around it, Olivia couldn't help but conclude that the destruction had originated from it. The buildings closest were mere rubble, and the level of destruction decreased in a wide circle. Back near the cavern entrance, the buildings were almost totally intact, and some of the tall ones even had thick glass still in the upper levels; perhaps they reflected the portal's light, and that's what Morgan had caught sight of down the road.

"I don't see anything moving in the cavern," Morgan offered, his eyes strangely black, almost like you were seeing into some bottomless depth.

"How good is that vision spell? Can you see through walls?" Bronwyn asked, leaning on the tall black spear Morgan had loaned her.

"I think I could pick up on strong Energy signatures behind normal walls, but no, I don't have X-ray vision." He chuckled as he continued to scan around.

"Do you think this goes to another world?" Olivia asked. She knew they didn't know but was curious about their opinions.

"No idea. I've been teleported a few times, but the one portal I walked through took me to that gargoyle world."

"The Summer Queen creates portals, but you can see the destination—or at least some hint of it—when you look through them," Bronwyn added.

"Well, I walked through a similar but much smaller portal to get into the dungeon at the academy. It was also a lot more colorful and frenetic in its shifting of colors." Olivia sighed and continued, "I don't think our experiences will tell us where this portal leads—we don't have enough data."

"Well, if it's a dungeon, we can probably leave once we get in. The dungeon Issa and I went to allowed you to leave from the entry area. Of course, the Crucible wasn't like that, but we did find escape tokens at one point."

"The Proving Grounds were similar, though I was given a recall item before even going in."

"So if it's a dungeon, we might or might not be able to leave easily." Bronwyn snorted.

"Again, our data set is too small," Olivia muttered, walking around the portal, wondering if something was different on the other side. The pulsing disc took twenty strides to get around, and she'd started near the middle. There was more rubble and a shimmer in the air on the back side, though no pulsing colors. "It's one-sided! How fascinating!"

Morgan followed her and reached out a hand before Olivia could say anything, waving it through the shimmery air. "Nothing," he declared.

"You dolt! What if it had pulled you through?"

"Well, the Energy is almost nonexistent on this side compared to the front; I felt pretty good about the risks," Morgan said, and Olivia realized his eyes were still affected by his spell.

"Fascinating." She took out one of her sketchbooks and started drawing the portal with an angled view. When she finished, she walked over to Morgan. "Can you draw what it looks like on both sides? Or at least try to sketch what you see?"

"Sure." Morgan took the box of colored pencils and the sketchbook, moving to the side and sitting down on a big chunk of rubble. Meanwhile, Olivia moved over to Bronwyn, still leaning on her spear and staring into the portal. "Any thoughts?"

"I think we should try crossing it. This world feels—I don't know, empty."

"Well, we've only seen a small piece of it, and most of our time has been spent in an abandoned city. It makes sense that it feels empty, no?"

"Yeah, I know. It's just my gut." Bronwyn's wild, red hair was half obscuring her face, and Olivia smiled, moving so she could peek under it. Bronwyn chuckled and pulled it back, fixing it into a ponytail. "I don't like this world," she said suddenly.

"Is it more than just wanting to get home? Something here is bothering you?"

"Yeah, it feels dead. I know it's not; there's Energy, small animals, giant creepy insects, and it makes sense the grass is all dormant for the winter, but something is just bugging me. It's like an itch I can't scratch."

"Here," Morgan called out at that moment, standing up with Olivia's art supplies.

When she looked at his drawing, she saw the pulsing, colorful waves of Energy that Morgan had added to her portal. His talent was a little surprising; Olivia hadn't thought he'd be artistic. The back side of the portal didn't radiate any Energy, just some spillage around the edges.

"It seems like a lot of Energy. Hmm, one second."

Closing her eyes and reaching out with her inner eye, Olivia felt for the threads of Energy around the portal. When she touched them, they felt violent and raw, and their weight promised to scour and tear apart her pathways if she tried to pull them in. "Wow! This portal is incredibly dense with Energy, and it's attuned to something I can't process. What about you guys? But be careful! I think it's dangerous to try to cultivate!"

She watched as Bronwyn and Morgan closed their eyes, and how Morgan's face grimaced slightly before he released an explosive breath, saying, "Dammit! I can't pull it. Even my Vortex Core doesn't want it."

"It's nothing I can work with," Bronwyn added, shaking her head. "Let's just vote. I say we go through it."

Morgan looked from Bronwyn to Olivia. "I think it's up to you guys. I can recall, remember? I don't have the same risk going through this that you two do."

"I want to go," Olivia said, glancing at Bronwyn before adding, "I just want to make sure it's not suicidal. Let me have a piece of fruit, will you?" Bronwyn shrugged and handed her a large, gray and yellow-spotted melon. Olivia gave it to Morgan. "Since you can recall, can you try pushing that into the portal and pulling it back? Try not to let your hand or fingers break the plane."

"Interesting idea," Morgan said, taking the melon, which seemed much smaller in his large, long-fingered hand. He stepped toward the portal and gingerly reached out, letting the fruit's rounded rind slip past the portal's swirling surface. The colors got brighter where it touched, and Olivia heard a crackling vibration that seemed to come from the spot, but when Morgan pulled it back, the melon looked exactly as it had before, no worse for the experience. "Seems fine," he concluded, handing the fruit to Bronwyn.

"Well? Do we try it?" she asked, taking a step forward.

"Let's go through together if we do," Morgan replied, moving next to Bronwyn.

"Alright," Olivia agreed, looking around the dark, dead city. "Hopefully, we won't be going from the cook pot to the coals."

She took Bronwyn's hand in hers, noting that her skin was smoother with fewer callouses, and saw her friend take Morgan's hand. Morgan counted down from three, and on one, they all stepped forward into the center of the portal.

Olivia felt a vibrating tug as her foot crossed the portal's plane before she felt like her entire being was being pulled down a drain to the center of the world. Less than a second later, it was over, and she stood on a smooth marble platform, looking down a long stretch of stairs that descended into a cavernous abyss. Bronwyn's fingers were still in her hand, and she turned to see both Bronwyn and Morgan looking about, eyes wide with wonder.

The darkness surrounding the platform and the extending stairs was profound and deep, though in the extreme distance, little twinkling lights reminiscent of stars in the night sky winked and flickered. Morgan stepped to the platform's edge and looked down the steep marble staircase. "There's a building down there, floating in the darkness."

"What is this? A strange world? A dungeon?" Bronwyn moved forward to also peer down the stairs. Olivia looked behind them, confirming what she'd suspected; the portal was nowhere to be seen.

"I don't know, but it looks like there's only one way to go." Morgan started forward, and Olivia moved to put a hand on his shoulder.

"Wait, let's observe for a minute. Those stairs are narrow, and I don't see a railing. What would happen if we fell? It's like we're floating in space."

"Clearly not. This is no vacuum," Morgan said, but he stepped back and waited.

Olivia noticed his eyes grow dark again as he looked around in a circle before focusing on the stairway. They all watched for a few minutes, but nothing changed, and finally, Olivia relented. "Alright, let's go. Agreed?"

"Yep," Morgan replied, starting down the steps. Bronwyn just looked at Olivia and shrugged.

Olivia followed after Morgan, noting how he held a hand to the hilt of his shiny sword, and for the first time in ages, she pulled the staff she'd bought in Tarn's Crossing out of her storage ring. In the academy, she'd come to learn it wasn't a great focus, but it made her feel more secure when she used it as a walking stick on the narrow, steep steps.

"If you fall, just do your trick where you turn your body into air and fly back up," Bronwyn spoke from behind her.

"I suppose that might work. Thanks, Bron."

She felt a comforting squeeze on her shoulder, and Olivia was suddenly glad that Bronwyn was there with her. Morgan was pleasant and competent, but his attitude about this whole situation was a little troubling—it was like he was trying to brute force his way through it.

Of course, he was worried about Issa and anxious to get back to her, and she couldn't really relate to that. She'd never been so single-minded about a person the way Morgan was with Issa. She sort of pitied him while at the same time feeling envious.

The descent was steep, and Olivia stopped counting steps somewhere in the two hundreds. Still, they finally reached the enormous white marble landing stretching from the base of the stairs to the flat, white marble double doors in the face of the structure's wall. Olivia estimated half an acre of marble lay between them and the edifice. The building itself had to be a dozen stories high, with a footprint that would put modern national capitols to shame.

"This feels like a dungeon," Bronwyn noted.

"Have you ever been in one?" Morgan asked.

"Not in person, but in plenty of VR games. I mean, this isn't a world. Maybe it's the house of a demigod or something. I don't know."

"Oh God, I hadn't thought of something like that," Olivia said. "What if some powerful being dwells here and doesn't want visitors?"

"Why leave a portal open, then?" Morgan shrugged. He started walking across the marble expanse, and Bronwyn followed him. Olivia sighed and brought up the rear.

They'd covered about a third of the distance when a soft, grinding sound resounded around them, and Olivia saw a square of marble rotate to reveal a statue on its reverse side. Looking around, she saw that more than ten other squares had done the same, and they now stood at the center of a ring of marble statues. Morgan lifted his sword into some sort of fighting position, and Bronwyn circled to put her back to his, her spear pointing out.

"Those don't look friendly," Morgan observed.

Olivia had to agree. The statues wore the shapes of nightmares: segmented bodies, scythelike legs, dozens of appendages along their spines with needlelike stingers, and all of them easily doubled the mass of even Morgan.

"Well, now's the part where they start moving and attacking us . . ." Bronwyn trailed off as the marble surface of the statues cracked and crumbled away, revealing the black, glistening creatures within which began to writhe and glide over the smooth floor toward the trio.

"I hate always being right," she groaned.

"I don't understand what I saw, to be quite honest," Oylla said, looking at Alyss and the auburn-haired Ghelli. What was her name? "Ah, hmm, Adeya, was it?"

"Adaida! Is Olivia all right?"

"Right, yes. Thank you for your help in locating her. Yes, she was alive. She was with two others of her kind. I'll tell you more, but first, I need both of you to assure me that you'll keep this knowledge to yourselves. Can you vouch for this student, Alyss?"

"You might have asked that before you used her connection to Olivia to scry," Alyss said primly. Then she cleared her throat and continued, "Yes, of course. Adaida, it could be dangerous if Olivia's detractors knew of her situation. We need to keep this quiet for now. Do you understand?"

"Of course! I wouldn't do anything to put Olivia in danger!"

"Good," Oylla said. Turning to Alyss, she continued, "She's on a world that is quite distant. My connection was very brief, even as I poured all of our Energy into it. It would be a rather monumental task to open a portal, but even if we wanted to gather the required materials and participants for such a ritual, I'm not sure it would be wise. When I glimpsed Olivia and the people she was with, they stood before another portal."

"What do you suggest?" Alyss asked.

"Olivia's nothing if not resourceful. Let's give her some time to figure things out and make her way back to us. We'll do another scrying in a few days. In the meantime, when people—including her professors—ask, she's on a special assignment for me. Understood?" Oylla looked each of the women in the eye until they nodded their understanding. "Excellent. Back to your studies, Adaida!"

# MORGAN

Morgan used Hollow Charge to tear over the ground toward one of the creatures, hoping to put some distance between himself and his friends so he could use his point-blank burst attacks. As he closed the distance, a red flash of light speared toward him, fired from the stingerlike tail of the abomination. His charge's secondary effect—protecting him from Energy attacks—came into play, and the red beam dispersed around him as Morgan felt some of the Energy course into his pathways.

As soon as his charging momentum let up, he swung his sword with a heavy hack and unleashed an Azure Burst. Bloodfang tore through one of the grasping, spearing appendages, and his Azure Burst expanded out in a sizzling ball of blue Energy, throwing the monstrosity back and catching two others in its blast. He moved forward, hacking down on the tumbled creature, shearing through its long, writhing torso, and sending its parts flopping away on the white marble, leaving streaks of black gore in their wake.

Three more of the creatures closed in on him as he finished it off. Firing off his Void Wave, reality ripped around him, expanding out in a rolling wave of nothing. The creatures screamed as their component flesh and parts began to disassemble, and Morgan felt and saw their Energy flare, trying to combat his attack and stave off the ravages of his spell. Still, they weren't up to the challenge, and as the wave passed by then winked out of existence, all that was left were piles of skinless, shelled, twitching organs and partially destroyed muscles.

Morgan scanned the battlefield and saw Bronwyn moving with a grace he hadn't witnessed before, her spear blazing with white light as she fended off three of the monsters. For her part, Olivia's form was encased in stone, chunks of rock circling her like orbiting planets, firing crackling blue plasma over a farther trio of monsters. They screamed and writhed and tried to flee the torrent of superheated, crackling liquid, but they were fully caught in the spray and dead before their brains registered the destruction of their bodies.

He turned back to Bronwyn and, using Void Step, appeared behind one of her assailants, where he began to hack it apart with his sword forms. With his distraction, Bronwyn finished off another one, then splitting its guard, they quickly dispatched the last of the monsters.

"Hey! I learned basic spear mastery," Bronwyn exclaimed. Dense motes of Energy began to gather on the corpses as she spoke and surged into the three of them.

Olivia walked over, still decked in stone.

"Very hostile, but not too dangerous, I'd say," she commented, then with a cloud of dust and a crumbling sound, her stone form fell away, and she stood there, looking like her usual self.

"That damn plasma spell you have really seems to annihilate monsters pretty well," Morgan said.

"You're talking about annihilating things? Whatever your void Energy is, it sure doesn't coexist with matter very nicely."

"Hey, if you two are done comparing notes, there's a chest in front of the doors now."

As Bronwyn started forward, Morgan saw she was right—a large, pink marble chest had appeared in front of the big, closed doors. Bronwyn strode toward it confidently, and Morgan, out of habit from his time with Issa, cast Guard Ally on her.

"Are you going to open it?" Olivia called, standing next to him.

"Um, yes. It's a reward for the battle, don't you think?" Bronwyn paused and looked back at the two of them.

"It makes sense," Morgan said.

"Yes, I got rewarded chests for winning fights in the Proving Grounds," Olivia added.

"Alright, I'll open it then."

Bronwyn leaned down, pushing at the heavy marble lid. As it slid away from the bottom half of the chest, a bolt of brilliant red lightning blasted out of the marble, illuminating Bronwyn with a terrible glow which seemed to expose her bones. She flinched in surprise, but it was Morgan who flew backward, bouncing and twitching on the marble ground until the arc of red lightning faded away from Bronwyn.

He groaned, his entire body hurting, and weakly flopped onto his back. His clothes were singed and smoking, and he knew his skin was raw; his insides weren't in much better shape. He'd grown incredibly resilient over the course of his adventures with his increased vitality and repeated racial evolutions, so he felt good about his chances of recovery. Still, it didn't change the fact that he was hurting worse than he could remember in a long while. "Ugh, anyone got a weak healing potion? I just have a couple of really good ones. They're not worth using for this."

"I have a potion of renewal," Olivia said, kneeling beside him.

"Wait!" Bronwyn called, trotting over. "First of all, why'd you get blasted instead of me? Hold on, hold on—you can answer that after you drink this. I killed a bad guy who had a dozen of these things, and he was trying to drink one to heal himself, so I think it will help you."

Bronwyn held out a small glass bottle with a bright orange liquid sloshing within. Morgan took the offering, pulled the cork out with his teeth, and downed it in one gulp.

Heat roared through his body, starting at his stomach and rolling out through to his fingers and toes and the top of his scalp. Sitting up, he took a sharp breath, feeling like he'd just been dosed with amphetamines. He stood up, stomped his feet, and shook his hands, trying to express some of the jittery Energy roiling within him.

"Damn! That's some potent shit, Bronwyn!"

"Uh, yeah, worked better than I thought it would," she said, eyeing him speculatively. "You alright?"

"Yeah." Morgan glanced around rapidly. He really felt like he was on speed or something. "I gotta burn this off. I feel like I'm dancing in my skin."

They both said something, but it didn't register, and Morgan started running around the marble square, sprinting from side to side like he was back in high school basketball practice.

Olivia and Bronwyn watched him with bemused expressions, then Olivia said, "Let's take a peek inside the chest; hopefully, he'll get whatever it is out of his system."

Morgan was only dimly aware of them moving, feeling nothing but the urge to act.

They'd been standing around the chest talking for a few minutes when, panting and sweating, he finally felt like he could stand still long enough to catch his wind.

"Damn! Bronwyn, those potions, they're more than just healing."

"Yeah, I figured after watching what you just went through. Sorry about that! The guy I had to kill was trying to drink one at the last minute. I'm glad I stopped him. Anyway, can you explain why the lightning hurt you instead of me?"

"Yeah." Morgan shrugged his shoulders sheepishly. "I got into the habit of using my Guard Ability on Issa when she opens chests. I just sort of did it on reflex when you reached for it."

"Well, shit. Thank you, Morgan! I feel like an idiot, putting you through that!" Bronwyn reached out earnestly like she wanted to grab hold of him, but she stopped short, maybe unsure of how he'd react, and ended up wringing her hands together in front of her.

"Nah, it's alright. My ability absorbs half the damage. At least you didn't get hit with the spell's full force, right?" While he explained the spell, Bronwyn's face blanched.

"I almost died, didn't I?"

"Um, maybe?" Morgan shrugged.

"Come and see the chest, Morgan. I think there's some good stuff," Olivia called, interrupting Bronwyn's flustered reply.

"Alright." Morgan walked toward them, wiping his sweating brow with his sleeve.

When he looked inside, he saw three items within. The first was a silvery helmet carved like a bird of prey. Morgan couldn't see any actual holes for the wearer's eyes, just the intricately designed screaming raptor. The next item was a crystal orb the size of a softball. Looking at the orb was like looking into the heart of a storm, shifting gray clouds and rippling lightning bolts and all. The final item was a red leather-bound book, large enough to mimic Morgan's grandma's dictionary.

"Three of us, three rewards." Bronwyn shrugged.

"Hold up," Olivia said, holding out her hands. "If this is a dungeon, which is seeming more likely, we might not be able to take all the items. In the Proving Grounds, sometimes I'd get chests with multiple items, but when I chose one, the others disappeared."

"Really? I don't think that ever happened in the Swordmaster's Citadel." Morgan frowned.

"Well, just in case, let's pick what item we want the most," Bronwyn suggested.

"Right. My vote is the book; we need knowledge more than anything," Olivia said.

"I think that helmet looks cool, but so does the orb, which might be a way to empower one of us. But I've got no good argument against that book. I agree with Olivia," Morgan said.

"Sure. Fine. Let's pick the book." Bronwyn looked at Olivia and gestured to the chest. "Be my guest."

"Hmm, okay." Olivia reached forward and gingerly picked up the heavy book. When she lifted it out of the cavity, the entire chest with its remaining contents disappeared in a cloud of pink mist that dissipated into nothing in the span of a heartbeat.

"Damn!" Morgan exclaimed.

Olivia thumped her book happily. "Told you, guys!"

"Alright, so what is it?" Bronwyn asked.

Olivia lifted the book and ran a finger over the runes on the outside, a slight frown turning the corners of her mouth downward. Opening the book, she examined the flyleaf, turned it, and read the first page, her frown deepening.

"It's not a book we can study; it's a System book. The person who studies it will gain knowledge of a spell called Mirage Double."

"All those pages for one spell?" Morgan asked.

"Perhaps the System just wanted to present the spell this way; I don't know if it really needed all these pages."

"Sounds like a defensive spell," Bronwyn pointed out.

"Yeah. Reminds me of someone Issa and I fought. She made copies of herself that attacked me while she tried to kill Issa."

"Damn," Bronwyn said, affecting a wince.

"Well, should we draw straws or something?"

"I can Energy Drain and have good mobility—one of you should take it." Morgan took a step back to emphasize his words.

"Well, I have a spell that gives me solar armor, but it's pretty expensive," Bronwyn said.

"I can change my form, as you both saw. This would benefit me, though, as that spell is on a long cooldown. Let's pick a number, and Morgan can arbitrate."

He thought of a number, and his mind settled on six. "Pick a number between one and ten."

"Seven," Bronwyn replied immediately.

"Three," Olivia said.

"Alright, it was six. Congrats, Bronwyn."

Olivia, to her credit, smiled and handed the book over to Bronwyn without a fuss.

"Should I read it now?"

"Yeah, might as well. You might need it on the other side of that door," Morgan replied.

Bronwyn nodded, flipped the book open, and stared at the first page. Nothing happened for a few minutes, but then a breeze seemed to roll out of the book, and the pages started to rustle. Bronwyn's long hair began to blow away from her face, and a dense stream of glowing runes surged off the pages now flapping in the breeze, flowing into Bronwyn's eyes with startling urgency.

Bronwyn jerked her head back, but the stream of runes followed her movement. She let go of the book, but it floated in the air, pages rippling as the runes surged off them. After a dozen heartbeats, the process stopped, and the book faded to a red mist before it was gone.

Bronwyn staggered, blinking rapidly, then smiled.

"This spell is pretty awesome," she said. "You wanna see?"

"Yes!" Olivia answered instantly.

Bronwyn closed her eyes, concentrating, and suddenly, she had a twin standing next to her.

"Punch me, Olivia!" Bronwyn urged.

"Are you sure?" Olivia gave the strange Bronwyn double a skeptical look.

"Trust me!"

"Alright," Olivia said, stepping forward and snapping out an impressive jab toward Bronwyn's shoulder. Her double smoothly stepped between them, knocking Olivia's fist aside.

"It will keep defending me until the Energy wears off or it's destroyed."

"Can you make it attack someone?" Morgan asked.

"Not yet. It's only at the basic level, though."

"Huh, cool."

"Well, c'mon. Let's see what's on the other side of this big door," Bronwyn prompted, turning and striding forward, her strange doppelganger on her heels.

# BRONWYN

The enormous marble doors had push plates at a natural height for human hands, so Bronwyn gave one a shove. The door glided open noiselessly with almost no effort. Another expanse of marble stretched before them, bordered by high marble walls, and Bronwyn realized it was a courtyard. Another door sat closed on the far side, about a hundred paces from where they stood.

"Should we keep going?" She turned to her friends, catching herself by surprise when her mirror self also turned to look at them.

"What else can we do?" Morgan asked, and Olivia shrugged.

"My Elemental Form is off cooldown. I'm ready."

"Okay."

Stepping forward, Bronwyn found that Morgan had increased his pace to stand next to her; Olivia lingered a few paces behind. As they took their second step into the courtyard, a smooth grinding sound reverberated throughout the square, and Bronwyn braced for more statues of freakish insect monsters to appear.

She was sort of right—a single gigantic square of marble spun in front of them, revealing a statue that resembled an enormous stone tick.

"A tick? You've got to be kidding me," Morgan complained.

The statue was the size of a passenger bus, though a bit wider and less lengthy. Still, Bronwyn didn't relish the idea of fighting something that size.

"Maybe it's not that big under all the marble . . ." she started but was interrupted by a resounding *crack* which echoed so sharply off the surrounding walls that the three of them clapped their hands to their ears in reflex.

Vast chunks of marble slid away from the massive, glistening carapace of the monstrosity. The slabs of stone, all larger than kitchen countertops, cracked and shattered as they landed in a horrific cacophony as the monster within began to stretch its six legs and two long, razor-tipped front limbs.

"How the hell do we fight something like that," Morgan said as he trotted to the side, splitting their group. Bronwyn knew it was a smart move—no point staying clumped—so she fanned out in the opposite direction.

The marble had stopped falling, and the giant, bulbous body of the horror quivered, starting to shimmy its legs so that it rotated, tracking Bronwyn with its huge, bulbous red eyes. Black, bladed pincers beneath its eyes snicked open and snapped shut with such a crack that Bronwyn felt the wave of sound ripple over her. It would shear them in half if that thing bit one of them; even Morgan with his improved bones.

Suddenly, a hissing jet of superheated steam tore through the air, impacting the monster just below its snapping mandibles. Bronwyn saw flakes of carapace chip away in a fine powder, and the monster shrieked, spinning to face Olivia and placing the thick chitin of its front claw in the path of her spell. A tremendous surge of Energy, palpable to Bronwyn, gathered near the creature's mandibles, a ball of orange light spinning rapidly there.

She started to shout a warning, but the ball lanced out in a beam, something like a laser, and flashed through the air toward Olivia.

The beam hit her square in the chest, but though it flashed and cascaded over her, it seemed harmless. Olivia backpedaled but appeared unharmed. That's when Bronwyn saw Morgan flopping over the ground, smoke rising from his black-clad body.

Activating Solar Shell, she started running toward him, hearing the monster's enormous feet clacking on the hard marble floor as it raced toward her; she heard and felt the air whoosh as it swung a claw, and though she didn't look, she flinched, waiting for the impact.

It didn't hit her, and she kept running. When she got to Morgan, she spun, putting the giant tick in her view, and saw her double dancing away from it, having distracted the creature for her. Bronwyn knelt, flipping Morgan onto his back. His shirt was burned entirely away from his torso, his skin was blackened and smoking, and he was utterly insensate, though not dead.

Bronwyn glanced back toward the tick still chasing her double while Olivia hounded it with attacks. One moment she was flinging a wave of plasma on its back. The next, she was trying to drill off one of its legs with a beam of smoking magma. Her attacks caused it to scream and redouble its attacks, but it didn't really seem all that hurt to Bronwyn's eye. She knew Olivia had a lot of Energy, but she couldn't have enough to keep this up for much longer, and if that thing fired that beam again, one of them was going to die.

She stood up to shout a warning, but then she felt a cold tug at her Core, and she realized she'd been so preoccupied that she hadn't realized her Mirage Double had been pulling Energy from her to maintain its existence through attack after attack. The tick had killed it several times already.

A quick glance at her status screen confirmed her fear—she was almost out of Energy. She bent, scooped up Morgan, and ran for the doorway they'd entered through. "Olivia, run! My double is about to be gone!"

Olivia turned to her, her face determined, but when Bronwyn's words registered and she saw Morgan's limp form, she ran for the door. Bronwyn got there a second before her double died again, feeling the tug and then the spell fading away when she couldn't provide the required Energy. Olivia was hot on her heels, and when they were both through, Bronwyn turned to see what the monstrosity was doing. There it was, sitting hunched in the center of its square, baleful red eyes staring right back at Bronwyn but unmoving.

She pulled another of the flasks she'd gotten from Thun out of her necklace and stooped to pour the fluid into Morgan's mouth. Heat flushed his cheeks instantly, and his blackened chest seemed to glow from within as the charred flesh fell away and pink, new skin took its place. His eyes sprang open, and he opened his mouth in a deep gasp, rolling over and springing to his feet. "Aaaaahhh!" he screamed into the air, looking around wild eyed.

"Easy, Morgan; we had to run away," Bronwyn explained, reaching out a hand toward his shoulder, but he shrugged her away and started running.

"He did it last time, too—I think those potions do a lot more than heal. It's like his body is filled with electricity." Olivia watched him dispassionately as he sprinted around, ran up the stairs a short way, and then jumped back down to repeat the climb.

"He got hurt saving your ass, you realize?" Bronwyn said.

"Really? I wondered why that beam didn't hurt, but I didn't see it hit Morgan."

"It was like when he guarded me against the lightning. I think his skill decreases the damage, but still, it seems crazy to take a hit like that on purpose."

"Well, I'm certainly grateful, but we need to develop a much smarter strategy if we're going to beat that monstrosity." Olivia turned and looked back through the open door at the hunched, glowering form of the giant tick.

"I'm not sure we can. One hit from its beam put Morgan out of commission, and if it snapped us with those mandibles, it would be lights out, I'm sure."

"My spells were hurting it, but not enough." Olivia rubbed her temples in a slow, rhythmic circle, then continued, "I burned through almost all of my Energy throwing spells at it while your double kept it occupied."

"We need to get smart. If I were leading a group against a boss, I'd plan the whole fucking thing out before we even set foot in the encounter. We're damn lucky the dungeon let us flee and didn't lock us in."

"Well, this isn't a game; hopefully, the unlocked doors are a reflection of that fact," Olivia replied.

Morgan came jogging up just as Olivia finished her sentence, red-faced and sweating, his long, lean torso shirtless.

"That was a nightmare," he said matter-of-factly.

"Yeah, it was. Thank you for taking that hit, Morgan. I'm not sure I would have lived."

"Me neither. My Guard Ability reduces the damage by half. I think a hundred percent of that beam would cook one of us."

"Perhaps. Maybe if it's fire-based, I might be able to take it with my Elemental Resistance. I'm happy not to test it, though."

"I don't blame you. It wasn't a picnic, and neither are those damned potions! I'm grateful to be healed, but those minutes of feeling like I'm on PCP are for the birds."

"Probably great if you chug it as a last resort during a fight, though," Bronwyn said, grinning.

"Yeah, true." Morgan's eyes were distant for a moment before a maroon shirt appeared in his hand. He shrugged into it, buttoning the front with little, audible snaps. "Well, I don't see many options other than camping here until Olivia figures out how to make a portal. We need to figure out a way to kill that thing."

"I agree, but there's one thing you guys should think about," Bronwyn said, making eye contact with them both. "That's the first boss in this dungeon. Don't you think things are just going to get harder going forward?"

"Then we'll need to get stronger and smarter, too," Olivia declared, turning to look at the glowering, red-eyed monster.

"Bronwyn, how long can you keep that double of yours going?" Morgan asked.

"A long time unless it gets hit or killed, in which case it draws a big chunk of Energy."

Bronwyn called up the spell and read the description aloud:

**\*\*\*Mirage Double—Basic: You use your specific Energy pattern to create a double that will act in your defense. Further mastery of this spell will allow for more functionality. Energy cost: 200. Cooldown: Medium.\*\*\***

She was still smarting a little from the realization that she hadn't gotten a class refinement at level twenty like Morgan and Olivia had. She was still a Summer Banneret, and she wondered if she had to get refinements from the fae now. Still, her stats had improved significantly.

She pulled them up and contemplated the math:

| Energy Affinity: | 5.6, Solar - 7.6 | Energy: | 1057/1057 |
|---|---|---|---|
| Strength: | 102 | Vitality: | 55 |
| Dexterity: | 48 | Agility: | 64 |
| Intelligence: | 44 | Will: | 36 |

"So basically, it can die five times before I'm out of Energy."

"I like that it can distract that thing, but it seems like you have to be targeted first, right?" Morgan pressed.

"Yeah, at least at the basic level."

"Have either of you tried to push a skill past basic with practice?" Olivia asked.

"Sure, I did that with spears, and swords to a greater extent." Morgan looked at Bronwyn, waiting for her answer.

"Actually, I've been too damn busy. Always traveling around the plains or busy with other stuff. I've just improved through real combat."

"Bronwyn, what if you and Morgan did some sparring, and you used that Mirage Double repeatedly? If you could get it to level, you might get a double that you can send in to attack."

"That's not bad!" Morgan said. "We could work on your spear mastery too, and I could use the opportunity to try to improve my Void Step. I'll use it as often as I can during our sparring."

"Meanwhile, I can keep studying spatial connections, and we can all keep cultivating to improve our Cores."

"Hah, so training montage time? Before we mess with big ugly in there?" Bronwyn laughed.

"Yeah, I think so. If we can use your double proactively to lure that thing away, we can set up a triple shot that might tear through its armor. Plus, we'll need all the strength we can get going forward, don't you think?" Olivia moved from the center of the field of marble toward the stairs, a blanket appearing in her hands.

"What are you doing?" Morgan asked.

"If we're going to be here for a while, I'll set up a camp. This floor isn't going to be comfortable to sit on."

"Damn, you'd think with massive magical containers, I'd have thought to pack some furniture. Why do I just have a bedroll and blankets?" Morgan asked, following Olivia.

"Keep it in mind next time you're looting a vanquished enemy's stronghold. At least I have a bunch of furs I took from Urghat we can sit on," Bronwyn said, summoning a loaf of the fae queen's travel bread. "Dinner's on me, but that means Morgan has to cook next."

# MORGAN

Morgan stared at the Heesporian plum and the wrapped package containing Randon's Core Cake. Issa had said he should wait until he was at the threshold of a new tier before using one of the two Core-improvement treasures, but he couldn't decide which one to use. Would one of them be enough to take him into the next tier? His Core had been sitting at base nine now for a few days, even with half a dozen hours of cultivating each night after he and Bronwyn had finished their daily sparring, so he felt it was time to break into one of these treasures.

"Which are you going to use?" Olivia asked, sitting across from him, her own Heart Crystal Core Breaker, as she'd called it, resting in her hands. She'd also gotten her Core to rank nine.

"I think I'll use the plum. I don't know if it has the longevity or potency of this cake, so I might as well see what I can get out of it." That said, he put the cake away in his ring and lifted the plum for a good sniff. It smelled like pure sugar to him. "I suppose if Bronwyn can get her Core to nine, I could give my other one to her. We need all the advantages we can get, right?" He glanced to the side where Bronwyn sat, some twenty yards away, silently cultivating.

"That would be very generous—my understanding is that treasures like these aren't commonly found."

"Yeah, well, let's see what happens. Here goes nothing," Morgan said, lifting the plum to his mouth and taking a bite.

He wasn't prepared for the burst of Energy that exploded from the pulp as he chewed, flooding his pathways and rushing directly to his Core. He gasped and had to brace himself to keep from falling over. He still held most of the plum in one hand, and he knew he'd need to eat more of it, but he was overwhelmed by the surge of pure Energy causing his Core to throb and spin at a tremendous rate.

"Everything alright?" Olivia asked, tentatively reaching out a hand.

"Fine, fine. It's just a lot of Energy in this thing. I'll have to process it in bits," Morgan grunted.

Olivia nodded and sat back, contemplating her crystal again. Morgan turned his mind inward, watching his Core, and it became clear what was going on: a massive influx of pure Energy had flooded the spinning arms of his Vortex Core, and as it spun, it was slowly processing part of that Energy into void-attuned Energy and letting it drift into its dark heart.

He closed his eyes and concentrated, applying the pressure of his will to increase his Core's spinning and absorption rate. When things equalized, it gave a satisfied pulse and then resumed its regular, sedate rotation, significantly brighter than he remembered it being. He took another large bite of the plum, reckoning he could finish it off in two more bites, and began the process anew.

By the time Morgan was processing the last bite of the plum, he felt like his Core was ready to burst out of his body, it was so dense with Energy and violently spinning. Sweating and shaking, he focused on pushing with all his might against the flaring, whirling maelstrom around his void Energy, trying to equalize the two forces.

As the pure Energy slowly converted to void Energy and bled out of the spinning arms, Morgan noticed a glorious heaviness and depth to his Core that hadn't been there before. He smiled at the feeling of potential and power that radiated from the center of his being, and couldn't help the satisfied chuckle that rolled out of his throat. When he opened his eyes, he had a notification waiting:

***Congratulations! Your Core has advanced to: Vortex Class—Improved 1.***

He called up his Energy status and studied the numbers.

| Core: | Vortex Class - Improved 1 | | |
|---|---|---|---|
| Energy Affinity: | 9.2, Void - 9.2 | Energy: | 7934/7934 |

He'd put more points in intelligence and will when he'd leveled, but his Energy had increased significantly from the Core improvements alone. "Nearly eight thousand Energy now," he whispered softly.

"Wow, nearly two thousand more than I have," Olivia said.

Morgan opened his eyes to see her sitting in front of him still, her crystal empty of light now, but she herself cloaked in a shimmering aura of blue flames.

"You broke through?" he asked, stretching his neck then turning to his storage ring, looking for the scroll he'd gotten so long ago in the Crucible; the cultivation manual for his Vortex Core.

"I did," Olivia replied, watching him closely as the scroll appeared in his hand. "What's that?"

"When I was in the Crucible, I got this as a treasure. It's a cultivation method for my Core, but it's improved, so I was only able to learn part of it with my basic Core. I'm hoping I can absorb the rest of it now and gain some insight into cultivating more Energy."

"Oh, that's quite fascinating."

"Here it goes," Morgan said, pulling open the scroll. Where before when he'd tried to pull the scroll open it had stuck partway, now it unfurled completely, and he could see the dense System runes on the whole thing. As usual, after he stared at them for a while, they started to shift and glow and then stream into his eyes, and understanding spread through Morgan's mind.

**\*\*\*Congratulations! You have learned the skill: Vortex Core Cultivation Drill—Improved.\*\*\***

"It's so strange," Morgan said. "Now I feel like I understand my cultivation drill a lot better, but the knowledge is just there, you know? Like I've known it all along. It's so weird how the System can just write things into our minds."

"Yeah, the level of control and power the System wields is hard to fathom. Think about how it created Fanwath from four separate planets. In our wildest dreams, humans never expected to do that with technology. We were happy to start figuring out terraforming."

"For sure." Morgan stood and stretched, trying to catalog what he'd learned about cultivating and what he'd already known. It was strange how it was all jumbled together now. He realized most of the new information had to do with concentrating Energy in his pathways as he cycled and how to feel out and separate attuned Energies in the world around him.

"Before you wander off, I wanted to talk to you about something, Morgan." Olivia had a certain tone she took when she wanted to talk about her teleportation research, so Morgan wasn't surprised when she continued. "I'm making some progress with my research, but the more I learn, the more I realize I don't know. One thing has become apparent to me: your particular brand of Energy, void, is unusually well-suited for making intraspatial connections."

"You mean interspatial?"

"No, I mean intra—within space. I know it's hard to wrap your mind around it, but what your Void Step spell is doing is creating a rip in the fabric of reality or space that connects you to another point. In the case of that spell, it's rather short-ranged, and targeting is accomplished visually."

"Alright, go on."

"Well, I think I've almost worked out a prototype pattern that expands on the Void Step spell. It creates a static portal, though."

"That's fantastic!" Morgan smiled down at Olivia, but her smile was a weak reflection of his.

"There's a lot more to do, and there are some problems involved. We have to find a way to target Fanwath, and we need an enormous amount of Energy. Something like a thousand times what your Void Step uses."

"Are you serious? That's a million Energy."

"Yes, and I'm not sure why my calculations are coming up with that number. I only needed a couple thousand to open the portal from your tower to the gargoyle planet."

"Probably because of the tower. An extremely powerful mage made it, and I'm sure it's got countless enchantments built into it. It probably focuses the portals somehow."

"That was my first thought, and you're probably right. I don't know how it worked, but I've still got a lot of research to do. I just wanted to give you an idea of where I'm at with the problem." Olivia looked upset, and it took Morgan a minute to realize she was worried about his, and probably Bronwyn's, expectations for her.

"Relax, Olivia. It's always been a long shot in my mind. You've already made more progress than I would have thought possible. I don't imagine there are very many self-taught portal masters in the world. Worlds."

"Right." Her smile brightened. "How's the work with Bronwyn going? Did she get any sign that her Mirage Double is improving yet?"

"It's hard to tell with a skill like that. With weapons, you can feel that you're getting close to a breakthrough, but with a spell that just sort of works, it almost feels like a surprise when it upgrades. At least that's been my experience."

"Yeah, I guess that's kind of been my experience too, though some of my upgrades came with levels or class upgrades."

"Right, same here. Speaking of upgrades, I'm going to work on my Void Step some more. I've done enough with my Core tonight."

"Okay, it's my turn to cook, so get ready for soup in a couple of hours."

"Yum!"

Morgan looked to the enormous marble door that led to the giant tick and cast Void Step. Reality ripped around him, and then he was looking through the door at the huge, sulking monster.

Was it sulking? It seemed so to Morgan, but he knew he was projecting. The thing just sat there, hunched and glowering, and Morgan couldn't even tell if it was breathing because it held so still. Its eyes moved, though, which was enough to keep him on this side of the doorway.

Standing there, staring at the monster for the hundredth time, Morgan wondered what the fuck he was doing. He should use his Token of Travel and get his ass back to Issa. Wouldn't she do the same?

"Yeah, right." He laughed. Issa would never abandon two friends in a hostile dungeon or world, and he couldn't either. Not without knowing his action would save Issa somehow, and for all he knew, she was perfectly fine, sitting at home, waiting for him.

He turned to look at his companions. Olivia was quietly reading her book, and Bronwyn was still sitting in the lotus position doing her cultivation drill. He was happy that Bronwyn was more cheerful and less full of self-doubt than when he'd last worked with her, but something felt strange about her whole encounter with the fae.

Was she working for them now? Was she compromised? Where exactly were her loyalties? He supposed he had to give some credit to her and her queen for coming to help him in the ziggurat, but still, something just felt off.

As the spell came off cooldown, he Void Stepped over to the stairway—their little camp—then drew his sword and started working through his forms. He'd made it through all of them when he felt his spell was ready, so he ported again, trying to perform his Crane Flutters Its Wings the instant he appeared at his destination. Imagining an enemy wizard standing there when he appeared, his sword arced through the air, trailing streaks of Energy. "Take that, you villain!" He laughed again at himself, then cast Void Step, appearing right in front of Bronwyn.

"Dammit!" She opened her eyes and scowled at him. "That fucking spell makes the creepiest noise. I'm just glad I wasn't watching you because the only thing worse than the noise is how it looks. It messes with my mind."

"So you keep saying! Get up, student! Time to work on your spear!" Morgan waved his sword in a flourish, a grin on his face.

"It's cultivating time! We already drilled today!"

"Come on! Let's mix things up—it's the best way to learn."

"Alright," Bronwyn sighed and hopped to her feet, the long black spear Morgan had given her appearing in her hands. "En garde, asshole."

## BRONWYN

Bronwyn read the description again, her excitement still flushing her cheeks: **\*\*\*Mirage Double—Improved: You use your specific Energy pattern to create a double that will act in your defense or attack a target that you designate. Further mastery of this spell will allow for more functionality. Energy cost: 400. Cooldown: Medium.\*\*\***

"I did it! Mirage Double Advanced to Improved, and I can use it to attack now! Um, but it costs twice as much? That doesn't seem like an improvement!"

"Maybe creating more complicated constructs that can act on your orders takes a lot of Energy." Morgan shrugged. "If all goes well, you won't need to cast it more than once for our plan to work."

"Hopefully." Bronwyn turned back toward their little camp at the base of the long stairway and saw Olivia busily sketching into one of her notebooks. "Should we give her the good news?"

They'd been working on trying to improve their skills for over a week, though time was challenging to track in the strange dungeon environment.

"Yeah, let's." Morgan strode over, hooking his shining sword onto his belt. He was so different than when she'd last spent time with him—not only was he physically larger, more lithe, and full of powerful, strange Energy, but he seemed terse, preoccupied, and even sullen much of the time.

"Probably missing his girlfriend," Bronwyn muttered, following a good distance behind him. When she walked up, Morgan was sitting down, stretching out his legs. "Hey, good news, sis. My double improved, and you were right—I can use it to attack now."

"Really?" Olivia looked up with a bright smile. "That's fantastic! I was worried we were wrong in our theorycrafting!"

"Hah, well, you never let on."

"Power of positive thinking!" Olivia sighed, smiling. "Speaking of which, I have some exciting news!" She turned to regard Morgan, who raised an eyebrow. "I've written out what I think is a proper spell pattern for creating a void-attuned gateway that will span any distance given enough Energy."

"Really? Did you solve the problem with targeting?" Morgan asked.

"Not yet, but I have an idea. My spellcraft text has the basics for a scrying spell, and I was hoping you could copy the pattern for your Void Vision spell. Using the two of them, I think I can make a spell that will allow you to scry someone you know. Like Issa!"

"Oh, now you're talking! I'll start on it tonight. Can I borrow your drawing supplies again?"

"Of course! That's only one part of the problem, though. We're also going to need a lot of Energy, and I mean a lot, unless we can find a way to amplify the spell as your tower does for the portals it houses."

"So we're screwed," Bronwyn scoffed.

"Not necessarily, but maybe. If only we had something that could store Energy in large quantities . . ." She trailed off as Morgan began to squirm in his seat, looking rather uncomfortable.

"I may have something." His face was red, and he continued, "I swear I just thought of this, so I'm sorry I didn't mention it before. I killed an ancient gem snake in my tower. It had hundreds of gems on its body that Tiladia said are very good for storing Energy. She said Artificers prized them."

"And you have them?"

"Yeah, but I don't know how to put Energy into them."

"It's trivial, I'm sure. I have my artificing text, and I'm sure I can figure it out. Let me see some of them, please!" She held out a hand, and after concentrating for a moment, Morgan produced a handful of darkly glittering gems, some yellow, some orange, and a blue one. "Do the colors do anything? Can they only store certain types of Energy?"

"Not according to Boris, but he'd planned to do more research. I never had the chance to follow up with him."

"We'll need to confirm they can hold void-attuned Energy, but that should be easily done after I come up with a charging device."

"You're a damn rock star, Olivia," Bronwyn said, favoring her friend with a bright smile. "You know, I'd like to hear more about your school—your classes, your friends. You know what I mean?"

"Yeah, Bron, of course." Olivia smiled at her, and Bronwyn's heart melted a little. She was so damn pretty!

"Hey, before you guys start reminiscing, can you pass me those drawing supplies? I want to get started on that pattern you asked for."

Morgan stood up and hovered impatiently while waiting for Olivia to pass him the pencils and paper. As soon as he had them in hand, he wandered off, presumably to find a quiet place to concentrate.

"What's with him?" Olivia asked.

"I think he's missing Issa."

"Oh, yeah, good point. He's desperate to get some news about her. You know, love and all that," Olivia said, almost wistfully.

"I can't really relate, I guess." Bronwyn frowned down at her feet, which were outstretched and crossed in front of her. She leaned back on her hands, basically looking everywhere but at Olivia.

"Really? I remember when we first met, I thought you had a crush on me. Or to be more mature, feelings for me."

Bronwyn's face suddenly felt very hot. Who was this woman, and what had she done with Olivia? She couldn't imagine her saying something like that so bluntly.

She started to say something at least four times before she managed to look at Olivia and put together a coherent sentence. "I'm not good at relationships! I don't know what I feel, to be honest."

"I think that's one of the reasons we were drawn toward each other, Bronwyn. I'm the same way. Or I was—I'm finding it easier to express my feelings these days. A side effect of merging a primal fire elemental with my soul, I guess."

Olivia chuckled, and Bronwyn, who was trying to avoid her eyes, found it very difficult—her friend was doing everything she could to look directly at her.

"Olivia, I felt like my feelings were just a crush, and then you were always kind of at arm's length. I think it's my fault, really. I tried hard to keep busy doing what I'm good at, which makes it easy to avoid things I'm bad at, like feelings."

"I know, sweetie, and I think we both settled on being platonic because it was easier, right?"

"Yeah, I think so."

"Well, let's stop being easy on ourselves! Let's confront our feelings and give things a chance to happen. What do you say?"

"So you didn't run off to the academy and get married?" Bronwyn chuckled.

"No! But some other students were definitely flirting with me," Olivia said with a giggle, batting her eyelashes at Bronwyn.

"Of course they were! You're amazing!"

"You know you are too." Olivia was all smiles and seemed very relaxed. Bronwyn didn't recognize this side of her friend, and it drove home just how much they both had changed.

"Well, tell me about your friends. Tell me about my competition!"

She scooted closer to Olivia, and they sat together talking about Fainhallow Academy for hours. All the while, Morgan sat on the other side of the marble platform and scribbled painstakingly onto the sheets of paper Olivia had given him.

\* \* \*

Issa knelt in front of the toilet, heaving her guts out. She was grateful for the perpetually running water in the smooth, clean bowl, but she wasn't grateful to be alone.

She'd made it back to First Landing just a few days ago, and she'd been getting sick every morning since she'd left Tarn's Crossing. She was not stupid or naive—she was pregnant. So far, the only person she'd confided in was Tiladia, and she'd sworn the dragon spirit to secrecy. What would she do if Morgan never made it back?

She'd heard the news about the portal and about Olivia and Bronwyn going after Morgan, so she felt better in that regard. The refugees had reported about Morgan and his exploits among the captives outside the gargoyle lair, and she knew he was giving them hell, as he would say.

Tiladia had warned her that she didn't have enough Energy to reopen the portal, but even if she had, the keystone that Bronwyn had supplied had begun crumbling shortly after the portal had closed, reduced to a pile of fine, warm sand by the time Issa had made it to the tower.

Finally feeling the nausea pass, she stood and gently rubbed her belly. Could it really be? Her cycle was a week overdue, and that, combined with the sickness, was clue enough. She loved Morgan enormously, and she was happy to be having his child, but it was something of a surprise; she'd been taking Shadow Lilly tincture since she was sixteen, which should have kept her infertile for another few years. Still, she'd been unable to continue with the doses while in the Crucible, and after Blake's bird creature kidnapped her, she'd missed a few days.

"But it's supposed to last for months or years," she said softly, looking at her profile in the mirror.

"Miss Issa, might I suggest that your racial enhancements most likely purged the tincture's residual effects."

"Tiladia!" Issa spun to see the misty, shimmery form of the spirit near the entrance to the bathroom. "You startled me! And, yes, I had considered that, and you're probably right."

"Lord Morgan will be very pleased, don't you think?" Tiladia chimed.

"I don't know! I know so little about his culture. I've been pushing him to adventure and gain strength, and now I'm throwing this"—she gestured at her stomach—"at him!"

"Oh, Issa, worry not about Morgan. He adores you and will be pleased, trust me."

"If I could hug you, I would, Tiladia," Issa said, walking toward the door. "Any news?"

"Miss Maria was here last evening tutoring Ykleedra. I told her you were resting, and she left after only two hours. Other than that, I've not heard from the other colonists."

"Thank you, Tiladia. I'll be going into town to meet with the council; I want to take a more active role around here while I await Morgan's return. It will be good for me to become more familiar with the human culture."

"That's a sound plan, Issa. I do hope Morgan returns soon; it's not right that you aren't in the master suite, especially in your condition."

"Nonsense; these rooms are more than adequate. Never you worry, though, Tiladia. Morgan will return, and he'll be ready to claim the rest of this tower when he does. I'm sure of it."

"Your confidence warms me! I can feel the hunt calling to my dragon heart," Tiladia said with a bright chime, taking on her dragon form and swooping around the bathroom as Issa walked to the bedroom door and out.

"Tiladia, I would like to invite the council here for a dinner. Do I have the authority to do so?"

"Yes! Morgan told me to, and I quote, 'give Issa full access to the tower.' If I'm generous in that interpretation, I think I can extend to you the permissions to invite others."

"Thank you, Tiladia. I'll buy supplies for the kitchen, and hopefully, you can help me get things working in there."

After making a list of the cooking instruments and ingredients she'd need, Issa left the tower and made her way over to where she'd staked Munch and Gopp near Olivia's mount, Blue. A young livestock tech had been taking care of Blue, but Issa had taken over when she'd arrived with the other two roladii.

"Good boys," she said, patting them and putting out fresh water for them. "I'm going to commission a stable for the tower. We'll get you boys nice and comfortable, don't you worry." Then she turned to the cobbled road and walked along it to the hilltop with the Town Stone.

She strode purposefully up the steps, happy for the warm summer morning and the fresh air. She loved the bustle of First Landing; the town wasn't nearly as populous as Tarn's Crossing, but it had a certain energy to it that filled the air with excitement and potential. Everyone was busy innovating, building, exploring, and learning. Nothing seemed stagnant or stale, and Issa wanted to be more a part of things here. She wanted to be one of the leaders of this place.

With those thoughts in mind, she rested her hand on the Town Stone and requested citizenship, making it her home stone. Her father would be upset that she was giving up her position on the Tarn's Crossing list of citizens, but who knew if she'd ever see him again. According to the refugees who'd made it through the portal, the odds were pretty grim.

Besides, she thought, gently pressing a hand to her stomach, she now had more important ties.

## Morgan

Morgan looked at the giant tick and then back at his friends. "We sure we're ready?"

"We could train forever or wait until we solve the rest of this portal problem, but I think we should give it another try. We know what to expect now, and we have a plan," Olivia said, pressing her lips together and nodding at her own words.

"Yeah, I'm ready. Sorry your spell hasn't improved yet, but I think the key is the strategy."

"Yeah," Morgan replied. She was right—he wanted his Void Step to improve and felt he was close, but it wasn't critical for this battle. "Alright. On you, Bronwyn." He hefted Bloodfang and primed his spells, ready for instant action. They all stood in the giant doorway, outside the threshold.

Bronwyn nodded and began to count.

"Three, two, one, go!"

She ran forward, her double right behind her, and Morgan and Olivia took opposite flanks. In response to some unspoken command, Bronwyn's double charged at the tick, driving its copied spear at its huge mandibles in a series of feints. The three companions hurried around the monster's sides, trying to get behind it, while it focused on battering and slashing the Mirage Double.

"That's one!" Bronwyn called out, indicating that her double had died once already. She could only maintain it for two deaths if their plan was going to work.

"Argh!" Morgan yelled, sprinting as hard as he could. He activated his combo when he was adjacent to the monster's rear legs: First, he cast Hollow Charge, smashing into the back of the giant tick's torso with his sword, then he instantly unleashed a Void Wave. As soon as the crackling, devouring hole in reality started to expand, he cast Void Step and appeared next to Olivia. She was already firing a narrow, focused beam of superheated steam, targeting the tick's torso inside Morgan's Void Wave.

"Go!" Olivia screamed at Bronwyn, and the red-haired woman held up her hands and called down a column of solar Energy with her Wrath of Summer spell. Morgan didn't leave anything to chance, spooling up a Vortex Lance and firing it parallel to Olivia's Pyrosteam Drill.

As the bright light and black ball of nothingness faded away, the giant tick wobbled forward on its four remaining legs, its mandibles open in a warbling squeak, gouts of yellow-red guts pouring out with the sound. Then, as it wobbled sideways, Morgan saw the extent of the damage they'd wreaked: the tick's fat abdomen was half gone, and its insides were tumbling out of it as it writhed in death throes.

"Yes!" Bronwyn whooped. She held up a hand, and Olivia gave her a high five. Morgan kept watching the tick, though, worried for some last-ditch attack. His fears were well-founded—it started to form a ball of red Energy at its leaking, trembling mandibles.

"Look out!" Morgan roared, watching to see which of them the tick targeted. Luckily for him, because he meant to take the blow again, the tick fired its beam at Bronwyn's double, killing it for the second time. After that, it collapsed with a massive shudder.

"Yes!" Olivia crowed, echoing Bronwyn's earlier celebration.

"Right on! Nice one, ladies."

Morgan started walking toward the corpse but stopped in his tracks. Huge purple motes of Energy were beginning to coalesce on the monster. They were volleyball-size and sparkled with silvery twinkles at their center. "Holy shit," he said, sensing the density of the Energy gathering around the corpse. As the motes gathered into a cloud around the gigantic carcass, it began to stream toward the three of them, a thick, pulsing river of purple Energy for each of them.

As the Energy pulsed into him, Morgan was astounded to be lifted off the ground, transfixed in the air. He arched his back and yelled with the sensation, and he heard Olivia and Bronwyn doing the same.

***Congratulations! You have achieved level 33 Void Adept, gained 8 Intelligence, 8 Will, and have 12 points to distribute.***

***Congratulations! You have learned the spell: Void Step—Improved.***

***Void Step—Improved: You are able to instantly travel between two points in space, provided you can see your destination. Energy cost: 1000. Cooldown: Low.***

"I leveled!" Bronwyn yelled, her face flushed with excitement and pleasure from the massive Energy influx.

"Me too!" Morgan and Olivia said at the same time.

"You owe me a Coke," Morgan told her, winking. "My Void Step leveled too. I knew it was close! The cooldown is the only thing that changed—it says 'low' now."

"Um, guys," Bronwyn called, pointing to the far end of the courtyard, past the huge corpse. Morgan followed her finger and saw that a large marble chest had appeared near the next door. "Treasure time?"

"Hell yes," Morgan said, striding toward the chest. He could hear Olivia's boots clicking as she followed, and Bronwyn trotted ahead. He felt glorious after that Energy infusion. On top of that, he knew Olivia was on the verge of finishing the pattern for a scrying spell, which meant that he'd soon be laying eyes on Issa. Or so he hoped.

"What a great day!" He smiled at Olivia as she walked up beside him.

"That's all it takes to get some smiles out of you? Killing a giant tick?"

"Hah! You know why I'm in a good mood. Now that this thing is done, we can rest a bit and maybe try that scrying spell, hmm?"

"Yes, Morgan." Olivia laughed. "I haven't forgotten!"

"Guys, should I open it?" Bronwyn asked.

"Just a sec! Remember the last chest, Bron? Sheesh!" Olivia hollered.

"I'm just kidding!" Bronwyn laughed, then sat on the ground, waiting for them to walk up to the chest.

"Alright, can we wait a little while to open this? I am very close to finishing Morgan's scrying spell. I also started working on another type of scrying spell for myself that will allow me to scrutinize items like this chest, assuming it works," Olivia said, sitting down in front of the chest across from Bronwyn.

"Seriously? You've been working on two spells?"

"I have about seven projects going right now, but yeah, I'm closest with these two. They're sort of related; I stole a piece of Morgan's spell to make mine, but it uses air-attuned Energy and only works on items I can physically see."

"How long?" Morgan asked, also sitting down.

"Not sure. Yours is almost done; give me a half hour to check my work?" Olivia pulled out one of her thick journals and a couple of her textbooks.

"I'll make us a snack!" Bronwyn announced.

"Right, sounds good." Morgan kicked out his feet and tried to keep his face relaxed. He was struggling to contain his excitement. If he could see that Issa was okay, it would be like taking a mountain off his shoulders. "I'll charge some gems while we wait."

Morgan rummaged in his storage ring, pulled the little copper plate Olivia had inscribed with runes, and set it on his lap.

The plate was only about the size of a coffee saucer, but Olivia had stamped dozens of runes into it. At its center was a circle—where he placed one of the gem snake's gems—and at the edge were two other circles where he was supposed to hold his thumbs while gripping the plate. That done, he channeled some void Energy along his pathways and into the plate, and Olivia's runes worked their magic. His Energy crackled along the lines between the runes then surged into the gem, slowly charging it.

It took about ten minutes for him to fill one gem, and they'd found that he could push around two thousand to seven thousand units of Energy into them. Some held more, some held less, and he couldn't discern what differentiated them. Regardless, it took Morgan about an hour of rest between gems. Considering they'd need two hundred or more to make Olivia's theoretical Void Gate spell work, he had weeks of charging to do.

When he finished up with the gem and stowed it away with the plate, Bronwyn offered him a sandwich packed full of sprouts, sliced veggies, and sharp cheese. The two pieces of bread were even slathered with something a lot like mayo.

"Damn, this is good! How lucky are we that food stays fresh in these containers?"

"Extremely lucky," Olivia muttered, still scribbling in her notebook.

"I have a pretty large supply left, and tons of the rations from the queen. What about you guys?"

"Well, I left my old dimensional bag with the refugees outside the gargoyle ziggurat. It had most of my supplies in it, but I've still got weeks' worth of dried meat and lots of water," Morgan said around a mouthful of sandwich.

"Mm-hmm, I have a lot of supplies still. We're fine for a long while," Olivia added, still only half paying attention to them.

Morgan continued to munch on his sandwich. He hadn't even been very hungry before Bronwyn had given it to him. Ever since he'd pushed his race into improved territory, he felt like he hardly ever got hungry.

"You know, Bronwyn, this is very good, but if we're worried about supplies ever running short, I probably shouldn't eat as much as I have been. I think my body thrives on Energy more and more as I advance my race. I hardly ever feel hungry."

"Really?" Bronwyn's cheeks were full of food, and she continued to chew while scrutinizing him. "I still get pretty hungry."

"It's true," Olivia interjected, looking up. "I probably could eat half what a normal person does, and I'm several steps below Morgan."

"Wow. I mean, that's cool, but I love to eat! You still like it, right?" Bronwyn seemed almost worried, like they were telling her she'd have to give up food if she kept improving her race, and it made Morgan chuckle.

"Don't worry! I can still eat plenty, and it's still as fun as ever." He laughed, holding a hand to his mouth to keep from spitting out crumbs.

"Morgan!" Olivia suddenly exclaimed. "I've got your spell ready. Why don't you study it and try building it in your pathway while I finish up mine?" She was holding a sheet of dense lines. When he looked at it, it seemed almost like a piece of art, but he could see the pattern, the design he was supposed to make with his Energy.

"It's pretty complicated. How long will it hold together?" he asked.

"It's not like weaving Energy together. You're just pushing a thread of void-attuned Energy into a pattern. It will hold as long as you concentrate. I mean, if you had a really low will score, you might struggle, but I think you said yours is high, right?"

"Well, a hundred and fifty-five."

"Damn!" Bronwyn exclaimed.

"Yeah, you should be good." Olivia chuckled, turning back to her notebook. She looked up suddenly and said, "By the way, my calculations for that spell's cost come out to around two thousand Energy. I think your void nature makes it cheaper to scry long distances because it opens a window between space. I'm not sure it would cost any more or less, no matter the distance."

"Huh, that's interesting. Why does the portal spell you're designing cost so much?"

"Moving matter is a lot different than opening a window, and we're trying to make a gate stable enough for all of us to pass through. I think I'm erring on the side of safety. I also think there might be a way to modify it so that only you go through. That would be a lot cheaper. One more thing, as you get close to finishing the spell, keep in mind the person you're trying to scry."

"Makes sense. Alright, will do," Morgan said, already starting to tune everything out while studying the spell Olivia had created. Thanks to his increased intelligence, he could memorize a good portion of it pretty easily, but he figured he'd have to stop and start the spell pattern quite a few times while he checked it. He closed his eyes and pulled a trickle of void Energy into his broad, central pathway, getting to work.

It took Morgan nearly an hour of concentration, of pressing his will against the Energy strand and holding it in place while he gently tugged it into the shape of the pattern Olivia had drawn. Several times as he completed portions of it, it pulsed and tried to solidify, pulling on the Energy in his Core. Morgan wondered if a lesser or partial spell had been completed and was ready to be cast. Still, he held back and continued to bend the thread to his will, twisting and folding it.

When he finished the last whorl of the pattern and it pulsed with dark void Energy in his pathway, Morgan finally released his hold on his Core and let the Energy flood out. He opened his eyes and thought of Issa.

With a disturbing crackle, like sound being erased, the area in front of his face split and opened into a black window. A moment later, an image materialized in the darkness—Issa stood in the foyer of his tower, speaking with Tiladia. He couldn't make out any sounds, but she looked animated and flushed and was gesturing about. He could tell by her mannerisms that she was laughing. Morgan started to laugh with relief at the sight of her, and tears began to well in his eyes. Then the window crackled again, a reverse of the un-sound he'd heard before, and it was gone.

***Congratulations! You have learned the spell: Void Window—Basic.***

***Void Window—Basic: You are able to open a window between two locations, observing a person or creature that you know well. Attempts to scry those you cannot easily picture will be met with failure. Energy cost: 2100. Cooldown: Long.***

As Morgan wiped his eyes, he realized Bronwyn and Olivia were standing behind him and laughing in celebration.

"It worked!" Olivia crowed.

"You guys could see through it too?"

"Yes!" Bronwyn exclaimed, slapping him on the shoulder.

"She's safe," Morgan said simply, flooded with relief.

"She sure is." Olivia also reached out and squeezed his shoulder. Then she said, "Now, how about this chest?"

## ~ OLIVIA ~

Olivia finished the last swirl of her new spell pattern with a flourish and smiled up at Morgan and Bronwyn. "Done!" she exclaimed, hopping to her feet. "Let's see if it works!"

She walked over to the chest, then looked at Morgan and asked, "What does your Void Vision tell you about this chest?"

"Hmm." Morgan's eyes became dark pools, and he studied the chest for a moment. "I see bright Energy signatures within, and maybe something shimmering around its surface."

"Alright, good to know for reference."

Olivia held up her spell design and studied it for a moment. She'd made it, so she was quite familiar with most of its shapes. Closing her eyes, she pulled a thread of air-attuned Energy out of her Core and quickly began to build the pattern in her pathway. She had to check her page a couple of times, but in just a matter of a minute or two, she'd created the spell, noting the pleasing pulse of Energy as it took shape. Olivia pushed more of her air-attuned Energy into it and let the spell run through her pathways.

A tingle in the back of her eyes let her know something was happening, and she studied the chest. She saw, highlighted in pulsing magenta light, tendrils of air tickling over the surface of the chest, slipping under the lid, and wrapping around the hinges. In their wake, Olivia saw tiny sigils brought to life, traceries of Energy flows, and a faint whisper on the wind that hinted at danger. As the spell faded, the System hit her with some notifications:

***Congratulations! You have learned the spell: Surveying Breeze—Basic.***

***Surveying Breeze—Basic: You animate the air to carefully inspect an object or area, reading the clues it leaves in its wake with enhanced vision. Energy cost: 200. Cooldown: Medium.***

"It's trapped," Olivia announced. She moved to the chest and produced a small engraving blade she'd purchased for practicing her artificing. Using the blade, she scratched through some of the sigils that were still highlighted in her vision, and when the Energy lines faded away, she knew she'd broken the trap. "It should be good now," she declared, looking back at Morgan and Bronwyn, who watched her with appreciation.

"Very cool," Morgan said. "I only felt a breeze. I take it you saw more as the spell's caster?"

"Yep, the wind showed me where the spell sigils were."

"That's awesome, Olivia!" Bronwyn exclaimed. "Can we open it?"

"Yeah, but I'll open it. I'm the one saying it's safe now. You both back up, please."

Morgan frowned but did as she asked, and Bronwyn nodded as well. She smiled at Olivia as if to demonstrate her confidence in her.

Olivia nodded once they were a few paces away and leaned down, putting both hands under the heavy marble chest lid, heaving it open. It swung easily on its hinges, and nothing terrible happened—no blast of electricity, fiery explosion, or lancing blade. She looked into the chest and caught her breath; it was filled with glittering items.

"Wow," Morgan said. "Quite a haul. You think we'll be limited to only one choice again?"

"I don't know. This time we killed a boss," Bronwyn offered.

"Just in case, let's study the items and prioritize," Olivia replied, pulling out a notebook. "Let's see. Do you all see that pile of silvery armor under that black cloth?"

"Yeah," Morgan said. "You think that counts as one item?"

"Let's hope so. Hmm, there's a black stone crown or tiara. What would you call it?" Olivia pointed to the delicate crown that seemed to be carved from obsidian.

"Just crown. Tiara sounds too girly," Bronwyn replied. Morgan snorted.

"There's like a thousand or more Energy beads piled in there. If we only get one item, we should avoid touching those." He pointed to the glittering, gleaming pile.

"Yeah, something tells me we aren't going to be limited to one item this time." Bronwyn nodded. "What about those axes?" She pointed to a pair of hatchet-size axes with broad, jade-colored stone blades.

"Nice." Morgan whistled. "Hang on," he said, and then Olivia saw his eyes turn black again. "I read strong Energy signatures from everything in there, but the crown is blazing like a sun."

"Oh, that's handy," Olivia replied. "Should we start with that, then?"

She glanced from Morgan to Bronwyn. He shrugged while she nodded, so Olivia reached into the chest and picked up the crown. It was cold and heavy, but she felt a deep resonance within her Core when she lifted it free of the chest.

"It's powerful; I can feel it in my Core. What about you guys?"

"Let me see." Bronwyn held out a hand, and Olivia reluctantly handed her the crown. Bronwyn frowned for a second or two but then shrugged. "Nothing."

She gave it to Morgan, who held it for a couple of seconds. His eyes grew dark, and he frowned.

"I feel something, but nothing much. Let's set it aside for now—the stuff in the chest didn't disappear." He nodded to the chest, setting the crown on the marble ground. Olivia felt her eyes drawn to it. "The next brightest aura is coming from those axes. Go ahead and pick them up, Bron."

He glanced at Olivia for any objection, but she just nodded. Bronwyn, grinning from ear to ear, reached into the chest and, clicking the two handles together, lifted the hatchets out with one hand.

"Nothing disappeared." Her voice was bright and excited as she gripped the handles in her fists. "These feel great." She turned away from the chest and chopped the two hatchets through the air a few times.

"Alright, dear." Olivia chuckled. "Set 'em down and let's finish."

Bronwyn laughed but set the hatchets down near the crown.

"Morgan, you pick up the armor," Olivia said.

"Yeah," Bronwyn echoed. Morgan shrugged and picked up the silk-wrapped bundle of clinking, silvery plates. Olivia saw it wasn't a complete armor set as he pulled back the silky wrapping. It was just an ornate, shining breastplate and two thick vambraces which looked like they were meant to protect a person's arms.

"Pretty light," Morgan commented. He set the bundle down next to the axes, then he looked back in the chest. "Just shitloads of Energy beads—all sorts of them."

"Looks like we get to take everything. Let's divvy up the Energy beads, and then we can talk about the real loot," Bronwyn said, and they all got to it, lifting out piles of beads and separating them into three roughly similar stacks. None of them cared enough about getting things exact to count them out. After they'd stowed their beads, Olivia leaned down and picked up the crown.

"I'd like to bond with this to see if I can tell what it does. Do either of you object?"

"Nah, it was pretty clear you wanted it from the start." Morgan smiled. "You might as well check out the hatchets, Bronwyn."

"Well, that leaves the armor for you, Morgan," Bronwyn said.

"Um, I'll be honest: I stopped wearing my armor all the time back when I hurt my arm. I kind of got out of the habit of it. It's so cumbersome, and I don't know if it would even save me from the kinds of things we've been fighting. I guess I could try this one; it seems like a lot less of a hassle, though it won't cover me as well. Are you sure neither of you wants it?"

"Not me," Olivia replied.

"Not this time; maybe the next armor we find," Bronwyn said, sitting down to study her new hatchets.

"Alright, then." He picked up the bundle of armor, then he too sat down to study his new items.

Olivia held the heavy, obsidian crown in her hands and turned it around and around, looking for some insight into it. She cast her Surveying Breeze spell on it, and though the tendrils of air wrapped around the crown, exploring its every nook and cranny, the only whisper that came to her ears was *Power*. She sat down and put the crown on her lap, resting a hand on the cool stone; then, she trickled some pure Energy into the item.

\*\*\***Crown of Nightmarch: Artificed item. Enchantments: 1. Durability**—**This item has been crafted from Heart Obisidian and enchanted to be incredibly resistant to damage. 2. Amplification**—**When fully charged, this item can magnify any spell's effects by a factor of ten. 3. Recharging**—**This item can achieve a full charge over the course of a day, less if kept in a high-Energy environment.**\*\*\*

Olivia lifted the crown to her head and smiled as the cool stone shifted to snugly but comfortably fit the shape of her skull. As it settled, it became almost weightless to her. "My crown is called the Crown of Nightmarch and is able to amplify a spell once per day."

"How much?" Morgan asked, looking up.

"The description says a factor of ten."

Morgan performed his low whistle of appreciation again. "Sounds nice."

"What about you guys?"

"Hatchets of the Jade Queen!" Bronwyn said, holding up the two weapons. "They're very sharp and made from something called living jade. They can self-sharpen, and they amplify Energy that's channeled into them. Do you think that would work with my Solar Arms spell?"

"They sound made for it," Morgan replied with a slight frown. "Anyway, nice weapons. This armor is called the Moonsteel Armor of the Keeper. I have no idea who the Keeper is or was, but it's supposed to be very strong, it's light, and more than that, it can mitigate Energy attacks. Watch this," he said, holding the armor to his chest.

As he held it in place, it seemed to ripple and flow over his shoulders, down his back, and then around his sides to connect to the breastplate. "Easy to put on and light. How can I complain?"

He slipped his arm through one of the bracers, which spread to cover his shoulder, leaving just a hair's breadth between it and the breastplate. He repeated the process with the other then flexed his arms, moving them around rapidly. "It's almost like I'm not wearing anything."

"That's awesome! Too bad there wasn't leg armor or a helmet." Bronwyn gestured to Morgan's head with one of her hatchets.

"Well, we're not done with the dungeon yet," Olivia said.

"True," Morgan replied. He stood up smoothly, his new armor gleaming in the strange perpetual twilight of the dungeon. "I know we've talked about this a million times, but do you guys think this dungeon is weird? Like, we have no idea why it's here, what the point of it is, why it had a portal in that dead city, all that stuff."

"Nope, no new insights. Sorry, Morgan." Olivia also stood.

"That's not totally true," Bronwyn said. "What about these items' names—Nightmarch, Jade Queen, Moonsteel, the Keeper?"

"Hmm, that's a great point, Bron. Maybe the items are telling a story. Maybe we'll learn more if we go deeper." Olivia pointed to the next marble door.

"Alright, let's keep going, but we need to take it slow. That tick almost did us in, and as far as we know, he was the easy first boss." Bronwyn gestured to the huge, seeping mound of a corpse on the far side of the courtyard.

"Right, but let's wait a few minutes. I'm close to being able to fill another gem."

"Alright, sounds good. I need to allocate my points from the kill anyway," Olivia added.

"Me too!" Bronwyn slapped a hand to her forehead.

Morgan laughed, then closed the empty chest, sitting down on top. He took out the charging plate Olivia had made and got to work, but not before he muttered, "Me too."

"Hah. Well, I'm putting my points into dexterity. I really struggled making those diagrams by hand. I think I could have done it much faster with a higher dexterity." Olivia sat down and pulled up her status sheet, doing precisely what she said she would, bumping her dexterity up to twenty-two. "I knew it played a factor in spell design, but until I felt my limitations, I didn't really put the credence I should have into my professor's words."

"Hmm, that's interesting. My dexterity is doing pretty well because of my last class, but my strength is lagging a bit. I'm putting my twelve points into that," Morgan said as he concentrated on pushing Energy into the gem on his copper plate.

"Well, since you guys are sharing," Bronwyn spoke, looking up, "I put five points into intelligence and then split the rest into agility and vitality. My strength is way higher."

"Okay, so we're all ready and primed for the next section! Let me finish this gem, rest a bit to get my Energy back, and we can see what horror is waiting for us."

They all chuckled, but when Olivia glanced over at the giant pile of remains, it drove the truth of his words home.

# BRONWYN

Bronwyn swung her hatchet at the clawing, frenzied giant centipede, splitting its carapaced head and sending it twitching to the ground. She stood behind Morgan, ready for the next insect to break past him. They'd been fighting their way through the long, downward-sloping marble hallway for what felt like hours. Every few minutes, a new wave of the black, giant insects would come rushing up the hallway, clicking against the hard floors and walls, squeaking, hissing, chirping, and clacking.

Morgan stood in front, with Olivia and Bronwyn giving him space so he could use his point-blank area attacks. Any creatures that broke through either met their fates on Bronwyn's hatchets or amid Olivia's devastating magic bursts. Morgan seemed to be in a frenzy, a glowing red claw enveloping his left hand as he hacked and slashed with his sword in the other. Every now and then, he'd let out a wave of void Energy or a blue blast of pure Energy, decimating the current wave of creatures.

"He doesn't seem to tire," Olivia said after they'd watched him working through the fourth or fifth wave of giant insects.

"He uses his Energy Drain to keep going. It's like he was designed for clearing hordes of weak enemies." Bronwyn shrugged. It was impressive, but she'd seen how much trouble the massive tick had given Morgan—he wasn't some sort of demigod.

"I keep wanting to step up and fire a blast of plasma into the horde, but I'm afraid I'll walk into his Void Wave or something. He's not exactly lucid when that wolf claw comes out. Have you noticed?"

"Yeah. Look at him! He's going berserk!" Bronwyn gestured, and sure enough, Morgan was screaming and hacking with both hands, driving deep into the wave of insects. Then, with its signature sound, worse to Bronwyn than fingers on a chalkboard, his Void Wave rippled out, obscuring everything in the hallway with its nothingness. When it cleared, Morgan was standing over partially obliterated insect corpses. He leaned over, hands on knees, breathing heavily with a grin plastered on his face.

"Having fun?" Olivia chuckled as she picked her way through the carnage to stand next to him.

"Actually, yes. I know I've said it before, but seeing that Issa was alright has taken a weight off my shoulders. I'm happy to take pleasure in exterminating some bugs."

"Let's hurry and make some progress before the next wave comes!" Bronwyn urged, striding past the two of them.

Olivia and Morgan started after her, but they'd only made it four or five steps before a surge of Energy flooded into their backs. None of them leveled, but Bronwyn felt like she had to be getting close. Sure, Morgan was doing more killings than she was, but he was also a higher level.

When she'd recovered from the influx, Bronwyn started jogging down the tunnel, hearing her friends' feet keeping pace.

"Yes!" she hollered when she saw a set of large marble doors up ahead. "We made it! No more waves!"

"Hell yeah!" Morgan cheered, catching her happy vibe easily. Olivia didn't say anything, but Bronwyn saw her smile when she caught up.

"I mean, it is kind of fun," Olivia said, perhaps voicing a conversation she'd been having with herself. "Killing giant bugs, flexing our spells and abilities, but let's not forget that tick could've killed us easily if we'd made just one more misstep when we met it."

"Killjoy," Bronwyn teased, grinning at her. She'd been a lot easier around her beautiful friend ever since they'd confronted their feelings about each other. Nothing was official, but it was nice to feel like there was some potential there, and that they both felt it.

When they arrived at the doors, Bronwyn saw they had handles to pull them open, much like the doors that had opened into the hallway. "Should I open one?"

"Why not? At least take a peek. Be ready to close it, though," Morgan said.

Bronwyn nodded and grabbed hold of a handle, pulling on the right-hand door. Like the doors above, it silently swung toward her with very little resistance. She pulled it open about six inches, and then she peered through. Morgan and Olivia crowded close to look as well.

A massive marble chamber opened up beyond the doors, well lit with shimmering white Energy lamps that hung from dozens of silvery chains attached to the high ceiling. The space reminded Bronwyn of a gymnasium or exhibition hall in its spacious, echoing enormity. On the smooth, white expanse of the marble floor, only one thing stood out: a colossal statue of a coiled centipede-like insect. Rather than just a head, mounted atop the long, multilegged body was a humanoid torso with six arms, all holding curved marble swords. The humanoid body had an insect-like head with gaping mandibles.

"That thing's ugly as hell," she muttered.

"Look," Olivia said, pointing high along the walls. Bronwyn followed her gesture and saw round holes evenly spaced around the room's perimeter, about twenty feet up.

"What are they for?" Morgan asked softly.

"I don't know, but I have a feeling that when we step in there, we're going to find out," Olivia replied.

"Well, it feels kind of like cheating, but I could send my double in. Hopefully, this is like the last boss, and it won't pursue us if we stay in the tunnel."

"It's not cheating! It's using our resources," Morgan scoffed. "We all full of Energy? Ready just in case?"

"Yeah, I was full as soon as that Energy reward hit us," Olivia replied.

"Same," Bronwyn said.

"Same." Morgan grinned. "Alright. Do it, Bron!"

Bronwyn nodded, motioning for Morgan and Olivia to give her some space. Concentrating, she cast Mirage Double, and after a surge of Energy flooded out through her pathways, a shimmer in the air heralded her double's appearance. Soon she was looking into the eyes of her twin Energy construct. Bronwyn pointed at the statue, and both thought and said, "Attack."

Without saying anything or even nodding, it turned to the statue and ran through the door. The three adventurers watched, holding their breath, as it charged over the marble floor. Nothing happened with the holes in the wall, but as soon as the double's hatchet struck the giant marble creature, it exploded in a shower of stone shards. Bronwyn grunted, feeling the pull on her Core as the double drew Energy to continue existing.

"It just died," she hissed through clenched teeth.

As the dust and debris settled, the whirling, sword-swinging insectoid resolved into clarity, and Bronwyn's double died again as a sword slashed her in half. Just then, a volley of orange flaming balls exploded out of the holes lining the room's walls. They burst into the double like a bomb going off, killing it again in a fiery conflagration. When the smoke and cinders settled, the heaving, black-chitoned monster was coiled back in its position with its blades splayed, staring at the doors to its vaulted chamber.

"Damn," Morgan breathed, rubbing a hand through his hair.

"Yeah, that looks rough," Bronwyn said.

"I wonder if those fireball cannons target the first person to enter the room? I could probably shrug them off in my fire Elemental Form."

"They didn't seem to hurt the big bug, either," Morgan noted.

"Yeah, he was caught in that blast but seems fine." Bronwyn pushed the door gently closed, then turned to her friends. "Ideas?"

"We could try a really fast blitz again. You know, stack up our attacks like on the tick."

"If those fireballs target us before it dies or after, we could end up with a rather Pyrrhic victory." Olivia frowned.

"True, or if our combined attack isn't enough to one-shot it," Bronwyn added.

"The door didn't close when combat started. Let's try this: I'll go in first; when the fireballs start shooting at me, send in your double. Let's see if they keep firing on me or split to attack it," Olivia said, her eyes distant as she envisioned the scene.

"You're not going in there alone!" Bronwyn grabbed Olivia's shoulder. The taller, black-haired woman smiled at Bronwyn, the blue flames in her eyes flickering brightly.

"I'm tougher than I look, Bron."

She gently pulled her hand away, and it reminded Bronwyn just how much the other woman had changed. She remembered being able to look down into her blue-and-silver eyes, and how she'd shyly suggested her adventuring days were over after the Yovashi cave.

"You sure, Olivia?" Morgan asked.

"Yep. Is your double ready?" She looked at Bronwyn's troubled face and forced her smile wider. "I'll be fine!"

"Yeah, give me a couple of minutes for Energy."

They stood there chatting for a few minutes about mundane things, as though to keep from thinking about the idea that Olivia was about to risk her life to test the mechanics of a monster fight. While Morgan lamented the lack of good cold beer in his dimensional containers, Bronwyn suddenly laughed. "This is fucking crazy! I swear, I fought through plenty of RPGs learning boss mechanics by trial and error—this is too surreal!"

"I know what you're talking about. I had friends who ran in raid guilds; they talked about that shit all day on patrol," Morgan said.

"Well, I have no experience with those things, but I can say this feels very gamelike. The System has its methods for encouraging growth, that's for sure. You ready, Bron?"

"Yeah, I'm ready. Be quick to run if that thing comes at you!"

"I will," she said. Seeing how Bronwyn stared at her, she repeated, "I will. Stand back, you two. I'm going to take my fire form."

Bronwyn reached out and squeezed Olivia's arm, looking into her eyes again before stepping back next to Morgan. Olivia smiled, turned away from them, and then erupted into flames. As Bronwyn's eyes adjusted to the glare, she realized it was more than that; Olivia's form under the flames was like a coursing, semisolid magma.

The heat from her roaring, flickering cloak of fire was difficult to bear even several feet away, and Bronwyn and Morgan both had their hands up to shield their faces and eyes while they waited for Olivia to head into the giant insect's hall. Olivia lifted one fiery, crackling arm, and it took a moment for Bronwyn to realize she was holding up a thumb. She then turned and drifted into the chamber.

Bronwyn hurried forward to watch, preparing her Mirage Double spell. Olivia hadn't gone far; she was gliding back and forth near the doorway, perhaps waiting for the monster or the fireballs to target her. Nothing happened for a few heartbeats until Olivia drifted just a bit further in, and suddenly, the boss stood up, fanning out its swords in outstretched hands. With concussive *thunk, thunk* sounds, fireballs started soaring through the air at Olivia.

"Now!" Morgan barked.

"Right!" Bronwyn's Mirage Double took shape as she ordered it to attack the enormous monster. It charged into the room, and Bronwyn looked to Olivia, relieved to see her gliding out of the fiery explosions, none the worse for wear. Meanwhile, another volley of fireballs launched into the air, again targeting Olivia. The insect monster had started moving toward her but turned its attention on the double, bearing down on it with stabbing legs and slashing swords.

Olivia glided to the far left-hand side of the vast hall and moved back and forth, waiting for another volley of fireballs. When they came, soaring through the air at her again, she shouted in a strange, disembodied echoing voice, "That's it! It works; I'm coming out!"

The fireballs exploded into her, and she emerged from the rolling, furious explosion laughing in that same strange voice. Bronwyn felt her double die, and once Olivia was through the door, she canceled the spell.

They backed away from Olivia. The flames surrounding her sputtered and winked out, and their friend was standing in front of the doorway with a wide smile. "Looks like it will work! I'll draw the fireballs; you two kill the boss."

"You say that like it'll be easy." Morgan chuckled.

"Nothing ventured, nothing gained," Bronwyn said, finding Olivia's confidence infectious.

# MORGAN

"Alright, Bronwyn, I'm going to let your double keep the attention as long as it can, then I'll take over. You're going to harry its flanks, trying to cut off those legs with your hatchets, right?" Morgan asked, peering through the half-opened door at the huge insect monster.

"Yes, as we discussed a dozen times now!" Bronwyn growled.

Morgan knew he was being irritating, repeating the plan over and over, but he was really just filling time while they waited for Olivia's elemental body spell to come off cooldown.

"How's it coming, Olivia?" Bronwyn inquired, turning to look at her friend.

"Just about ready," Olivia said calmly, not opening her eyes or projecting any stress or annoyance. She was sitting with her back against the wall, not cultivating but concentrating on her Core. She said it helped her relax and focus her thoughts.

Morgan gripped Bloodfang tightly, squeezing his palm into its hilt's rough, dry material. He knew the weapon was conscious—it certainly chose when it wanted to aid him and seemed to get excited when he fought, but it never spoke to him. In a way, he was jealous of Issa having a weapon that gave her advice and pointers, but in another, he was glad Bloodfang was quiet. He wasn't sure he'd like the things the sword had to say.

"Let's do this," Olivia spoke, holding out a hand for Bronwyn to haul her to her feet.

"How long will your fire shape last?" Morgan asked.

"I should be able to keep it going for nearly ten minutes," she replied.

"That's a long time in a fight—we should be good." Morgan nodded.

"Yeah, let's hope so." Bronwyn flipped her hatchets and caught the handles in each hand. She said she still only had basic axe mastery, but with her agility and natural fighting skills, she seemed to be doing just fine; at least against the smaller insects they'd faced in the hallway. "When you're ready, Olivia. My double will be hot on your heels."

Morgan and Bronwyn stepped back while Olivia moved up to the door. She gave them both a quick look, then nodded her head and burst into flames. Her fiery, smoldering form slipped through the door, and just as Morgan was about to say something, Bronwyn's double took shape, moving to attack the insectoid. Morgan nodded and rushed into the hall, following a few paces behind.

The centipede-like monster was already barreling over the ground toward Olivia, but when the double came into range, it turned to swipe one of its many swords at it. Morgan cast Hollow Charge, surging over the smooth marble floor to smash his blade into one of the many limbs on the monster's left side. Bloodfang bit deeply, shearing through the carapace and nearly removing the appendage altogether. Yellow-green ichor sprayed from the wound, but Morgan didn't stop to examine the damage he'd done. He cast Azure Burst and then Void Stepped to the far, rear side of the monster.

It was surreal coming out of his teleportation to see the tail end of his Azure Burst still expanding and blasting against the monster. Several of the legs on that side of its body were destroyed, and Morgan could see flames licking along the cracked carapace on its thick, contorting body. The monster hadn't noticed Morgan's new location; it was twisting back toward the mirage double, or what Morgan thought was the mirage double. Both versions of Bronwyn were busily hacking at the monster's limbs with gleaming jade hatchets.

Morgan lunged forward, driving Bloodfang into the monster's tail and casting Void Wave. Crackling, reality-distorting black Energy expanded from him, completely obliterating several of the monster's legs and mangling a wide swath of its rear quarter. Morgan knew the attack would get the creature's attention, so he backed up, lifting Bloodfang into the Crane Defends the Nest. The massive creature whirled its segmented body with a whoosh of displaced air and brought three of its sword arms down at him with a combined smashing strike.

Morgan's defensive form dealt with two of the blades, but the third slipped under his guard and smashed into his ribs. He was sent sprawling over the marble floor but felt almost no pain—his new armor had mitigated the blow nicely. Morgan rolled to his feet, eyes on the colossal monster, watching as it moved toward his new position.

The creature wasn't nearly as nimble as it had been. Its tail end was in ruins, and its oozing yellow-and-green guts were still leaking from the partially destroyed segments. More than a dozen of its legs had been hacked short and were spreading ichor all over the floor, and while it was fixated on him, Bronwyn and her twin were hacking apart more of them.

Morgan pointed his sword at the approaching horror and wound up a Vortex Lance. Just as it lifted its swords to strike at him again, the spell finished and blasted out in a percussive hammer blow to the monster's top left shoulder, ruining the joint and causing one of its sword arms to fall limp. Morgan waited for the last second as the blades started to descend on him again before he Void Stepped to the rear quarter of the monster, just above the ruined portion.

He saw Olivia on the far side of the hall from his new vantage, moving slowly back and forth while fireballs chased her, exploding harmlessly around her. With his big-hitting spells on cooldown, Morgan cast Energy Drain and started to hack into the creature with Bloodfang.

His vigor surged as he pulled a thick stream of black-tinged, caustic Energy into his pathways, devouring it with his Vortex Core. Hunks of chitin and meaty insect innards began to fly as Bloodfang really went to work and carved a huge gouge out of the monster's abdomen before it finally broke away from whatever distraction Bronwyn and her double had caused and brought its remaining swords to bear against him.

Morgan used his crane forms to block most of the sword blows. His silvery armor saved him from many gashes, but one of the blades smashed his sword aside and glanced off his skull, leaving a deep cut that hurt and bled like hell but didn't crack the bone. By then, his Azure Burst was off cooldown, so he cast it again, the blue wave of fiery Energy catching the boss insect's humanoid torso and most of its sword arms in the blast, destroying chitin and flesh and knocking the massive creature back.

Something tickled the back of his mind, and Morgan used Hollow Charge to streak away along the monster's flank just as it reared up and smashed its girth against the space where he'd been standing. It struck so hard that the marble cracked with a thunderous concussion, and it seemed to have dazed itself. Just then, with a sizzling explosion of blazing light, Bronwyn brought the might of the Summer fae to bear, and the enormous, chitin-covered monstrosity writhed in the burning beam. The column of sunlight seemingly erupted from the ceiling of the high hall, shining down on the centipede man and cooking its shell and the innards within.

In the stillness that followed, the whoosh and impact of the fireballs on the far side of the hall became a lot more noticeable. Morgan knew then the creature must not be dead, or those would have stopped. He jogged forward to the toppled front half of the monstrosity, lifting Bloodfang for a coup de grâce, aiming to relieve the horror of its round, bug-eyed head.

Just as he brought the blade down in a mighty hack, the giant insect stirred and snapped out with its mandibles, catching the blade in a death grip. Bloodfang's edge cut deep into one of the pincers, but the creature held fast and pummeled Morgan with sword blows from its three remaining arms.

He held his left arm up, trying to block the haphazard swings from the dying monster at least enough to protect his head, while he jerked on his sword, trying to pull it loose. He knew the smart move would be to release the blade and dodge back out of the monster's reach, but he stubbornly held on. He jerked and pulled, and then a smoking, whistling missile tore into the chitin of the monster's head, smashing a fist-size hole through one multifaceted eye and bursting out the back in a shower of yellow droplets. The missile clattered over the marble floor, and Morgan realized it was a smoldering black hammer.

The sword arms twitched and fell limp, and the mandibles released Morgan's sword. He looked back over his shoulder to see Bronwyn whooping and pumping a fist. She held out her right hand, and with a loud smack, she was holding the smoldering hammer again. Morgan turned to Olivia and saw her gliding over the ground toward them, still in a fiery form but no longer bombarded by fireballs.

"Hell yeah! Nice shot, Bronwyn!" he yelled, backing away from the enormous corpse while waiting for the sign that Energy was gathering.

Just as Olivia and Bronwyn approached, he saw it: little twinkling lights gathered around the body, slowly growing into large orbs of purple-gold Energy that merged to form a cloud. The cloud began to flow toward the trio, splitting into three thick streams, then Morgan was impaled by one, lifted off his feet, and flooded with euphoria and vitality.

\*\*\***Congratulations! You have achieved level 34 Void Adept, gained 8 Intelligence, 8 Will, and have 12 points to distribute.**\*\*\*

"Did you guys level?" Bronwyn asked.

"Yep," Morgan said.

"Me too!" Olivia's face was flushed and excited, back in her human form.

"Damn, Morgan, what are you up to?" Bronwyn asked.

"Thirty-four." Morgan walked to the side, skirting the giant corpse. Sure enough, a large chest had appeared near the far doors. "Chest time!"

"Guys, I'd like to take some time to rest and go over attributes and talk strategy. I think I'll try to destroy this corpse as much as possible so we're not camping by a giant, rotting body." Olivia gestured toward the chest. "Why don't you go over there while I cook this thing? I'll try to drive the fumes away with Wind Gust."

"Right, but we won't open it until you've checked it out," Bronwyn said.

"Yeah." Morgan nodded, doing his best to avoid stepping in any yellow bug guts.

He looked at his attributes and decided to spend his extra points on vitality. His strength and dexterity were nicely balanced and at decent levels, and his agility was outstanding. He seemed to keep getting himself into positions where things were beating on him, so he figured being sturdier could never be bad. That done, he turned to Bronwyn and asked, "What attributes are you focusing on?"

"Well, the Summer Queen talked me into improving my mental stats. I mean, she told me how they affect my Energy levels and kind of taught me a lesson through experience about how important will is. I'm taking a break from boosting my strength and agility and pushing those up a bit."

"Sounds smart."

"I mean, don't get me wrong. I'm still putting some points into my fighting stats, but my will and intelligence are getting a big chunk every level now."

"How many free points do you get?"

"All of them. Twenty-eight."

"Holy shit! That's cool! The class is one designed by the fae?"

"Right!"

"Seems like a big benefit. What do you give in return for all that?"

"Oh, come on! We've talked about this. I'm working for the queen." Bronwyn's face grew flushed and irritated, like she was expecting Morgan to start lecturing her about something.

"Relax." He held out a placating hand. "I'm not judging. I just want to know more about you and your situation. What if she asked you to kill Olivia?" Morgan sat on the marble floor in front of the chest and watched while Olivia sprayed crackling, flaming blue plasma all over the corpse of the giant sword insect. "Speaking of swords," he muttered, then yelled, "Olivia! Don't destroy the swords!"

"Morgan, that was an asshole question!" Bronwyn said, finally. "The Summer Queen wouldn't ask me to do something like that. She promised she'd never ask me to do something that would go against my heart."

"Your heart?"

"She has a way of speaking; it's almost like poetry. Anyway, she wouldn't do that."

"Alright, I believe you. You're not worried she might lie, though?"

"Didn't I tell you guys the fae can't lie? They can hold back information or tell you truths that serve their interests, but they can't directly lie."

"How do you know?"

"She told me. I know how that sounds." Bronwyn sighed explosively and sat down. "I felt it, though. I can't describe it any better, but I knew she wasn't lying."

"Alright, alright. Goddamn, those spells are impressive," Morgan said, watching as Olivia's plasma reduced the corpse to a bubbling black puddle and she drove the fumes away with gusts of wind. Every so often, she would stoop to pick up one of the swords, tossing it to the side on a large charred expanse of marble she'd already "cleaned."

He stood up. "I'm gonna go check those swords out, okay? Don't be mad about my dumb questions, all right?"

"I'm not mad. I hope you can meet her someday, Morgan. You'll see what I mean."

He nodded and walked over to the pile of swords, careful that Olivia could see him so she didn't spray any fire his way while she cooked the guts and insect blood splattered all over that side of the hall.

## OLIVIA

Olivia cast one last Wind Gust, driving the fumes and smoke toward the far side of the hall and out through the open doorway. The bubbling black tar—all that was left of the massive corpse—had cooled enough to stop smoking. Sighing happily at a job well done, she turned to Morgan.

"Are they any good?"

"Hmm?" He swung one of the six identical swords back and forth. "They're tough and sharp. I'm not sure what metal they're made of, but they don't seem to be enchanted. I'll take them to someone who knows more, I think."

"Sounds good. Shall we see about that chest?" She glanced over to where Bronwyn sat eating a sandwich beside it.

"Yeah, I'll charge another gem while you check it out."

He strolled over to sit near Bronwyn while Olivia followed. Once again, her Surveying Breeze revealed hidden runes and lines of Energy on the chest, and she carefully used a sharp knife to scratch out some of the runes. When the Energy pathways faded away and she felt it would be safe to open, she sat on the chest and waited for her friends to finish what they were doing. Bronwyn had made her a sandwich, so she picked up the little wooden plate and started munching on it.

"This is good, Bronwyn, thank you," she said around a mouthful of sourdough, veggies, and creamy sauce.

"No problem. I'd say we earned a hearty lunch after that effort." She nodded toward the black pool on the far side of the chamber.

"Rald would love this bread," Olivia commented, taking another bite.

"He's the big Shadeni in your cohort?"

"Right." Olivia frowned slightly. "I'm going to be really late getting back to school. I hope they don't give my spot away or kick me out."

"Fat chance, you goofball. They're lucky to have you, and they know it. Didn't you say the headmistress or whatever was going to change your schedule so you could get more one-on-one time with higher-tier professors?"

"Yeah, she did. And, not to sound conceited, but I think you're kind of right about them not wanting to lose me—I earned a lot of points with the administration when I completed the Proving Grounds."

"Exactly! You'll be fine, but I bet your friends are going to miss you. Especially Adaida," Bronwyn said, smirking slightly and giving Olivia a crooked smile.

"Oh hush, now." Olivia took another big bite, throwing Bronwyn an exaggerated scowl.

"God, how am I supposed to concentrate with you two carrying on?" Morgan chuckled, picking up the charged gem from his plate and storing it away. He looked around, disbelief on his face. "You didn't make me a sandwich?"

"I was going to! I just got distracted eating mine and watching Olivia while she tickled that chest."

"Tickled?"

"Yeah, with your little wind fingers." Bronwyn giggled and pushed her loaf of bread and ingredients toward Morgan over the blanket she'd spread out.

"You should be a writer, Bronwyn! You have a very figurative way of viewing things," Olivia said.

"Well, better a writer than a chef because this is terrible service," Morgan joked, scooting over to the sandwich supplies.

"Morgan, when you're done eating, can you scry Arthur? I want to see what's going on in First Landing," Olivia changed the subject.

"Yeah, sure, but what if he's in the bath?"

"Oh God!" Bronwyn burst into laughter.

"Great point!" Olivia shook her head, smiling broadly. "You look first and close the window if you see something like that!"

"Oh, so I have to sacrifice my sanity? I get it."

Morgan looked at his sandwich piled with veggies and slathered with Bronwyn's creamy dressing, then snapped his fingers. He stared into space for a minute and produced, presumably from his storage ring, a package of sliced, smoked meat. He piled it on top of the veggies.

"Hey! You're ruining your veggie sandwich!" Bronwyn glared at him.

"Well, not really. The veggies are still there."

"How many gems do you have now?" Olivia asked.

"That one makes thirty-two."

"Gosh, we'll need to stop and really buckle down on those if we ever want to get out of here. I think you'll need more than two hundred if you're ever going to cast that portal spell."

"Do you have the spell done?" Bronwyn asked.

"Almost. I just need to integrate his scrying spell with the portal to give it a target location."

"Well, if it takes me an hour per gem, considering my regeneration rate, and we do it for twenty hours a day, we could be ready to try the spell in less than ten days."

"Yep. I say we take a vote after we loot this chest. We could camp in this room, gather the gems necessary, and portal home, or we could continue into this dungeon, risking God-knows-what," Olivia said, looking from Morgan to Bronwyn and meeting each of their gazes.

"Alright, after the chest." Bronwyn nodded, standing up and brushing crumbs from her pants.

"You sure you got the trap?" Morgan asked around his half-eaten sandwich.

"Yes, there were two more runes to deface than the last chest, but I'm sure I got them all." She stood and turned to look at the chest. "I'll open it. You two should back up for safety, just in case."

"Alright," Morgan grunted, standing up, sandwich in hand. His shiny metal armor was so flexible that it didn't seem to restrain his movements at all. "Guarding you anyway," he said, walking back a few paces.

Olivia didn't think he needed to, but she figured it was better safe than sorry. He'd only take half of whatever damage came her way if his explanation of the skill was accurate. Bronwyn also moved back, and Olivia turned to lift the lid of the chest.

It didn't surprise her when it opened with no explosions, but the contents were another matter. She caught her breath as she saw the glowing silver orbs hovering over several intriguing items.

"What are those?" Bronwyn asked in a hushed voice, having quickly slipped beside her when the chest failed to explode.

"I don't know!" Olivia replied.

"They look like advancement orbs, at least in their shape and the way they hover. Issa and I found some in dungeons; they give you an instant level. The ones we found were golden, like pure Energy, though," Morgan explained, quickly grabbing Olivia's wrist as she reached for one of them. "Hold on. You can't move or store them if they operate like advancement orbs. Once you touch it, the effect hits you."

"Alright, well, let's see here," Olivia said, pulling her hand back and leaning to scrutinize one of the orbs closely. "It's silvery, and within are tiny motes of black that are in constant motion. I don't detect any runes. What does your Void Vision tell you, Morgan?" She glanced at him; his eyes were black as he stared into the chest.

"First of all, there's a rainbow of bright Energy in that chest. The orbs are . . ." he trailed off as he leaned closer. "The orbs are brimming with potential, but their actual Energy signature isn't that bright. I get a feeling of . . . possibilities."

"That's weird," Bronwyn said.

"Well, who wants to touch one first? I'll go," Olivia offered.

"Hold on! You're always risking yourself; you're not responsible for us, you know," Bronwyn said, stepping forward and looking Olivia in the eyes.

"I know," Olivia sputtered. "I never meant to give that impression. I just . . . I don't know. I just care."

"You're not the only one," Bronwyn replied softly, reaching out to squeeze Olivia's wrist.

"Ahem," Morgan interrupted. "Well, what do you want to do? Draw straws?"

"No need," Bronwyn spoke with a wicked grin, reaching into the chest and grabbing one of the orbs.

"Bronwyn!" Olivia reached out but was too late.

Bronwyn suddenly straightened, her eyes focused a million miles away, as silvery Energy flooded through her arm and into her body. Olivia watched as it spread, illuminating her exposed skin and shining out of her eyes. Bronwyn started to topple backward, but Morgan caught her and gently laid her on the marble. He and Olivia stood over their friend, watching as her body began to vibrate, and steam started to rise from her in thick white-gray gouts.

"Is her race advancing?" Morgan asked.

"Is that what it looks like? I've felt it but never watched anyone; my cohort and I all did it together."

"Sort of. I definitely remember the steam and the passing out part. Issa said the steam is impurities leaving your body."

"It's so fascinating! The first thing I'm doing is checking out a book on this subject when I get back to the academy!"

"Gimme a pencil, quick!" Morgan said, holding out his hand. Olivia called out a pencil from her ring and handed it to him. Morgan began tracing Bronwyn's figure on the pale marble floor with a mischievous grin on his face.

"Haha, good idea!"

She bent down and put a hand to Bronwyn's forehead, hoping that she and Morgan were right about what was happening with her. Her skin was strangely cool on the surface, though a tingling buzzing sensation came to her from deeper inside. She wasn't sure if she was actually feeling something or if she perceived some sort of Energy activity.

She straightened up and looked at the line Morgan had drawn—was it possible Bronwyn was already growing over it or had Morgan angled the pencil under her?

"Jesus, she's already outgrown my line!" Morgan said, taking the pencil and starting a new outline.

Olivia watched Bronwyn's face, happy to see that the red-haired woman looked peaceful, her skin smooth and untroubled, even serene. While she watched her eyelids, noting the darting movement of her eyes beneath them, something caught her eye, and she reached down to pull Bronwyn's hair back from her ears.

"Holy shit!" she exclaimed, "Her ears are pointed!"

Ykleedra was stressed out. Her sisters' eggs had grown warm and started to form soft hatch lines along the hard shells, but her brother, *oh*, her brother's egg was something else. It was now more than twice the size of her sisters' and still coated in a thick, hard shell over every square centimeter. Would she be able to handle him when he finally emerged? If her sisters came soon enough, maybe they would be able to help her.

Part of Ykleedra wanted to ask Tiladia or the lovely blue lady for help, but she was still scared of what they'd do. Everyone seemed nice to her, but she'd read about how her people had been treated by the other races of this world. What if they killed her siblings out of fear?

She glided between some damp ferns, several large, ripe fruit clutched in her tentacles, and slipped down into her burrow. She ducked to avoid the big root sticking out of the roof of the short tunnel leading to the den and smiled when the cool blue light of her Energy orb came into view. The color was so much easier on her eyes than the yellow of the artificial sun in Morgan's atrium.

Her siblings were tucked into soft black soil along the back wall, and Ykleedra placed her burden around the eggs, piling them on top of other overripe fruit and soft, decaying meat—it was good to have a meal waiting and tempting her siblings forth. She'd read that in one of the texts also.

She moved over to the little bed of soft fern boughs she'd made for herself and settled down, folding her legs under her. The pouch Morgan had given her filled with magically fresh meats sat beside her, and she pulled out a large, raw, featherless bird.

Holding it between her hook palps, she lifted her robe with her tool tentacles and fed the fowl to her nether beak. It crunched through the flesh and bone, and a comfortable warmth spread through Ykleedra, originating from her lower abdomen. She sighed in pleasure and watched her siblings, wondering which would be the first to join her.

# BRONWYN

"What do you mean my ears are pointed?" Bronwyn slapped a hand up to her head and felt; sure enough, her ears were tapered to a definite point at the top.

"Not just that! Your eyes are . . . I don't know. The irises seem bigger and brighter; they're absolutely gorgeous!"

Olivia was kneeling in front of her, smiling broadly, and though Bronwyn found her beautiful and sweet, she was too stressed out to have her trying to placate her. She pulled away and scrambled to her feet, freaking herself out more when she saw her long, slender fingers and stood up to her full height, now only six inches or so shy of Morgan's towering height and slightly taller than Olivia.

"What the fuck?" she exclaimed. "Do either of you have a mirror?"

"Of course." Olivia pulled a hand mirror from her copper ring.

Bronwyn took it and stared at herself. She looked sort of like one of the tall, elflike fae. Her nose was a bit narrower than it used to be, but it still had its slight upward tip. Her lashes were lush, and her eyes were big—they glimmered a greenish yellow in the bright light of the hall. Her hair was fine but dense, and the color shimmered when she shook it out.

"Holy smokes," she said, pulling her full, pink lips back and exposing her teeth. They were white and straight, but her canines were longer than they used to be. "I look like a fae."

"Could it be your class? Your pact with the queen?"

"I don't know. She indicated that humans are somewhat descended from the fae. Maybe my racial advancements are drawing that out?"

"How many ranks did you get?" Morgan asked.

Bronwyn slapped her head before pulling up her status sheet.

Her eyes bulged at what she saw:

| Name: | Bronwyn Tallow |
|---|---|
| Race: | Human (Fae Bloodline) - Improved 2 |
| Class: | Summer Banneret - Epic |
| Level: | 22 |
| Core: | Summer Class - Base 6 |

"I gained a full ten ranks. I'm Improved Two now, and it says I'm a human with fae bloodline."

"Ten ranks?" Morgan's voice rose an octave in disbelief.

"Fae bloodline?" Olivia's tone was more interested than shocked.

Bronwyn started to pace, which is when she saw the outline of a person in concentric rings on the marble floor, each one showing a longer body.

"You guys were drawing lines around me? What the hell?"

"For science!" Olivia said, grinning.

She stepped forward to Bronwyn, gently putting her hands on her waist and forcing her to look into her eyes. Bronwyn, as always, calmed down when she saw those flickering flames behind her irises, and she felt a slow smile spreading on her lips as warmth radiated into her from Olivia's touch.

"Would you relax? This is good! I don't know everything about racial advancement, but I know you're going to be healthier now, you can gain more levels, and you'll live a very long time. Right, Morgan?"

"Yeah, that's right," Morgan replied. He'd moved over to the chest, eyeing the other two orbs with interest.

"Thanks, Liv," Bronwyn said, using the nickname she'd told her about from the academy. She impulsively leaned forward and kissed her on the forehead, and Olivia sighed softly, leaning into it.

"Well? We gonna take our medicine, Olivia?" Morgan asked, still staring into the chest. Olivia looked into Bronwyn's eyes and smiled, favoring her with a wink before she pulled away and walked over to the chest.

"I suppose so. Bronwyn can watch over us. I'm a little worried, though—these seem incredibly potent, and what if it digs out more of my elemental nature?"

"Aren't you still like ninety-nine percent human?" Bronwyn asked.

"I've no idea the exact amount, but I'd say my human percentage is overwhelmingly in the majority." She stood next to Morgan. "I won't shy away. This new reality we're all facing has dangers that we'll need to face if our people are going to thrive. Part of gaining power is advancing in every way we can; at least as long as we aren't harming others. Morgan, you go first. Bronwyn and I can help you lie down, and then I'll touch mine."

"Sounds good to me, and for the record, I agree with what you just said. I need to talk to you about a title I have, but we can discuss it later. Bronwyn knows what I'm talking about."

He glanced at her, and she smiled, giving him a brief nod.

Reaching into the chest, he touched his orb. Silvery light flared brightly, and then it was coursing into his body. He stood up straight and grew very still, and Olivia and Bronwyn each grabbed hold of his shoulders, gently lowering him down.

"I'm curious if he'll grow any more. He said he hardly did with his latest advancement," Olivia commented, drawing an outline around him with her pencil. He was steaming, but not nearly as much as Bronwyn had. She handed the pencil to her and said, "Do me, okay?"

"Oh, talking dirty?" She giggled, and Olivia blushed.

"Oh my gosh! You're bad, but save it for another time." She smiled, then leaned forward and stole a quick kiss. Bronwyn was about to say something but just sputtered instead. Her lips were like soft, warm pillows, and Olivia furiously blushed when she pulled away.

She reached into the chest and grabbed the orb, almost like she was using it to run away. Bronwyn hurriedly took hold of her shoulders and gently lowered her to the marble.

She took the pencil Olivia had handed her, and while steam—more than what was coming from Morgan—began to rise from her body, she outlined her. Bronwyn was distracted by the emotions and excitement she was feeling at Olivia's show of affection, but she couldn't help marveling at her fingers holding the pencil; they were so long and graceful, and her nails were so perfect and . . . sharp.

She sat down, legs crossed, watching her friends go through their processes. While she stared at Olivia, imagining what it would be like to snuggle up to her or hold her hand while they walked, her eyes were drawn to her copper ring. She started to get a feeling in the bottom of her stomach; it was a particular brand of dread, and it reminded her of one thing: Thun. She didn't know why, but something about Olivia's ring of storage called to mind the Winter Court. Was it the ring?

"Or something inside it?" she asked softly.

Suddenly, her thoughts were interrupted when Morgan cried out. He arched his back, eyes wide and mouth open in a silent howl, and then with an eruption of white steam, he was flung over onto his stomach, where he writhed as though he were in terrible pain.

Bronwyn jumped to her feet and went over to him, wondering what was going wrong, when she saw the steam was billowing from the center of his back. As she watched, it spread out into two long gouts of roiling white-gray clouds, but then it darkened at its center.

As the steam continued to darken, Morgan stopped thrashing, settling onto his stomach, his face now calm and turned to the side. When the steam lifted away, two massive black-feathered wings hung out and down, sprouting from the silvery plate armor at Morgan's shoulder blades.

"What the actual fuck?" Bronwyn knelt to feel one of the long, glossy black feathers, wondering if they were real or some kind of illusion. Sure enough, it was real. "You lucky jerk."

"Ykleedra?" Issa called, looking around the lush atrium. When the girl didn't reply, she started down the path toward the burbling sound of the little stream she knew was just ahead. When she came to the sitting area with the stone benches, she called again, "Ykleedra!"

"Yes, miss?" Ykleedra asked, her long legs pulling her out from between some ferns.

"Ykleedra, I'm going to have a dinner party tonight. I'd love it if you could come."

"Oh, a party?" The girl's odd, gray face didn't show much emotion, but her voice sounded intrigued.

"That's right! With lots of good food and people for you to meet and talk to!"

"Tonight? How long will it last, Miss Issa?"

"Just a few hours. Can you come?"

"I have . . ." The girl paused and looked around. "I have a project I'm working on and am afraid to leave it unattended for long. Could I leave early?" She ducked down on her long multijointed legs so she could bow her head before Issa.

"Of course! I want you to come and enjoy yourself, and you can leave whenever you want! I think Morgan would like to know you were meeting new people."

Ykleedra straightened up at the mention of Morgan, and Issa thought she saw a hint of a smile on her rigid face.

"Thank you, Miss Issa! I will come. Please have the dragon spirit tell me when it's time."

"I will, Ykleedra. Is there anything else you need? Do you need help with your project?"

"No, no." She shook her head, swaying on her front legs, and Issa was glad the female Yovashi wore robes; she'd heard their tentacles were rather disturbing to behold. "Thank you. I'm fine."

"Alright, see you tonight then."

Issa waved and turned, walking back out toward the exit. She heard a soft rustling sound, and when she looked back, Ykleedra was gone, just some twitching ferns betraying her passage.

\* \* \*

"Captain Gella, please wait here. Lord ap'Gravin will be with you in just a few minutes." The secretary gestured toward a plush couch near the bay window of the reception hall, and Gella nodded his thanks, sitting down with a heavy sigh.

He'd been on the ground less than an hour and could really use a good meal and a long night's sleep. The *Shrike* had been wind tossed and drenched for most of the night, and he was Ancestor-damned tired from wrestling with her rudder.

The couch was comfortable and the air warm, so Captain Gella found his chin nodding and his eyes growing heavy as he sat waiting in the silence. He shook his head and tried to stimulate his mind by thinking about what he'd say to Lord ap'Gravin. He dug his fingers into his tight uniform collar, trying to let some blood circulate through his itchy, strangled flesh. He was shifting uncomfortably, stomping one foot to get at an itch on his heel, when the receptionist finally returned and cleared her throat.

"Lord ap'Gravin will see you now."

"Thank you," he said, rising to his feet with a grunt. She led him down a short hallway and gestured to a partially open ornate door. Gella had been to see ap'Gravin many times, though never with such momentous news. He cleared his throat in advance of entering the lord's office, then stepped in.

"Close the door," ap'Gravin indicated sharply as soon as he passed the threshold.

"Yes, Lord." Gella turned, pulled the door closed with a heavy *click*, then turned to face his employer. Ap'Gravin was an imposing figure—an Ardeni man, well into the advanced racial ranks; he stood well over six feet in height. His eyes gleamed a bright, shimmery red, and his long mane of red hair hung down around his shoulders, glistening like cut Amber Ore. He'd also developed an interesting bloodline trait—sharp, gleaming black horns stood out from his forehead, and long, black nails tipped his elegant fingers.

"Well, let's have your report. Did you find the village that whelp at the academy came from?"

"Yes, Lord, and I bring good news!" Gella hurried forward and ducked his head in respect, waiting for the command to keep speaking.

"Go on; I don't want to drag it out of you." Ap'Gravin sat down, motioning with his hand in the universal sign to keep going.

"There are close to five thousand of the humans in their settlement. They were very open about their abilities, resources, and so on. They have a significant militia with rather ingenious weapons, but the highest among them wasn't yet tier two. I don't think things will remain that way, though, Lord. Our survey of more than three hundred revealed an average Energy affinity of nearly six." He paused to let that sink in.

"An average of six? They told you as much?"

"Yes, they were almost universally open about their attributes when we interviewed them. We, of course, helped them relax their guard by sharing false information about our own attributes and classes, and couched the interviews as a means for us to determine how best to help their community."

"How very intriguing. So this little phenom at the academy might not be all that unusual, eh?" Lord ap'Gravin tapped a black claw against one of his canines as he grinned.

"Yes, Lord. I had some thoughts on how you might capitalize on this situation—"

"Nonsense. I won't need strategic advice from you, Captain. I might require your services to transport my agents again, though."

"Of course, of course. My apologies."

"You say their most powerful representatives are still in tier one?"

"At least the ones present in the settlement. They spoke of 'heroes' who fought off an Urghat invasion, but they weren't present. Even so, I gathered only one of them was even tier two."

"Yes, I think a few tier four representatives should make recruiting rather easy. How many passengers can your ship carry?"

"Twenty comfortably, sir. Forty or so uncomfortably."

"That won't do. I'll need you to pilot one of my grand clippers. I won't be happy unless we take their top thousand. No, two thousand."

"I think that should be doable, sir, especially if you send some of your high-tier agents to demonstrate their might. Promises of wealth or knowledge will work on many."

"I said I won't need your strategies, Captain." A slight growl entered the lord's voice.

"Apologies," Gella said quickly, bowing low enough to scrape his forehead on the desk.

"Very well, Captain. Enjoy a short break in the city. I'll send word when one of my larger ships is in port."

"Yes, Lord!"

Gella pivoted on a heel and smartly strode from the room. Once his back was turned, his lips curled into a smile, and his mind raced with visions of wealth. He'd managed to stay on the mission, and now, he'd be part of the recruitment. He'd be assured a portion of the bounty for each *recruit*.

# ॐ MORGAN ॐ

Morgan stood awkwardly, trying to figure out his balance with two enormous, completely foreign appendages sprouting from his back. He glanced over to where Bronwyn and Olivia sat, talking animatedly about their experiences. Olivia glanced at him, smiling reassuringly when she caught his gaze. She'd come through the racial advancement with only a few noticeable changes—her eyes smoldered more brightly, she was a little taller—though still shorter than Bronwyn—and just more beautiful overall.

"Lucky," he muttered, barely catching himself as one of his wings twitched without warning.

He looked at his status sheet again, wondering why he'd gotten a bloodline designation and Olivia hadn't. Right there, under his name, it said, "Human (Anemoi Bloodline) - Advanced 2." He didn't even know what *Anemoi* meant, but Olivia said it had something to do with Ancient Greek mythology. She couldn't remember their role in the pantheon precisely, but she thought she remembered them having something to do with the wind.

They'd talked in circles trying to make sense of everything. Maybe Olivia would get a bloodline at Advanced rank. Maybe not. Perhaps it only came out if it was particularly strong in an individual.

Were the Anemoi really a type of human or fae hybrid? Were they some other elder race? Were other mythological beings rooted in reality, originating from a time when Energy was on Earth? All they had were questions, though Olivia said she thought she'd be able to find a lot of answers back at the academy. If they ever got back.

Morgan concentrated again and tried to flex his wings. He could feel and move them, and they were incredibly strong—nothing like you might imagine new, never-before-used limbs would be. The problem was in controlling them. He supposed it was like getting your first pair of legs as an adult. Trying to walk might come as a challenge, and the wings were no different.

When they were furled, folded on his back, they were alright; he felt like he had a living backpack on. When he unfurled them and spread them, if he didn't anticipate their movement, they knocked him off balance. When he flapped them and drifted off the ground, his heart raced, and he wobbled and panicked and fell to the marble floor. He'd only tried once.

"Morgan, you wanna see what else is in the chest?" Bronwyn called.

"Yeah, but shit! I need to get a feel for these wings. At least enough to keep from knocking myself over every time I accidentally twitch one." He growled, almost doing exactly that when he turned to reply.

"Alright, we can wait awhile!"

Bronwyn sat back down next to Olivia, and they held their heads together, talking quietly. Morgan couldn't hear them, but he saw the smiles on their faces, and a paranoid part of himself wondered if they were laughing at his predicament. Another part of him was glad they were happy.

"All right, you unruly bastards," Morgan told his wings, bracing his legs and slowly unfurling them. They had to be impressive, each stretching ten or so feet from behind his shoulders. He decided to try walking around with them wide open, then in every state between open and furled. Once he managed pacing back and forth in the enormous hall, he changed things up, doing the same thing with only one wing at a time, and so on.

Morgan realized he was taking a long time, but he couldn't imagine going into another fight and having to worry about twitching a wing and knocking himself over. Bronwyn and Olivia had moved on to their own distractions and didn't bother him, so he decided to keep working on it.

Hours later, when his shoulders and back were aching from the efforts and his stomach was starting to growl, Morgan decided to take a break. He was confident he could, at the very least, keep his wings folded and not worry about involuntary spasms. He'd even managed a few gliding leaps, covering dozens of feet and catching quite a bit of air. He was starting to get excited about the potential the wings symbolized.

When he walked back over to the chest and his two friends, Olivia looked up and said, "That was looking a lot better, Morgan!"

"Yeah, it's going to take some work, but I'm starting to see the possibilities."

"Do you think you'll be able to, like, really fly?" Bronwyn asked, looking up from her hatchet. She'd been adorning the haft with a glimmering, multicolored Energy bead that Morgan knew was one of Olivia's.

"Yeah, I think I will. I'm scared to flap again while I'm in the air, but eventually, I'll have to get the nerve to practice it."

"Do you think you're lighter than before? When that orb drew out your bloodline, did it make your bones hollow or something?" Olivia asked.

"God. Good question. I don't know." Morgan shrugged.

"Come here," Bronwyn said, standing up. Morgan looked at her quizzically but took a step over to her. She smiled at him, then wrapped him in a hug. He wasn't sure where the affection was coming from, but he wouldn't complain. He reached his arms around her to hug her back, but then her arms tightened and she grunted, lifting him off the ground. "Good lord, he might be lighter than a normal person his size, but it wouldn't be by much!"

She dropped him back to the ground and let go, laughing.

"Jeez! I thought you were going to hug me!"

"Awe." Olivia laughed. "Poor guy!"

"Alright, alright. Let's see what's in this chest." Morgan walked past Bronwyn and looked into the marble chest. He noticed, right away, another piece of the armor he was wearing—a helmet. Next to the helmet was a glittering, multifaceted blue gem the size of a baseball, and next to that was a folded bundle of silvery chain mail.

"What do you think?" Olivia asked from where she sat. "I'm interested in the gem, not any of the armor."

"I figured I'd check out the chain mail since the helmet looks like it matches your armor, Morgan," Bronwyn added.

"Sounds like you guys have it sorted out. I'm fine with that," he said. "Who wants to go first?"

"Bronwyn," Olivia said.

"Olivia," Bronwyn spoke at the same time. Morgan looked from one to the other and snickered.

"You go, Bron! If we only get one item, you need armor more than I need a gem!"

"But—" Bronwyn started, but Morgan gave her a shove.

"I agree. Get some armor other than that shitty spiked leather stuff you've been wearing. I'm always afraid I'll bump you and get a tetanus infection."

Bronwyn sighed and tucked her long hair behind an ear, moving hesitantly to the chest. She looked from Olivia to Morgan again, then reached in and lifted out the gleaming chain mail. It was silvery and sparkled in the white lights shining above them. She let it unfold, hanging from her hands, and Morgan saw that it was just a hauberk, though it had long sleeves and looked like it would protect her all the way down to her thighs.

"Good news, the other items are still there," she announced.

Tugging the chain mail hauberk on, she struggled to pull her thick mane of hair through the neck hole. After it was hanging loosely off her shoulders, she held a hand against it and concentrated. It glimmered and shrank to fit her body, forming itself around her curves. "Moonsteel Chain Hauberk," she said. "It has similar enchantments to your plate, Morgan. I can barely feel that I'm wearing it!"

"Nice." Morgan leaned into the chest and picked up the helmet. It was light and looked like it would cover the top of his head, making him worry about how it would stay put, having no strap or anything. He studied the mirrorlike metal finish and the silky blue padded interior, and reckoned it would be comfortable if nothing else.

"That armor is gorgeous, Bronwyn," Olivia complimented, still looking at her friend.

Morgan shrugged and put the helmet on top of his head. It was too small. Touching a hand to the top, he channeled some energy into it, and it immediately slid down over his skull. He felt it expand down the back of his head, over his ears, and remarkably, over his face. The only thing he noticed as it covered it was a slight dimming of the bright overhead lights and the faintly hollow sound of his breathing.

"Morgan! That's cool! Your whole face is covered by metal, even your eyes. Can you see?" Bronwyn asked.

"Yeah, I see just fine, and hear too. Does it look cool?"

"Oh my gosh, he's worried if he looks cool, Bronwyn." Olivia giggled.

"Yeah, it looks cool, Morgan," Bronwyn replied, also laughing.

Morgan chuckled at himself, then felt around his neck where the helmet met with his breastplate. Sure enough, the two pieces had melded together, just as his vambraces and breastplate had. Like with the other parts, he had an intuitive feeling for how it worked now that he'd bonded with it. He touched the smooth faceplate, gesturing upward, and it receded away, leaving his face exposed.

"Now we can see your pretty blue eyes," Olivia said with a teasing grin.

"Watch out, or I'll tell Issa you're flirting with me," Morgan replied, deadpan.

"Oh, she knows better than that," Olivia dismissed, nonplussed.

"Yeah, good point. Well, see what your gem is!" He gestured to the chest and held out a hand to help Olivia up.

She grabbed it, and he pulled her to her feet before backing away, watching as she picked up the big blue gem. She turned it over a few times, studying it closely, then shrugged. Morgan, watching with Void Vision, saw her trickle a little Energy into the item. Her eyes went very distant, and she stood still for a long time. Morgan saw as gold bursts of excitement emanated from her before he turned off his Void Vision and watched as a slow smile crept over her face.

"Well?" Bronwyn asked, leaning close to her.

"It's a history. It's filled with images and narratives about the city where we found this dungeon. Guys, it tells about the peoples' destruction and why this dungeon is here."

"Thank you for accompanying me back to the atrium, Tiladia. I had a wonderful time at Miss Issa's party," Ykleedra said as the spirit whirled about her, following her to the entrance of her burrow.

"You're quite welcome, Miss Ykleedra. I wonder why you felt you had to leave so soon?"

"I'm working on a project, and I didn't want to leave it unattended. I hope to surprise Morgan with it when he returns."

"Perhaps I can be of some assistance?"

"No!" Ykleedra hissed, then recovered herself. "No, Tiladia! I want to surprise you too. Please wait until it's ready before you come in. I'll tell you when, okay?"

"Of course, Miss Ykleedra. Please call upon me if you need anything at all."

With that, the spirit spun and departed the atrium, and Ykleedra sighed, turning back to her burrow. She felt terrible about deceiving Tiladia; the dragon spirit had been nothing but kind and respectful and had taken painstaking measures to be sure never to intrude on Ykleedra's privacy. Was she doing the wrong thing by not telling her about her siblings?

"No, I don't think so," she whispered as she examined the eggs.

No, eggs were too easy to destroy. People would be more sympathetic when they had to look into her sisters' eyes and hear their cries. Let them come into this world, and then Ykleedra would seek guidance from someone, perhaps Tiladia, or maybe the human woman, Maria.

She wondered about Tiladia. How much could she sense? She was part of this tower and seemed to know when someone was outside the door. Were the eggs too inert to draw her attention? Would she notice when the children came forth from their shells?

"If so, I'll beg her to be discreet. I'll explain my love for you. She'll understand—she told me about her children and how she'd guarded her eggs with her life . . . does she already know about you?"

She gently felt the eggs with her tentacles, gauging their warmth, trying to sense her sisters' moving within. One of them felt warmer than the others, and Ykleedra held onto it for a long while, thinking positive thoughts and hoping she'd be able to make all of this work somehow.

She was just turning to go to her nest when the egg shuddered and, with a delicate crackling sound, a wet, sleek, black bit of chitin poked through the shell.

# ⚛ BRONWYN ⚛

"Wait, so what are these creatures called again?" Bronwyn sat cross-legged in front of Olivia, drawing on a sheet of paper while listening to the stories and descriptions Olivia read from the blue crystal.

"The first ones to arrive on the planet were called 'Rehavash,' which was a colloquial term that meant walking nightmare." Olivia's eyes had a blue glaze over them as she looked into the crystal. She said it was like a fancy database UI with folders filled with images, firsthand accounts, and even histories of the people that used to live in the world where they'd found the portal.

"And they killed everyone?" Morgan asked, eyes closed as he charged another crystal.

"No. Are you two listening? It started when some mages from Unu, the world where we found this dungeon, were trying to open a permanent gate to another world. They had allied with the people from Inisellia and wanted to have a standing portal for trade and travel, rather than using the City Stones and paying the exorbitant fees the System extracted. They, um, missed and opened the portal to what they called Ruqeel, which is a term that's synonymous with hell."

"Then what?" Morgan asked.

"Well, the first thing to come through was one of the flying Rehavash, a big one. The person who wrote the report said it was tier eight. Morgan, that thing you thought was a dragon was probably one of them."

"Oh, shit."

"Yeah. It destroyed the city and killed everyone who didn't flee, and they had some strong Energy users. After that, more and more of the creatures flooded through, and the high-tier ones were smart; they started attacking other cities, breaking the System City Stones. The more powerful people who could create portals or afford the System rates to travel off world fled ahead of the Rehavash. Those unable to flee were slaughtered."

"And the city we found?"

"That's where things get really interesting. There were some heroes there, in the city of Nightmarch—high-tier Energy users that built wards into the walls and held off the Rehavash for a long time. They used most of their wealth to help citizens flee the world through their City Stone, but some of them, led by—get this—Keeper Te'quil refused to abandon their world."

"Keeper? Like my armor?" Morgan knocked his knuckles on his breastplate.

"Exactly, and my crown—Nightmarch."

"Well, keep going!" Bronwyn urged. "What did they do?"

"Alright. Ahem, Keeper Te'quil and dozens of others created this dungeon after they'd evacuated as many people as possible. They *literally* put their souls into it. The monsters are creatures that came from Ruqeel, and the treasures are gifts from the heroes. This gem has kept track of time since the dungeon was made; it's been thirty-eight thousand years."

"Is there more?" Bronwyn asked, her voice hushed. She suddenly felt like she was sitting in a cemetery.

"There's so much more! This gem holds accounts of tens of thousands of years of history for the various peoples of Unu. I'm barely scratching the surface of the most recent entries—the narratives of their destruction." Olivia's eyes lost their blue sheen, and she blinked rapidly, apparently done reading from the gem for now. "We're so lucky the Rehavash were mostly dormant or gone when we showed up!"

"Yeah, no shit!" Morgan agreed, popping his newly charged gem into his storage ring.

"Why a dungeon?" Bronwyn asked.

"It was a way to get the System to help protect their legacy, I'd guess," Olivia answered.

"Makes sense," Morgan said. "I mean, the System will help them generate or duplicate loot and keep the dungeon from disappearing. I doubt we're the only adventurers who will ever pull one of those history gems from a chest."

"Which brings us to the next big question: do we stay here and watch Morgan grind out more Energy crystals so we can make a portal home, or do we keep exploring the dungeon?" Olivia looked from Morgan to Bronwyn, and Bronwyn felt like she knew what Olivia wanted to do.

"You want to keep exploring, don't you?" she asked.

"I do. The people who made this dungeon were far more powerful than anyone I've met on Fanwath, and they gave up everything to create this legacy. I'm curious."

"I feel better about extending our stay now that I know Issa's doing alright, but I still want to get back. I'm torn," Morgan said. He was sitting on the chest, his folded wings hanging behind it. He'd had a small fit when he'd tried to sit on the ground and the wings kept getting in his way.

"What about a compromise?" Bronwyn suggested. "We could camp here, practice our skills, and give Morgan enough time to fill as many gems as we'll need. Then, we can try to push on into the dungeon. If things are too hard, we can just leave."

"It would give you a chance to get better with your wings, too, Morgan," Olivia added.

"Yeah, that sounds good, actually. Nice plan, Bron." Morgan's smile seemed forced, but Bronwyn could tell he was relieved.

"Can you scry Arthur now? I want to get a look at things back home," Olivia asked Morgan.

"Yeah, hang on. It takes two thousand Energy, and I'm still low from that gem I filled," Morgan said, standing up and stretching. "Gimme like twenty minutes."

"C'mon, Morgan. Let's spar a little while we wait." Bronwyn stood up, brandishing her two hatchets.

"Sounds good; I can use the exercise."

"Just weapons! No Energy," Bronwyn admonished, flipping her hatchets in the air and deftly grabbing the handles.

Morgan just nodded, and then they were at it. Bronwyn knew he was holding back; his sword skill was at the Advanced tier, and she still hadn't moved past Improved with her hatchets. Still, she gave him a good run for his money, making him work hard to stay out of reach of her dual blades.

Fighting with two hatchets seemed like a no-brainer; she blocked with one, hacked with the other, or alternated them in hacking motions. She kept wondering if she'd get a dual-wield skill, but so far, she hadn't. Either it didn't exist or she hadn't gotten good enough to trigger its acquisition. Maybe there was a specific type of movement she needed to do, but she wouldn't know until she spoke to an expert or found a manual on the Town Stone back home.

After a good sweaty workout, Morgan announced that he had more than enough Energy to do the scrying spell. Olivia stood up and came over as Bronwyn hung her hatchets on her belt. They watched Morgan while he concentrated for a moment, then the weird crackling destruction of air, sound, and light filled Bronwyn's ears and she grimaced, moving to look over his shoulder.

In the space between Morgan's outstretched hands, she saw Arthur sitting at a tavern table, drinking from a foaming mug. Maria Rios sat across from him laughing, the corners of her eyes crinkling with lines while she rocked back and forth.

"Huh, who knew Arthur could be so funny?" Morgan smirked.

"Well, at least we know things must be going okay. I doubt Arthur would be drinking and laughing it up if the colony was burning down," Olivia said.

"Yep!" Bronwyn smiled before moving away. She didn't want to be close by when Morgan closed the window; she hated that sound almost as much as when he opened it.

\* \* \*

Issa walked along the smooth brick pavers leading from the cobbled road to the new clinic the humans had constructed. She admired the rows of flower beds some green-thumbed volunteers had planted along the path.

It was quieter over here, on the western edge of the colony, and she was glad to be out of the bustling, jostling crowd that seemed ever-present around Bronwyn's Hill. She smiled at the name—the council had officially named the hill in commemoration of when Bronwyn had planted the Colony Stone.

She liked the idea of a clinic—a place for doctors to gather to see patients in one area. In Tarn's Crossing, doctors had their own offices, and while that worked fine most of the time, she thought it was nice to have one central location for those who needed medical attention. This way, if the doctor someone wanted to see was busy, maybe there'd be someone else to help. Or, in Issa's case, if she had no idea who to speak to, hopefully the right person would be at the clinic.

The glass-paneled double doors were propped open to let in the fresh summer air, and as Issa walked into the lobby, she was greeted by a friendly dark-skinned woman with a name tag on her shirt reading Sherlene.

"Hello," Issa said, unintentionally putting a hand on her belly before catching herself. She nervously moved it to her hip, sliding her palm on the fabric while she continued, "Um, is there a physician I can speak to about childbirth?"

"Childbirth?" The woman stood up and moved around the corner to approach her. "Are you pregnant, miss?"

"Issa, my name's Issa, and yes, I think so."

"Issa, I've heard that name! Aren't you one of the heroes who saved us from the Urghat?" The woman warmly took her arm and directed her over to the little grouping of sofas on one side of the reception area. "Don't you worry, sweetie. I'm going to go and find just the right doctor to speak to you."

"Thank you," Issa replied with a relieved smile. She sat on the mustard yellow couch, admiring how it was firm but giving, and just the right depth for her long legs. She grew up being average-size, at least for an Ardeni, and her new height had taken some getting used to, especially when it came to furniture and doorways.

The woman disappeared through swinging double doors in the back wall, and Issa sat quietly. She closed her eyes, letting the sun warm her face and breathing in the rich fragrances of grass, flowers, and the occasional whiff of food being cooked that drifted on the breeze through the doors. She was startled out of her reverie when a soft, feminine voice spoke.

"Issa?"

"Oh, yes?" Issa's eyes popped open, and she blearily blinked up at the small, black-haired woman. She wore a white coat over tan-colored pants and a pale blue blouse, and had an exceedingly friendly smile on her rather plump, round face.

"I'm Dr. Cho, Issa, and I'll be so happy to answer your questions today. Won't you come with me?"

"Yes, thank you!" She stood, towering over the little woman.

Dr. Cho held out her hand, and Issa took it, gently returning the squeeze.

"This way," she indicated, leading Issa back through the swinging door, down a short hallway, and into a small room with a tall, padded table and two chairs. Dr. Cho pointed to one.

"Have a seat. You can speak freely here; this room is quite private." She then shut the door and sat down in the other chair. "So, tell me, what brings you in?"

"Well, as I was telling your receptionist, I'm fairly sure I'm pregnant, and I'm not sure you know, but my mate is human. Morgan Hall."

"Oh?" Dr. Cho's eyes widened, but her smile didn't falter. "How exciting! Imagine! How strange that we'd be so compatible considering the vast distances between our worlds!"

"Yes, but I'm very happy for it," Issa said softly.

"Of course you are! Of course! Still, we should be sure of things, don't you think?"

"Yes, that's why I came here. I also wanted to talk to you about help with the birth when the time comes."

"I wouldn't have it any other way. Now"—Dr. Cho reached out and took Issa's hand—"I don't have half the equipment I used back on Earth, but I do have some exciting new skills. I spent a lot of time tending to injuries and helping with exposure to poisons and toxins in our new environment here, and when I reached level ten, the System gave me a Healer class. One of my skills allows me to diagnose my patients. Would you mind if I used it on you?"

"No, of course not. That's why I came," Issa said.

"Right. Okay, dear, let's get you up on the table."

She stood up and motioned to the tall, padded table.

"You want me to lay down up there?"

"Yes, I want to do a physical examination as well. Nothing invasive, sweetie; I'm just going to press on your abdomen a little."

Issa stood and awkwardly hopped up on the surface, lying flat on her back with her legs still hanging off the edge.

"This table is such a nice work of craftsmanship—far nicer than the mass-produced stuff we had back in my old clinic. Watch this," Dr. Cho said, then she slid out a recessed extension under Issa's legs so they were supported comfortably. "Isn't that nice?"

"Yes. Did someone craft that here?"

"Yes, one of our very own—Tom Hollins. He's making quite a name for himself, crafting furniture. Alright, relax now while I get a look at you. Sorry if my hands are a little chilly."

Dr. Cho gently lifted Issa's blouse and rested both of her warm hands on her belly. She moved her fingers around very gently, pressing into her abdomen slightly. A moment later, Issa felt the telltale warmth of Energy being used, and then Dr. Cho's faint smile grew very wide, her bright teeth gleaming as she leaned over Issa.

"Oh my goodness, sweetheart! You have two very healthy little babies growing inside you!

## OLIVIA

While Morgan and Bronwyn sparred for maybe the thousandth time in the last week, Olivia sat on her pile of animal furs—Morgan and Bronwyn both had a disturbingly large supply of them—and practiced expanding and retracting her fiery aura. Ever since she'd received the massive boost in her racial levels from the silvery orb, she'd felt the fragment of her elemental nature far more clearly and had a great deal more control over its aspect.

Not only was she able to expand the aura, but if she really concentrated, she could increase the shimmering flames' temperature. She wasn't doing that now—Olivia had no desire to scorch the furs protecting her butt from the ubiquitous marble flooring.

The whole racial advancement thing was fascinating to her. Morgan and Bronwyn had both gotten bloodlines added to their racial status, but Olivia hadn't. She didn't know if it was because of her connection to the primal elemental within her or if her ancestry was simply more mundane than her friends'.

Other factors were also creating more questions than answers. For instance, she still had several ranks more than Bronwyn, but Bronwyn had grown taller than her. Was it her fae bloodline? Were they all simply reaching a certain peak, determined by their DNA? Morgan hadn't grown any taller but had gotten wings and seemed leaner. Olivia could only imagine all the possible variations humanity had buried in their genetic code.

With thoughts like those buzzing around her mind, Olivia had started keeping a log of the changes she and her two companions had gone through during their various racial advancements. It had been interesting hearing Morgan's account of creating the elixir that had advanced him to Improved and how he'd been out of commission for so long. The orbs the three of them had absorbed must have been extremely potent, and Olivia wondered if it had to do with the dungeon being so old and created by such powerful people.

Bored with her current activities, Olivia shrank her aura down to nonexistence and pulled out her Spellcraft textbook. She'd been working through all of her texts in the hours they'd spent in the large, bright hall. While Morgan charged gems with Energy, and he and Bronwyn sparred, Olivia studied. She still got in some exercise—Bronwyn was a very competent hand-to-hand combatant and took an hour or two each day to help Olivia practice grappling. She didn't fancy herself a fighter, and she never expected to win a fight that way, but she figured it never hurt to exercise, and it gave her an excuse to spend more time with Bronwyn.

She glanced over at the tent they'd set up, and a smile flickered over her lips. It had been Bronwyn's idea to put up tents; they had no control over the bright lights in the hall and, as such, needed the structures overhead to get any sleep. It didn't hurt that she and Bronwyn shared one while Morgan slept on his own. Her smile turned to embarrassment as she imagined Morgan listening to the soft sounds that must have been coming from her tent while she and Bronwyn perfected their make out game—embarrassing but worth it.

After Olivia managed to get focused on her book, she read through a chapter or two before switching to artificing. The last third of the book dealt with magical contracts, which Olivia found fascinating. The idea that you could create a contract signed with each party's Energy signature that magically enforced the terms brought to mind a great many possible applications. Employment contracts, lending contracts, sales contracts—the possibilities were endless.

Of course, it also raised a lot of concerns. What if the two parties were at a disparate level of status or means? Would it be possible to trap a needy employee into an unfair contract enforced by magic? Was there any oversight or regulation on such things?

While practicing writing Energy contracts and other spell diagrams, she'd grown frustrated with her ability to actualize the images in her head, and she realized her dexterity attribute was holding her back. She added her free attribute points to dexterity, but didn't know if it would be valuable in the long term—would she need to create spell patterns and magical documents when she was high level? She hoped so because she rather enjoyed it.

She'd practiced making one of the magical contracts with Morgan and Bronwyn; they'd made an agreement about who would make dinner for a week because Olivia wanted to practice adding in an expiration component.

It had been strange to feel the tug of Energy on her Core when the time came for her to make her meal, and she'd tried to resist it. A shiver of cold had started to clamp on her Core, and the longer she held out, the more severe it became. She'd given in after postponing for an hour, just to see what it felt like. None of them had been able to resist the contract terms for long; once you'd grown accustomed to Energy and had it coursing through your body—quite literally sustaining it—that deprivation became almost like having air denied to your lungs.

Morgan had found the experience valuable and commented that it was good to know what it was like. He'd also added that he couldn't see himself ever entering into a binding Energy contract. Olivia was inclined to agree, but she didn't need anything right now. What if someone offered her a valuable bit of knowledge in exchange for a task or short-term employment?

"It's possible," she told herself.

"What's up, bookworm?" Morgan asked as he and Bronwyn approached their makeshift camp. They were both sweaty and breathing heavily.

Morgan took his usual seat on the fur-covered chest; he still hadn't figured out an easy way to sit on the floor with his wings furled. He'd gotten a lot more comfortable with them, though—taking short flights around the room and agilely using them to leap and dodge during combat practice.

"Just reading about more complicated contract provisions," Olivia replied, smiling and lifting her chin as Bronwyn leaned down for a quick kiss. Morgan, to his credit, didn't say anything. Instead, he held his hands out in front of himself and created a rip in reality so he could look at Issa.

"You know, every time you do that, you're adding more time to your Energy regeneration. Which, you know, adds more time before you can see her for real," Bronwyn said, plopping down on the furs near Olivia.

"Yeah, but I'm only human!" He narrowed his eyes at them. "No cracks about my wings, alright?" Looking back at his scrying window, his brow furrowed. "She's in that doctor's office again. You guys think something's wrong with her?"

"Do they look upset?" Olivia asked, just as she had the first time he'd seen Issa on the exam table.

"No, they're smiling and laughing." Morgan nodded, his face more relaxed.

"She's an alien to the people in First Landing. Maybe she volunteered for them to study her or something," Olivia added.

"Yeah, she's fine, Morgan."

Bronwyn had spread a towel out in front of herself and was setting down sandwich-making supplies.

"Sandwiches again, Bron?" Olivia sighed.

"Hey, it's my turn, and I like sandwiches!"

They'd all agreed to share one meal a day, even though Morgan had said he could probably go a week between meals. They had plenty of supplies left, and an end to their exile was in sight—Morgan had more than two-thirds of the gems charged up and ready to try with Olivia's portal spell. Meanwhile, she'd spent some time over the last week perfecting the pattern, polishing its design by removing redundancies, and streamlining it.

"Speaking of which," Morgan said, closing his window with a crackling snap. "I've got to use the restroom." He stood and walked to the far corner of the hall where they'd erected a makeshift curtain around a hole that Olivia had blasted through the marble with her Pyrosteam Drill. When she'd cut through the marble, they'd all been rather weirded out by the black expanse that opened just a foot or so beneath the dungeon's structure.

"Don't fall in." Bronwyn laughed.

"Good one," he drawled, flapping his wings and scattering Bronwyn's lettuce away from her as he bounded into the air.

"Jerk!" she called after him. She turned to Olivia and said, "Those wings are turning him into a monster!"

"Oh, come on, he's just messing around." Olivia flipped her text closed. "Now tell me, what kind of sandwiches today?"

"Arthur?" the woman asked, stepping up to his table at the tavern. She was wearing the uniform of the standing militia, the ones guarding the gates.

"Yes?"

"A man has come in through the northern gate; he's one of the ones who went missing back in the early days, and he has an entourage. He wants to meet with the council."

"Entourage?"

"Yeah, a bunch of those thin, winged folks, the, um, Ghelli."

"Oh? Who is the man?"

"Cal Jennings? Does it ring a bell?"

"No, I'm afraid not. Well, did you bring them to the council building?" Arthur wiped his mouth with his napkin and pushed aside his half-finished bowl of stew.

"Oh no, sir, but Sergeant Childs did. They're probably already there."

"Very well, thank you. I'm sorry, I've forgotten your name . . ."

"Kennedy, sir. Corporal Kennedy."

"Very good. Thank you, Corporal."

Arthur stood and briskly walked out of Green's Tavern. He turned to the right, waving to people who called out greetings, then marched up the street to the new council building.

When he arrived, he found Maria Rios already sitting down at the council chamber, speaking to a bearded, dark-skinned man with a cheerful face and gleaming white teeth. More to Arthur's interest, though, were the others seated around the table: a Ghelli woman next to the man Arthur assumed was Cal, an older, more petite Ghelli woman, and three Ghelli children—a toddler and a young boy and girl.

"Ahem," he said, walking up to the empty seat at the head of the table. "Pleased to meet you all; I'm Arthur Ballard."

"Well, hey there, Arthur! Long time no see! I'm Cal Jennings, one of the livestock techs from the *Pilgrim*. I've got a lot to tell you, but let me start by introducing my wife, Lysee, and her family."

"Yes, have a seat, Arthur," Maria said. "This is Lysee, her mother, Vella, and let's see if my memory holds up—Gelyss, Bren, and Vonna."

"Exactly so! Thank you, Miss Maria," the woman Cal had indicated as his wife said.

"Excellent. I'm pleased to meet you all." Arthur sat down, clearing his throat again and looking at Cal. "We assumed you were dead, I'm sorry to say, Cal. I'm so happy to have you prove us wrong! You must have quite a tale to tell."

"Well, I sure do! I was just getting started telling Maria, here. I can rewind, though!"

Cal had a genuine, effusive manner, and it made Arthur want to smile along with him.

"I was snatched up by a big ol' girl named Whitestar. She's one of those Urghat. She was going to bring me to her people and probably throw me in the stew pot, but over the course of a few days, I think my winning personality started to wear her down. She ended up dumping me in a forest up by those mountains north of here. That's when Lysee and her people found me."

He sat back, lifted the glass of water on the table, and took a long pull.

"Well, I'm certainly glad you won free of the Urghat. We've had some luck dealing with some of them, but they seem quite combative for the most part," Maria said to fill the air.

"Yes, quite," Arthur agreed.

"Right, well, I didn't really win free. Whitestar's an okay sort, I think. I hope she didn't wind up dead in the battle you all had."

"I wish I could tell you, Cal. Unfortunately, many Urghat died assaulting our walls, and I have no idea what any of their names were. It's really quite tragic." Arthur drummed his fingers on the table as he spoke, feeling a slight resurgence of the stress he'd lived through during the battle.

"Well, some hope is better than none," Cal said. Then, as Lysee reached up to gently squeeze his wrist, he continued, "Anyway, Lysee and some others were out foraging when they found me. They brought me back to their village, Shady Lee, and treated me real fine. I was kind of out of it for a while, having been nearly swallowed by a great cat monster."

"He was quite a mess, but his friend, Whitestar, had treated his wounds; he would have lived without our help," Lysee added.

"Well, long story short, Arthur, I ended up falling for Lysee here, and when I married her, of course I married her whole family. Well, I've finally talked them into coming 'round to meet my people, and I think we might settle down here for a while. I've begun to make a name for myself among the Ghelli as a Spirit Singer, and I think my talents might be appreciated here in First Landing."

# BRONWYN

Bronwyn lay on her side, watching Olivia sleep. She wanted to reach out and touch her cheek or gently fiddle with her hair, but she didn't want to wake her. She'd never been as close to anyone as she felt with Olivia, which was both wonderful and terrifying. She was starting to understand the agony Morgan had been in when they'd first been stranded by the teleporting pyramid. She could only imagine her stress if she were forcefully separated from Olivia and didn't know if she was safe.

Her eyes moved from Olivia's face to her pale shoulder and down her exposed arm on top of the blanket. They came to rest on Olivia's copper ring, and once again, Bronwyn felt a disturbing chill when she saw it. Something about that ring was antagonizing the fae in her.

She gently reached out and brushed a fingertip along Olivia's eyebrow.

"Mm, good morning," Olivia said, her eyes opening almost immediately at the touch.

"Hey," Bronwyn whispered, then leaned down to kiss her. Her lips were unbelievably soft, and just as always, Bronwyn felt an electric tingle at their touch. "I need to talk to you about something that's been bugging me."

Her face an inch from Olivia's, Bronwyn could tell the other woman was trying not to breathe with her so close. She smiled and pulled back.

"What?" Olivia's eyebrows turned down as her expression grew serious. "Something's wrong?"

"No. I don't think so . . ." Bronwyn wasn't exactly sure what to say, so she decided to trust Olivia with the simple truth. "You know I have a strong connection to the fae." She reached up and touched one of her ears. "I mean, more than just my bloodline—I'm connected to the Summer Court."

"Right . . ." Olivia sat up, pulling her legs in and crossing them under the blanket.

"Well, I told you about Thun, right? The agent of the Winter Court I killed? I told you about how nasty he was and how he had a dimensional container full of fae corpses."

"Yes. What are you getting at, Bron?" Olivia's face fell into a frown.

"Alright, well, he made me feel a certain way. Like, I knew he was my enemy just from being near him." Bronwyn paused for a minute, gathering her thoughts. "There's something about your copper ring that gives me the same feeling."

"What? My cohort ring?" Olivia reached down and twisted the band.

"Yeah. It's your dimensional container, right?"

"One of them," Olivia said, pointing at one of the two rings on her other hand.

"Do you think there's something in there that's connected to the Winter Court?"

Olivia narrowed her eyes, staring into the distance. A few seconds later, her eyes opened wide, and she produced—as if by magic—a dark blue piece of paper, slightly larger than an old-fashioned business card.

"Professor Somhairle gave me this! He told me he was descended from the fae! He approached me late at night once in the library, and the more I think about it, the creepier it seems!"

Bronwyn recoiled involuntarily from the card, leaning back away from Olivia. She hissed, "That's it! Liv, it's bad. I feel disgusted when I see it, and I can feel the cold seeping out of it! Don't touch it!"

"It doesn't feel cold to me." Olivia raised one eyebrow, studying the card. Then she looked at Bronwyn's face, eyes narrowed, and she drew her lips together. She held out her other hand, and suddenly, a crackling, roiling ball of blue electrical fire appeared above it.

"If it upsets you that much, I don't need to hang onto it." Very deliberately, she fed the card into the blue plasma ball, and it dissolved into wisps of blue smoke. A thin rime of frost formed on the fabric as the smoke hit the top of the tent. "There, that's done."

"You're so fucking amazing, Olivia!" Bronwyn said, leaning in to kiss her again.

The pressure of ill intent from that card had made her want to flee from it, and now it was gone, utterly destroyed by this remarkable woman just because Bronwyn had said it bothered her. Olivia returned her kiss, and they fell together onto the piled furs, Olivia giggling softly, probably worried they'd bother Morgan.

Captain Gella stood atop berthing tower eighteen and watched as the massive ship approached. She was a grand clipper class transport and certainly did justice to her name, *Skybreaker*. His own ship was a child's plaything in comparison, and he had to admit some excitement at the prospect of taking her helm.

A dozen dockhands were standing by, waiting to catch her tie-downs, and Gella marveled at the smooth precision with which her Energy cones kept her level as she glided up to the tower. Five hundred and forty feet, bow to stern, and seven decks, it was hard to imagine the Energy required to control such a magnificent ship.

He'd done plenty of jobs for Lord ap'Gravin, but he had to admit some surprise that he'd been given such an opportunity. Was it really his knowledge of the human colony that had earned him this spot, or was it his willingness to do as he was told and not ask questions?

He chuckled to himself—the answer was obvious.

The ship drew along the square berthing tower on her port side, and the deckhands threw her mooring lines over to the dockhands. They pulled the huge ropes, each thicker than a strong man's arm, over to the mooring winches. As they fed the lines into the Energy-driven mechanisms, they were pulled taut, and the massive ship was made snug against the padded tower dock.

With a shudder, the propulsion cones powered down, and the clipper sank a few inches as just the lift cones took over, holding her in place. The dockhands wheeled the boarding ramp over, and suddenly, the tower top was bustling with activity.

Gella stood there, his captain's jacket and tall black hat setting him apart from the sailors and dockworkers, and he waited for the ship's captain to find him. It didn't take long before a rather portly Ardeni fellow with a sloppily untucked shirt under his too-tight captain's jacket hopped down from the ramp and walked over.

"Captain Gella, I presume?"

"Good! Word reached you."

"Of course. *Skybreaker* has a powerful communication array."

His face was badly shaven, and his bloodshot eyes betrayed his previous night's activities. Gella handed him his commission paperwork, and the disheveled captain gave it a bleary-eyed review before handing it back.

"Very good, she's all yours. I can use the vacation." He turned to shout at a couple of deckhands who watched from the top of the boarding ramp. "Right! Gentlemen, bring my trunks! Make it smart, and first round's on me!"

He looked back at Gella and asked, "Anything else, Captain?"

"Well," Gella cleared his throat and pondered the colossal ship, "is there anything I should know about her?"

"Rear port thrust cone is charging ten percent slower than spec. I'd have it looked at before you leave; I think some of the Energy stones might be cracked. First Mate Reeja knows all that business, though. Really, just put in your orders, and the crew will run things smoothly. She's a hell of a vessel, and they're proud to call her home."

"That's what I like to hear, Captain. Enjoy your vacation; any idea what ap'Gravin has for you next?"

"No, I don't. I've been doing passenger runs so long that I'm a bit out of the loop on his other affairs. We'll see. I've been working for the ap'Gravin family for forty-three years, and they've never left me without a post for long. Good luck, Captain Gella."

With that, the frumpy, hoarse-voiced man turned and started for the lift, barking at the crewmen to "make smart."

"So you're Gella, hmm?"

A cold shiver ran down Gella's spine at the words, and he spun around to see the most striking Ghelli man he'd ever laid eyes on. He wore a tailored black suit with silver buttons, complete with a stylish bowler hat, and was tall, towering over Gella's five-foot-nine frame. His wings were stunningly large and glittered with the telltale sparkles and motes of Energy that signaled the man's advanced race. He could fly with those wings. More striking than his wings or height, though, were his eyes—pitch-black orbs that seemed to see through Gella.

"I am. Baron Finneal, I take it?"

"My reputation precedes me?"

"More so than mine does me, I'm sure. Lord ap'Gravin told me to expect you and a few others."

"Oh, please don't tell me I'm the first to arrive?"

"You are. I wasn't actually expecting any of you until this weekend. You must have made good time."

"Oh, I always make good time. Very well, I'm assuming you haven't sorted out the accommodations yet?"

"No, I haven't even boarded yet! I've got to go through the manifest and move some crew around. I'll be sure to give you a proper suite, sir." Gella knew better than to antagonize a man like Finneal.

"Yes, that will be good. I'll return on the morrow; I've business I can see to tonight." He didn't wait for a response, lifting lightly into the air and trailing a streak of glittering Energy behind him as he descended toward Gelica proper.

"Must be nice," one of the dockhands said, watching the man fly away.

"Watch what you say and what you look at with that one," Gella warned. "He's killed more people than you or I could count."

"Aye, Captain," the man replied. "Seems you always have to be careful around them high tiers."

"Just so," Gella said, walking toward the boarding plank. "Just so."

Ykleedra was panicking. Her sisters were more than she could handle, and she needed help. Her only question was who to ask for it. What if Miss Issa grew angry at her for deceiving Morgan? What if she threw her out of the tower? Could she ask Tiladia for help? Would the spirit know what to do? Would she report everything to Miss Issa?

Maybe she was overreacting. Things would get easier as they grew and began to communicate properly.

She looked at the mewling little creatures, their nether beaks lunging and snapping for more food. They were insatiable! She'd fed them a considerable portion of the meat Morgan had left for her already, and they weren't interested in the fruit she'd harvested. Why was that?

Ykleedra couldn't remember when she'd started eating fruit, but she thought she'd enjoyed it even as a little child.

"Hush now!" she scolded the mewling pack of long-legged little sisters. "You've eaten plenty already, and I've had to wash you all three times today!"

Every time she fed them, it seemed like they had to void immediately, and Ykleedra was starting to have trouble getting the smell out of the burrow. She'd had to replace the nesting material twice and rinse the area several times with water from the little stream, but it was a constant battle. What would it be like when her brother finally hatched?

Ykleedra was rummaging through the dimensional container Morgan had given her, looking for a suitably small treat for her sisters, when she felt a blinding pain from one of her tentacles. She yelped and hopped back, only to find one of her sisters had snuck up beneath her robe and snapped at her tentacle with her nether beak.

"You little monster!" she hissed, then hurried out of the burrow, leaving the mewling, crying creatures to their own devices. She didn't know where she was going or what she was planning, but Ykleedra knew she needed a moment alone.

She stopped by the little stream to dip her wounded tentacle into the cold water. As the wound grew numb and she felt some relief from the pain, Ykleedra felt her eyes filling with tears, and a sob escaped her.

She was in trouble, and she knew it. She couldn't keep things quiet here much longer, and she needed more food. Maybe she should take her sisters and her brother and flee. She could hunt outside—if she had a nice roladii carcass, that would keep her sisters busy for a full day.

"That's how I'll do it. I'll ask for help, and if Issa wants to hurt my sisters, I'll beg her to let us leave."

# MORGAN

"Morgan?" Olivia's tone was concerned, and her voice was loud. Morgan snapped his eyes up from the text and groaned.

"Ugh, this journal is disgusting, but it's like a car crash; it keeps pulling my attention. What did you say?"

"I said it's about time for you to charge another gem, right? What kinds of things are in there, anyway? It's the one from that guy who kidnapped Issa, right?"

"Yeah, let me get a gem started, then I'll tell you about it." Morgan fished another gem out—number one ninety-five, if he wasn't mistaken—and began charging it. He looked at Olivia, glanced over to where Bronwyn was napping, then cleared his throat. "Well, I started reading the journal hoping to find out where Blake was from or what sort of person he was. Like, you know, his race or species or whatever. He really did look human, and he referred to holbyis as sheep."

"But you're sure he wasn't?" Olivia asked softly, also glancing toward her sleeping girlfriend. Morgan wasn't sure that was the correct term, but they seemed like girlfriends to him.

"I don't think so. The more I learn about advanced races and bloodlines and all that, the less sure I become, though. But my main clue is that the System didn't recognize humans when it spotted our ship. I remember it saying something about 'integrating non-System entities.' The people we rescued said he'd been there for years, so yeah, unless he could hide from the System, I don't think he was human."

"Okay, and the journal?"

"Yeah, the journal. It's not about Blake but about his experiments. He's got detailed logs of all his attempts to isolate and distill racial traits. He was trying to make elixirs that he could use on himself to improve his race. He had some success over the years, and I think that's why I had such a hard time killing him."

"Success? How did he distill racial traits?"

"That's the horrific part—he treated people like livestock, breeding them, and when he saw a promising trait, he used alchemy to strip it, often killing the subject. I'm not going to go into more detail. Trust me; you don't want me to."

"How awful." Olivia shook her head, her eyes distant. "It brings to mind the evils committed during the Holocaust."

"Yeah, and the worst thing is, I think I have one of his 'successes.'" Morgan told her about the bottle of perpetually warm liquid he'd found with the journal.

"Oh, God! What are you going to do with it?"

"Well, I want to destroy it, but then I think, 'How many people died to create this thing?'" Morgan shook his head, frowning. He regretted ever finding and reading the journal.

"Down that road lies madness, Morgan. I think we should bury it, have a funeral for Blake's victims. Let's do it when we get back to First Landing. In the meantime, I'm happy to help you burn that journal."

Olivia's eyes flashed, and Morgan saw blue flames leaping behind her irises.

"God, that sounds good, but I have a thing about burning books. Although I've never had a journal from a psychotic, evil man before; I guess I could make an exception." He slipped the journal into his ring, though, and said, "Later. Maybe when we get back, eh? I wanna talk to Issa about it too."

"Hmm, alright." Olivia glanced down at the copper plate he'd set down to pick up the journal. "Done already?"

"Yep. A few more hours of this, and we'll be either trying to make a portal or going deeper into the dungeon."

"Well"—Olivia glanced at Bronwyn's sleeping face again, then back at Morgan—"I kind of want to get back. I'm nervous about what's happening with my status at the academy." She spoke softly, and Morgan got the idea she didn't want to admit as much to Bronwyn just then.

"You know how I feel. The sooner I can get back and tell Issa I'm alright, the better." He nodded toward Bronwyn. "When she wakes up, let's talk about it."

"Alright." Olivia sighed and sat back, leaning on her elbows. She had her legs outstretched and crossed at the ankle. She'd told Morgan about her boots and robe, and he had to admit—she looked like the real deal. She looked like a bona fide sorceress, ready to challenge a demon or something. He snorted softly to himself and closed his eyes, waiting for his Energy to regenerate.

Ykleedra gave her sisters another pair of skinned feyris, noting how her dimensional container was almost empty. She'd wanted to hold out as long as she could to give her sisters a chance to grow and gain control of their impulses before showing them to Issa, and she'd made it another few days, but the meat was almost gone.

She'd finally given in and named them, choosing the names of her mother's sisters and cousins. She'd never met any of them, but she'd heard many tales.

She studied her sisters while they ate, starting with Tvalla, admiring her pale blue-gray skin. Then her gaze fell upon Gvon and her natural black nails and nether beak. They were sharp and hard, harder than Ykleedra's. Pkril chirped and purred her soft growl while pulling a piece of thigh meat away from Gvon. Finally, there was little Ykerli, calmly waiting for her larger sisters to back away and see what they had left her. Ykleedra liked her the most, and it wasn't just because of her similar name.

Ykleedra sat back and smiled. She could almost do it. If she just had a little more help, she was sure she'd be able to raise these girls. Time was up, though. She could feed them once or twice, and then they'd start to starve, and what kind of sister would allow that?

Time to face her fears.

She watched Ykerli clean up the scraps, including the bones, and smiled. The others didn't know what they were missing; bone marrow was the best part.

A sudden crunch from the other side of the burrow startled her, and Ykleedra glanced toward her brother's enormous black-and-red egg. There, wagging slowly in the warm air as if to gauge the quality of the air, was a shiny, taloned forelimb.

Her brother was coming.

"Bron, c'mon!" Olivia said, stepping after the angry redhead. She grabbed her wrist and pulled until Bronwyn stopped stalking away.

She whirled on her, eyes flashing.

"I know! I'm being stupid. Of course we should go back. I just . . ." She glanced at Morgan, then huffed out a breath and continued, "I was having fun! Okay? I'm selfish. I know when we get back, you're going to leave. You'll be back at the academy, and who knows what the Summer Queen has planned for me next."

"I get it." Olivia reached up and put a hand behind Bronwyn's neck, pulling her head down to her shoulder. "I'm sorry, Bronwyn. I'm having fun with you, too. We can't put the rest of the world on hold, though. It's not fair to anyone."

She said other things, too, but Morgan couldn't hear without really trying, and he didn't want to be a creep. He could understand Bronwyn's feelings. She was here with someone special, and they were basically getting an extended time-out away from all the other demands and pressures they felt. Suddenly feeling impulsive, he cleared his throat.

"Hey, how about one more? Let's just do one more boss, then get the hell outta Dodge."

"Really?" Bronwyn pulled her head away from Olivia's shoulder and looked at Morgan with wide eyes. "You don't mind?"

"Nah, I just watched Issa taking a nap; things are good with her. What's another couple of days?"

"What do you say, Liv?" Bronwyn looked back at Olivia, but the answer was clear—Olivia wore a bright smile, and she met Morgan's gaze for a moment before hugging Bronwyn.

"Okay, I like the idea of one more. Maybe we'll learn something important from the Keeper and his friends."

"Great!" Bronwyn said, pulling away. "Let's go in the morning, then!"

They'd taken to calling the time when they woke up "morning," even though there wasn't any night or day in the dungeon.

Morgan and Olivia agreed, and he resigned himself to another evening of meditation while he tried not to look bored as Olivia and Bronwyn got lost in each other. On the bright side, he'd gained another two levels to his Core, and he was pretty sure Olivia and Bronwyn had only gained one.

He chided himself for being petty.

"Hey, how about I cook a specialty?" he spoke. "It's a stew Issa taught to me when we first entered the Swordmaster's Citadel. I have just enough of the ingredients."

"Oh, that sounds good, Morgan. It's not your turn, you know?" Olivia said, always the stickler for routine.

"Yeah, I know. I want to do something nice for you two—we're not going to be stuck together much longer."

"Thanks, Morgan!" Bronwyn exclaimed, pulling Olivia to sit next to their camp stove on a thick pile of furs.

"My pleasure, but you guys have to provide the entertainment. I heard a rumor," he said, utterly deadpan.

"What rumor?" Olivia asked, and Morgan knew he had his victim.

"I heard you could sing. Like really well."

"What? Who told you that?"

"Hmm, I don't hear you saying it's not true," Bronwyn piled on.

"Well, my only extracurricular was the choir. But I don't like performing on demand! Morgan, how'd you find this out?" Olivia looked outraged, and Morgan started to laugh.

"I made it up! Lucky guess. Well, c'mon, what are the odds someone from your social strata never took a music or voice lesson?"

"My parents weren't rich!" Olivia's voice cracked a little at her perceived betrayal.

"Don't tease her, Morgan!" Bronwyn said, pulling Olivia in under the crook of her arm.

"Oh, come on! I'm just guessing and making shit up. Don't be mad, Olivia. If we promise to sing along, will you lead us?"

"Yeah, please, Liv?" Bronwyn asked, nuzzling her forehead into Olivia's hair.

"Oh, alright, but you two have to sing with me!"

"Better pick a popular song, then." Bronwyn grinned and gave Olivia a little shove to give her space.

---

Captain Gella looked down from the bridge of the *Skybreaker*, his gaze passing along the main deck, past the escape buoys, and falling upon the trio of ap'Gravin's high-tier agents—Baron Finneal, Haku-dak, and Tanna ap'Cilla. Any one of them could kill a hundred tier-two Energy users like him.

"Them types make me nervous, Captain," Reeja said, running a thumb under his belt to give his prodigious girth a little breathing room. Gella looked around to be sure no one else was within earshot, then nodded curtly to the first mate.

"They should, Reeja. They should. Do yourself a favor and don't let others hear you talking about them. Too many empty pockets need filling these days, and I wouldn't be surprised if a harmless complaint like that got back to them with a few embellishments."

"Right. Just so, Cap'n, just so. They'll be debarking for the mission in a couple of days anyway, eh?" He gave Gella an exaggerated wink like he had some idea what was going on.

"Aye, and we'll be sticking around to give 'em and our new passengers a lift back, so don't go burning any bridges."

"What's this First Landing like, anyway? I never been this far out into the frontier—ain't much cause for passenger vessels out here."

"It's a frontier town, really not a bad place at all. The humans seem to know what they're doing when it comes to setting up a civilization. They're friendly and have good food, too."

"Right, right." Reeja drew a few of his long whiskers between his thumb and forefinger. "And what do we need the big hitters for?"

He gestured to the trio standing out on the deck, watching the clouds rush by.

"That's above my pay rate, which means it's way above yours, Reeja. Go holler at the chef, will you? I'm hungry for fowl this evening."

"Right, Cap'n. Been meaning to stop by the kitchens anyhow."

He rubbed his belly as he grinned, lumbering in his peculiar rolling gait toward the stair leading to deck two. Gella smiled; the man seemed oafish, but he was well-liked by the crew and knew the ins and outs of the *Skybreaker*. He was glad to have him along.

Once again, his eyes drifted to the trio of tier-four mercenaries out on his deck, and he shook his head. If only he could say the same about them.

# MORGAN

Morgan stood, panting and sweating, over the corpse of the blade abomination. Thanks to Bronwyn's tracking, he knew they were called something else, but they looked like giant ants with swords for legs and humanoid heads. Blade abomination seemed to fit just fine. He and his two companions had been clearing passage after passage of the monsters, so many that they'd already each gained another level.

"God! I hope that's the last of them. Where's the next boss, anyway?" Bronwyn groused, kicking at the monster's four-foot bladed leg.

"I don't know, but I could use a break. We've been at this for hours. Days?" Olivia leaned back against a white marble wall, rubbing her forehead, the incinerated remains of another blade abomination just to her left.

"No, definitely not days. Close to a day, though," Morgan said. He was feeling alright and knew Olivia was being dramatic—she had nearly as high an Energy affinity as he did, so she'd be replenished from victories just like he was. "How's the map looking? Any idea what we're missing?"

He walked over to her and waited while she pulled out the notebook where she'd been mapping the corridors they were clearing.

"Let me see." She traced the neat lines with her finger. "This area here is suspiciously blank. There's a door up this hallway we haven't been through; it might lead down there."

"All right. So back this way"—Morgan pointed to the map—"then up those steps and to the left." He sighed and stretched. "Let's have a sandwich before we get moving, hmm?"

He looked around for an argument, but neither of them said anything. Bronwyn was already putting a hand to her necklace, presumably looking for her sandwich ingredients.

"Yeah, while we snack, let's go up the ramp a bit, away from these stinking corpses."

Morgan led the way, and they all sat at the top of the sloping passage, taking turns with the ingredients to build their lunches. "Hah, I keep thinking of this as lunch. I guess because we've been working hard and we're taking a break. It feels like a lunch, doesn't it?"

"I guess. If people worked forty-hour days." Bronwyn snorted.

He chuckled and wolfed down his sandwich before waving his hand over his face to activate his helmet's visor. Standing up, he leaned against the wall, Bloodfang in hand, waiting for Olivia and Bronwyn to get the hint and finish. He'd agreed to fight one more boss, but the process was taking a lot longer than he'd intended, and he was starting to get anxious.

"I'm going to scout a little ahead," he said, voice echoing out of his helmet. "Meet you at the junction up this way."

Olivia nodded, and he moved off—better to give them a little space than stand around, making everyone tense. They'd already cleared the area, so when he got to the junction where another abomination's corpse slumped against the wall, he sighed and cast Void Window, concentrating on Issa.

The sizzling, popping gap in reality opened between his hands, and he saw her standing in his tower, near the atrium, talking to Ykleedra. Ykleedra had grown. Not a lot, but even with her legs folded in close, she was as tall as Issa.

Not for the first time, Morgan wished he could hear what was being said through the scrying spell. Still, it was good to lay eyes on Issa, and he was pleasantly surprised to see Ykleedra looking healthy; he hadn't spared many thoughts for the young Yovashi, but he did feel some responsibility for her.

"I ought to, seeing as I killed her family," he said, gripping his sword with a grimace.

While he watched, Issa's head jerked toward the atrium glass, and her eyes widened. She looked at Ykleedra, and it looked to Morgan like she was yelling or exclaiming. Ykleedra backed up a step, shaking her head and lowering her front legs in a show of obeisance.

"What the fuck?" Morgan asked, watching the silent drama unfold. Issa moved forward to Ykleedra, still speaking vehemently.

"Spying on your sweetie?" Bronwyn asked as she and Olivia traipsed up the hallway.

"Uh," Morgan let the window close, then he turned to Bronwyn. "Yeah, I guess so. She was having an argument with Ykleedra, I think."

"Your pet Yovashi?" Bronwyn scowled.

"Bron! She's a person!" Olivia admonished.

"I know, I know. I'm sorry, but I'll never forget that monster in the cave."

"That's like hating all humans because of, oh, I don't know, Dahmer or Perez."

"Jesus, do you have to bring Perez up?" Morgan asked. Even as out of touch as he'd been as a teen, he remembered the nonstop footage of the trial—Perez, the butcher of Europa Station.

"Well, it makes the point, doesn't it? You can't judge an entire species based on the actions of an individual or two." Olivia frowned from Morgan to Bronwyn.

"Of course, you're right. I'm sorry, Liv." Bronwyn reached out a hand, facing Olivia, and the other woman took it. They stood staring at each other for a minute, and Morgan sighed, turning to walk toward the unexplored doorway.

He found that he could remember details better now than ever in his old life. He could picture Olivia's map in his head, so he followed the turns back to the corridor with the three marble doors, one of which they hadn't opened yet.

He only had to wait a few minutes for Olivia and Bronwyn to catch up. They seemed to be done with their little dialogue, walking briskly and silently up to him.

"Ready?" he asked.

"Yeah, all set," Bronwyn replied, hefting her crescent moon–shaped green hatchets.

Olivia nodded, and Morgan leaned into the door, pushing it open. Like all the others before it, it slid silently and smoothly on invisible recessed hinges. A sloping marble corridor led up into the distance.

"My spatial awareness is pretty good, and I don't remember going up in that direction before," Morgan said, gesturing.

"Yeah, this is promising," Olivia agreed, peering up the slope.

"Alright, fingers crossed."

Morgan strode forward, his gleaming sword ready and his Core primed. He climbed the slope for a hundred meters before it leveled off, and he saw a massive double door ahead. Standing before it were three blade abominations, still too distant to react to the companions' presence.

Morgan didn't want to give them a chance to notice his approach, so he cast Void Step, suddenly appearing in their midst, then unleashed a Void Wave. He felt them struggle against its destructive Energy, fighting his assault with their will. They weren't a match, though, and their chitin began to crumble, flesh beneath dissolving, and their will to fight faded as the wave of nonexistence washed over them.

By the time Olivia and Bronwyn reached him, he was standing over the twitching creatures, draining their Energy. Bronwyn quickly moved among the broken, weak creatures and dispatched them with her hatchets.

"I'm not trying to take the glory if that's what you're thinking," Morgan spoke, looking between the two women. "I'm just sick to death of these damn things and wanted to kill them quickly."

"No complaints from me," Olivia assured him. Then she glanced at the doors and continued, "Those look like boss-room doors."

"Hell yes," Bronwyn said.

A surge of Energy from the dead abominations filled Morgan's reserves. A stream went to Bronwyn, and Morgan was surprised to see a thin ribbon flow into Olivia as well. It wasn't the first time he'd noticed that the System seemed to share out Energy to people working together, even if one or more of them didn't really participate in a fight.

"Well? I'm ready to see what's next. What about you guys?"

He looked from Olivia to Bronwyn.

"I'm all set. I have a little surprise for this one," Olivia said, tapping her black crown.

Morgan grinned and nodded. The crown was a very cool item, he had to admit, and it looked impressive. With her improved race and elemental highlights, Olivia looked like some sort of sorceress queen or fantasy demigoddess with that crown.

"Bronwyn?" Morgan asked.

"Yeah, sec," Bronwyn replied, concentrating, then her double shimmered into being right next to her. They both raised a hatchet, and the original said, "Ready!"

Morgan nodded and pushed open the left-hand door. Another massive marble hall appeared before them, and in the center stood a titanic marble statue of a bulky humanoid. Morgan glanced around the room, wondering if there were more fireball-launching tubes or other statues to be aware of. He didn't see anything on the floor or along the walls, but metal lines crisscrossed the ceiling, looking suspiciously like rails or tracks for something to slide along.

He followed them with his eyes and, tucked against the walls, so surreptitiously that one might mistake them for ornamentation, were little orbs with downward-facing tubes at their center. He saw a dozen on the left and a dozen on the right.

"You guys seeing those?" Olivia asked in a breathy whisper.

"Yeah," Morgan replied while Bronwyn grunted an affirmative sound.

"We've got this," he said. "Be aware of those things on the ceiling and be ready to dodge. Let's light this thing up."

"Literally." Bronwyn grinned.

She pushed the other door open, and with a nod from Morgan, she sent her double at the colossal statue. It towered forty feet in the air, each long arm the size of a tree, and Morgan knew they couldn't afford to let it hit them.

The three of them stepped into the room, and as Bronwyn's double closed the distance, the marble encasing the giant started to crack and fall away.

As massive sheets of stone crashed to the ground in thunderous cracking concussions, Bronwyn called her double away, afraid it would be crushed before even engaging with the monster.

"Good call!" Morgan yelled over the din.

"I'll send her back in after it's done shedding!"

"I'm going to flank! Watch the ceiling!" Olivia warned, moving to the left.

Morgan strode forward, watching the revelation of the monster. It didn't have skin; at least not like a person. Its exposed flesh was dark brown, spotted with black shiny patches—chitin or something between chitin and skin. Its head was bulbous and round, and a dozen wet, black eyes of varying sizes dotted its forehead. Pincers jutted from its wide jaw, and snapping claws were revealed when the marble fell away from its hands. This was some sort of humanoid relative to the giant tick they'd fought before. It made sense. Olivia had said the dungeon was populated with creatures from the same world.

As the marble stopped crashing to the ground, Bronwyn urged her double to attack. The titanic boss roared as it saw the little red-haired figure rushing toward its oversized, clawed feet. Morgan pointed Bloodfang at the center of the monster's round, smooth head and charged up a Vortex Lance. With a concussion and a swirl of Energy, the speeding projectile smashed into the titan's left cheek, blasting a hole in the thick skin and rocking its head back several feet. It roared again, whirling to face Morgan.

It took a ponderous stomp toward him, lifting a hand to deliver a hammer blow that would reduce him to a pulp. Morgan targeted its back foot and cast Hollow Charge. Racing over the ground, avoiding the smashing impact, Morgan held out Bloodfang, slicing a deep groove through the titan's heel and cutting deeply into its tendon. It screamed and lifted its foot to stomp, and Morgan used Void Step to relocate himself to the back side of the room.

He watched as Olivia suddenly swirled with wind and lightning and took on her air form, he wasn't sure why. Perhaps to boost her mobility. She fired spell after spell into the massive torso of the giant, blasting away bits of chitin and causing it to stumble and roar in pain.

He turned to Bronwyn and her double, no longer sure which was which; both were laying into the feet and ankles of the giant, carving long grooves and hunks of flesh away with their hatchets while dodging away from the stomping feet and slow, slapping blows. The giant roared and screamed in angry, pained outbursts.

Morgan was starting to think the battle would be easy, considering the monster's ponderous movements, but then something happened: a loud clicking report sounded from the ceiling, and the orbs were suddenly sliding along the tracks, bright beams of Energy shooting from their nozzles. They looked like magenta laser beams, and though they didn't tear up the marble, they didn't look like they'd feel good against the skin.

"Watch out!" he bellowed.

Bronwyn danced back from the giant, no longer hard to distinguish from her double which kept hacking at the titan's left foot. The beams were converging on the center of the room where she stood, and Morgan couldn't see an easy path around them. He cast Guard Ally on her and prayed she'd avoid most of the beams. Bronwyn's double suddenly disappeared, and Bronwyn's body flared with bright, golden light—her shield spell. Morgan hoped it would help.

He watched with white knuckles as she danced between the flashing, sliding beams of Energy, avoiding most of them by less than a hair's breadth. One of the beams grazed her arm, but her golden armor of light seemed to deflect most of the damage. The rest came through to Morgan and flashed brightly against his armor. He didn't feel any pain and grinned, realizing Bronwyn would be okay. As the beams began to slide toward the room's edges again, Morgan began to plan his next assault on the titan.

That's when things went sideways.

Her attention on dodging the last of the beams as they raced past her toward the room's perimeter, Bronwyn didn't notice as the titan lifted a massive foot to stomp her. Olivia screamed, and Bronwyn whirled, seeing the gigantic appendage falling toward her.

Suddenly, she stood up straight, her hatchets outspread, and shouted with the voice of crashing thunder, so loud that Morgan thought the world was breaking.

The entire room vibrated with the sound. Chunks of marble broke from the ceiling and crashed down while the titan stumbled back from the palpable sonic attack, flailing its huge arms for balance. A beam of crackling, blinding plasma the size of a telephone pole speared through the giant's chest, annihilating its flesh and organs and scorching the marble wall behind it.

Morgan followed the beam's trajectory to Olivia, who stood with her palms outstretched and her crown blazing with high white flames that shone like a supernova. Her eyes sparkled like little suns were burning within them, and her mouth was twisted in a snarl. He glanced back as the titanic abomination slumped against the far wall, gouts of black fluid pouring and bubbling from its quivering mandibles, and Morgan could see the insides of its chest where Olivia had hollowed it out. The titanic boss shuddered and jerked, then fell still.

Morgan looked from Bronwyn to Olivia and could only say, "Holy shit!"

# OLIVIA

Olivia fell to her knees and clutched her hands to her chest. She felt like her body was about to either burst into flames or explode. She concentrated on taking deep, slow breaths, even if the air burned her throat as though she were breathing fire. She could hear Morgan and Bronwyn talking, maybe to her, but it sounded like they were far away, and the roaring in her ears made their voices indistinct.

Ever so slowly, she felt the roiling, rampant Energy coursing through her body start to return to her Core or burn off into the air. Her breaths began to cool, the bright sepia of her vision returned to normal, and she sat back on her butt with a sigh of relief.

". . . okay?" Bronwyn asked, and Olivia became aware of her kneeling before her, gingerly holding out her hands like she wanted to grab hold of Olivia but didn't want to cause further harm.

"I'm okay, I'm okay," she said, her voice weak and hoarse. "The crown's surge of Energy was more than anything I've ever felt. It took me a minute to cool down."

"More like three or four," Morgan spoke. Olivia turned to see him standing just a bit to her left, a potion in his hands. "I was about to try forcing this down your throat."

"No need, no need. I'll be okay."

Olivia stood up, holding out a hand so Bronwyn could steady her. Bronwyn rushed to her, putting an arm around her for support.

"Brace yourselves," Morgan said, pointing to the slumped body of the titan. Orbs of purple-gold Energy were starting to form all over the gigantic surface of the monster.

Despite the proportion of the damage done to the titanic monster was in favor of Olivia, when the streams of Energy rushed toward the trio, they looked fairly similar in size. Olivia and Bronwyn were pulled apart as the surging Energy lifted them into the air, flooding their pathways. As always, the System-generated Energy was pleasing, even euphoric in nature—nothing like the coarse flood that had come from her crown.

Olivia closed her eyes and let the renewing effect of the Energy pour through her, filling her pathways, replenishing her Core, and permeating the cells of her body.

**\*\*\*Congratulations! You have achieved level 24 Elemental Paragon, gained 12 Intelligence, 12 Will, and have 12 points to distribute.\*\*\***

When she settled back to the ground, much relieved and refreshed, she said, "I leveled! Did you two?"

"Yeah." Morgan stooped to pick up the potion he'd dropped and put it away.

"I did!" Bronwyn announced, retaking Olivia's hand.

Looking into Bronwyn's bright eyes, Olivia suddenly remembered her under that giant's foot.

"How did you shout like that, Bron?"

"Yeah, you almost brought the whole place down!" Morgan said with a chuckle.

"It's one of my boons from the Summer Court. I can 'speak with the voice of thunder in times of great need.' Pretty cool, huh?"

She squeezed Olivia's hand, and Olivia pulled her into a hug.

"I thought you were about to be smushed!" she whispered, her throat growing tight with emotion.

"Is that why you blasted him to kingdom come?" Bronwyn asked, kissing her three times on her cheek, the corner of her eye, and the side of her forehead.

"Olivia, that crown effect was certifiably badass," Morgan said. "And Bronwyn, please, never yell at me like that." He laughed, turning toward the large marble chest that had appeared near the closed doors.

Winking at Bronwyn, he jumped and flapped his wings, launching himself into a glide toward it.

"What a show-off! Do you want to go see what we got?" Bronwyn asked her, squeezing her again.

"Yeah, I'm feeling a lot better. Come on, let me inspect that chest before Morgan blows himself up." Olivia took Bronwyn's hand and started after the tall figure in shining armor.

"It's not fair that he can fly," Bronwyn pouted, though a hint of a giggle hid beneath her words.

"Who knows what you'll get when you hit advanced race, though." Olivia squeezed her hand and smiled, glancing sideways to make eye contact.

"Doubt I'll have a flame aura like you."

"Hey, I can control it now; I hardly let it show!"

"Yeah, that's what you think."

"What? Really? I thought I had it suppressed most of the time now."

"Oh, you do. Except when you're casting or startled or moving fast or dreaming or embarrassed or—"

"Dreaming?"

"Yeah, when you're having a particularly interesting dream, the flames really start up!" Bronwyn's grin was wicked, and her eyes were glittering with amusement.

"You're lying!" Olivia stopped and stared at Bronwyn, trying to gauge if she was teasing or not.

"You'll never know!" Bronwyn laughed and pulled Olivia's hand to get her to start walking again.

When they stepped up next to Morgan, Olivia cast Surveying Breeze and saw that the chest, once again, was trapped with some sort of elemental blast. She spent some time defacing most of the runes until all the lines of Energy were dull, then she nodded. "I think it's safe now. Let's be cautious, though. Morgan, do your thing."

"Yep." Morgan nodded, backing up a bit. "I'm guarding you, Olivia."

"Back up, Bronwyn!" Olivia nudged her away.

"Alright, alright." Bronwyn moved back several feet to Morgan's left.

"More," Morgan said, giving her a push away from him.

"You guys are paranoid!" Bronwyn said but backed away even more.

Olivia nodded then lifted the chest. Nothing exploded and no lighting erupted, but a shower of needle-tipped darts erupted from the chest and tore toward her. As they impacted her, they flashed with blue light, and Olivia heard Morgan grunt as his silvery armor pinged a dozen or more times. Olivia whirled to see if he was okay, but he stood there, grinning, clearly unharmed.

"Paranoid, huh?" Morgan gave Bronwyn a pointed stare.

"Alright! I've officially learned my lesson." Bronwyn was holding both hands to the sides of her head, clearly dismayed by the additional trap.

"No harm done." Morgan strolled forward to peer into the chest, and Olivia did the same. Most of the chest's contents were obscured by three golden orbs about the size of golf balls hovering near the top of the opening.

"Are those what I think they are?" Olivia asked.

"Yeah, those are advancement orbs. It looks like we're getting another level before we go home."

"Really? They're an automatic level?" Bronwyn asked.

"All the times I've seen them, yes," he replied. "You can't save them, either. Once you touch them, the effect takes place."

"Well? Shall we?" Olivia asked.

Morgan shrugged, and Bronwyn nodded, so they all reached out for one of the golden orbs. Olivia felt the warmth of pure Energy enter her fingertips and then rush into her pathways, instantly suffusing her body. She arched her back, and a groan escaped her as the dopamine-like burst of well-being rolled through her.

***Congratulations! You have achieved level 25 Elemental Paragon, gained 12 Intelligence, 12 Will, and have 12 points to distribute.***

"Well, that was a fast level," Bronwyn said.

"You're not kidding." Morgan leaned forward to look into the chest. "Aha! Are those what I think they are?" He pointed to some shiny pieces of armor on the left-hand side of the chest, and Olivia thought they were probably the leg armor to match the rest of his suit.

"Yeah, I think so," she replied. "There's a book too, and what is that? A wand?"

"I think so." Bronwyn's voice was hushed, peering into the chest. "Morgan, you pick your armor first. Just in case."

"That alright with you, Liv?" Morgan asked.

He and Bronwyn had been using her nickname more and more frequently. She liked it, though it reminded her of Adaida, and she felt a pang of guilt thinking about the sweet, friendly Ghelli. She'd have to have a real heart-to-heart with her when she got back to the academy.

"That's fine. I think we'll be able to take all three rewards, anyway, seeing as this was a boss."

Morgan nodded at her words, then reached in and lifted out his armor. As he pulled it free of the chest, the container dissolved into a cloud of pink mist, proving her words entirely wrong.

"Oh shit!" Morgan cursed, a panic-stricken look in his eyes.

"It's not your fault." Bronwyn shrugged. "At least we all got the orbs."

"True. It's okay, Morgan—we all agreed you should get the armor. I hope it completes the set." While she spoke, Morgan's eyes went glassy, and she knew he was bonding with the new armor pieces.

"Yeah, it did! The description says 'complete set' now. Hang on." He held the steel shin guards to his legs. As soon as they were in place, they stretched and flowed over his thighs, upper feet, and groin, connecting to his breastplate with a tiny, flexible seam.

"Jeez, you're a regular knight in shining armor now." Bronwyn stepped forward and rapped her knuckles against Morgan's breastplate.

"Heh. Well, all these levels and treasures make me almost want to keep exploring this dungeon. *Almost*. A deal's a deal, though, right? You guys ready for me to make that portal?"

"Easy there, tiger," Olivia said. "I need to create the pattern on the floor, place all the Energy gems, and then you need to scry a safe location to open the portal to. It might take some trial and error."

"Safe location?"

"Well, your portal is based on void-attuned Energy. I'm not sure the opening of the portal won't be destructive to, you know, everything. I think you should scry Issa or Arthur until you catch one of them outdoors. Then I think we should watch that location until there isn't anyone around. As I said, it might take some trial and error."

"Damn! I hadn't thought of that. I don't think I'd like to rip a hole in my tower or a crowd of people," Morgan said, smiling despite the slight setback.

Olivia figured he could see the light at the end of the tunnel.

Arthur Ballard stood on Bronwyn's Hill, watching the enormous airship anchor and settle near the northeast corner of the colony's wall. The captain, Gella, had come down earlier on a much smaller flying ship to announce their desire to dock the *Skybreaker*. He'd assured Arthur and the council of their peaceful intent, saying the airship was here with representatives who wanted to offer opportunities to the citizens of First Landing in the Ridonne Empire.

Arthur was skeptical, but the ship didn't appear geared for war—no visible cannons or other devices were aboard, and Gella had insisted it was a passenger vessel.

Arthur still felt troubled, despite Gella's assurances. Why such a large vessel? First Landing couldn't spare a significant number of people. Everyone was needed in a frontier town, especially if their people were meant to prosper. Things were going so well, and people were happy. He didn't think many would want to leave, even if the council didn't urge them to stay.

The colonists had, by and large, been chosen for their drive and willingness to work toward a common end. How would Gella's representatives react when very few humans took them up on their offer?

Several of the ship's crew had come down to prep the squat tower at the wall's corner. They'd worked some sort of Energy magic to plant reinforced girders around the structure, the tops of which had huge metal eyelets for the ship's anchor lines. Everything seemed to be holding up fine; all twelve lines were tied down, and the ship seemed quite stable, floating near the rampart.

Still, it made Arthur nervous—some anxious part of his mind kept waiting for the ship to get blown by a stray gust into the tower, or for one of the lines to snap, creating some sort of Hindenburg-like accident.

He watched for a few minutes longer before the ship was tugged into the correct position for the boarding ramp to be deployed. Before it could be set down, though, a tall figure approached the ship's railing and launched himself over.

Arthur caught his breath, wondering if he were leaping to his doom, but then he saw his fluttering wings and the stream of glittering motes that trailed him as he flew past the wall to land in the grass, not far from Morgan's tall, iron tower.

"Huh, I didn't think Ghelli could fly. Is he a Ghelli?"

## BRONWYN

Bronwyn watched while Morgan stared into his scrying window. He'd been casting and recasting it for two days now. Sometimes, he'd catch his target indoors or in a crowded area and sigh and cancel the spell, only to target another individual in First Landing. If he saw someone outdoors, he'd watch the location for as long as he could keep the window open, hoping that everyone would disperse, and they'd have a safe site for the portal target.

So far, he hadn't been lucky.

Prior to Morgan's efforts, Olivia had taken three days to create the spell's pattern on the marble floor. First, she'd drawn it with a thick charcoal pencil, then she'd painstakingly etched grooves along the lines with a little chisel and hammer. She'd had to make little circles for all two hundred and eleven Energy gems she and Morgan had calculated they'd need. In Bronwyn's opinion, the whole thing looked really impressive, like some sort of ancient ritual pattern.

She laughed, realizing it was a ritual pattern, just not ancient—they now lived in a time and place of real magic.

"Something funny?" Morgan growled, glancing over at her.

"No, relax! I just thought it was funny how I still catch myself thinking of magic as a thing from stories sometimes."

"Ingrained perceptions take a while to die," Olivia commented, looking up from her notebook. She was going over her calculations and spell design for the thousandth time.

"This is no good," Morgan said. "I caught Arthur outside, but he was standing near the tavern, and there's constant traffic. By the way, some very interesting-looking people were walking with him—some guy in a military-style uniform with a high hat and a very tall Ghelli with huge, luminous wings."

"Most Ghelli gain the ability to fly with enough racial ranks, or so my friends at the academy tell me," Olivia said.

"Oh?" Morgan asked, his wings twitching. Bronwyn wondered if it was involuntary.

How strange it must be to have new appendages!

"Yeah, and some Shadeni too. The head of first-year students, Oylla-dak, has them. They're almost as big as yours, Morgan."

"Well, maybe I can meet her sometime, and she can tell me how to sit in a normal chair with these things." He let his hands drop, canceling his spell. "Let's see here; I'll check up on Maria. She's outside a lot."

Morgan was standing in the circle attached to the spell pattern that Olivia had drawn for him. She'd said he'd need to be in that position when he activated the complicated spell he'd been drawing over and over for weeks.

"So this portal spell has two parts? The pattern Morgan makes in his pathways to create the spell, and then this physical pattern on the ground?" She only asked Olivia, really, to make conversation; she'd already heard the explanation before.

"Right. The physical pattern on the ground is just there so Morgan can draw on the Energy in all these gems. The real spell takes place inside of him."

"I got it! Come look!" Morgan yelled.

Olivia and Bronwyn jumped to their feet and hurried to peer through the window between Morgan's hands.

"Maria was walking through the grass behind the tavern, heading north toward where Arthur's house is. There's nothing around for a dozen yards, and I don't see any other people."

"Yeah, it's just grass," Bronwyn agreed.

"Are you ready, Morgan?" Olivia asked, though it sounded like she was the one who might not be prepared to see the fruit of her labor.

"Relax, Liv. You did the spell right," Bronwyn said, reaching out and squeezing her hand.

"I'm doing it, guys. Back up if you want."

Morgan closed his eyes, taking deep, steadying breaths. Olivia backed up several steps, pulling Bronwyn with her. That's when the fireworks started.

Morgan spread his hands out, then his wings, and black, flickering lines of Energy began to flow out of the gems near him, gliding along the grooves in the ground to enter the circle Morgan stood in. When the strange, crackling, jumping Energy crossed the line, it started to fill the space, obscuring Morgan's feet. As more and more gems began to pour out their contents, the weird void Energy filled the invisible cylinder around Morgan, climbing to his knees, then his hips. Morgan's hands began to vibrate, still outstretched, and a weird whistling, popping sound began to emanate from him.

As the void Energy climbed past his lower back and up to the base of his wings, Morgan suddenly yelled, and two streams of black, crackling Energy shot from his outstretched palms toward the center of the spell pattern. With a horrible rending of reality, a doorway started to rip open.

Bronwyn slapped her hands over her ears, but it didn't stop the sound, the destruction of sound, or whatever was happening with that terrible, strange Energy.

The void Energy kept flowing out of the gems toward Morgan, and he kept channeling it out through his hands into the nascent doorway. His spell was burrowing between reality itself, and the strain of the effort was evident. Morgan's yell had become an unending scream, and standing behind him, Bronwyn was glad she couldn't see his face because it sounded like his soul was being torn asunder.

"Will he be alright?" she tried to yell, but her voice was swallowed by the surplus of void-attuned Energy in the air.

She felt something tickling at her flesh, and when Bronwyn looked down at her arms, she thought she saw wisps of black Energy pulling away tiny motes of her skin and hair.

"What the fuck?" she yelled, but again couldn't hear herself. Suddenly, Olivia was yanking on her arm, pulling her further away, and Bronwyn stumbled after her. They ran away from him and the spell, and when they were at the far end of the enormous hall, Bronwyn started to feel normal again.

"We were too close," she heard Olivia speaking. "He's channeling more Energy than any of us have ever seen, and it's void Energy!" She hissed. "I'm such an idiot! I should have realized how dangerous it was."

"Will he be alright?"

"I think so! He has a void affinity, after all!"

They were fifty yards from Morgan now, and still, the un-sound and strange quality of the air was enough to disorient Bronwyn.

"How long will it be?" she yelled.

"I don't know! I'm trying to see which gems are depleted, but I can't focus on anything in there!"

"Same here! It's like looking at a flickering black hole or something!" Bronwyn yelled.

It was true—she could catch a glimpse of Morgan and his wings every now and then, but the space within the ritual circle was awash with void Energy, and things kept blinking in and out of existence, at least as far as her eyes told her.

The black hole in reality or whatever that portal was continued to grow, its edges spinning and throbbing. Through it all, Morgan's unending scream echoed around the chamber.

"I couldn't hear myself near him; why can we hear Morgan?"

"I don't know. Maybe that sound is stuck or being reechoed by the spell or the weird way his Energy is manipulating the physical reality and space."

Just as Bronwyn feared the spell or its bizarre effects would be the end of her sanity, Morgan's scream rose to a terrible crescendo. The pooled void

Energy rushed out from around Morgan toward the black gateway, and then, with an audible popping rip, the edges of the portal steadied, and a perfectly round opening about two meters across appeared. Bronwyn could see through the doorway to a grassy meadow on the other side.

Morgan was leaning forward—hands on his knees—heaving for breath, a small pool of blood on the white marble at his feet. He stood as she and Olivia ran to him and turned to grin at them. He had streaks of blood on his cheeks under his eyes, and blood still flowed from his nose, but he looked happy.

"It worked!" he grunted, voice hoarse.

"Yeah! Will it close soon?" Bronwyn asked, looking from Morgan to Olivia.

They answered at the same time.

"I think so," Olivia replied.

"Not for thirty minutes," Morgan said, far more definitively. He smiled at Olivia. "I can feel it, and also, I gained a new spell and its description."

While he spoke, Bronwyn saw huge motes of golden Energy start to coalesce in the air around Morgan before they all surged into him. He arched his back and sighed, smiling even more broadly.

"Profiting off of my hard work, I see." Olivia laughed.

"Another level! That spell was a doozy," Morgan laughed too as the rush faded.

"At least your nose stopped bleeding. We don't have to worry about an aneurism," Bronwyn said, punching his shoulder. "Are you going to spend your attribute points before we go through?"

"Might as well. Say your goodbyes to this place while I sort things out, please."

Morgan's eyes went glassy as he contemplated his status screen. Bronwyn snorted and shook her head. She and Olivia had talked about their recent levels, and Olivia had helped her confirm her decision to keep improving her speed and mental attributes. Olivia, on the other hand, had brought some of her languishing physical attributes up a bit, saying that her class gave her plenty of mental improvements.

Bronwyn stepped toward the portal, looked through, and laughed when she saw a crowd starting to form on the grass. "We better get going before they start coming this way."

"Right, I'm ready," Morgan said, stretching his wings and then pulling them in close. "After you, ladies." He gestured to the portal with a flourish. "I'll be right behind—just going to gather these empty gems so I can reuse 'em."

"Why, thank you, sir." Olivia laughed and took Bronwyn's hand. "We'll go through together," she said more softly.

Bronwyn nodded, unable to stop the thrill of joy that ran through her heart. She felt so full of love and luck to have come to an entirely new world and still manage to meet and grow close to someone like Olivia.

She pulled Olivia toward the portal, squeezing her hand tight, excited to see what might come next for them.

Issa stood outside the burrow and called out, "Ykleedra!"

While waiting for the young Yovashi, she listened, wondering if she'd hear the little ones. She'd been upset with Ykleedra at first for keeping such a huge secret, but then she'd started to think about how lonely and scared the girl had been, and she couldn't help feeling some joy at the prospect that she now had sisters.

Imagine! One minute, Ykleedra had been alone, not knowing where or if any of her other kind might live, and now, she had four siblings.

She wondered if Morgan would be upset, but she knew how guilty he felt about Ykleedra, and hoped it would bring him some peace, knowing she had some surviving family. Even better, these children knew nothing of their people's horrible history; they were a blank slate and would hopefully grow to become happy members of their community.

"Yes, Miss Issa?" Ykleedra scampered out of the burrow to stand before her.

"I've brought you more food," Issa spoke softly, unsure if the babies were sleeping. "Are they sleeping? I want to meet them!"

"Oh, they're sleeping, miss, and my burrow isn't suitable for someone like you. Can I bring them up to meet you another time?"

"I suppose. Maybe later today? Just tell Tiladia when they're awake, and she can come get me. I think it's important that they get used to other types of people, don't you?"

"Yes, of course, Miss Issa!"

Issa nodded and handed the storage bag to Ykleedra.

"There's a lot of meat here, just like you asked. Also, I spoke to Tiladia, and she told me that while reading a text from your home, she learned that infant Yovashi will begin to eat other foods as their upper stomachs form. She said it usually takes around three months."

"Oh, wonderful! I have so much fruit I gathered!" Ykleedra reached out, took the bag, and with a tremulous voice, said, "Thank you, Miss Issa! I was so worried that you'd make us leave, but you've been nothing but kind."

"You're wel—"

"Lady Issa!" Suddenly, Tiladia was there, her tinkling voice high with excitement.

"Yes?"

"He's returned! Maria was just here! Morgan is back, and some sort of confrontation is taking place in the colony!"

# MORGAN

Morgan picked up the last of the spent gems, stuffed it into his ring, then jogged back to the portal. He'd only taken a few minutes, and he knew the portal would stand open for another twenty or so, but he still hated being the only one left in the dungeon.

That said, as soon as he was on the correct side to cross the crazy void doorway, he stepped through. Unlike other portals Morgan had experienced, this one offered no feeling of travel or time loss—as soon as his foot went through, it set down in springy grass, followed by the rest of his body. His void magic literally connected the two distinct points in reality.

As the bright blue sky hit his eyes, Morgan was overwhelmed by a chaotic scene. A huge, burly, red-skinned man had hold of Bronwyn from behind, pressing a curved axe blade against her neck with one hand while he squeezed her arms to her sides with the other. Olivia was writhing on the ground, red bands of Energy wrapped around her limbs constricting her with bright flashes of Energy, and colonists were running back and forth, screaming various things.

Morgan moved to draw Bloodfang, saying, "What the fuck?"

Just as his fingers closed around the hilt, something crashed into him, sending him tumbling over the grass. He flopped once and flipped to his back, ready to spring back up, when a weight crashed down on him, and he saw his assailant. A tall, thin Ghelli man with glittering wings knelt on him, pressing a cold, blue dagger to his neck.

Morgan narrowed his eyes as they grew black like the depths of space. Then, with the noise of air and sound being annihilated, he was gone.

The man who had attacked him spun around, looking for his target, but Morgan had Void Stepped into the air a hundred feet above his attacker, and now he streaked back down, his massive black wings folded behind him. Just as he was about to crash into the Ghelli, still looking around with his knife held out at the ready, Morgan flapped his wings and brought his feet up so they smashed into the man's back with tremendous force. Morgan's boot crunched one of his fragile, glittering wings and sent him tumbling head over heels through the grass.

Morgan whirled on the two assailants attacking Bronwyn and Olivia, jerking Bloodfang through its metal loop with a resounding, clarion ring. He started to channel Energy Drain and advanced toward his struggling friends.

Just then, a tremendously loud horn blew, and a man rushed up from behind the huge Shadeni who was squeezing Bronwyn, shouting, "Stop! Stop! They aren't invaders! They live here!"

He was joined by Arthur and Alec, also calling for everyone to stop fighting.

The big Shadeni let go of Bronwyn, shoving her forward and backing away, but the mage holding Olivia was too engrossed in her efforts, her face strained and pale. Morgan saw that Olivia's flaming aura was growing and turning from its usual blue to white.

"You better back off, or she's going to annihilate you!" Morgan yelled, jogging forward.

The Ardeni woman casting the red fetters that held Olivia finally registered what was being said around her, and she opened wide eyes to stare as Morgan drew near, Bloodfang still naked in his fist. However, Morgan didn't get a chance to intervene before Bronwyn tackled the woman, knocking her to the ground.

"Ahh! Help me, Haku-dak!" she screamed, rolling in the grass with Bronwyn clinging to her back.

"Back off," Morgan growled as the big Shadeni started moving to the struggling women. Olivia had regained her feet, and her eyes were blazing with white flames.

"Please stop! There's been a terrible misunderstanding!" Arthur yelled.

"Yes, Ancestors-damn it! Stop!" the Ardeni man in the fancy uniform screamed at the women rolling in the grass.

"Fuck that!" Bronwyn snarled, holding the woman by the neck, a gleaming hatchet blade poised to strike.

"Bron," Olivia's voice was filled with raw power, and it crackled and echoed strangely. "Bron, it's okay. Let her go—she's not fighting."

It was true; the woman had stopped struggling and looked toward Olivia with wary eyes, though she seemed more intrigued than fearful. At that moment, though, Morgan thought only a fool would underestimate Olivia.

He felt a tickle at the back of his neck, and he whirled to see the tall Ghelli in the fancy suit walking toward him over the grass. He looked ruffled and annoyed, and Morgan could see he wasn't used to being hit back.

Morgan spread his massive black wings and held his sword ready, scowling at the man. The Ghelli dusted off his hat, placed it back on his head, and made a show of putting his blue dagger away before bowing. "Baron Finneal at your service. My apologies—we thought this community was being invaded when the portal appeared. My colleagues and I simply moved to intervene on behalf of the citizens here."

"Yes, yes. Please release Lady ap'Cilla," the uniformed man said. "I'm Captain Gella of yonder airship."

He gestured to his left, and Morgan took in, for the first time, the massive airship floating above a reinforced wall tower. It was hundreds of feet long and hung over the wall with half a dozen levels of windows or ports visible. Enormous beams were folded along its side, and furled wings or sails were visible against the hull. Cones of glass or some other shiny material pointed in various directions, pulsing with Energy. Morgan thought those must be what held it aloft and propelled it.

"Please!" the man continued, pleading with Bronwyn. "Stop this! No harm was intended!"

"If this bitch touches Olivia again, I'll take her hands off," Bronwyn snarled, letting go of the woman and hopping to her feet.

She spat a wad of bloody saliva into the grass and walked over to her girlfriend. The flaming raven-haired woman held out a hand for Bronwyn to take, watching the Ardeni woman as she clambered to her feet, clearly not used to a physical tussle.

"Morgan!" a new voice called out, and he turned to see Issa charging over the grass toward him. He smiled, his anger at the trio of would-be defenders forgotten, and without even thinking about it, he flapped his wings, gliding over the grass to grab Issa into an embrace. She caught him in a hug, and all was right with the world for a moment.

"Wings, Morgan?" She laughed into his neck, squeezing him close, her arms just below where his new appendages sprouted from his back.

"I know, I know. They're ridiculous, but at least I didn't grow a tail!" He laughed, his eyes watering up, the momentary conflict with the strangers completely forgotten. Issa kissed him softly, oblivious to the people staring, and then she gently pushed him back, making a show of peering around his broad shoulders.

"What's going on here?"

"A misunderstanding, I think," Morgan replied, turning to look at the crowd still standing in front of the portal.

Bronwyn was glowering furiously around, her nose and chin bright with blood—had the large warrior struck her while they grappled? Olivia's flaming aura had calmed considerably, but her eyes still blazed as she spoke with Arthur and the airship captain. The Ghelli, Baron Finneal, stood off to the side next to the sorceress, staring at Morgan, though his face wasn't openly hostile.

"Probably should go talk to them."

Issa's hand in his, he walked toward the growing crowd, just catching the tail end of what Olivia had been saying, ". . . finally managed to open a portal, and you know the rest."

She gestured vaguely, indicating the area where they'd had their brief confrontation with the strangers. Then her eyes fell on Bronwyn's face, and she frowned, reaching up to gently rub at the blood under her nose. Wispy smoke lifted into the air around where she touched, and the blood was gone when she pulled her hand away.

As Morgan and Issa returned to the gathering crowd, Arthur cleared his throat and spoke loudly. "Allow me to introduce our new arrivals. You've all just met Olivia Bennet—one of our world's premier scientists. This is Morgan Hall, and Bronwyn Tallow is the woman with the, um, hatchets. I'm sorry it led to such a violent misunderstanding, but we do appreciate you trying to defend our community." He addressed the ship captain, but his eyes flicked to the other three while he spoke.

Several people were calling out questions and greetings to Morgan, most focused on his wings. He waved, and when Boris came out of the crowd to clap him on the shoulder, Morgan smiled broadly and shook his hand. "Not only got your arm back but a couple wings too? What the hell, man?"

"Yeah, it's been a crazy couple of months."

Morgan fielded a few more questions while watching the Ghelli and sorceress from the corner of his eye. He knew Olivia also had an eye on them while she spoke with the council members who had come running in the aftermath of the dustup. He was telling Boris about the racial advancement potion he'd had made in Tarn's Crossing when, with a rush of air like a miniature tornado, the portal snapped out of existence.

Startled murmurs broke out in the crowd, but Olivia called out, "It's just the portal expiring, relax. By the way," she said loudly enough for most everyone to hear. "We're all exhausted and wouldn't mind a chance to get cleaned up and get settled."

It was Captain Gella who responded first.

"Of course, of course! It was wonderful to meet you all, and I hope that we'll have a chance to grow better acquainted during our visit. Come, let's give these heroes some space!" he urged, directing his voice to his three companions.

Baron Finneal tipped his hat to Morgan and then launched himself into the air, soaring away toward the airship with a glittering trail of Energy. The others simply walked away, and Olivia and Bronwyn came, still hand in hand, over to Morgan and Issa.

Issa took her arm from around Morgan's and rushed to hug Olivia and Bronwyn. They smiled and laughed, and Morgan heard them start to catch up on all that had transpired as they walked toward the tower. He couldn't concentrate on their words, however, because something about the colossal airship and the violence they'd met from its occupants had him unsettled and his mind wandering.

"Pathetic!" Tanna ap'Cilla hissed at Haku-dak as they walked ahead of Gella toward the airship. "How could you let that bitch loose to tackle me like that?"

"I heard the captain calling for peace," Haku-dak said with a shrug, glancing back toward Gella. Gella, for his part, smiled nervously at the mighty warrior.

"So you just let her knock me to the ground and hold a blade to my throat?"

"Well, I didn't think she'd take you down—she wasn't that strong." He shrugged again.

"Oh, I see. So I manage to subdue my target, Finneal gets thrown like a rag doll, and you just let your opponent loose? I see."

Gella could see she was furious; her hands kept sparking with red light, and little crystals of ice were dropping from her fingertips into the grass as they walked.

"How is that bitch so strong? Not the one with the axes, the other. I could barely hold her and felt like she was about to let something loose. I thought they were only tier two?" She turned to glare at Gella.

"That's the intelligence we have," he replied with a shrug.

"Well, if she's tier two, she's unlike any I've ever met. Isn't she the one who's supposed to be at the academy?"

"That's right," Gella said. "With any luck, she'll head back there now that they've found their way home."

"What about the tall one with the wings?" Haku-dak asked. "I could feel his aura. That ain't no tier two. Did you see his armor? I'm not looking forward to dealing with him."

"Yes. The way he shrugged off Finneal—I've never seen that Ghelli so embarrassed." Tanna laughed, an icy, brittle sound that sent shivers down Gella's spine, though some of the fear was mixed with admiration—she had a beautiful voice.

"With any luck, we won't have to worry about him. We need to polish our pitch and get the contracts right, and hopefully, we'll get plenty of volunteers," Gella said, though he felt like he was only fooling himself, especially when Tanna snorted in derision.

# MORGAN

On their way to the tower, Arthur caught up to Issa, Morgan, Olivia, and Bronwyn, breathless from the short jog. "I hope we can count on you to come to the council meeting tomorrow night! We'd love to hear about your experience and fill you in on what's happening around here."

"Of course they will," Issa said before Morgan or anyone else could reply. "I'll be there too, Arthur. Don't worry."

Morgan smiled at him and was about to echo Issa's sentiment when Olivia spoke.

"Yeah, we'll be there, Arthur, but I'm late returning to the academy, so it might be the only meeting I attend for a while."

"Yes, of course. Very well, you all look quite road weary. Have a good rest."

He waved awkwardly then turned back toward the town center. Bronwyn giggled, still holding onto Olivia's hand, and Morgan saw Issa's eyes linger on the two women. She cleared her throat, let go of Morgan, and moved next to Bronwyn.

"Did you know they named the hill at the center of town? It's Bronwyn's Hill now."

"What? Really?" Bronwyn's eyes opened wide in surprise, and Morgan figured the woman might have been prepared for any sort of news other than that.

"Yes! They named it after you because you're the one who planted the stone and named the colony."

"Well, wow. I didn't think I had enough support around here for something like that."

"Don't be ridiculous, Bron," Olivia said. "You were famous before we even came here."

"Yeah, but . . . well, never mind. I'll take it!" She smiled, and Morgan was struck again by how much she'd changed.

As they drew near the tower, Issa continued. "I'd like to make dinner for you all, but for now, I have a lot of catching up to do with Morgan."

"Yes! That sounds nice. I need a bath and a nap," Olivia replied while Bronwyn just smiled and nodded. They entered the tower, and Tiladia was quick to greet them all, hovering with little agitated flips and dips while they gathered near the stairs.

"Tiladia, thank you for keeping the tower in order and for being helpful to Issa while I was gone. I'm assuming you were helpful?" He looked at Issa with an arched eyebrow.

"She was wonderful!" Issa said, and Tiladia spun around, making a loop in her dragon form.

"Thank you, Issa! Yes, Morgan, things have been hectic here, especially with the new children!" Tiladia's voice was clear and musical, like silver chimes.

"Children?" Morgan looked around.

"I'll explain everything," Issa said, moving between him and Tiladia and pulling Morgan to the stairs. "Let's go to our rooms, and I'll fill you in." She looked him up and down and added, "And you can fill me in. Do I need to know about any other appendages? Are you sure there's not a tail hiding in those trousers?"

Bronwyn snorted in laughter, and Olivia's eyes widened.

"You know, he was always careful to make sure no one was around the potty hole when he visited it. I hope he's not hiding any surprises for you, Issa," Bronwyn teased, and Olivia almost choked, slapping a hand over her mouth to hide her expression. Issa took it in stride, laughing and pulling again at Morgan's hand.

"You guys are always in such a good mood when I'm the butt of the joke, eh? Well, don't worry—I know this all stems from jealousy. Your barbs won't tarnish these feathers, though." Morgan spread his wings and made a show of preening one of his long, black feathers between his fingertips.

"All right, enough teasing. Come," Issa urged, walking backward to the stairs, pulling at Morgan's free hand again.

"See you later, ladies." He folded his wings and followed Issa onto the stairs. Just three steps later, they were walking onto the landing and down the hallway to their chambers.

"I really do have a lot to tell you, Morgan," Issa said as she opened their door. "You have to promise to stay calm and not be angry about any of it."

"What? How can I promise that without knowing what any of it is? Are we talking bad news?"

"No, I don't think it's bad news, but some of it might be startling or alarming. I'm not worried about you being angry at me but at someone else, so will you trust me and promise you won't be angry?"

She closed the door and steered Morgan over to their bed, pushing him to sit on the edge so she could look into his face more easily. Morgan had learned to tilt his wings slightly to allow for easier sitting, though it had taken him some practice.

"You know, you are just taking it for granted that I can sit like this. I had to work very hard to figure out how to accommodate furniture made for wingless people."

"Morgan! Be serious for a few minutes, please?" She leaned forward and kissed him softly, but before he could pull her in for a more passionate embrace, she pulled back and stared at him for a minute. "I'm going to start with the easiest news, I think."

"Alright, relax, Issa. Nothing you say is going to upset me. I'm too thankful to be back home with you." He reached out and took her hand, dread in the back of his mind because he still hadn't told her about his utter failure with regard to finding her father.

"Okay, first of all, many people came here through the portal Bronwyn and Olivia made. They all told us how you attacked the invaders and fought their entire garrison, allowing them to flee to the portal. You saved a lot of people, Morgan, and you should be proud of that. I spoke to the Ardeni survivors; I know my father's probably gone for good. I've come to terms with it, and I don't want you to feel guilty about it."

"How did you know that's what I was thinking about?"

"I know you, Morgan, and of course the only thing on your mind right now is how you think you've failed me. You did more than anyone could hope for. Those invaders killed my father, not you!"

She didn't choke up or cry, and Morgan knew she must have faced those emotions already. Her apparent acceptance gave him the courage to add what he knew.

"Issa, I think I was about a day too late for Roald. I saw what they were doing to the captives in their base or hive or whatever you call it, and none of them survived, but it was fast and, hopefully, without much suffering. I'm sorry, Issa."

She leaned forward and hugged him around his neck. He held her like that for several long moments, and then she pulled back, wiping at her eyes.

"Now, the next subject: Ykleedra lied to you."

"Huh? Ykleedra?" That caught Morgan off guard; the young Yovashi hadn't been on his mind at all. Though he supposed it was a little strange that she hadn't greeted him when they'd returned to the tower.

"Yes, Morgan. Her siblings' eggs weren't destroyed or whatever she told you. She snuck them into the tower under her robe when you first brought her. What's more, they've hatched, and she now has four little sisters living with her in the atrium."

"Four! Sisters?" he asked, hoping he'd heard right regarding their gender.

"That's right!" Issa's face stretched into a smile. "Isn't it wonderful that she isn't alone? I've met them too, Morgan. She's very protective, but she needed help feeding them. When I insisted on meeting them, she brought them up out of the burrow she dug, and I saw them. They're actually kind of cute, and they won't have any bad influences—we can see to that!"

"Alright, alright. Now I see why you made me promise not to be angry. Don't worry—I won't hold it against Ykleedra. She's a child herself. How could I expect her to trust me right away when she'd seen what I did to the adults in her family? I'm glad she came to you for help, Issa, and I'm sure you're doing the right thing."

She smiled and hugged him again, more briefly this time, then pulled back and said, "Now, the biggest news. Are you ready?"

"Yes." She stared at him as though he hadn't convinced her, and he repeated, "Yes!"

"Alright. I've spoken to a lot of humans while you were gone, and I've learned some things about your customs. First of all, I want you to know that I'm very happy about this news, and if you aren't happy about it, that's okay. We'll figure things out, but I want you to be happy, Morgan. Please tell me you're going to be happy."

"What is . . . ?" Morgan wasn't a stupid man, and he connected the dots before he could finish the question. A huge smile spread on his face, and he leaned forward, pulling Issa into a hug. He stood, still holding her tight, and lifted her off her feet. "Of course, I'm happy, Issa. Oh my God! I didn't dare to hope it was possible!"

"I haven't even told you what it is," she said softly, nuzzling into his neck.

"You gave me enough clues." He set her back down on her feet, turned her in his arms to hug her back against him, and gently caressed her stomach.

Issa sighed, resting her head back into him, then she grinned, squinted her eyes in amusement, and said, "Morgan, they're twins."

"Brother, I wish you'd let me introduce you to Miss Issa." Ykleedra nervously glanced at the dark figure of her newest sibling. He crouched in the furthest corner of her burrow, clinging to the shadows and glaring at her through dark, fathomless pools.

"No, sister. You've done well, but you must have faith in my judgment; I was entrusted with the memories of our people for a reason."

His voice was harsh and sharp, and though he spoke softly, it grated on Ykleedra's mind, stirring some deeply buried memory and causing her to wince. When he'd come out of his egg and started speaking to her, she'd thought she was going mad, but then he'd begun to explain things to her.

Yovashi males were born with a selection of memories—not their own but those of their people—enough to carry on their fight against their true enemy: the System.

The prospect terrified Ykleedra, and his insistence on keeping him a secret deeply troubled her. He'd encouraged her to ask Issa for help with acquiring food but sworn her to secrecy about himself. Ykleedra felt like she'd come clean and been forgiven for one lie, only to dig herself deeper with a much bigger one.

"How long will you hide here? Aren't you worried about going mad as our father did?"

"I'll hide until I'm strong and until the opportunity arises when I can slip free of this tower without incurring the wrath of all these Energy users you consort with. As for madness, it is subjective, and you can believe our father wasn't as mad as people claim. I know I never met the man, but I have plenty of information up here"—he caressed his head with one of his long tentacles—"that explains the so-called madness and all the other lies the System has propagated about our kind. I don't want to harm these people you call friends, but their suffering or lack thereof is irrelevant in the context of the great war."

"What if they could help you? Morgan is very powerful, brother!"

"Power and the perception of it is another subjective matter. You have a very limited frame of reference and know so little of what our people have worked toward. I must find my contemporaries, few though they may be, and continue the great work."

"But you won't hurt anyone here, right?"

"Not unless it cannot be helped. You must begin working on your plan as well, sister. It's imperative that you and our siblings, as soon as they're able, remove yourselves from this lair of foreign Energy users. You must make your way to an isolated location, set up a proper brooding burrow, and await the sires I send your way."

"Yes, you've said as much, brother. How long, do you think, until you're ready to make your . . . exit?"

"Sister, do not seek to hasten that which is beyond your control. The answer is, and shall remain to be, when I'm strong enough. Now, I could use some more meat. Did that woman give you anything with some bones in it?"

# ❦ OLIVIA ❧

"It's not bad!" Bronwyn said, licking the edges of her cone and scooping up all the dripping vanilla ice cream.

"Not bad? It's better than any ice cream I ever had on Earth!"

Olivia leaned back on her left hand, enjoying the cool scrunch of the springy grass under her fingers. She savored the treat, happy that the colonists were starting to grow comfortable and settled enough to begin exploring non-essential goods and services.

They sat on the northwestern slope of Bronwyn's Hill, watching the crowds outside Alec's tavern. A colonist from Idaho, of all places, had built a cart with a built-in, Energy-powered freezer and was selling cones to passersby.

"Well, are you going to tell me what it said?" Olivia asked, gesturing to the tiny roll of paper Bronwyn still clutched in her free hand.

They'd only been sitting for a minute or two when one of the long-tailed, brightly colored birds commonly found sweeping through the air over their pond had landed with a flutter at Bronwyn's feet. Olivia wasn't sure how, but Bronwyn had immediately seemed to realize it was there for her, and she'd snatched the little rolled parchment from its talon. The funny creature had made a *cheep-chirp* sound before launching back into the air.

"I'm trying to pretend I didn't read it." Bronwyn took another long lick of her ice cream, then closed her eyes and held her face to the warm sun.

"Well, that's not going to solve anything. Come on, what did it say?" Olivia made a grab for Bronwyn's hand, trying to pry her fingers apart, but Bronwyn squeezed her fist tight. "Are you going to make me cast a spell on you?"

"Oh, fine. Read it!" Bronwyn relaxed her fingers, and Olivia took the little paper. She unrolled it, turned it front to back, and frowned.

"It's blank."

"No, it isn't!" Bronwyn snatched the paper back and held it open, reading, "'Daughter, there is one in your community named Cal Jennings. He seeks a friend, and it is vital that he is successful in his quest. Aid him.'"

"First of all, that paper is blank. Second of all, who is Cal Jennings? Oh, and third: daughter?"

"I have no damn idea, but I'd rather have some time off to spend with you." Bronwyn blew some loose strands of red hair out of her eyes.

"That answered one of my questions," Olivia pressed.

"I don't know why you can't read the paper. Maybe the queen didn't want others to see my message. She calls me daughter sometimes. Usually 'daughter of Summer.'"

"That's sweet!" Olivia laughed and bumped her shoulder into Bronwyn's, jostling her enough to make her stretch out her hand, holding her ice cream precariously, to maintain her balance.

"Are you trying to start a food fight? Because this is how you start a food fight!" Bronwyn held her cone threateningly.

"No! No, please!" Olivia held up her free hand in mock surrender and took another big lick of her cone.

"Alright, sheesh. I wish you'd get a little serious, though—I feel like I have to do what it says here, which means I might be out of touch for a while."

"Bronwyn. Sweet, fiery Bronwyn," Olivia spoke, reaching out to run her fingers along Bronwyn's jawline, pushing her breeze-blown hair back. "You know I have to go back to the academy, right? We'll see each other soon, but in the meantime, I think we both have important things to do. That's alright, isn't it?"

"Yeah, of course, but that doesn't mean I like it," Bronwyn said, leaning forward to kiss her.

Olivia returned the kiss, enjoying how Bronwyn's lips were cold and how she tasted like vanilla. She reached a hand up and gently caressed Bronwyn's ear, rubbing the pointed tip between her thumb and forefinger. Bronwyn groaned softly then pulled away, her cheeks flushed.

"You're going to start something else if you're not careful," she warned, lying down in the grass. She rested the back of her head on Olivia's thigh and continued eating her ice cream.

Olivia had just crunched the last bit of her cone when Bronwyn growled and sat up with a deep scowl. "Damn it! I feel like I have ants in my pants. I feel like I have to get going to figure out what's up with this Cal guy. It's driving me crazy! I'm sorry, Liv."

"Alright, it sounds like you're on a quest. I'm planning to activate my teleport back to the academy tomorrow morning. If I don't see you before then, don't beat yourself up about it, okay? I'll make sure I visit again soon. Besides, Morgan is working on something—he said he might have a way to connect his tower to the academy. Told me I should be sure to speak to him before I leave."

"When did he tell you that?"

"After dinner last night, when you were in the bath."

"Ugh, dammit! I gotta get going. Olivia, if I miss the council meeting, please explain that I'm doing something important!"

She hugged Olivia again fiercely, and they kissed for a long moment, then Bronwyn turned and ran down the hill toward the tavern. Whatever purpose the Summer Queen had put into her seemed to be affecting her palpably.

"Not too sure I like that," Olivia murmured, wondering just how much the queen could make Bronwyn do. Maybe it wasn't so much direct control but a feeling of urgency that she somehow shared with Bronwyn? "I wonder if I could meet this patron of hers someday." Olivia sighed and stood up, brushing the dew and grass from her robe.

She'd planned to spend the day with Bronwyn and still had hours to kill before the council meeting. She was clean, rested, and had a full belly.

"What to do," she asked aloud, then looked north at the activity around Morgan's tower. Issa had contracted some builders to make a stable and corral on the grounds nearby. "I guess I could go say hi to Blue." She walked over to the steps and lightly descended. She was sad that Bronwyn had been called away, but was overall very happy with how things were going for her.

Morgan's new stables were about half built, and the wood being used was kind of rough and a natural reddish brown. Olivia approached one of the workers, a short-haired woman in a gray smock. "What kind of wood is this?"

"We don't know what the natives call it, though I suppose there's plenty of them around to ask. Anyway, we just call it new cedar 'cause it smells like it and seems to hold up good to weather." She shrugged.

"Really? Is it plentiful?"

"Yeah, half the trees in the Gresh Woods are new cedar. You wouldn't know it, looking at them—they're tall and skinny with white bark and blue leaves."

"Things are so colorful here, aren't they?"

"They sure are, ma'am." Olivia was taken aback by the woman's deferential tone. She'd earned a lot of respect in academia but rarely had strangers treat her that way. Was it her advanced race? Her clothing?

"Oh, you can call me Olivia."

"Olivia Bennet, right?"

"That's right."

"Well, I've heard of you. I mean, I knew about your name before we even left, what with the cryo-pods and all. Still, I've heard you've been giving the locals and monsters the business, so I appreciate you standing up for us humans and doing us proud."

"Oh, I . . ." Olivia didn't really know how to respond. Finally, she just settled on, "Well, thank you. What's your name?"

"I'm Heather. Um, Heather Taylor." The woman looked embarrassed for some reason, and Olivia decided to leave her to her work.

"Nice to meet you, Heather. I'm going to go visit my feathery friends over there." She pointed to the three roladii staked not far away in the grass.

"Oh wow, one of them is yours?"

"Yep! They're very sweet and easy to train. You should get yourself one!"

Olivia waved and walked around the new construction toward the roladii. Blue perked up when she drew near, sensing her even before she entered his field of vision. She produced a brush from her storage ring and began to scrub at his rough, gray skin, scraping away flakes of loose, dry skin from around his feathery mane.

Munch and Gopp started edging their way over when they saw the attention Blue was getting, and Olivia laughed. "Oh, you want some loving too?" She began to rotate her attention among the three roladii, laughing at how they jostled for attention.

"They'll take up all your time if you let them," a woman's voice said from behind her. She turned, smiling, only to see the woman who had chained her with Energy when they'd first stepped through the portal.

Her smile fell away.

"Oh, hello." She straightened and put the brush away, resting her hand on Blue's rump.

"I wanted to apologize for the way we met yesterday."

The woman came another step closer, and Olivia regarded her carefully. She was an Ardeni, though shorter and slighter than Issa. She had dark hair, but her eyes were bright green, which was unusual. Most of the Ardeni Olivia had met had eyes that reflected their hair coloring. She wore a silky black blouse with glittering turquoise buttons up the middle. The top two buttons were loose, and the shirt had fallen open to the left, exposing the smooth curve of a breast. She was, all in all, a beautiful woman.

"Well, you thought you were protecting our town. I'm just glad things didn't escalate more." Olivia let the words hang for a minute, allowing the woman to make her own inferences about what Olivia meant.

"Yes, of course. I'm happy as well. Um, Olivia, wasn't it?"

"Right, and I'm sorry, but I'm not sure I heard your name."

"Oh, it's Tanna ap'Cilla."

"Ap'Cilla? I'm new to this world, but I've learned it's customary for Ardeni to take their father's name as a surname."

"Well, in some cases, we choose to honor our mothers." The woman's lips smiled, but her eyes didn't reflect it, and Olivia wondered if she'd overstepped.

"That's very interesting. I'm actually quite glad to hear that—patriarchal customs don't always reflect the best interests of women."

"Quite. Tell me, Olivia. You've been studying at Fainhallow, correct?"

"That's right," Olivia replied, noting the quick change of subject.

"Are you due to return soon?" she asked, glancing around at the stable construction and the tower.

"Yes, I'm afraid so. I'll be visiting regularly, though." Olivia wasn't sure what made her add the last part, but something about this woman, her companions, and their gigantic airship troubled her, even with the rosy apology she'd just received.

"I wanted to tell you that I was impressed by your ability to resist me. Of course, I didn't know who you were when you came through that portal, but when I later found out that you were Olivia, a tier-two student from Fainhallow, I was flabbergasted. Did you have some sort of defensive item which helped you resist my bonds?"

"Hmm, something like that," Olivia replied, remaining cagey. She felt a slight surge of Energy, so small that she probably wouldn't have noticed it had she not been so familiar with the affinity—water. She glanced toward the source and saw a few flakes of frost trailing off Tanna's fingertips, quickly dissipating in the warm summer air. "Oh, a fellow Elementalist?"

"What?" Tanna looked startled, then shook her hands and said, "Ugh! My emotions tend to come out through my pathways. I've always had that problem. I do have a strong water affinity, though. You as well?"

"Mm-hmm. Yes, I have a water affinity." Olivia smiled, nodding.

"Well, I've never been good at explaining things, or I'd offer you some pointers. I'd never make it as a teacher, I'm afraid."

"Pointers? Oh, that's kind of you, but I have good instructors at Fainhallow. Don't worry yourself."

"No. No, I won't." The woman suddenly seemed distracted, and Olivia followed her gaze to the dark gray iron tower behind her. "I wonder, where did that winged fellow acquire this tower?"

"I believe he earned it as a reward in a dungeon." Olivia knew exactly where Morgan had gotten the tower, but she didn't feel like giving this woman a straight answer. Something about her was really starting to rub her the wrong way.

"Interesting. He's of a higher level than you and the others, isn't he?"

"Oh, yes, a bit."

"And his wings? How fascinating. Do all humans gain such as they advance their race?" Tanna leaned closer, and Olivia became aware of her perfume. It was cloying and sweet, and if she liked the woman, she might have enjoyed it, but with her bias, it reminded her of overripe fruit and the flies that fed on it.

"We're really not sure, Tanna. Not many of us have advanced our race appreciably."

"I see. I wonder, do you think you could give this to Morgan?" The woman produced a small envelope sealed with a dollop of violet wax.

"What's this?" Olivia asked, not reaching for the envelope.

"Nothing harmful! Simply an invitation to dine at the captain's table aboard the *Skybreaker*. I'd have invited you as well, Olivia, but the dinner is in two days, and I thought you'd be gone by then."

"Oh, alright." She reached out and took the envelope. The woman held onto it briefly as she pulled at it, but when Olivia looked into her bright green eyes, she just smiled and let go.

"Well, it's been nice to meet you properly, Olivia. I hope we can . . . talk again. Perhaps when you've finished your studies." She smiled, but to Olivia, it looked more like a smirk.

She turned and walked away.

Olivia watched her go. When she was out of sight, having meandered toward the center of town, she turned to the steps leading up to the tower door, muttering, "You better hope we never have reason to do more than talk, bitch."

# MORGAN

Morgan looked at the little envelope with the purple sealing wax.

"Purple?" he asked, raising an eyebrow.

"It's actually violet," Olivia replied. "That woman really rubbed me the wrong way, Morgan. If you go, keep your guard up."

"You think there's something off about them too, eh?" Morgan activated his Void Vision and studied the envelope—it seemed to be totally mundane. Shrugging, he slid a finger under the wax, peeled it away from the paper, and pulled out the little card within.

*Morgan Hall,*
*Please join us for dinner at the captain's table this Thursday, the 27th of Tanewik, aboard the* Skybreaker. *Naturally, we'd love for you to bring a guest.*
*Warm regards,*
*Tanna ap'Cilla, Baroness of Shattered Crag,*
*Together with,*
*Captain Gella and his esteemed guests.*

"Huh. Baroness?" Morgan handed the card to Olivia. She read it and scoffed, handing it back.

"Well, as I said, keep your guard up. I'm heading up to my room. We've got some time to kill before the council meeting."

"All right, thanks for delivering this," he said, waving the card before slipping it into his storage ring. He had plans of his own and meant to deal with them before someone came along to provide another distraction. He watched as Olivia disappeared up the stairs then called out, "Tiladia?"

"Yes, Morgan?" the tinkling voice of his tower's spirit responded almost immediately. He looked around for her and saw her gliding toward him from the library.

"Is Issa still out?"

"Yes, Issa has yet to return from her excursion into town."

"I'm going to the sixth floor—time I cleared out this tower."

"Morgan, I think your chances with the next guardian are quite good."

"Yep, I think so too. Anyway, you know where I'm going."

Morgan took a moment to pull his armor from his ring and apply each piece, allowing it to encase his body in a flexible, silvery layer of rune-inscribed protection. He waved his hand over his face, sliding the visor into place, drew Bloodfang, and stepped onto the stairs.

Concentrating on the sixth floor, Morgan strode up the steps. Before he knew it, he was walking out onto a landing that was made logically impossible by what he knew of the tower. Perforated metal grates made up the flooring, and high above, tall, narrow windows filled the space with light. Wide archways led away from the landing on the left and right, opening into huge workshops lined with high tables and cabinets.

Still more massive windows lined the walls of the workshops, filling the entire space with bright sunlight. Morgan activated Void Vision and scanned around. He couldn't see anything of note in the central landing, but a bright flare of Energy from off to the right caught his attention, and he slowly stalked toward the workshop in that direction. A glimmering orange aura, reeking of fear, pulsed in the room's far corner. Morgan stalked toward it, readying a Vortex Lance as he pointed his blade toward the hiding creature.

When he stepped through the archway into the room, he saw that the aura emanated from behind a tall glass-door cabinet.

"I'm here, guardian," Morgan said, his voice echoing hollowly from his magical helmet. With a burbling, wet belch, a mound of animated green-and-yellow ooze surged from behind the furniture, streaking over the ground toward him. Morgan took a step back in surprise but didn't hesitate to release his Vortex Lance.

His sword recoiled slightly as the projectile spun through the air at supersonic speed. It struck the mound of slime dead center and tore through it, spraying half the creature's mass in a neon splatter over the floor and onto the wall behind it. The splashes of ooze rapidly trickled back to the main body, and Morgan realized he hadn't harmed it at all. He reasoned his sword would have a similarly ineffectual impact on this monster.

He looked around for the widest open area in the workshop and slowly backed toward it as the oozing mound followed. Once it drew within a dozen paces, Morgan cast Energy Drain, pulling a thick band of pulsing orange Energy into his pathways. It was warm and cloying, and he willed his Vortex Core to spin faster in order to clear it from his pathways as quickly as possible. The Energy kept surging out of the monster, and it hurried its pace toward him.

As soon as it was within a step, and dozens of probing slime tentacles had sprouted from its bubbling surface, Morgan cast Void Wave. He smiled at the now-familiar sound of reality splitting as his dark Energy poured forth, annihilating light, air, sound, and everything else. As the wave struck the mound of ooze, Morgan watched through his Void Vision as the creature's will and Energy fought against the destructive force.

Bright flashes of orange battled the consuming darkness, and Morgan knew that if he hadn't been drawing a torrent of the monster's Energy, it might have withstood his attack. As it was, the creature couldn't deal with his two-pronged offense, and it started to dissolve in the face of the void-attuned Energy. As its will and store of Energy faltered, great chunks of its slimy structure simply ceased to be.

When the wave faded away, Morgan kept pulling with his Energy Drain until the stream faded to a trickle, then nothing, and only a thin puddle of oily-looking gray fluid remained on the metal floor, slowly draining through the built-in grates. Morgan scanned around with his Void Vision, making sure no other Energy signatures were lurking nearby, ready to pounce.

He didn't know if it was infallible or, more precisely, avoidable, but his vision didn't reveal anything hiding. Morgan knew it was over when golden motes of Energy drifted up from the metal floor to surge into him. He wasn't surprised when he didn't level—things had gotten slower in that department unless you counted dungeon bosses and advancement orbs. For the first time in a long while, he searched through his System menu to look at his quest objective:

**\*\*\*Quest: Defeat the guardians of Vormendion's Iron Tower 6/8. Reward: Access to each guardian's level and Vormendion's Reliquary.\*\*\***

"Well, that was fast," he said. He'd barely been on this level for five minutes and was a hundred percent ready to keep going.

"It was, Morgan. I felt you were equal to this challenge back when you were missing a limb and had a much less potent aura."

Morgan jerked around, his heart hammering in his chest. "Tiladia, you scared the crap out of me. Can you please, like, float into view before you speak like that?"

"My apologies, Morgan."

"It's nothing. Let me see here. You said the portal stones are on the final level, right?"

"They are, and Morgan, should you best the guardian of the seventh level, you'll be able to access part of the eighth, even before facing the final guardian."

"Really? It doesn't guard the whole level?"

"No, just the reliquary. There are unguarded spaces before that chamber."

"What about this level? Anything here I should know about, other than these workshops?" Morgan looked around at the cabinets and countertops in the bright, high-ceilinged room.

"These laboratories are stocked with some rather difficult to acquire alchemy and enchanting paraphernalia. You'll find distillers, centrifuges, scanning arrays, engraving tools, and myriad other instruments and tools within these cabinets. Vormendion put the most powerful and difficult to attain crafting supplies and tools in his reliquary, however." Tiladia looped around in a large circle, indicating the room and the one on the other side of the landing with expansive gestures of her amorphous form.

"Well, I guess I'll have to invite Boris up here to check things out."

Morgan started walking toward the stairwell. Tiladia spun after him, rushing around to get between him and the stairs.

"What are you planning next, Morgan?" she asked, and he stopped to regard her.

"I'm going up to the next level."

"Morgan, the guardian of the seventh floor is a significantly more powerful opponent than the one you just vanquished."

"That's alright; I hardly broke a sweat." Morgan gestured toward the nearly drained puddle behind him with Bloodfang.

"Yes, well, I don't count your chances as insignificant, but . . ." she trailed off in a very uncharacteristic show of not knowing what else to say.

"Relax, Tiladia. I'm feeling good about my chances. Talk to you in a few minutes, okay?"

Morgan started walking around her again.

"Morgan, do be careful. Miss Issa needs you to be okay." Tiladia's voice was small and distant sounding, and he wondered what sort of memory she was reliving with those words.

"Let's have a nice long talk tonight, Tiladia. I'd like to know a lot more about you."

"That would be nice, Morgan." She drifted out of his way, and Morgan started up the stairs.

"Hello, Professor Somhairle. To what do I owe the pleasure?" Oylla-dak gestured to one of the plush, sky-blue chairs in front of her desk. Somhairle smiled and sat down, his knees poking up as his long legs folded.

"I was wondering if there was any update on your student, Olivia Bennet. Have your scrying attempts born fruit?" His long, pale, angular face stretched in a strange, uncanny attempt at a rather unctuous smile.

"Oh, funny you should ask, Professor. This very morning, my scrying spell suddenly had success and at a much-reduced cost of Energy. Olivia is back on Fanwath, and I daresay, I'll be surprised if she's not back here in the next day or so."

It was true—Olivia had returned, and Oylla had happened to catch her talking to her tall, beautiful fae friend about having to return to the academy.

It was a fortuitous glimpse and had set her mind much at ease. Now that she thought about it, was it a little too far-fetched to believe that Somhairle's interest in Olivia was simply coincidental with her friendship with the fae woman?

Even with the strangeness of the circumstances, Oylla didn't see a reason why she should hide the information from Somhairle—he'd come to her with news of Olivia's disappearance, after all. Following that line of thought, she continued, "You didn't notice her return to our world? Strange, after you so quickly noted her departure."

"Hmm. Not so strange as you might think. It was mere chance that I noticed her leaving. No, my fae heritage has its quirks. I'm not surprised at all. Thank you so much for the good news. I'll look forward to meeting with her upon her arrival."

"Interesting. Does Olivia have something to do with the fae? You're a professor here and have been so for a very long time, so I don't question your motivations, but you did mention your heritage. As to your request for a meeting, I'm sure she'll meet with you, though I *do* have quite a few professors lined up to talk to her about apprenticeships. Were you interested in such? I wouldn't mind adding your name to the list."

Oylla opened a drawer and made a show of pulling out a pad of paper and a silver quill.

"Ahh, there's a list? I surely wish you'd have let me know," he said, still affecting that unctuous, red-lipped smile. Were his lips overly red, or did they just stand out because of his pale skin, so white it tinged toward blue? "Olivia's people come from a world where my ancestors once thrived. That's the extent of any connection between Olivia and my . . . heritage."

"Never fear, Professor; there's always room to add your name. I'll be sure you're given an interview. Though, with Olivia's inexperience and great potential, I'll be helping her represent herself in these meetings. That won't be a problem, will it?" An involuntary twitch flicked through Oylla's wing, and the motion seemed to unsettle Somhairle.

"No, no. That should be fine."

He stood, sketched a very shallow bow, then turned to the door. "I'll look forward to hearing from you," he said, quickly slipping through without waiting for a reply.

Something about him bothered Oylla, but she couldn't decide what it was exactly—something to do with his fake affectations or perhaps the strangeness of his heritage.

"Still, we can add him to the list. No reason why Olivia shouldn't be allowed to make informed decisions."

## ⚭ BRONWYN ⚮

"Cal? Yeah, I know him! He just got back to town a couple of weeks ago! He was one of the original missing colonists—you know, the ones we thought were taken by Yeksa or boyii hounds." Alec spoke enthusiastically, wiping out a mug and draping his ever-present dish towel over his shoulder. "Why?"

"I heard he needs help with something, so I'm trying to track him down." Bronwyn drummed her fingers on the bar top, looking around Green's Tavern.

"Well, did you check his house?"

"No, do you know where it is?"

"Not exactly, but I think it's in the newer neighborhood in the southwest corner." Alec gestured behind Bronwyn to her left as if she could look through the tavern's walls to see where he pointed.

"Alright, thanks, Alec. Hey, can you let him know I'm looking for him if he comes by?"

"Sure, no worries. Wait a sec, though, try this out." He turned to the counter behind him, bringing a tray forward. Little wedges of pastry were arrayed on the shiny serving tray, each piled with a creamy filling and several fresh berries. "Mini tarts! Let me know what you think—I'm trying to up my menu game to compete with the new restaurants in town."

"I just had ice cream," Bronwyn protested weakly, but she was already reaching for one of them. She plopped it into her mouth and was surprised when the chilled pastry and filling melted in her mouth with a tangy sweetness. "How is it refrigerated?"

"Haha, magic serving tray! I just feed it a little Energy, and it will keep things chilly for an hour or more."

"Well, they're delicious. Thanks, Alec." She pushed away from the bar before he could ask her to try something else.

"Sure! Come back for dinner, hmm?"

"Yeah, if I'm still in town. Things are a little crazy right now. See you!"

As she exited the tavern, Bronwyn reflected on her words. Things *were* crazy! She felt like she had a buzzing, burning need to find Cal and help him out, and she wasn't pleased about it. She hadn't wanted to leave Olivia so suddenly, especially since she'd be going back to the academy tomorrow. Still, when Bronwyn had read the message from Queen Aestasia, she'd been filled with anxiety, like the queen's urgency had become her own.

"Is it just her sense of how important this task is, or is she controlling me?" Bronwyn didn't know if the distinction mattered—either way, she felt she had to do what the queen asked.

She strode quickly along the cobbled road to the south, then took the right-hand branch that led toward the newer residential area. These homes had brick walls and a little more space between them. There weren't any tall dormitory-style buildings around, just lots of one and two-story homes with grass and cobbled paths between them.

Bronwyn flagged down a harried-looking woman with wild, gray-shot brown hair as she walked by. "Excuse me!"

"Yes?" The woman stopped short, backing away from Bronwyn, eyes wide and confused.

"Hi, I'm Bronwyn. Have we met?"

"Bronwyn . . . oh! I know who you are! You look different than I remember. Oh my, that was rude. I'm sorry!"

"It's not rude to notice the obvious! Don't worry. I'm sure you'll learn more about it as humans gather knowledge about this new world, but yeah, I've advanced my race a few times, and it's brought out these traits." Bronwyn gestured to her face, assuming the woman was referring to her pointed ears and bright eyes.

"Oh my, it's fascinating, isn't it? Oh, my manners! I'm Charlene Post. Charlie. I'm sorry to be in a rush, but I'm late for a class—I'm supposed to be teaching the Krystree an English class."

"What? English? Who's Krystree?" Bronwyn reached out a hand, putting one long arm in front of the woman to keep her from walking away. She didn't mean to be so pushy, but she was intrigued and didn't want the woman to scurry off.

"The Krystree—they're a race of birdlike people that Olivia and, um, *you* rescued through the portal."

"Oh! Right, right. Why do they need to learn English? The System Language Integration skill doesn't cover it?"

"That's the most interesting part—their Energy affinity is very low, and we speculate the System didn't deem them worthy of including. They don't have the skill! I'm really sorry, but I have to go!"

The woman started to push past Bronwyn's arm.

"One more question: I'm trying to find a man named Cal Jennings. Do you know which house is his?" She pulled her hand back, out of Charlie's path.

"Read the directory!" Charlie said over her shoulder, pointing to a small structure a short way down the cobbled road that reminded Bronwyn of a bus stop.

"Thanks! Nice meeting you, Charlie," Bronwyn called after the woman, but she was walking so quickly that she'd almost broken into a jog. She felt a little bad about making her late, but it wasn't like Charlie was trying to save the world—the Krystree could wait a few minutes for their next English lesson.

Bronwyn hurried up the road to the little three-walled brick structure with a sloping roof, and saw that the back wall was dominated by a corkboard listing people's names in alphabetical order, their house numbers posted next to them.

She scanned the list for the *J*s and found Cal Jennings. "D Street, number four. Gotcha!"

She hurried down the cobbled path, looking at the conveniently posted little street signs and the numbers on the houses, all made from pyrographed wood. When she turned down D Street toward the six houses along the little lane, she saw some activity taking place outside one of them.

A dark-skinned man, wearing a huge backpack reminiscent of an old-school hiking backpack with a bedroll, pans, and ropes hanging off it, was hugging a Ghelli woman while some other Ghelli stood around wearing long faces. Bronwyn walked toward them, knowing somehow that this was Cal.

"Hush now, Lysee! I'm just going to find my friend—you heard about what happened with the invasion. She probably needs help, don't ya think?"

Bronwyn stopped a few feet from Cal's back when she saw the other Ghelli had taken note of her. One of the smaller ones, a little girl, pulled her hand away from an older woman and ran past Cal and the woman he hugged, straight toward Bronwyn.

"Hello, fae lady!" She giggled and curtsied, her little wings bobbing up and down.

"Oh, hello, little one," Bronwyn replied, leaning down to look into the little girl's olive-colored eyes. "But I'm not really fae," Bronwyn frowned in consideration, then added, "Well, not a pure one, anyway."

The girl only giggled in response, and then Cal turned and cleared his throat.

"Hello, um, ma'am. Can I help you?"

Bronwyn liked the energy Cal projected. He had a genuine smile and eyes that were kind and patient. She stood up and walked past the little girl, gently trailing her fingers through her blonde curls as she passed by, impulsively wanting to feel their springy warmth.

"Hello, I'm Bronwyn. To tell you the truth, I came here to offer you some help, Cal." She reached out a hand, and Cal looked up at her warily as he reached out to grasp it. His skin was warm, his grip firm and pleasant, and Bronwyn smiled, looking into his eyes.

"Help me?" He sounded a bit disconcerted as he glanced back at the Ghelli woman he'd been hugging and then over at the older one.

"Yep! You're about to embark on some sort of journey or something, right? I've kind of had a calling to aid you. I know it sounds crazy, but consider all the crazy things you've seen in this world. You can trust that I don't want to cause you any harm. Exactly the opposite, in fact."

"Well, that's mighty nice of you, but I've got things under control here. I'm just heading up north to see if I can find a friend, and maybe not one you'd care to meet. You see, she's an Urghat."

"An Urghat?" Bronwyn blew out her breath in a soft chuckle. "I happen to have quite a few Urghat friends, and I'd like to check in on them, too."

"Really?" the woman asked from behind Cal. "What do the fae want with Urghat?"

"It's interesting that you and this little sweetie"—Bronwyn tousled the blonde curls of the little girl again—"marked me as fae. I'm not really fae, though. I just have a strong connection to them through my bloodline."

"Right . . . Bronwyn! Bronwyn Tallow?" Cal said with a snap of his fingers.

"That's it!"

"So you're human?" the older Ghelli woman asked.

"Yep! Do you folk have dealings with the fae?" Bronwyn asked, her interest in the subject pulling her into the tangent.

"One of their Way Trees opens into our grove. We see and speak with them from time to time," the older woman explained.

"Ah, I see. Well, Cal, I'm here to help you, so you'll have to get used to it. I'll follow from a distance if you don't want my company!" Bronwyn shrugged, feeling the buzzing tension in her gut ease for the first time since she'd read the Summer Queen's message. "It's not really something I can help."

"Is it a quest?" the woman behind Cal asked.

"This is my wife, Lysee," Cal introduced, stepping back and putting an arm around the woman's waist.

"Nice to meet you, Lysee," Bronwyn said, then continued, "It's very much like a quest, yes."

"This is good, Cal," Lysee told him, her voice high and musical. "You're not a fighter, love. I'll feel much better knowing you've got someone so powerful along with you."

Bronwyn opened her mouth to ask why the woman thought she was powerful, but then she stopped. Any competent Energy user would be able to feel her aura, and the fact that she'd advanced her race so much wasn't something she could hide. Instead, she said, "That's right, Cal. I'll help you deal with any trouble on the way, and we'll find your friend; maybe even see some of my friends in the process. What's your friend's name, by the way?"

The little boy, still clutching the older Ghelli's hand, piped up, "Whitestar! She's a great Urghat hero!"

"Oh? Whitestar . . ." Bronwyn ran the name through her mind and tried to remember if she'd heard it before. "Well, she sounds amazing. What's your name, little hunter?"

"I'm Bren, but I'm not a hunter! I'm going to be a keeper like my mom!" Bren said, taking the tone that only a child could pull off without sounding petulant.

"Oh, I'm very sorry for making that assumption." Bronwyn laughed, enjoying his outraged expression. "Keeper sounds very good, indeed. Your mother must be very proud. What about you, others? What about you, sweetie?" Bronwyn asked, gently tousling the little blonde-haired girl's hair again, enjoying the way she'd stayed next to her through the whole conversation.

"I'm going to be a Spirit Singer like Cal!" she informed, looking up at Bronwyn with big eyes and a bright smile.

"Oh, a Spirit Singer?" Bronwyn raised an eyebrow at Cal.

"Aye, little Vonna's shown some real talent already." Cal nodded, smiling.

"I'm Vella, and this quiet one is Gelyss," the older woman said, waving from behind Lysee.

"Quite a family you have here, Cal. What a lucky man!" Bronwyn exclaimed, and she meant it. How fortunate he was to have so many who cared about him in this strange new world!

"I am lucky, Bronwyn. I'll take your arrival to mean my luck's still holding."

"Yes! The roots are smiling on you, Cal. We'll all sleep better knowing Lady Bronwyn is with you," Vella said, squeezing the quiet girl in a side hug.

"Alright, well, I'm sorry to have you meet my family only to pull you away from them, but I'd meant to be on the road by now." Cal nodded down the path, turning with his arms spread for one last hug.

Everyone but Vella rushed into a group embrace, and Bronwyn smiled as she watched him kiss the tops of each of their heads.

"Nice to meet you all. I'll bring him home safe; don't worry!" Bronwyn waved and laughed as the little blonde-haired Vonna squeezed her around the knees.

"Will you bring us a present when you come back?" the quiet Gelyss called after Cal as he started to walk away.

"You know I will, sweet thing," Cal called back, then he turned and hurried down the cobbles, a spring in his step and Bronwyn right beside him.

# MORGAN

The landing on the seventh floor reminded Morgan of a VR ad for an exclusive hotel—marble flooring in a circle around the stairs, wide banks of windows providing expansive views in four cardinal directions, and a semiopen floor plan with wide archways connecting the various parts of the master suite.

He surveyed the area with his Void Vision, looking from the spalike bathroom with showers, a walk-in tub, and lush, green beds of succulents to the kitchen and dining area with its strange appliances pulsing with Energy, to the bedroom and sitting area.

He didn't see any sign of the guardian, so he did like before and called out, "Guardian! I'm here to challenge you."

Morgan heard the unmistakable sound of a door opening and turned toward it, seeing a French-style door leading to a balcony he'd completely overlooked. A man stepped through, and Morgan, so unused to the changes that had occurred in his appearance over the last few months, didn't recognize himself for several long heartbeats.

The man was tall, thin, but strong looking, with wiry muscles cording his bare arms. When it clicked that he was seeing his double, sans the wings, he snorted in laughter and said, "This old bit? I have to face a copy of myself?"

"No, no. Nothing so mundane. I took this form because I find it amusing to see people die as they stare into their own eyes." His voice sounded strange, as it always did when he heard it outside his head.

"So, a guardian and a psychopath, hmm?" Morgan held Bloodfang in a middle guard and walked around a plush, white sofa, stepping to a broad, clear area covered in woven, Berber-like carpet.

"Psychopath. I like the term, thank you." The man wearing Morgan's face shimmered briefly, then he was gone. His voice came from behind him. "Any particular rules of engagement you'd like me to observe?"

"What?" Morgan whirled, putting Bloodfang between himself and the eerie copy of himself. The guardian didn't wield a weapon and was dressed in simple white linen, not armor, but still managed to appear menacing as he stared at Morgan from just a couple of feet away.

"Rules of engagement. I see you wield a sword. Shall I as well? Pause after hits or an all-out brawl? To the death or to the blood? I mean, in your case—you'll have to kill me to claim this floor."

"Since you seem talkative, do you mind answering a few questions before we fight?"

"Why not? It's been ages since I spoke to someone from outside the tower. Before you ask—no, I don't know how long. I'm sure the busybody dragon fragment has explained that time is strange for us who are bound to the tower."

"Fragment?"

"Soul fragment. What's the world come to when a challenger for this tower knows so little? How fare the Yelestivians?"

"The who?"

"Oh gods, it's worse than I thought."

"How did you come to be bound as a guardian?" Morgan saw no reason to rush the fight and wondered if this talkative creature would provide a window into Vormendion's time.

"It's the oldest tale in the library, my friend. I loved a woman, Vormendion took a fancy to her, and a threat led to a duel which led to part of my soul being bound here as a slave."

"So he got the better of you, then?" Morgan took a step back and to the side, uncomfortable with the guardian so close.

"Oh, yes, challenger. Painful to admit, but Vormendion was twice the Energy weaver that I was."

"Do we have to fight? It seems the other guardians thought so, but is there no way I can claim this floor without destroying you?"

"Do you care for my feelings, young one? Fear not. This is just a hollow echo of me." He gestured up and down his body. "If Vormendion wasn't overly cruel, my soul fragment will escape this place and join with the whole. Assuming a challenger is able to conquer me, that is."

"Overly cruel?"

"Yes. He could, conceivably, have designed this tower to entrap my soul fragment even after this guardian duty ran its course. I've seen no evidence of that, however." He took several steps to the left and sat on the back of another sofa, still facing Morgan. "Anything else?"

"How many challengers have you faced? I'm assuming you can remember that, if not the time between."

"Impossible as it may seem, Morgan, you are my first. No one has claimed this floor of the tower since Vormendion departed this plane."

"So when you said you enjoyed watching people die while 'looking into their own eyes,' you weren't talking about your duties as a guardian? You fought like this before Vormendion captured you?"

"Why yes. I've always been handy with shape-shifting." He feigned a yawn, covering his mouth with the back of his left hand.

"You know this tower isn't on the world where Vormendion created it, right? That's why I've never heard of that . . . um, that name you said earlier."

"Really? Now, that is a bit surprising. When I came to this tower, it stood proudly from the craggy top of Mount Tyn. The views it commanded were something to behold. I knew something was off when I started to see these odd, purple meadows off the balcony. Tell me, are those little people below related to you? They don't bear wings like you."

"They're humans, like me. Speaking of wings, why didn't you copy that?" Morgan spread them to elaborate his point.

"Ahh, well, my shape-shifting is good, but I've never had wings and didn't want to flub it up. How embarrassing would that have been?"

"Alright, if there's no way to get you to back down, I'm going to have to fight you now. I need to get up to the next level, you see?" Morgan cast Void Vision, and his eyes turned into black pools with distant stars flickering in their depths.

"Very well. To the death, then?" The man held out his hand, and a beam of crackling white Energy extended from it, forming a glowing, sizzling sword blade, dripping liquid lightning that hissed and smoked as it fell into the carpet. The sword looked like it could cut through steel like butter, and he hoped Bloodfang was up to the challenge.

"I guess so. I'm not usually good at winning a fight without getting hurt, so I don't think first blood will cut it." Morgan was acting lackadaisical, but he was priming himself inside, preparing for a flurry of motion. The guardian had already shown him that it could teleport, so he primed his Circle of Combat spell and said, "Count us down; we'll start on one."

"Very well," his double replied, smiling. "Three, two, one . . ." He'd barely said the word when Morgan disappeared with a ripping sound, and the guardian faded away in a shimmer of light. Morgan reappeared where the guardian had been, and the guardian appeared behind where Morgan had stood. The guardian smiled, but then, directly behind him, dark swirls of Energy erupted from the ground, spinning into the walls of a black vortex.

"Let's keep things personal, hmm?" Morgan said, putting his back to the wall of his dueling circle and pointing Bloodfang at the guardian. He smiled and started forward, but Morgan was a step ahead and activated Hollow Charge, racing over the small space and ripping his sword into a pattern of cleaves, using his form, the Crane Flutters Its Wings.

The guardian was a competent swordsman; more than that, he was fast and precise, and his sizzling blade of liquid lightning tore through the air, knocking aside each of Morgan's cleaves and leaving black scorch marks on Bloodfang's silvery surface. Morgan didn't mind, though—he was testing the guardian and trying to occupy it while he set up his more powerful attacks.

Just as he finished the last of his series of cleaves, he cast Void Wave, and the black pulse of destruction ripped apart the air and light as it washed over the guardian.

Still looking through the black eyes of his Void Vision, Morgan watched as the guardian's will and Energy did battle with the destruction of the Void Wave. Morgan pushed out the void-attuned Energy through his pathways, trying to bolster the spell with his own will, and the clash of his dark Energy with the bright, lightning-like Energy of the guardian was like the explosion at the tip of a welder's torch.

Morgan cast Energy Drain and grabbed onto the guardian's hot, pulsing Energy, trying to yank it straight from the creature's Core. As the torrent hit him, he was surprised at how easily it flowed through his pathways and into his Core; it felt almost like it was pure Energy, though he knew it was different. While he pulled and pushed and the guardian struggled against his spell, Morgan lost track of his sword and let his guard down, and that's when the guardian proved it could multitask better than he. It lashed out with its terrible popping, crackling Energy blade and hacked into Morgan's leg.

Morgan screamed and stepped back, but realized he'd been anticipating seeing his leg cut off and had reacted reflexively rather than from pain. He was completely unhurt; his armor had deflected the blow, nothing but a black scorch mark on the shiny metal to show he'd even been touched.

"Sure you can't concede?" Morgan growled, yanking more of his opponent's Energy into his hungry Core.

His Void Wave had petered out, but not before it had taken a terrible toll on the guardian; Morgan's double looked wan, shrunken, and singed. His pressed linen outfit was frayed and tattered, and his hair was jagged as though part of it had been dissolved. It probably had.

"Stronger than I anticipated, but no, there will be no easy way out for you or me."

The guardian shimmered, faded, and reappeared beside Morgan, its crackling Energy blade slicing through the air in a deft series of feints, hacks, and thrusts.

Morgan's swordwork was more than a match, though, and he deflected the blows with Bloodfang. Droplets of plasmalike Energy flew off the guardian's blade with each clash and splattered against Morgan's armor, sizzling little black spots into the shining metal. As his opponent brought its blade back for another strike, Morgan cast Azure Burst.

Blue Energy blasted forth from him in an explosion of roiling flames that filled the entire space of his dueling circle. In the weird, semi-grayscale tones of his Void Vision, Morgan saw his Azure Burst engulf and toss the guardian back to slam into his roiling vortex wall and then smash down onto the ground.

The flames died away, and Morgan's tormented double struggled to stand, pushing himself up with shaky, blackened arms. His Energy blade was nowhere to be seen, and Morgan took the opportunity to dart forward, plunging Bloodfang through the side of the guardian's singed, reddened neck.

He stepped to the side, and pulling hard on Bloodfang, he drew an edge against the other's throat, severing tendons and arteries in a dark blue splatter. The creature may have made itself look human, but the illusion hadn't extended to its blood.

Morgan stepped back to observe, waiting to see if it died. The guardian twitched and clawed at the blackened, stained carpeting, and Morgan reached out with another Energy Drain, pulling in sporadic spurts of hot, yellow Energy. When nothing more came forth, and the body ceased moving, golden motes of Energy began to coalesce around it and then flow into Morgan.

**\*\*\*Congratulations! You have achieved level 39 Void Adept, gained 8 Intelligence, 8 Will, and have 12 points to distribute.\*\*\***

"I don't think he fought you with everything he had, Morgan," Tiladia said, gliding toward him from the stairwell.

"Really?"

"I say that not because I want to shame you but because I knew him well, and Lenethar was a master duelist. I think he wanted to feel your strength, and deciding you were worthy, he didn't wish to remain in this tower any longer."

"He threw it? You think Vormendian would allow that?"

"Vormendian was powerful but also vain, and may have underestimated this fragment of Lenethar." Tiladia sounded downbeat and almost melancholy.

"What's the matter, Tiladia? I'm not upset that you said that—whether he gave it his all or not, I won, and that's fine by me."

"No, it's just that . . . Lenethar and I were friends. I spent many, many days in these chambers conversing with him to pass the strange time in this tower." She slowly spiraled toward him, flowing over the body of the odd shape-shifter.

"Shit. I'm sorry, Tiladia."

"I'm not upset that you beat him. I'm actually glad that his fragment is free and may find its way to the real Lenethar. I'm only sad that my friend is no longer here in this tower. I have other friends and people now, though. I'll be fine, Morgan." She tried to prove her mood had improved by taking on her dragon form and flipping in a backward loop.

"You do have other people now! Don't forget it, and don't be afraid to tell Issa or me if something's bothering you, okay?"

"Thank you, Morgan. My connections to you, Issa, and Ykleedra are growing stronger day by day, and it makes me feel grounded and more real. I'm sad to see the last of Lenethar, but I'm happy for the memories I have of him. I'm even happier for the memories yet to come from you and your friends and family."

"Likewise, Tiladia! Lots of good times are ahead!" Morgan looked around the spacious master suite then back to the stairs. "I'm excited to show this place to Issa, but first, let's do something about your friend's body. Should we bury it?"

"I appreciate your sentiment, Morgan, but he's long gone from that vessel. Let us simply deliver it to an incinerator chute."

"Alright. Oh, what about those portal keystones? Could you show me those real quick? I want to talk to Olivia about them after the council meeting."

"Of course, Morgan. If we go up the stairs, there are three rooms you can access on the eighth floor. The fourth and largest room is the reliquary, and you'll need to face the final guardian before gaining entry."

"Got it. After you, Tiladia," Morgan said, gesturing to the stairwell.

# OLIVIA

Olivia looked around at the council table and the assembled faces of her peers. A lot had changed since she'd last sat at a full meeting. The table was new, a long oval of dark, polished hardwood that would have been an impossibly expensive antique back on Earth. There were chairs along the wall, away from the table, where various government functionaries and secretaries sat to listen to the proceedings. Strangest of all was the deference and respect people in the administration building had shown her as she walked through the foyer, the short hallway, and into the council chamber.

A seat to her left was empty—Bronwyn's spot. She sighed heavily, realizing her friend, her love, had been right about needing to leave the colony. "Oh, Bronwyn," she sighed softly. "I'm going to learn a spell to send you messages as soon as I get back to the academy."

"What's that?" Maria asked from the seat to her right.

"Just talking to myself," Olivia replied, favoring her with a smile.

"I can't get over how all of you have changed," Maria said, gesturing across the table to where Morgan sat, towering over the people nearby with his wings jutting up behind his shoulders. Issa was in a chair along the wall behind him, talking softly to a short, black-haired woman.

"Yeah, it's really something, isn't it?"

"These, um, changes are all due to remnants in your DNA that the System brought forth?" Maria asked, clearly referencing a conversation she'd had with others.

"Mostly, though in my case, there are external factors—things to do with my class and my affinities. I'll document everything when I have some time and make sure the colony gets a copy."

"That would be very welcome." Maria nodded.

"We're all here. Shall we start the meeting?" Arthur spoke up from Olivia's right.

He sat near the end of the oval table, and his voice carried clearly throughout the room, though he didn't shout or raise it. Olivia saw his palm resting on a smooth polished stone inset in the tabletop. Every seat at the table had a similar one in front of it.

"Does that stone amplify his voice?" she asked Maria.

"Yes," she whispered. "Simply rest your hand on it, and it will do the same for you."

Olivia nodded and waited while the conversations around the room died down, and Arthur cleared his throat to speak again.

"We have a lot of new business to discuss today, and we're nearly at a full council for the first time in a while. Bronwyn Tallow was called away on important business, but Ms. Bennet has her proxy. Is that right, Olivia?"

"That's right." She looked around the table at the other council members and continued, "She sends her regrets, everyone. She really wanted to be here."

"Thank you, Ms. Bennet. Please use the speaking stone should you need to address the table again—we'd like everyone to be able to hear and record your words." He gestured to the people around the edges of the room, and for the first time, Olivia saw the airship captain sitting in a chair near the far door. Olivia just nodded. "Very good. Let's begin with old business and updates."

Arthur and the regular council members spent a good hour discussing day-to-day things in the colony. There were updates from engineers on various construction projects, including, apparently, a road between First Landing and Tarn's Crossing. Olivia was interested to learn that a full-blown sewage system had been installed throughout most of the colony, and that land claims were being offered as rewards for contributing to the settlement. The claims were for farming, mining, and logging rights, and Olivia began to realize how out of touch she'd grown with the goings-on in First Landing.

"Before we move on to new business, I'd like to give our guest speaker, Captain Gella, a chance to address the council. He's on the schedule for next week's meeting, but I thought today would be opportune, considering Ms. Bennet, at least, might be leaving shortly. Any objections?"

Arthur looked around the table, but everyone's eyes had fallen on the captain, who stood with his tall uniform hat in his hands before him.

"Thank you! Thank you so much for letting me sit in on this meeting and for giving me the chance to address you all. I might say, I'm very impressed by the egalitarian approach you humans take with governance."

"Are things not democratically decided where you're from?" Olivia had spoken without thinking, putting her hand on the stone to amplify her voice.

"Ah, well, the Ridonne Empire is a quasi-democracy, I'd say. We do have a ruling class, though they are limited by the Imperial Charter, and local governments such as this council are not unheard of in our smaller towns. Merchants and their organizations operate with great autonomy and often hold more sway on local economies than the empire." He looked at Olivia to see if she had a follow-up question, but she sat back and waited for him to continue.

"Well, the reasons I'm here are manifold. One, I'm serving as a sort of liaison between Ridonne and your new community. Two, I represent the interests of a very powerful family, and Lord ap'Gravin has authorized me to offer opportunities to your populace. Three, we—myself and those I represent—are eager to learn more about your people and customs."

"Ap'Gravin?" Olivia interjected again.

"Ms. Bennet, please do hold your questions until the good captain has had a chance to speak," Arthur said, clearly worried his guest would become offended by the interruptions.

"No, no, that's quite alright, Mr. Ballard. Um, Ms. Bennet, was it? Yes, my sponsor and the owner of the *Skybreaker* is Lord ap'Gravin—the head of the Mercantile Guild in Gelica."

"Is he related to a professor ap'Gravin at Fainhallow Academy?" Olivia couldn't stop the scowl from drawing her eyebrows down, nor the slight flare of blue fire in her eyes.

"Um, why yes. That would be Lord ap'Gravin's second son." He cleared his throat and continued when Olivia didn't respond. "I'd like to discuss some of the opportunities I have to offer your people if you wouldn't mind."

"Of course, please continue," Arthur said.

"Well, Lord ap'Gravin has many businesses—hundreds of them. Additionally, he has close dealings with all of the guilds in Gelica, a city of more than a million souls. He's sent me with authorization to enter into contracts with the citizens of First Landing. I have opportunities for apprenticeships in nearly every industry, as well as military, exploratory, and privateering contracts. He's offered generous signing bonuses and relocation stipends. We want the human race to thrive here on Fanwath, and Lord ap'Gravin knows that your growth can't happen in a vacuum. He wants to take this early opportunity to earn your friendship."

"Thank you, Captain Gella," Arthur spoke once the man fell silent. Then he looked at the table and asked, "Any questions for the captain?"

"How many people are you looking to take away, Captain?" Maria asked before anyone else could speak up.

"*Skybreaker* has room for more than two thousand passengers. I'm authorized to call for another ship should demand be high enough."

"What?" Maria exploded. "How can we function as a society if you take away half our people?"

"Your people would be stronger and in a more secure position should you all integrate with our society and gain valuable knowledge and skills in your new positions."

"So your goal is to dissolve our populace into the cities of the Ridonne Empire?" Olivia scoffed.

"I wouldn't say that's my goal; more like a side consequence. Why struggle out here in the frontier when you could join our great society, given a leg up by Lord ap'Gravin and his generous contracts?"

"Arthur," Olivia said sharply, touching the stone in front of her chair, "I'd like to speak about the . . . opportunities the captain has brought before us, but I'd like to speak freely."

"Yes." Morgan finally broke his silence. "I second that. Captain, thank you for your words, but I think we'll continue this discussion in a closed meeting. Anyone object?" Morgan looked around the table, allowing his eyes to fall on Arthur.

"Of course," Captain Gella replied, bowing. "Please keep in mind that my purpose here is to benefit your citizens."

"Yes, thank you, Captain," Arthur said. "I'll find you at Green's Tavern later to give you an update."

"Great choice!" Alec Green spoke. "Captain, you'll enjoy the menu tonight—it features my mom's meatloaf recipe."

"I look forward to it. Thank you all."

The captain bowed again, then exited via the door. When it clicked closed behind him, the table exploded into chaotic conversations.

A shrill whistle stopped the noise, and everyone looked at the source: Morgan.

"Listen, we all have a lot to say, but I want to start with Olivia." He looked at her before continuing, "What do you know about this ap'Gravin family?"

"I know that the professor is a creep. He's aligned with a student who was giving me trouble and tried to help her frame me for a crime. It's a long story but suffice it to say that if the father is anything like the son, I wouldn't want to do business with him."

"Alright, so that's one anecdotal problem. Another I see is what Maria brought up: do we want First Landing to thrive? Do we want human autonomy, or do we want to disappear into the masses of Ardeni, Shadeni, or whatever society?"

"This conversation smacks of racism," Dr. Kerns said, clearing his throat. "Do you really worry about the different races we might 'disappear into'? I'd have thought you'd have a different outlook, considering your relationship with Issa." He nodded toward the woman sitting behind Morgan, and she scowled at him.

"That's not what I meant, dammit!" Morgan growled. "I mean, we, as humans, have a history. We have an obligation to make sure our people thrive here and don't disappear. If millions of us were on this world, I'd have a different perspective, but less than five thousand? Aren't you all worried that we could disappear, that our descendants won't even know about Earth in a few generations?"

"Of course that's a real concern!" Maria exclaimed. "If Gella took two thousand of our people, we'd have a hard time maintaining a viable community. It would be catastrophic! We're already dependent on nonhuman citizens to maintain our current growth."

"Aside from all that, we should be worried about the contracts," Olivia said. Everyone stopped talking and looked at her, waiting for further words. "If he's using real artificed contracts, people need to read them carefully and ensure they understand all the clauses. If you make a mistake, you could—quite literally—become enslaved by a contract in this world."

"Which brings up another concern," Rene Bisset added. "What do we know about this Ridonne Empire? Do their values coincide with ours? Is slavery allowed there? Indentured servitude? Do they value personal liberties? Rights to privacy, speech, personal autonomy?"

"Issa?" Morgan looked over his shoulder at her. "Do you know much about Ridonne?"

"Probably as much as Olivia." Issa shrugged. "We're deep in what they call the frontier or the borderlands. I've heard about wars they've been in, and I've heard about some of their cities, but I've never been."

"Thank you, Issa." Arthur cleared his throat. "I'll repeat her words for those who couldn't hear." He carefully repeated almost exactly what Issa had said, using his amplified voice. "Olivia, anything to add?"

"Yes, I do. First, Fainhallow is outside the empire, but many of the people there are from Ridonne. Second, it was my understanding that Gelica is a border city, just on the edge of the empire. If this Lord ap'Gravin operates from Gelica, you have to wonder what people from deeper in the empire will think of us. I know the Ridonne Empire is constantly in conflict with its neighbors, including rather large, powerful city-states on their eastern border. I know there is most definitely a class system in place—the wealthy live very different lives from the common folk.

"I'm afraid I don't know much more than that, but I have access to histories and experts at the academy. I just wish I could communicate with you all more easily. If I could, I'd return in the morning, do some research, and fill you all in."

"That might be possible," Morgan said, touching his amplification stone. "I've cleared more of my tower, and I have the means now to semipermanently open a portal to different locations. I could send one of my portal stones with you, and you could set it up on your end. Then we could easily stay in communication."

"Really?" Olivia's heart lurched in her chest.

Did that mean she'd be able to visit regularly? Better yet, did that mean that Bronwyn could visit her?

Other conversations started to break out around the table as people took in the gravity of Morgan's words.

"Morgan," Arthur spoke. "How many such portals can you make? Does this mean we might have access to a larger city?"

"My tower has six portal gateways, so yeah, I imagine so. I mean, as long as someone traveled there and set things up in a secure space."

Once again, conversation broke out, with people loudly speculating and others shouting for them to return to their discussion of Gella's presentation. Olivia sighed and sat back, realizing this meeting wasn't going to be over anytime soon.

# MORGAN

Morgan listened, irritated by all the tangents coming up, while the council bickered, ranted, and at least to some nominal degree, discussed the issues facing First Landing.

He was itching to get back to his tower to explore the possibility of opening a portal to Fainhallow Academy with Olivia, anxious to finish the quest to fully take charge of his home, vanquishing the final guardian, and excited to get back with Issa and ask her about her latest appointment with Dr. Cho. These thoughts battled for his concentration, and he found himself tuning out much of what was being said around the table.

"So, we're agreed?" Arthur's voice jerked Morgan out of his reverie. "We'll issue a statement urging citizens to remain with the colony, warning them of the dangers of binding Energy contracts, and offering a legal review of all contracts for those citizens tempted by Captain Gella's offer?"

"Yes, I can make a copy of the relevant pages in my text. I'm sure we have plenty of people familiar with contract law and the relevant legalese that would take up quests if the council authorized them at the Town Stone. Also, I'll draft a pamphlet describing the dangers of revealing one's affinities, especially their general Energy affinity. At the very least, I'll explain that the people of this world keep such information rather closely guarded," Olivia said.

"I have a proposal I'd like to bring before the council," Tanya Delgado spoke up, filling the silence as people considered Olivia's words.

"Go ahead." Arthur turned to her.

"It seems we're always down a council member or three. I propose we have a special election so we can fill a standing alternate position. In other words, we'll have a tenth member that only serves to break ties in the event we have absent members. For instance, today, we have eight members present. If we had a tie vote on something, what would we do? Wait for Bronwyn to return before we can make a decision?"

"I have Bronwyn's proxy," Olivia reminded her.

"Still, I think it'd be a good idea in the event that wasn't the case," Tanya pressed.

"That's a fairly standard practice on boards, and I wouldn't be opposed to it," Dr. Kerns agreed.

"Any objections?" Arthur asked.

"Will the position be open to any citizen?" Olivia asked.

At first, Morgan thought she was looking at him, but he realized her eyes were staring over his shoulder toward Issa. Did Issa want to run for council? As far as he was concerned, she could have his seat.

"Yes, I don't see why it wouldn't be," Tanya replied, looking around at the assembled faces.

No one objected.

"Very good. I'll schedule the election later today. Tanya and Maria, will you walk to the stone with me after the meeting?" Arthur asked, and both women agreed. "Any other business?"

"I have a piece of business," Morgan said. "Kind of strange business, but I promised Bronwyn I'd bring it up when we got back to First Landing."

"Go on, Morgan," Alec prompted, nodding encouragingly.

"Well, this issue goes back to the very first day we arrived in the solar system. You're all aware that the Noah unit woke me up to troubleshoot the scanners, right?" He glanced around the table, meeting everyone's eyes as they nodded or otherwise affirmed his statement. "Well, the System noticed I was awake and sent me into the Crucible. You all know that. What I never mentioned is that it also gave me a title. I think I didn't mention it because it's kind of embarrassing; I mean, it's so pretentious sounding. Anyway, it labeled me Human Champion."

"Oh?" Alec asked with a chuckle. Olivia raised her eyebrow from across the table.

"Yeah, and it's a pretty significant boost—it increases my Energy use efficacy by fifty percent. What it boils down to is that my spells and abilities are a lot stronger than they would be without that title."

"That's great and lucky for you, but why bring it up to the council, Morgan?" Maria Rios asked.

"Because it's a transient title—it can be moved to different people somehow, probably at the Town Stone."

"And you're worried you don't deserve it?" Olivia had a half smirk on her face.

"Well, more like I think it's presumptuous of me to hang onto it. I mean, do you all think the populace should have a say in who holds the title? That's kind of what Bronwyn and I concluded."

"You helped save us from the Urghat! You found us our closest allies! Shit, man, you just dove through a portal to try to save some innocent folks," Rene

Bisset said. He looked at Olivia. "Not that you're the only one, but I sure don't have a problem with you holding that title."

"Nor do I, Morgan," Olivia added, smiling at Rene.

"I move to have Morgan hang onto his title for now, and that this matter be revisited in one year," Alec proposed.

"Seconded," Arthur answered immediately. "All in favor?" The table resounded with people saying "Aye," and Morgan sat back with a warm flush in his chest.

"Any other business? I've got ribs in the smoker," Alec said, pushing his chair back slightly. No one had anything else to bring up, so Morgan stood, turning to find Issa already walking toward him.

"That went well." She reached out a hand for him to take.

They walked out of the building and stood to the side under a flowering purple-leafed tree in a brick planter surrounded by little shrubs. Morgan watched the people leaving the building for Olivia, and when he caught sight of her, he called her name. She strode over the cobbled courtyard toward them, her lengthy black hair iridescent in the sunlight.

"What a meeting, huh?" she asked, blowing out a big breath.

"Yeah, I'm not sorry to have missed so many while we've been gone."

"You two should be more enthusiastic about the chance to govern yourselves! The same families have dominated the council in Tarn's Crossing for generations, and nothing ever changes. I wish we had open elections like you do."

"You don't?" Morgan was surprised.

"Not really. Candidates have to be approved by the council, and newly elected officials are held on probation for years, with their votes only counting as half a normal vote. It's very difficult to affect change because, even with the backing of the people, by the time a new council member gains full voting rights, their driving issues may have been forgotten or lost momentum."

"Yeah, I don't like the sound of that." Olivia shook her head.

"Exactly! Do you think I would stand a chance if I tried to run for the new alternate position?" Issa asked, looking from Olivia to Morgan.

"Hell yes," Morgan said automatically.

"I think you have a good chance, Issa. My only concern is that people might think you being with Morgan puts you two into a conflict of interest."

"Then I'll step down." He shrugged.

"You've been itching to get off this council from day one." Olivia laughed.

"Can you blame me?"

"Come on! You heard Issa. We need to appreciate our civic privileges."

"Well, seriously, I know Issa would be twice the council member that I am. If it comes down to it, I'll step down if people have a problem with you running."

"It might not be an issue. I mean, I know for a fact married couples are serving on the same boards and town councils back on Earth. There is precedent! And you guys aren't even married; at least not yet," Olivia said, grinning at Morgan's red face.

Issa didn't say anything, just stared at Morgan with a big, sweet smile, and he stuttered for a moment before he could form any words. Issa bailed him out, turning to Olivia.

"I have some news that we haven't told anyone. Can I tell her, Morgan?"

"Sure. I'd like to tell everyone in the world, so yeah." He reached an arm around Issa's shoulders while she reached forward to take Olivia's hand in both of hers.

"I'm pregnant, Olivia! Morgan and I will be parents!"

"Oh my God! Seriously? Issa!" Olivia pulled her into a hug, lifting the smaller woman into the air and pulling her away from Morgan. "This is fantastic! Do you know what this means? We must share common ancestors! The fae, maybe? This means we can stop worrying about our population so much, Morgan! We're not going to die out!"

"Yeah, I wanted to say that when Kerns accused me of being racist. I'm not trying to keep humans *pure* or some bullshit; I just don't want us to lose sight of our history, our roots, you know?"

"Yeah, I know. I don't know who Kerns was trying to impress with that little line, but trust me; no one thinks you're racist, Morgan." Olivia reached out and squeezed his shoulder. "Do you guys know what you're having? I bet it's a little girl!"

"No, but we're having twins!" Issa's grin was so wide that Morgan could have counted all of her teeth.

"Oh, wow! You're kidding! I can't wait to tell Bronwyn. I can tell her, right?"

"Yes, of course. I hope you'll both have a part in our children's lives," Issa said, still clasping Olivia's hand.

"I'm at a loss! I can't even think of what I was going to do right now. All I can think about are cute little pale blue babies." Olivia had tears welling in her eyes.

"Oh God." Morgan shoved a hand through his hair and looked away. "Really? Let's not get all teared up, alright?"

"Oh, hush!" Issa shushed him. "They're going to be so cute, Olivia! I can't wait!"

"Yeah, yeah. They're going to be the talk of the town for sure. Come on, I know what you need to do now, Olivia—we need to go over how the portal stones work with Tiladia because I really want to set up a permanent connection to Fainhallow."

"That would be so great! I'd love for my friends to come visit, and if we have a portal, we could come every weekend! I could see Bronwyn all the time. And you guys, of course!"

"And the twins!" Issa added, gripping Olivia's hand and pulling her along the cobbled walkway toward town. "Let's stop for a snack on the way back?"

"Yes! I'm starved!" Olivia agreed, walking along briskly.

As Morgan stood in the shade of the flowering tree, watching them leave, he realized they'd completely forgotten about him. He sighed loudly and started after them.

He could grouse and complain about being bored in a council meeting, but really, he had it very good. Issa was happy, healthy, and making good, solid connections with the people in his life. He'd almost cleared his tower of guardians, and the only existential threat to the town seemed to be a slightly overzealous recruiter. Things could be worse.

He stretched his wings, fluttering them lightly in the sunlight. They'd grown cramped after sitting in the council chamber for hours, and the air and light felt terrific. The feathers were like hair—they didn't have sensation—but the part where they sprouted from the skin was very sensitive, and as the breeze fluttered them, it made him want to flap them and take off.

"Why not?" He laughed, and his wings cracked as he launched himself into the air.

At the apex of his upward momentum, he flapped again and really rocketed up. It was thrilling, and the wind whistling by his ears and through his hair and feathers was like a drug—he wanted more.

He opened his wings, angling his body so they caught the air and slowed his progress, and tilted to the right, banking into a slow, wide spiral, looking down at the cobbled path and Issa and Olivia. They'd stopped and were watching him, and Issa raised a hand to wave. Morgan waved back, then tucked his wings and dove toward the ground.

As he came near, he opened his wings, slowing his descent and angling into a curve so that he zoomed by, parallel to the ground, then back up into the air. He flapped a few times and was suddenly much higher than he'd ever flown. Morgan laughed, enjoying the feeling of ultimate freedom as he explored the sky above First Landing.

As he slowly made his way toward his tower, happy to let Issa and Olivia have a little time together, his eyes drifted toward the enormous airship docked at the northern edge of town, and he wondered if he should pay it a visit or just wait for his dinner appointment the next day.

# OLIVIA

"So I put this stone here, and Olivia uses the other one to set up the target portal? Does she need to prepare the location somehow?"

Morgan was holding two smooth, dark gray stones, both of which looked more like metal than actual rock. One was wedge shaped, similar to the stone Bronwyn's patron had given them to open a portal to find Morgan. The other was rectangular and about three times the size. They were both carved with runes and had an identical symbol inlaid with silver that Olivia recognized to mean simply One. She wasn't sure if she'd learned the symbol in one of her texts or if the System was translating it for her.

"That's right, Morgan. Yes, Olivia will need to choose a location that won't be disturbed by traffic or construction. The space should be ten by ten feet with a vertical clearance of twelve feet. It's best to activate the anchor on bedrock or some similarly solid surface out of the elements. It's imperative that she not place the anchor portal within twenty feet of any other dimensional or spatial-magic structures."

"So don't put the anchor stone on top of the teleport pad at the academy. Got it," Olivia said, reaching out for the larger stone. Morgan handed it over, and she felt the Energy resonating within the heavy object. "Will the gateway be present all the time, or will I need to activate it?"

"The gateway will be present, but the portal will remain inert until activated. Only people who Morgan gives permission to will be able to open it." Tiladia paused for a moment, collapsing and expanding in a tinkle of chimes and an explosion of mist, then resumed speaking. "That's not entirely true—someone with enormous power could force it open, but they'd have to be able to overpower the tower itself, which not even Vormendion could have done. He designed this building to withstand entry by beings far more powerful than even he."

"I gave you permission when you touched it, Olivia," Morgan clarified, nodding. "I'll be sure to give Bronwyn permission too so she can use the portal whenever she's around."

"Thank you, Morgan!" Olivia smiled. "Is it safe to put this in my ring?"

"I'm sorry, but no, Miss Olivia. This anchor stone is a spatial container in itself—it will expand into a gateway when you activate it."

"Oh, it's alright. That'll incentivize me to set it up quickly—don't want to carry it all over the place, do I?"

"Do you have a bag you can carry it in?" Morgan asked.

"Yes, don't worry. I'm going to gather my things and get going. You'll know when I get this set up, Tiladia?"

"Yes, I will. This portal will illuminate once the anchor is set as well."

"Alright, well, Morgan, I'll hopefully be seeing you soon. Be careful at that dinner tonight, and make sure Issa comes to watch your back. You know how distracted you are by good food." Olivia laughed as she pulled Morgan into a hug.

"Right, well, take care of yourself, and yeah, now you should be able to come back anytime you want. So if things don't go well, or they've . . . you know, expelled you, come on home, alright?" He squeezed her tightly, and Olivia felt a real sense of fondness for him—they'd grown close during their shared exile.

Not wanting to prolong the goodbye, Olivia turned and stepped onto the magical stairway, thinking about going to the guest quarters. Three steps later, she was on the landing leading to her rooms. She'd already said her goodbyes to Issa, and Bronwyn was nowhere to be found, so nothing was holding her here other than her lingering guilt about abandoning the council and the community again.

Olivia supposed she felt guilty mainly because she was eager to return to the academy while having niggling fears about the airship and the captain who worked for ap'Gravin. Perhaps she could find some more information about the professor's father while at the academy, though.

As far as the council went, they were handling things quite well, in her opinion. If she lost her seat at the next election because of her absenteeism, that would be fair. She could always campaign and try to regain it sometime down the road when she was ready to spend more time at First Landing.

She looked around her quarters, making sure she hadn't left anything she wanted to bring back with her. Most of her belongings, especially the ones she truly valued, were in her storage rings. After talking to Issa, she had taken her advice, splitting her belongings up between her rings—if she lost one, she wouldn't lose everything.

Walking around the room, she scooped clothing and toiletries into her ring, laughing to herself when she realized more than half the discarded garments were Bronwyn's.

Olivia sat at the edge of her bed and sighed. She really was disappointed that Bronwyn had left so suddenly.

"What's the deal with this Summer Queen bitch, anyway?"

She sighed again and shook her head. Bronwyn had been so open and happy while they'd been together on Unu and in the dungeon, but she definitely had a leash attached to her neck, and Olivia didn't like it. That thought always brought with it other, even less pleasant ones, like what exactly were Bronwyn and Olivia to each other? They certainly enjoyed each other's . . . company. They'd professed their fondness for each other, but was it really love? Was there a future in it?

Olivia sighed again, heavily.

Thinking about her relationship with Bronwyn brought up another worry—how would she treat Adaida? They'd been growing close, and Olivia was excited to see her, but would she need to keep her at an arm's length now?

"Maybe she's assumed I'm dead or not coming back, and she's forgotten all about me."

Olivia stood and gathered up Bronwyn's clothes, folding them and setting them on the bed before moving in front of the mirror inside the armoire door and giving herself a good once over. She held a finger to a little cluster of runes at the hem of one of her robes' sleeves, concentrated for a moment, and the garment shifted from burgundy to gray. She'd spent some time in the dungeon learning to add the runes to her magical robe, taking it a step further than Oylla had suggested—not only could she make them gray to fit in at the academy, but she could imagine nearly any color, and the fabric would shift to match it.

Her hair looked good, as always these days; one of the perks of having an evolved racial status. She smiled to herself, wondering what people would think if she strode back into the school wearing her Crown of Nightmarch. The crown was beautiful but intimidating, and it certainly sent a signal.

"Who wears a crown all the time?" She supposed that if she was adventuring or worried about having to use magic in combat, it would be wise to keep the crown on, but was it really appropriate for school? "Maybe if I were a princess or something."

Her boots were shiny and clean, as always, and Olivia could find no reason to keep delaying her departure. She'd already spoken to Arthur, giving him copies of the pages from her text on Energy contracts. She'd said goodbye to Morgan, Issa, Maria, and even Ykleedra. Ykleedra! How strange it was to see the little Yovashi nurturing her four little sisters!

Morgan had yet to speak to the girl, and she'd begged Olivia to put a good word in for her. "Poor thing." She shook her head, smiling. "If she knew what a softie Morgan was, she wouldn't be worried."

Olivia slung a small cloth satchel over her shoulder and slipped Morgan's teleporter anchor stone into it. It was heavy on her shoulder, but she'd only have to endure it for a little while.

With a final glance around her room, Olivia took out the teleportation token Oylla had given her, activating it. With a shimmer and a faint *pop*, she was gone, engulfed by darkness. A heartbeat later, bright sunlight shone in her eyes, and a cold mountain breeze ruffled her hair.

Surprisingly, Olivia wasn't alone on the academy's teleportation platform. A young man wearing a very dapper gray suit was walking down the steps in front of her, but when she arrived, he stopped and turned. Upon seeing Olivia, his red-skinned face brightened, and he lifted a hand to tilt his black bowler-style hat.

"Hello! Newly arrived?"

"I am, as are you, I take it?" Olivia stepped forward, enjoying the cool, fresh air. The academy towers, on the other side of the arching bridge, had pennants flapping and snapping in the stiff breeze. She wondered if a storm was on its way.

"Yes, ma'am! I'm Carlu of Persi Gables—I've been dispatched to investigate the murders."

"Murders?" Olivia hurried down the steps to walk beside Carlu, and they both continued their way to the bridge.

"Oh, you hadn't heard?" He held out a hand as though to help her with the steps, but Olivia smiled at him and waved it away.

"No! I hate to hear someone has died, but I dearly hope it wasn't one of my friends! I've been gone a while," Olivia said, unable to dissemble in her genuine concern.

"I hope not! I'm afraid my summons was a bit light on the details—I only know two students have been murdered in the last week. Hmm, a second-year and a third-year student. I didn't catch your name, ma'am."

"Well, I hadn't offered it yet. I'm Olivia Bennet, and I'm grateful for the information. Selfish though it might seem, I'm relieved—my friends are first-year students."

"It's the nature of social creatures, ma'am. We tend to care about those in our circle but have a hard time empathizing with faceless others."

When they reached the paved walkway to the bridge, Carlu produced a shiny black cane and gently tapped the cobbles with it as they walked along. Olivia thought it was funny, in a way, that he presented such an affected style, but then she reminded herself that she'd never been to Persi Gables. Maybe canes and suits were in fashion there.

"It's rather alarming that students are being murdered, isn't it? I've only been here part of the year, but I hadn't heard of anything like this happening."

"Oh, I would imagine so, though if it were something they could solve in-house, I wonder if anyone would ever hear about it. Forgive me. Your, um, presence is making me rather free with my words, and I'm sure the chief inspector would have me on citation duty if he heard me speaking in such a way."

"My presence?"

"Well, I've never been so close to someone with such a striking appearance. May I ask, are you from off-world?"

"I am, though my people have recently settled on Fanwath. I'm sorry, Carlu, if my presence is disturbing you," Olivia said, favoring him with a smile.

She was a good deal taller than the young Shadeni, but she'd reined in her fiery aura. Still, she knew her features were rather remarkable since she'd undergone so many racial advancements, but she'd never thought her mere presence might fluster a stranger.

"Oh no, no! You aren't disturbing me, Miss Bennet. Again, my mouth is simply running away from me. My chief has often scolded me for being too friendly with those I interview. Oh, he scolds, but would he admit that my closure rate is higher than his ever was? I think not."

"I see." Olivia glanced over the bridge into the thick clouds below them. "So this is an interview?"

"Oh dear, that's not what I meant! You see? My mouth isn't consulting with my brain! No, I think I should simply say it was a pleasure to meet you, and I hope we can speak again while I'm here."

They'd reached the tunnel leading under the wall, and Olivia could see the guard leaning against his station, sipping from a steaming mug.

"Well, it's been nice to meet you too, Carlu. I wish you the very best of luck with your investigation."

Olivia held out a hand for him to shake, but he clasped it with both hands and gently squeezed her fingers. It was unlike any handshake Olivia had ever had, and she wondered if she needed to check out a book on social etiquette from the library to see if she was supposed to curtsy or something.

Though she felt awkward, she could feel the sincerity in his warm, gentle touch, so she smiled at the investigator, looking into his bright, red-flecked green eyes, and then turned to walk quickly through the tunnel, stretching out her long legs.

The guard didn't challenge her as she walked by, and she waved at him with a bright smile, her cheeks rosy from the chilly air.

"The summer is surely shorter here than back at First Landing," she muttered, pushing her way through the crowds on the market street and hurriedly making her way toward the main academy building.

If a murderer was afoot, she had even more reason to find her cohort and see what she'd missed.

# OLIVIA

The academy was as busy as always on a Thursday. Olivia strode through the crowds in the central, open hallway, quickly passing through and taking corridors and stairs that would lead her directly to Oylla-dak's office. She saw faces she recognized, but none of her cohort members or the others in her class. This time of day, they were all probably in Spellcraft.

Olivia passed through the reception area for the administrators' offices, walking so surely and quickly that no one called out to her or asked where she was going. Oylla's door was closed and it looked dark, like the shades had been drawn, but Olivia gave it a knock anyway, standing back from the door in the dim hallway.

She only waited a few minutes before the door opened and a small, pink-skinned woman with tiny Ghelli wings stepped out. She was wearing a silky blue blouse with a gray skirt, and Olivia thought she recognized her from one of the registrar's desks. She looked at Olivia wide eyed and nodded toward the open door.

"She's at her desk," she said, then hurried down the hallway.

Olivia walked into Oylla's sitting room, took a right through the open double doors to her office, and said, "Hello, Professor. I'm very sorry to be so late coming back to the academy."

Oylla was sitting back in her chair, her feet on her desk, massaging her temples. Her eyes popped open at Olivia's words, and the tiny starlike lights in their dark, glittering depths glinted in the dim light. Her lips spread, revealing enormous canines, and then she was on her feet, striding to Olivia, arms spread wide.

"Olivia! I knew you'd be here soon, but didn't expect you this early!" She pulled her into a hug, and Olivia reached under her arms to hug her back, surprised to be nearly at eye level with the formidable woman. "You've been through a lot, haven't you?"

"I've certainly learned a lot! I've been keeping a journal and have some amazing discoveries to share with you!"

"Oh? I'll look forward to spending some afternoons with you, then. We have much, and I mean *much* to discuss, Olivia! Sit down, please. There are a few things we need to settle right now. Excuse me," Oylla said as she reached down to her desk to touch a polished stone. "Bina? Please cancel my next appointment."

Olivia sat in one of the plush chairs in front of Oylla's desk, and to her surprise, Oylla sat in the chair next to her, not behind her desk.

"I'm sorry to make you miss your appointment—"

"Not at all! I should be thanking you for getting me out of that meeting! Who wants to sit down and listen to a stuffy accountant whine about expense reports? Now, tell me a little about your experience. Just the broad strokes, though—we can get into the details in our next meeting. I can tell by your aura that you've gained some significant power."

"Well, I should start by saying I'm level twenty-five now," Olivia began, and Oylla's eyes widened. "I gained a new class at level twenty—Elemental Paragon. You see, a friend of mine fell through a portal while defending against an invasion from another world, and another friend managed to find a way to open a portal to him, so we staged a rescue. That's where things sort of went off plan. We got teleported to a different world entirely, and we had to spend several weeks learning how and preparing to open a gateway back to Fanwath. That's the much-abridged version of events."

"You opened your own gateway?" Oylla raised an eyebrow.

"Not just me. I figured out the spell for my friend, who has an affinity for void Energy. Luckily, he had the means to store a lot of Energy. That's what took the longest."

"Void Energy, hmm? That's rather uncommon, Olivia. I'd like to meet this friend of yours sometime."

"Well, that's another matter we should talk about." Olivia lifted Morgan's anchor stone out of the satchel she'd set next to her chair. "This is an anchor stone for a portal in my friend's tower back home. He's asked me to seek permission to place it here, at the academy. With this in place, I'd be able to visit First Landing more frequently, and so would you or others from the academy. Obviously, it would also allow Morgan or others to visit this place."

"That's impressive, Olivia. I've seen the like, and we have several similar gateways on the grounds. They're extremely costly, though, and usually only very wealthy, established families from the empire maintain them here." She took the stone from Olivia and examined it. "Very sophisticated work. Did your friend create this?"

"No, he earned his tower from the System when we first came to this world. He had to fight the guardians within in order to claim these stones and activate his portals; he only managed to do so recently."

"Fascinating. I'll grant your request if only to satisfy my own curiosity about your friend's tower. What did you say his name was?"

"Morgan. Morgan Hall."

"Alright, when we're done with this meeting, I'd like you to speak with Mrs. Poyle at the administration front desk. She'll assign you a plot in the Travel Pavilion where you can place this anchor. Have you seen the pavilion? It's west of the flower garden, around the other side of the main academy building."

"I think I have seen it, but I didn't know there were gateways there. We never had cause to go inside. I mean, my cohort members and I."

"No, it's not usually a subject for first years. Alright, that's settled. Now, I have important matters to discuss with you regarding your studies." She paused to look at Olivia, waiting for any objections or questions, but Olivia stayed silent. "I want you to continue your classes with Professors ap'Rall and ap'Rek. The rest of your days will be spent working with an advisor. A mentor, really."

"Oh? While I was gone, I worked a lot on my artificing and wouldn't mind learning more—"

"Time for that when you've perfected your spell knowledge. Trust me, Olivia."

"I do trust you," Olivia said, nodding.

"Good! Now, this is where you get some more input—we need to choose your advisor. I've had more than a dozen tenured professors come to me with an interest in you, and I've narrowed the list down to five. We'll interview them together. How does that sound?"

"Um, it sounds good, Oylla. Thank you for helping me with that."

Olivia frowned slightly, and Oylla reached out a long-fingered red hand to take hold of Olivia's.

"You're wondering how I narrowed the field. Let me say that I have extensive knowledge about the professors at this school, and although I'm the head of first-year students, that wasn't always the case. Heads of class rotate with their cohorts. Next year, I'll be head of second-year students, and the third-year head will move to first year. I know all the professors, and only Headmaster Jaxin-dak outranks me on these grounds.

"So you see, I recognized many of the parties interested in you for their true intent. Professor ap'Gravin, for instance, would seek to recruit you to his family's service, perhaps in an unfavorably binding contract."

"Ap'Gravin was interested?" Olivia couldn't help the way her voice rose in alarm.

"Oh yes. You may have bested his protégée early on, but that won't keep him down. No, he sought to save face by taking charge of your future learning. I rebuffed him for you, of course. That's just one example. Professor Yizshin would bury you in research and keep you locked away in his alchemy laboratory for the next several years—not a good way to foster your natural talents and love of learning, trust me."

"No, that doesn't sound ideal . . ." Olivia said, imagining a dark basement filled with bubbling beakers and cauldrons.

"So, I'll start scheduling the interviews. We'll begin tomorrow. Does that sound alright?"

"Yes, that's great. Should I attend Spellcraft and Cultivation tomorrow?"

"Oh yes, I'll be sure to schedule around those two classes. Now, about your accommodations, you're technically still part of Copper cohort. However, you've outstripped the growth of all the other first-year students, and I'm not sure it would be kind to keep you housed with them, especially when your advisor will no doubt expect you to work on projects in your own space."

"Oh, Oylla! I really want to stay with my cohort, at least for the rest of this year. I can imagine they're going to be peeved that I'm not in all their classes as it is. How will they react if I get my own room?"

"Alright, alright. We can make that part of the interviewing process. Let's see which professor will be willing to give up some of their space so you can have an office!" Oylla smiled rather wickedly, then continued, "I think that settles most of the most urgent matters. Why don't you go talk to Mrs. Poyle, and then you can see if you can find your cohort? I'm sure you're eager to reunite."

"I'll do that, but first, Oylla, could I ask you about the investigator that's come to the academy? I ran into him on the teleportation platform when I arrived. Should I be concerned about the murders?"

Oylla's smile faded, and her eyes drew into a narrow scowl.

"So you met this investigator on the platform, and he immediately told you about the murders, hmm? Not very discreet, is he? Well, I'm glad to hear he's arrived. I imagine he's meeting with the headmaster as we speak. No, don't worry, Olivia. We'll sort this out soon. Of course, it's troubling that students have been killed, but if you stay with your cohort, you should be safe." Oylla looked at her for a moment with a measuring gaze. "Actually, I should say your cohort will be safe so long as you are with them. Now, on you go. We'll talk again tomorrow. Someone will be 'round with your appointment schedule."

Olivia thanked Oylla again, then stood and made her way back to the front administration office. Mrs. Poyle was sitting behind her desk as usual, though she was sipping from a teacup and eating a biscuit, and was surprised when Olivia came walking out of the hallway behind her.

"Hello, dear, I didn't realize you'd gone by. Did you need some help?" she asked, putting her cookie onto a delicate plate with blue inlaid paisleys.

"Yes, thank you, Mrs. Poyle. I was speaking with Professor Oylla-dak, and she's approved me putting a portal anchor stone in the Travel Pavilion. She said you'd be able to give me directions to an approved location." Olivia sat in the wooden seat in front of Mrs. Poyle's desk.

"Oh yes. My, that's an unusual request. Let me see here." Mrs. Poyle turned and studied the shelf of books and binders behind her, running a finger over the spines as she muttered the names to herself. ". . . commons permits, room assignments, office space, lab requisitions, aha! Travel Pavilion!" She pulled a black leather-bound binder from the shelf and plopped it onto her desk. "Haven't had to assign a new space in there for a few years!"

"Are there many gateways active?"

"No, no, only a handful, but there are some dormant ones, and this little map"—she flipped the binder open to show a rectangular grid with blank and shaded-in squares—"shows exactly what spaces are open." She ran her finger over the page and asked, "Would you like your space to be near the door or further in?"

"Um, I don't think it matters. Near the door, I guess?"

"Good. Alright, here we go, A3. Yes, space A3, dear. Can you remember that?"

She didn't bother to wait for an answer, taking a small piece of card stock from her drawer and neatly printing A3 on one side. She handed the paper to her, and then she shaded in the spot on her map. Mrs. Poyle flipped a few pages back in the binder and started to write.

"Olivia, what was your last name?"

"Bennet," she replied, holding up her copper ring. "I'm in Copper cohort."

"Right, right. And where will this gateway open?"

"To First Landing. Um, it's near the Chebli Sea."

"Perfect! That should do it, Olivia. Be sure to talk to Professor Oylla-dak about permissions after setting things up. Don't make her come find you!"

"Oh, I'm meeting with her tomorrow; I'll be sure to take care of it."

"Good! Care for a cookie?" She pushed her plate over the top of the desk, and Olivia reached forward to take one of the three little sugar cookies.

"Thank you!"

She bit into the cookie, enjoying the sweet, buttery flavor, then smiled and waved. While she chewed, she walked out of the administration building and into the hallway. She vacillated about going straight to the dormitory or setting up the anchor stone, but ultimately decided to go to the Travel Pavilion first; she was tired of hauling around the heavy object.

## ⚭ MORGAN ⚭

"We don't have to go, you know," Morgan said, watching Issa study herself in the mirror. They'd moved into the master suite of the tower, and the bank of mirrors near the closet was proving to be one of Issa's favorite features of their new accommodations.

"You're joking, right? Have you ever been on a skyship? I haven't! I've never even seen one as big as the *Skybreaker*. I want to see what the inside is like!"

"Yeah, I suppose it will be neat to see what it's like inside."

Morgan walked over to the northern windows and looked out over the grassy field to the colony wall and the huge airship tethered there. Because of the tower's height and position at the top of a gentle slope, Morgan felt like he was looking down at the vessel's deck. "It's kind of cool to know these windows aren't visible from the outside. I can stand here staring at the little people out there and not worrying about who might see me watching."

"Rather suspect behavior!" Issa said with a laugh.

"Yeah, I guess so." Morgan chuckled. "Hey, I want to see Ykleedra before we go. I've been putting it off, and I'm already dressed and ready, so how about I meet you downstairs in fifteen minutes?"

"Sure, I could do without you staring at me for a while."

Issa walked toward the closet where she'd hung some of her extra clothes. Morgan had thought the bedroom-size walk-in wardrobe rather superfluous, given their dimensional containers, but Issa had been thrilled to look at all her clothes hanging next to each other, saying something about being able to picture her outfits more clearly.

He headed to the stairwell and, atrium in mind, started downward. He stepped onto the landing a moment later and turned to regard the warmly lit garden through the paneled glass wall. Morgan had definitely been putting this off, he realized, a sinking feeling of dread in the pit of his stomach. He wasn't scared or worried about Ykleedra's eggs. No, he was worried about facing the girl who was so fearful of him that she'd held onto such an important secret. She'd been afraid he'd destroy her eggs, according to Issa.

"How do I respond to something like that?"

Shaking his head, Morgan walked up to the atrium door and stepped inside. It was warm and the air moist, and he resolved to talk to Tiladia about adjusting the light so it wasn't quite so hot and bright in there during the artificial day. If he was going to have a bunch of young Yovashi living in the atrium, he should make it more comfortable for them.

"Ykleedra?" he called out.

"Morgan!"

Ykleedra came out of the nearby foliage almost immediately, and Morgan wondered if she'd been on her way somewhere or if her burrow was that close. Should he ask to see her burrow? Was that overstepping?

She stood there, head poking out of the ferns, her eyes slightly downcast. Though her face was devoid of typical human emotion, Morgan thought he saw trepidation writ there.

"Hey, Ykleedra. I'm sorry I've been gone so long. I'm sorry I haven't been here to help while you were going through such a tough time."

He took a step forward, and Ykleedra brought two feet out of the foliage, drawing herself out of the shadows. She still wore the same silvery robe she'd had on when Morgan had met her; he realized it must be enchanted because it fit her still even though she'd grown, and it was shimmering and clean.

"Morgan, I'm so happy you're okay. I was distraught when I heard about you being lost through an enemy portal." She ducked her head shyly, her long, spiderlike legs bent and curled in to make her seem smaller than she was.

Was this a defense mechanism? Was she making herself small so he'd feel more sympathy for her? Morgan hated himself for analyzing her that way, and it made him realize that he still harbored doubts about the Yovashi, even Ykleedra.

He determined to make up for it.

"Ykleedra, I heard about your sisters, and I want you to know that I'm not upset. Well, I'm not upset with you. I'm a little upset at myself for not making you feel welcome or comfortable enough to trust me with your secret. I hope you believe me when I say that I want your sisters to be safe, and I want you all to stay here. I can help you in any way you need, all right?"

"Really, Morgan?"

Her head came up, and she looked into his eyes for the first time. The fathomless black pools of her eyes looked moist, and Morgan was happy to see that they squinted slightly, showing more emotion than he'd thought she was capable of. Even her thin lips stretched into a slight smile, revealing her pointy white teeth. Had he seen her smile before?

He stepped forward and held out a hand, part of him dreading what he was about to do.

"Take my hand, Ykleedra," he requested, standing before her. Towering over her, really.

"Take your hand?" She tilted her head quizzically.

"Hold my hand. With one of your . . . uh, tentacles." The girl's head tilted even more, and she stared at Morgan for a second, but then a thin, gray tentacle snaked out from beneath Ykleedra's robe and curled around Morgan's hand.

He forced himself to remain still, and when the warm, dry appendage curled around his wrist and hand, he closed his fingers around it, holding it softly. "In my culture, sometimes people shake hands as a show of sincerity. I want you to know that I trust you and that I'm never going to hurt you or your sisters. I won't let anyone hurt you. Do you trust me, Ykleedra?"

"You're the first person I've touched, Morgan. Other than my family, I guess."

The tentacle gently quivered as the tip advanced along his wrist, holding onto him more firmly. Morgan was dismayed to see liquid pooling in Ykleedra's eyes and then tears streaming down her cheeks. Her words hit him so strongly that his own eyes filled as well, and he pulled her toward him, leaning down to wrap his other arm around her very humanoid torso, squeezing her into a hug.

"I'm sorry, Ykleedra," was all he could say as the girl leaned her head into his shoulder and her tears soaked his white dress shirt. After a time, he stepped back, happy to see that she still held onto his hand. Another tentacle reached up through the top of her robe to wipe at her face. "You going to be okay?"

"I am, Morgan. I'm so sorry I didn't trust you." A sob caught in her throat. "I'm sorry my father killed your friends, and I'm sorry my mother and grandmother were hostile to your kind. I wish they could have learned what you were really like." Tears continued to stream down her face, and she continued to wipe them away.

Morgan opened his mouth to argue, to say he'd been the aggressor in her home, but she was right—they'd had a dead human in the house, and the grandmother had been teaching Ykleedra how to kill and butcher him.

"Let's try to forget the past and move forward, alright? Now, what can I do for you and your sisters? Do you want me to hire some workers to help you build a proper home in here? Issa says you're all living in a burrow?"

"Could you really do that? The atrium is big, but would you be okay with a house here?"

"Hell yes, I'd be okay with it!" Morgan laughed. "How cool would that be? A house in the atrium of my tower? I'll talk to the council, see who's doing the best building, and I'll hire them, alright?"

"Thank you, Morgan!"

"What about food?"

"Miss Issa has given me a vast quantity. We'll be fine for a long while, Morgan." Her tentacle, still in Morgan's hand, pulsed and flexed softly with her emotion, and Morgan found he was enjoying her gentle, warm touch. It was nothing like he'd feared it would be. Still, he slowly disengaged his grasp and pulled his hand back, letting it fall away.

"I have to go to a dinner meeting, Ykleedra. I'll be back tomorrow, okay?"

"Yes. I will await you. Would you like to meet my sisters tomorrow?"

"Of course! I was going to ask if I could!" Morgan smiled and reached forward to gently squeeze Ykleedra's shoulder where one of her front spider legs protruded. The junction where the hard chitin-covered appendage met her softer humanoid shoulder was strange under the fabric of her robe, but Morgan kept his smile in place before waving and turning to leave.

"Morgan, your new wings are impressive," Ykleedra spoke as he neared the atrium door.

"Hah, thank you, Ykleedra. Would you like to hear the story of how I got them? When I visit tomorrow, let's do some catching up, alright?"

"Yes, I'd like that very much." Ykleedra's voice seemed small, disappearing in the thick growth of the atrium. Morgan almost didn't hear it as he began descending the steps.

Morgan found Issa already waiting for him in the tower foyer. She wore a blue sleeveless dress, several shades darker than her skin, and though it fell to below her knees, it was made of sheer fabric that clung to her in all the right ways.

"Goddamn, you look good," he complimented, striding over and leaning down to kiss her gently. She barely allowed their lips to touch, clearly worried he'd mess up her pink lips. Her eyes were also shadowed with pink makeup, and Morgan had to admit the color looked amazing against her natural shading.

"What happened to your shirt?" she asked, running a palm over his chest where it was still damp.

"God, I just had a very emotional talk with Ykleedra. I hugged her, Issa, and it was the first time anyone's touched her since her family was killed. Can you imagine that?"

Issa's face fell at his words, the smile leaving her face and eyes.

"No, I can't, Morgan. Ancestors! Are we monsters?"

"I don't think so! I don't know, though. I mean . . ." Morgan looked around, then nodded to the door. "Let's go outside, hmm? We can talk while we walk." He led Issa out of the tower, and once they were walking over the blue, twilit grass toward the northeastern tower, he continued his train of thought. "I never had an urge to touch her, and she always kept her tentacles tucked away, you know, keeping her distance. I thought she was sort of reclusive and standoffish, but maybe she just recognized in our eyes—my eyes—that there are things about her that are . . . ugh, I don't know, strange, unpleasant?"

"The tentacles? The spider legs? The dark, emotionless eyes?" Issa said softly, clearly also feeling guilty.

"But they aren't emotionless, Issa! I thought so too, but tonight, when I spoke to her, I saw fear, joy, relief, and warmth. She cried!"

"Right, we need to start helping her acclimate more. We need to spend more time with her, and I'm going to hug her when I see her next. Ancestors!"

"I told her I would have a house built for her and her sisters in the atrium. There's got to be a couple of acres of space in there, and I think a dwelling like her old home would be good. I don't like her living in a burrow, especially with little children."

"That's a wonderful idea. I'll speak to Alicia—her team did a great job on the stable, and if you describe what you want, I'm sure they can do it."

"Alicia? What's her last name?"

"Um, something long, like Watertown. I'm really not sure."

"No worries. You can introduce us, and I'll ask her," Morgan said, looking toward the ship growing larger as they approached. "How about I fly us up there? We can arrive in style."

"In this dress? I don't think so, love." Issa laughed, shaking her head.

# MORGAN

When they'd reached the top of the northeast tower, Morgan realized that the visiting airship crew had spent some time reinforcing the structure and adding a more comprehensive wooden platform to the top. A semipermanent walkway connected the new platform to the midship boarding port on the enormous airship. When the crew members waved Issa and him forward, it felt like they were walking into a building—everything was so steady and solidly constructed.

"It almost feels like we're on the ground," Issa said, a hint of disappointment in her voice.

"Yeah, I guess with a ship this large, you don't really notice the fact that it's in the air. Maybe if we were flying through the clouds, though . . ." Morgan trailed off as he noticed Tanna ap'Cilla approaching down the wide, wooden hallway. She wore a black gown with a deep, open neckline that stretched all the way to her waist. Her pale blue skin glittered in the yellow-white light from the Energy globes mounted along the walls, and Morgan wondered if it was some racial enhancement or if she had actually put glitter on herself.

Issa straightened next to him, and Morgan smiled, lazily putting an arm around her shoulders as they waited for their host. Issa leaned into him, and he could feel her shoulders loosen up as she relaxed.

"Greetings! Thank you so much for accepting my invitation. I'm Tanna ap'Cilla, and I already know your names, Morgan Hall and Issa ap'Roald."

She wore a genuine-seeming smile that was reflected in her eyes as she reached out a hand to Issa. Morgan wondered at that choice. Was she trying to win Issa over by showing her extra respect?

Issa reached forward to take the smaller woman's hand.

"Pleased to meet you, Tanna. I've always wanted to see an airship like this." The two women smiled at each other for a moment, then Tanna released Issa's hand and held it out to Morgan. He took it, and though she held it with her knuckles facing upward, he squeezed it in a normal handshake. He wasn't about to try kissing her hand or whatever she'd intended.

"Good to see you again, Tanna. Any chance we could get a tour of the deck later? I'm also interested in this vessel," Morgan said.

"Absolutely. Follow me to the captain's table for now, though. They're getting ready to start service." Her fingers were cool, and as she withdrew them, she let their grip linger, sliding along Morgan's palm and fingers. Morgan couldn't help his nervous glance at Issa because the touch hadn't been benign. Issa's face was impassive, however, and she reached up to take hold of Morgan's upper arm, walking together as Tanna led them down the hallway.

Morgan admired the craftsmanship of the vessel. While it was steady and spacious, the tooled wood and round, brass-lined doorways were constant reminders that this was a master-crafted construct, designed for sturdiness in motion. There were no loose bits of furniture, and strange sounds vibrated through the wood: faint rumblings and hisses and the occasional shouted order echoed through the hallways they bypassed.

"Does the airship use a lot of Energy to stay docked like this? It seems the crew is awfully active for a vessel at rest," he asked as they traversed a short, elegantly crafted spiral staircase.

"These vessels require constant adjustment, and yes, we have a full crew responsible for charging the propulsion rings. They're on light duty while it's docked, but they still have to maintain the charge, keeping her ready for departure or maneuvers at a moment's notice." Tanna glanced back while she spoke, her bright green eyes glinting in the light.

"Tanna, was one of your parents Shadeni?" Issa asked suddenly.

"My grandfather," Tanna replied, turning her gaze to Issa but still smiling. "It's why my hair is black, I imagine."

"I thought as much; one of my good friends had black hair, though her eyes were a shade of orange. Her father was Shadeni." Issa's voice was friendly, but Morgan was wondering if there was some subtext to this conversation that he was missing.

"You know, there are scholars who claim the Shadeni and Ardeni are the same race. That they simply favor different bloodlines." Tanna didn't wait for a response to that statement, gesturing to a large open set of double doors. "The captain's table!"

The dining room of the *Skybreaker* would have been impressive in a manor or vineyard estate. The fact that it was on a floating ship made it stand out even more so. In Morgan's estimation, the room was around a hundred by fifty feet, and the ceiling was high enough that he could have jumped using his wings for a boost and not touched it. Waitstaff stood to the sides of the opulently appointed room, all wearing white jackets over black pants, with towels draped over their forearms.

At the head of the long, rectangular table sat Captain Gella, his navy-blue uniform impeccable with brass buttons glinting in the bright lights. He wasn't wearing his hat, and his long mustache and beard puffed out as he spoke to the man standing to his left, whom Morgan didn't recognize. He was one of the large, otterlike people—Vodkin, if he remembered correctly. He did, however, recognize the others seated at the table: Baron Finneal, the man he'd tangled with outside the portal, and Haku-dak, the huge warrior that had wrestled with Bronwyn.

"Good evening, everyone. Might I present Morgan Hall and Issa ap'Roald?" Tanna introduced, smoothly speaking over the conversations. The room stilled, and everyone's eyes turned to the trio coming through the door.

"Wonderful! Come, come," Captain Gella said, standing up in front of his chair. The Vodkin he'd been speaking to bowed slightly before departing through a door on the other end of the room. Haku-dak and Baron Finneal also rose.

"Thank you all. No need to stand," Morgan said, walking forward with Issa still holding his arm. He headed to the two vacant chairs on the captain's right, pulling one out for Issa before taking the other. As soon as she sat down, everyone else did the same, Tanna taking the empty seat across the table from Morgan.

The captain spoke again. "I'm so pleased that you were able to join us, Morgan and Issa."

"Thank you for having us," Issa replied.

"It's truly my pleasure." He paused and motioned to one of the servants, who stepped forward with a tray of delicate tall glasses. "I'd like to propose a toast," the captain continued, watching as each of his guests took one of the slender glasses filled with pale orange-red liquid.

When Morgan lifted his glass to his nose, taking a sniff out of habit, he knew it wasn't wine but some sort of liquor. It had a smoky aroma, and a thin sheen of oil sat atop the liquid.

"Beneset bitters with House ap'Anua gin," Captain Gella said, nodding to Morgan.

"A toast?" Morgan asked, prompting the captain to continue.

"Yes, to new friends and profitable ventures."

He lifted his glass, and as the others followed suit, so did Morgan and Issa. Morgan took a tentative sip of the liquor and was pleased with the dry, rich flavor—berries and herbs with a smoky aftertaste. Issa made a soft, happy sound, and Morgan smiled at her.

"Excellent, Captain," Morgan said.

"Thank you! Please drink up; my chefs have prepared several pairings to go with tonight's meal." He made himself an example by finishing off his glass and nodding around the table as his guests did as well.

"Captain, wasn't there some business to discuss before we eat?" Haku-dak asked, his baritone rumbling over the table.

"Oh, Haku, so quick to charge into the fray." Tanna tsked.

"Well, he's right, I suppose. Morgan, I did have some things to discuss with you while you're at the table with me, but Haku, we can certainly eat and talk business at the same time, no?"

"Naturally you can, Captain," Baron Finneal spoke, glaring at Haku-dak.

Morgan took the opportunity to look at the man, noticing more than his glittering wings for the first time. He was tall and lean, with pale skin and orange-red hair, and had wide, dark eyes that glittered with tiny pinpricks of light. He was undoubtedly a Ghelli, but his appearance reflected a lot of racial advancements or an unusual bloodline. He wore a suit much like the one Morgan had first seen him in, but this one was a deep shade of ocher that somewhat complimented his orangish hair.

While he'd been distracted looking at the baron, the captain had indicated to a servant to proceed with the service. In short order, servers were swarming into the room, depositing delicate gold-leaf plates in front of the diners with paper-thin wafers of some sort of fried root with a thick, creamy dollop of herbed cheese. Other servers deposited another type of fizzy cocktail in front of each guest.

"Ahh, wonderful, pateen root with herbed cheese from Volai. Let me know what you think!" the captain said, scooping some of the soft cheese onto one of the root slices and plopping it into his mouth. Morgan followed his example, taking a bite. The cheese nicely complimented the salty, sweet root.

He tucked into the little dish, and so did Issa.

"Bah, this isn't enough for a man," Haku-dak complained, quickly munching down the tiny serving.

"Patience, friend," the captain said. "We have several more courses!"

"Delicious," Issa complimented.

"Isn't it, though?" Tanna asked, smiling at her.

After a moment, Morgan asked, "What sort of business are you wanting to discuss, Captain?"

"Ahh, well, you realize we're here to offer recruitment opportunities to the citizens of First Landing, yes? We have a lot to offer on behalf of Lord ap'Gravin. I even have an opportunity that might be fit for someone of your stature." He looked at Issa and added, "And yours, of course, Miss ap'Roald."

"Ahh, I don't think that's going to work for us. Thanks, though, Captain. No, I've been gone a while, and I'm eager to spend some time here in town, and so is Issa."

"That's right. I'm working to become more involved with the community here," Issa added.

"Oh? That's a shame. One of Lord ap'Gravin's exploratory teams has recently found the entrance to an ancient ruin. He believes a dungeon lies within."

"Ahh, that sounds exciting, but this isn't the right time for us. If things change, I'll be sure to get in touch with you."

"We could have you in Gelica within a week, and from there, you could be to the ruins in another week. If you didn't like what you saw, you could teleport home—you have the means to make a portal, don't you?" Tanna asked, and though she was smooth, Morgan felt like the line was rehearsed.

"Hmm, yes, I do. But no, I'm not interested right now. Thank you again."

While he spoke, Issa reached a hand under the table to rest on his thigh, indicating, he thought, that she supported what he was saying.

Morgan took a sip of his new cocktail; it was crisp and sweet, with a hint of alcohol under the fruity flavor. "Are you having much luck with your recruiting?"

"Oh, not nearly as much as we'd hoped. I'm afraid your council has poisoned the well somewhat." The captain's usual smile faltered, and Morgan saw his eyes dart toward Tanna and Finneal.

Was that subconscious? Was he worried about them? Who was really calling the shots here?

"Poisoned the well?" Issa asked.

"They've issued statements discouraging your citizens from leaving and warning about unfair contract practices," Finneal responded.

"Well, that's hardly poisoning the well. You have to understand the need for a fledgling community to have a growing, local citizenry. The people of First Landing are also quite new to the System and Energy use—it's perfectly normal for the council to give them information about contracts, don't you think?" Issa said, scoffing lightly.

"Yes, but so many opportunities abound. Think what your citizens could return with if they spent some years learning and working for a thriving merchant empire like ap'Gravin's," Finneal countered.

"Just so," the captain agreed, nodding. He gestured, and servants began to clear away their dishes. "Let's switch subjects. I trust you'll let me know if you change your minds, Morgan and Issa. Meanwhile, Morgan, pray tell us about that amazing tower of yours!"

# ⪦ MORGAN ⪧

"That was truly an amazing meal, Captain," Morgan said, reaching out to shake Gella's hand. The captain took it warmly, pulling his pipe away from his lips with his other hand and gesturing to the deck of his enormous airship.

"Sure you don't want to stay aboard a bit? We could take a tour over the mountains to the north, and I could show you the encampments of those Urghat that were giving you all trouble."

"Thank you for the invitation, Captain, but Morgan needs to get me home," Issa replied, helping Morgan to bow out.

He was exhausted and grateful for Issa's intervention—it felt like he'd been playing defense all night, avoiding one invitation after another from the captain, Tanna, or Baron Finneal. The only member of the dinner table who didn't seem to want Morgan to do something or go somewhere was the hulking Haku-dak. Even now, the big Shadeni leaned against the far railing, sipping a crystal goblet of brandy while seemingly unconcerned about anything but the mysteries at the bottom of his glass.

"Yes, rest is important for those in your condition, Lady Issa," Tanna said, leaning close and speaking so softly that Morgan almost didn't hear her. Still, he stiffened at the sorceress mentioning Issa's pregnancy—they hadn't brought it up to anyone yet.

Gella must have seen how his brows furrowed because he cleared his throat and gestured toward the colony.

"You and your people should be proud, Morgan. The design of your burgeoning city is elegant yet simple—commerce will thrive here."

"Thanks, Captain. I'll pass your compliments along to the planners. Thanks again, all. I'm sure I'll be seeing you again before you leave."

Morgan didn't wait for a response; he simply stepped next to Issa and pulled her close, like he was going to hug her. Instead, his massive wings snapped out, and he leaped over the railing, gliding into the night sky and down toward the grassy field near his tower. Issa, for her part, didn't cry out or act surprised; she just hugged him tight and put her face into his chest. Once they were down, she let out a shaky breath.

"A little warning would have been nice!"

"Sorry, it rattled me when that woman mentioned your pregnancy. I couldn't think past getting us out of there." Morgan unwrapped his arms from around Issa and took her hand, walking with her the short distance to the steps leading up into the tower.

When they were passing by the new stables, he said, "Nice job on those, by the way. Are Munch and Gopp happy?"

"Yes, and Blue. Don't worry about Tanna, Morgan. She was trying to get a rise out of you—they were pushing you all night, in case you didn't notice."

"Oh, I noticed, all right."

"The only one with any real brains is the quiet one, Haku." She climbed the steps ahead of him, and Morgan held onto her hand, pulling until she looked back at him.

"What do you mean by that?"

"The others were feeling you out, trying to gauge you somehow. He'd already taken your measure just by observing you, and knows he wants no part in any trouble with you."

"You got all that by observing his . . . what, his silence?" Morgan pulled her close so she was looking into his eyes, two steps up from where he stood.

"His silence, his sidelong glances at Tanna and Finneal, his heavy sighs at their clumsy attempts to rile you. I'm not sure what game they're playing at, but he's eager to be away." She leaned forward and rested her forehead against his. Morgan savored the warm tingle where their skin met.

"He might be eager to be away, but I worry about their sponsor, ap'Gravin. It can't have been cheap to send a ship that size out here. Imagine the normal business they're missing out on by being here. They won't be happy to leave empty-handed," he said softly, finishing his words with kisses, first on her chin, then her nose, and then against her soft, warm lips.

"Well, you didn't show any weakness. They know they'll have to tangle with you if they're going to do anything underhanded with their contracts or anything else. Not to mention Olivia's probably setting up the portal to the academy as we speak."

"Right. I get the feeling Olivia would like an excuse for another round with Tanna." Morgan allowed Issa to pull him up the steps, inhaling deeply of the night air. "Well, at least the dinner was good."

"Ancestors! Wasn't it amazing? I didn't know there were so many spices in the world!"

She pulled the door open, and they walked into the tower. "Let's go to bed, Morgan. I know you're considering exploring the top of the tower some more, maybe even having a go at the final guardian, but can we just have a night to ourselves? You can talk to Tiladia about it tomorrow, okay?"

"Yeah, all right. I really do want to finish opening up the tower, though. Do you think it's a bad idea? I kind of already talked to Tiladia about it—she's not able to give me any information about the final guardian."

"Well, you tell me," Issa said, still guiding him toward the stairs. "You mentioned the seventh guardian wasn't that difficult."

"That's just it. I think it was supposed to be a lot harder, but he'd grown fond of Tiladia, and I have the feeling he was pulling punches in our fight."

"What? You didn't tell me that. Tiladia and the seventh guardian were friends? That's awful, Morgan! She lost a friend?" They walked onto the steps, hand in hand, both thinking about their suite on the seventh floor.

"Yeah, Issa. I feel so sorry for Tiladia, and that's one of the reasons I want to finish this quest. I want to have full access to everything about the tower, including the basement and the automated systems, and God willing, whatever is holding Tiladia here. What if there's a way for me to free her?"

Morgan glanced around, suddenly wondering where the dragon spirit was. Was she listening to them talk about her? He didn't want to call her because he'd rather not cause her distress by mentioning things that might be sensitive topics.

"Anyway, let's talk about it tomorrow. Tonight, I'd like to spend some time just talking about things that are important to you. Let's start with your doctor's visit this morning—I want you to tell me everything Dr. Cho had to say."

"Come on, then," Issa said, leading the way off the landing and into the sitting area of their room.

"Let's go out on the balcony. I haven't had a chance to enjoy our view from these rooms."

He led the way through the bedroom and opened the glass-paneled door leading to one of the balconies that surrounded their suite. Comfortable wicker chairs provided a spot to lounge and look out over the bustle of First Landing. From this particular balcony, they could see Green's Tavern and Bronwyn's Hill, and Morgan sighed happily as he sat down next to Issa, still holding her hand.

"She says their hearts are strong, and she offered to tell me their sexes. How do you feel about that, Morgan? Do you want to know?"

"Why? Did you let her tell you?" Morgan's heart began to race, and he squeezed her hand even more tightly.

"No, silly! I didn't want to know until I spoke to you first. I'm scared! What if they're girls? I don't know how to deal with girls, Morgan!"

"Oh God." He laughed. "I don't know; I think a couple of sweet little girls running around the tower are just what this place needs."

"Seriously? You know Ykleedra has four baby sisters in the atrium, right?"

\* \* \*

"Well?" Baron Finneal asked, watching the man with the enormous dark wings glide down to the grassy field below.

"Well what?" Tanna ap'Cilla asked back.

"Don't play coy, bitch," he growled.

Haku-dak snorted from where he gazed over the rail a few feet away, and Captain Gella walked over, holding out his hands.

"Let's not fight among ourselves. We've enough problems, don't we?"

"Well, tell your witch to be more forthcoming," Finneal said, spitting over the rail and twitching his large, luminous wings.

"I'm nobody's witch, Finneal, and you know it! Least of all this little whelp of an airship captain."

"Please, please! Can we just get down to business? Were you able to get a read on his signature? Can it be done?"

"Yes and yes," Tanna relented. She touched the round blue crystal hanging from her neck. "I have his readings here, and given enough time, I can construct wards around his tower. I should be able to hold him within, even prevent him from using gateways or teleportation tokens. For a time, anyway—he's stronger than he should be."

"We should cut our losses," Haku-dak said, his low voice rumbling over the airship deck.

"What?" Captain Gella asked.

"If you try to lock him in and he gets out, I don't want to be around when he figures out what happened," he spoke matter-of-factly, and Gella stared at him open-mouthed—he'd never seen the huge Shadeni admit to fearing anyone.

"Frightened?" Baron Finneal sneered.

"Smart. I'd think you'd be smarter still having felt his strength, however briefly."

"So he threw me off; I had plenty more ready for him."

"You really that slow?" Haku-dak snorted again, drawling his words. He reached into his vest for a tin of yiil weed, making a production of stuffing a large wad into his lip before he continued. "You think that guy didn't have a few tricks ready to go also? Forget tricks. You saw his armor. That suit he wore was tier-five gear at least! You didn't think to wonder where he got it? Do you think they fought some Urghat to get gear like that? You saw the crown the Elementalist was wearing. Speak true, Tanna. I know you felt the heat of it!"

"The brutish warrior speaks reason," Tanna admitted, gazing at the tall, dark spire of the human's tower. "He speaks what we're all thinking but are too stubborn to admit—we might be higher level than the human champions, but there's something off about them, something that makes them more dangerous than their level would imply."

"Are you going to explain to Lord ap'Gravin why we returned empty-handed, then?" Captain Gella asked. "Because, believe me, I'd much rather avoid a conflict and just head back tonight, but I'm not going to be able to stand up to him. You know what he's like. There's a reason you're all in his debt!"

"Just start working on your wards, ap'Cilla," Finneal said sharply. "If Haku-dak and you are afraid, I'll deal with Morgan Hall should he find his way free before we deliver our cargo. There's a reason I was known as the Scourge of the Nine Towers."

"Right, because slaughtering Bogoli children and merchants has prepared you to face a deadly alien champion. Makes sense," Tanna replied, smirking.

Finneal wasn't amused, however. Dark, shadowy winds began to whip over the deck, gathering around him as his eyes grew dark to match while his outstretched hands lengthened into black talons.

"Stop it!" Captain Gella shrilly said. "Ancestors! How am I supposed to succeed in this mission when my assets are constantly at each other's throats?"

"Yes, you should stop," Tanna warned, her entire body frosting over. Clinking droplets of ice fell to the deck around her, and red sparks danced in her eyes.

"Fools," Haku-dak said with a final snort, spitting a black wad of yiil weed juice to the deck and turning to walk below decks.

"He's got a point. I'll save my Energy for a real fight," Finneal sneered, launching himself into the air with his glittering wings. He trailed motes of Energy as he flew toward the center of the human settlement.

"He'll go and drink with the humans and be back to his normal self by morning," Gella said, walking closer to Tanna. "Are you sure you can make the wards?"

"Yes, and please don't ask again. I'll need some time, however. A few days at least. Please keep Finneal out of my workshop."

She followed in Haku-dak's wake, and Captain Gella stood alone on the deck, rubbing his temples.

"What an absolute circus," he muttered, pulling a silver flask from his vest pocket and taking a long pull of the sharp liquor within.

He could only hope Tanna wasn't just boasting and that she could craft the wards in the time she promised. That would mean a few more days of playing nice, and then they could begin their plan B.

Lord ap'Gravin may have wanted thousands of volunteers signed into iron-clad contracts, but he'd be happy with a few hundred special "volunteers" whose futures would be entirely moldable by the Lord's interests delivered beneath the usual channels and available for special assignments.

## MORGAN

Morgan stood before the large bronze-colored double doors that Tiladia had led him to. "These are the only doors I cannot pass by or see beyond," she said, moving her crystal-shard parts in a slowly oscillating spiral.

"So that's where the final guardian is, hmm?" He stepped up to the door and put an ear against the cool metal. He didn't hear anything other than the faint background hum that seemed ever present in the tower's structure.

"Yes, though I have no information about it."

Morgan pulled up his quest from so long ago, taking a look at the wording:

**\*\*\*Quest: Defeat the guardians of Vormendion's Iron Tower 7/8. Reward: Access to each guardian's level and Vormendion's Reliquary.\*\*\***

He laughed when he saw the old System message, and Tiladia made a questioning sound.

"It's weird. When I got this tower and set it up, I wasn't surprised that the System gave me the quest to explore it and fight the guardians. Back then, I thought the System was constantly watching me, judging me, and giving me opportunities to . . . oh, I don't know, prove myself or fail to do so. Since those early days when I was in the Crucible, however, I've hardly heard from the System. If it weren't for me gaining levels, I'd almost forget it was there."

"The System is not omniscient. There are limits to its ability to focus on multiple beings or locations in its controlled space," Tiladia said, once again surprising Morgan with her breadth of knowledge.

"What, seriously? It seems pretty much everywhere all the time to me. Like if thirty people gained a level at once in First Landing, the System would know to give them all their level-up message."

"Those are automated activities. When you were new to Fanwath, the System was probably fully conscious of you. Only as it became familiar with you and your people and the things you were capable of did its focus shift. Does it bother you that the System is not consciously focusing on you now?"

"No, not really. I mean, honestly, I'd rather not be watched all the time."

"That is wise, Morgan. When the System brought its focus upon my world, we fought it. Dragons had been masters of Energy long before the youngling System thought to try to control us."

"Were you successful?"

"Oh yes. We rebuffed the System and its attempts. It was younger then, and I've been away for millennia, but I would wager my people still freely roam the skies of Aradnue."

"That's your homeworld, right?"

"Yes, the mountains and moons of Aradnue are home to my people, though we've spread to a hundred thousand worlds."

"But Aradnue is the first home of dragons? And you lived there?"

"That's correct!" Tiladia spun and flipped in the air, taking on her misty dragon form.

"That's incredible. Did you say your people flew around the moons?"

"Yes, Morgan! I used to lead my sisters on merry chases between the moons and down to the high peaks."

"So you could fly through space?"

"It was trivial for an elder dragon—I could create currents of Energy that made even the highest peaks seem calm in comparison!"

"And I'm guessing the temperature and lack of air didn't bother you, huh?"

"That's right!" Tiladia spun again, this time whirling around Morgan in a circle.

"I wonder if I could learn something like that. I'd like to fly up there and see if our ship is still around."

"There are dozens—no, hundreds of races that have learned to use Energy currents to fly through space, Morgan. I'm sure you could learn something, especially since you've already gained the gift of flight! I knew you were special when I first met you!"

"Really, Tiladia?"

"Well, I hoped. The truth is, you were the first person I'd spoken to, other than some of the guardians in the tower, since Vormendion left."

"Yeah, that sounds more like it." Morgan chuckled. "Well, I'm going to see what's behind this door." He stepped forward, drawing Bloodfang and readying his mind for a fight. "Maybe stand back or something? I don't know."

Tiladia didn't say anything, but her ethereal, tinkling form spun in another loop and then faded away toward the stairwell.

"Here goes," Morgan said, putting his hand on the large, round push plate at the edge of the left-hand door. He gave it a good shove, and the door swung silently inward.

The door's arcing swing revealed an ever-broadening swath of the room beyond—an oval chamber of gilt wood, rich marble flooring, and a high domed plaster ceiling. The far wall wasn't a wall so much as a metal cage beyond which Morgan could see rich furniture, overflowing bookcases and shelves, racks of weapons, piles of rugs and furs, and display cases filled with ornamented dishes and glassware.

Standing before the brass-colored cage door was a naked humanoid being, probably eight feet tall and molded from tan-colored flesh that was smooth and devoid of blemish. Its arms were long, with enormous fingers and claws nearly touching the marble floor, and its face was without expression, marred only by two slits for a nose and two black marbles for eyes. It was utterly motionless, though Morgan had the feeling those smooth black marbles were taking him in.

"Creepy," he muttered, moving his eyes up and down the smooth, fleshy being, more bothered by its lack of genitalia than he thought was probably reasonable.

So far, the fleshy monster hadn't moved, and Morgan wondered if the encounter wouldn't commence until he stepped into the room. He'd already tried to get Issa to come up to the tower's eighth floor, but she hadn't been able to traverse the stairs past level seven.

"So I'm on my own, just like with every other guardian," Morgan mused aloud. It didn't matter if he had to step into the antechamber to start the encounter; he was the only person with a physical body on this floor, and it would remain so until he won.

He took a step back from the door and contemplated the guardian. Was he ready to fight it? Issa had given him her tacit approval, indicating that she trusted his judgment when he said he was coming up to locate the final warden of the tower. But what if he died up here? The only being who would be able to look upon his corpse would be Tiladia. She'd no doubt let Issa know what had happened, but it would surely end his career as an adventuring champion of humanity with a sad little fizzle.

"You're not going to kill me, are you? I'm going to go in there and beat the tar out of you."

Morgan squeezed Bloodfang's hilt, feeling how the rough, absorbent leather fit the contours of his callouses. He'd grown more and more familiar with the weapon over the course of his exile on the icy planet and in its mysterious dungeon. Not only had he killed countless Rehavash, but he'd sparred for seemingly endless hours with Bronwyn. The heavy broadsword felt like an extension of his arm, and he knew the blade was stronger and sharper than any other weapon he'd seen, save maybe the blade that Swordmaster, Von-dak, had used. "But he gave me you as the price for the flesh of my own arm. That's got to mean something, right?" Morgan asked the silent weapon.

Not for the first time, Morgan was glad the sword didn't speak to him. He could only imagine the types of things it would say, and he didn't relish having a bloodthirsty berserker spirit growling murderous thoughts directly into his mind. Still, he liked the sword. Sharp and true, it had never failed to cut his enemies, and it had resisted the attempts of mighty creatures to break or bend it.

Morgan caught himself thinking about how much he liked his sword and shook his head ruefully. What was he doing? Stalling?

"Yep," he told himself and the silent flesh monster. "If I'm going to be the champion of this budding civilization, I'll need to be the master of my own home, don't you think?"

Morgan pulled his helmet out of his storage ring, put it on his head, and waved his hand in front of his face, sliding the visor down. Completely encased in the shining, reflective Moonsteel armor and with Bloodfang in hand, he stepped into the circular antechamber of his tower's reliquary and watched as the lanky flesh monster quivered and came to life.

"He's started the battle, Miss Issa," Tiladia said softly from the doorway.

Issa was pacing back and forth in the music room of the tower, trying to keep herself occupied because she knew Morgan would do what Tiladia had just confirmed. He'd said he was going to "check out" the eighth guardian, but Issa had known what that meant. She had to come to terms with the fact that Morgan had grown significantly while he'd been away on the invaders' world. No, not the invaders' world; the one after it, and the dungeon therein. It didn't matter. He'd already been outpacing her due to his high affinity, and now he was more than double her level.

"He's strong enough, don't you think, Tiladia?"

"He's stronger than anyone I've ever met at his level. He's not as powerful as Vormendion, but the old master didn't expect someone to match his power just to unlock the tower. I think Morgan has what it takes to conquer the eighth guardian, though my knowledge of him is nonexistent."

"He's like no one else on this world, Tiladia. He'll win. I have to accept that he'll be going places and taking risks that I can't help him with. His growth is beyond anything my people have ever seen, even in the legends of heroes like Asyr-dak or the Crag Queen."

"The mate who stays with the hatchlings makes a sacrifice paid for in blessings the fighting mate cannot fathom." Tiladia swooped closer to Issa, performing a double loop in her misty dragon shape.

"You have children, Tiladia?"

"Yes! Seven from three different broods. My first time, I grew to resent my hatchlings because I saw the battles my mate participated in and how his scales thickened and shimmered with the metals he ate. Still, after my daughters took wing and began to bring home prizes, who do you think they showered their affections upon? Not Yong the Dread Horn!"

"Yong the Dread Horn?" Issa couldn't keep the amusement out of her voice.

"Oh yes! His nose horn was long and deadly! Many met their ends, thrashing their guts out upon it."

"Ancestors!" Issa's amusement was instantly replaced by horror. She changed the subject. "Can you see how Morgan is doing?"

"No, I'm sorry. The door closed when the fight commenced. I cannot bypass it or hear anything from within."

"I hate this. Let's go to the atrium! Talk of your hatchlings has me wanting to see some children, and Ykleedra has four of them!"

Issa walked with purpose out of the music room, through the landing hall, and into the bright, green atrium. The plants were so foreign to her—not a single leaf or blade of grass was blue. Still, she loved the fresh smell of the air and the soothing sounds of the brook that babbled through the middle of the space.

A rustle in the nearby ferns announced Ykleedra's presence, and she poked her head out to ask, "Is something wrong, Miss Issa? You seem troubled."

"Morgan is battling with the final guardian. I was hoping to see your sisters, Ykleedra—some new life would do wonders to distract me."

"Of course, Miss Issa! Please wait, and I'll bring them up."

Ykleedra ducked back into the ferns, and Issa heard her scurry away toward her burrow. Moments later, she heard her coming closer, speaking in soft clicks and coos. She reemerged from the ferns, one tentacle trailing behind her, clasped tightly around another smaller tentacle. Then her sisters appeared, one after the other in a little train, each holding tightly to the one behind.

Issa's eyes filled with tears at the sight of the little creatures sweetly holding onto each other, staring around with big, liquid black eyes, ducking and jostling to hide behind their big sister.

"Oh, sweeties, don't hide from me. I'm not here to hurt you!" Issa said, crouching low and reaching out with her hand. Tiladia made similar sounds, taking on her dragon shape but slinking along the ground with a gentle chiming melody. "Can they understand me, Ykleedra?"

"They can't speak yet, but they're learning some words. Pkril is the most vocal—she likes to ask for more whenever I feed them. She's the one with the red in her hair. Ykerli is the opposite. She's the quiet little one that's still hiding in the ferns. Come here, you little hidgii! Miss Issa wouldn't hurt you!" Ykleedra snaked out another tentacle and wrapped it around her littlest sister's long foreleg, tugging at it.

"They're adorable, Ykleedra! You've done such a wonderful job with them so far! Speaking of which, I heard Morgan offered to have you a home built in here. Has any work been done yet?"

"No, but a lady named Mrs. Washington came to do something called a survey."

"Yes, I gave her permission to enter at Morgan's request," Tiladia said, still tinkling around on the ground near one of the young Yovashi.

Issa lost track of her worries while she sat on the grass in the atrium, getting to know Ykleedra's sisters. She was so engrossed with them that she'd almost, but not quite, forgotten about Morgan's challenge. She was holding onto a smooth, gray tentacle, trying to get the sister named Gvon to say, "Issa," when a tremendous gong sounded, seeming to reverberate through the metal shell of the tower.

The ground shook, the ferns and trees in the atrium quivered, and the artificial sun dimmed and brightened. Tiladia, who'd left at some point during Issa's visit, streaked into the atrium, larger, brighter, and more dragonlike than Issa had ever seen her, and announced, "It's over!"

## MORGAN

The door closed behind Morgan with a reverberating clang. Sidestepping, he eyed the flesh monster as it shuddered and flexed, leaning forward with its flat, expressionless face, nostrils widening as though it were taking a huge sniff.

He didn't see any point in letting the monster ramp up an attack, so he fired a Vortex Lance as he circled the creature. The Energy shot rang out, echoing around the circular chamber and leaving its spiral trail hanging in the air. With no mouth to cry out, Morgan was surprised but not shocked to see that the monster didn't seem particularly harmed by the blast, though it punched a fist-size hole through its right shoulder.

Some bits of flesh and a spray of dark blood splattered the wall behind it, but it moved as if it hadn't noticed the attack, loping straight at Morgan with its long, clawed arms raking the air as though it were swimming toward him. Morgan waited for it to draw near, then cast Void Step, placing himself directly behind the monster before unleashing a Void Wave. His movement and subsequent attack were almost instantaneous, and the flesh monster swept its claws through the space he'd occupied at the same time that Morgan's black, reality-ripping wave washed over it from behind.

Morgan watched with grim satisfaction as his spell engulfed the creature, feeling its will struggling against his attack. The monster's skin began to dissolve, but Energy, thick and red, pulsed up out of the creature's Core and pushed back Morgan's Void Wave. Once the spell had passed, Morgan saw he'd damaged the monster, but only superficially. Its will or the Energy sustaining it had proven stronger than his void Energy, more so than any enemy he'd hit with it in the past. Morgan was so stunned by the lack of effectiveness that he barely got Bloodfang up in time to block the swipe of the claws that tore through the air, leaving a trail of red steam.

The monster's three long talons rang like steel against Bloodfang's edge, and Morgan was thrown back by the ferocity of the attack. While his blade was occupied, the flesh monster's other claws came swiping from the side and tore into his shining cuirass, biting through the metal and digging into the flesh of his shoulder. Morgan cried out and cast Azure Burst, hoping to give himself some space by blasting the creature back.

With him at its center, a rippling wave of crackling blue flames exploded outward. Morgan saw the monster flinch back, and before it could regain the initiative, he reached out with Energy Drain and pulled with all the might of his Core, yanking on a thick stream of the hot, red Energy that pulsed within the monster. He felt the torrent of potent Energy enter his pathways and yanked even harder, pulling it into his Core and sending it out to mend the gashes on his shoulder. Meanwhile, he circled the monster as it regained its balance, its blackened flesh sizzling and smoking as it turned its eyeless face to track Morgan's movements.

"Didn't like that one, did you?" Morgan asked, waiting for it to make a move. His Vortex Lance was off cooldown, so he primed it, trying to aim more carefully while pointing his sword tip at the monster's head.

A red wave of Energy began to emanate from the guardian, rippling along its flesh. Morgan knew it was about to do something, so he fired his Vortex Lance, doing his best to place the shimmering bolt of Energy through the center of the fleshy creature's face.

The supersonic missile cracked through the air, and Morgan's aim was good, if not perfect. The creature started to move just as Morgan released the shot, and though it hit its head, it only tore through the left upper quadrant, shearing away a thick groove of flesh and whatever matter made up the inside of the guardian's skull; it didn't look like brains. The shot and the trail of gore continued past the monster to smash into one of the walls with a reverberating clang.

The creature clearly felt no pain because it didn't so much as flinch at the blow. The red aura that suffused it had started to pulse rapidly, and the creature moved like it had been charged with electricity, twitching through the space between it and Morgan as though it were skipping part of the distance. Morgan, anticipating an attack, fell back into the Crane Defends the Nest. Just as he channeled Energy into the form, he felt a dozen slashes smash into the Energy barrier that had enhanced his guard.

The creature's swipes were coming so fast that Morgan couldn't see the individual swings, doing his best just to backpedal and block with his parry form. Just as he was about to be driven into the wall with nowhere else to retreat, he felt Void Step come off cooldown. With a crackling rend in reality, he winked out of existence and reappeared directly behind the monster. It was his turn then to unleash a flurry of cleaves as the monster's back was completely exposed.

Bloodfang went to work, cutting huge, terrible rends into the guardian. Morgan didn't feel any bones, just the tough naked flesh and the sinewy tendons and muscles that thickly lined its torso as his sword cleaved through those dense, ropy viscera. Dark blood sprayed left and right with Morgan's heavy, powerful blows. The monster tried to turn during Morgan's combo, but his slashes were so heavy and cut so deeply that it was pressed into the wall, unable to turn to interpose its long, hard claws between Morgan's sword and its body.

Just as he finished the Crane Flutters Its Wings, Morgan felt Void Wave come off cooldown. When he unleashed it this time, the creature's will and Energy stores were insufficient to negate the spell, and Morgan felt it struggle for a moment before his wave of nothingness washed over the monster, consuming its flesh with much greater effect than the first time.

Morgan saw a red pulse of potent Energy surge up from the monster's Core, but it was just a quick burst, easily overwhelmed by his spell. Morgan's Energy stores were nearing ten thousand, and apparently, this creature couldn't compete with such reserves.

When the wave of his dark, void-attuned Energy faded away, the guardian sat slumped against the wall, most of its flesh gone, revealing a thin, steel-colored skeleton covered in shreds of viscera, skin, and a light coating of blood. A fist-size skull sat atop its metallic shoulders, a dimly pulsing pink gem mounted at its center.

Unsure what surprises the guardian might have in store, Morgan didn't hesitate, stepping forward with a heavy cleave aimed at the narrow, wirelike neck of the construct. Bloodfang didn't disappoint, shearing through the metal with a pinging crunch. The little skull fell to the floor, rolling in a sad spiral, and the gem pulsed more slowly, its light gradually fading away.

As Morgan stood over the ruined warden, panting with exertion, a gong boomed, deeply resounding through the metal of the tower. In fact, Morgan felt the sound before his ears registered it. His entire body shook, as did the tower, and then a surge of Energy unlike any he'd ever encountered flooded his body, lifting him from the ground, pushing into his pathways like an electrical torrent that spread all six of his limbs. Still, the deluge of Energy came, filling his Core and pushing out through his pathways until golden Energy began to erupt from his mouth and eyes.

Morgan lifted his head and screamed, unable to do anything else as the surge coursed through him. The Energy poured up from the floor, through him, and out to the ceiling of the circular room. He was like a circuit in a massive electrical connection, though it was pure Energy that flowed through him rather than voltage. When it finally ended and he fell to the floor, limp and weak beyond measure, he struggled to open his eyes and was greeted by several System messages.

\*\*\***Congratulations! You have achieved level 40 Void Adept, gained 8 Intelligence, 8 Will, and have 12 points to distribute.**\*\*\*

*\*\*Level 40 Class refinement. Class refinement is permanent. Human Energy cultivators will next be offered a Class refinement selection at level 50. To view your options and make your selection, access the menu through your status page.\*\*\**

*\*\*Congratulations! You have completed the quest: Defeat the guardians of Vormendion's Iron Tower 8/8. You have gained access to each guardian's level and Vormendion's Reliquary. As the new master of the Metalline Tower, you will have full access and control of all its aspects.\*\*\**

Captain Gella stood on the deck of his ship—well, Lord ap'Gravin's ship—and watched the lights of First Landing. Tanna stood beside him, much more pleasant to be around when she wasn't sniping with Baron Finneal. He wanted to look at her but didn't want her to catch him admiring her glittering flesh or the cut of her blouse. Instead, he continued to stare down toward the hill they'd named after the missing heroine, Bronwyn.

Seizing on an interesting topic, he said, "A shame for the humans that one of their heroes seems to keep disappearing. You haven't heard anything more about Bronwyn, have you?"

"No, but that's fine with me. One less person to worry about."

Tanna leaned forward, suddenly staring down toward the tall iron tower that rose up from the nearby field. Gella took the opportunity to glance sideways at her, drinking in the sight of her elegant neck and the way she'd swept her hair up into a bun, leaving just a few tendrils to hang down over her pale blue skin with its countless little sparkles, only really evident if you looked for them. Gella had never seen an Ardeni with such a strange but beautiful bloodline. He wanted to ask her about it but feared her acerbic tongue.

"What's happening down there?" she asked, completely unaware of his attentions.

"What?" Gella tore his gaze away from the beautiful sorceress and looked down toward the dark finger of metal jutting upward. "Not so dark as I remember it," he muttered as he saw swirls of bright Energy moving around the base of the structure, pulsing through the iron in bright brass-colored loops.

"I don't like this," Tanna said. "I was just starting to relax about that tower, having finished one of the ward stones. That's a lot of Energy surging around in it. Can't you feel it?"

"I—" Gella started, straining to feel what she was talking about but unable to. His affinity was just too low. "I can see it, but no, I don't feel anything," he admitted. Suddenly, the swirls of Energy in the dark iron tower grew brighter and connected to each other, forming a solid, looping band around the base which slowly began to grow brighter and brighter.

Tanna sucked in her breath, and then Gella *did* feel it: a pulse of Energy so strong that his exposed flesh tingled with the sensation of it as it rushed out. The bright band of Energy shot up the length of the tower, coloring the metal from dark iron to bright brass, and then a beam fired from the top into the heavens, a great searchlight that speared into the starry sky.

"Ancestors!" Tanna breathed, her knuckles white where she gripped the rail of *Skybreaker*. The beam of Energy started to fold down onto itself, and then an image took shape atop the now shimmering brass tower—the projection of a man in shining silver armor with a gleaming broadsword held victoriously over his head. It was a titanic projection of Morgan; Gella would recognize that armor anywhere.

"What the bloody shit is this?" he muttered.

"He's worked some sort of ritual or gained some sort of new power over that tower. I don't know, but it's like a dormant giant has awoken. I can feel the Energy fading, though; I don't think this enormous surge is permanent. I hope I can still find a way to ward it to hold him within, but this certainly complicates things."

Tanna gradually relaxed her grip on the railing, sighing as the enormous projection of Morgan Hall began to flicker and fade. The two of them watched for several more minutes, but the new brass-colored aspect of the tower didn't completely fade, settling on a less shiny bronze. Still, it was a good deal brighter than its previous dull, iron aspect.

It was like Tanna had said—the structure had been sleeping, and now it was awake.

## BRONWYN

"I see more Urghat tracks leading up this ridge," Bronwyn pointed out, turning back toward Cal and shading her eyes from the sun hanging low on the western horizon.

"Too bad you can't see their names," Cal replied, looking up the steep ridgeline.

"I think it's just one, but yeah, it would be nice to know who. This little adventure would go a lot easier. You up for the hike?"

"Well, I ain't got your endurance, but I think I got a little pep left in my step." Cal, still wearing a large backpack despite Bronwyn's offer to put it into her storage necklace and wielding a gnarled walking stick he'd been whittling on during their camp time, started up the rocky trail.

"Good to know, Cal." Bronwyn laughed and continued up, a few steps ahead of him.

A short while into the hike, Cal started to hum one of his magical songs. This one had become quite familiar to Bronwyn—it energized her muscles, making walking or, in this case, hiking seem easier and faster. He called it his travel song. Bronwyn followed the Urghat tracks up the ridge, noting the long stride and figuring it was a pretty big one.

They were two days north of First Landing, a bit to the east of the plains, following a lead they'd gotten from a lone Urghat hunter who had claimed to have heard of a new Urghat clan being formed in these hills. So far, they hadn't run into any other Urghat or had any luck tracking them down. Bronwyn's skill was helpful, but there were so many tracks on the northern plains from all the Urghat that had passed through in the last weeks that it was difficult to find any that panned out.

The ridge trail was steep, but Bronwyn found it easy to climb, especially with Cal's song. Every so often, she'd stop and look out at the scenery to wait for Cal. The view was something to see, really. People back home would've killed for such a vista. The plains stretched out as far as the eye could see to the west, and if she turned to the north, she could see verdant forests and tall, purple peaks that put the Rockies to shame. She knew that somewhere deep in those mountain ranges was the little mountain valley where she'd fought Thun.

"I wonder how long it would take to hike that far. A couple of weeks?"

"What's that?"

"Oh, the fae queen sent me into those mountains with a portal. I was wondering how long it would take to get there by foot."

"It's just a few days' hike to the mountains," Cal replied while he leaned on his knees, catching his breath.

"Yeah, I know. I don't mean the foothills. Those mountains go on and on, Cal. Even after the queen sent me into the middle of them, I hiked north for over a week, and I didn't saw any sign I was through them."

"Oh, gotcha. No, I've never been into them. The Ghelli wood is just a bit northeast of these plains."

"And you got to level fourteen just hanging around their village?"

"Well, not just hanging around! I was singing for my supper for a long while at one of the inns, even after I married Lysee."

"I bet they loved having magical songs to entertain them! I don't suppose you sang your travel song, though, did you?"

"Nah, I learned a few others. I have a song that helps you relax and rest. I have a song that helps you dance and laugh—that was the most popular one—and I have a song that makes cleaning and working easier. I used to sing that one for the crew at the inn after hours."

"Pretty cool, Cal. Are all your skills and spells songs?"

"Yeah. Elder Tryllie, back at the Ghelli Wood, also had a Spirit Core. She told me that having a spirit attunement made other spells harder to learn and that I ought to focus on what I was good at."

"Spirit Core, huh? I haven't heard of it." Bronwyn shrugged, taking a deep drink from her canteen.

"Yeah, the Ghelli said it's pretty uncommon among them too. Tryllie had attunements for fear and resolution—you can imagine they had pretty different effects."

"Wait, what? So what are your attunements?"

"I just have the one—harmony."

"Those are pretty interesting-sounding attunements, though. Every time I start to think I'm getting a grasp on things, I learn there's a lot more to this world and System than I thought."

"Definitely! When I saw you, I learned there's a whole lot about humans I don't know!" Cal laughed, touching his ear to indicate he was talking about Bronwyn's elfin appearance.

"Right." She laughed as well, then turned back to the path. "Well, this ridge isn't going to climb itself!"

"That's a fact!" Cal agreed, straightening up and nodding. "Ready when you are."

They followed the trail for another two hours, and as the sun was starting to sink in a glorious red and orange display, they finally reached the top. The Urghat tracks led along the high, rocky ground toward a distant structure: a jagged stone tower.

"Now, that's what I call a place with a view!" Cal said, coming up behind Bronwyn.

"Yeah, I wonder who built it. Maybe Urghat?"

"Hard to know. Lots of people have come and gone from these lands, according to the Ghelli. There were people living here even before the worlds were joined."

"Well, the tracks lead to the tower, so let's go check it out. Stay behind me in case they have a bow or something." Bronwyn touched her necklace, and suddenly, she was holding her two half-moon hatchets.

"Those are pretty," Cal commented with a low whistle.

"Thanks." Bronwyn winked at him and started along the trail toward the tower. When she got within fifteen meters or so, she saw that the tracks led through the broken doorway. She called out, "Hello? Whoever's in the tower, I want to talk to you. We aren't here to fight!"

A few seconds passed, and then a darkly furred head poked out around the hanging timbers of the doorway.

"Underclaw?"

"Ironhide!" Bronwyn said with a relieved laugh. "Come here, you big oaf!" She strode forward, lowering her hatchets.

"I was wondering if I'd ever see you again, Underclaw," Ironhide said as he squeezed through the broken, nearly petrified wood. "Who's this little hairless one with you?"

"Ironhide, you know we're called humans. Don't be rude. This is Cal, and he's been a friend to Urghat."

"Sorry, Underclaw," Ironhide said, chagrined. "Is there something different about you? You seem longer and pointier."

"Just some racial advancements. Where's the rest of the band?"

"Off doing your bidding—delivering the Underclaw rings, looking for family members, seeking a life after the fall of the Ur-clan."

"Nice to meet you, Mr. Ironhide!" Cal said, finally finding a place to step into the conversation.

"Er, uh, nice to meet you," he rumbled, smiling at Cal in a way that looked almost like a snarl.

"Ironhide, you can let the rest of the members of our little band know—First Landing isn't on a war footing anymore. If you guys come with empty hands and indicate you aren't there to fight, they'll leave you in peace. We can build a longhouse, as you guys talked about. It doesn't have to be in the town itself—there's lots of room in the plains nearby or the woods."

"I think it would just be me at this point, Underclaw. You were gone a long time, and there are some new Underclaws now that you sent out those rings. I haven't heard from Shadoweye or the twins. I think they joined the Underclaw Shadoweye made with the ring she had."

"Really? And Heartseeker? Fangripper?"

"The same. They went north, into the hills. I haven't heard from them. It seems that the new Underclaws are happy to take them in despite their oaths to an outsider. Probably helped that they had the Underclaw bands to bargain with."

"Well, that's fine, so long as they followed my instructions to give the rings to good candidates; Urghat leaders who wouldn't seek to make an Ur-clan and attack the humans."

"Aye, I think they did a good job in that regard. The new Underclaws have been at odds with each other, not seeking to unite anything."

"Hey, um, sorry to interrupt, but I was wondering if you knew an Urghat named Whitestar?" Cal interjected, clearly anxious to hear about his missing friend.

"Whitestar? Yar, she's the one that Shadoweye and the twins joined. She's a new Underclaw in the hills north of here."

"Really? That's kind of a big coincidence." Bronwyn looked from Ironhide to Cal, raising an eyebrow.

"I ain't surprised," Cal said. "If you knew Whitestar, you wouldn't be, either. She ain't no follower, if you know what I mean."

"Does she have a clan home yet?" Bronwyn asked Ironhide.

"I heard she was trying to take the Hollows back from the trolls." Ironhide spoke like his words would be universally understood, but Bronwyn and Cal both looked at him with quizzical expressions.

"Hollows?" Cal asked.

"Trolls? Like forest trolls?" Bronwyn asked at the same time.

"Er, the Hollows used to be a clan home for Urghat, but some swamp trolls killed most of the Urghat there and chased the rest out. I heard this Whitestar whelp thought she had what it takes to root them out." He shrugged and spat into the rocky dirt.

"You think she's delusional?" Bronwyn asked.

"We need to help her!" Cal said, making a fist.

"Swamp trolls ain't no pushover," Ironhide growled.

"Relax, Cal. I told you I'd help you find your friend, and I intend to see it through. Come on, Ironhide. Time to quit hiding out in old ruins and earn your name." She thumped the burly Urghat on the shoulder.

"Gah! I weren't hiding! I was just spending some peaceful time up here."

"Right, right." Bronwyn laughed. "I mean, at least you have a nice view; the sunset can't be beat!"

"Ain't that the truth!" Cal said, turning to admire the last purple-red streaks along the western horizon.

"Well, we can't go anywhere tonight. Let's set camp here, and we'll get going in the morning, all right, Ironhide? You can guide us to these Hollows?"

"Aye, I can," he grumbled. "Well, do you at least have something good to eat, Underclaw?"

"Of course I do!" Bronwyn grinned. "In fact, I have some rations that I guarantee you're the first Urghat to taste, and you're going to love them."

"Why's he keep calling you Underclaw?" Cal asked, looking between Ironhide and Bronwyn. She pointed to the ring on her arm.

"I earned the title by dueling one of their Underclaws. Ironhide was one of the first to follow me."

"Har, only after you whooped me real good. You think Whitestar will be willing to deal with another Underclaw? What if she wants to challenge you to start working toward an Overclaw title?"

"Well, then I'll have to straighten her out. I hope that's not why I was sent here to help, though. I hope Whitestar is as smart and good as Cal says." Bronwyn reached out and put a hand on the man's shoulder. "I don't have any intentions of hurting your friend, Cal."

"I can tell you ain't lying, Bronwyn. Don't worry. Whitestar's as good an Urghat as there ever was."

"Come in the tower if you want," Ironhide said. "The chimney still works, and I have wood for a fire. I'm hungry!"

"Ha, always thinking with your stomach, Ironhide! I'm truly glad to see you, and I'm happy to hear we'll be seeing more of Shadoweye and the twins!"

"If the swamp trolls didn't eat them yet," Ironhide replied with a snort, turning to squeeze his thick, furry body back through the broken boards in the ancient tower.

Bronwyn looked at Cal and shook her head.

"They aren't dead. Don't worry, Cal."

"Nah, I think I'd feel it or something. I think you're right; it feels to me like we'll get there just in time." Cal smiled, his bright white teeth shining in the dim light, then stepped through into the tower. Bronwyn followed, looking in her necklace for the fae rations.

# MORGAN

Morgan sat on the marble floor, looking around the antechamber to Vormendion's reliquary, and tried to take in everything that had just happened. The wave of Energy that had coursed through him had done more than give him a level—something had happened with the tower too, like it had woken up and made a connection with him. He couldn't exactly *feel* the tower, but he was somehow aware of it. For instance, he simply knew that it had taken on a bronze aspect on its exterior. He also knew he could change it to look like almost any sort of metal.

"Vormendion was a grumpy old guy, huh? Making this place look like a cast-iron finger of doom." He shook his head and took a moment to realize he was still alone, several minutes after defeating the guardian. He looked over his shoulder and saw the doors were still closed, realizing he *knew* they were locked. He decided to keep it that way for a minute to take a few breaths all to himself before he had to explain everything that had happened.

Morgan waved the notifications from the System out of his vision and opened his status screen with some anticipation, touching the Class Refinement tab and reading over his options, which numbered fewer than he'd ever seen:

***Class refinement option 1: Void Master—Legendary. Prerequisites: Affinity with void-attuned Energy, certain criteria with mental attributes, and exceptional Energy affinity. You have developed new and powerful means of piercing the void. Continue down this road and gain further mastery of your rare affinity. Class attributes: Intelligence, Unbound.***

***Class refinement option 2: Anemoi Cloud Warden—Legendary. Prerequisites: Exceptional Energy affinity and the strong presence of the ancient Anemoi Bloodline. You have unlocked a partial connection to an ancient bloodline. Utilize this connection to develop class abilities and spells that complement the secrets of your ancestry. Class attributes: Intelligence, Agility, Dexterity.***

***Class refinement option 3: No Refinement—You are pleased with the path on which you find yourself and choose to continue until your next refinement option.***

"Guess I should think about this for a minute. Maybe Issa or Tiladia will have some advice," Morgan said, for some reason talkative in his postbattle, post-Energy-surge state of limp relaxation. With a grunt, he hoisted himself to his feet, unconsciously using his wings to provide momentum. He was growing more and more used to the new appendages, so much so that he hardly thought about them anymore.

He walked to the door, and it unlocked at his approach. When the tumblers clicked, it swung open almost immediately, and then Issa rushed through the opening and smashed into him like a guided missile, grabbing him around the waist in a tight hug.

"Hey." Morgan laughed, hugging her back.

"You did it! I knew you would, but I was still worried. Isn't that dumb?" Issa asked, looking up at him with moist eyes.

"Were you crying? Of course that's not dumb! I'm sorry you were worried!" Morgan kissed her upturned brow, gently smoothing the moisture away from her cheeks with his thumbs. A tinkling shift in the light reminded Morgan that Tiladia was there, and he turned to face the dragon spirit. "I have a connection to the tower now. I can sort of sense you too, Tiladia. I think I can free you if you want. It might take me a minute to figure out, but I feel like it's possible."

"Free me? But my body is long gone, Morgan." She whirled into the shape of her misty dragon, opened her jaws, and roared out a plume of white mist.

"Well, yeah, I guess I'd be freeing you to, I don't know, do what spirits normally do."

"I'm not ready for that yet! There are too many things happening that I'm interested in, Morgan! Please let me stay!"

"Oh God, Tiladia, I wouldn't force you to, um, move on. You tell me what you want to do when you want to do it, and I'll help you make it happen."

"We love having you here, Tiladia!" Issa said, turning to the floating dragon spirit.

"Good!" Tiladia declared, voice chiming in a happy tinkle. "I'm glad to help you as I have been, as long as so many good and interesting people are coming and going. The tower is brighter now, Morgan. I'm glad that you've inherited it!"

Morgan looked at Issa and said, "It is, like, actually brighter. Wait 'til you see the outside."

"What about this?" Issa gestured to the bronze gates closing off the rest of the reliquary.

"Yeah, should we check it out?" Morgan turned and walked over to them, stepping over the creepy, wiry skeleton of the guardian, still covered in dried blood and bits of flesh and sinew. "Uh, watch your step."

He gestured to the mess.

"What was the guardian like? Was it difficult to beat, Morgan?" Issa asked, stepping around the unmoving wire feet.

"I can sense the residue of immense Energy in that crystal affixed to the construct's head," Tiladia said, floating over the weird, apple-size skull.

"Yeah, it was covered with flesh and had plenty of muscle when we started fighting, but that tiny head and the wiry bones are weird as hell. Was this thing created somehow by Vormendion, do you think?" Morgan prodded the skull with the toe of his boot; when it didn't move or react, he squatted down to pick it up. It was heavy and dense, and though it was inert, Morgan could feel the potential in it, like when he held a powerful natural treasure.

He slipped it into his storage ring with a shrug.

"I believe so," Tiladia was saying. "Vormendion was a talented Artificer, and his mastery extended to the capture and forced servitude of spirits, as I'm testament to."

"There was a spirit in this construct, you think? It's not still there, is it?"

"There may have been—most of his guardians were enslaved spirits. It will have departed upon the vessel's destruction, however, just like the others you conquered.

"It seems an evil practice," Issa said. "I'm sorry Vormendion took you, Tiladia." She reached out a hand as though to touch Tiladia, but her fingers passed through her misty form. "I wish I could hug you."

Tiladia, in response, swirled around Issa, starting at her hips and moving up until she spun around her shoulders, still in her misty dragon shape, then she puffed out a cool cloud of air on Issa's neck, eliciting a giggle.

"Was that a kiss? Thank you, Tiladia!" Issa's eyes were bright with cheer.

Morgan, watching her, noticed her stomach poking out under her blouse, her pants a bit tight for her. He wanted to grab her into a hug right then but instead held out his hand and, when she took it, pulled her toward the gate to the reliquary.

"Let's see what's in here," he said.

They spent hours exploring through the considerable trove of items that Vormendion had stashed away in the massive space. Not for the first time, Morgan marveled at how weird it was to know the physical size of the tower's exterior and yet walk around a chamber that was several times too large to physically fit in its footprint.

They found artwork of all sorts: paintings, sculptures, crystal figurines, vases, woven rugs, carvings, and myriad other intricate, beautiful things that Morgan struggled to classify. There were stacks of books, hundreds and hundreds of them, and Tiladia said they belonged in the nearly empty library. Along one wall, they found huge wooden crates, and when Morgan opened one of them, he saw what looked like laboratory equipment. "These must belong in the workshops on the sixth floor?"

"That's right, Morgan. Vormendion had equipment that rivaled any of his peers. He was a better Artificer than many of my dragon kin."

"Dragons craft things?" Issa asked, and Tiladia let out a harsh, discordant ring of outrage.

"Of course! Dragons aren't just fire-breathing brutes, you know! We're among the oldest of peoples, and with our ability to shift our shapes, we could easily take on a form that could work even the most delicate of instruments."

"I'm sorry, Tiladia. I just don't know much about dragons; there aren't any on Fanwath. At least, I don't think so." Issa looked crestfallen at the idea that she'd hurt the spirit's feelings.

"You shift your shapes?" Morgan asked, trying to take some of the heat off Issa.

"Only with a conscious effort of will, and it's tiring to do. Fledglings can't do it—it requires too much Energy. When a dragon begins to mature, we start accumulating enough Energy to maintain a different shape for longer and longer periods of time. Morgan, I could have been a beautiful human for months and months if I'd wanted to!"

"Oh?" Morgan wasn't really sure where Tiladia was going with that, and he glanced nervously at Issa. She was smiling, looking rather pleased that he was suddenly uncomfortable. "Um, I'd have loved to see that, Tiladia."

Tiladia didn't say anything more, though. Rather, she continued her swooping perusal of the vault, Issa's unintended slight apparently forgotten. Morgan looked at Issa and offered her a wink. Her smile broadened, then the two of them continued exploring.

"I'm going to have to hire some people from town to help me move this stuff around the tower. Now that the labs will be fully equipped, I should invite Boris and some of his friends to work in them. I bet they'll be better than anything the town can come up with for quite some time."

"That's a good idea, Morgan. We should see if anyone wants to work in the tower. We could use a cook, you know."

"Yeah, I suppose so. I mean, we have a ballroom and that big dining room. We should be having some parties. I'd like you to meet more people, too. I bet you aren't the only pregnant woman in First Landing! Wouldn't it be good to have friends to talk to about what's happening with you?"

"Well, I have you. And Doctor Cho," Issa said, but she looked pensive. "But I would like to meet more people. I haven't told you this yet, but I used the Settlement Stone to make myself a citizen of First Landing."

"Really? Is it that easy? Should I make myself a citizen of Tarn's Crossing?"

"No, it doesn't work like that. The System only allows you to be an official citizen of one settlement. You'd have to give up your citizenship here to join the rolls at Tarn's."

"Oh, shit. So you're not a citizen there anymore? What about your fam—" Morgan cut himself off and slapped his forehead. "I'm sorry, Issa. Of course you should be a citizen here. Your family is here now."

She smiled and nodded. "That's right, it is. So you see why I want to meet more people. Our family needs to grow in influence, and I'd like to be a part of that."

"Influence." Morgan scratched his chin. "Right. I think I see where you're going with this. Like how in Tarn's Crossing, there were certain families who had more influence or power in the town or on the council than others. You don't want to be at the mercy of a family like Swent's."

"It's not just about not being at someone's mercy, Morgan. This is the first town, soon to be a city if I'm not wrong, that humans have founded on Fanwath. It's going to be the center of a great civilization someday; I'm quite sure of it. I want to be a part of that. I want our family to be a part of that." As she spoke, she put a hand on her stomach, and Morgan knew what she meant.

"I hadn't really thought about that, Issa." Morgan reached forward and gently placed his hand next to hers. "I see your point. I'm glad you're thinking about these things."

"Morgan!" Tiladia called, swirling over the crates back toward them.

"Yeah?"

"I found the inner vault. I believe Vormendion left his inheritance items within."

"Inheritance items?" Morgan and Issa asked in unison.

## MORGAN

"This tower is part of Vormendion's inheritance, but there's more to it. Before he departed this part of the universe, he chose certain treasures to bestow on the one who conquered the challenge of his guardians. I don't know more than that, though I can feel the Energy emanating from the inner vault," Tiladia explained as Morgan and Issa followed her through an extensive collection of musical instruments covered with dust shrouds. Morgan looked at Issa with raised eyebrows. She smiled, eyes scrunched with excitement.

"I admit, I was excited to see what a powerful wizard had in his reliquary, but I didn't expect something like this," Morgan said.

"Well, we haven't seen it yet. Don't count your kisses before the Fling," Issa replied.

"The Fling?"

"Ancestors! Don't you people do anything fun? The Spring Planting Gala? The Seed Fling?"

"Ahh. Gotcha. Well, we'll have to get something like that started around here, hmm?"

Issa began to answer, but they'd come upon a portion of the wall obscured by crates, and Tiladia said, "The door is behind those boxes of linens!"

"Vormendion put the extra linens in his reliquary?"

Morgan shook his head with a bemused smile before he started moving the boxes. They were heavy, but he was strong and large, and it wasn't much work to clear a path to the bronze-colored metal door set into the formerly iron wall. There was no handle, knob, or dial that he could see, but a flat, shiny plate about the size of a person's hand was set into the center of the door.

Something in his connection to the tower told Morgan that if he pressed his hand to that plate, the door would open, so he stepped forward, still holding Issa's hand, and reached out to press his palm to it. Warm Energy pulsed under his flesh, and then, with a tremendous click and a hiss of pressurized air, the door swung outward a few inches. The air that gushed out of the room was cold and devoid of scent, and it caused the metal of the door and the tower wall to frost over with icy condensation.

Morgan and Issa stepped back, waiting for the foggy, hissing air to stop pouring out of the opening.

"Was the room refrigerated?" Morgan asked as the cloud of cold air finally stopped and pooled around their ankles.

"It seems so," Tiladia replied, swooping closer to the door and disappearing through the gap. Morgan glanced at Issa and, with her reassurance, reached forward to pull the door open further. It was heavy but swung easily on its perfectly crafted silent hinges. Once it was fully open, pale white lights flicked on, illuminating the vault's interior.

It was a round, bronze room about ten paces across, and the back wall, opposite the door, held four recessed shelves, each containing a dark wooden box. Tiladia was flitting around something to the right, and when Morgan took a tentative step into the vault, he saw that it was a pedestal with a bronze humanoid head sitting atop it. Once he stood before it, wondering what Tiladia was doing, the bronze eyelids snapped open, revealing glowing orange orbs.

"Hello, mortal. Congratulations."

The head spoke in a dry, inflectionless deadpan, moving just as a living person would, its wrinkled flesh flexing with the articulation of its jaw, and its glowing orange eyes tracking Morgan as he moved closer.

Morgan had seen talking objects before. This wasn't a shock or even the strangest thing to happen that day, but he still did a double take at the weird head. It was bald, had pointy batlike ears and angular eyes under a heavy, brooding brow. If Morgan had to guess at the age of the subject, he'd say it looked like a man in his late middle age.

"Uh, hello," he said, glancing at Issa and shrugging.

"That head is meant to look like Vormendion," Tiladia informed, flitting away from it. "I've determined it is not him, however."

"Correct, spirit. I'm a mere shard, a tiny splinter, of the great Vormendion."

"I'm a whole spirit of a mighty dragon, and I should eat you here and now for what your creator did to me!"

Tiladia streaked toward the bronze head, opening her misty jaws and letting loose a burst of cloudy breath. The Vormendion's bust widened its eyes and stretched its mouth in a startled cry, but he was unharmed when the foggy breath poured over him. Tiladia banked her flight and spun away, a tinkle of laughter following her form.

"She doesn't like you," Morgan said.

"I'm not responsible for what my greater version did to her! I've no memories involving dragons or their spirits!" the bronze head protested.

"She won't hurt you." Morgan paused and watched the dragon spirit flying in arcs outside the inner vault, swooping over the crates and furniture in the larger space. "I don't think."

"I have information for you, mortal, now that you've inherited this great structure."

"Tell him, then," Issa said, frowning at the skull. Morgan gave her a questioning look, and she continued, "If he's really a fragment of the mage that built this place, he can't be a very nice person. Look at what he's done to Tiladia and all of the guardians!"

"It's a valid point." Morgan moved a step closer to the bronze head.

"Again, I was created for a purpose, and the great Vormendion did not include very many superficial memories. As I said, I'm just a tiny fragment of his soul, and there wasn't room for much beyond speech, vocabulary, a bit of personality, and the knowledge I need to impart upon you." The bronze head sounded pained, irritated, and also a little fearful. "Trust me; you'll want me to carry out my duty!"

"All right, well, what is it you need to explain?" Morgan asked, now standing directly in front of the head.

"This room contains items of immense power and potential. A gift from Vormendion to the one who inherits his legacy: this tower and its contents." The bust's glowing orange eyes moved from left to right, and Morgan felt like, if it had arms, it would be gesturing expansively at the shelves with their cases on the far wall.

"Why would Vormendion do this?" Issa asked, coming to stand next to Morgan. "He doesn't seem like the altruistic sort. Why leave these gifts for someone to find?"

"The Great Vormendion had many motivations! How dare you impugn him so? He was more than charitable in his time on this plane!"

"I thought you said you didn't have many memories?" Morgan leaned closer to the head, scowling.

"No! I don't! I'm sorry, but it's my imprinted personality. It seems I'm very eager to defend Vormendion, the greater portion, from insult."

"All right, but the question stands. Do you know why Vormendion left this 'legacy'?"

"Yes, I have some of that knowledge. Part of it was pride. He'd spent more than a thousand years on this plane. He didn't want to leave without a trace, so he turned his home, this tower, into his legacy, making it a challenge and reward all in one. He also struck some . . . *bargains*, so certain conditions were placed on the creation of this legacy. I'm afraid I cannot explain those motivations—the knowledge simply isn't there."

Morgan looked at Issa. She shrugged, so he said, "Okay, tell us about this inheritance."

"Finally! My purpose will be fulfilled!" The head smiled, revealing even bronze teeth. When it began to speak again, Morgan caught a glimpse of the bronze tongue within its mouth, and he did a double take—it was forked like a reptile's. "There are four items that the Great Vormendion left for the one who claims his tower. You are that person, Morgan Hall—"

"You know my name?" He interrupted.

"Of course. I am of this tower, and you have bonded with the tower." The head paused to stare at Morgan, waiting for him to nod. "Now, the four items in the inheritance are somewhat related to each other, at least most of them. However, they may be used separately and by people of your choosing. Each one is powerful and rare.

"On the first shelf"—the bronze head moved its gaze in the general direction of the indicated object— "you'll find a tome containing knowledge that will grant the reader a class change. Not just any class, though! The reader will receive Vormendion's third class refinement, the epic-rated Prime Artificer class!"

The bronze head paused, staring at Morgan and Issa as though waiting for a reaction.

"So anyone who reads that tome will instantly gain that class? They'll become a, what was it, Prime Artificer?" Morgan asked.

"That's right! The only prerequisite is that the individual must have reached the appropriate level for their species to obtain a class. In most cases, that would be level ten."

"Will they gain skills and spells as well?" Issa inquired.

The head looked at Issa with a frown, but when it saw Morgan's expression, its demeanor returned to neutral, and it replied enthusiastically.

"Of course! Depending on the level of the person who reads the tome, certain skills and spells will be granted. As the individual gains further levels, the tome will provide additional rewards, the last being granted at the attainment of tier seven."

"Sounds valuable," Morgan commented. The head frowned, apparently hoping for a more exuberant response. "Well? What's next?"

"The second shelf"—again the head gazed in its direction—"contains a scroll with a copy of one of Vormendion's signature spells! If you have the requisite Energy and will, the Imbue Soul Shard spell will allow you to bind a captured or willing spirit to an object.

"The scroll is the result of all the knowledge Vormendion gathered through thousands of trials, allowing the one who studies it to create imbued constructs with as much or as little physical and intellectual detail as desired. Why, this is the spell that the Great Vormendion used to infuse me into this fine, bronze vessel."

The head stopped speaking, its grandiose presentation ending rather abruptly as it looked to Morgan for a response.

"Uh." Morgan glanced around, suddenly glad that Tiladia wasn't in the room. "So it's a way to enslave spirits?"

"Not exactly! First, you must capture the spirit, or as is my case, create a shard of your own spirit. Or you might find a willing spirit! Any of those cases will work with this spell."

"You use the terms *spirit* and *soul* interchangeably. Are they the same?" Issa asked.

"In my mind, they are, which tells me the Great Vormendion thought they were synonymous." The head answered Issa quickly this time, without looking at Morgan first.

Was it learning? Could it learn? Was it alive? Morgan didn't like the implications and questions this situation was stirring up in his mind.

"So I could take a spirit and put it into any object?"

"No! The object must be properly prepared, which brings me to the third shelf and its contents! The Great Vormendion has left a tome containing one of his most sought-after, difficult-to-obtain skills! The person who reads that tome will learn the skill Prepare Vessel!" The bust was practically yelling in the enthusiastic delivery of its information.

"Are these skills and spells not granted by the class tome?"

"No! These are custom, self-taught abilities that Vormendion spent nearly a hundred years perfecting!" the bust answered Issa.

Morgan was growing tired of the bust and its faux enthusiasm. He was beginning to count himself very lucky that he'd never met the real Vormendion.

"All right. What's in the last box?"

"Yes, yes. On with my duty! The final object in the Great Vormendion's inheritance is a portal stone which will connect this tower to the dwelling that Vormendion built on Aradnue. There, you will gain access to even greater mysteries! For your safety, the box containing the portal stone will not open until you have achieved tier seven."

"What?" Morgan exclaimed. "The world where Tiladia is from?"

"Ahh!" the bronze head exclaimed. "Ahh!" Its eyes were beginning to glow more and more brightly, and little orange veins started to spread from them. "My duty is done! I am released!"

The orange veins spread until the entire bronze head was glowing orange, and then it simply burst into a cloud of black smoke. When it cleared, the pedestal on which the head had rested was empty.

"Goddammit!"

"What?" Issa seemed glad the head was gone; her shoulders were more relaxed, and she was breathing more calmly.

"I should have questioned that thing a lot more before I let it finish its duty. Now it's gone."

"We know what we need to know, and I was starting to fear that evil man's spirit would be in this tower forever. I'm glad it's gone."

"Yeah, but now we need to figure out what to do with all these things." Morgan gestured to the shelves and their boxes.

"I have some thoughts about that," Issa replied, walking over to the shelves.

"I'm glad to hear that because I feel pretty damn overwhelmed right now. I also need your advice about my class. I hit tier four."

"Oh!" Issa turned to him with wide eyes. "All right. Let's go somewhere quiet and comfortable to talk. You can lock this vault up for now, right?"

"Right," Morgan said, happy to put the inheritance on the back burner.

He took Issa's hand and led her out of the vault. Closing the heavy door, he pressed his palm to the plate until, with a hiss and a resounding click, it sealed shut. He'd deal with this mess after he and Issa sat down and figured out his class refinement.

As they started toward the stairs, he called out, "Tiladia! Come with us, please. I'd like your advice too!"

## ❦ MORGAN ❧

Morgan, Issa, and Tiladia settled down in the library, sitting in one of the comfortable arrangements of leather chairs and couches while Tiladia hovered in the air nearby. Watching her misty, crystal form gliding and spinning, it occurred to Morgan that the spirit was never still. She never seemed at rest.

"Tiladia," he said on an impulse. "What if we could make a different body or vessel for you? One which allowed you to interact physically with things and people."

"Do you think such a thing is possible?" Tiladia asked, her form shifting to that of the misty dragon she seemed to prefer. It hovered in the air, long, smoky neck arched so her crystal eyes could stare at Morgan.

"Were you listening at all when that Vormendion bust told us about the inheritance?"

"No, I'm sorry. I found his voice and demeanor brought up repulsive memories." The misty dragon coughed a cloud of vapor in emphasis of her words.

"Part of the inheritance seems to be the ability to craft vessels for spirits. I think we might be able to do something like that for you."

"I would love to be able to interact with things more, Morgan!" The dragon spirit's voice rose in excitement.

"Alright, well, let's not get ahead of ourselves. I think it's something to explore, but I don't want you to get your hopes up too much. I'm not sure I fully understand the inheritance, okay? I'll look into it soon, though, I promise."

Morgan sat back, stretching his long legs so his feet rested on a nearby ottoman.

"I'll try not to allow my emotions to run wild, Morgan, but you've stirred up a lot of thoughts I'd held locked in a tiny corner of my mind!" Tiladia looped in the air, flapping her little misty wings so she surged through the motion with an eruption of tinkling crystal.

"I think it's good to hope, Tiladia, and I think you have reason to! I heard the description of the inheritance, and I think what Morgan suggested will be possible." Issa smiled at the dragon as she curled her legs under her, leaning comfortably into the corner of the sofa.

"All right, let's focus on one thing at a time, okay? Right now, I want to decide what class to choose for my level-forty refinement. Let me describe them to you both, and then you can tell me your opinions. Sound good?"

He paused, and Issa nodded.

"Thank you for including me, Morgan!" Tiladia said.

"I should have been including you in a lot of decisions, Tiladia. I don't think I really appreciated how significant it was having an actual dragon, an elder being, living in my home. I'm sorry if I haven't given you the respect you deserve." Morgan leaned forward, earnest, trying to look into the dragon's crystalline eyes. Once again, he wished she had a more solid form, if only so he could see her expressions better.

"Thank you." Tiladia surged forward to flow around Morgan's shoulders and neck before moving back in front of the sofa. Her mist was cool but left no residue where it touched him.

"Well," Morgan started, turning to include Issa. "I only have two choices. Three, if you consider I could keep my current class. Both of my options say they're legendary. I'm assuming that's the progression after epic?"

"I've never heard of a legendary class . . ." Issa's words trailed away as Tiladia spoke.

"Vormendion had a legendary class when he visited Aradnue. He worked for centuries afterward to gain the next rarity, going through several more refinements before he succeeded. That's when he created his inheritance and left this plane."

"What was the next rarity?" Morgan asked.

"While he pursued it, Vormendion used terms like *divine* or *mythical*, but he didn't see fit to tell me what the System called it once he succeeded. By that time, he spent very little time in this tower, and when he did make an appearance, it was usually to retrieve an artifact or, later, to prepare his guardians."

"I see," Morgan said. "I guess that's not important right now. Well, let me describe the classes for you." He paused, looking at Issa, whose eyes had grown distant. "Something wrong, Issa?"

"No. I'm just thinking about how small my world was before you came. Well, before I went into the Crucible, I guess. I thought an Advanced class was impressive when I was growing up. I was so proud when I got my Battle Witch class. I used to think traveling up the Rill Catcher to Gelica was a great journey and an impressive goal, but here I am, talking to beings from other worlds, one of whom is my mate! I guess I'm just a little overwhelmed but also very excited about what's in store for us. For our family." She rested a hand on her stomach and smiled, clearly trying to reassure Morgan that she was okay.

He reached out a hand, resting it atop hers, and smiled, staring at her for a few heartbeats. He felt like he could stare into the bright, golden-yellow irises all day, but Tiladia, shifting in the corner of his eye, brought him back down to solid ground. He cleared his throat.

"All right, well, one choice I have seems to be a progression of my current class. I'm a Void Adept right now, and the new refinement is called a Void Master. I don't think it was automatic that I received this refinement, though. In the description, it mentions that I've 'developed new and powerful ways of piercing the void.' I think the scrying and Void Gate spells that Olivia helped me learn opened up this class."

"What attributes does it focus on?" Issa asked.

"Intelligence and unbound, so I'll have some freedom in that regard."

"What is your other choice, Morgan?" Tiladia inquired.

"It's called Anemoi Cloud Warden. It sounds interesting, and I'm sure it's being offered because of my bloodline—the description says I'll learn skills and spells that complement the 'secrets of my ancestry.' The class attributes are intelligence, agility, and dexterity." He glanced from Issa to Tiladia. "Any thoughts?"

"I like the idea of a warden-type class for you, Morgan," Issa spoke. "I think it fits your personality. However, I think the other class sounds more powerful."

"If you're being offered the Cloud Warden class because of your bloodline, Morgan, you can be fairly confident that this option will not go away. You'll see it at each refinement going forward. It might change to suit your skillset or to reflect a further connection to your bloodline, but some form of it will persist." Tiladia swirled closer to him and said in an airy whisper, "I'd go with the Master class. You're bound to learn some powerful skills and spells."

"Why do you think the Void Master class sounds more powerful, Issa?" Morgan asked, trying to cover his surprise at Tiladia's strange behavior.

"Your void Energy is powerful, Morgan, more so than any affinity I've ever seen. This class is promising you mastery of greater uses for it. You'll also have unbound attribute points at every level. The Cloud Warden sounds interesting, but it seems like it's trying to push you into a box. I feel like the other class will teach you how to break boxes."

"Your mate is perceptive, and I agree with her," Tiladia said, swooping again around Morgan, trailing her cool mist around his neck. Was she being friendly? Affectionate? Morgan found himself trying to imagine the dragon spirit's motives and emotions and shook his head.

He really hoped he'd be able to help her into a form that suited her better, one with a face that could express itself and vocal cords rather than tinkling crystals.

"So you're both in agreement? This was easier than I thought it would be. I thought, with two legendary offers, I'd be stuck deliberating for days."

He looked from Issa to Tiladia again, giving them each a chance to voice any sort of doubt or change of mind, but they both returned his gaze. Issa nodded, smiling, and Tiladia simply didn't say anything.

"All right, then." He pulled up his status sheet and selected the refinement page.

"You didn't tell us what you thought," Issa noted.

"I was leaning toward Void Master, just because I love the idea of teleporting, and Void Wave is the most devastating spell in my arsenal. It's a known quantity, whereas the Anemoi Cloud Warden is a complete mystery."

He shrugged, then selected the Void Master option on his screen and sat back, eyes losing focus as System messages scrolled into his vision.

\*\*\***Congratulations! You have refined your class: Void Master. Class spell gained: Void Missile—Basic. Class spell gained: Void Step—Advanced.**\*\*\*

\*\*\***Congratulations! World-first Void Master! Feat awarded.**\*\*\*

\*\*\***World-first Void Master: Feat granted: Void Drifter—While in a natural void, a vacuum devoid of matter, you will passively cultivate void-attuned Energy.**\*\*\*

\*\*\***Void Missile—Basic: Conjure forth an orb of pure void Energy and hurl it at enormous velocity, undoing your target's material connections to the physical plane. Energy cost: 200. Cooldown: Minimal.**\*\*\*

\*\*\***Void Step—Advanced: You are able to instantly travel between two points in space, provided you can see your destination. Energy cost: 1000. Cooldown: Minimal.**\*\*\*

"Wow," Morgan said. "It seems like this class is gearing me up to travel in space?"

At Issa's puzzled expression, Morgan described the feats he'd gained for his world-first achievements, both for Void Adept and this new class.

"Is space a void?" Issa asked, her eyes going distant once again.

"It's a kind of void," Morgan replied.

"It is indeed," Tiladia agreed. "When I flew between worlds, not even sound could reach me in the great black."

"Yeah, but I mean, you can see things in space. Light travels through it. My Void Wave seems to destroy everything, even light."

"Your void-attuned Energy is the pure form of the concept, Morgan. Voids in nature might not be so pure, but that doesn't mean they won't work with your abilities," Tiladia said, speaking matter-of-factly.

"I should have spoken with you a lot more in the past, Tiladia. Thank you for your guidance and help." Morgan felt Issa's fingers snake between his, and when he looked at her, he saw her smiling at him, almost like she was proud.

"What?" he asked.

"Nothing. I'm just happy that I'm with such a considerate man."

"I'm happy too, Morgan. You begin to grasp the edges of true power. Certainly in this world, but even in some of the older worlds, you'd be regarded as having great potential. I'm happy you remain humble and kind. I couldn't imagine anyone else I'd prefer as the master of this tower." Tiladia's tinkling voice rose and fell, and Morgan knew she was trying to add emotion to her words.

"Morgan, I think you should use part of Vormendion's inheritance. The spell and skill, at least. I think you should do it for two reasons," Issa said, squeezing his fingers.

"What two reasons?"

"One, so you can help Tiladia into a better body, one with a voice and a face and limbs that can interact with the world."

"I would love that!" Tiladia surged forward to curl around Issa in what Morgan was starting to realize was her only means of touching someone: brushing her cool mist over their skin.

"The other reason is that I don't trust anyone else not to do evil things with those spells. Vormendion made slaves. Someone else might do so, too, no matter how well you know them. People change with power. You've proven that you can handle it and still be a good man." Again, Issa squeezed his hand, and Morgan found himself struggling to figure out how to respond.

His thoughts spun at her and Tiladia's earlier words.

Was he a good man?

He tried to do what was right and think about how other people would feel when he spoke or did something, but he wasn't anything special. His success on Fanwath revolved around a lot of luck: He'd been lucky to be the one awake when the ship had entered the solar system. He'd been lucky to find Issa in the Crucible, and lucky to have a strong Core and a high Energy affinity.

He sighed heavily and decided it was stupid to dwell on it. Why not just be glad that he'd been so fortunate?

Morgan kissed Issa's fingers and looked into her eyes, saying, "I might do good things and maybe even be good, but it's because I've had good people around me and a lot of lucky breaks. Without you, I'd have died in the Crucible, and my story would have ended pretty abruptly, despite some of my lucky breaks. Most of the good things I've done were because of you, Issa. If I were to trust anyone with those inheritance items, it would be you." He paused then, staring at her eyes, feeling an impulse he didn't want to second-guess.

Before he could doubt himself, Morgan said, "I love you so much. I don't know how things are done with the Ardeni, but will you marry me?"

Issa's smile was brilliant, her lips pulling back from her teeth, exposing her sharp canines, and making her eyes twinkle. "Yes, Morgan! Of course I will, but I'm fairly sure that your custom says you're supposed to give me a ring. Isn't that right?"

"Oh God! Who have you been talking to? Of course, I'm supposed to have a ring, but . . ." his words trailed off as Issa launched herself into his lap and smothered him with kisses.

Tiladia had erupted into a cascade of tinkling crystals, swooping around the sofa like a miniature hurricane. Morgan simply laughed, returning Issa's kisses and savoring the joy in his heart.

# OLIVIA

The Travel Pavilion was quite a structure, and Olivia wondered why she'd never wandered inside during her explorations of the campus. It blended in well with the architecture of the area, sort of a white-washed, marble museum feel. Manicured lawns and hedges surrounded the structure, and the wide, open archways that served as doorways allowed for easy ingress and egress, both for people and the flower-scented breeze.

When Olivia climbed the steps at the end of the cobbled pathway and walked through the eastern archway, she saw dozens of platforms and several fountains, but no gateways. She supposed they wouldn't be open and active all the time. Upon a closer inspection, she realized there were a few different archways on certain platforms. She walked toward one made of long, woven branches and saw a metal placard embedded in the marble platform that read A7.

"Aha," Olivia said, noting that all of the platforms held similar placards. She moved to her left, and reading the numbers as she progressed, found the open platform labeled A3. She hefted the heavy keystone for Morgan's portal and looked around at the raised surface. "All right. Where do you go, hmm?"

She scanned the smooth marble for any indication and saw a slight indentation on the far end where the platform approached the wall of the pavilion. Not knowing what else to do, Olivia set the heavy, tapered rectangle of dark grey metal—why it was called a stone when it was clearly made of the same stuff as Morgan's tower was beyond her—on the indentation before stepping back from it. Nothing happened.

"Oh, of course."

She stepped forward to put a finger on top of the stone. She pushed out a tiny trickle of Energy, watching as the metal soaked it up, slowly changing from inert, dark gray to the smoldering orange of an ember, though it gave off no heat. The stone started to vibrate and push forth gouts of white steam, so Olivia backed off, watching the process unfold.

As the keystone glowed and steamed, it started to expand, almost like it was unfolding from itself, and as Olivia observed, it grew into the exact same shape as the portal archways in Morgan's tower. The dark metal ticked and hissed as it cooled, settling into its new form. Olivia walked up to the metal, touching it, and UI menu opened in her vision with three options:

**\*\*\*Vormendion's Tower Portal #1\*\*\***
**Open Portal**
**Lock Portal**
**Assign Permissions**

"Well, that's easy enough." Olivia figured she'd need to give Oylla permissions, but for the moment, she didn't think she needed to do anything.

Dusting her hands against each other with a satisfied smile, Olivia turned to the nearest pavilion exit and started on her way back to the main academy grounds.

As she walked through the gardens, Olivia passed near a small group of the strange, floating Onaghi, and though she'd seen several of them in her time at the academy, she didn't know how to communicate with them. Still, she waved awkwardly, and the weird, billowy creatures waved their jellyfish-like tentacles her way. She smiled, wondering if they'd understood her after all.

Watching them float away, she found herself wondering how Bronwyn would react to such strange people, which brought on other thoughts about the woman she'd professed to love not long ago.

"Why'd you have to get mixed up with the fae?" she asked the air.

She wasn't so much worried about Bronwyn. No, the woman had proven her resourcefulness enough times that Olivia was willing to give her the benefit of the doubt. It was more like she was worried she might never be as high a priority for Bronwyn as Bronwyn was for her. There was always a sense that part of her wasn't being shared, wasn't being fully open to Olivia. There was a connection between Bronwyn and the Summer Queen that Olivia couldn't touch or even fathom.

"Believe me, I tried plenty," she muttered, resorting to her old habit of talking to herself now that her mind was idle and she was alone.

Thinking of their relationship and her complaints, Olivia wondered if it was fair for her to expect to share in every aspect of Bronwyn's life.

"Maybe not fair, but something I'd like. It's not like I'm holding anything back from her."

The most annoying part about Bronwyn's relationship with the fae was that she seemed to have given up some of her autonomy and was apparently completely fine with it.

Olivia realized she'd been so deep in thought that she hadn't noticed her entire walk back to the commons. She paused to watch the student groups socializing, exercising, and relaxing in the warm afternoon sun, and a smile brightened her face when she recognized some of Copper cohort sitting in a circle near the Alchemy Pavilion.

Olivia hurried over, nervously smoothing her beautiful gray robes and glancing at her boots to ensure they weren't scuffed. She ran her fingers through her hair and briefly contemplated putting on her crown but laughed the idea off—they'd never let her live it down if she walked up to them wearing a crown!

Rald, Veena, and Shani were sitting in a loose circle, passing around some sort of card. Olivia caught them by surprise when she barked, "All right, you lazy pups! Get up and give me twenty deadfalls, and then I'll see you take turns with arm throws!"

Her own laughter broke the spell as Shani looked up in a momentary panic. Rald joined in, saying, "Ancestors, Liv! You don't sound anything like Grobak!"

"Olivia!" Veena exclaimed, her white-painted face breaking into a huge smile.

"Hi, Veena! Rald, Shani! I missed you guys! I'm so happy to be back! Where's Adaida? Hanwol?"

"Well, speaking of Grobak." Rald chuckled. "He kept them after class. He said Adaida was talking too much, and that Hanwol could earn some extra credit throwing the beanbags at her while she climbed ropes."

"God, seriously? I was just joking, invoking the old grump; I didn't think he was really still terrorizing you all." Olivia glanced toward the main campus and the basement gymnasium where Adaida was, apparently, going through some rough extra lessons.

"Why don't you head to the gym," Rald suggested with a wink. "I bet Adaida would cheer up real quick if she saw you waiting on the sideline."

"Yes, Olivia! Go meet Adaida. We'll see you in the dorm a bit later!" Shani chimed in, standing up to hug her. "Roots, Olivia! You're even bigger than I remember. Did you advance your race? You seem so dense with power; it's almost like standing next to Professor Oylla-dak!"

"She's right, Liv," Rald said, standing up and moving close to her, using his hand to measure his height against hers. "What level are you now?"

"Well, um, I gained a lot of levels in the Proving Grounds, you guys know that, right? And when I got home, I had to go through a portal to another world to help rescue a friend, and things weren't exactly peaceful there. I gained a few more levels, and yeah, advanced my race a bunch. I'm level twenty-five now."

"Twenty-five? Orla's bones, Olivia! How are we supposed to compete with that?" Veena's eyes looked like storm clouds brewing, and Olivia knew she'd triggered her competitive streak.

"You're not, Veena! I'm on your team, remember? I spoke with Oylla, and she promised me I could stay in Copper."

"You're going to feel pretty bored in our classes, Liv." Rald snorted.

"I'll be in Spellcraft and Cultivation. The rest of the day, I have to work as an apprentice to some old professor or another."

"That makes sense," Shani said, seeming to take everything in perfect stride. "Well, go find Adaida, will you? She's been talking about you constantly."

"All right. See you guys a bit later. I'm still me, okay?"

"Yeah, sure, Liv. See you at the dorm." Rald waved, and so did Veena, seeming to warm a bit but struggling to come to grips with the fact that she didn't have to compete with her.

Olivia turned and started walking to the gym, excited but also nervous and harboring a pit of guilt at the center of her stomach for some reason. Why did she feel guilty?

"Because I'm wondering what Bronwyn would think of me going to see Adaida. I'm wondering how Adaida is going to react when I tell her about Bronwyn."

Olivia knew she was right, but saying her thoughts out loud didn't really help because she knew she wasn't telling the whole truth. There was another option she was leaning toward, if she was being honest: she was contemplating not mentioning Bronwyn to Adaida. She was thinking about putting things off until she'd visited home again and spent some time talking to Bronwyn about the things in their relationship that were bothering her.

Maybe it was a moot point. Maybe Adaida was happy just staying friends. Olivia had been gone quite a while, after all. First, she'd been in the Proving Grounds for weeks, and then she'd gone home for a vacation that was supposed to last a week or so, but she'd disappeared for months.

"Right, no doubt she's forgotten all about her old crush on me."

Olivia looked up and saw she was in the last stretch of the wide hallway that led to Grobak's gym. When she walked in through the open double doors, she almost laughed aloud at seeing how many poor students Grobak had working on remedial training. He must have been in a very bad mood, indeed. Shouts and grunts echoed around the high walls, and Olivia was surprised to feel her heart rate increase; the room stressed her out.

She scanned the enormous indoor space, glad to see that Grobak was on the far side screaming at some students from Bone cohort. She looked to the left, where the ropes hung from the high ceiling, and sure enough, there was Adaida climbing and leaping between swinging ropes, dodging the beanbag missiles that Hanwol was firing at her with maniacal glee. Adaida was proving to be a difficult target, but how easy was it to dodge a seemingly endless supply of beanbags while straining to climb and swing on ropes? Hanwol struck home several times while Olivia watched, to the frustrated outcries of the auburn-haired Ghelli.

Olivia leaned against the wall and surreptitiously tried to help her friend with some well-timed Wind Gusts, throwing beanbags off target and eliciting curses from the little Bogoli. Olivia was starting to worry about Adaida as she struggled to hang onto the ropes, but Grobak finally relented, blowing his whistle and telling all the detained students to get out of his sight. She watched as Adaida let go of the high rope and used her wings to break her fall, gently fluttering to the gym floor.

"Nice one, Adaida!" she called out.

Her two cohort members jerked their gazes her way, and then Adaida was running toward her. Olivia's face split into a beaming smile, and she held her arms out, eager to hug her friend. Hanwol followed after at a more sedate pace, but he fell away from Olivia's conscious mind as Adaida's thin frame crashed into her and they embraced.

Adaida's thick hair smelled familiar and good, and the way her narrow frame pressed into her brought heat to Olivia's cheeks. Suddenly, she was overwhelmed by guilt again, and she gently took hold of Adaida's shoulders to push her back. "Nice to see you too, Adaida!"

"I missed you so much, Liv! I was afraid you'd never make it back to our world! Did you know it was me who helped Oylla scry you? My connection to you made it possible! She said she'd never have been able to get such a clear image without my help!"

"She did mention you helped! I missed you too! I missed all of you," Olivia added, smiling at Hanwol, who stood behind Adaida with his white-gloved hands folded in front of his robe.

"Glad you're back, Olivia," Hanwol said. "It's good that you're here. Have you heard about the murders?"

"Mother of Trees, Hanwol! That's how you greet our friend? With talk of murder?"

"I have heard, yes. Come on, you two. Let's go to the dorm. I think we all have more catching up to do, hmm?"

"All right," Adaida agreed, then added, "But I want some time alone with you soon. I have a lot to share with you, and I want to hear all about your time away."

"Of course, Adaida." Olivia smiled, though there was a pang of dismay in her heart.

# OLIVIA

Olivia lay in her bed, savoring the sounds of her friends sleeping around her. How strange it was to be back among them, listening to their soft night sounds and finding comfort in them. At first, she'd thought she'd find the communal space annoying after so many nights with just her and Bronwyn sharing a space. Even in the dungeon, Morgan had kept to himself and rarely bothered them once they went into their tent. Now she was here, three feet away from the softly snoring Veena and just across the aisle from Shani and Adaida, and her eyes felt heavy with the desire to close and drift away.

She turned over and allowed her sleepy eyelids to fall, replaying the conversations they'd had before going to sleep. Rald had insisted on sharing some liquor he'd brought from home—some kind of Ridonnian whiskey. It had been harsh and smokey and made the cohort's rebonding experience easier and more fun than Olivia would have thought possible. Rald had moaned endlessly about how he needed Olivia's help with women, having struck out with not one, not two, but three relationships while she was gone. Of course, this opened him up to more teasing from Veena and Shani, and Hanwol had simply snorted and opened a book to peruse while he deemed the subject unworthy of his attention.

Olivia smiled into her pillow as she remembered how Veena hadn't let Hanwol slide so easily, landing a perfectly placed barb about his recent "date" with Gwinna. Apparently, they'd been studying how to manipulate certain states of matter together—they shared an affinity for something called bonding Energy, which Olivia found intriguing on its own. Not only were there different types of affinities, but there appeared to be different states of Energy within those affinities. The revelation drove home how much she'd missed in their Spellcraft class.

Smiling at the memories, Olivia felt her eyes grow heavier, and sleep pulled her into oblivion. Though she dreamed quite a lot, when she woke to the hushed conversations of her cohort getting ready for their first class, they fled her mind, and she had no recollection of any of them.

"Mmff," she grunted, rolling over onto her back and pulling her pillow into a ball beneath her head. "Is it time to get up already?"

"Guess you've been getting lazy in your time away from the academy, huh?" Adaida teased, coming over to sit on the side of her bed. "Must be nice not to have to go to most of your classes!"

"Well, I have to go sit with Oylla-dak while we interview people vying to be my new taskmaster!" Olivia scooted up, both enjoying and feeling the familiar pit in her stomach at Adaida's proximity.

Just as she opened her mouth to say something, a piercing scream sounded from the hallway. Suddenly, Olivia's pleasant, fuzzy demeanor shifted, and she veritably flew out of bed, her nightgown-clothed body blazing like a white-blue torch.

"Get back!" she commanded Adaida and Veena, the only other members of her cohort near the door, then she summoned a ball of crackling blue plasma and pulled the door ajar, peering into the hallway.

A student, Ulya ap'Tine from Wood cohort, was standing with her back to the wall, a hand over her mouth, her entire body shaking while she gazed upon the scene of a slaughter. Olivia stepped into the hallway and took the girl's wrist, guiding her into the dorm to Adaida and Veena; then she went back into the hall, pulling the door closed behind her.

Some of the other dormitory doors opened a few inches while other students peered into the hallway, trying to see what the scream was about. They quickly closed them when they saw Olivia's torchlike figure standing amidst the carnage, and what carnage it was! The remains of a female student were strewn up and down the hallway. Viscera and blood liberally painted the walls and floor, and even the ceiling dripped with the fleshy matter.

Olivia wouldn't have been able to identify the remains as a person if not for the perfectly intact headset purposefully in the center of the hall. Olivia studied the floor, noting the sprays of arterial blood and the footprints left by Ulya as she'd stumbled into the scene.

"How did she get so far into it before she realized what she'd come upon?" Olivia carefully tiptoed through the mess, looking up and down the hallway but not seeing any sign of the aggressor. Realizing the authorities weren't anywhere near yet, Olivia moved back to the center of the slaughter and the decapitated head that sat there, surveying the scene of its own massacre.

"Poor thing," she said, squatting down to peer into the cloudy violet eyes. The victim had long white hair, the ends of which were painted crimson by the blood on the floor. Smooth, pale blue skin and tiny antennae told the story of the girl's heritage—part Ardeni and part Ghelli. Olivia glanced at her face more closely, a thought like a thunderbolt running through her, and then she saw it. "Oh God! Shathi . . ."

She hadn't known the girl well, but there were only so many cohorts, and they had several classes together; of course she should recognize her! Olivia had thought the girl from Silver cohort was beautiful and sweet and hadn't ever had cause to complain about her. She wasn't overly competitive. She never gossiped out of turn, and in fact, she'd once helped Olivia with one of her alchemical recipes after she'd been in detention.

"Stand slowly and turn to regard me!" The voice was firm and loud but very calm, so Olivia didn't overreact. She just rose to a standing position and slowly turned toward the voice, still holding her ball of crackling plasma. When she saw Carlu, the investigator, still wearing blue-and-white striped pajamas, she relaxed.

"Hello, Inspector. What a horrible thing to wake up to, wouldn't you say?"

She ended her spell, and the sizzling ball of Energy winked out, reduced to a wispy line of blue smoke that shortly faded into nothing.

"Oh, Miss Bennet." Relief was evident in his voice. "I was alerted to the scream of a student and feared I might have stumbled upon the killer."

"No sign of the killer to my untrained eye. The girl who screamed is in Copper cohort's dorm here." Olivia gestured to the closed door between them.

"Well, let me see what I can find. Please don't move for a few moments—the less you stir up the Energies before I can do some scrying, the better."

"Oh, I should have thought of that. Did I ruin the scene? I, um, wouldn't mind getting into some different clothes." Olivia was suddenly self-conscious about standing in the hallway in her white, silky nightgown.

"I beg your patience," Carlu said, fiddling with a pair of brass goggles. They sprouted a half dozen different springy antennae and emitted a buzzing, crackling sound as he powered them up. Olivia watched as he slowly moved his gaze over the hallway, lingering on this spot or that and seemingly staring at her feet for a long couple of minutes. After darting his glance here and there, he reached up and turned a dial on the side of the goggles until visible electrical currents began to arc between the antennae. Then he knelt and stared down the length of the hallway, seemingly forming some sort of impression.

Olivia folded her arms over her chest and frowned, tapping a foot, glancing at the various dormitory doors that opened and closed as curious students poked their noses out. Finally, Inspector Carlu seemed to finish, and he reached up to click off the weird goggles, pulling them from his face.

"Thanks for putting up with that; it was good that you weren't mixing more of your Energy signature with the killer's. While I had you standing there, I was able to isolate the signature of the victim and, I believe, a trace of the murderer. We're looking for someone with a Spirit Core and an affinity for death Energy."

"A Spirit Core? Death Energy?" Olivia repeated, sounding almost like an echo.

"Not a common combination in civilized circles, I'm afraid, though that might work in our favor. I'll deal with the administration if you'd like to return to your dormitory now, Ms. Bennet. Thank you for so bravely coming forth in the defense of your fellow students."

"Oh, well, you're welcome. Thanks, Mr. Carlu," Olivia said, pleased that the investigator was giving her the benefit of the doubt.

She quickly tiptoed between smears of blood to her dormitory and went inside.

"Liv! What in the roots? Why'd you run out there?" Adaida asked the instant she came inside.

"Why? I was hoping to catch the killer, of course."

"Hah, of course she was. Conqueror of the Proving Grounds that she is!" Rald slapped his hands together. "Is it true?" He gestured to where Ulya was sitting on Veena's bed, sobbing into her hands while she spoke softly to Shani and Veena. "Was it Shathi?"

"Yes," Olivia said with a sigh. "Poor thing. If I could pick anyone from the first years who didn't deserve to be killed like that, she'd be on the list."

"This is hitting rather close to home, isn't it?" Hanwol's voice was even more morose and sonorous than usual.

"This is terrible! Poor Shathi! She reminded me of my sister, and not just because their names are similar." Adaida sat at the foot of Olivia's bed and stared into space, almost like she was in shock.

Olivia glanced at Shani and Veena, still comforting Ulya. She supposed the blonde Ghelli was similar in features to the victim, but Shani was far more acerbic and outgoing than Shathi. Still, there was no accounting for how other people felt, and if Adaida felt they were similar, who was Olivia to judge?

Rald opened the door and poked his head out, only to have a school official bark at him to wait within until they were cleared to leave. "Looks like we're missing Enchantment today."

"Is that all you can think about?" Adaida asked, her eyes beginning to well with tears.

"No! Come on, you know me better than that! I liked Shathi, too, all right?" Rald sat down on the wooden bench that flanked their doorway. Olivia often used the bench to put her shoes on, and she wondered if Shathi had used a similar one to put hers on that morning. She cleared her throat and walked over to Ulya.

"Did you see anything, Ulya? How'd you get into the middle of that mess?"

"What?" Ulya looked up at Olivia, her blue face swollen and her eyes bleary and red.

"I mean, the hallway was a disaster. How'd you get so far into that mess without realizing it was a murder scene?"

"I was running! I stayed with Garnet last night! I was hurrying back to the dorm to change."

"Oh?" Olivia prodded.

"Yes, if you must know, Pirk and I were . . . studying last night."

"What?" Veena spoke. "You slept with him in their dorm? I hope you didn't mind the audience!"

"It's not like that! Haven't you been to the gemstone dorms? They all have separate rooms that open into a hallway."

"What?" Rald asked, stunned. "That's hardly fair!"

"It's called money," Ulya replied, sniffing loudly. Just then, a loud knock sounded on the door before it opened. Inspector Carlu stood there with a black-robed administrator whom Olivia had never met. He cleared his throat, stepping forward with a short bow.

"Pardon me, but you did say the witness was within, is that right, Miss Bennet?"

"Yes, Ulya is from Wood cohort. She's the one who screamed."

"I didn't witness anything! I just stumbled on that horrible mess!"

"Nothing to be upset about, Miss ap'Tine."

"How do you know my name?" She sniffed loudly, wiping her nose on the back of her sleeve.

"Oh, I took it upon myself to memorize the current rolls. Would you mind coming with us, please? I have some scrying spells I'd like to use to try to jog a few details loose in your memory. Things you might have noticed without realizing it."

"Yes, come along, Ulya," the administrator indicated. "You all may head to your class now; we've finished with the hallway. I would encourage you all to stay together and avoid spreading rumors. Very little is known at this point, and speculation will only cause harm to the academy. Is that understood?"

"What?" Hanwol stepped forward in a very uncharacteristic show of confrontation. "You have the nerve to ask us not to speculate when our classmates are being slaughtered wholesale in the hallways?"

"That's exactly the kind of talk we'd like to avoid, Mr. Fenash! Would you like the alumni to pull their funding? Would you like the great families to call their children home? The academy doesn't exist in a vacuum!"

"In that case, you should work to solve these murders, sir. It's hardly our fault this is happening," Hanwol replied, not backing down even an inch.

Olivia smiled, watching the interaction. Hanwol's blue-painted face hid all of his emotion, but his red-shot eyes were steady and unblinking. Hadn't he said something about wanting to be a solicitor or something? Perhaps he felt a calling to stand up to authority.

"As I said, please refrain from spreading rumors," the administrator concluded, turning and exiting. Inspector Carlu took Ulya's elbow and guided her out of the room, and then Rald stood up and gave Hanwol a thump on the back.

"Nice one, Han! Don't let them push us around!"

"It's easy to be brave when you have Olivia watching your back, eh, Han?" Adaida added. Olivia hadn't noticed, but she'd moved close to her again, and now she reached out to, quite literally, hang onto her shoulder.

"Listen, you guys, I promise, anyone who comes into this dorm looking to hurt any of you is going to get reduced to slag, but I can't be with you all the time, so please, please stay together, as the professor said. Do you all promise me?" Olivia looked around the dorm, meeting eyes with each of her cohort members.

"Say it! Promise me!"

She stood in front of the door with her arms crossed until they each promised her to stay with the others.

"What about you?" Adaida asked, still clinging to her arm.

"I'll be fine. I'll stay on high alert, alright? I'm on my way to see Oylla as soon as you all leave, anyway. I don't think anyone will mess with me as long as I'm with her, right?"

# OLIVIA

"Come in, Olivia! Sit down! I heard about your morning. What a terrible thing to wake up to. Your cohort was lucky to have you around." Oylla motioned for Olivia to come into her office, gesturing to the pair of couches over by the window, which, uncharacteristically, had its curtains pulled wide, allowing bright morning light to fill the office.

"What makes you say that?" Olivia asked, sitting on the indicated couch.

"What? That your cohort was lucky you were there?" Oylla sat next to her, a foot or so between them. "I suppose I was thinking of worst-case scenarios, if the murderer were still present or seeking further victims. You have more raw ability and power than nearly any other student on the grounds; few professors would try to match you in pure Energy potential. I think the killer would have been rather startled had he tried to murder you the way he did poor Shathi."

"Is it? A man? Or are you just using that term generically?"

"Inspector Carlu seems convinced the killer is a man, but he did allow for some small doubt. Now, I know this topic is burning through the hallways of the academy, and I'm sorry to add fuel to the fire. Still, we need to focus on a different matter today: you and I have interviews to conduct, and the first prospective mentor-advisor will be here in just a few moments. Are there any concerns or questions you'd like to go over with me before she arrives?"

"Who's the first interview with?" Olivia sat up straighter, reaching for the cup of tea that sat on the coffee table before her.

"First up today will be someone you know. She indicated to me that she was the one on duty to greet new students when you arrived: Professor Yunsha."

"The Bogoli woman? Can you explain why some Bogoli, like my cohort members Veena and Hanwol, have surnames and others don't?"

"It's not that Professor Yunsha doesn't have a surname; it's a matter of her choosing not to use it in public. Some Bogoli believe there's power in a name and avoid sharing their full name with the general public."

"Is that true? Should I be guarding my name?"

"It's true if you believe it. It's one of those things which seems to be affected by one's perceptions. If you build up the power of your name in your mind, you open yourself to the possibility that someone can use it against you. If you, however, tell everyone your name and don't dwell on its importance, it's difficult for anyone to use it against you."

"What would be the benefit of believing like Yunsha, then?"

"Well, having that secret allows for rituals that involve trust. If Yunsha shares her intimate name with someone, that person can work certain magics designed to take advantage of her full trust. It's difficult to explain, but it might be something you learn about if you accept Yunsha as your mentor."

"Will we have time to discuss the interview before the next one?" Olivia sat back on the little couch, smoothing out her robes, trying to avoid any of her usual nervous ticks.

"Oh yes. I've tried to keep the pressure on by only scheduling fifteen minutes for each meeting." Oylla smiled and leaned forward, picking up her cup of tea. Olivia took a sip from the cup she held and smiled at the smooth, tart taste. It was remarkably like Earl Grey with a hint of lemon in the aftertaste.

"Good tea," she said.

She was tempted to remark about how strange it was that people on Fanwath drank tea in the same way they did on Earth, but she knew that rabbit hole would lead to a more extended discussion than they had time for at the moment. Instead, she set down her cup and closed her eyes briefly, clearing her mind for the upcoming meeting. Oylla sipped from her cup, set it down, and, at just that moment, a delicate knock sounded on the door.

"Come," Oylla said, sitting back and crossing her long, red legs, her knee exposed through a slit in her black, silky robes. The door opened, and Yunsha came into the office, walking quickly to the couch opposite Olivia and Oylla.

"May I?" the Bogoli asked.

Olivia noticed the woman was quite a lot taller than Veena or Hanwol, though she didn't seem to have advanced her race as much as Gwinna; her eyes were still natural looking, though the reds of her sclera and the glitter of her bright blue irises were striking, nonetheless.

"Of course," Professor Oylla-dak said, gesturing with a palm toward the couch. Yunsha sat and cleared her throat, reaching for the cup of tea nearest her.

"I know I only have a few minutes, so I thought I'd get straight to the point, Olivia. You should allow me to take you on as a mentee because I'll be able to teach you things about manipulating spatial Energy that most professors can only theorize about. I've heard you've had some luck creating spells which allow scrying and even teleportation, though I can assure you, there is much you don't know. I'm a master—the only master at this academy—of such types of magic."

"I can confirm that Yunsha speaks the truth. She is peerless when it comes to spatial manipulation," Oylla said with a slight nod, sipping from her tea.

"Oh, that's very interesting, Yunsha. I am extremely keen to learn more about that sort of magic, though it doesn't necessarily match my talents." Olivia wasn't just trying to be polite—she really did find the use of Energy for instantaneous travel to be one of the most fascinating subjects she'd learned about so far.

"Nonsense. Just because you've an affinity for elemental Energies doesn't mean you can't learn to use raw Energy to fold space. Among other things."

"So that would be the focus of my study under your tutelage?"

"That's correct. With your raw talent and reserves of Energy, I think we could make some great strides in that area." Yunsha nodded primly, her face neutral but held in such a way that made it seem like she was bending every rule in the book by paying such a compliment to a potential student.

"And what would my life be like? How do you see a typical day or week going for me as your mentee?" This wasn't the first time Olivia had been recruited by professors, or more broadly, universities. No, she'd been recruited in academia and outside of it many times. She knew she held the cards right now.

"Well, you'll spend time reviewing patterns that we develop, running tests, and gathering data. You'll have a large backlog of my academic papers and texts to familiarize yourself with. You'll need to help me research materials for the conduction and storage of Energy."

"I understand that those are the sorts of things we'll be working on, but what about my day? My time? I, of course, would value your work as a mentor, but I'd have my own projects to work on, and I'd like to maintain a healthy work-life balance. There are classes I still need to attend and recreational activities I would like to participate in."

"Oh?" Yunsha's eyes narrowed, and Olivia could see she was straining to form a sentence that didn't include any sort of rebuke. "You realize the opportunity I'm putting before you? Do you have any sort of idea how many third-year students are vying for a spot on my team?"

"She's well aware, Professor. She's also aware that she can work circles around any of those third years. What do you say, Olivia? Have you heard enough?"

"I suppose—" Olivia started to say, but then Yunsha spoke again, leaning forward earnestly.

"Wait," she interrupted. "Olivia, you have a great talent, it's true. You're going to hear things from some of the other professors looking to recruit you for projects that make my offer seem rather dull. Still, you need to know something about me, and I think that Professor Oylla-dak will confirm my honesty." She glanced at Oylla, who nodded solemnly.

"I don't answer to anyone, Olivia. I wasn't lying when I said my expertise in spatial manipulation is without peer. You might learn quite a lot on the subject without me, and you may even grow to be an expert someday, but I can help you leap years or decades of trial and error on the subject. This sort of magic is powerful and very sought after. The things we discover could help you and your people solidify their foothold on Fanwath. Keep that in mind while you're speaking to the other potential mentors, would you?"

"I will, Professor. Thank you so much for your honesty and your interest in helping me grow."

Olivia stood and held out her hand, and Yunsha stood to shake it. Her white-clothed hand was small but strong, and Olivia felt genuine warmth in the connection. She smiled and remained standing as the Bogoli walked out of Oylla's office.

"She's truly a great Energy worker, but she plays political games that leave even me scratching my head from time to time," Oylla informed after the door clicked shut.

"Do you think my life would be miserable working under her? That's a question that begs another one: how long will I be expected to commit to the mentor we select?"

"Regarding the first question: you won't be miserable, but you'll be very busy; however, it could be quite rewarding if you find common interests with the woman. As far as the duration goes, you'll be expected to commit the rest of your three-year student tenure. After that, you'll be free to pursue other interests or not, depending on how things are going. You might find you want to spend the next part of your life furthering your work with your mentor."

"Well, my thoughts about Yunsha are mixed. Maybe I'll be able to solidify my opinion after meeting some more potential mentors. Who do we have next?"

"Next up is a rather strange but influential fellow, Professor Somhairle." Oylla seemed to be holding a carefully neutral expression while she spoke, though Olivia got the feeling she was watching her very closely for a reaction.

"The fae?" Olivia couldn't help allowing some distaste to enter her voice.

"You know him?" Oylla raised an eyebrow.

"I met him briefly in the library. It was a strange meeting, and I always felt like I lost some time—like he and I spent more time together than I realized. I'm going to be very honest, Oylla; he sort of creeps me out."

"Very interesting. I should tell you that he was the first person to alert me about you leaving this world. How do you imagine he knew you'd gone through that portal?"

"Good question! Now I'm even more creeped out. Actually, you know, he gave me some kind of calling card. My friend, Bronwyn, said that it bothered her; she could feel something from it that she had trouble explaining to me, and so I burned it up."

"Even more intriguing!" she said, a slow smile spreading on her lips.

Olivia didn't like the idea that Oylla was gaining some sort of political points by using her mentorship as a sort of leverage.

"Oylla, I know the realities of institutions like this, the politics involved. But I hope you aren't steering me wrong so you can see the reaction Somhairle has during our meeting."

"Olivia! I promise you I only have your best interests at heart, though I will confess that I relish the idea of learning more about the mysterious Professor Somhairle. He was hired directly by the headmaster, and I've had a harpy of a time getting any concrete information about the man. Let's see what he has to say, hmm? I promise I won't push you into his clutches."

"All right." Olivia shrugged as she spoke.

It wouldn't hurt to try to learn something about the professor; she had nothing against helping out Oylla, and she had her own questions, like why had Bronwyn reacted so strongly about his calling card? What sort of connection did he have to the fae? Why was he interested in Olivia?

In her heart, she had to admit that she hoped that learning more about him might help her understand Bronwyn better.

# OLIVIA

When Professor Somhairle entered Oylla's office, the first thing Olivia noticed about him was that his previously intimidating presence was much less so. He no longer seemed larger than life. Sure, he was tall, but he was so thin with such long, awkward limbs that he seemed more at odds with himself than imposing. Additionally, his otherworldly appearance was a shadow of what Olivia remembered. Perhaps it was because she'd spent so much time with Bronwyn after her racial advancement.

Somhairle had pointed ears, but Bronwyn's were far more pronounced. He had big, mysterious eyes, but they were nothing compared to Bronwyn's, Oylla's, or if she were being honest, her own. Still, he gave off an aura of cold, dark depths, and Olivia wondered if he had an affinity for water Energy.

"Hello! Wonderful to see you again, Olivia, Professor," he greeted with a stiff little bow aimed primarily at Oylla-dak.

"Yes, good to see you, Professor. Please take a seat." Oylla indicated the couch opposite them, where Yunsha had been just a few minutes earlier.

Somhairle sat down, his knees jutting up awkwardly, and said, "Olivia, you seem rather different from when we spoke last. You've had some opportunities for growth?"

"Oh yes. Quite a few, I'd say. When was it that we spoke? That time in the library, late at night? I think it was around the time I was accused of attacking that girl in the hallway. A bad time for me, all told."

"Oh! I'm sorry; I didn't mean to drudge up bad memories."

"Not at all. It does seem like a very long time ago, though, doesn't it? Anyway, we have a full schedule today, Professor. Did you have some sort of interest in mentoring me?" Olivia could tell she was unsettling him by driving the conversation, and she appreciated Oylla remaining silent thus far.

"Well, yes. I noticed your potential quite some time ago, and when I learned you were moving into a specialized program of study, I thought I'd be able to offer you some unique opportunities."

"Such as?"

"Well, after doing some research, I've learned that your people, uh, humans have a strong connection to the fae. Do you recall how you seemed to think my name sounded familiar to you? It turns out my ancestors spent some time on your homeworld!"

He spoke like he was revealing a great mystery, and Olivia couldn't help the smile that crept onto her face.

"That's right, Professor. I've learned quite a lot about the fae over the last few months. One of my dear friends has awakened a bloodline which has her looking a good deal more fae than you, yourself."

"Truly?" Somhairle's eyes darted from side to side, giving tell to his nervous energy.

"Yes. However, it seems I've very little of the bloodline. I'm something of a pure human, it would seem, though I've picked up some elemental aspects through an exposure of a different kind. In any event, I'm not sure I could benefit much from your specialized teachings, and even if I could, I'm not so sure our interests align. You see, I've learned a thing or two about the different Fae Courts. I'm not so sure your goals for my people align with what we intend for ourselves."

"You've had dealings with the Summer Court, then?" Somhairle's lips pressed together in a barely contained sneer. "Is that why my calling card is no longer in your possession?"

"What an odd question," Oylla said, finally choosing to speak.

"Very odd. Were you using that card to spy on me somehow? What makes you think I don't have it any longer? This seems very irregular. Is such a thing appropriate, Professor Oylla-dak?" Olivia did her best to act scandalized, holding one of her hands in front of her mouth, widening her eyes, and scooting back on her couch, putting more distance between her and Somhairle.

"Professor, do you have something to say for yourself? What was the nature of this *calling card*?" Oylla leaned forward, affecting the opposite of Olivia's body language, her lips curling back in a snarl to reveal her long, needle-sharp canines.

"This meeting hasn't gone at all how I intended! My tongue seems to have run away with my brain. My calling card had a simple enchantment which would allow the holder to contact me at a mere thought. Naturally, such magics come with a connection to the caster; otherwise, it wouldn't work. I can assure you I had no nefarious ulterior motive when I gave the card to Olivia."

"Do you mind me asking, Professor," Olivia interjected, "just how much fae blood do you have? Would you call yourself half fae? A quarter? I don't mean to pry; there's a reason for me asking."

"Not nearly so much. I know I appear much like the tales describe the fae, but as far as I know, my grandfather was half fae. Might I ask as to the reason for your inquiry?"

"Well, my friend." Olivia paused and almost threw herself off by wondering why she was describing Bronwyn as a friend. She shook her head and soldiered on. "The one with the fae bloodline? She's spent quite a bit of time with true fae, and she told me they aren't able to lie. That rule doesn't apply to you, does it?"

"Are you implying that I'm being duplicitous at this moment?" Somhairle looked from Olivia to Oylla, then shook his head, his face reflecting feelings of naked disgust. "I can see someone has poisoned this well ahead of me. This meeting won't go anywhere productive. Good day to you, ladies."

With that, he stood and stalked out of the office. Oylla didn't try to stop him or even reply to his statement. When the door closed violently behind him, she looked at Olivia and grinned.

"You really pushed his buttons! I've never seen the mysterious Professor Somhairle lose his poise like that! What a fruitful meeting!"

"I'm sorry if I was a little too aggressive. I was hoping to throw him off balance, but I didn't think he'd storm out!" Olivia smiled sheepishly, shifting back to a normal sitting position.

"Oh, he didn't like the question about lying, that's for sure. I wonder if it's true about fae. Your friend really believes they can't lie?"

"Yes, she does. It's been the source of a lot of disagreements between us."

"Speaking of your friends, Olivia, should I expect visitors from the new portal? I have a report from the caretaker of the Travel Pavilion indicating that you've set it up."

"Yes, I did! I'm sorry, Oylla. I meant to tell you this morning and assign you full permissions, but the murder in the hallway sort of jumbled my mind!" Olivia leaned forward earnestly; she wanted Oylla to believe her.

"Nothing to worry about, dear. We'll finish these interviews and then take a walk over to the pavilion."

"Who's next?" Olivia poured herself another cup of tea from the little decorative pot, admiring the delicate orange and violet flowers that covered its surface.

"Another professor you should know, Gan-dak. I rather like him." Oylla held out her own teacup for Olivia to refill, watching her to gauge her reaction.

"Gan-dak? I don't think I remember . . . *oh!* The man who evaluated me when I first came to the academy?"

"That's right!" Oylla made a show of pulling out a delicate crystal-and-silver device from a pocket in her robe and staring into it. "He should be here in just a few minutes. Do you have any thoughts?"

"He seemed really nice! When he saw what I could do with channeling multiple affinities, he warned me not to allow professors to recruit me immediately. Hah, I wonder if he was just looking out for his own interests or if he really wanted to protect me?"

"Probably a bit of both, if we're being honest," Oylla replied with a sly grin. "Give him a chance. He's well-liked in the academy and among the nobles of Persi Gables. You could do worse than having him as a benefactor."

"I'll keep an open mind."

Olivia didn't have a hard time being pleasant with Gan-dak. He was as affable as the day she'd met him, and spent most of his fifteen minutes complimenting Olivia on everything she'd accomplished. It was getting near the time when he'd have to leave when Olivia finally pushed the subject for which they'd made the meeting.

Looking up into his bright mauve eyes, she asked, "Professor, I find you easy to talk to, and you're one of the nicer people I've met at the academy, but what sort of work would you have me do if I took on your mentorship?"

"A wonderful question! I was wondering when the interview portion of this meeting would begin!" Oylla laughed openly at that statement, but he just grinned and continued, "Olivia, I will help you to perfect your spellcrafting. Our affinities don't align, and I can't teach you much about elemental magic, but I can teach you to craft clever, delicate spells which will leave your peers staring in wonder, their mouths agape as they struggle to understand what you've done. It's all about discipline and the manipulation of threads in creative ways, and I'm quite good at it, you see. If you want to move beyond the simple cudgels that you wield now and learn to manipulate Energy into clockwork mechanisms so fine that a spider would be jealous, why, then I'm the mentor for you."

"Cudgels, Gan-dak?" Oylla asked with a chuckle. "Hyperbole won't win Olivia over to your side. Some of her spells are quite elegant already."

"Oylla! You undermine me!" He smiled wolfishly, reaching up to smooth back his long black hair.

"I find your argument quite compelling, Professor," Olivia said politely. "I've had ideas for spells that are far more complex than the ones I currently wield, and I'm not sure how to go about creating them. You're saying you could help me with such ideas?"

"Absolutely. Even Oylla will admit that my spellcrafting is an art unto itself!"

"He is talented; I won't deny it," Oylla replied, still smiling. Was she flirting with Gan-dak? Olivia did a double take, watching how the two of them grinned at each other. "Well, that's your time, Gan. We'll have a decision before the end of the week. Thank you for coming in."

"Nice to see you again, Professor," Olivia said, standing to shake his hand. It was strange, being able to look him in the eyes. She remembered how intimidating he'd seemed when she first met him, so tall and his red skin and long canines so otherworldly.

He reached out and took her hand, smiling warmly.

"Regardless of your decision, Olivia, I hope you'll come to me with some of your spell ideas. I'd love to help you figure them out!"

He departed the office quickly, and she sat down with a loud exhalation.

"Well, that earned him some points!"

"What? How he offered to help you, regardless of your decision? Come, Olivia, it's one of the oldest tricks in the book. He's a good man, but he has plenty of personal projects he needs help on. You'd be invaluable to him as a colleague if not a mentee."

"Still, he's so charming . . ."

Olivia looked at Oylla, hoping to see some hint as to her feelings for the man.

"Sure, he is. A true gentleman, too, I might add. Now, you're down to your last two interviews, and they're both with people you don't know. Shall I tell you a bit about them?" She paused, and Olivia nodded.

"The first is with a young professor named Pria Peele. She's a Ghelli who earned a name for herself similarly to you, though not so spectacularly. She has multiple affinities and gained the respect of most of the professors here when she was a student. Afterward, she successfully located and delved into a large dungeon near the Bogoli city of Zancryst. She brought back some of her findings and earned a professorship here. She's the youngest tenured professor at Fainhallow."

"She sounds impressive!"

"She is! The final interview will be with a man you might describe as Pria's opposite. Chol ap'Vun is the oldest living professor at Fainhallow, and I wouldn't have thought him a good candidate for your mentorship except that he approached me and said he was interested. I haven't seen Chol interested in, quite literally, anything for several decades. To be honest, most of us tend to forget he even exists. That isn't to say he wasn't impressive in his day. No, that wouldn't be right at all. When I was a girl, I was endlessly fascinated by tales of Chol ap'Vun and his exploits in various wars and dungeons."

"You're not going to make this decision easy for me, are you, Oylla?"

"No! What kind of professor would I be if I didn't make you pull out a hair or twenty?"

# OLIVIA

"Hello, Olivia!" Pria Peele greeted, striding forward and extending a hand. Olivia stood quickly and reached out to take it.

Pria was, as Olivia was starting to expect from successful people on Fanwath, a striking figure. She was clearly a Ghelli with an advanced race, her broad, dragonfly-like wings glittering with motes of Energy that continuously fell away from them, bright but fading as they descended like sparks or embers drifting away from a flame. She wasn't short, but she seemed so in the presence of Olivia and Oylla. Her silvery hair was cut in a sort of bob, framing her youthful face with its upturned nose and bright green eyes rather strikingly.

Olivia found the professor quite beautiful and was instantly jealous of the sharp gray suit she wore. Her jacket was short and open, revealing a silky white blouse, and her pants were tapered at the ankles, showing off delicate, open-toed black shoes that would have made any Manhattanite jealous.

"Pleased to meet you, Professor Peele," Olivia replied, feeling like a giant, ill-dressed oaf looming over the woman.

"The pleasure is mine! I've heard a lot about you, Olivia. Please, sit down," she said, turning to find her own seat. Olivia admired how Pria had taken control of the meeting almost instantly. She glanced at Oylla as she sat back down and saw one corner of her mouth had quirked up in an amused, sideways grin. Olivia steadied herself with a deep breath and determined to take back her command of the interview.

"Professor, I've heard some impressive things about you, but I wonder what sorts of activities did you see me fulfilling under your tutelage?"

"Ahh, right to the point, I see. Have I come at the end of a long list of suitors?" She chuckled slightly at her choice of words. "No need to answer that. I'm happy to explain what I have in store for members of my graduate team, which you'll be a part of, even though you have years of basic instruction to attend. I'm new to research, other than what I did in service to older professors." She paused and gave Oylla a smile and a nod.

"No, when I finished my studies, I didn't have the desire to sit around trying to figure out new and novel ways to cast spells. I wasn't interested in spending more time poring over old texts and trying to improve the enchantments on powerful artifacts, or even to copy them." She leaned forward and picked up a teacup that Oylla had filled while she spoke. She took a delicate sip before continuing. "I sought power. I sought to enhance my race. I sought to find and explore the secrets of the world. Well, it's been ten years of that, and I'm ready to work with a team to figure out some of those secrets I uncovered."

"Figure out?" Olivia prodded.

"Yes. I've come away from my explorations with dozens of artifacts that work in ways that baffle modern understanding. Some were planted by the System, treasures from worlds with more advanced Energy users than Fanwath. Some are mysteries left over from one of the worlds prior to the Joining. Some are natural wonders that defy explanation. I'm back at the academy to utilize its facilities and assemble a research team." Again, she looked at Oylla and smiled. "For a share in whatever I discover, of course."

"Naturally." Oylla smiled back and took a long drink of her tea.

"That sounds fascinating, Professor, but I have my own growth to consider. Would helping you figure out mysterious artifacts be the best path forward for me?"

Olivia sat back and crossed her legs, taking a moment to smooth the fabric of her magical robes and ensuring that her magical boot hung just near the edge of the table. If she were being honest, she might admit she was trying to compete with Pria's style, or at least demonstrate that she wasn't a typical novice. She didn't think about it, though, perhaps acting mostly subconsciously.

"Of course, Olivia," Pria said, smiling, her eyes indicating that she'd taken the clue: Olivia had seen a dungeon or two herself. "I've a lot to teach you concerning spellcraft and Energy usage. Much of our time together would be spent with demonstrations of such and assignments from me to help focus and hone your skills."

"So I won't just be a full-time researcher working for peanuts?"

"Peanuts? Should I assume that's a colloquial term meant to indicate a small amount? If so, then no, I won't expect you to be my research slave." She laughed good-naturedly. "You can expect some field expeditions to test theories and devices and to gain some practical knowledge. I assure you, your time on my team will be rewarding." Pria paused and added, "What sorts of activities were you hoping for?"

"Well, much of what you said sounded good to me, Professor. You seem like a very successful woman, and I'm sure I'd enjoy learning from your experience."

"I think you would as well, Olivia. I believe we have much in common."

Olivia considered her words for a moment, her mind taking her to rather fanciful places where she studied mystical relics, explored ancient tombs, and tested theories on battlefields from bygone eras.

"I'm very intrigued by your proposal, Professor. I surely appreciate you taking the time to come here today, and I'll be sure to give what you've said the consideration it deserves. Is there anything you'd like to add?"

"Only that I'm more interested in working with you than ever. This meeting has been . . . enlightening." Pria stood. "Don't stand; it's fine. I'll show myself out, ladies. I look forward to hearing from you, Olivia." She turned and nodded to Oylla. "Professor. Thank you for the time."

"I'll speak with you soon. Thank you, Pria."

Olivia smiled as she watched the professor leave the office before she turned to Oylla and said, "You weren't kidding! She's impressive!"

"Yes, on many levels. Do you think she'd be your first choice as of now?"

"I don't know! I'm intrigued by Yunsha and Professor Gan-dak also!"

"Good! I don't want this decision to be easy. That would mean I didn't do my job well when I selected the candidates." Oylla looked like she was about to say more, but a knock sounded on the door, and someone pushed it open. A small man poked his bald head through and cleared his throat noisily.

"Oylla? I saw that Peele girl leave and figured I might get in a bit early. May I come in?"

"Professor ap'Vun!" Oylla glanced quickly at Olivia and winked. "Please do come in. How fortunate that you saw the opportunity to come in early!" Oylla stood up and walked forward, reaching out with one arm to guide the stooped old fellow in.

Olivia wasn't sure she'd seen anyone on this world who looked as old as Professor ap'Vun. He couldn't have been more than five and a half feet tall, and his back was stooped in a permanent, forward-leaning hunch. He had tufts of white hair around the sides of his head, but the top was utterly devoid of it.

He wore intricate spectacles consisting of several lenses, the left side of which she noticed had two lenses standing out on wire hinges, whereas the right side had all the lenses aligned. Behind the spectacles, his bright yellow eyes peered sharply, though, and Olivia resolved then and there not to underestimate his intelligence just because he acted a bit like a doddering old-timer.

"Greetings, youngster." He sat down on the couch with a heavy sigh. Peering around at the coffee table, he tsked, saying, "Tea? No biscuits?"

"Of course I have biscuits! I was saving them for your visit, but you came early, didn't you?" Oylla asked, standing and walking over to her desk. She returned with a filigreed tin. Carefully pulling off the top, she set the container on the table. Even from where she sat, Olivia could smell the sugary, buttery scent of its contents. "Butter cookies from Flower Wheels in Persi Gables."

"Ahh!" He smacked his lips and smiled, lifting his round blue cheeks with the expression. "That's more like it! Good lass!" He reached out, took a flakey cookie from the tin, and took a bite, crumbs falling down his chin as he chewed noisily. He saw Olivia and Oylla watching him, and he motioned to the tin. "Well? Don't make me eat these alone! They're too good to waste them all on an old man!"

"Thank you," Oylla said, reaching down and taking one of the cookies. Olivia marveled at her show of respect, and she, too, reached down and took a cookie, biting into it and savoring the rich, buttery flavor and the way it practically dissolved on her tongue.

"God, that's good!" she let out, unable to contain the exclamation.

"Hmm, God, is it? What deity do you serve, girl?" Professor ap'Vun asked, squinting at her over the tops of his glasses.

"Oh, um, it's an expression from my world. I'm not very religious."

Olivia had noted how the various races in this world seemed to have different belief structures, but very few of them spoke of any sort of god. She didn't know how they would receive a discussion of Christianity, and didn't feel like she was the type of person to broach the subject. Olivia hadn't been to church since she was a child, when her grandmother had taken her to Christmas Mass.

"Oh yes, you're the girl who traveled here through the stars, yes? With your people? Most visitors from other worlds come through the System Stones. I was impressed to hear that your people flew here through space. Now, let's see here, why was it you wanted to work under my tutelage?"

Olivia started to speak, then stopped and looked at Oylla for clarification. The older woman's smile was broad, and she simply shrugged at her, her star-filled eyes glittering with amusement.

"Professor, my mentors, including Professor Oylla-dak here, have determined that I need a specialized course of study. I'm trying to find the best professor to study under."

"Excellent, yes, yes. Now, I haven't taken on an apprentice for some time. Not since old Orthal. I decided to come here and have a sit-down with you when you started showing up in my scryings."

Again, Olivia glanced at Oylla, but the professor wasn't any help, simply raising her eyebrow as if to indicate she was as confused as she was.

"Scryings, Professor?"

"Yes, surely Oylla's told you of my talents for augury? I've predicted three of the last four disasters to strike the empire!"

"And I'm showing up in your . . . um, auguries?" Olivia scooted forward in her seat, leaning toward the old professor.

"Oh yes, but not as part of any sort of disaster. Relax, girl. I've seen myself dealing with a few strange things, however, and you were present, helping me with this or that. The images weren't terribly clear, but I'm quite sure it was you. Yes, I'd recognize that pale skin and those burning eyes anywhere."

"Burning eyes?" Olivia held a hand up to her eye self-consciously. She'd thought she had her elemental effects more under control than that.

"They're not burning right now, Olivia," Oylla said helpfully.

"Oh? They look ablaze to me!" Chol ap'Vun shrugged. "I see more than the average person, though."

"What sorts of things would I do if I came to work as your apprentice, Professor?" Olivia asked, trying to steer the conversation back on topic.

"Oh, learn to wield massive amounts of Energy, craft sophisticated spells, investigate rumors, and deal with deadly phenomena. You'll need to get along with my team; I don't always accompany my apprentices in the field, so you'll often be working with one of my senior mentees." He turned to regard Oylla before continuing, "The other professors here probably don't even know what I do most of the time, but there are a few who understand the importance of my work. I'm confident I'll be hearing from you, Olivia. You might do yourself a favor when you report to my offices and bring a tin of these biscuits."

"I . . ." Olivia's mouth fell open. For the first time in a long while, she was unable to think of something to say.

She glanced at Oylla and was further flummoxed to see the powerful professor staring at Chol ap'Vun with a look of abstract confusion.

The old man stood up, picked up the tin of cookies, and smiled broadly, revealing even, white teeth with very pronounced canines.

"Ladies! Thank you for the visit. I'll speak to you soon, I'm sure."

He turned then and walked out of the office.

Oylla looked at Olivia, and she could tell the professor was struggling to find words. Finally, she said, "That was surprising. I thought he was just an old, nearly retired professor biding his time by lingering around the place where he spent most of his life. I don't know anything about any team who works under him, and I surely didn't know anything about his auguring ability. My mind is so frazzled right now that I'm only just realizing that I'm babbling to you about things I don't know. Olivia, I must ask that you don't mention this to anyone while I work to figure out what is going on with that man."

"I don't even know what I'd say, Professor," Olivia said. She meant it, but one thing was for sure: the meeting with Chol ap'Vun had eclipsed the ones with the other professors in her mind, and she was having a hard time thinking about anything else.

# BRONWYN

Ironhide gestured to the branch in the path. "Down here, through this swampy wood, we'll reach the valley with the Hollows in a day or two. This is the part where I'd warn you about trolls setting ambushes in the trees and that we shouldn't venture in, but I guess if Whitestar is fighting for the old home, we should be able to get into the valley, at least. Hopefully, we'll learn what's going on before we get surrounded and eaten."

"God, Ironhide! I don't remember you being this dramatic," Bronwyn said, shaking her head and starting down the indicated path. She could see hundreds of old Urghat tracks, so many that they completely obscured any other she might have noticed, whether troll or the little rodentlike feyris.

"I'm not dramatic, Underclaw! I've seen the remains of a hunting party ambushed by trolls. Not a pretty sight!" the big, dark-furred Urghat grumbled, following behind her and Cal.

"Well, I, for one, am glad to have you two to travel with. I'm glad I didn't have to try to hunt down Whitestar all on my own. If I'd heard a rumor she was down in these parts, I'd have surely come here on my own, and I'm not too thrilled at the idea of meeting a troll," Cal said before launching into a whistling tune which seemed to energize Bronwyn's legs.

She smiled at the happy, lilting song and tried to hum along with it.

"Not bad, Bronwyn!" Cal laughed, pausing. "I think we'll make a Spirit Singer of you yet!"

"Hah, not likely. My Core's a hundred percent solar Energy."

"So the fae helped you change your affinity, huh?" Cal had heard the story around the campfire, but apparently, he was still interested in the details. Bronwyn sighed and tried to explain.

"Well, when I went through their trial to become an agent of Summer, I managed to find a Summer Source, and when I touched it, everything about my Core and affinities changed. I could feel the Source accept me, and when I embraced the solar Energy, all my old affinities, skills, and even my class were removed."

"I don't like it, Underclaw. You humans always smelled good, but now you smell like a fae. I'll have to fight off the other Urghat to keep them from trying to eat you."

"Hah!" Bronwyn laughed at Ironhide's words. "You big goof! Don't worry about me. If any Urghat want to challenge me, they'll realize pretty quickly that it's a bad idea." Bronwyn tapped the ring on her biceps. "You know how many I've beaten already, right? Well, I'm a lot stronger now."

"Right, Underclaw," Ironhide grumbled.

"I've got a song or two that help people calm down. If things start to get heated, I'll try to diffuse things." Cal resumed his whistling, and Bronwyn smiled at him with a nod. She wasn't worried. If she had to make an example out of an overzealous Urghat, it wouldn't be the first time.

The woods they walked through were composed of stunted, twisted trees with gray bark and long, flat, blue-green leaves. The undergrowth was thick, and though the path was firm, hard-packed dirt, Bronwyn could see that the ground to her right, where it fell away down a slight slope, was dark and moist. "What's the deal down that way? It looks like the ground is getting wetter and wetter."

"Aye, I said as much. The Hollows are bordered by a swamp. There's a big, low lake in these hills, fed by some kind of underground river, and it fills the nooks and crannies of these hills with moisture. Eventually, the waters feed into the Gorge Cutter and flow out over the plains, splitting the north half. We crossed it twice when you were going around challenging Urghat. Remember?"

"Yeah, I remember crossing a river, but I didn't realize it came out of these hills. Makes sense, I guess."

Bronwyn trudged along, her mind wandering back to her time on the plains, when she'd traveled from one Urghat camp to another, fighting the ones who wanted to challenge her. It seemed almost crazy now, looking back. It also seemed like a very long time ago; like she was a totally different person now. What had she been trying to prove? She'd gone north, saying she was going to scout the Urghat, but she'd ended up fighting one after another, killing dozens in the process. None of them had been much of a challenge, either. It almost felt like her behavior had been evil, though she had tried to give the challengers every opportunity to back down or to follow her.

The more she thought about it, the more she realized she was being hard on herself. The Urghat traditions had been in place long before she'd come around.

"Ironhide, do you resent me? For going around and accepting challenges from all the Urghat camps? Should I have just kept to myself?"

"Nar, Underclaw. You were learning about our ways, building up a following. You know, there were a lot of Urghat who never joined the Overclaw's army because of you. That's a lot of Urghat that didn't die who might have if they'd gone along with his foolish plan."

"Thanks, Ironhide," Bronwyn said, determined to stop dwelling on her past, whether she'd made mistakes or not.

Instead, she spent time thinking about Olivia while they hiked. She had been sweet and full of kisses when Bronwyn had parted ways with her, but she knew the other woman was worried about her sudden departure, if not a bit irritated. Bronwyn was irritated about it; how could Olivia not be? Still, Queen Aestasia wouldn't have called her to this mission if it weren't necessary. Besides, Olivia had a teleportation token from her professor or whatever, right? She'd see a lot more of her than before. Olivia would have to accept that Bronwyn had important things going on in her life, too.

Bronwyn sighed heavily as that last thought went through her mind. She wasn't being totally fair; Olivia's experience at the academy was of tangible benefit to the humans. Bronwyn had a mysterious patron whom no one had met that expected her to drop everything and jump when she wanted something done. Was it really fair for Bronwyn to expect people to be understanding?

She hoped this mission would make explaining herself easier. She wished she was doing something that would have a real, clear benefit for humanity here on Fanwath.

"It would sure be nice to know for sure."

She'd picked up the pace, putting some space between herself and Cal. Ironhide was a good ten paces behind the man, so no one had heard her speak, and she smiled at the memory of her time in the Summer Trial when she'd talked to herself almost nonstop as a way to keep her sanity. Had that really been why? Or had she just been having some fun? She'd never felt like she was on the verge of losing it when she'd been in the trial, even after the swarm had given her its blessing.

"Hello, Underclaw," a raspy, clipped voice came from behind a nearby tree. Bronwyn stumbled in surprise, coming to a halt and turning toward it. She was tempted to call forth her jade hatchets or cast Solar Shell, but the voice was familiar and had called Bronwyn *Underclaw*.

"Hi, Shadoweye! I've missed you," she said, waving to the deep shadows between two twisted trees. A darker one detached from the depths of the hollow, and Shadoweye's shape took form as she stepped into the light. Cal and Ironhide came up behind Bronwyn just as the stealthy, leather-clad Urghat scout slipped out of the tree and came forward.

"Huntress!" Ironhide greeted, reaching out a big paw to grip the wiry scout's arm.

"Ironhide. You've lost weight," she said with a dry, raspy chuckle.

"No one to cook for me these last months. Lucky the Underclaw found me when she did. I was about to fade away." He grabbed at his still prodigious girth with a mock-sad face.

"Shadoweye, this is Cal Jennings. He's friends with an Urghat named Whitestar. You know her, right?"

"Aye, Underclaw. I hope you won't kill me for it, but I've sworn myself to her. You were gone so long . . ."

"Of course I won't kill you! I never expected you to serve me forever, Shadoweye. I hope we can stay friends and see more of each other than we have these last few months, but I understand I'm not an ideal Underclaw, what with the way I keep disappearing and with all my other responsibilities. Still, I don't want to give up my ring just yet. There might come a time when humanity will have to deal with our Urghat neighbors, and I'd like to make sure we come to a peaceful resolution and maybe even some sort of partnership."

"Aye, you said as much back when we traveled the plains. The twins will be happy to see you. You *are* coming to Whitestar's camp, aye?"

"Yes, we are. Cal has been wanting to see his old friend, and I have a feeling she could use some help with something. How are things?"

"Grim," Shadoweye spat, her long white fangs somehow making the gesture more vehement. "Whitestar says she has visions telling her to retake the Hollows, but we struggle to gain any footing inside the valley, let alone the Hollows. The trolls are vicious, and something drives them forth, organizing and corrupting them even more than nature has done."

"I knew we were coming at the right time," Cal said, smiling and stepping forward. "Shadoweye? Did you earn that name for the black fur around your eyes?"

"Nah, it's 'cause I can see in the dark and pull shadows around myself. My fur is white around my eyes, but I like to rub charcoal in it." Shadoweye spoke without a hint of humor, but Bronwyn knew she was lying—the Urghat had black fur and no white spots that she knew of.

"Don't tease him, Shadoweye! He's a friend to Urghat, and your people can use all the friends they can get these days. Have you heard what happened to the Urghat in the Deep Down?"

"The Deep Down? No, that clan is too far to worry about!" She looked at Bronwyn with a raised eyebrow as if to ask what kind of nonsense she was getting at.

"They're almost all dead! Invaders came and killed most of them. Only a few dozen escaped when my people attacked the invader's camp."

"Really?" Ironhide asked. "The Deep Down clan was huge. All dead, you say? Then Urghat truly are in dire straits."

"The reason I bring it up, Shadoweye, is that Cal is a good guy who only wants to help. Me too, by the way. So can you lead us to the camp? If Whitestar thinks she needs to reclaim the Hollows, maybe we can help."

"Aye, Underclaw. You don't have to ask twice. I'd bring you to her even without your horror stories about the Deep Down. If you think I'm smart, wait 'til you talk to Underclaw Whitestar."

"Smart!" Ironhide scoffed. "Wasn't it you who had half the Overclaw's army chasing you through the woods when all you were supposed to do was scout them out?"

"I saved Underclaw Bronwyn's village, you immense boar!"

"Alright, alright! Yes, I know you're smart, Shadoweye. Let's get to your camp, and then you and Ironhide can have a contest to see who's the smartest."

"Aye! Let's make sure it includes an eating portion. I can eat better than you any day, Shadoweye!"

"Eating?" Cal asked, looking searchingly at Bronwyn.

"I think Ironhide would try to include eating in any contest he got involved in." Bronwyn laughed.

Shadoweye snorted and turned up the trail, motioning for everyone to follow her. "We'll be in the forward watch camp in just an hour or so. Whitestar's main camp is a day's march beyond that. I had the outside watch, but we'll send the middle watch to take my spot. It's Bright-tooth, Underclaw; he'll be thrilled to see you!"

"Oh, really?"

"Yes, he's grown and gained a class. Whitestar has been a good teacher for the twins, helping them uncover their potential."

"That's great, Shadoweye!" Bronwyn was genuinely happy that the twins were doing well. They'd been the strangest members of her band by far, and she'd worried about them ever fitting in with the Urghat again.

"Yes, it's good, but Soft-fur has a strange curse. It's one of the reasons Whitestar wants to take the Hollows back from the trolls. The girl will die if she doesn't bathe in the Well of Ancestors."

"What?" Bronwyn asked, her voice rising almost comically.

# OLIVIA

Olivia sat alone, looking out over the commons at the academy. After showing Oylla to the portal stone and setting her permissions, she'd still had a large part of the afternoon to herself, as she wasn't expected to attend any of her classes until the next day. There were quite a few students on the lawn, but Olivia could sense some tension in the air, and none of the students moved about by themselves. Everywhere she looked, students were paired up or in larger groups.

"Except for me, that is."

She leaned back and turned her face to the sun, enjoying the warmth in the early autumn breeze. She imagined the academy would get some snow soon, up in the mountains the way it was. She glanced over the rooftops toward the tall peak where the teleportation pad was, and she saw that it, indeed, was clothed in a thick blanket of white. If it had been snowing on such a nearby mountain, surely the academy should have some on the ground. "Is the weather warded somehow? I bet it is."

"Talking to yourself?"

Olivia turned to see Adaida, Veena, and Shani walking up behind her. "Took you guys long enough! Did you get in trouble again?"

"No, but Grobak wanted to lecture us about one of his battles, and he got a little long winded. Stupid Rald kept asking him questions, too." Adaida was scowling as she sat down on the bench next to Olivia.

"We're going to the library," Veena said. "We just wanted to escort Adaida out here, considering the murders . . ." she trailed off, perhaps uncomfortable with the subject.

"Speaking of that," Adaida said. "Why are you out here alone? You promised us you'd be careful!" She poked Olivia in the shoulder.

"To be honest, I didn't really think about it until I was out here waiting for you guys. Frankly, I wish the jerk would try me! Someone needs to put a stop to this! Poor Shathi!"

For some reason, the image of the dead student's remains came back to her, stronger than when she'd stood amidst them that morning. A tremble entered her voice as she continued. "Whoever did it was trying to terrorize us! They put her head in the hallway, perfectly intact, staring at her scattered remains!" Her eyes began to fill as she spoke, and she hurriedly wiped at them with her sleeve, frustrated by her quick show of emotion.

"Are you okay?" Shani asked. Adaida opened her mouth to speak but stopped, closing it again like she didn't know what to say.

"No, I guess not," Olivia replied. "I was full of adrenaline this morning, and then I had to go straight to Oylla's office. I don't think I had a chance to really think about what I saw. I'm sorry, you guys." She laughed ruefully at herself while wiping at her eyes.

"We should have been more aware of your feelings, Liv." Adaida reached out to hold her hand. "I think we all kind of think of you as some kind of phenom and forget you're a person who feels things just as much as the rest of us."

"Sorry, Olivia." Veena reached out a small, gloved hand and rested it on her shoulder.

"Thanks for sharing your feelings, Olivia," Shani said. "I'm freaked out about the murders too, and I didn't even really see the scene."

Olivia sniffed and laughed, squeezing Adaida's hand before pulling hers free. "I appreciate you all so much! Now, you two get going! I don't want to make you late."

"Well, Professor Brince is probably waiting for us, so I guess we should go," Veena said, though she seemed reluctant to pull her hand away from Olivia's shoulder. "You'll stay with Adaida? Promise?"

"Yeah, of course." She forced a smile.

"See you later at the dorm, then."

Shani and Veena walked off together toward the main doors to the academy. Adaida scooted sideways a little so she could look at Olivia better and smiled, though her expression was off, almost pained. Her pale face seemed wan under the smile, and Olivia could see signs of stress: dark skin, almost like bruises, under her bright amber eyes and worry lines between her brows.

"Now, you tell me what's the matter," Olivia prompted. "I came clean, even cried in front of you all. What's got you so stressed?"

"I think you know," she replied softly, looking down so her thick chestnut hair fell forward, partially obscuring her face from Olivia.

Olivia felt her heart speed up. This was it—the confrontation she'd been dreading. Her stomach started to twist, and her mouth got suddenly dry. She licked her lips, trying to formulate the right words. "Have I seemed different? I mean, in the way I act toward you?"

"I don't think you'd ask that if you didn't know the answer. What changed? You never used to pull away from me so fast, and you tried to spend more time with me whenever you could. Now you slip away whenever possible, and when we're alone, it's like you're trying to get back to the others as fast as possible." Adaida sniffed, and Olivia could see she was the one fighting back tears now.

"It's not that my feelings are different! I still want to be with you, to spend time with you, but . . . well, while I was gone, I got very close to another person. She and I were never really together before, but we sort of were forced to spend a lot of time alone, or almost alone, and things happened.

"Don't get me wrong, I don't regret being with her, other than how it makes me feel when I'm with you. I just feel sick inside. I don't know how to explain it, Adaida, but I still care about you. I still want to be close to you, but I don't want to hurt Bronwyn. I don't want to hurt anyone!" She reached out and tried to take Adaida's hand, but the Ghelli pulled away, and when she lifted her head to look at Olivia, her eyes were narrowed, angry.

"I guess we didn't have anything really going on when you left, did we? It was just flirting and hints. Why should I expect you to keep me in your heart while you were away?"

She started to stand, but Olivia grabbed her wrist, holding her.

"Please don't go! Let's talk this out."

"What's there to talk about? I've made a fool of myself, as usual. I can't believe how I've been fawning all over you since you got back, and all the while, you were wishing I'd leave you alone. You should have said something sooner!" She jerked her hand, and Olivia let go, not wanting to overpower the girl. When she saw the anger in Adaida's face, saw the tears in her eyes, and heard the pain in her voice, her own eyes filled with tears, and she let out an involuntary sob.

"Please, Adaida! I didn't want to hurt you. Let me explain! I don't know what the future holds with Bronwyn and me . . ." she trailed off, realizing she was just babbling.

Adaida was already stiffly walking away, clearly embarrassed and upset. Olivia watched her depart over the lawn, walking toward the cobbled path that led around the academy's main building and between the Alchemy Pavilion and Gardens. Suddenly, Olivia imagined Adaida's head sitting amid a scene of slaughter, and her heart raced, her palms began to sweat, and she leaped to her feet to chase after her.

"Adaida!" she called, running over the grass, but Adaida quickened her pace, slipping through the gate to the gardens and out of Olivia's view. She raced over the last thirty yards of grass onto the cobbled path then took the right turn through the open wrought-iron gate. The Alchemy Gardens covered an acre or two of ground, and plants sprouted from raised beds and hung from trellised, hanging pots which made it hard to look beyond the row you were standing in.

"Adaida?" Olivia called again. She saw movement to her right, so hurried that way, only to run into a trio of second-year students. Olivia, her face panicked and eyes blazing with blue flames, grabbed their attention easily and asked, "Have you seen a Ghelli come through here? Just a minute ago? She has long, auburn hair."

"No. Nobody has come through recently. Is something wrong?" one of them asked, a tall Ardeni with gray-blue hair. He stepped back to regard Olivia with wary eyes.

"I hope not," Olivia said, turning and running the other way, barreling around the corner. Again, she called out, "Adaida! Please! It's dangerous to be alone!"

She raced around another corner and then another, and soon, she was deep in the gardens, unable to hear or see any other students. "Goddammit! Why haven't I learned any scrying spells, a locating spell, or some other damn thing!"

Olivia felt like she was close to losing it, she was so fraught with worry. She thought about her spells, thought about Surveying Breeze and how she might use it or modify it to survey the gardens quickly, but her mind kept jumping to the imagined scene of Adaida's slaughter, and she found she couldn't concentrate on the spell pattern. Tears started to spring into her eyes, her breathing grew ragged, and she called out again, her voice hoarse with emotion, "Adaida! Please!"

"Hush! You're going to get the whole campus up in arms!" Adaida scolded, poking her head around the corner. Olivia raced over to her, tears in her eyes.

"You could have been murdered! Do you know what that would have done to me? To your sister? I couldn't pick a better place for some creepy killer to be lurking about!" She reached out as though to grab Adaida's shoulders but stopped short, pulling them back with a frustrated growl. "Can we please talk? I didn't want to hurt you, Adaida! You're the sweetest, kindest person I've met here! I'd rather . . . oh, I don't know! I'd rather walk over coals or something than hurt you!"

"Well, you did! I know I don't have a right to be upset or hurt—as I said, I know we weren't together—but I had hoped. I spent my whole break, and then the whole time you were missing, thinking about you. I'm struggling with my courses because of it! When you came back, all I could think about was how glad I was, how I wanted to spend more time with you, tell you how I really felt. I feel so stupid!"

"You're not stupid! I had—*have* feelings for you too! I didn't mean for something to happen between Bronwyn and me. I thought she and I had settled on being friends!" Olivia wiped at her eyes, annoyed by her emotions overwhelming her. She wanted to tell Adaida her feelings. She wanted to be open and make her feel better, but still, there was that pit in her stomach, that twist of guilt. She'd been so happy with Bronwyn in the dungeon. They'd shared everything and felt so close. How could she betray all that now, just because Adaida was here in front of her, her big eyes filled with tears, her nose red, and her lips quivering with emotion . . .

Suddenly, Olivia leaned forward and kissed Adaida. She pressed hungrily against Adaida's trembling, tear-salted lips and felt her hot breath quicken. Adaida kissed her back, reaching up to grab her neck and pulling her closer, her tongue searching for Olivia's. Olivia pulled her in, passion clouding her mind and sending her hands down to clutch and grope at Adaida's body.

When Adaida pulled back, panting, and started to kiss and bite at her neck, Olivia opened her eyes and stared out into the garden. Though passion-drenched emotion was filling her with heat, she couldn't stop her mind from drifting away to Bronwyn's smiling, laughing face as she lay next to her in their tent. She couldn't stop remembering how they'd held hands for hours and shared so many secrets, whispering to keep from bothering Morgan in his tent.

She sobbed again, letting go of Adaida's back and reaching up to gently push her shoulders back. "Wait," she said.

"What? Just kiss me some more." Adaida leaned forward, reaching her mouth, her hungry lips, toward Olivia's neck again. Her breath was hot, and Olivia almost broke again, but she firmly pressed Adaida back.

"Adaida!" she hissed, her voice thick with emotion. "I can't do this yet. I need to settle things with Bronwyn. I need to figure out my feelings. Can you give me some time?"

"Yes," Adaida replied softly, allowing Olivia to push her back. "Yes, I can. Thank you."

"Thank you?" Olivia asked softly, reaching up to stroke Adaida's thick, soft hair.

"Yes, for letting me know I wasn't the only one with feelings. I don't feel as stupid now. I can wait for you to figure things out, okay? Just don't make me wait too long. You need to make a decision, all right?"

"Yes," Olivia said, smiling and sniffing. "You're not stupid, Adaida. Anything but."

She was about to pull Adaida into a hug when she felt her stiffen and saw her eyes grow wide, looking at something behind Olivia.

# ~ OLIVIA ~

Adaida's face looked so disturbed, and it was such a sudden shift in emotion that Olivia didn't hesitate to cast Elemental Form, taking on her earth-attuned aspect. With a soft, grinding rumble, her flesh hardened, and rocks lifted from the ground, erupting out of the soil to orbit her and Adaida, whom she still held close. Just as she finished the spell, she felt pressure on her back and heard a clanging scratch as something slid over her hardened flesh.

Adaida screamed and fell back, blood spraying from one of her hands. She'd been holding onto Olivia with her arms wrapped around her sides, her fingers resting just under Olivia's shoulder blades. Whatever had struck Olivia had sheared through them, and the girl stumbled back in pain, her face grimacing while her other hand squeezed her wounded digits.

Olivia's eyes blazed with rage as she whirled, holding out one stony arm and summoning a globe of plasma. A masked figure stood before her holding a curved, sicklelike blade. His form seemed masculine to Olivia, though she couldn't be sure. He was clad in black robes, not unlike the ones worn by the professors, and his mask completely obscured his face. It seemed to be made of wood and was rectangular, painted to look like a leering reptile with green skin and bright yellow stripes.

Olivia hurled her plasma ball at the figure, who danced back, holding up a hand to create a blazing blue shield that stopped the attack, though it crackled and flared. The man had to continue to retreat, clearly straining to maintain the shield, as Olivia held out her hand again and cast Pyrosteam Drill, driving a beam of superheated steam at the center of the killer's shield.

He grunted and backed up once more, his shield blazing with bright blue light, still refusing to break despite Olivia's onslaught. She pressed the attack, driving more Energy into her drill and simultaneously motioning with her free hand, sending her orbiting rocks to streak through the air at the masked figure. Just as the first smashed into his shield, causing him to stumble and noticeably weakening his spell, he lifted his other hand and threw an object at the ground.

Bright blue flames erupted in a wall, completely obscuring Olivia's view, and though she kept pressing with her Pyrosteam Drill and throwing rocks through the sheet of blue flames, she couldn't see her target. A few seconds later, the flames flickered and died away, and the killer was nowhere to be seen.

Olivia started to turn back to Adaida when she noticed two pale digits on the ground in front of her. She stooped to pick them up before hurrying over and helping the ashen, teary girl to her feet. "Come on, let's get you to the infirmary. Nurse Tyliste will fix this up, just you watch!"

"Was that . . ." Adaida began, but a sob cut her off. Olivia, still in her Elemental Form, hoisted the Ghelli into her arms and stomped out of the garden.

"Hush," she said as she walked. "You're fine. That worm ran away, and he better pray I don't find him. I have a feel for him now, Adaida. I felt his Energy. I'm going to figure out a spell to scry him out, then we'll see who's hunting whom." Olivia had never felt rage like the hot, searing fury running through her at that moment.

She allowed her Elemental Form to drop once they'd cleared the garden, continuing to carry Adaida, hardly noticing the lithe Ghelli's weight. The sun had begun to set, and though the lights around campus were coming on, their magical sensors detecting the darkening sky, it was quiet and dark, with hardly a soul moving on the paths or over the commons.

Olivia hurried without concern for the attacker, knowing he was off licking his wounds, probably raging about how a student had sent him scurrying. Once she reached one of the main doors, rather than set Adaida down to free up a hand, she kicked at its base, staring through the glass at a passing student. He hurried over and opened it, and Olivia brushed past him with a quick, "Thanks."

Adaida had turned into her, resting her cheek against her shoulder, her face, still moist with tears, pressed into Olivia's neck. Olivia clutched her two severed fingers in the hand underneath Adaida's knees. The other held her tight against her chest as she strode through the academy, brushing past the light traffic in the hallway, ignoring the looks and questions. She had a mission: get to the infirmary. Get to nurse Tyliste.

When she walked into the room, the dim light of sunset illuminating its high windows, she scanned the beds, looking for the nurse. She saw one of her aides giving medicine to a patient before her eyes fell on the sparkling wings of the advanced Ghelli. Olivia strode toward where she leaned over a bandaged male student, holding a light to his eyes and flicking it away.

"You'll be fine, Sorl. I don't see any signs of a concussion," she was saying as Olivia approached.

"Excuse me, Nurse. We were attacked by the killer, and Adaida needs seeing to." She had tried to keep her voice calm, but it'd come out strident with a hint of hysteria.

The nurse stood and spun to face her.

"Attacked? Where? Put her on the bed here," she indicated, gesturing to the empty bed next to the bandaged student.

"In the Alchemy Gardens, but I sent him running. I have no idea where he is now. Here." Olivia gently laid Adaida on the bed before holding out her hand with the severed fingers.

"Roots! Poor thing! I can fix this, don't you worry," Tyliste said, resting a hand on Adaida's forehead and smoothing her hair back. "Shh, time to sleep, sweet one."

Olivia felt a surge of Energy and saw a pulse of light under the nurse's palm, then Adaida closed her eyes and began to breathe steadily. Nurse Tyliste nodded, took the digits Olivia had handed her, and lifted Adaida's wounded hand. "At least they were clean cuts, and you got her here quickly, didn't you?"

"As quickly as I could," Olivia replied. She heard a commotion at the entrance to the infirmary but didn't look away as she watched Nurse Tyliste work. The amazing, glowing-winged Ghelli was holding one of Adaida's severed fingers to the stump on her hand and concentrating with her lips pressed into a firm line. Olivia saw a pulse of Energy around her fingers and felt a huge surge of it from the nurse herself. Then Tyliste smiled and laid Adaida's hand down, picking up the next digit.

"That went very well. In just a few moments, I'll have enough Energy to try this one."

"Try?" Olivia asked, her voice strained with worry.

"Well, it's not a sure thing, but I have a very good feeling."

"Olivia?" Oylla-dak's unmistakable voice cut across the infirmary, and she spun to see the tall Shadeni professor walking toward her with storm clouds in her eyes. Inspector Carlu followed several paces behind her, like he didn't want to get in Oylla's way, a contrite look on his face.

Olivia turned back to Adaida, wanting to see if Tyliste would be successful with her second attempt, but the nurse said, "I'll need another couple of minutes to rest. Speak to your professor." She kept her voice low, and Olivia wondered for a moment if the powerful Ghelli could read her mind.

"Olivia," Oylla repeated her name, now just a few feet away.

"Yes, Professor," Olivia replied. She took Adaida's whole hand in hers before turning to face Oylla and Carlu.

"Were you attacked? The academy is abuzz. Something about a magical battle in the Alchemy Gardens? What's happened to your cohort member?"

"Yes, the killer attacked us. He severed two of Adaida's fingers before I could send him running."

"You saw him?" Carlu asked from behind Oylla.

"You hush!" Oylla growled, spinning to face the inspector. "You've been here for days, and all you do is look at the crime scenes. How about doing something proactive?" She turned back to Olivia and the nurse. "Tyliste, will she be all right?"

"She'll live, for sure. Give me a moment, and I'll let you know about her finger. I've already reattached one of them."

"Olivia, tell me what happened. In more detail, please," Oylla requested, reaching out a hand to gently squeeze Olivia's shoulder.

"We were standing in the garden talking when he attacked from behind me. Adaida's eyes widened in a look of horror, which alerted me. I used Elemental Form to avoid his blow, but he hit her hand." Olivia spoke while staring at Adaida, unwilling to look away from her injured friend. "I turned on him and went on the offensive, but he had some kind of shield spell, and once I started to break it, he threw up a wall of blue flames and ran."

"What did he look like?" Carlu asked, stepping around Oylla so he could look directly at Olivia. Oylla glared at him but didn't object to the question.

"He wore robes like a professor and had a wooden mask painted to look like a yellow-striped green reptile."

"Did he speak?"

"No. Oylla"—Olivia turned from Adaida to look at her mentor—"I felt his Energy. Can someone here teach me a scrying spell? I want to find him and put an end to this."

"I would have to object—" Carlu started to say, but Nurse Tyliste held up a hand.

"I'm going to attempt to fix this finger now. Please be silent."

She lifted Adaida's wounded hand, and Olivia saw the forlorn, bloody stump of her ring finger. She felt hot tears sting her eyes again as the nurse pressed the pale, bloodless finger Olivia had recovered to the stump and began concentrating. Again, Olivia felt the Energy around Tyliste's hands and then the deep, powerful surge from the nurse's Core. She let go, and Adaida's finger remained where she'd placed it, though the nurse wore a frown.

"Is something wrong?" Olivia asked.

"The flesh is rejoined, and she'll keep the finger, but it may not be as functional as it was. She may have lost feeling in it. Well, nothing a few racial advancements won't fix!" She smiled and, once again, smoothed Adaida's hair. "She should rest now. No small amount of Energy for the healing is drawn from the patient. Do you all mind moving your talk of murderers to a different venue?" She turned and smiled crookedly at Oylla-dak.

"Yes, follow me back to my office, please, Olivia. You may come as well, Inspector." She turned and began marching out of the infirmary.

Olivia didn't follow immediately. First, she leaned forward and kissed Adaida's forehead, pleased that her skin was warm and her eyes seemed untroubled. She knew firsthand that the nurse was good at making people relax.

She turned to her and smiled.

"Thank you, Nurse Tyliste. I knew you could help her."

"You're welcome, Olivia. Thank you for bringing her so quickly. If you go after the one who hurt her, please be careful. I can fix many things, but I cannot restore life to the dead." The nurse's face was impassive, like she spoke about things like that all the time. Olivia nodded, attempting a reassuring smile.

"I'll be careful, but there's no way I'm going to sit around and wait for him to hurt another student. Something has to be done, and I have to help if I can, right?"

"Yes, I suppose I agree with that. If you can prevent another death or injury, you must help. Let me know if I can help, dear. Now, you'd best hurry—Oylla's not known for her patience."

She gently reached out and took Olivia's shoulder, steering her away from the bed. Olivia nodded and started walking after the inspector, who was clearly dragging his feet to avoid being alone with Oylla.

"No, she certainly isn't," she said under her breath, lengthening her stride to catch up with Carlu.

## MORGAN

"So, yeah, I think you and your assistants should come to check out the lab. I'm cool with you guys working there as much as you need. Seriously, man, the equipment I uncovered is way beyond anything you guys are using. It's beyond anything at Tarn's Crossing, even." Morgan was leaning against Boris's workbench. He and Issa had just had breakfast at Alec's tavern, and she'd gone to visit with Maria, saying she wanted to talk to her about human wedding traditions.

"That's really generous of you, Morgan. You sure you want a bunch of crafters traipsing around your home?" Boris sat back, lifting the strange, glimmering spectacles he wore up to his forehead.

"Well, I mean, let's start with just you and your team, all right? I can set permissions on the stairs so—no offense—you guys can only access the floor with the workshop and lab." Morgan chuckled, imagining one of Boris's helpers stumbling into his master suite.

"Ahh, that's cool! I'd give my left arm—" He laughed, glancing at Morgan's perfectly whole appendage. "Well, maybe not! Anyway, I'd love to see the enchantments on that tower. I wouldn't know where to look, though. Maybe when I level up enough."

"Yeah, the tower is something else, for sure. I'm not sure where I'd begin trying to figure out where all the enchantments are. I sort of gained a connection to it when I beat the final guardian, and I still don't know how it all works. It's like getting the operating codes to a new interceptor, being able to fly it and work all the fancy equipment but having no clue how it all works."

"Yeah, that makes sense. Well, here's hoping I can learn as much as the guy who built it, eh?" Boris absently tapped one of his fine, metal inscription tools against the piece of steel he'd been working on.

"There are some things he knew that you don't want to know, my friend. He did some messed up things while he was around." Morgan shook his head, his eyes going distant for a moment.

Boris cleared his throat uncomfortably.

"Right, well, you know, I'm just trying to learn how to make life easier for us on this planet."

"Of course! Anyway, I'll need the names of your assistants. Actually, to make this easier, can you all just come by the tower first thing tomorrow? I'll give you permissions with the door and stairs so you can access the labs."

"Hell yeah, Morgan! Thank you! Is there anything I can do for you?"

"Yeah, actually, there is. I was hoping you'd ask! I knew if I offered you access to my labs, you'd feel obligated, muahahaha!" Morgan mock laughed and rubbed his hands together. Boris laughed along with him, and Morgan reached out to clap his shoulder. "So, are you good at making rings?"

"Man, I'm an Enchanter, not a jeweler! Why?"

"Well, I proposed to Issa and sort of did it without a ring." Morgan rubbed at his head, sighing. "She's the best thing in my life, and I want to make sure I do things right, you know?"

"Well, I can help you, buddy. Several jewelers work in the Crafting Pavilion, and I'm pretty sure they all owe me favors. Let's start with the best, though, Gina Brooks. If we get her to craft the rings, I'll do some enchanting for free, alright?"

"That's great, Boris. I have some materials I'd like to use. Is she here yet?" Morgan glanced around the pavilion, and Boris turned toward the far corner.

"Yep, there she is. Let's go talk to her. Congratulations, by the way, Morgan! That's great shit!"

"Thanks, Boris." Morgan clapped him on the shoulder again as they started walking. Boris reached up to pat Morgan on the back but stopped short.

"Dude, the wings. How am I supposed to pat your back?"

"Sorry, Boris." Morgan shrugged. "They get in the way more than you think, but I'm getting better at living with them."

Once they reached Gina's table, she lifted her head from her project, large magnifying lenses making her eyes look huge. She was a small woman with short, curly black hair. She tucked a tiny pair of pliers into one of the dozen pockets on her gray overalls and smiled broadly when she saw Boris.

"Hey, cutie! Coming to try to make another deal, hmm?"

"Oh, gosh!" Boris actually blushed, and Morgan snickered. "Come on, Gina, don't embarrass me in front of my friend! This is Morgan, and he happens to have a commission for you!"

"*The* Morgan Hall?" Gina asked in a mocking tone. "You think we don't notice your big friend coming in here to make secret deals with you, Boris? About time you shared some of the attention!"

"Uh, nice to meet you, Gina," Morgan said, offering her a hand to shake.

"You too, Morgan." She took his hand and squeezed, her short fingers only making it halfway around his palm.

"I need some rings made. I have the materials, and I can pay. That sound like something you could do?"

"Straight to business! I love it. Boris usually bores me with a story or two about his latest achievements before he tells me what he wants." Her voice was high and a little scratchy, and Morgan found her demeanor instantly amusing. She reminded him of someone he'd watched on VR, but he couldn't quite pin down the memory.

"I'll pay extra, but I need at least the first ring done as quickly as possible. You see, I proposed to my, uh, girlfriend, and she said yes, but I don't have the ring yet."

"Oh, an engagement ring, hmm? And you'll be wanting wedding rings, too, I suppose?" She grinned at him, and Morgan noticed a wide gap between her front teeth, though he found it hard to see anything other than her enormous, magnified eyes.

"Yeah, that's right. I have this metal I want to use . . ." Morgan pulled out the bar of Amber Ore he'd been hauling around. He figured he could spare a tiny portion for some rings and still have enough to use in a new blade if he wanted to. "This is Amber Ore. Have you worked with it before?"

"No, I sure haven't," the woman said, picking up the heavy bar. "God, it's dense! Feels similar to gold, but"—she set it down and scratched at it with a sharp metal tool—"hard as hell!"

"It also holds enchantments really well, Boris," Morgan added, turning to his friend.

Boris whistled. "Do you think you can work it, Gina?"

"Oh yeah, I've learned a few spells for cutting and shaping metal. If anything, I might have to use a power stone or two to supplement my Energy." She looked up from the bar of metal to Morgan, squinting. "Where'd you get it anyway? Seems like it would be valuable, even in this magical world."

"Adventuring, and yeah, it's damn valuable, so I'll need most of it back. I'm going to have a sword or something made with it eventually." Morgan didn't mean to let some steel enter his voice, but it did, and Gina physically flinched at his change of tone. "Sorry, I don't mean to sound threatening. It's a byproduct of my class and titles and racial advancements—you get the idea."

"Sure. Sort of. Anyway, if you let me keep enough of this metal for just one extra ring, I'll make yours for free. You'll still be getting more than ninety percent of this bar back."

Morgan thought about it for a minute, then nodded. "Deal."

"Nice! Payment all sorted! Now, let's talk about the style of the engagement ring. Are you thinking you'd like a stone in it? Simple band? Delicate flowers? I can do all sorts of fancy work!"

"I have something," Morgan said, scanning through his storage ring.

When he and Olivia had been preparing for the portal spell in the dungeon, he'd noticed something about the stones from the gem snake. Of all three hundred plus stones he'd gathered from the creature, only one was colorless, and it had reminded Morgan of a diamond when he'd first seen it in his pile. What was more, it had held quite a lot more Energy than any of the other stones. He set the gem, about the size of a golf ball, on the workbench.

"This is a rare stone from a rare animal, and I don't know if it can be cut, but if it can, I think it would be nice to use."

"Let me see." Gina lifted the gem and held it in front of one of her lenses. While Morgan watched, the lens in front of her left eye turned opaque and started to sparkle with silvery motes of Energy. A moment later, she smiled and set it down. "I can cut this. I can cut several large, beautiful stones out of it. When I'm done, they'll each have the Energy storage potential of the original, a byproduct of my gem-cutting skill."

"You can tell all that with your lens?"

"Sure! Combined with my Analyze skill, these lenses allow me to see more about gems, metals, and other stones and materials than any set of microscopes or even a mass spectrometer could tell me back on Earth."

"All right, one more request," Morgan said, waiting to continue until Gina nodded. "You know what the flowers in the Chebli Sea look like?" He produced one of the flowers he'd picked and stored in his ring during his last journey through the sea with Issa. "I'd like one carved from the Amber Ore on either side of the stone."

"So, like the flowers are kind of holding up the stone?"

"If you can do that so it looks good, yeah," he replied.

"All right, can do. The other two rings are just bands, right? One to fit your huge finger and one for your bride's?"

"Yeah, that's right. You can measure my finger now, and I have this"—Morgan pulled one of Issa's rings from his pocket—"for you to measure Issa's size. She let me borrow it this morning."

"Sister," Tkron hissed from his dark corner of the burrow. "What goes on without? The noise has increased tenfold. How am I to concentrate and gain my full strength?"

"Morgan is having a new home built for me and my sisters, Tkron," Ykleedra said, looking to the ground, afraid to make eye contact with the large, pale Yovashi, worried that her answer would enrage him again.

"Why indulge his fantasy? We'll all be leaving soon."

"How soon, Tkron?" Ykleedra asked, knowing the question would lead to him dismissing her in an irritated huff.

"Again, you ask?" His voice clicked, indicating he was speaking with emphasis from his nether beak. "When I've gained enough strength to break free of this prison!"

"Tkron, why won't you let me speak to Morgan on your behalf? I'm sure he'd allow you to leave?"

"Wouldn't you like that? Wouldn't you love to see me slink away into the forest while you and my sisters play nice with the humans, forgetting your history, forgetting your culture, and abandoning your people? The five of you are important for our race! Our numbers dwindle!" He lurched toward her on his long, black-and-red chitin-covered legs, looming over her, already nearly twice her mass.

"Tkron," Ykleedra said, shrinking back, afraid he'd strike her or worse. "I'm sorry! Of course we'll slip away as soon as possible. I only allow Morgan to build this home for us to keep him happy and to avoid causing suspicion. How strange he'd think it if I insisted I didn't want a house modeled after my mother's and that I enjoyed living in a filthy burrow!" Her words seemed to calm Tkron, and he moved back to his dark corner.

"Enough, I need to cultivate. Your contributions to the compost pit are starting to bear fruit; the levels of decay Energy are rising in this . . . *filthy burrow*. Begone, now. See to your sisters, for I need peace to accomplish my drill."

With that, Ykleedra was dismissed, and she knew better than to linger around him when he'd made such a declaration.

She exited the burrow and followed the winding path through the ferns to the large clearing where Miss Washington's people were working. Her sisters were obsessed with the activity, and she'd left them playing nearby. As she walked, she let her mind wander back to Tkron—she'd stopped thinking of him as a brother—and his behavior.

He was becoming more and more brooding, and his attitude and language toward Morgan and his people were increasingly hostile. Ykleedra had struggled with the problem for a long while, but the more he changed, the more aggressively he acted, the easier he made things. His hostility, his threats—especially toward her sisters—were pushing Ykleedra to act.

She'd already decided what action she would take: she'd seek out Morgan and tell him everything. Morgan could solve this problem.

## MORGAN

Morgan sat on Bronwyn's Hill, a few feet from one of the stairs leading up to the Town Stone. His hands were out behind him, resting on the warm, blue-tinted grass, and his face was toward the sun. It wasn't hot, there was a definite hint of coolness in the breeze that tickled his exposed skin, but the sky was cloudless, and the bright midday sun felt wonderful.

His wings were partially splayed behind him so he didn't sit on them, and he marveled at how they soaked up the sunlight and the amount of sensation he had at the base of each of his thousands of feathers.

He'd finished his ring order, sampled some cider someone was selling from a cart near the Crafting Pavilion, and now he was simply waiting for Issa.

"Nothing else on my plate," he said, enjoying the feeling.

He opened his eyes and looked to the north, a smile quirking his lips when he saw his tower. It had gone from an imposing, brooding place to a bright, almost inspiring edifice. It reminded him of something you might see in a fairy tale or fantasy novel.

"Should I keep it bronze? Maybe I should try steel or silver. Maybe gold?" He chuckled at himself, realizing he'd find something even shinier to be too garish. Who was he to live in a golden tower?

While staring at it, he realized he was still sort of aware of its presence. He could feel movement within, and when he concentrated, he came to understand it was the work crew that Alicia Washington had brought in to work on Ykleedra's home.

He wondered how far he could be from it and still sense things within. Would he be able to do so from anywhere? Would it fade away as he moved further afield?

"Something to experiment with, I guess."

He'd started to relax again, closing his eyes, when he felt a surge of Energy darkly tainted with something like death from within the tower. "The hell?"

He opened his eyes and concentrated again, searching through it with his mind, almost like he could see the inside of his storage ring. There, near the middle, he could sense Ykleedra and her sisters, the human work crew not far away. He couldn't see the source of the Energy surge, but there seemed to be a dark shadow near the bright, warm signature he associated with Ykleedra.

Morgan stared at the obscured space, trying to pierce its veil, and with an effort of will, he started to unravel the shadows. As they fell away, he became aware of another Core, another being with the same kind of dark, decaying Energy he'd felt surge up. As he tugged more of the shadows away, it surged again, and Ykleedra's warm, familiar Core signature dimmed.

"What the fuck?" Morgan leaped to his feet, his wings cracking as he launched himself into the air.

He winked out of existence in a rip through reality, reappearing much closer to his tower. He dove toward the door atop its short set of stairs, casting Void Step again and crashing into the door with a resounding gong. He wasn't fazed by the collision, however, yanking the door open and charging into his tower.

---

"I know. Hush, now." Ykleedra softly ran a tentacle along the back of Pkril's head, gently smoothing her long, silky hair. "He's mean and short tempered, but we won't have to deal with him much longer. When Morgan gets back, I'm going to confess everything to him. He'll know what to do about Tkron."

Pkril just sniffed, pushing her face into Ykleedra's stomach, and not for the first time, Ykleedra wondered at the trauma Tkron was visiting upon the little ones. She wondered at the wisdom of her mother and grandmother in raising her away from her father.

She stretched out another tentacle, gently rubbing at the hairline crack in Pkril's chitin. If Tkron had hit her much harder, he'd have caused a severe injury. "This will heal soon, Pkril. Little sweet one, just keep your distance from him, all right?"

The little girl sniffed and nodded, a testament to her quick and clever mind. She'd been the earliest talker and could already clean after herself when she voided.

"Is that so, sister?" a deep, hoarse voice asked from the shadows of the nearby ferns. Ykleedra's heart nearly stopped, and she scurried to face the voice, pushing Pkril back behind her.

"Tkron! You shouldn't be out here! What if someone sees you?"

"You mean before you have a chance to report me to your human? Before you ask him to slay me?"

"I'd never, Tkron! If I spoke to Morgan, it would be to ask him to help you leave! To help you find a home away from the humans!"

"Is that right?" Suddenly, a surge of Energy erupted from Tkron, and Ykleedra felt a horrible pain in one of her tentacles, the one she'd been pushing Pkril back with. She yanked it back, tucking it under her robe, but not before seeing the open, rotting sore Tkron had inflicted with his decay-attuned Energy.

"Brother!" she cried, using the word for the first time in weeks.

"Now I'm *brother*? Not Tkron?" He lurched forward, crashing out of the ferns, his long, powerful, front walking legs digging into the turf as he stomped toward her.

Ykleedra cowered, hoping to assuage his wrath with a show of submission. It usually worked, allowing her to escape his anger with just an injury or two, but he'd never used his decay Energy on her before. As she bent low, folding her own walking legs so she seemed even smaller, he lifted his front forelimb and smashed the hard, chitin claw into her back, driving her down into the soil.

"Brother," Ykleedra said again between sobs, struggling to pull in air. She'd never learned any spells for fighting; her mother had deemed her too young, and she'd hardly cultivated any decay, not even forming an affinity for it. No, she had just a weakly throbbing Core of simple Energy and knew nothing but a few utility spells that the human teacher had taught her. What good was a ball of light when your giant brother stomped you into the soil?

"You call me *brother* only when you want something, *sister*!" he sneered. "I think your influence on my other sisters has turned sour. I think it's time we all left and I taught you some respect!" He pressed down on the heavy, sharp claw, driving her into the ground and pushing out more of her air before he turned to the cowering Pkril. "Fetch your sisters, runt. Hurry!"

Pkril scampered back but didn't leave, looking from Ykleedra to Tkron with wide, tear-filled eyes.

"She . . ." Ykleedra gasped. "She can't . . ." Again, Tkron pushed down on her back, driving out the breath she'd managed to steal.

"She can't what?" he asked, twisting his foreclaw back and forth, grinding it into her back and ripping through her silver robe.

"She . . ." Ykleedra wheezed, unable to pull in enough air to complete a sentence. She gasped, desperate to pull in more air, when suddenly, the weight was gone. A weird sound, like the air was eating itself, erupted above her, and Tkron was crashing through the ferns to smash into a narrow-trunked plum tree, cracking the wood and making the branches thrash back and forth, sending half-ripened fruit flying in every direction.

"Who the fuck are you?" Morgan growled, his gleaming broadsword in one hand, and his wings spread wide. Even Tkron's oversized body seemed insignificant before him, his long legs scrabbling in the dirt for purchase as he worked to stand.

Morgan looked at Ykleedra and her cowering little sister, and if his eyes were angry before, they turned to pure molten rage now. He strode toward Tkron, sword held high as a wave of pure murderous intent poured out of him.

Ykleedra saw the demise of her people in that wave, saw the ruined bodies of a million Yovashi, and she cried out in despair.

Tkron, the direct focus of Morgan's rage and aura projection, fell flat, uncontrollable sobs pouring from his throat. He might have been born with memories and knowledge, but he was still a child, and none of his racial memories could have prepared him for a confrontation with Morgan, the furious bane of Yovashi.

"Morgan," Ykleedra said, coughing with the effort. She tried again, raising her voice, panic driving her as Morgan closed the distance and she saw his arm flexing, ready to bring his sword down. "Morgan!"

Morgan stopped, stiffening, and turned, glancing at her over his shoulder and wing. "Ykleedra?"

"Morgan, please don't kill him. He's my brother."

"He . . ." Morgan stood there, chest heaving, staring at her. After several heartbeats, he made a visible effort to calm himself and lowered his sword. Ykleedra could feel his aura, his murderous intent, starting to fade away as he turned to Tkron. "Don't move. If you threaten Ykleedra or her sisters in any way, I'll take you apart." He looked away from the figure cowering in the ferns in much the same way Ykleedra had been cowering before him, and said, "Ykleedra, what's going on? You had a brother? How'd he get into my tower?"

"He was one of my mother's eggs, Morgan. I didn't know, I swear! I didn't know that male Yovashi are born with memories. I didn't know any of it!" She sobbed then, unable to contain her emotions. Guilt, fear, and relief warred for dominance in her mind, and she cried, tears pouring out of her dark, fathomless eyes. She felt the warm, gentle caress of Pkril's tentacles as her little sister curled up underneath her, also crying.

"Ykleedra, it's okay," Morgan tried to console her while he stood guard over Tkron at the same time. "Tiladia!" he called. Suddenly, the tinkling, misty form of the dragon spirit was there, whirling over to him.

"Morgan?"

"I need you to tell me what the fuck is going on here!"

"I don't know, Morgan! Are you referring to that Yovashi cowering before you? I didn't see what happened! Was he your guest?"

Morgan sighed heavily. "No, Tiladia. He wasn't my guest." His voice was calm now, resigned, and the rage seemed to have left him. Ykleedra loved that about him. She'd never seen him carry anger for long. "Can you please watch this guy? I need to talk to Ykleedra."

"Of course, Morgan. Should he move even an inch, I will alert you." Tiladia took on the misty dragon form that Ykleedra loved so much and began to swoop and swirl around the cowering Tkron. Then Ykleedra felt warm hands and arms curling around her, and she was lifted into the air, her long walking legs dangling loosely.

"Come on, um, Pkril, right? Follow us," Morgan said as he carried Ykleedra further into the atrium, away from her burrow and toward the large clearing where the house was being built. "I think I heard your sisters over there."

"That's right. They were playing. Pkril wandered off and angered Tkron. I was comforting her when he heard me say that I was going to tell you about him. Then he attacked me!" Ykleedra wanted to tell Morgan everything now, but she was gasping for air still, and her words were pained and slow, accompanied by breathy wheezes.

"Shh. Hold on."

Morgan jogged along the path, making quick work of the little trip to the clearing and her sisters, who were playing amid the piled lumber that Alicia's people had left. Morgan set Ykleedra down in the grass nearby then handed her a small vial.

"Drink this."

Ykleedra did as he said, swallowing the warm, sweet liquid. Heat flooded through her pathways, and suddenly, her ribs expanded with an audible *pop*, and she could breathe easily again. She glanced at her tentacle, noting with relief that the decay-filled wound had also healed.

"Thank you, Morgan," she sobbed, reaching out a tentacle to gently grip his wrist.

"Hush, it's fine. You can tell me everything later, but for now, just tell me what you want me to do with your brother." Morgan knelt in front of her, the rage and murder in his eyes completely gone. He smiled, reaching out to gently rub her shoulder. "You're okay, Ykleedra. He'll never hurt you again, no matter what you say."

"I don't know what you should do, Morgan. I don't know what is right. I don't want him to die, but he's grown more and more unstable in just the few months he's been out of his egg. What will he be like in years? There's something wrong with the magic that gave him his memories and made him mature so quickly, I'm sure of it."

"Huh. So if I let him go, send him away, he could end up hurting innocent people." Morgan scratched at his chin, eyes going distant. "Well, I'll tell you this because you're his sister, Ykleedra. The wizard who built this tower wasn't a nice guy. He had something like prison cells in the basement. I can feel them. Would it be okay if I put your brother into one of them until we figure out a better solution?"

"Yes! I think that would be best, Morgan! He's become violent and unpredictable."

"Alright, Ykleedra. You stay here with your sisters. Don't worry about a thing, all right? I'll come talk to you after I get things settled, and I'll bring Issa.

Would that make you feel better? She'd love to talk to you about this, to help you sort out your feelings. No matter what, you don't have to worry; you're not in trouble. I'll never make you leave or anything like that, okay? This is your home." He gestured to the clearing and the foundations sticking out of the soil. "Isn't that right, little ones?" he asked the gathering of Ykleedra's little sisters, all trying to squeeze closer and closer to her, somehow sensing her distress.

Ykleedra, feeling too emotional for words, just nodded to Morgan, and he smiled.

He stood up and waved, then stalked away through the garden, back the way they'd come. Ykleedra watched him go, and though she knew he wasn't going to kill her brother, she'd already started to think of Tkron as gone. She'd be fine if she never saw him again.

## ॐ BRONWYN ॐ

Bronwyn looked down the hill at Whitestar's camp and breathed out a soft, "Holy shit." The Urghat had built a log palisade around their camp, and there had to be nearly fifty tents and a dozen wooden structures within. "It's more like a town or village than a camp," she said more loudly.

"Aye, Underclaw. Whitestar's attracted a decent-size force, and she knows what she's doing," Shadoweye replied.

Bronwyn took in the wider vista of the vale, the twisted forest crawling up the hills and the rocky ground covered with scraggly brush at the center. Far off, beyond the encampment, she could see the ground slope further down toward a deeper canyon between two hillocks, and she knew that in those shadows were the cave mouths that led into the Hollows—a deep, partially natural cave system which used to serve as the home for thousands of Urghat.

"Well"—she glanced over her shoulder at Cal and Ironhide—"we ready to head down?"

"Yeah, I'm hungry," Ironhide said, sniffing the woodsmoke in the air.

"Of course!" Cal replied, walking past Bronwyn.

Shadoweye gave Bronwyn a pained look and hurried to walk in front of the lanky, travel-stained man. She chuckled and followed, happy to let him have this moment. The journey hadn't been particularly hard, but Cal had put up with quite a lot and ventured into the unknown to find his friend. Why not let him lead the party into the camp?

They received a lot of hostile glares from the Urghat outside the walls. Some were digging trenches, and others were working to clear brush away; further out, Bronwyn could see crews chopping trees and cutting logs. When they came to the palisade gate, which was open, five burly Urghat wearing heavy armor and wielding thick, brutal weapons like hammers and axes stood around the opening. The biggest one stepped forward with a growl and held his cleaverlike axe in their path.

"What's the meaning of this, scout?" he growled at Shadoweye.

"Important people to see the Underclaw." She stepped back and pointed at the band on Bronwyn's arm. "Best move out of the way and let them through."

"Huh." The big, grizzled Urghat stepped closer. He was large, but nothing like Spineripper or his Underclaws, and Bronwyn had gained a lot of power since she'd last faced an Urghat in battle. She stood up straight and summoned her hatchets, pouring some solar Energy into them with her Solar Arms spell.

"Back away," she snarled, staring into his bloodshot, rust-colored irises between the gray plates of his helmet.

"I feel your mark, Underclaw," he growled, backing off the path. "If you challenge Whitestar, don't expect us to swear to you." He spat into the dirt, and all the Urghat around the gate followed his lead, spitting wads of phlegm and saliva into the path in front of Bronwyn.

"Relax," she said. "I'm not here to challenge anyone. I want to help her."

"You know where she is, hunter," the big Urghat told Shadoweye, then stepped out of their way.

As they passed under the gate and moved a dozen steps beyond the guards, Cal turned to Bronwyn. "They don't seem to like you much."

"Urghat usually aren't happy when an outsider takes one of their Underclaw titles. Ironhide and Shadoweye didn't like me at first, either. Still, they respected me—at least enough not to challenge me. By the way, I doubt they like you much either, Cal."

"Yeah, I wasn't getting any warm and fuzzy vibes from that crew." He chuckled.

Bronwyn snorted in reply, striding alongside Cal as Shadoweye led them toward the center of the encampment. She kept her hatchets in her hands, but she'd let the solar Energy fall out of them. They were impressive weapons, and with her silvery chain mail and improved race, she knew only an Urghat like Spineripper would dare to challenge her for her Underclaw title. She also knew an Urghat like him only came around once every few generations.

She was impressed by the layout of Whitestar's camp and by the industrious nature of the Urghat who followed her. She didn't see any of them lazing about drinking near their tents as she'd so often encountered when she'd visited the encampments on the plains. Every single Urghat seemed either alert, acting as a guard, or busy improving the fortifications or managing the day-to-day upkeep. Shadoweye led them down a hard-packed dirt road to a wooden structure that reminded Bronwyn more of a Viking longhouse than anything else.

They approached the wooden doors of the building up a short flight of steps. The two armored Urghat standing guard spoke to Shadoweye for a moment, giving Bronwyn, Cal, and even Ironhide dirty looks, but one of them went inside, indicating that they had to wait. A few moments later, the door was swung wide from the other side, and a different Urghat stood there. She was unlike any other Bronwyn had seen, from her narrow, expressive face to her strange—for an Urghat—attire.

She had dark fur, but the white patch over her eye gave away the origin of her name. Whitestar was the first Urghat Bronwyn had ever seen wearing robes. She was tall and lean, and Bronwyn knew the Urghat Underclaw had improved her race a time or two. She reminded her a little of Bloodfang, though she wasn't quite as large as the Urghat Blood Caster who had first challenged Bronwyn. Still, it was clear that Whitestar had managed to gain a much higher affinity to Energy than most of her race, her aura pushing out of her as she smiled wolfishly at Cal.

"Human! So the Ghelli didn't eat you?" She laughed roughly and grabbed Cal in a bear hug, lifting the much smaller man into the air and clapping him roughly on the back. When she set the wheezing man down, she laughed again and said, "Did you come to sing me some pretty songs, human? Don't worry. We won't eat you. Maybe I'll eat this pretty Underclaw, though."

She pushed Cal aside with one long, furry arm and stepped close to Bronwyn, putting her snout with too many long teeth sticking out right in front of Bronwyn's mouth. She stared into her eyes, and Bronwyn couldn't help noticing how pretty the Urghat's honey-colored, red-flecked irises were as she took a deep, exaggerated sniff.

"Bronwyn," she growled. "I've heard your tale from Shadoweye and the twins. I suppose I can let you visit if you aren't here to challenge me."

"I'm not, Whitestar. I'm here as a traveling companion to Cal and to see if there's any way I can help you with the trolls in the Hollow."

"You are this softling's mate?" Whitestar asked, resting a long, furry hand on Cal's shoulder.

"No, Whitestar!" Cal said, faster than Bronwyn could.

The Urghat chuckled at his words, a deep, throaty sound, and jostled him with the hand she'd wrapped around his shoulder.

"Still can't find love, human?"

"Whitestar! You left me with the Ghelli, and I married one of them. I have you to thank for a lot, but that's the most important part." Cal reached out, putting a hand on Whitestar's outstretched forearm, and the tall, wiry Urghat grunted, her wolfish smile twisting awkwardly as she pulled her hand back.

"Good!" she growled. "Come inside then," she told the group. "We'll have some food and talk about how I can get this strange Underclaw to leave." She gestured at Bronwyn before turning and walking back into her longhouse.

"Now, Whitestar, that's no way to talk about someone who's come a long way to help you out," Cal admonished, following the Underclaw through the doorway.

Shadoweye turned to shrug at Bronwyn and Ironhide, and the three of them stepped through. The guard who'd gone to fetch Whitestar was standing within; he glared as they walked by but stepped out, pulling the door closed behind him.

The longhouse was much like Bronwyn had imagined: high wooden beams held up the peaked roof, and a firepit in the center of the structure provided dim, orange-tinted light to the space. Smoke drifted in the air, though most of it drafted toward the square opening at the center of the roof. Bronwyn squinted, her eyes stinging, and looked around at the crude benches and tables, noting that they were all empty. Apparently, the Underclaw didn't allow her followers to loaf about inside her longhouse during the day.

Whitestar headed to a table placed along the far wall and sat down in a heavy wooden chair at its head, gesturing to the benches along the sides for the rest of them to sit. Bronwyn followed Cal to the table's far side, sitting near Whitestar. She didn't mind the rude behavior of the Urghat thus far; she knew what they were like and that they viewed her as a threat to their traditions. She'd had plenty of fighting over the weeks she'd spent in the dungeon with Morgan and Olivia, and as far as she was concerned, she'd take a lot of shit to avoid hurting or killing one of the Urghat.

As images of her battles in the dungeon flashed through her mind, she thought about Olivia, and a little dip of vertigo or dizziness flashed through her. She couldn't really explain the sensation, but one thing was sure: she'd hardly thought about Olivia since she'd left First Landing.

That wasn't normal, was it? Weren't they in love? Hadn't they been passionately kissing when the Summer Queen had sent her the message to help Cal? Had her feelings faded so quickly?

"I've just been busy and distracted," she muttered, her voice covered by the loud conversation taking place between Cal and Whitestar.

". . . made you want to seek me out?" Whitestar was asking Cal.

"Well, I finally managed to move my family to First Landing; you know, the human settlement. I've always told my wife and my adopted kiddos that I woulda died out there in those plains if you hadn't decided to help me get free, and I felt like I owed it to you to follow up. You know, see how you're doing, and let you know I made it. I'm still alive!"

"You have a strange memory, Cal. Wasn't it I who took you from the humans? You'd never have needed saving if not for me." Whitestar chuckled, scratching at the table with one of her long claws.

"That's true, Whitestar, but I'd never have met my wife nor would I have ever been able to join her family and earn the love of those wonderful kids then. I owe you pretty much everything I'm happy about. I think fate threw us together in a way. When I decided to come find you, Bronwyn here showed up to join me. Now, we've learned you might need some help with yonder trolls"—he gestured vaguely in the direction of the Hollows—"and, I don't know if you know this, but Bronwyn is a pretty tough cookie. She'll help you!"

"It does feel like that's what I'm meant to do out here, Underclaw," Bronwyn said, using the title in a show of respect.

"You assume I need help?" Whitestar asked, arching one of her heavy brows.

The expression made Bronwyn imagine a wolf or bear sitting there talking to her, face animated like a person's, and it threw her off for a second. The Urghat she'd spent the most time talking to was Ironhide, and she couldn't remember him ever making an expression like that, despite his colorful personality.

"Not necessarily need, but maybe you wouldn't mind it? I mean, I always enjoy an extra pair of hands on a task," Bronwyn replied with a shrug.

"Well, you'd have been correct if you thought I needed it. I do. The trolls are more brutal, resilient, and organized than I expected. If we don't take back the Well of Ancestors in the next few days, Soft-fur will die."

"Shadoweye told us something similar, but she said she didn't know anything about it. Some kind of curse?" Bronwyn leaned forward, hating the idea of the sweet, strange Urghat child dying.

"She is cursed with a certain type of Energy. None in her clan understood it, unsurprisingly. I had to read about it in an ancient text I stole from Spineripper's lair after his army moved out to attack your people. She was born with a role to fill; as she gained level ten, she became a Clan Heart. Something quite rare, Underclaw," Whitestar said, returning Bronwyn's show of respect.

"What's that got to do with her Energy? With her being near death?"

"She must release her Energy periodically into the Well. It maintains our link to our ancestors and makes it possible for our traditions to continue." She tapped the ring on her arm, one that matched Bronwyn's. "If she doesn't enter the Well, her Energy will destroy her."

"There's no other way? A spell she could cast or something? You know, to release some of the Energy?"

"No, Bronwyn." Whitestar chuckled. "I have tried everything." The big Urghat paused for a moment, eyeing her, then said, "Come. While these others wait for our meal, let me take you to Soft-fur. She's spoken much about you, and I think it would do her good to see you again. You can tell her you've come to help."

Bronwyn shoved her bench back, dragging Cal's feet over the floor, and stood,

"Yes! Please, Whitestar. I'd like to see her very much."

# OLIVIA

Olivia sat in Oylla-dak's office next to Inspector Carlu, feeling like she was in trouble for some reason. Perhaps it was the deep scowl that Oylla wore, or perhaps it was because Carlu was fidgeting nervously, and Olivia was mentally associating herself with him. She crossed her legs, folded her hands in her lap, and stared at Oylla, her eyes ablaze, daring the professor to try to blame her for anything that had happened.

"Carlu, do you have a scrying spell you can teach Olivia?" Oylla asked, surprising both of her guests. Carlu sputtered for a moment, glancing from Olivia to Oylla. "If you don't, we can find something in the library, I'm sure. I know some scrying spells, but nothing quite right for this purpose."

"The killer does a fairly good job of shielding himself. I've only ever found traces of his Energy signature, never enough to track him down. His image is always obscured. Just a blurry shadow," Carlu said, answering the question in a way which made it seem like he was thinking aloud.

"I felt his Energy very clearly," Olivia spoke. "I can still feel it, almost like a dirty taste on the back of my tongue."

"In that case, I have a spell we could probably modify fairly easily to help lead her to the killer. I don't have my texts with me, so I'll need to write the pattern by hand before we can alter it. Do you want me to do that now?" Carlu produced a neat, leather-bound notebook and a quill.

"Yes, start writing it, and I'll call Professor ap'Rall to help with the modification. We could do it, but she'll be faster." Oylla touched a black stone on her desk. When it began to glow with a soft orange light, she said, "Have Professor ap'Rall report to my office immediately." Olivia couldn't hear the response, if there was one, but Oylla lifted her hand from the stone and nodded. "Olivia, tell me everything about your encounter with the killer. Try to describe his spells to me."

"I already told you pretty much everything. He snuck up on Adaida and me in the garden; Adaida saw him coming. When I saw the look in her eyes, the way she stared over my shoulder, I just cast Elemental Form out of reflex."

"You anticipated his attack from a look in Adaida's eyes?" Oylla, someone Olivia had always thought of as a kind of mentor, sounded more skeptical than she would have liked.

"That's right. When I chased Adaida into the garden, I'd already been fearing the worst. It seemed like the perfect place for an ambush, for a killer to hang out."

"You chased her?" Oylla raised an eyebrow, and Olivia heard Carlu's breathing slow, almost stop, as he waited for her response.

"Damn it, Professor! We were arguing, and she stormed off. I'd promised not to let her wander alone, so I feared—rightly—the worst!" Olivia couldn't help the frustration in her voice or how her shoulders, and probably her head, started to flicker with ghostly blue flames.

"Relax, Olivia," Oylla said. "I'm sorry if my questions seem harsh, but I'm trying to get to the bottom of things." Her voice was soft, and she spread her hands out, palms down on her desk, almost like she was speaking to a dangerous animal, which had the effect of throwing tinder on Olivia's smoldering irritation.

"Relax? I was attacked in the gardens of this school! My classmates are being slaughtered! Adaida's fingers were cut off! I'm done *relaxing*, dammit! Get me this spell and let me go put this killer down!" Olivia heard the anger in her voice, the frustration, and knew it wasn't really all about the killer. She'd been emotional and frustrated even without his appearance. She wanted to scream, wanted to ask Oylla, Carlu, anyone, what she was supposed to tell Bronwyn.

She felt tears start to spring up in her eyes, and she scrubbed them away with an irritated growl.

"Olivia, you will not be rushing after the killer as soon as we prepare this spell. Is that understood?" Oylla asked, leaning forward, her star-filled eyes growing bright. Olivia didn't respond immediately, so she continued. "When we're done, you will scry out this person, and we'll go together, the three of us. Now answer me, is that understood?"

"Yes," Olivia replied softly. She couldn't argue with those words; surely, the three of them would have an easier time, and Olivia was just happy to not be sidelined.

Just then, after a quick knock, the door was opened, and Alyss strode into the office. She looked at Oylla and followed her gaze to Olivia.

Her eyes widened.

"Olivia! I knew you were back, but I didn't realize you'd . . . changed so much. How are you?"

"You'll have to spend some time catching up later, Professor," Oylla interjected. "We've a bit of an emergency on our hands." She stood, pulling a chair from against the wall over to her desk, next to Carlu's. "Please sit down."

Alyss looked from Oylla to Olivia to Inspector Carlu, still furiously scribbling in his notebook, then shrugged and sat down. "Am I in some kind of trouble?" she asked in a small voice, and Olivia couldn't help the snort of laughter which escaped her.

"Of course not, Professor!" Oylla exclaimed. "Why would you ask that?"

"Well, everyone seemed so serious, and I saw the inspector here, and . . ." she trailed off, cleared her throat, and continued, "It doesn't matter, Professor. What can I help with tonight?"

"Olivia's had a run-in with the killer, and we need your help to modify Carlu's scrying spell. She's going to track him based on a strong sense of his Energy."

"Excuse me? *Olivia's* going to track him?"

"Yes, but we'll be with her, of course."

"I think I should also accompany her! This isn't exactly a safe activity for a student!" Alyss said, and Carlu grunted in agreement while he worked.

"Alyss, Olivia Bennet could utterly dominate most of the professors at this institution. She'll be fine."

Olivia had never heard Oylla speak so frankly about her power. She'd hinted at Olivia being stronger than most students and having more raw potential than many professors, but to have her say that she could *dominate* most of the professors gave her a strange, torn sensation. She wanted to be proud, but she felt a sort of shame instead. It almost felt like she was an imposter. What had she done to earn such power? Was she really as strong as Oylla thought?

"Really?" Alyss glanced at Olivia, at the flames that still flickered along her shoulders and on her head like a blue, living crown. "I'll come along in any case. I insist."

"Almost done here," Carlu informed, and for the first time, Olivia noticed how fast his quill was flicking over the page of his notebook. If the marks he was making were accurate, then he had quite a talent for scribing.

"Was anyone else harmed?" Alyss asked, looking up from Carlu's work.

"Adaida, but I think she'll be all right," Olivia answered.

"So he didn't get anyone? That's good news, at least!" Her orange eyes widened as she breathed a sigh of relief. "I didn't want to hear that we'd lost another student with tomorrow's announcements."

"I don't want him to get anyone else, either," Olivia said. "That's why I have to do something. I got a really good feel for his Energy, Alyss. I can still taste it, like a cold, sickly oil on my tongue."

"Tut, Olivia—that's professor ap'Rall to you." Oylla narrowed her eyes at her, and Olivia realized she wanted to keep Olivia's familiarity with her and Alyss between them.

She still didn't completely understand the decorum and power structure at the academy, but the more she learned, the stranger it all seemed. Everyone seemed to keep secrets from each other, and that thought made her realize that it was part of the problem with catching the killer. None of the professors seemed to wholly understand what any other professor was up to.

"Finished!" Carlu announced, rubbing at his strange, red-flecked green eyes blearily as he looked up.

"Good, please hand it to Professor ap'Rall. Professor, we want to modify this scrying spell so that Olivia can focus on the sensation the Energy of our target has given her."

"I gathered as much. Let's see here. Can you describe how the spell normally works, Inspector?"

"Yes, normally the caster would focus on the person, and this spell would create a trail of Energy visible to the caster leading to the target."

"Mm-hmm, yes. This is perfect. I'll just need to change this section here which provides the target. Oylla, do you have a copy of *Karn's Energy Divinations*?" Alyss looked up, squinting at the bookshelves behind Oylla.

"Not here, but I'm sure I do in my study. One minute, Alyss." Oylla stood and stepped through a sliding pocket door at the side of her office. Alyss looked at Olivia and reached out a hand to take hers.

"Are you okay, Olivia? This can't be easy!"

"I'm fine, Al—Professor," Olivia said, mustering a smile.

Oylla strode back into the room, then, and handed Alyss a thin, black-bound book.

"Yes, this is it." Alyss flipped through the pages. "He wrote a spell which was supposed to help find residual Energy in a person who'd had their Core damaged. I think I can take a part, modify it, and add it to the inspector's spell. Yes! Here it is."

Alyss scooted up to Oylla's desk, ripped a fresh page from Carlu's notebook, and began writing a spell pattern. Olivia wanted to watch, wanted to see the process as she modified the spell, so she leaned forward and observed as the diminutive professor painstakingly worked out the spell.

Alyss was quick with her work but very precise, and her artistic ability was far beyond anything Olivia could muster. She added shading to empty portions of the pattern, and some of her lines looked like they were written in three dimensions, making the whole thing sort of seem to lift off the page as Olivia watched. "This is beautiful," she breathed, leaning forward to watch.

"Professor ap'Rall has quite a talent for spell design. If you went to more of her classes, you'd be learning a thing or two, I'm sure," Oylla said archly.

Olivia flinched at the words and glared at the powerful Shadeni, wondering if she was putting on some sort of show for Alyss, Carlu, or both.

"It's almost like people and events are conspiring to keep me from your classes, Professor," Olivia spoke, still glaring at Oylla. To her relief, both professors smiled at her words, though Oylla struggled to control her lips. She turned her gaze back to Alyss's work and watched as the woman seamlessly began to incorporate a modified portion of the spell from the textbook into Carlu's spell. Oylla might have been teasing her, but she couldn't disagree; she'd learn a lot if she spent more time with Alyss.

Either a few minutes or an hour later—Olivia couldn't have been more accurate in her assessment than that, so absorbed was she in Alyss's process—the professor finished and set her quill down. "That's it. I'm quite sure it will work, though if you can build the spell in your pathways but it doesn't pulse with Energy, it will mean I've made a mistake. Are you ready to try?" She looked at Olivia, her eyes saying much more than her words. She was worried and would be willing to support her if Olivia wanted out of this.

"Yes, I'm ready," Olivia said, reaching for the spell.

No one else in the room spoke or objected, and she held the pattern in front of herself, studying every line, angle, and whorl. She'd already been doing so while Alyss worked, so she had a good, general understanding of the shape, but all the little details would take a few minutes to get right in her pathways. Still, it was a masterfully designed pattern, and she could easily understand the gist of the spell.

Olivia closed her eyes and teased a thread of wind-attuned Energy from her Core. She wasn't sure why she chose wind; perhaps because she felt like it had a natural predilection for searching and finding things, and she could imagine its tendrils poking around corners and tracing over clues.

She built the first part of the pattern, then opened her eyes, holding the tendril in place with her prodigious will. After memorizing the next section, she closed them again and repeated the process.

A few moments later, she said, "I'm about halfway there."

"Halfway?" Alyss said. "Ancestors, Olivia, what's your will attribute up to?"

"Nearly two hundred," she muttered, closing her eyes to complete another section of the puzzle.

If she'd been paying attention, she'd have seen the other three in the room exchanging looks and Oylla nodding smugly at Alyss. Not five minutes later, Olivia finished the pattern and was rewarded by a pulse of Energy in her pathway as the spell formed before the System confirmed what she already knew:

\*\*\***Congratulations! You have learned the spell: Hunt Energy—Basic.**\*\*\*

\*\*\***Hunt Energy—Basic: Casting this spell while concentrating on a well-known Energy signature will create an animated breeze, visible to the caster, that hunts for the source of the target Energy. Energy cost: 400. Cooldown: Medium.**\*\*\*

Olivia grinned broadly, concentrated on the dirty feeling of the killer's Energy, then allowed her Core to flood the pattern, finishing the spell. From the periphery of her vision, she saw magenta swirls of air rush into view, whipping around the room before slipping under the door. She stood up and rushed toward the door, shouting, "Come on! They're on the hunt!"

## OLIVIA

Olivia burst through the door, the professors and inspector on her heels, and ran down the corridor, the tails of her magenta hunting winds just in sight as they whipped around the corner.

"Can you see them?" she called over her shoulder, face flushed with excitement and the high that always accompanied the surge of Energy from casting a new spell.

"No!" Carlu replied.

"The spell is designed to let you see the trail, not others," Alyss added, breathless from trying to keep up with the much longer-legged Olivia.

Olivia hurried after her winds, wondering if they'd truly leave her behind if she didn't try to keep pace, but not wanting to risk testing it. They flew down a set of stairs, then another long corridor, and then underneath a door which Olivia had never been through. When she pulled on the handle, it was locked.

"Stand aside," Oylla said, producing a key that glimmered with red and silver motes of Energy. She tapped it on the handle, and the door *clicked* as it unlocked. Olivia pulled it open, and a small room with a narrow descending stair greeted her. One of her magenta breezes was swirling around the top of the stairs, and when she approached, it whooshed down the steps.

"It waited for me!" Olivia laughed, hurrying down the narrow stairway. It ended after twenty or thirty steps in a cramped stone tunnel with a dozen or so brass pipes lining its ceiling. Olivia had to duck as she stepped off the stairs.

"Olivia! I know you're excited about the spell, but you must be cautious. These maintenance tunnels aren't frequently traversed, and we could come upon our quarry," Oylla said, a bright orb of yellow light flaring to life near her head.

"Right," Olivia replied. "I can see my hunting breeze swirling around a junction about fifty feet ahead."

"You used air-attuned Energy? Interesting . . . and clever!" Alyss nodded her approval. Olivia smiled at her professor before hurrying down the corridor, now brightly illuminated by Oylla's spell.

At the junction, she turned to the right, following her churning breezes, and soon they came upon another locked door, this one made of iron and rusted around the edges.

Carlu cleared his throat and spoke up. "When I conducted my survey of the grounds, I wasn't shown this door."

"The academy is a very big place, Inspector," Oylla said, stepping forward with her magical key. She tapped it on the door's handle, and its bolt noisily slid open. "We showed you more than many of the board members wanted to."

Olivia tugged the door open and was pleased to see her brightly colored gust of air swirling around a circular stone staircase that descended yet again. It had no railing, and the stones looked damp and patched with mold. "Where does this go?" she asked, gingerly stepping into the small, circular room, afraid she might slip into the open stairwell.

"Ancestors know," Oylla replied. "I've not been this deep beneath the academy in ages, and never via this stairwell."

"Watch your step," Olivia told the others, suddenly remembering her magical boots and the fact that she wouldn't even notice if the steps were slippery. With that foreknowledge, she strode confidently down the narrow, damp steps, following the winding curve of the open stairwell. She didn't want to look over the edge for fear of triggering some sort of vertigo, but just then, a sputtering red light fell down the shaft, illuminating its depths.

The red light bounced and sizzled as it fell into a puddle at the bottom, and Olivia reckoned they were about halfway down.

"Carlu, it's nice to see what's down there, but if the killer had been lurking, you'd have given away the chase," Oylla said.

"I think our progress is noisy enough to belay such worries," he replied.

Olivia quickened her pace, taking two steps at a time, enjoying the confidence her boots gave her. "Don't hurry!" she called back. "I have magical boots! I won't go far ahead."

"Olivia! Stay in sight!" Alyss answered from quite a ways behind her. Olivia splashed down into the puddle where Carlu's red flare sputtered, sending up steam and smoke. The stairway was shaped like it was following the inside of a deep well, and the room at the bottom was round to match. A low tunnel, seemingly carved into the stone of the mountain, led away, and Olivia could see her magenta breezes swirling around in the tunnel about fifty yards ahead.

She crouched, summoned an orb of crackling plasma and, holding it before her, started into the tunnel. She'd made it about halfway to her hunting winds when Oylla called after her, "Olivia! Wait for us."

Olivia wanted to hurry. Her heart raced with excitement, and she guessed it was the feeling everyone who ever talked about "the thrill of the hunt" must have meant. She forced herself to calm down and stop, waiting patiently for Oylla and the others to catch up.

"Glad you waited," Alyss said from behind Oylla. The petite professor hardly had to duck to be in the tunnel, whereas Oylla and Olivia were nearly bent double. Carlu crouched in the back, looking a bit out of sorts though still maintaining his usual decorum. He reached up to press his spectacles into place and nodded as Olivia made eye contact with him.

"Are we all ready, then?" she asked. "My winds are swirling around something about thirty feet ahead."

"Yes, for the love of knowledge, please hurry. My back can't take this tunnel much longer," Oylla hissed.

Olivia nodded in sympathy and turned to hurry forward, her boots splashing in the thin layer of water on the stone. When she caught up to her breezes, swirling and swooping in the air, she saw that a round, metallic door had stopped them. It reminded her of an airlock door you might see on an old ship or submarine. The metal wasn't iron; it had more of a dull gray appearance, and there wasn't any sign of oxidation. She reached forward and gave the wheel at its center a tug, but it didn't move.

"What's this?" Oylla said as she approached, straightening up in the wider space before the large metal door.

Olivia shrugged and pointed. "It's locked. Will your key work?"

"Let me see." Oylla pulled out her sparkling key again and tapped it on the wheel, but nothing happened other than some sparks flying off the key and it clicking against the metal. "This isn't an academy door. Someone added it without the knowledge of the board. At least without all of the board's knowledge."

"Let me try," requested Carlu, stepping forward. "I know a spell or three for getting into places criminals don't want me poking around." Olivia watched and listened as he tried one spell after another, his hands glowing with his brand of silvery Energy, and she wondered what his affinity was. After around five minutes, however, he backed up, shaking his head. "No luck. It's warded rather powerfully."

"All right. Back up," Oylla-dak said, pulling her shoulders back and motioning for the three others to move into the tunnel. "I don't like to use this affinity, but I have a spell which might breach this door."

Olivia followed Alyss into the tunnel, Carlu close behind, and as they crouched down, watching Oylla, she asked, "What affinity is she talking about?"

"She has an affinity with abyssal Energy. She rarely uses it, focusing on the pure portion of her Core."

"Abyssal?" Olivia raised an eyebrow.

"It's not well understood, but the Energy found at great depths beneath the earth or deep in the trenches of the oceans gains characteristics which are more destructive than normal Energy. I believe your professor found her Energy affinity while exploring a cave system under the World Breaker Mountains to the north," Carlu replied before Alyss had a chance.

"Earth," Olivia echoed, once again noting the use of the term despite their world being called Fanwath. She wondered if he was using a different word, but the System Language Integration made her hear "earth." Before she could ask another question, Oylla hissed, holding out her hands to form a ball of blazing violet-tinged yellow Energy. Olivia couldn't see her face, but Oylla's shoulders were hunched, and chords on her neck stood out with the strain of containing her spell.

A moment later, as the ball of Energy grew bright enough that Olivia had to shield her eyes, Oylla screamed, and a beam of blazing Energy surged toward the metal door. Olivia watched, between squinted eyelids, as it smashed into the door and seemed to be absorbed by the metal. The entire surface of the barrier began to glow with heat, and just as Olivia thought it might break or burst or melt to slag, Oylla's spell ended, and she fell forward in exhaustion.

Alyss rushed toward her in the heat and light of the glowing doorway and helped Oylla to stand. "Are you all right?"

"I'm fine; it's just an exhausting spell. Whenever I work with the abyssal Energy, I feel hungover for days." Oylla stared at the door, her starlight eyes narrowed in frustration, and said, "If it could absorb that much Energy, I don't know if we can get through. At least not without assembling a full cohort of professors."

"Why don't you let me give it a try?" Olivia stepped out of the tunnel, straightening up.

"Olivia, I know you have some destructive spells, but I don't think you can match what I just threw at that door." Oylla squeezed her shoulder. "I'll make sure you're present when we attempt again."

Olivia reached into her storage ring and pulled out her Crown of Nightmarch. "I know I don't have more power than you normally, Oylla. This crown lets me do something rather extreme once per day, though. Why don't you step back into the tunnel, please."

"Ancestors! Olivia, I can feel the Energy in that crown from here!" Alyss exclaimed, allowing Oylla to drape an arm over her shoulders.

"Yes, it's quite an item. I've only used it once, and . . . well, it was like riding a lightning bolt."

Olivia lifted the crown to her head, smiling at the familiar, comforting weight. She'd worn the thing for a rather long while in the dungeon; she felt stronger, more powerful, and more prepared when it was on her head, and wished she had the confidence to wear it all the time, even around the academy. She briefly imagined her cohort's reaction to her strutting around with a crown, and when she pictured Adaida, the smile on her face faltered. What had she gotten herself into with her?

"Olivia, be careful," Oylla warned, allowing Alyss to guide her back into the tunnel where Carlu still watched, thoughtfully regarding Olivia and her crown.

Olivia tuned them and their low, whispered conversation out, focusing on the metal door. She contemplated using Pyrosteam Drill, but she didn't want to punch a hole in the door. She wanted it gone. "Plasma Wave it is," she said, priming the spell in the pathway nearest her Core. Before, when she'd used the crown to destroy the boss monster that had been about to crush Bronwyn, she'd acted in a sort of reflex.

Olivia's heart raced suddenly, and panic made her stomach flutter. Could just the thought of Bronwyn do that to her?

No, it wasn't Bronwyn who did it. It was Olivia's betrayal. How was she going to explain that she'd been away from her for just a few days and had already been so disloyal, already developed doubts about her feelings for the beautiful, funny, brave woman?

"Are you all right, Olivia?" Alyss asked, jerking her out of her introspection.

"Yes, just bracing myself. Stay back. It's going to get very hot in here."

Olivia took a deep breath and stretched her hands out, mentally feeling for the additional pathway the Crown of Nightmarch built as a bridge to her when she wore it. When she cast her spell, she channeled it through the crown and back into herself, now massively magnified, before firing it out at her target, just as she usually would.

Olivia had seen news stories about flash floods and how water surged down dry gullies to sweep away bridges and cars. That was what her Plasma Wave was like as it erupted into the air before her. It was a crackling, superheated torrent that smashed into the metal door and nearly instantly filled its Energy-absorbing qualities to bursting. The door flared from red to orange to yellow to blinding white in just a second, and then it was gone, blown to shreds of glowing metal droplets in the fury of Olivia's onslaught.

As her spell ended, Olivia heard a high-pitched, keening wail and realized she was screaming. She fell to her knees, breathing heavily, her vision blotted out by the white afterimage of her spell, and her pathways scoured and raw from the torrent of Energy she'd channeled. Still, she felt better than the first time she'd done it, and she wondered if it was something that would continue to get easier. Was she damaging herself, or was she making herself stronger?

These thoughts raced through her mind as she knelt there, but then she felt hands on her shoulders and her companions' soft, distant voices, and she allowed them to help her stand. When she blinked her eyes and the bright image of her spell began to fade, she realized there was a System message in her vision:

\*\*\*Congratulations! You have learned the spell: Plasma Wave—Advanced.\*\*\*

\*\*\*Plasma Wave—Advanced: Prerequisite: Affinity—Fire, Affinity—Air. You conjure forth a surging wave of pure plasma. Your experience with overcharging this spell has allowed you to create more destructive and malleable plasma than usual. Energy cost: 300. Cooldown: Minimal.\*\*\*

"That's nice," she said, reading the description of her spell improvement.

"Olivia?" Oylla asked, gripping her chin and turning her eyes up to her face. "Are you all right? Ancestors! I've never seen a person channel that much Energy!"

"I'm fine, thank you, Professor," she replied, allowing Carlu to help her to her feet. "My spell improved from Basic to Advanced. I was just reading the description."

"You cleared the path, Olivia," Alyss said, peering through the space where the door used to be. Splatters of molten metal, still glowing from the heat and ticking like a thousand little clocks as they cooled, coated the tunnel for the next thirty feet or so. Beyond that, Olivia could see flickering blue lights.

"That blue—it's the same as the killer's Energy." Olivia stepped forward, an orb of plasma floating before her. She'd summoned it so effortlessly that it was almost like taking a step or flexing a muscle. "I'm sure he's running. Come on!"

## ॐ OLIVIA ॐ

When Olivia, the two professors, and the inspector made it to the flickering blue lights at the end of the tunnel, they found a stone-walled room, bereft of inhabitants but full of objects.

"Damn it!" Olivia hissed, peering into the room with its flickering sconces, overturned tables, and messy cot but no sign of her quarry. "Why would my spell lead me here? It was supposed to target his Energy!"

"And it did," Carlu replied, approaching her. "Please stay in the corridor while I examine this space." He took one step into the room, then produced his clockworklike goggles with their intricate lenses and put them on. Olivia glanced at Oylla and Alyss, and they both nodded encouragingly. If something could be found in the room, Carlu would find it.

"Patience, Olivia," Oylla said, her eyes lingering on the crown that Olivia still wore.

"I'm sure your spell worked," Alyss encouraged. "How else would we be here? Do you see the state of this room? I think the killer was here and rushed to depart or hide. Hopefully, he's hiding somehow, and Carlu will sniff him out!"

"Right."

She nodded and watched the inspector work. He slowly scanned the room, looking left to right and top to bottom, frequently switching the lenses he looked through. Olivia could hear them, standing this close to him; they hummed and buzzed and clicked, and she wondered what sorts of clues they were revealing.

After several minutes of standing in the doorway, Carlu advanced into the room, cautioning the others to stay back. He reached into a pouch and hurled a fistful of white dust into the air. As it floated out in a cloud, it shimmered and spread and fell in an unnatural flat plane, like a blanket, covering every inch of the room. Again, Carlu spent several minutes scanning with his goggles, flicking through various lenses.

It wasn't Olivia who ran out of patience. Sometime after ten or fifteen minutes, Oylla-dak said, "Inspector, have you found anything at all?"

"Oh yes!" He turned back to the trio standing in the doorway. "You can come in now. I'm just double-checking my findings."

"Well?" Oylla asked, striding up to the smaller man and looming over him.

"There is residue from a teleportation spell. I'm afraid it was rather sophisticated work, and I cannot discern the destination, though it seems to have been stored in an object—the Energy signature is very different from the killer's." He indicated the flickering blue sconces.

"Damn it!" Olivia barked for the second time.

"Don't despair, Miss Bennet," Carlu said. "You've put the scoundrel on the run, and he's had to leave a great many clues behind. Why, with a few days' study of these objects, I do not doubt I'll be able to truly scry him out. It's only a matter of time now 'til he's brought to heel."

"A matter of time?" Olivia growled. "How many deaths will there be in that time? How many students' lives cut short?"

"I'm in agreement with Olivia's frustration," Oylla interjected. "However, I recognize it's time for you to do your work, Inspector. Olivia, you've been a great help tonight; let's let the expert take it from here."

"I'm really not happy to just walk away. I need this creep to be stopped, Oylla! After what he did to Adaida, what he tried to do? I won't be able to rest." Olivia made to walk further into the room, heading to an overturned table where broken glassware and some stained parchments littered the floor.

"I'm sorry, Olivia," Oylla said, putting a firm hand on her shoulder. "I'll have to insist. Leave this to the inspector and me, and if there's anything we need help with—another massive door that needs melting, for instance—we'll call upon you. Thank you." She exerted a bit more pressure on Olivia's shoulder, steering her toward the doorway. Olivia didn't resist; she couldn't exactly fight Oylla-dak so she could stay. "Alyss, please walk with Olivia back to her dormitory."

"Of course, Professor." Alyss reached out to take Olivia's wrist and gently tugged her toward the tunnel. "You've done a lot, Olivia. Time to trust in the professor and the inspector, all right?"

"It's not really all right, no," she replied, though she allowed Alyss to guide her away down the tunnel. "We were so close!"

"We were, and now we're closer still. I think Inspector Carlu is well skilled in divination. He has enough of the killer's belongings now that he'll be able to sus him out."

"I hope he does it before someone else dies."

"Do you really think the killer will strike again? After we came so close? I feel he's probably on the run. If it were me, I'd seek out a City Stone and travel off-world! Assuming he has the funds, that is."

"Do you think he'll do that? Will we lose any chance at justice?"

"The empire has long arms, and Carlu has a network of investigators he can call upon. I think there's an excellent chance that this killer will be run down." Alyss, who still held Olivia's wrist, let go as they approached the spiral stairs leading up. "You go first. I'd hate to fall on you."

"Really, Alyss? You're not going to fall. Come on," Olivia urged the smaller, older woman to start climbing. "If you stumble, I'll catch you."

"If you're sure," she said, heading up.

"I'm sure. These boots make it almost impossible for me to slip or stumble, and you'd have to really work at it to knock me down," Olivia explained as she followed the woman up the narrow, slippery steps. Alyss did slip a couple of times, but Olivia was quick to steady her, and soon, they were walking through the upper tunnels and out into the main hallways of the academy.

"You really don't need to escort me, Alyss."

"Nonsense. I'll walk with you to your hallway. My quarters aren't very far from there."

She didn't give Olivia a chance to argue, leading the way through the quiet, dimly lit hallways. After they'd climbed the stairs to the second level, she turned to Olivia. "You should keep that crown on, Olivia. If, however unlikely it might be, the killer tries you again, I'd like to hear that you melted him into a puddle."

Olivia had almost forgotten the crown was on her head, and she reached up to touch it self-consciously. "Well, I need to keep it out of my ring for a day, at least, so it can recharge."

"Right." Alyss nodded, and Olivia thought she saw something like relief in the woman's eyes. "Well, do so! Wear it all the time. If another student tries to trouble you about it, send them my way."

"It's not that I think they'll give me trouble," Olivia said, her face flushing a little at the silliness of her concern. "It just . . . well, it seems presumptuous to wear a crown around. I'm not a princess or something!"

"Olivia, that's absurd. You have a potent artifact there; one which you earned! There are plenty of students at this academy decked in magical equipment that someone handed to them. You'll wear that crown, and you'll do so proudly. Do you hear me?" Alyss, walking beside Olivia now, reached up and squeezed her arm in emphasis.

"Well, if you're saying I have to, then what can I do? I won't argue with my favorite professor!" Olivia smiled and nodded.

"Good! Am I, though? Still your professor, I mean? Have you spoken to Oylla about your schedule?"

"Well, I still have to choose a mentor, but she said I'd be able to continue with your course and Sange—um, Professor ap'Rek's."

"Oh, that's wonderful! I have so much I want to teach you and so many questions I'd like to ask! Will you come tomorrow? You should!" Again, Alyss squeezed her arm, still holding it above the elbow.

"Yes, Alyss. I'll be there." Olivia slowed and pointed. "That's my hallway. Thanks for walking with me, Professor."

Alyss nodded and, somewhat reluctantly, let go of Olivia's arm. "Very well. Tomorrow, then, Olivia."

Olivia waved then started down her hallway, glancing back once to see Alyss still watching her. The woman had on a pensive, quizzical expression, and Olivia couldn't figure out what to make of her. In her opinion, Alyss had certainly been acting strange, but was she really good at noticing things like that? She knew the professor well, had spent a lot of one-on-one time with her, and had never felt the woman act so . . . clingy.

She decided to chalk it up to Alyss being overprotective and worried about Olivia. They'd certainly been involved in some dangerous matters that night.

When Olivia walked into the dormitory, she was swarmed by her cohort members. Before she could utter a word, Shani practically screamed, "What happened? They won't let us into the infirmary!"

"Oh God, Shani! I'm sorry! I should have insisted someone come and explain everything to you guys! Adaida is fine. She got hurt by the killer, but then I—"

"Hurt how?" Rald interrupted.

"It's true, then; you ran into the killer?" Veena asked at the same time. Hanwol sat at the foot of Olivia's bed, the one closest to the door, clenching his hands closed and open repeatedly, his eyes distant. Olivia stopped what she was about to say, looked at her stressed-out cohort, and opened her arms, pulling Shani into a hug.

"Adaida's fine! Nurse Tyliste fixed her up. I'll tell you everything, but that's the first thing you all should know." She pushed Shani back, looked into her big eyes and the smears of tears and makeup on her cheeks, and continued, "Come on. Let's all sit down, and I'll start at the beginning."

She pulled the Ghelli along with her, walking to the couches. Rald and the others followed.

Sometime later, after she'd told them the story of the killer attacking her and Adaida in the garden but leaving out the stuff that happened prior to that, she paused to answer questions.

"So you just blasted him with spells until he ran?" Hanwol's eyes were bright with excitement, and he looked into the distance as though picturing it.

"Her fingers?" Shani asked.

"You haven't said what the story is with that crown," Rald said.

"Then what happened?" Veena pressed, urging her to ignore the others.

"All right, all right," Olivia said. "Yes, her fingers, but don't worry! I carried her to the infirmary, and Nurse Tyliste fixed them." She turned to Rald. "This crown is an artifact I found in a dungeon. I used it to help me melt a doorway that the killer was hiding behind." She held up a hand, forestalling another question. "Let me start at the beginning! So, when I was standing in the infirmary, watching Tyliste work on Adaida's hand, Professor Oylla-dak came into the room, and you should have seen her face! Poor Inspector Carlu was trailing behind her..."

An hour later, once she'd finished the story and everyone was yawning and out of questions, Veena suggested they all get some sleep. Olivia nodded and added, "Yes! We should be rested tomorrow so we can help Adaida. I'm sure the nurse will release her for classes, and we'll want to be able to keep things positive for her. I hate that the killer got away tonight, but Professor ap'Rall thinks he's probably on the run for good."

"Okay," Shani said, nodding to the others. "Let's sleep. Can anyone put a ward on the door?"

"I've learned a good one," Veena said. "It'll make the sound of a barking hound if anyone opens it."

"Can you teach me how to do that, Veena?" Olivia asked.

"Of course, come and watch me," she replied.

Olivia smiled and followed the diminutive woman, marveling at how the thought of learning something new about Energy and its uses seemed to banish her exhaustion.

As they walked to the door, Veena pulled out her Energy-powered pyrography pen. "First, you need to have a way to burn some runes into the door. It doesn't matter how small they are, either. You can put wards on doors that are almost impossible to spot..."

## BRONWYN

Bronwyn looked down at the nest of blankets and the furry, raggedly panting form within, and her heart tore. "Oh, Soft-fur! What's happened to you?" She knelt and took the Urghat's soft, hot hand, gently rubbing her thumb against the fur on the back of her knuckles and looking into her eyes. They were bleary and bloodshot, and her soft, yellow-brown irises were cloudy and obscured by puslike fluid.

"Underclaw?" Soft-fur said in a scratchy voice, the black flesh of her lips barely parting beneath her damp, tan fur.

"It's me, Soft-fur! I didn't know you were so sick! I'm here to help you, okay? I'm going to help you get where you need to go."

"The Energy, Underclaw, it's so hot! It's burning me. I have to get it out . . ." she rasped, her voice trailing off as she closed her eyes and let her head fall back into her furs.

"She can't speak for long," said Whitestar, reaching a large, clawed hand to Bronwyn's shoulder. "You should let her sleep now."

"She can't last long like this!" Bronwyn exclaimed, standing up to face Whitestar.

"That's right! Why do you think I'm pushing so hard to take back the Hollows? But each day, while we fight, I lose good Urghat. How many lives is Soft-fur worth?"

"It's not just about her life, though. You said the Energy she was building up needed to go into the Well in order to maintain your traditions!"

"Yes, that's true, and that's why I can keep my Urghat trying, despite our losses. Still, we're not making progress as fast as we need to." She gestured to Soft-fur's fitful slumber and continued, "Come with me, and I'll show you a map."

Bronwyn leaned forward and gently squeezed Soft-fur's paw again, then followed Whitestar out of the little room. Soft-fur was in one of six bedrooms with doors opening directly into the longhouse, and when they walked out, she saw Cal drinking and laughing with Ironhide and Shadoweye, a large steaming platter of meat between them. Whitestar didn't spare them a glance, however, walking to the far end of the hall and through another wooden door.

When Bronwyn caught up to her, Whitestar was leaning over a large square table with a map spread over it. It was drawn in charcoal, but it was detailed enough and skillfully shaded in a way that gave depth to the page. Whitestar pointed to a square between some hills and said, "This is where we are." Bronwyn nodded, and the Urghat drew one of her long nails from the square through a depiction of trees and then into the shadows of a deep gorge. "Here is the entrance to the Hollows. We have fought our way this far several times, but each time, we're thrown back."

"The trolls have fortifications?" Bronwyn asked.

"No, but the terrain favors defense, and they are savage and strong. They move as though they can see each other's minds. When we kill one, a dozen more come from the nearby tunnels."

"Hmm." Bronwyn wanted to say something about the irony of hearing an Urghat call something else savage, but she held her tongue. She wasn't in the mood for jokes after seeing Soft-fur. "How do they fight? Throw rocks? Jump out from behind trees?"

"They have burrows all along these hillsides, and when we push our way in, fighting off the ones in the trees, they come out and surround us. If we didn't retreat, we'd be cut to pieces."

"Have you killed any?"

"Yes! But they are hard to kill, Underclaw." Whitestar smashed a fist into her palm in frustration, using Bronwyn's title as a way to cover her annoyance, perhaps. "We can kill them in small numbers, but as soon as they begin to congregate, we lose ground."

"I fought a troll once, and I agree; they are hard to kill. I have Energy that suits the purpose, however, so I think I'll go out and take a look for myself. Would that be all right with you?"

"You may be stronger than they are, Bronwyn, but they are fierce and have numbers you wouldn't expect. Don't let them surround you."

"Whitestar, I appreciate your concern, but if we're going to figure this out in time to save Soft-fur, then I think I need to get a look at the problem. Will you keep Cal here and safe?"

"Yes, and I hope you bring back many troll teeth!"

Whitestar held out a hand, and Bronwyn took it, wrapping her long, fae-touched fingers around the strong, wiry hand of the Urghat. She wondered if it was the first time two such bloodlines shook hands. She saw Whitestar's eye narrow, then her lips pulled back from her fangs.

"I think I know what you're thinking. You smell good, Underclaw, but not like meat I should eat. No, the fire is too hot with you, and I think my stomach knows better."

"Good," Bronwyn said, returning the smile. "I'll be back soon, I hope." She didn't wait for a reply, just walked back out to the central hall and straight to the table where the others sat.

"Bronwyn," Cal called, pointing to the platter of cooked meats. "Get yourself some of these ribs! They're falling off the bone!"

"Maybe later, Cal. I'm going to go scout around these Hollows the Urghat are trying to move into. I'll be back later or tomorrow, maybe."

"Oh?" Cal asked while Ironhide scooted back the bench he was sharing with Cal and stood.

"We leave now, Underclaw?" He reached for the axe haft jutting up over his shoulder.

"Not *we*, you old softie. I need you to stay here and keep Cal and Soft-fur safe. I'm going to be moving in a way you can't keep up with, old warrior. Can you accept that?"

"Aye," he grumbled and sat back down. "I knew you'd outgrown my help, Underclaw, but if you say to fight, I'll be there, and I'll have my axe sharp."

"Good. Shadoweye? Don't let him sneak out after me."

"I won't, Underclaw. I'll keep him too full of mead. He's already behind by a full tankard, too." She lifted her mug, and Ironhide's eyes bulged out.

"That's a lie, Underclaw! I've had just as many drinks as this whelp!"

"Hah! Cal, why don't you sing them some drinking songs? I'll see you all later," Bronwyn said, turning to stride toward the doors. She was out before any of them could voice more concerns, and that was how she wanted it. She didn't have a plan, exactly, but she knew she had to get an eye on the Hollows and the trolls protecting them. She couldn't wait because seeing Soft-fur like that had nearly broken her. The innocent little Urghat had never fought or killed anything in her life. She'd been abused from the moment she and her brother had been taken by Goretusk.

The Urghat in the camp regarded her warily as she passed by, but none of them said a word until she strode through the gates leading to the narrow valley where the Hollows lay. "Trolls that way, Underclaw," the lanky, red-furred female Urghat warned.

"Yeah, I know." Bronwyn kept walking, and the Urghat moved aside.

"I saw you fight Ironhide. It was right what you did for him—let him swear to ya," the Urghat said in her scratchy, thick voice.

"Oh? Yeah, he's a good man, Ironhide. He's in camp now; if you know him, you should go say hello." Bronwyn slowed to look at the leather-clad woman. She had a patch over one eye and several long scars on her elongated snout.

"He is? I would like to see him!"

"He's in Whitestar's longhouse. I'm sure he'll be there all evening because he's already drinking."

"Har!" the Urghat barked. "I'll visit him soon. Thanks, Underclaw."

"Yep." Bronwyn waved and continued her steady, long-legged pace downslope into the narrow valley. As she moved past the clearing and into the stunted but heavily leafed trees, she saw the path the Urghat had been clearing and the thousands of stumps they'd left behind in their efforts to thin out the dark forest.

There was a tree that stood out from the others. It was taller and broader, by far, than the trees around it, and its bark was dark and smooth. Its long branches extended out, forming a canopy that blotted out the sun and created a clearing of sorts around its thick, straight trunk. When Bronwyn saw the leaves hanging from those branches, how their blue-white coloring was segmented by their blood-red veins, she heard a voice, deep in her spirit, that said, "Umbrilak."

"How do I know what you're called?" she asked as she walked toward the mighty old tree. No voice answered her, but when she grew nearer and felt the depth of the Energy within, she knew it was something special.

She reached up a palm and rested it on the smooth, dark bark, catching her breath at the sensation of buzzing, stinging electricity under her palm. A moment later, with a wet, ripping sound, the bark parted beneath her skin, and a narrow, deep tunnel lined in the dark wood of the Umbrilak opened before her.

"Wow," Bronwyn said, looking into the deep tunnel. It went on far longer than the tree's diameter should allow, and she knew some sort of dimensional magic was at play. She wondered if she dared enter the tunnel to see where it led when a lilting, distant voice echoed out of it.

"*Daughter,*" the voice called, "*come into the Umbrilak. I must speak with you.*"

"Queen Aestasia?" Bronwyn's voice was trepidatious, almost whispering so as to avoid anyone hearing her. She glanced over her shoulder, suddenly worried that she was being ambushed, but nothing stirred in the thinned-out grove.

"*Come, daughter,*" the queen's voice repeated. Bronwyn felt the familiar compulsion in her gut and knew it really was the queen. She sighed and entered the Umbrilak. Once she'd taken a few steps into the woody interior, she heard the same wet, stretching sound. When she looked over her shoulder, the opening had already closed.

"Lady?" Bronwyn said, walking forward into the tunnel.

"*Just a bit further, daughter. You're almost here.*"

This time, the queen's voice was much stronger, and Bronwyn confidently strode forward. Soon, an expansive space opened before her, and she stepped into a high, round chamber, roughly walled with the wood of the Umbrilak, diffuse sunlight somehow filtering in from above. Queen Aestasia sat on a chair of Umbrilak roots, her legs crossed and her silken, yellow gown falling away from her perfect pale knees.

"I'm sorry to pull you away like this, Bronwyn, my child. I have news which is urgent beyond measure, and I had to guide you to me."

"You guided me to that tree? I thought I stumbled upon it."

"Did you not feel a desperate urge to travel in its direction?" the queen asked with a sly half smile.

"Yes, but I had good reason!"

"The urge was from me, but the motivation was from you. The best sort of compulsion."

"I'd love to talk to you about that!" Bronwyn said, some mettle entering her voice. "You drove me away from Olivia at the worst possible time!"

"I'm sorry, daughter, but at that time, I felt the need to help Cal, and his Urghat friend was of incredible importance." The queen uncrossed her legs and leaned forward, her glittering crystal crown brilliantly reflecting the sunlight coming from above.

"At that time?" Bronwyn asked, noting the way the queen qualified her words.

"That's why you're here now, Bronwyn. Something has changed, and I fear I must ask you to abandon this quest. We cannot allow the Urghat to drive the trolls forth from the Hollows." She stood as she spoke and took a step toward Bronwyn, her eyes reflecting the pain she knew her words would cause.

"That's bullshit!" Bronwyn replied, the words coming unbidden. "I'm sorry, but Soft-fur is dying! You swore you'd never make me do something which caused me pain in my heart! If I don't help Soft-fur, I'll never be able to live with myself!"

"Daughter," the queen spoke, resting her warm, powerful hands on Bronwyn's shoulders. "How proud I am of you! I watch your progress, and my heart sings. Do you think I would ask this of you if it weren't the only way to spare you something worse? Believe me, your *heart* is the only thing driving this change of plans."

"My heart?" Bronwyn asked, wondering at the strange way the queen had emphasized the word.

"Your heart, daughter. Olivia." The queen pulled Bronwyn into her arms then, pressing her tightly in a hug that would have brought comfort if not for the panic racing through Bronwyn's mind.

# ❦ MORGAN ❦

Morgan touched the bronze pad next to the heavy, airtight door made from the same metal and mentally selected the Viewport option beneath the Open option on the menu that appeared in his vision. A large section of the door crackled with electrical Energy and then he could see through it, just as if it were a perfectly clear window. He knew, from testing, that it was a one-way view; on the other side of that door, it was still a solid, magically reinforced bronze barrier.

Inside, the rectangular chamber was walled, floored, and ceilinged in the solid bronze of the tower. Glowing runes stood out on the metal, and Morgan intrinsically knew their purpose: anyone using Energy outside of their body in that chamber would be drained of it. The tower would pull the Energy from their Core and leave them weak and debilitated until the sparse ambient Energy in the cell slowly restored them.

Tkron was slumped in the far-right corner of the cell, obviously drained. He must have ignored Morgan's warnings and tried to turn his Energy against the enclosure. He had fracture lines on his two front spiderlike legs, and Morgan figured he must have been pounding on the door or walls, which were incredibly sturdy. When Morgan had tested them, even Bloodfang hadn't been able to leave a mark.

Morgan glanced down the hallway, wondering why Vormendion had needed six cells like this. "Who am I kidding? I know exactly why he had them."

He shook his head, imagining the experiments Vormendion had conducted on subjects that were most likely quite unwilling. He turned back to the cell in front of him and contemplated Tkron. The Yovashi hadn't been inclined to say anything to Morgan when he'd brought him here. He'd refused to answer any questions, even when Morgan had let some of his Yovashi Bane aura start to bleed forth.

"Let's see how you respond now that you've drained yourself."

Morgan touched the pad again and used the other option to open the door. He stepped through and left the door open behind him. He'd learned that these cell doors operated much like the tower's stairway. If someone without permission attempted to pass them, they'd find themselves walking back into the room they thought they'd exited. The cells had doors because some Energy users had a powerful will or an ability which would make the redirection enchantment ineffective. Tkron wasn't such an individual.

"My tormentor arrives," the Yovashi said, his voice slurred and soft.

"You brought this on yourself," Morgan replied, staring down at the pathetically crumpled form. Tkron's long walking legs were curled up like a dead spider's, and his tentacles were splayed out beneath his torso on the cold, bronze floor. "I can activate a bed for you and some bathing facilities, but first, you need to agree not to try to harm yourself."

"Hah," Tkron coughed, spitting some black blood-tainted phlegm onto the floor. It sizzled and began to dissipate immediately—the cell wouldn't abide a mess. "You'd like a nice, calm pet in your cage, hmm?" the Yovashi asked, glaring at Morgan with his saucerlike, fathomless eyes.

"What's your suggestion, Tkron? What would you have me do with you? Are you able to look objectively at yourself? Can you see your erratic behavior and violence toward your sisters? Do you think those are things I can tolerate?" Morgan leaned forward, aware that the Yovashi could be dangerous but confident that he outmatched Tkron in every way, from speed to strength to raw Energy.

"My suggestion? My suggestion is for you to prostrate yourself before me. Allow me to end your life quickly before you come across a crueler, more powerful member of my species."

Morgan snorted and straightened up. "I'll let you stew on it for a while. Don't worry; I've supplied the cell with protein, and it will dispense a meal for you every eight hours. The toilet and bathing facilities will appear twice a day for twenty minutes. This cell will alert me if you do anything to harm yourself, so please behave. I don't want to spend my time coming to restore your health repeatedly."

Tkron didn't reply, turning his face away from Morgan and clamping his mouth shut. Morgan walked away, and once he'd stepped through the door, he turned and said, "Tkron, when you feel like you can speak to me civilly and work on a solution for your predicament, simply say so. Tiladia will let me know when you're ready to cooperate."

With that, Morgan put his hand on the bronze plate and closed the door. It slid down from its recession in the ceiling and sealed with a *hiss* that smacked of finality to Morgan.

He headed out of the hallway housing all the cells and into the central basement. From this room, a stairway led up to the kitchens, a hallway led to extensive food and wine cellars, and a third one led to the furnace and laundry.

The only hallway with a door on it was the one where he'd left Tkron. Morgan figured Vormendion used to keep a guard posted there because next to the door was an inset alcove housing a little desk and chair.

"Tiladia?" he called.

A moment later, Tiladia swirled into view, seemingly from the stairway leading to the kitchen. "Yes, Morgan?"

"Can you please ask Issa to meet me up in the reliquary? She'll know what it's about."

"Yes, I will," Tiladia said, then sped away up the stairs. Morgan followed after her at a more sedate pace, figuring Issa would take a little while to start on her way. She was with Ykleedra and her sisters; she'd been spending a lot of time with them since the day he had first confronted Tkron.

When Morgan had asked Tiladia about Tkron, about why she'd never told him the male Yovashi was present, the dragon spirit had claimed she'd never been fully aware of him. She said that she'd felt the strange shadowy obstruction to her senses coming from Ykleedra's burrow but had assumed it was something Ykleedra had done to maintain her privacy. Morgan didn't feel worried about the breach in his tower's security; it was a pretty novel and probably unique set of circumstances which had allowed it to happen.

He didn't figure many enemies of his would be able to convince him to allow them access to his home to hide some self-obscuring magical egg which would someday hatch, producing a hidden enemy with memories and motivations already installed.

No, he didn't think this situation would repeat itself.

He walked through the kitchen, now looking much more . . . *used* than when he'd found it. Copper pots and pans hung from hooks above the stove, herbs in bundles were tied to shelves filled with crockery and dishes, and a large cast-iron pan sat on the stove, still dirty from the breakfast he'd cooked for Issa. Morgan smiled, sniffing the bacon and eggs still in the air. He passed through the dining hall to the central stairs, and then, four steps later, he was on the landing leading to the reliquary.

He entered the ample space, nodding to himself when he saw the vast vacant areas where furniture, books, and lab equipment had already been cleared and moved into other parts of the tower. His library was now properly filled with thousands of books, and Morgan had every intention of exploring the volumes as soon as possible. "If I can ever get a few minutes just to relax," he muttered.

Footsteps approaching caught his attention, and he turned to see Issa walking toward him. She wore the engagement ring Morgan had ordered just a few days ago, and when he saw it glittering on her hand, he felt an involuntary smile spreading from ear to ear. Boris had enchanted it in such a way that the gemstone was accessible as a store of Energy for Issa as long as she wore it. It held quite a lot, too—nearly three thousand. When Issa had said it nearly tripled the amount she could usually draw upon, Morgan had been reminded just how different he and Olivia were from the average Energy user.

"So you're ready to deal with this legacy, love?" Issa asked as she leaned up for a kiss.

"Yes, and I think you're going to put up a fight," Morgan replied, letting his forehead linger against hers for a moment after their kiss.

"What do you mean?"

"I mean, I've been thinking about that class and those tomes. I think it's foolish for the same person not to use them all."

"You think you want to take the Artificer class?" Issa asked, frowning.

"No, silly. I'm thinking you should use them all."

Morgan had thought long and hard about the inheritance, and he couldn't think of anyone else he trusted with those abilities. He figured he could possibly see himself allowing Olivia to take them—she'd shown that she could handle immense power without corruption—but, well, Morgan knew how humans could be, and just because Olivia seemed level-headed and reasonable now didn't mean she'd always be so. He supposed the same was true of Issa, but dammit, he loved Issa, and that had to count for something, right?

"I'm a Battle Witch, Morgan," Issa said, her voice soft and her eyes suddenly downcast.

"I want you to know something, Issa," Morgan started. "I thought about this for a long time, and I thought about your feelings. I know your dad wanted you to be an Artificer, and I know it's kind of shitty of me to tell you I want to give you this class because I'm sure it's bringing up all kinds of memories and pressures. So, the first thing I want to assure you of is that I only want you to think about this. I mean, give it a fair chance. Think about the pros and cons; if you decide you don't want it, that's fine. No pressure from me, okay?"

"Then why do you mention it, Morgan?" Issa asked, taking a step back and frowning up at him.

"Because I love you, and I think this is a good option. Will you hear me out?"

"I will listen." She folded her arms in front of herself, still frowning.

"You're almost level twenty, right?"

"Yes, I'm sure I'm just a little cultivation away. Or a kill or two." Her frown turned thoughtful, perhaps seeing where Morgan was going.

"If you took this class, you'd be a Prime Artificer but still have the experiences, attributes, spells, and skills you learned from your time as a Battle Witch. I'm sure you'll level to at least twenty when you learn the skill and spell in the inheritance. That means you'll be offered another refinement almost immediately! You might get some exciting options with all you've been through, *plus* the Prime Artificer class!"

Issa was silent for a long time, rubbing her chin and pacing away from Morgan in a slow, circular walk. When she returned to him, she nodded, her face serious and her voice slightly tremulous. "You are a smart man, Morgan. It's good that I love you." She grabbed him about the waist and squeezed him tight, her arms crossing beneath his wings.

"Will you be angry if you don't get a class refinement that interests you?" Morgan asked, breathing deeply of her flower-scented hair.

"I won't be angry," she said into his chest. "I would be lying if I didn't say the class had interested me. I was stubborn, avoiding saying I wanted it because of how I acted in the past with my father."

Morgan pushed her back so he could see her face. "Really?"

"Yes. I can't keep up with you adventuring. I need a new way to advance, to increase my strength. For our family and our people, I need to be strong. I think this inheritance will help me achieve it, and I can work here, in our home, with our children."

"I . . ." Morgan started to answer, started to say some placating nonsense about how she could still go with him or how he could stay home, but he knew it was bullshit. He'd chosen his path, and he knew he could be called away for any number of reasons. While he'd been in the dungeon with Bronwyn and Olivia, he'd imagined battling some of those creatures with Issa and had been struggling with the realization that he couldn't—no, didn't *want* to face dangers like that with her. Now that they were going to have children? He couldn't imagine it. He revised his words and said, "It's not fair."

"What?" Issa looked at him, confused, like he hadn't understood her words.

"Why are you the one who has to give up adventuring? You wanted it as much as I did—maybe more. I can stay with the kids, you know." He wasn't sure what made him say that. Was he trying to say the "correct" thing? Did he really mean it?

He realized he did. He'd be perfectly damn fine staying home with their kids and dealing with town issues. He knew what Issa would say, however, before she said it.

"It's not your fault that the Ancestors"—she tapped on his chest—"blessed you with such gifts. You gain levels quickly. You have powerful Energy and a class which isn't suited to sitting at home. Morgan, your gifts are wasted if you don't use them. You can become a great champion for your people, and it's your duty to do so. For us," she said, pulling his hand to her belly. "It's the same reason I'm going to take this inheritance, and I'm going to make the most of it.

"Come," she continued, still holding his hand and pulling him toward the inner vault. "I want you with me when I go through this."

Morgan couldn't think of a proper argument, so he just shut his mouth, held Issa's hand, and thanked the Ancestors who had guided him to her so long ago in the Crucible.

# MORGAN

Morgan watched as Issa lifted the box from the first niche in the inner vault and set it on the pedestal where the Vormendion bust used to rest. The box was made of dark, grainy wood, beautifully crafted, and nearly seamless where the boards joined. When she pressed down on the cover, it clicked and then lifted on tiny brass-colored hydraulic arms, exposing a velour interior on which a heavy-looking leather-bound tome sat.

The tome was unadorned save for an elaborately written *V* and the numeral One. "How uncharacteristically unpretentious. I mean, he still included a *V*, but he didn't write something like *Vormendion's Stupendous Inheritance Manual Number One*." Morgan chuckled, but Issa seemed too nervous to see the humor in his words. "Hey, don't worry about it. Look at it like a dungeon reward."

"It's not, though. It's from a mysterious ancient mage with questionable morality." Issa frowned down at the book.

"You know, I never thought about it that way. Do you think this book could mess with you somehow?" Morgan asked, stepping closer. Issa looked at him and smiled, opening the front cover of the tome.

"Don't worry, Morgan. I'm sure it's fine. Vormendion was working with the System in some regard when he made this inheritance, which is why you got the quest for it. I doubt the rewards would be cursed." She flipped the page, and her eyes unfocused as she stared at the symbols on the paper.

"Cursed?!" Morgan exclaimed, but she wasn't listening to him. His excitement had turned to dread as he watched her stare at the page and then saw the dense, glowing glyphs start to lift from the book and flood toward her eyes. Hundreds of characters poured into her, the page turned as if blown by a breeze, and hundreds more started streaming toward her faster and faster. The pages continued to turn, also at an increasing pace, until they were flipping one after the other, and a dense flood of symbols poured into Issa.

Morgan watched, unable to breathe from the stress, and several moments later, the flood tapered off, leaving Issa blinking rapidly and leaning forward, hands gripping the edges of the pedestal. Morgan gently rubbed her back and said, "Everything all right?"

"Yes, just . . . a lot," Issa answered haltingly. She reached up and started touching the air in front of her face, and he realized she was reading through System notifications. "It replaced my class, but I still have my skills and spells from Battle Witch. The tome granted me four Artisan skills and two spells, Morgan! And there are sections for me to read at every tier up to seven!"

"Well, that's pretty good, isn't it?"

"It's amazing! I feel like I know so much. I want to get into a workshop and try out some of these concepts!" Issa's eyes were still distant as she finished reading through her System messages. "I didn't think about how it would be suddenly having nineteen levels in a new class! Morgan, I understand things I didn't even know I wanted to know . . . I can't explain it!"

"Well, how do you feel about those?" Morgan gestured to the other inheritance boxes, and as Issa's eyes followed the motion, they widened with excitement.

"Yes! I understand so many concepts related to the creation of highly cognizant objects and tools. I'm very curious to see how Vormendion's spells work. I want to learn how to help Tiladia!"

"All right, let's do the skill first?" Morgan asked.

"No, I feel it's important to learn them in the order that Vormendion placed them in the inheritance. I'm not sure how I know that, but I feel like some concepts from the spell are important for fully learning that skill."

Issa started toward the shelves, placing the box with the class tome back in its place before lifting out the second box.

"Really? I thought the two skills weren't related to the class, but it seems like maybe they are?" Morgan mused, voicing his thoughts as a question.

"I don't think the class is necessary, but I think anyone learning these two skills would certainly benefit from being an Artisan of some type. I also don't think it would have harmed anything to learn the skill before the spell, but I think I'll gain more this way." Issa lifted a similarly bound book out of the second box, this one with a numeral Two next to the *V*.

"You sure you're ready?" Morgan asked, a little unnerved by Issa's sudden enthusiasm.

"Yes, Morgan! Don't worry!"

Before he could question her further, she opened the book and started reading the runes on the page. The way her eyes darted from side to side made Morgan wonder if she could actually read them now rather than just staring at them while waiting for the magic to work. In just a moment or two, brightly glowing runes were streaming into Issa's bright, yellow irises.

Once the stream faded away, a different sort of light started to gather around Issa. Bright golden motes of Energy began to form in the air, then they flowed into her. Issa stood up straight, receiving the influx of Energy as it flooded into her chest, and when it ended, her face was aglow with the usual euphoria following an Energy surge. With unfocused eyes, Issa waved her hand in front of her face, obviously reading more System messages. She blearily focused her eyes on Morgan and said, "Level."

"Is that all you're going to say? What else?"

"The spell is amazing, Morgan. It's a dozen times more complicated than anything I learned as a Battle Witch. Also, I can't believe how many attribute points I gained having this epic class! I mean, I know what you told me about your class, but it's still hard to grasp! I'm not looking at my class selection options until I learn the skill, though. I don't know if they're already set or if I can influence the options still, but I want to learn it first, anyway. Do you think that's wise?"

Morgan released a long breath he didn't realize he'd been holding. He was immeasurably relieved that Issa had calmed down enough to ask him his opinion. She'd seemed so manic and voracious that he'd begun to worry if the new class had altered her personality in some way, but it seemed the flood of Energy had balanced her out a bit.

"Excitement," he said to himself, nodding, then he looked into Issa's eyes. "Yeah, why not? Learn the skill before you look at the options."

Issa closed the spell book and put it back in its case. "It's empty now, but I'll put it back on the shelf for now, all right?"

"Yeah, sure." Morgan watched as she carefully placed the beautiful wooden box back in its niche before lifting out the third box. The skill tome she grabbed from inside was twice as thick as the spell tome had been. When Issa held it in her hands, she looked at Morgan, demonstrating its heft by lifting it up and down with a grin.

"There's a lot in here, Morgan. More than just a simple skill. I think it will lay many foundations for concepts needed to craft amazing vessels for spirits like Tiladia. I think this is the skill that Vormendion used to make all of his guardians too."

"Yeah, but we still agree that it's not okay to do things like that, right? I mean, with unwilling or even unknowing spirits?"

"Yes, of course, Morgan! Just because I appreciate the knowledge and the skills required doesn't mean I think what Vormendion did with them was okay!" Issa frowned at him, but then she set the book down and moved closer to Morgan, reaching out to take his hand. "I'm sorry, love. I'm sorry if I'm acting crazy. I just . . . I never thought I'd be so excited to learn these sorts of things. I'm so happy I didn't make a mistake and refuse. Morgan, I have a million things I want to try to do. I have a thousand things I want to craft for you, for our family, for our home!" She lifted Morgan's hand and kissed his knuckles, smiling impishly.

"Oh, well, you should know by now that this is the best way to get me to do or say anything you want." Morgan laughed, leaning over to kiss her forehead. "All right, go learn that skill."

"Thank you, Morgan. Thank you for everything," she said, turning back to the pedestal and opening the leather cover of the book. A moment later, she was gripping the sides of the pedestal while a stream of brilliant runes and symbols held her transfixed as they flooded into her eyes. This tome took more than twice as long to divulge its secrets, and when the runes finally trickled away to nothing, Issa fell forward, gasping while holding herself steady on the bronze pillar.

"You all right?" Morgan asked, rushing over to rub her back gently.

"Yes, just—" She was cut off by a torrent of large Energy motes coalescing around her before smashing into her from every angle, not even forming a stream first. Issa shook and groaned, and her smile fell away as she gasped, her eyes rolling back in her head.

"Issa?" Morgan asked, concerned only because he'd seen her level and gain Energy many times and hadn't seen a reaction this strong from her.

"I'm okay!" she gasped. "I'm okay. It's just . . . it's just so much." She stumbled back toward the wall, and Morgan followed, holding one of her wrists as she slid down to sit on the cool bronze floor of the inner vault.

"Maybe we should have spread this process out over a few days, hmm? Look at me, Issa. Let me see your eyes." Issa had been shaking her head slowly back and forth, looking at the ground between her knees, but when Morgan asked her to, she looked up and focused on him. Once they made eye contact, Morgan squatting before her and holding her shoulders, she steadied and took a deep breath.

"I'm all right, but you might be right! This is an awful lot for one day. Morgan, I feel like my mind has expanded so much. I understand so many concepts, and I feel so sure about how to do so much! It's . . . it's hard to explain. This tome I just learned had so much more than a skill in it. It had all the underlying prerequisite abilities. Morgan, I could carve a lifelike bust of you out of solid bronze, just like that Vormendion bust."

"God, please don't." Morgan laughed, gently rubbing Issa's shoulders.

"I won't," she breathed with an exhausted but pleased smile. "I leveled again, too, and now I have a class refinement to look at!" She shook her head ruefully.

"No. Let's hold off on that, all right? I'd like you to rest a bit, hmm?" He stood and closed the now blank tome, putting it back in its box and then into the niche from which it came. "Come on. Let's go get some lunch, and then we'll see how you're feeling. All right?"

He looked back at Issa and saw she was glassy-eyed, looking at System messages.

"Hmm?" she asked absently. "Just a sec, Morgan. I'm reading these messages."

Morgan sighed heavily, realizing she hadn't heard a word he'd said. He supposed he couldn't be angry or annoyed—would he have waited to go and have lunch if he had something so exciting happening to him?

"Well, maybe," he muttered, "but it would have to be a pretty good lunch, and I'd need to be hungry."

Again, Issa said, "Hmm?" but didn't look up, scanning through messages that Morgan couldn't see. He sat down with a sigh, half splaying his wings out in the odd fashion he'd learned was the only comfortable way for him to sit on the floor, and waited.

When her eyes finally refocused, staring into his, they twinkled and gleamed as she said, "One of my options is legendary, Morgan!"

# MORGAN

"Heartsong Artisan, hmm?" Morgan mused, taking another bite of Alec's "famous" meatloaf. He'd managed to get Issa to come up for air and a bite to eat before deciding for sure what class refinement to take. They sat in a rear booth at Green's Tavern, eating the special of the day. It had been rather hard to resist Alec's new hire, an infectiously jovial Cadwalli who had wandered into First Landing looking for work. He'd claimed to be from west of Tarn's Crossing, from a village near the Great Marsh.

"That's right. It says my experience *putting my heart into my chants*, combined with my Artificer abilities and knowledge has opened this path for me." The corner of Issa's mouth was smeared with grease and Alec's very popular homemade ketchup, and Morgan smiled at the earnest, excited look in her eyes when she spoke about the class option.

"God, you're cute," he said, receiving a scowl in response.

"Be serious!"

"It sounds like the best option, Issa. I don't see a downside, at least. I mean, you're going to receive more attribute points from a legendary class, and I can only imagine the amazing things you'll learn to do."

"I know, Morgan! I already know so much! The things I learned from Vormendion's class tome and then from the two abilities . . . it's like I have a million things going through my mind which I want to go work on all the time. I'm even struggling to sit still here and eat this delicious loaf!"

"Well, that's wonderful, Issa, but please don't tell me you're going to turn into some sort of mad scientist in your lab, forgetting about your boring old husband and children, right?"

"Husband? I don't think I have one of those . . ." Issa laughed at Morgan's stricken expression.

"Seriously! Let's talk about that for a moment. Do you really want a traditional wedding based on my culture? What about yours?"

"Weddings are small affairs among my people, a family ceremony that's not binding in any sort of legal sense. I wasn't really interested in the whole thing at all until Bronwyn teased me about when the wedding was."

"Bronwyn!" Morgan growled jokingly, smacking a fist into his palm.

"Hah! It's a good thing she did so because when I started asking her about your traditions and then spoke to some other people here, I realized I simply couldn't live without a big ceremony!" Issa laughed, licking her fork as she studied Morgan's face for a reaction.

"That means we need to invite your friends and family," Morgan said, his face turning serious. "You must have some cousins or distant relatives, no?"

"Yes, of course. I have fourteen people I'd like to invite from Tarn's. That's enough, don't you think?"

"Yeah, I think I'll struggle to come up with that many. You know I don't have any family here, right?"

"Oh, nonsense! Half of First Landing will want to come see you get married!"

"Yeah, I guess. Should we do it outside? We can have the reception in the tower." Morgan looked up, his eyes going glassy as he imagined the scene—big pavilions, lots of music and dancing, magical fireworks. He laughed and shook his head. "I'm getting excited now. This will be great, Issa."

"Of course it will! Let's not get too ahead of ourselves, though. We have a lot of planning to do, and I still need to have a dress crafted. Oh! Maybe I can make it myself! Of course, it'll need to be enchanted so I don't look pregnant!"

"Oh God! Who told you that? You can look pregnant if you want!" Morgan sighed, planting his forehead into his palm.

"No one did! Don't you think I know what looks good in a dress?" Issa tsked and shook her head, wiping her face with her napkin. "Now, silly man, I'm going to go somewhere quiet and take this class refinement, and then I'm going to begin work on my first project. Can you guess what it will be?"

"Something nice for the man who loves you?" Morgan grinned.

"In a way. I'm going to help the poor spirit that's been ensorcelled to help you in the tower. I'm going to craft her a body with more capabilities. I'll include her too, let her tell me what she wants."

"Really? You're ready for something like that already?"

"I have the skills and knowledge to do it, yes. I hope my new class refinement will give me further tools to make it even better." She slid out of the booth and stood up, leaning to give Morgan a kiss on the cheek. "Come visit the workshop later. I'll tell you all about it."

Morgan wanted to say he'd go with her, that he'd keep her company while she took the class refinement, but he got the feeling she wanted some peace and quiet for the process, so he just smiled and nodded.

"I'll be up in a few hours, all right?"

"Perfect! That'll give me time to interview Tiladia. By the way, will you stop and get more meat for the children?"

"Yeah. Already, hmm?" Morgan knew she was talking about Ykleedra and her sisters.

"Yes, they prefer small game to fowl," Issa said over her shoulder as she made her way out of the tavern. Morgan sighed and motioned for Grus, the new Cadwalli server, to come over. He wasn't necessarily hungry, but he could go for another helping of meatloaf.

"Before you ask," Tanna ap'Cilla said as Gella walked into her workshop, "I'm almost finished. Another day and I'll have the final ward stone."

Gella took a moment to compose himself before he replied. He looked around the workspace, noting the long bench behind Tanna covered with all manner of crafting paraphernalia and debris. He saw smelting pots, snips for cutting metal, fragments of carved stone, and a hundred other remnants from her activities.

"Do you think they'll work?" Gella asked for the hundredth time. He knew it irritated Tanna, but he couldn't help it. Everything was riding on this operation. He'd been getting increasingly hostile communications from ap'Gravin, and he knew he'd be ruined if he didn't return to Gelica in success.

"You didn't just ask me that again, did you?" Tanna glared at him over the top of her workbench. She didn't look any better than Gella felt. Her hair was pulled back in a sweat-stained leather band, her eyes were red and bleary, and the white apron she wore while working on projects was stained with oils, food, sweat, and Ancestors knew what else. She'd been toiling night and day for nearly a week on these stones.

"I'm sorry, but you know what ap'Gravin's like. I just finished speaking to him, and I'm telling you, we'll all be working in the mines if we don't pull this off." The memory sent a shudder down Gella's spine. Ap'Gravin had been livid, as usual, but his threats had been far more specific than the norm. He'd even brought up Gella's son in Persi Gables and how he relied on the apprenticeship that ap'Gravin had arranged.

"Oh, I don't know about that," Tanna said softly while she carefully carved a rune into the side of the slatelike gray stone before her. "Airship captains aren't so hard to come by, but a tier-four Storm Sorceress with ten levels of rune-carving experience? I think I'll pull through this alright, even if you bungle everything. As for my colleagues, they can rot, especially Finneal. That man has been nothing but a hindrance." She blew some stone dust away as she finished speaking.

"If I bungle? I wouldn't be so sure about things, Tanna. Haku-dak is convinced that ap'Gravin will be the least of your troubles if your wards don't hold that man in his tower."

"Perhaps this isn't the best plan, then. Perhaps we should be working on taking him unawares—killing him outright?" Tanna smirked because this conversation had already played out a dozen times among the tier fours and Gella.

"You know it's too risky. We don't know enough about him, and he's had his guard up ever since that dinner. He rarely even comes out of that tower. When he does, it's in the middle of the day, and he's constantly looking around like he's hoping someone will do something untoward!"

It was true. Gella had people watching the tower, watching for Morgan, at all hours. Just the other day, they'd seen him sitting in the sun, then, according to reports, he'd erupted into flight, jumping through space with his potent Energy as though responding to some sort of threat. Gella's man had claimed that Morgan had traveled from the hilltop to his tower faster than a person could count to five.

"You mean Finneal and Haku-dak are afraid to fight him openly. Don't mince words with me, Captain," Tanna said, standing up to roll her neck with a sigh. "Halfway done with this side." She gestured to the slate she'd been carefully carving.

"May I?" Gella asked, moving around the bench to look more closely at her work. She rarely spoke about what she was doing, and he'd taken the statement of her progress as an invitation of sorts. He knew it was hopeful. He knew she would likely scream at him for encroaching on her space or curse him for rushing her again. Still, his heart was a demanding master, and it often put him into compromising positions. Why would that stop now?

Over the weeks, he'd come to learn that Tanna ap'Cilla's bark was a lot worse than her bite, and while she'd openly tell Finneal to get away from her, she rarely dismissed Gella. She was acerbic, yes, but seemed to tolerate his presence much more than the others. Was he deluding himself? Did he think he had some sort of a chance with the woman? Perhaps, but he was a man who enjoyed his delusions. It was conceivable, he mused, that in her exhausted, stressed state of composure, he might win some favor by uttering something as simple as a soft compliment. "Your work is exquisite!"

Gella leaned over the dense, black slate, admiring the glittering silver-red runes that Tanna had been carving in neat, tiny lines upon its surface. She stayed still, not pulling back from his nearness, and she even let her arm linger on the bench when his ever so slightly brushed up against it.

The faint touch was like an electric shock to Gella, and the hairs stood up on the back of his neck in his excitement. Bloody Ancestors! He wanted so badly to reach out and grasp her hand, to pull her into his embrace. His fear of her reaction, his fear of *her*, kept him still, however, hardly daring to breathe while he stood next to her.

"Well?" she asked, breathing the word next to his ear so her hot breath tickled over his flesh.

Gella panicked, then, wondering what she was referring to, and he sputtered, trying to think of the proper response. "Um, well . . ." he began to babble before, to his horror and abject glee, she ran a warm, pale-blue finger over his hairy forearm. Again, it was like lightning ran through his body, and he felt all of himself respond to the touch.

"Well?" she asked again, this time speaking so close to his ear that he felt her lips brush against it.

"Uh . . . well, what?" he choked out, barely able to form the words in the shudder of anticipation that ran through his body.

"Well, are you going to do anything about this?" she said, pressing her lithe, warm body against his side as she spoke into his neck, her hot breath making his flesh contract and convulse in pleasure.

Gella gripped the workbench, his muscles tingling and spasming as blood rushed into his ears in a thunderous avalanche. When he finally managed to speak, he realized she'd moved away from him to the door and was giggling as she slipped out, leaving him there, shuddering with unspent urges.

## BRONWYN

Bronwyn pushed against the queen's hips, trying to get out of her embrace, and though Aestasia's arms were strong and resisted her at first, she felt them give and release, and Bronwyn pulled away. She looked up into the impossible perfection of the Summer Queen's eyes and said, "What does any of this have to do with Olivia? What do you mean?"

Aestasia frowned, somehow becoming more beautiful with the show of emotion. "Is it not enough that I warn you? That I tell you to do this in order to benefit your love?"

"No! If I can't understand the reason, I won't be able to live with myself. If it means killing Soft-fur, maybe I don't deserve love all that much." Bronwyn felt tears spring into her eyes at her suddenly fatalistic thoughts.

"I will explain then, but only because I favor you greatly, daughter." She reached out a hand, and Bronwyn took it. Standing there, looking up into the queen's eyes, she couldn't help but marvel at the warm tingle of fathomless Energy beneath the flesh of those fingers. "When you slew the villain Thun, you corrected an imbalance on Fanwath. His departure from this plane and your emergence brought us into equilibrium with the Winter Court."

Bronwyn had questions. She wanted to ask what the queen meant by *this plane*, but she held her tongue, waiting for more explanation. The queen continued. "Should you slay the troll matriarch and allow Soft-fur to fulfill her birth quest, it would be a great victory for Summer. I won't explain how, but it is something I want you to do with all my heart."

"Then why shouldn't I?" Bronwyn asked, tears slipping down her cheeks as she pleaded.

"Winter is aware of your presence here, and they have parleyed with me. They've shown me they have an agent in place, working to trap the powerful human, Olivia Bennet. They intend to take her and twist her to their cause. Failing that, they will slay her in a drawn-out, horrific ritual which will ensure her spirit knows no rest. The offer was made: leave the trolls to their business, and their agent will withdraw from the scheme involving Olivia."

The queen spoke softly, matter-of-factly, but her words hit Bronwyn like a hammer.

Bronwyn dropped her gaze, staring at the ground, tears of frustration and despair dripping down her nose to splash against the rich, wooden interior of the Umbrilak tree.

"Is there . . ." she started but shook her head. She wanted to ask if there was any other way, but she knew there wasn't. She was stuck in some sort of a ritual—no, a game that the Summer fae played with the Winter fae. "If you know Olivia's in danger, why won't you help her? Let me help Soft-fur, and you help Olivia."

"Should I do that, what would stop my counterpart from waltzing into First Landing and slaying or taking every human? We have rules for a reason, daughter."

"Isn't there . . ." Bronwyn took a ragged breath, squeezed her eyes tight, brushed the tears away with the back of her hand, and tried again. "Isn't there a chance Olivia will win? That she'll see the trap and destroy the Winter agent? She's strong, Queen Aestasia! She's so much stronger than I am!"

"In terms of raw power, perhaps, but you have some growing to do yet. To answer your question, daughter, there is always a chance. Humans are surprising creatures; it's one of the things we love so much about you." The queen let go of Bronwyn's hand and reached up to grasp the sides of her head, turning her face so they were staring into each other's eyes again. "There is a third option, though it will likely bring you pain. Would you like to hear it?"

"Yes!" Bronwyn replied, desperate for any way out of the dilemma.

"I can bargain for one day. You are of greater value to me than the Winter Court's agent is to them. In that one day, if you can stop the trolls, perhaps by slaying their matriarch, then your friend, Soft-fur, will be saved."

"Really? You can do that?" Bronwyn wanted to rage, wanted to ask why this option wasn't offered to her first, but she just focused on the release of stress. One day. She could do it.

"I can, but there will be a price." The queen's words brought Bronwyn crashing back to the ground.

"What price?" she asked warily.

"I'll be gaining a day while the Winter Court will take their agent off the board immediately. They'll want a price. They'll want you off the board for a time."

"Off the board? This really is a game to you, isn't it?" Bronwyn's emotions were surging, and she couldn't figure out how she should feel. She'd gone from despair to worry to euphoric relief to anger, and with each shift, some of the prior emotions lingered, and she was starting to feel insane. She reached up and pulled at her hair, her eyes red and strained.

"What the fuck have I done?" The thought came out of her mouth, and she focused on it—would any of this be happening if she hadn't made a deal with the fae? If she hadn't agreed to work with them? Would this be happening if she hadn't killed Thun? Was the Winter Court targeting Olivia because of her?

"It's a cruel way to speak, Bronwyn. I'm sorry. We try to maintain a balance, though the heroics or horrors our agents—for lack of a better word—perform can tip the scales for a time. If I strike this bargain, if I allow you a chance to save the Urghat scion while asking the Winter Court to keep their agent at bay, then they'll want a price: both of our agents off the board for a time, mine for much longer."

"How long," Bronwyn asked, her voice a bare whisper.

"Ten years. This isn't what I wanted, Bronwyn."

"So you already explored this option? You already made this bargain? You knew I wouldn't be able to let Soft-fur die?"

"I wanted to come to you with options, child. I'm trying to protect your heart. I feared—no, I knew you wouldn't take the first option. I knew you would rather lose your love than permit a child to die, even one as disparate from you as an Urghat. So I made the best bargain I could. Winter knows how much I value you, Bronwyn. They know I'm losing a great deal by having you leave Fanwath for ten years. Far more than they are losing, believe me."

"And if I leave your service?" Bronwyn sniffed, allowing some of her anger to seep into her voice.

"Then I will lose everything. I will lose a daughter that I love. I will lose my ability to bargain with Winter in this affair, and they'll run amok with their plans. I suppose you could still challenge the troll matriarch, though you'll be much weaker, having lost all you've gained in my service. You could try to race to Olivia to warn her, though it will take days. Even this I cannot help you with—our conversation is made possible because the Umbrilak and I have bent time. Nearly nine days will pass before you walk out of this tunnel."

"What? What the fuck? Nine days? Even if I agree to your *bargain*?" Bronwyn turned, pacing back toward the tunnel she'd come through. She threw her hands up and growled in frustration, turning around and stalking toward the queen.

Queen Aestasia remained still, watching her movements without any hint of judgment. Once Bronwyn stood before her again, she said. "Yes, Winter and I circle each other warily while we bargain. After you and I have spoken, the decision will be made known, and things will commence apace."

"Make it two days," Bronwyn said, sniffing and wiping her eyes a final time. She stood up straight and stared at the queen, daring her to argue.

"Two days?" The queen raised an eyebrow, her eyes unfocused in contemplation, but before Bronwyn could break the silence, she continued, "I can do that, Bronwyn. As payment, I'll need to keep you away from Fanwath longer, but I can arrange it. Why, may I ask, do you want another day?"

"One day to kill this troll matriarch, and another to say goodbye to Olivia. Where will you send me?" Bronwyn almost didn't ask the last part; she almost didn't feel like she deserved to know. She was so angry with herself, so upset that her involvement with the fae was the probable cause for all this trouble, and her heart was torn at the realization that her time with Olivia was almost over. "Over before it started," she muttered as the queen began to answer her.

"If you truly wish to see your love again before you leave, I'll need to help you facilitate that. I will do so." She nodded archly, as if she'd offered to do something utterly benevolent and kind. "As for your other question, I will send you for more training, daughter. I will help you become a great heroine, and when you return, the world will shake with your presence. Winter will rue this price they've extracted from us."

"Well, Arthur, I wish I could say it's been a successful journey for me and the *Skybreaker*, but it looks like we only were able to recruit a handful of your people to come and work with Lord ap'Gravin." Gella stood at the flat area on top of Bronwyn's Hill. He'd asked Arthur to meet him there, preferring not to get bogged down in a lengthy discussion in the council chambers. He wore his uniform and had the collar buttoned smartly, happy that the weather had turned and the sun, though high and bright, wasn't doing much to warm the light chill in the air.

"I'm sorry to hear about your troubles, Captain, but as I told you before, our populace is rather driven to create a successful colony here. We were selected for that purpose on our homeworld, so it doesn't surprise me that most want to stick around. I'm sure you'll have more luck with the next generation! Why, we have quite a few expecting families already!" Arthur hooked his thumbs in his belt and arched his back, stretching it with a slight groan of pleasure as he slowly surveyed the town, a proud father looking at his children as they built sand palaces on the beach.

"Well, Lord ap'Gravin is a very long-lived man, that's true. His vision stretches beyond what I could imagine, and he might very well take you up on that. I, myself, will hopefully be retired before that recruitment drive!" Gella laughed good-naturedly and rubbed at his belly. He'd put on twenty pounds over the last month, eating his stress.

Thank the Ancestors for magically resizing clothing!

"Is there anything the council can do to ease the burden of your empty vessel? We're happy to entertain talks of trade agreements or delegations between your employer and us. I'm sure I could find a representative willing to make the journey with you. Perhaps you needn't leave completely empty-handed . . ."

Arthur trailed off, gazing over Gella's shoulder at the long line of crew hauling crates, sacks, and barrels toward the *Skybreaker's* berth at the northeast tower.

"Ahh, yes. I see you've noticed we're taking on a lot of supplies. I'd like to throw a party for your town, Arthur. Not many of your people have been aboard the ship, though many have expressed interest. We'll be hosting a deckside feast and gala in a few days for any of your people who would like to come by. How does that sound? We'll be hoisting sails and heading home the next day. Come, Arthur; surely you'd like to see what our ship is like. From what I hear, it might not be long before your engineers make one of their own!"

"Hmm." Arthur rubbed his chin with a thoughtful smile. "Why, yes, I think I would enjoy a tour of that vessel! I've heard good things about your kitchens as well!"

# OLIVIA

The morning after Olivia's hunt through the depths of the academy, she was the first to rise, having tossed and turned and slept very little. Her mind kept racing through the many troubling thoughts at its disposal. Why couldn't she get to the killer before he fled? Was he truly running, or was he hiding? Would he strike again? Why were his targets closer and closer to Olivia? Hadn't he been at it while she was away? So why kill someone in her hallway and then attempt to strike her and Adaida directly?

When her mind wasn't chasing after the unanswered questions regarding the killer, it was trying to wring some logic from her feelings about Bronwyn and Adaida. While she couldn't make sense of her heart, she had no trouble coming up with plenty of guilt. She kept running through her mind how she'd speak to Bronwyn, tell her about Adaida, and try to solve her torn feelings based on how Bronwyn responded. None of the imagined conversations went well—Bronwyn was fiery. She was emotional. She did everything with her heart in the open for all to see. Olivia felt like a snake.

She heaved out a heavy sigh and threw her blankets off. The air in her room was chilly, and she saw that one of the bay windows was open a crack. Rald liked cool, fresh air while he slept, preferring to snuggle in his covers than to have to kick them off, as he put it. Olivia tiptoed on the cold planks to the bathroom, where she took a few minutes to get cleaned up and dressed. As she'd promised Alyss, she wore her crown, and its weight was comforting.

When Olivia left the bathroom, mildly surprised that none of her cohort had come in while she'd been getting cleaned up, she found them all clustered around Adaida near the two sofas.

"Hey, Liv," Adaida said, her face rather wan but with a true smile reflected in her big, amber eyes.

Olivia took a step closer, glancing nervously at Shani and Veena, the two sitting closest to Adaida. "Are you feeling better? How are the fingers?"

Adaida held up the hand in question and wiggled her fingers. "They work! Thanks to you, Liv. My ring finger is a little numb right down the center; it's kind of strange, but Nurse Tyliste said it'll clear up as I gain more levels, especially if I advance my race at all."

"That's great, Adaida. Are you going to classes today?" Olivia took a step closer, wanting to take her hand, to look closely at the scars, to kiss them, even. She hesitated, however, and lingered at the periphery, looking over Rald's shoulder as Adaida spoke.

"No, I think I'll stay in the dorm today. The nurse wrote me a pass, and I'm going to take advantage. Maybe you could—"

Adaida was cut off as the door to the hallway burst open, and the sound of dogs barking echoed throughout the dorm room. Oylla-dak stood there, eyes squinted in irritation before she touched the door, and the noise stopped as a cloud of woodsmoke rose into the air.

"Olivia, you need to come with me." Oylla's voice didn't brook argument, and the urgency of her words sent a shiver down Olivia's spine as she hurried toward her.

"What is it? Is it the killer?"

"You all stay here," Oylla ordered, and Olivia realized that her entire cohort, including Adaida, had followed her to the door.

"What's happened?" Rald asked. Olivia had to smile at his protective tone—he'd spoken with a much deeper note than he usually did.

"I'll go with Olivia," Adaida said.

"No, you won't. Every one of you will stay here. This cohort is on lockdown. Any of you so much as poke your heads through that door, and I'll have you expelled. Am I clear?"

Olivia had never seen such anger in Oylla's eyes, even when she'd stormed into the infirmary the night before. She took a step back.

"What's going on, Professor?" She asked, putting some steel of her own into her voice.

"The time for explanations will come. Now, follow me."

She turned and strode out into the hallway with a swirl of her black robes.

Olivia turned to her friends and shrugged. "I'll tell you guys what's going on when I get back. Be careful and stay together!" She spared one last look into Adaida's eyes before she followed after Oylla. The professor was already down the hallway, and Olivia hurried to catch up. "Can't you please tell me what's going on?"

"Olivia," Oylla said, her voice catching slightly, "something terrible has happened."

She shook her head, clearly struggling with what she had to say, and turned down a corridor Olivia hadn't traversed before—it led to the part of the academy where some of the professors and graduate students had private rooms.

"Professor, you're freaking me out!" Olivia hissed, grabbing the tall Shadeni's arm above the elbow and pulling her to a stop, forcing her to face her. To Olivia's horror, there were tears in the powerful woman's eyes, their blue-black depths and glittering starlike lights obscured by the pools of salty liquid.

"I'm sorry, Olivia," Oylla said, shaking her head and reaching out to take her hands. "I don't want you to see this, but the inspector thinks it's important. He thinks there's a message for you in it. Obviously, he's right, but I still don't want you to see it."

"See what, Professor?" she pressed.

"There's been another murder, and this one will hit you hard, Olivia. I'm so sorry. I wish I could spare you from it. I wish I could cancel the semester and, when everything's over and we all come back, tell you that Professor ap'Rall has gone on sabbatical. I thought about that, you know? I almost did it." Her hands were warm and gentle, and as the shock of her words finally resonated in Olivia's mind, she sagged backward. Oylla had to fight to hold her up, moving one hand from her wrists to her waist.

"Alyss . . ." Olivia felt the hot tears pouring down her cheeks, and though a part of her wanted to collapse and cry for real, another part of her noted that the tears weren't just hot—they were like boiled water that turned to vapor nearly as soon as they left her eyes. She focused on that heat and how it came from her center, near her Core. She allowed it to flow through the rest of her, and soon, Oylla was letting go of her and taking several steps back. Olivia was alight with blue, flickering flames that radiated away from her, making the air shimmer.

She looked at Oylla, and the fury blazing in her eyes caused the professor to take another step back. "Where?" Olivia's voice was harsh, distant, reverberating strangely like it was echoing on itself. Oylla-dak thought it sounded like the voice of a fire.

"Follow me, Olivia, but please, don't burn the school down."

She strode down the hallway, took a turn, and stopped before the third door where two black-robed professors Olivia didn't know stood watch. They stepped away when they saw Oylla coming. Olivia struggled to rein in her flames, tried to quell the heat that wanted to explode out of her, burning everything to cinders. By the time she stood before the door at Oylla's shoulder, she'd managed to reduce her aura to pale flickering flames along her shoulders and crown.

Oylla looked back at her and said, "I'm sorry for this, Olivia. Please only look at it as long as you must. See if the message means anything to you, and then we'll get out."

She didn't respond, and Oylla nodded, turning to open the door. Olivia's nostrils were immediately hit with the coppery scent of blood and the unpleasant odor of exposed bowels.

Olivia didn't realize she was doing it, but she cast Elemental Form, taking on the form of fire, and suddenly, the smells were just a distant itch in her nose and easily ignored. Everything took on a sepia tone, and it was with that filter, that bit of distance between herself and reality, that Olivia took in the scene of her favorite professor's murder.

Alyss didn't have extravagant quarters. Inside the door, on the hardwood floors, a round woven rug greeted visitors. A couch sat across from a comfortable, overstuffed leather chair, and a small wooden coffee table stacked with books sat between them. Bookshelves lined the room, and Olivia could see Alyss's bedroom through an open archway. She walked forward and, with Oylla beside her, headed over so she could see into it.

Alyss was in her room. All over it. Entrails, fine bits of flesh, and splattered blood coated every surface except the wall behind the bed. Alyss's head was intact, sitting in the center of the mattress, and one of her pale blue arms was carefully placed next to it. The fingers of her hand were arranged so they pointed to the wall where a bloody message in the absurd form of an acrostic poem had been scrawled on the white plaster. Olivia took a ragged breath, her lungs sounding like a fire being blown by a bellows as she read it:

*Obedient*

*Love,*

*In*

*Vain,*

*I*

*Ache*

"What the hell?" she hissed. The message didn't mean anything to her. Obedient love? The only thought that kept repeating in her mind was that she'd been anything but obedient with her love. "In vain, I ache?" She stepped forward to the bed and gently smoothed Alyss's forehead, squashing the flames in her hand with an effort of will. "Poor Alyss. I'm so sorry this happened to you. I don't know what this means, but I'll figure it out. I'll punish him, Alyss."

"Just so," said a familiar voice, and Olivia whirled to see that Inspector Carlu had come into the room, standing behind Oylla with a strangely out-of-place smile. Olivia thought it looked almost smug. She noticed that Oylla also looked surprised to see the inspector, and that her eyes bore more than a hint of irritation.

"Don't sneak up on people, Carlu," she scolded before stepping forward, reaching toward Olivia but stopping short of touching her flaming arm. "Olivia, let's get out of here. You've seen what the killer left for you, and now you can mull it over in a place far removed from this."

Olivia nodded and headed out of the room. She didn't want to remember Alyss this way, so she didn't look at her again, didn't look at the mess of the room hiding behind the odd tint caused by her Elemental Form. Still, she mulled over the bizarre poem and wondered what it had to do with Alyss. It was undeniable now, to her, to Oylla, to anyone, that the killer was somehow involved with her; that he wanted something from her or wanted to punish her somehow.

As soon as they entered the hallway, Olivia concentrated on her memory of the killer's sickly, cold Energy and cast her Hunt Energy spell. She wanted to hope that it would work and believe that she'd be able to track down the killer, but she wasn't surprised when the winds swirled into being, several individual magenta gusts wafting back and forth in front of her, before promptly dying out.

"Damn it," she said.

"You tried to track his Energy?" Oylla asked.

"Yes."

"I was going to suggest it." Oylla frowned when she realized the inspector had followed them out of the room. "Carlu, shouldn't you be inspecting the crime scene?"

"Oh, I have, Professor. I was hoping to interview Miss Bennet."

"You'll have to hope for something else. Olivia will be with me for the day. Perhaps I'll read your questions to her if you write them up. Come, Olivia." The professor again reached for Olivia's arm but pulled her hand back from the flames. "You could drop that form now, don't you think?"

"Yes," Olivia replied, doing so. She felt distant; felt like she was outside herself. Everything seemed somehow fake or fabricated, even herself.

When she felt her normal aspect return and her vision clarified with the full spectrum of color, she allowed Oylla to guide her down the hallway away from the crime. The only thought that kept playing through her mind was that this couldn't be real.

Nothing felt real.

Even herself.

## OLIVIA

After they left the scene of Alyss's murder, Oylla tried to get Olivia to come with her to her office, but failing that, she urged her to return to her dorm. Olivia argued, saying she wanted to be alone, her voice ringing with the finality of the statement. This led to a rather long and tedious discussion about Olivia's feelings, her fragility, and the fact the killer was obviously targeting her in some way.

"It's not me you should be worried about!" Olivia snapped. "You should be protecting the people that I'm close to. My cohort, for instance! I feel like the more time I spend with anyone—you included, Professor—the more of a target is put on their back!"

"Well, if you won't come with me, and you won't go to your friends, I need you to promise me you'll stay in a public area. I also expect you to check in with me this afternoon when you've had some time to process your feelings." Oylla's face looked sour at the compromise, but Olivia nodded, already turning as she responded.

"I agree to your conditions. I'm going to the library."

As she walked away, Olivia couldn't help comparing how a serial killer on campus would be handled at a university back on Earth to how it was being handled at Fainhallow. There would be crisis counselors, canceled classes, news reports, political intervention; the list went on and on. Things were very different in this world, in this remote mountain academy for training Energy users.

When Olivia arrived at the library, she looked around, seeing her favorite chair and the other students talking in hushed voices over their projects at the widely scattered tables, and a strange, profoundly uncomfortable feeling came over her as she thought about how she'd spent time studying her spellcrafting for Alyss's class in much the same way. Olivia sighed and moved to a chair by one of the bay windows, staring out at the gray fall skies and the cloudy mountaintops outside the distant academy wall.

Olivia had known people who'd died, of course, but something about Alyss's death—no, *murder* was hitting her especially hard. She wondered about the need for her to witness the murder scene. If she were being honest, she thought Oylla had made an error in judgment. There was no need for her to see Alyss that way. Oylla could have broadly described the scene and told her about the ridiculous poem.

"She said Carlu wanted me to see it," Olivia told herself under her breath. "I wish she'd told him to . . ." She sighed and rubbed at her head, seeing no point on that train of thought.

"Obedient love?" she whispered, looking out the window again. Was the poem referring to her? To someone she knew? To the killer? "Who's obedient?"

Was the killer mocking her for pulling away from Adaida in the garden? Surely he'd seen her and Adaida before he attacked. Had he listened to their conversation? Had he watched them kissing? "In vain, I ache?"

Suddenly, her mind turned to Alyss, and she wondered if the poem had been about her. The poor woman's hand had been pointing at it, after all. Had Alyss been in love? Had she obediently avoided acting on it, aching in vain?

"God, did she have feelings for me?" Olivia didn't believe it, and the more she wracked her brain, the more she wondered if the killer was just messing with her mind, trying to make her crazy. "Poor Alyss, were you killed just to get at me?"

If so, Olivia had to wonder why. Why had the killer set his sights on her? Had she always been the intended target of his actions, or had she put herself into his crosshairs when she fought him off in the Alchemy Gardens? She decided it didn't matter. She'd been determined to find and stop him before, but now it was all she would think about. If he wanted her obsessed, then he was going to get it.

Olivia stood and moved to the part of the library where professors' and other scholars' published spell patterns were shelved. There were thousands of volumes, taking up several rows of bookshelves along the far wall of the first floor. Alyss had cautioned her students about delving into those tomes too early or without guidance.

None of them were off-limits, but it was a widely held belief that many of the patterns were inelegant or ill-suited for most people's purposes. Alyss had said they needed a few years of proper basics and a slow ramp-up of understanding before they went exploring through those esoteric books.

"Well, I don't have Alyss to guide me anymore, do I?" she said, eyeing the rows and rows of books. Most were thin, containing what a professor or visiting scholar deemed to be a clever application of Energy or, in some cases, what they viewed to be their greatest work.

Some of the tomes had matching bindings, and she knew they were spells written by the same author over a number of years. Many shelves had empty spots where books were out on loan, but the vast majority were in place, and many were dusty with disuse.

"Poor things. Students too busy learning their curriculum to come looking for more?"

Olivia wanted to learn more magic. She wanted to learn spells like the one Morgan had, allowing a form of teleportation, flight, or anything to make her more mobile. She wanted to learn spells to bind criminals or render them helpless. She wanted to learn magic to find people more effectively or at least differently than her Hunt Energy spell. She wanted a way to put her prodigious Energy pool to use, protecting her without having to take on her Elemental Form. There had to be spells to make shields like the one the killer had used to block her attacks.

Olivia reached up to touch her crown, wishing she'd been wearing it that night in the garden. If she'd ended the killer then and there, Alyss would be teaching her class today.

"All right, where to begin?"

The shelves weren't organized by spell type or Energy affinity. No, they were arranged by authors; alphabetized names that meant absolutely nothing to her. "I need a spell to find the right kinds of spells." Her attempt at humor did nothing to lift her spirits, and she didn't even smile as she ran her finger along the dusty tomes. Not having a better idea, she closed her eyes and walked back and forth along the long, back row of books, allowing her fingertips to brush the spines gently as she passed.

When she felt a slight tingle at the tips of her fingers, either real or imagined, she stopped and pulled out the fat, dusty tome. The cover was black leather with no identifying marks; not even the author's name. She blew off the dust and opened the heavy cover, and after turning the flyleaf, she saw a handwritten note.

*Reader,*

*Within, please find some of my most elegant applications of Energy. Should you enjoy them, I'd appreciate a note letting me know how you used them or if you made any improvements.*

*—Tuzrical of Tharcray*

"All right, Tuzrical. Let's see what you got up to."

Olivia took the heavy tome and walked back through the stacks to the bay window and her favorite chair. She sat down to read, and for the first time in days, her mind didn't wander to thoughts of the killer. She flipped to the first spell pattern, read the description, and flipped to the next. She repeated this process several times, not seeing anything of interest until she'd made it to Tuzrical's seventh spell, something called Flesh Wards.

Olivia's eyes widened as she looked at the diagrams expertly drawn of a humanoid shape with tattoolike markings at key points—one at the throat, one at each wrist, one just above the pubic region, at the base of the belly, and one at each ankle. She read through the text and found that Tuzrical had "perfected" a method for turning a person's flesh into a sort of artificed item, powering the enchantment with Energy in the person's Core.

The following several pages had the main spell pattern with variations for different effects; things like resistance to heat or cold, physical damage, or even enchantments to shrug off decay or acid. The more complicated the pattern for the initial spell, the more complex the corresponding tattoos on the flesh had to be, and the more Energy their maintenance would require. According to Tuzrical, he'd enchanted his flesh to resist blades, and found the Energy draw tolerable, though it did slow his overall recovery rate by nearly twenty percent.

"How badly do I want to make myself resistant to damage? Enough to put tattoos all over my body?" Olivia asked herself as she sketched the patterns in one of her notebooks. She truthfully didn't really care about the tattoos, and the prospect of having passive defenses appealed to her, but to feel safe, she'd want several effects. Could her passive regeneration keep up? Would there be a way to turn them off if she wanted to recover her Energy more quickly?

While copying the various patterns, she started to recognize their similarities, and an understanding of how the spell worked and how it tied into the tattoos, much like a warded item, began to click in her mind. "Tuzrical, I think I see a mistake in your process already," she breathed as she held two patterns up next to each other, one to resist heat and one cold. They were essentially identical, just a tiny section on one pattern was a mirror image of the other.

At first, Olivia couldn't figure out why the mage had created different spells for so many effects. Why create a pattern for cold and another for fire and yet another for decay and so on when you could just make one with a generic resistance to Energy? Then it had occurred to her that not everyone was worried about defending themselves from hostile Energy. Someone might want protection from actual fire or freezing temperatures.

"Well, not me, Tuzrical. I just want to resist hostile spells."

With that in mind, Olivia began to sketch out the spell but altered the specific resistance sections to have only two branches: one to resist hostile Energy and one to guard her flesh from cuts. As she finished sketching the double-pronged pattern and the corresponding glyph tattoos, a thought occurred to her. She altered the part of the spell that would activate the tattoo at her neck and added a third prong, one which would shield her from concussive forces.

Olivia triple-checked her work, comparing her new designs to the ones in Tuzrical's book, and felt confident they'd work.

"The only question is how much Energy these things will draw. Will I cripple myself? Will they draw more Energy than I can maintain?"

She thought about what would happen if that were the case. She'd eventually run out of Energy and be unable to replenish her Core so long as the wards were trying to draw from her. Olivia wondered what would happen then. Would it be like being hobbled, unable to maintain her body because she had no Energy to spare? She figured she could deface the tattoos to ruin the spell, saving herself if it came to that, but she wanted a more elegant solution.

Olivia pulled up her sketches and thought about what she'd learned while studying artificing. She thought about how some items were activated by trickling Energy into them. What if she could design the markings so they didn't work unless she turned them on? All it would take was a small addition to their design, a trigger she had to consciously trip by priming it with a tiny stream of Energy from her Core. When she wanted to turn them off, she could stop the flow of Energy to the trigger. Best of all, if she ran out of Energy, the shutoff would be automatic, and her normal regeneration would resume.

While she made the changes, Olivia wondered if she was acting too hastily. Tuzrical's book was the first one she'd picked up, and she'd only read through the first few of several dozen spells. Did she want to go through this process before exploring more options?

She glanced through the stacks toward the rear wall decked with thousands of spellbooks and realized that if she took the time to be genuinely thorough, the killer would be an old man before she was decided.

*No*, Olivia thought; she needed to learn. She needed to get things done, and this was a good first step. Tuzrical's patterns were elegant, and though she hadn't wanted to use the first few spells she'd read, they'd been quite clever; better than anything in her class texts. She didn't believe in fate, but she certainly had a more open mind about the mysteries of the universe than she did back on Earth. It felt right, somehow, that she'd found Tuzrical's book so quickly.

She still wanted to know more—she needed to find the spells which would help her locate and catch the killer—but this one would make her a lot tougher.

"I'm sorry it won't help you, Alyss, but I hope he tries to stab me again. I'll give him a surprise," Olivia hissed as she stood up, tucking the book under her arm. She walked out of the library, striding purposefully toward the main academy exit. She needed to find a tattoo artist or, failing that, get her hands on a needle and some ink.

# OLIVIA

Olivia had a destination in mind as she walked into the cool, windy air outside the academy. One of the restaurants she and her friends had frequented during her first weeks at the school was managed by a Ghelli woman with bright, lifelike tattoos of flowers on her neck and arms. Olivia remembered asking Veena if they were magical or if they were just drawn by a particularly talented artist, but Veena had scoffed, saying she didn't know anything about tattoos.

"Well, same here, Veena, but I'm going to learn."

The main market square inside the academy walls was bustling, despite the crimes taking place in the school and despite the chilly, windy weather. When Olivia had noticed how so many people were wearing thick, collared cloaks and puffy jackets, she'd looked down at herself, still wearing her magical gray robes, and taken a moment to remember that she didn't feel the elements as a normal person might. She could probably stand naked in a snowstorm and not feel much discomfort thanks to her Elemental Resistance feat. Still, she could *notice* the weather, breathe in the fresh, cool air, and appreciate the change in seasons.

She crossed the square and proceeded up one of the handful of streets inside the walls wide enough to accommodate more than one-way traffic. Soon, she was standing before Nalla's, a simple soup shop boasting a counter for ordering and two rickety wire tables with matching chairs. She remembered how Rald had bent one of them by leaning back in it, and how the rest of them had laughed when he'd fallen on his butt. Olivia didn't smile at the memory; she just frowned and stepped into the shop.

The smells of rich broth and meat being seared at the bottom of a stock pot instantly hit her nose, and Olivia felt saliva gather in her mouth. She swallowed it away, her frown deepening. How could she think of enjoying some soup right now while Alyss was gone, her body defiled as a macabre message?

"Hello, love, need some warming up inside?" Nalla heard the door and came to the counter. She wore a pale blue, long-sleeved shirt under a stained, off-white apron, and her hair was pulled back in a messy bun. Olivia had always liked the breezy nature of the woman, and she allowed herself to smile as she stepped forward.

"Hello, Nalla. No, I'm sorry, but I haven't time to eat right now. I have a question for you which I hope doesn't offend you."

"Oh? Now, that's the most interesting thing a customer has said to me today! Well, out with it, then! Want to know how many lovers I have?"

"*Oh.*" Olivia felt her face redden, and she hurriedly said, "No! I mean, I was just wondering where you got your tattoos done! They're beautiful, and I need some work done . . ."

"Oh, roots! I'm sorry if I embarrassed you, sweetie. My tongue gets away from me sometimes! Now, my tattoos, hmm? I'm sorry, but my artist is back in my hometown: Twilight Home. I know someone here who does work, though, and he's not half bad."

"Really? That would be very helpful, Nalla! Do you think he'd see me today?"

"A big hurry, is it? He does ink work on the side, a way to make extra money, and he's usually eager for a new customer, so I bet he would."

"Well, would you mind giving me his name? Where can I find him?"

"Oh, right, right. His name's Barnt, and you'll find him standing watch at the main gates; he's the big guard who works for the academy."

"Barnt . . ." Olivia said, tracing through her memories, trying to remember the guard at the gates, and then it clicked: the enormous otterlike Vodkin who'd first greeted her. "He's a Vodkin, right?"

"That's right! Don't let his size fool you; he's very clever with those little needles of his!"

Nalla smiled and leaned forward, and Olivia caught a glimpse of her somewhat stunted wings. Adaida's and Shani's were much more prominent, though they had a long way to go to get to Nurse Tyliste's level. She figured Nalla hadn't ever improved her racial rank, and her mind started down an irritatingly unnecessary tangent, wondering just what percentage of people in this world ever saw anything beyond a base-one status. What was the average? Were people with high racial levels like long-lived demigods to the shopkeepers and labor class of the world?

She shook her head, forcing her mind back to reality. "Thank you so much, Nalla. I promise I'll bring my cohort here soon for a big lunch!"

"You're welcome, sweetie. Tell Barnt I'm making a nice meaty stew, would you? He'll probably buy the whole pot, and that's enough to pay the bills for a couple of days!" She laughed and waved as Olivia opened the door.

"I will! See you soon!" Olivia said over her shoulder as she hurried back toward the square before turning down the main avenue toward the gate. The crowds were a little denser as the morning began to turn the corner toward noon, and she had to wend her way around slower-moving groups and a couple of wagons, but soon she saw her target.

Barnt was visible, leaning against the inside of the gate tunnel, from a hundred yards away, and as she got closer, Olivia began to remember why the big man had imprinted on her memory. He was close to seven feet tall, and his girth had to put him at more than four hundred pounds. More than that, he wore an enormous, heavy-looking chain-mail vest, a round pot helm, and boots which looked like they could squash a child into paste. Barnt's thick, sleekly furred arms stood out from his vest, and his hands, decked in fingerless leather gloves, were hooked in his thick, heavy belt by their thumbs. A toothpick large enough that Olivia could imagine using it as a chopstick hung from his black lips, and his whiskers quivered as he smiled at her approach.

"Hello, Miss. Heading out?"

"No, Barnt! I'm here to see you, if you wouldn't mind the interruption," Olivia replied as she stopped just inside the gate tunnel, a few feet from the big man.

"Oh? Did I do something wrong? No! Don't tell me; someone came in that shouldn't have! I knew I shouldn't have given my shift to Venda yesterday! My stomach was bothering me, you see—"

"No, no! Barnt, it's nothing like that! I'm here to ask you a favor!" Olivia interrupted the poor man before he could confess any other imagined sins. "Well, more like to hire you. I'm looking to get some tattoos done."

"Oh, Great Sharks!" Barnt rubbed his forehead like a human might to remove sweat, even if Olivia couldn't see any moisture through his sleek, dark-brown fur. "I don't know why I feel so guilty all the time! It's like I don't belong here as a guard captain; like I should still be serving in the legion, taking orders about what and when to eat, where to march, and how deep to dig the latrines."

"Relax, Barnt. It's called imposter syndrome, and many, many successful people feel that way. I felt that way for much of my career back home. I still feel that way sometimes!"

"Is that right? Really?" Barnt looked down at her, his slightly protruding snout twitching while his lips pulled back in a half smile. "Even someone like you?"

"What do you mean like me? I'm just a person, Captain." Olivia made sure to use his title now that she knew he was a guard captain and was self-conscious.

"Well, I mean someone so successful, with magical artifacts, and, erm . . . well, so lovely and advanced . . ." he trailed off, looking down, and Olivia knew that if she could see his skin under that fur, it would be furiously flushed with embarrassment.

"Oh, hush, Captain! I'm just a student here that's had some good luck in her life. I promise you: I feel inadequate most of the time. Now, how about we forget about our insecurities for a little while and talk business? I need six rather complicated tattoos. I heard from Nalla that you're very good with your needles. Do you think you'd have time to help me today?"

"Oh?" His lips twitched up into a broad smile, revealing his pointy white teeth. "Nalla said that? Have you seen her tattoos? I wish I could make colors like those."

"She *did* say that. Yes, I've seen them, and I don't need anything quite so bright; you also don't have to come up with the pattern; I've already done that. Oh, and before I forget, Nalla was hoping you'd come by to try her new stew. She said it's very meaty."

Barnt clapped his hands together, rubbing the leather half gloves in anticipation. "That's wonderful! I only have to work until noon, Miss, so I'll stop by Nalla's after that. I work the dawn shift because most of my guards like to stay up late and sleep away the morning. They'd never make it in the legion, I can tell you that!"

"My name's Olivia, Captain. Please feel free to call me that. Do you think you'll have time to do my tattoos today?"

"Oh, yes, yes. I can surely get started. I'll need to see the patterns to figure out how long it will take, erm, Olivia."

"I have them here, Captain." She pulled her notebook out of her ring and flipped to the tattoo sketches she'd made in the library. "This page and the ones after it. They're shaped like rings because they need to be drawn around parts of my body."

"Oh, these are lovely. You're a good artist, Olivia. I can't read this language, but they look like fancy letters and, what's the word . . . gleffs?"

"Glyphs, and that's right, Captain Barnt. These are System runes meant to interact with a spell I've designed, so the tattoo has to match the pattern exactly. Do you think you can do that?"

"Easy as eating a pastry, Miss Olivia. I've done more complicated things. I'd show you some of my own work, but I've let my hair grow in over them."

"You have tattoos?" Olivia wasn't sure why she was surprised—he was an artist, after all. She supposed it seemed strange to her because they wouldn't show under his fully furred body.

"Aye. I got started with them in the legion. My unit kept track of our deployments with tattoos. I've got seventeen of those, and then some of us started making art to symbolize some of our best battles. I've thirty-nine of those. Most of them are on my arms, but my mates helped me to put a few real beauties on my back. Here, I've got one I can show you!" Barnt peeled off the glove on his left hand, holding out his dinner plate–size palm so Olivia could see the tattoo on the smooth, furless skin.

The tattoo was simply stunning in its detail and depth. It pictured a pile of skulls on a field littered with broken spears, and in the distance, a crooked stone tower stood before a mist-covered moon. The moon seemed luminescent, and the skulls were not only white but had scraps of decaying flesh upon their bloodstained, real-looking bone surfaces.

"The battle of Rook Tower. Nine thousand legionnaires died on that field, and my unit was sent in to root out the insurrectionists in the tower itself, mostly Shadeni led by a Golemancer. We had to fight some abominations made of flesh and bone, and they didn't want to die, let me tell you!" He chuckled, causing his prodigious belly to bounce up and down under his heavy chain vest as he pulled his hand back.

"That's . . . amazing work, Captain. I think I forget there's a whole empire of people nearby, living in cities and fighting wars. I'm from deep in the frontier."

"Aye, easy to forget about civilization in a world this big, Miss."

"Is a Golemancer what I think it is? An Energy user who creates golems—cognizant or sentient constructs?"

"That's right, and this one had some rather horrible ideas about what a golem should look like and what kinds of body parts he should attach to them. I won't say more than that, Miss Olivia."

"Barnt! How's the day so far?" a new voice asked. Olivia turned to see a short Ardeni woman wearing similar clothing, albeit much smaller, to Barnt's. She had short, buzzed pink hair, and her eyes gleamed out from under her heavy brow with the same color.

"Tash! Is it time already?" Barnt asked over Olivia's head.

"Aye, you're done for the day, Captain. Go get yourself some food! I bet you're hungry. Hello, Miss, I'm Tash," the woman greeted as she stepped closer to Olivia and Barnt.

"Hello. Olivia. So, Captain, does that mean you might be able to get started on my request?"

"Aye, Miss Olivia. Let's get some food in our bellies first, as Tash suggested. I think your job might take me a few hours, and I won't last that long unless I get some sustenance." He rubbed his belly, making his chain vest jingle and clink. Olivia smiled, the first genuine amusement she'd felt since the horror she'd faced so early that same morning, and she nodded.

"All right, Barnt. I can't deny a man his sustenance."

She waved to Tash as Barnt started to lumber up the street to the square. Following him, she noted his rolling gait and the surprisingly agile way in which he stepped around much smaller people. She tried to imagine the horrors he'd faced fighting in distant wars. She tried to imagine the loss of Alyss multiplied by tens or hundreds of dead companions, and she wondered at his ability to carry on with his life.

# MORGAN

"Are you going to attend the *Skybreaker* crew's gala?" Boris asked when Morgan ran into him at the base of his tower's stairway.

"Tomorrow?" Morgan knew exactly what Boris was referring to but asked anyway.

"Yeah, tomorrow night."

"Nah, I don't think I'll go. I had enough of those people when Issa and I had dinner with the captain."

"What if Issa wants to go? It's supposed to be quite a send-off they're throwing for themselves, breaking out supplies they won't need, including some of the captain's own liquor."

"Well, the booze won't interest her, but yeah, she does like a party. We'll see what she says. She's been so busy with her project for Tiladia that we haven't even spoken about it."

"Have you seen her work? God, man! She's talented as hell, and she's using tools and devices in your workshop that the rest of us don't even understand. Here's hoping she'll give us some lessons as she gets less busy!"

"Yeah, she will, I'm sure. You'll also learn some of that stuff just by leveling your class, don't you think?" Morgan leaned against the bronze balustrade, curious to hear Boris's response.

"Oh, no doubt! Depending on if our classes focus on those types of skills. She's the only one I've seen making casts and molds for statue parts!"

"Statue parts? I think maybe I should go see what she's doing; it's been a couple of days." Morgan straightened up and gave Boris a pat on the shoulder. "I'll talk to you later, all right?"

"Yeah, man, of course. See you later. If not here, then at the party!"

Boris laughed and gave him a wink, then turned and continued toward the tower door. Morgan chuckled and stepped onto the staircase, focusing on going to the shop and laboratory on the sixth level. In three steps, he was striding out onto the landing, and the clamor of people working and the smells of various concoctions coming from the lab assaulted his senses.

Morgan figured Issa would be in the workshop, not the alchemy lab, so he turned to the right and walked into that space, his mind reeling from the changes Issa and the earthling artisans had wrought in the last two days.

Workbenches still dominated the center of the vast hall, but Morgan could see and hear the workings of a forge in the far rear corner. An Energy-powered smelter had been set up nearby, and Morgan saw rune-covered steel machines that he had no idea the purpose of, quenching barrels, stacks of ingots, large piles of lumber of all shapes and sizes, and huge chests, likely holding other materials.

He saw table saws, drill presses, and lathes, some of which seemed large enough to craft industrial-scale parts. Morgan whistled in admiration—he'd had no idea there were these many tools up in the reliquary. He'd only opened a few crates, which had primarily held alchemy gear.

"Morgan!" Issa called out from a large workbench near the smelter.

"Hey," he replied, walking toward her. She was positively glowing, her yellow eyes brighter than ever, and her face flushed with excited energy. He knew he was probably projecting a little, knowing she was pregnant and doing something she enjoyed. She was pretty damn beautiful and luminous all the time thanks to her racial advancements, but he thought there was something more to it today.

"I'm so glad you're here, Morgan! I figured out what I want for a wedding present!" She stepped up to him, gripping his wrist and looking up at him with her eyes wide and her smile as mischievous as he'd ever seen it.

"Oh? Seriously? No wonder you were happy to see me! Well? What are your demands, m'lady?" Morgan laughed at her enthusiasm, and he had no concern about what she'd ask—if he had it and she wanted it, then he'd give it to her; there was no question about it.

"Tiladia and I have been working hard designing her a new body. She wants to use silver, and I have enough of that. I used some treasure and also bought some with Energy beads. The problem is, if I want to make a vessel capable of everything I want—you know, showing expression, lifelike movement, self-repair, and most importantly, capable of forming and containing a Core that Tiladia can use to work Energy—I'll need to make the silver into an alloy, and I'll need a powerful natural treasure which I think you have."

"Okay, I have quite a lot of stuff in my ring. What are we looking for?"

"You have a large bar of Amber Ore, right? You also showed me a piece of horn that we both sensed was rich in Energy but didn't know what it was. You still have those, don't you?"

"Well, I have most of the Amber Ore. You're wearing a bit of it on your finger, there." Morgan pointed at her hand, but then he sighed and dug around in his ring for the rest of it. If they ever set a date, he already had the wedding bands ready for their big day, so he lifted out the rest of the heavy, mostly whole bar. He'd learned over the process of having the rings made that this ore was very pure and often cut into an alloy.

"I'm sorry, Morgan! I know you wanted to use this to make a sword of your own. I promise we'll come up with something better someday."

"Yeah, it's okay, Issa. Bloodfang and Heartspark are both in good shape, and I think I have some growing to do before either of them seems inadequate."

He handed her the heavy bar of lustrous orange-yellow metal, then dug around in his ring until he found the hard, polished black horn. It was about six inches in length but only about two wide at its thickest point. Morgan felt the Energy stirring within, knowing it was powerful and would cost a fortune to purchase. Still, he didn't even know what it was or what a person would use it for. He handed it to Issa, and she took it in her hands reverently.

"Sheesh, you already stowed away my Amber Ore?" he teased.

Issa wasn't listening, though, and he felt a little surge of Energy as she cast some sort of analysis spell on the horn. Her smile broadened, displaying her long canines and the sharp teeth behind them. "The horn of a calepsii! It's alive, Morgan, and full of Energy. This will work wonderfully to build Tiladia's Core!"

"It's alive?"

"Yes! Calepsii are a kind of sea serpent. They never stop growing, and if you harvest parts of them, you can use them to create some very potent artifacts—artifacts like a spirit vessel with a living Core!"

"Seriously? I imagine it has other great uses, too . . ." Morgan trailed off, his voice growing wistful. He was teasing; if anyone had suffered enough and deserved this treasure, it was Tiladia. Still, he wanted to milk this situation to earn some points with Issa.

"I'm sorry I'm asking so much, Morgan! But don't you think Tiladia deserves it? She had her real body stolen and was forced to be a slave to an evil wizard! Trapped in this tower for millennia!" Issa's eyes welled with passionate tears, and Morgan instantly felt guilty for making her plead her case, even if he'd been very mild about it.

"Of course, Issa. Of course. I think it's wonderful what you're doing for Tiladia, and I'm so excited to see her. What sort of body did she want, anyway?"

Issa's face crinkled mischievously, and she shook her head. "Uh-uh. Sorry! Tiladia wants it to be a surprise."

"Really? I just figured she'd want to look like a dragon again. I guess if you're making her body out of silver and Amber Ore, it won't be a very big dragon . . ." Morgan imagined a miniature, dog-size silver dragon roaming around his tower, and he grinned at the thought.

"I think you'll be surprised! Also, the body parts won't be solid silver and Amber Ore, just the shell, and the enchantments I'm putting within will allow it to take on a more living aspect. That's why I wanted the ore—it's much more capable in that regard."

"That's very neat, Issa. I didn't know you could do that!"

"Well, I can! I'm halfway done stamping the internal rods with the enchantments, and I've already made the forms to cast the parts. Now I have your ore, and I can start mixing the alloy." She gestured to the nearby smelter.

"Hey, I just had a thought," Morgan said. He'd imagined Tiladia in her dragon form with an actual Core and solid body, and he wondered if she'd even have to stay in the tower anymore. "Will Tiladia still be bound to the tower? Will she be able to leave? Do we need to worry about her going on a murderous dragon rampage of revenge?" Morgan half joked with the last question, but it wasn't a ridiculous fear—Tiladia had been a member of an elder race, and she'd been terribly wronged. What if she had a vendetta that he didn't know about?

"You'll have to release her spirit from the vessel Vormendion has it in—those bits of enchanted glass that swirl around within her misty form. Once you do that and she has her new vessel, then no, there won't be restrictions on her movement. Do you think there should be?" Issa asked the last question with a scowl.

"No, of course not. She should be free! I just voice my worries out loud sometimes."

"Well, I agree. If she wants to seek revenge, the only person in danger is Vormendion, and he's long gone, Morgan. Don't you feel you can trust her? I do!"

"How strong will her new Core be?" Morgan asked, trying a different tack.

"I'm not sure. It could be in the improved ranks because of the strength of that horn, but Morgan, Tiladia won't instantly be all she was when she was a dragon. I'm not sure what level or class she'll even be. She may be at base-zero, even. She might have to level up like a new person. I told her that, and she was fine with it. She wants to be autonomous again. She wants to have a real body and be able to leave this tower when she wants to, but she insisted that she likes us and wants to stay with us—she thinks of us as family and this as her home."

"Well, shit. I can't begrudge her any of that. Take the horn and take my Amber Ore with my blessing. Is there anything else I can do to help? Anything else I can get to make it even better?" Morgan pulled Issa into a hug, feeling emotional all of a sudden.

"No," Issa said into his chest. "I have everything I need. I'm going to make her a vessel which will put any of the ones Vormendion crafted to shame. He didn't have my class, Morgan, and I'm so grateful I got it. I'll be able to sing true life into it! Especially with this horn you gave her. She's going to have a second chance, Morgan!"

"How much longer will it take you?" he asked the top of her head, still squeezing her into his chest, soaking in the warmth of her.

"With these tools and with the abilities I gained from the inheritance? I think I can be finished in less than a week." Issa pushed on his chest, pulling back so she could look into his eyes. "I think we should have a party for her when it's done. I think we should reintroduce her to the people of First Landing. They should know she's a new citizen and a real person."

"Absolutely. We'll do it in a week or so. We can announce our wedding too, don't you think? We can set a date and invite the whole town."

Issa didn't answer, she just slid her arms back around his waist and pulled him into a tight embrace, and Morgan could feel, the way she folded into him, that she was happy.

# MORGAN

The morning after he'd spoken to Issa and given away two, apparently great, treasures to help Tiladia's cause, Maria Rios paid a visit to Morgan's tower. He met her in the little study with the map table, and the two of them sat in the chairs in front of the desk. He hadn't spent much time in that room, but he had the idea it would be nice to fix it up and have someone alter the map to be relevant to this world.

"So, how are things going? I've hardly spoken to you since you've been back!" Maria sipped her coffee, which she'd brought with her, along with a cup for Morgan. It was rich and had a generous splash of cream in it.

"I'll answer that, but first, you have to tell me where you found coffee beans!"

"The Contribution Store. More and more options open up as we advance the town. There are a lot of plants and seeds available from Earth now. Well, let me take that back—they're available from *somewhere*. They could be analogs from very Earthlike planets or things created from the information the System stole from our minds or the ship. Who knows where the System gets the things it puts in the store?"

"Well, it's a pretty nice treat. I used to be an addict; six or eight cups a day."

"Hah, happy to help you feed that particular demon! So, how are things?"

"Um, what do you want to know? Things are hectic! You know about Issa and the babies, right?" Maria nodded, and he continued, "Well, she's been nothing but incredible, but we've decided to get married, and we're talking a lot about the future, so yeah, it takes up a lot of time. Then there's Ykleedra and her sisters . . . and brother. Did you hear about him?"

"Yes, Ykleedra told me all about it. The whole thing is horrifying. I think it's good that you didn't hurt him, but I hope you'll seek guidance from the council and some behavior specialists in the colony about what to do with him. Do you think he can be rehabilitated?"

"I really don't know! I can't get much out of him. Whatever magic his people worked so the males of their species would be born with advanced genetic memories or whatever seems to have made them very emotionally unstable. I appreciate your suggestion, however, and I think that's a great idea. I'll bring it up at the next meeting. Maybe we can get a team of specialists to work with him. We could at least figure out if he's beyond help, if what they've done to themselves is something we can't help."

"I'm glad you're open to the idea. Ykleedra told me something similar about him, about his emotional instability. Speaking of her, Morgan, I'm here to ask your permission about something." Maria set her cup down on the desk and leaned forward.

"Oh?"

"Yeah, I was speaking to that Captain Gella fellow from the big airship. You know about the party they're throwing tonight, right?"

"Oh, I'm sure I've heard about it a time or three." Morgan chuckled.

"You're not going?"

"Nah, things were kind of tense when Issa and I left his last get together, and I'm not really interested in hanging out with those people again. Issa's very wrapped up in a project, too. She told me she was glad to stay home." He shrugged.

"Well, I was speaking to him, and I mentioned that I'd been coming to your tower regularly to give lessons to Ykleedra. He was fascinated at the prospect of a—as he put it—*civilized Yovashi*. He practically begged me to bring her to the party tonight."

Morgan had a sinking feeling; every bad VR he'd watched where someone different was mocked in "polite" society ran through his head. "I don't think that's wise. Those people have very deep-seated feelings about Yovashi. What if they mock her, or worse, what if one of the crew freaks out and attacks her?"

"I think the experience will be good for her, Morgan, and she'll be able to leave anytime she gets uncomfortable. I'll stay by her side the whole time, I promise! Don't you think it would be good for Gella and his crew to see that all Yovashi aren't murderous cannibals? That at least the females shouldn't be hunted to extinction?"

Morgan thought about it, imagining Ykleedra's glee at being on an airship and eating fancy foods among people she admired. It sounded nice, but he was still apprehensive about how the people on the airship would behave. "Gella said he wanted her to come? Did he offer any assurances?"

"Yes, of course! He swore that he'd prepare the crew and that no harm would come to her."

"All right, I'll tell you what: you can take her, but I'd like her home early. How does two hours sound? That should be enough for her to see the sights, sample some things, and be able to leave before everyone starts getting drunk."

"Perfect, Morgan! I agree; that would be just right for her." Maria's face lit up with excitement as she continued, "I'm going to come early so I can help her get ready. She has such beautiful hair, and I love her silver robe, but I wonder if there's something else she'd like to wear!"

"I'm not kidding, Maria. I'll fly over and get her if she's gone more than a couple of hours." Morgan's voice was stern, but he was smiling, imagining Ykleedra sampling hors d'oeuvres. He'd made plenty of mistakes in his life, and he felt like he was making one now, but he trusted Maria and her judgment, so he decided to let go of his paranoia. She had a level head and had done a lot to impress him in the past months.

"I can see you aren't kidding, Morgan, don't worry," she said with a snort. "No need to draw that sword or spread your wings threateningly!"

"Oh, come on! I only do that to bad guys!" Morgan laughed, lifting his coffee mug and taking a sip of the liquid, expecting it to be lukewarm by now but pleasantly surprised it was still hot. "Insulated?" he asked.

"No—enchanted! Get used to it, Morgan. Our people are coming up with all sorts of amazing things!"

Maria left not long after that, and Morgan spent most of the morning practicing his sword forms in the dueling hall. He'd yet to find a sparring partner among the colonists, and he wondered if there was some sort of a job or help-wanted board.

"Is there a newspaper?"

The thought suddenly sprang into his mind, and he had to imagine someone was working on a printing press. As he wiped the sweat from his brow and stowed away his armor, he decided there were too many things he didn't know about First Landing.

He figured his visit with Maria was part of the source for the thought; if they had coffee now and enchanted mugs to keep it hot, what else was he missing? He'd seen plenty of new buildings, from restaurants to clothing stores, and he figured many interesting things were being made and sold that he had no clue about.

"Time to remedy that," he grunted, refastening his belt.

Bloodfang on his hip, he strode down the steps and out of his tower, walking purposefully toward Bronwyn's Hill. If anyone could fill him in on the current projects and achievements of the people of First Landing, it was Alec Green. He knew just about everything about everyone, from their favorite drink to whom they spent the night sleeping beside.

Morgan laughed as he caught himself walking over the grassy field between his tower and the town proper. "What am I doing?" he chuckled as his wings cracked out, and he launched himself into the air.

"You placed them?" Finneal asked Tanna as they watched the tall, winged warrior fly toward the town center.

"Yes. The wards are buried around the tower; they'll activate at my command. I'll wait until tonight when the party's in swing and we can be sure no one will be visiting him." Tanna looked tired, her pale blue skin marred by deep purple circles around her eyes.

"You don't look great. Are you sure they'll work?"

"Yes, fool!" she snapped. "I've done them properly! They'll stop anyone from entering that tower who's under tier two, and they'll specifically stop Morgan and Issa from leaving, no matter their current tier. I perfectly matched their Energy signatures."

"I heard he has portals in there. They'll stop those?"

"This again? How many times will you idiots bring this up? They won't stop the portals, but they'll keep Morgan or Issa from traveling through them. My wards will create a shell that stops any sort of travel, be it dimensional or physical."

"That doesn't make sense. He uses void-attuned Energy. You saw the portal he made when they returned! How can you stop him from connecting two disparate points of space? If we've gambled on these wards, and you've overlooked something so—"

"Enough!" Tanna snapped. "You can't begin to comprehend what I've done, you fool! There will be no void Energy manifesting in that tower, not while my wards hold. Now be silent! Take your doubts and play with them in your quarters! I'm trying to enjoy the air after being cooped in my workshop for two weeks!"

"I always thought they called you the Ice Queen because of your affinities, but I can see it's mostly because you're a colossal bitch," Finneal sneered as he marched away from her toward a nearby stairwell.

Tanna smirked at his words, not bothering to reply or even watch him leave. She knew she'd won that engagement, as usual. When he resorted to name-calling and retreated with his "last word," it was over in her mind.

"A weak, preening simpleton. Should he ever try more than words, I'll deliver him a lesson which will alter his life."

"He's dangerous, Tanna," Gella spoke softly from where he'd walked up to her side, similarly softly.

She almost jumped from the start. How had that portly, lustful dolt snuck up on her? Rather than give away her surprise, however, Tanna took a slow breath and forced a smile.

"Am I not also dangerous, Captain?"

"Yes, but I think he's mad." Again, the captain's words were softly spoken; anyone more than a foot away would have trouble hearing them.

"Do you fear he'd hear you, even now? He's long gone, Captain, no doubt harassing some crew member in a mop closet."

"Perhaps, perhaps," Gella said, drumming his fingers on the rail while looking out over the human colony. "I heard the tail end of your conversation. I wasn't trying to eavesdrop; you were both speaking rather loudly. I'm impressed with your work, you know, and I've already given a report to ap'Gravin about all you've done while those other two lounged about."

"Oh, dear! Are you still trying to earn favor with me, Captain? Well, as remarkable as your bootlicking is, the most impressive thing you've done in all the time we've been on this tedious mission, is to make me not want to kill you. How exactly have you done that?"

"I don't know. Persistence?" The captain chuckled, and Tanna couldn't help the little thrill of amusement in her chest. He was simple, and he was weak—only tier two—but something about his gruff nature and the way he kept coming back for more was intriguing. He never seemed daunted by her rejections, no matter how cruelly she teased him.

"Well, for your honesty, I'm going to give you some advice: write another missive to your lord and give some praise to those other two layabouts. Make something up if you must. They're cutthroat, and if ap'Gravin dresses them down for a lack of effort, they'll find a way to make you suffer for it."

# MORGAN

Morgan sat on a tall workshop stool and watched Issa preparing the smelter to create the alloy for Tiladia's new body. Issa had asked him to keep her company, and since she wasn't casting any of the body parts yet, she wasn't worried about spoiling the surprise Tiladia wanted.

"Are you excited?" Morgan asked the dragon spirit as it hovered, her shards of tinkling crystal swirling in an agitated manner. Well, Morgan reflected, the movements seemed agitated, but he wasn't sure.

"Extremely, Morgan! I still can't believe I'll be unbound from this tower. It's been . . . millennia!" Tiladia exclaimed, swooping close so her cool mist brushed his neck.

"Yeah, but what about the new body? I'm curious to see what you and Issa came up with!" Morgan didn't look at her while he spoke, still focused on Issa's strange preparations. She'd created a copper tray on which she'd scribed scores of runes and piled a dozen bars of silver next to the large bar of Amber Ore he'd given her.

Before Tiladia could answer him, Issa looked back at him with a pleasant smile and a look on her face that seemed to say, "Watch this!" She put her hands flat on the copper plate, and Morgan felt a surge of Energy, warm and wonderful, blaze to life, coming directly from her. He watched, waiting to see what the Energy would do, but before anything could happen, he heard a haunting, lilting hum, and he realized Issa was singing.

Tiladia drifted away from him toward Issa, her conversation with Morgan lost in the sound of Issa's melody. Morgan couldn't blame her—he had a hard time thinking of anything while that sound grew louder and the notes stretched and folded on themselves, sending shivers down the back of his neck and raising goose bumps on his arms. A deep golden-blue glow began to emanate from Issa's hands, and Morgan stood, trying to see what was happening.

The glow was spreading from where her palms touched the copper, and as it traveled over the sheet, it ignited the runes Issa had inscribed, following a pathway Morgan hadn't noticed before. When the Energy had traveled through all of the runes and they all glowed brilliantly, one stream went to the silver and the other to the Amber Ore. Issa's song grew louder and faster, her high soprano rippling in a dozen different notes at once. Morgan felt the surge of Energy coming from her mount in intensity, more than he'd ever felt from one of her spells before.

The different ores began to glow then, taking on the gold-tinged blue light that had suffused the copper plate and all of its runes. As Morgan watched, the runes faded away, and the ore seemed to pulse with the Energy before it subsided, absorbing the magic that she had infused in it. Issa stopped singing and sighed happily, clapping her hands and rubbing them together before she moved to inspect the silver.

"That was so beautiful, Lady Issa," Tiladia complimented, hovering around Issa and bathing her shoulders in the mists that held her essence.

"Thank you, Tiladia, but you promised not to call me 'Lady' anymore!" She laughed, gently rubbing her fingers over the bar of silver and closing her eyes.

"I'm sorry!" Tiladia chimed, though she didn't seem sorry—more amused, if Morgan were any judge.

"That was something else, Issa," Morgan said as he moved closer, trying to see if he could detect any differences in the silver or Amber Ore. They looked the same to him, though he imagined he'd be able to feel the Energy if he held one of the bars. On a whim, he cast Void Vision and examined the metals. They blazed brightly in his enhanced view, a deep aura around them which matched the Energy Issa had put forth, a sense of potential and . . . *beauty* coming from them.

"Thank you! Can you help me with the next part? I need to carry all of this silver to that big crucible." She pointed to a large bucket-shaped piece of equipment suspended from a chain near the smelter.

"Yeah, sure," Morgan said, moving over to the pile of silver bars and carrying them, four at a time, to the crucible. They were smaller than the Amber Ore bar, but all together, he thought the mixture would be something like ten to one. When he'd piled all the silver bars in the bottom half of the big crucible, Issa handed him the Amber Ore.

"Put this on top, please. I need to get a stool in here!" She stood on her tiptoes and watched him place the ore. "Now, I need to smelt this for a while, and I'll work some more spells into it while it cooks. After that, I will pour it into the molds for Tiladia's body parts!"

"So you're banishing me?" Morgan asked with a grin.

"Right! I'm going to get the molds out and set them up while this is cooking, so . . . begone!"

She laughed and pushed him toward the exit. It was Saturday, and none of Boris's people were working, especially with the big gala on the airship starting soon, so Issa had the whole shop to herself.

"Well, I'm going to talk to Ykleedra about what I need to do with her sisters. I got stuck with babysitting duty while she goes to that party."

"What a nice man," Issa teased, favoring him with another smile, but then she went back to her crucible, clearly too excited and distracted with the process to spare him much thought.

Morgan laughed and hurried on his way, using the stairwell to step down to the atrium level.

"Ykleedra?" he called as he strolled down the path toward the fountain. He knew she and the children had been spending a lot of time at the build-site for their future home, but sometimes she was down in the burrow she'd made. He found the fastest way to get her attention was to call out for her and wait on one of the benches.

He'd only just sat down and started daydreaming about tackling some of the texts in his library when he heard footsteps and laughter. He turned toward the sound and saw Maria and Ykleedra walking in his direction from further into the atrium. He slapped his head and said, "I forgot you were here, Maria!"

"I came to help Ykleedra with her hair. Don't you think it's lovely?" Maria asked, perhaps leading him a bit too obviously.

"Oh!" Morgan stood up and took a good look at the young Yovashi. Her silvery-white hair—usually straight and tied back in a ponytail—had been curled and trimmed, and it fell like glistening ribbons on the sides of her head. Morgan didn't have to lie when he exclaimed, "Oh, Ykleedra! It looks beautiful!"

Ykleedra looked down shyly, and her long walking legs folded slightly, making her appear smaller. "Thank you, Morgan. Maria taught me how to use a special iron for my hair!"

"Well, you look great. I hope you have a lot of fun tonight," Morgan said, giving Maria a pointed look. Ykleedra wore her usual silver robe; Morgan knew she didn't own anything else. It was a pretty garment, though, and suited her well. He supposed he should see about getting her some different robes, regardless of the usual Yovashi customs. He was trying to steer her away from those traditions, anyway. "Where are the little ones?"

"They're playing near the new house. They shouldn't need much watching, Morgan. They mostly crawl around the piles of lumber and explore in the grass, pretending to hunt each other. They'll feel sleepy and want to curl up together in a few hours. We've been sleeping out here; I haven't wanted to go into the burrow since you took Tkron." Her voice grew soft as she told him the last, and Morgan stepped forward, concern in his eyes.

"Is everything all right?"

"Yes!" Ykleedra said, attempting a humanlike smile with her stiff facial features. It came out looking more like a grimace, but Morgan knew better. "We enjoy the atrium at night—the smells and sounds. It's nice to be away from the decay pit that Tkron had been building. I'm letting the atrium retake the burrow. It's starting to fill with roots, and the ground slowly shifts back to where it was when I started digging."

"Ahh, I imagine that's the tower's self-repair function." Morgan nodded, scratching his chin. "So, are you two heading out?"

"Yes, we are!" Maria replied, and Morgan took a moment to look at her, noticing her carefully coiffed hair and the shimmering material of her navy-blue blouse.

"You look very nice too, Maria."

The woman was a good ten years his senior, but like many of the colonists who'd worked to improve their levels, she looked much younger and more vibrant than when they'd first arrived. Morgan wondered at that. How different would their culture become with much longer-lived citizens and a lack of significant disease? How much would it change as their species began to mingle more and more with the others on this world?

"Thank you, sir." Maria curtsied with a giggle.

"All right, all right." Morgan chuckled. "I'm going to find those little rascals. Have fun. I wasn't joking earlier, though—I'll come looking for Ykleedra if she's not back in a couple of hours."

"Oh, all right, you grouchy old man!" Maria said with another giggle, and then she reached out a hand, and Ykleedra wrapped a tentacle around her wrist. Morgan felt some tension inside him release when he saw the physical contact. Maria would look out for Ykleedra.

Captain Gella was exceedingly pleased with the party. Hundreds of the humans had accepted his invitation, and everyone he'd seen had partaken of the foods, or at least, the drinks. His crew had put together a band of sorts and were playing some lively tavern music on the quarter deck. Lieutenant Bekira had proven to have a lovely voice, and the humans seemed to enjoy the fast-paced string music—they had some novel ideas when it came to dancing, and Gella rather enjoyed the chaotic energy he saw on the dance floor they'd set up on the main deck.

"Captain," First Mate Reeja called, sauntering up from below decks.

"Yes, Reeja? Do you have a report for me?"

"I do. All of the soporif—" he began, but Gella cut him off.

"Quiet, fool! You needn't spell it out!" Gella turned and walked up the short steps to the first aft deck, motioning for Reeja to follow him. He backed up until he was pressed against one of the Energy crystal housings and said, "We can speak here, but keep your voice down."

"Erm, yes," the Vodkin replied, looking over his massive round shoulders in the least surreptitious manner Gella could imagine. "Well, all of the special dishes have been dispensed, and the *cook*"—he winked obnoxiously at the word—"is ready to activ—*er*, mix up the final ingredients whenever you give the word."

"Ancestors, man," Gella sighed. "Well, did you ask the crew if anyone saw that"—he glanced around and spoke under his voice—"*Yovashi* eat any of the *special dishes?*"

"Aye, sir! Many!" Reeja grinned.

"Excellent. Let's prepare to"—again, he looked around—"end this farce. Send my go-ahead to the cook, but first, check with Tanna to ensure her project is in play. Tell Finneal and Haku-dak to stand by for any resistance."

"Captain!" Arthur Ballard called, walking up the short flight of stairs to aft deck one, a noticeable wobble in his step. Gella had been pleased to see that more than half the human council had decided to come to his party, and many of the engineers and crafts folk as well. He might be coming back with a lighter haul than ap'Gravin had wanted, but the quality of the cargo was undeniable.

"Yes, Arthur! Please come on up; tell me what you think of the food!" Gella exclaimed, affecting a smile and nudging Reeja to get moving.

# ❦ MORGAN ❦

Morgan watched the little Yovashi sisters move together into the mound of blankets Ykleedra had created for them. They hadn't had to go far from where they'd been playing; their new "nest" was situated near the edge of the same meadow where they'd been playing all afternoon. As the atrium began to go dark, starlike flickering lights took over from the false sun that normally hung in the sky. Watching the children curl up under the dim stars, Morgan realized that now that he had full control of the tower, he could adjust the sun and other lighting effects to suit them better.

He thought about it for a minute, and though he was tempted to dim the sun for Ykleedra's comfort, he wondered if it was wise to get her and her sisters used to circumstances which were different from the world in which they lived. There were also the myriad plants and trees to consider—he didn't want to initiate an inadvertent foliage die-off in the atrium. He decided to hold off for now; he'd consult Maria and some of the psychologists in the colony before acting on impulse.

"Sleep well, little ones," Morgan said as the sisters nestled together, ferns surrounding part of their makeshift bed, with cushions and pillows making little walls around the rest of it. He wondered where Ykleedra had gotten the pillows, but he knew the answer without asking: Issa. She'd spent a lot of time with Ykleedra after Morgan had taken Tkron away, and the atmosphere in the atrium reflected it. Things just seemed happier, more idyllic.

The construction of the Yovashi home was well underway, and Morgan was impressed by Alicia Washington's capabilities. The solid stone foundation was set, and the framing was all but complete. More than the efficiency of her crew, though, Morgan was impressed by the talent displayed. The beams that made up the frame for the walls curved up and seemed to become part of the ceiling without any sort of joints or nails; just long spans of timber that stretched up then bent into rounded corners, meeting at the center of the dwelling where he knew Alicia was planning to build the kitchen.

"Tiladia?" he called softly, knowing the spirit would hear him.

"Yes, Morgan?" her tinkling response echoed up the path as her misty form streaked into the atrium, moving much faster than her normal, sedately floating pace.

"How long has Ykleedra been absent from the tower?" Morgan had the itch of a worry starting to form in his gut.

"Two hours and seventeen minutes. Are you concerned about her?" Tiladia asked as she floated between him and the sleeping children.

"I am. I am, Tiladia. Will you please watch her sisters until I return with her? I'm going to go hurry her along." Morgan turned and started walking as the dragon replied.

"Yes, Morgan. I shall be sure to alert Lady Issa if the children need anything."

"Hey." Morgan paused and watched as Tiladia took on her misty dragon form and curled up in the middle of the little Yovashi huddle. "How is Issa? Is everything going well with her project?"

"Yes! She was thrilled when she finished the alloy smelting. She created a named alloy and said it'll be even more versatile than she'd hoped." Tiladia's response was soft, barely a whisper, but Morgan heard it like she was speaking into his ear. Part of the connection to the tower he and Tiladia shared, he supposed.

"Named alloy?" he asked, starting once again down the path, confident that he and Tiladia could keep speaking despite the increased distance.

"Yes! When she sang her song to increase the bonding efficiency of the disparate metals, her efforts bore wondrous fruit: a new alloy was created. The reward from the System helped her to gain a new level!"

"Wow!" Morgan exclaimed, striding toward the stairwell. "What was it called?"

"Luster Ore! Doesn't it sound wonderful? It's beautiful, Morgan, and Issa says it will make her enchantments more effective."

"That's great, Tiladia," Morgan said as he strode off the staircase and into the entry hall. He walked to the tower door, touched the handle so it unlocked, and pulled it open. "I'll be back soon," he said, then stepped out into the night air. Or he tried to step into the night air. His foot encountered a rubbery resistance, and he almost fell on his ass from the strange sensation.

"What the fuck?" he blurted.

"Is there something wrong, Morgan?"

"What's going on with the door? I can't walk through."

Morgan didn't wait for an answer. He pushed a hand through the opening, but it felt like he was trying to push against a stiff, rubber membrane, though he couldn't see anything there, just empty air. He drew Bloodfang and stabbed it into the opening, and the sword slipped out through the doorway as if nothing was there. He tried to follow the blade with his arm, but his knuckles hit the weird membrane again, and he growled, pulling his sword back in.

"I don't see anything amiss, Morgan. Nothing is wrong with the tower."

"Goddammit." Morgan cast Void Step, aiming for the grass at the base of the tower. He felt the spell take form in his pathways and rush out of him as it always did, but nothing happened. Morgan felt his void-attuned Energy leave his body and dissipate as though the air were absorbing it somehow. He cussed again, trying a more basic spell—Void Vision—but it also refused to take effect, even when the Energy clearly left his pathways.

"What the . . ." Morgan's question died in his throat when an explosion suddenly lit up the night sky outside his tower.

Maria was having a wonderful time watching Ykleedra experience the party. The music, food, and courteous conversations with dozens of new people kept the Yovashi in a constant state of pleasure, as evidenced by the gentle clicking of the short, hard-tipped tentacles she kept under her robe. During one of their first lessons, Ykleedra had explained to her that Yovashi expressed emotions with the sounds they could make with those hidden appendages, and a rapid, quiet clicking denoted joy.

Ykleedra leaned close, swaying to the music coming from the front of the ship, and said, "Don't you want to try one of these?" She held a little wooden plate with smoked sausages in a buttery, flaky batter, one of her dexterous tentacles gripping the plate.

"No, no! You go ahead, Ykleedra! I've been to many parties in my time, and I always get food in my teeth. No, I want to smile with confidence!" She laughed, looking around at all the interesting people, especially the smartly dressed crew members. She sipped at her drink, nervous about overindulging. Maria hadn't been lying; in fact, she'd been minimizing. She'd made a fool of herself at quite a few company parties over the years, nearly losing her catering company after one particularly bad incident involving a lawsuit for lewd conduct.

No, she'd start this new life on the right foot.

"What kind of meat is it, anyway?" she asked, watching Ykleedra take another bite.

The young Yovashi had just begun to chew when her gray eyelids closed, and she fell to the deck, her long, walking legs curling around her body. "Ykleedra!" Maria yelled in alarm. Then a wave of fatigue hit her so hard she stumbled forward and nearly fell, but she shook it off and stood up, looking around at the sounds of breaking glasses, clattering plates, and thuds of bodies hitting the deck.

"Grab that one," a harsh voice came from behind her, and she spun to see a crew member rushing toward her with a black piece of metal in his hands. Baron Finneal stood nearby, surveying the chaos as more and more crew members came up from the lower decks and began snapping those metal bands around everyone's necks.

"What—" was all Maria could get out before the Shadeni man was on her, grabbing her arms and trying to snap the collar around her neck. Was that really what it was? Were they putting collars on everyone? Why had everyone fallen asleep at the same moment?

"Let me go!" she screamed, jerking back and kicking at the man's groin. She must have made contact because he grunted and stumbled back, and then Maria was running, sprinting toward the center of the deck where the stairs led down to the boarding corridor.

She ran past people she knew, people lying stupefied on the deck. She wanted to stop, to shake them, get them to come with her, but she knew she had to get away. She had one thought in her mind: get Morgan. He could stop this. He would stop this. He wouldn't let them hurt Ykleedra. She ran, jumped, and nearly made it to the door leading below when suddenly, her legs stopped listening to her. When she looked down, she saw why: a wide, glistening silver blade was sticking out of her stomach.

Baron Finneal yanked his broadsword out of her spine and said, with very little emotion, "Should have taken the collar."

Maria gasped, still unable to make her legs do what she wanted. The ship lurched, then, and she stumbled and fell toward the port railing. Finneal didn't strike her again or try to stop her, and though she couldn't control her legs, something kept her from falling on her face as she moved toward the railing. Once it struck her midriff, she tumbled over the top of it and fell.

Maria flopped through the air for twenty or thirty feet, smashing onto her back, the impact driving the air from her lungs. By some miracle, she'd landed on a canvas sack of something and hadn't hit her head, though she could see by the contorted nature of her legs that she was grievously wounded. She gazed around, her chest spasming as it tried to suck air in to fill her empty lungs. Stars swam in her eyes, most from lack of oxygen, but some were real. She saw stone parapets and great metal eye hooks.

She was on top of the northeast tower.

"Ma'am, are you all right? What happened?" a panicked voice asked. She rolled her head to the left, and there, dressed in a standard militia uniform, was a young man with one of the new Energy rifles.

Her mouth tried to form words, her lips moving in and out like a dying fish, until finally, she managed to grunt a coherent sound. "Stop them!" As the words came out, she finally managed to heave half a breath and said, with more clarity, "Stop that ship!"

The effort had been enormous, and the pain of her broken ribs and the trauma to her body overcame her. Even though Maria struggled, the blackness at the edge of her vision came closing in, and she fell into it.

"Get us aloft and moving east! Now!" Gella hollered to his helmsman. He stood in the high, glass-walled bridge of the massive ship and watched over the decks as his crew went among the insensate guests and slapped the control collars on their necks. After they finished, they could take their time bringing them into the reinforced cabins, of which he had plenty. The ship could hold thousands, and in his estimate, they'd captured four or five hundred of the humans.

"Status?" he barked to Reeja as the big Vodkin came rolling into the bridge. "Why aren't we aloft?" he shouted to the helmsman before Reeja could answer.

"We're moving, sir. The deckhands are pulling in the ties, so she's lifting slowly and listing to port."

"Just get us moving!" he growled.

"Sir, nearly all of them went down when the potion was activated. I saw Finneal dealing with a few—rather brutally, I might add—who didn't fall asleep, but I'd say it was just a handful," Reeja said as he came puffing up beside him.

"Brutally?"

"Aye, he's cutting 'em down with his blade."

"Could he not just subdue them?" Gella grunted angrily, scratching savagely at the stubble of his beard. The blue flesh around the whiskers was irritated and raw, and he knew he was having some sort of outbreak due to stress. "And Tanna? Did her wards hold?"

"Aye! She says they're doing the job."

"Excellent." Gella felt the tension start to bleed out of his shoulders. He'd been more than mildly apprehensive that something would go wrong.

As the massive ship started to lift more noticeably and the prow turned to the east, he walked to the rear of the bridge and looked out the glass toward the colony.

"I wonder what they're thinking right now. Maybe they're naive enough to assume we're taking the partygoers for a tour." He chuckled softly, still not quite believing they'd pulled it off.

"What are they doing, you reckon?" Reeja asked, pointing to a few now distant figures pushing around some large black objects on the wall.

"I don't know—" he started, but then a blinding light erupted from one of the objects, and he had to squint against the glare. "Battle stations!" he roared as the ship lurched, and a fiery explosion burst into the black night from the aft keel area.

"Sir! We've lost the main aft impeller!" a panicked Ardeni flight operator howled.

"Full ahead! Ancestors-damn it! Why didn't we know about those weapons?"

As he spoke, the ship lurched forward at much greater speed, though she listed badly, the other impellers having to make up for the blown one. They'd cleared another mile when a second brilliant light lit up the top of the human's wall.

"Brace!" he roared before a fiery explosion flared from the starboard flight mast, and the outer third of it fell away, ripping the wind sail in half.

"Captain, we've lost—" the Ardeni started, her voice quavering.

"I know it! Push everything to the lift rings! Keep us in the air and keep us moving! When we've put some mountains between us and that town, we'll set down for repairs."

## ◈ MORGAN ◈

"The town was firing on the ship?" Issa asked as she ran after Morgan toward the stairs.

"Yes, dammit. I need to get out there. Something's very wrong!" Morgan snapped, his nerves frayed and his frustration mounting with each second. "I hope whatever they've done is only holding me!" He charged onto the stairs and was back in the lobby before he'd finished speaking.

"Just walk through the door?" Issa asked, charging out of the stairwell behind him. She looked toward the tower's still open bronze door. Morgan had already explained what was going on with his inability to leave and the strange way his void-attuned spells weren't firing. He'd tried Azure Sight, and it had worked fine, so he knew it was something explicitly blocking his void magic, which gave him hope that whatever was keeping him from leaving was also targeting him specifically.

"Yeah, I already tried flying off a balcony—same shit is happening. Try the door."

Issa nodded, running toward it while Morgan followed, ready to catch her if the strange barrier threw her back. It was good he took the precaution because once she crossed the threshold, panic and anger for Ykleedra in her eyes, she rebounded toward him as if she'd run into the surface of a giant balloon.

Morgan caught her in his arms. "Goddammit!"

"Let go of me a minute here," Issa said, struggling against him. Morgan let go, and she stood up, producing a large round lens. She began to peer at the doorway through it. "Someone has placed wards around this tower. I can see the lines of their influence. Give me a few minutes to study this."

"You can understand what's going on?" Morgan wanted to look with his Void Vision and again cursed when he remembered he couldn't cast the spell. Azure Sight didn't show him much at all, just a sheen of Energy around the doorway.

"Yes. This is the work of an Artificer. It's thorough, Morgan. I don't think anyone without a very strong will and a lot of Energy will be able even to approach the tower, and I can see the barrier keeping us inside is designed to block you and me entirely. Cast a void spell. I want to see something," she said.

"All right." Morgan cast Void Vision, not surprised when the Energy left his pathways but did nothing for his sight.

"Ahh, yes! I see it now! Morgan, whoever made this trap is stealing your Energy to reinforce it! Each time you cast a spell, it gets stronger."

"Oh, great!"

"We need to get someone to go out, between the tower and the barrier keeping people away, and find the wards. They have to be physical runes with large Energy stones. I don't think they could have carved them into the tower, so there are probably stones, crystals, or something like that placed around it."

"There's just us," Morgan said, but then he snapped his fingers. "Ykleedra's sisters!"

"Morgan, they can't even speak yet. I think it would be dangerous to send the equivalent of toddlers out there to try to mess with the wards. The runes might have dangerous defensive mechanisms . . ." Her eyes unfocused, staring into the distance, then she frowned and looked Morgan in the eyes. "What about Tkron?"

"No fucking way," Morgan replied. "You haven't spoken to him, Issa. If we let him loose, I can promise he'd just leave. We'd still be stuck, and I'd be worried about what kind of evil shit he was doing out there."

"Right." Issa paced in a small circle, thinking.

"I have an idea," Morgan continued. "What about the portal? I could take it to the academy, then use my talisman to recall to First Landing!" He started running for the stairs, but Issa called for him to stop.

"Morgan, I'm sure the wards will block regular teleportation. The portal doesn't connect two points in space like your void magic does; it just sends you, very quickly, along a magical . . . river, for lack of a better word. I'm sure the wards will prevent that."

"I'll still try it. Won't hurt, will it?"

"No, it won't, but I have another idea. I'll be in the workshop. Come let me know how it goes." Issa surprised him by hurrying past him and going up the steps before he could reply.

Morgan started to follow her, but something caught his attention—movement outside the tower door. Turning to head back to the open doorway, he realized someone was approaching over the grass.

A soldier, a militia member, was running toward them, her blonde hair flying out behind her in the wind, and Morgan knew she was running to him for help with whatever was going on out there. He stood in the doorway, willing her to make it, willing her to charge up those steps and help them out of their predicament. She saw him standing in the doorway, and she started to yell something, but as she came within a few feet of the base of the steps, she simply collapsed.

She fell like a rag doll, flopping and bouncing along the grass to lie, unmoving, at the bottom of the tower steps.

"Fuck!" Morgan hissed. He thought—hoped—she was still breathing. The wards wouldn't be lethal, would they? What kind of madman would kill random people like that?

Morgan turned and ran up the steps to the portal level, stalking directly to the one connected to Olivia's academy. He trickled some Energy into the archway, knowing exactly how to activate and control the portal now that he had full mastery of the tower. He felt his Energy go into the arch and saw the portal stone start to glow, but as the swirling gateway started to form, it sputtered and stopped. "I wish you weren't right so often, Issa."

"Morgan?" Tiladia's chime caught him by surprise. He turned to see the spirit floating near the stairway.

"Tiladia, we've got a problem!"

"I sensed as much from your words earlier. The children are sleeping soundly. Is there aught else I can do?"

"Yeah, follow me to Issa's workshop. She said she had an idea."

Morgan hit the stairs, and when he walked out, striding to where he'd last seen Issa working, Tiladia was right behind him. He found Issa not by the smelter, which was cold, but working at a long workbench covered with dozens of thin, bronze-colored rods of various lengths. She held an etching tool in one hand and her special lens in the other, and appeared to be carving tiny runes into one of the rods.

"The portal didn't work?" Issa asked without looking up.

"No, you were right. What are these?"

"These are the rods that go inside the cast body parts I made for Tiladia. They'll act as bones and muscles, and also the pathways for her new Core."

"Oh shit," Morgan said. "I think I can guess your idea!"

That got Issa to look up, and she grinned at him. "Yes! I can finish her body in a couple of days if I work really hard and if you help me. I still need to craft her some organs, but if I show you how to etch these rods, you can do it, can't you? I've seen your notebook—you have excellent fine motor skills. You don't need to understand any of it—just copy my designs." She pointed to a sheaf of papers next to her.

"Yeah, I can do that. I can sure as hell try, anyway."

"Here." Issa pushed the top page to him. "See? I wrote the length of each rod and the rune pattern next to it. You can measure them with this"—she held up a metal stick that looked very much like a ruler—"to ensure you etch the right pattern on the right rods." She set down her etching tool and stood up.

"I'm going to start working on Tiladia's heart and the housing for her Core. I'll check on you when I'm finished. Tiladia, come with me; I have some questions to ask you before I make your heart!"

"Um . . ." Morgan stopped talking because Issa had already rushed away, back to one of the workbenches near the forge. He sat down, picked up the etching tool, and looked at Issa's notes. There were nearly a hundred rods, some as long as his forearm and some shorter than his pinky. He flipped through the pages and saw that each rod needed somewhere between three and several dozen runes inscribed. "This is going to take a while," he breathed.

A hissing, whooshing noise signaled the forge being brought online, and Morgan picked up the first rod, settling in for some serious busywork. He tried to take heart, though—if they finished Tiladia's body, she could, in theory, go out and disable the wards. Still, there was always the hope that someone outside would manage to figure something out. Maybe Olivia would come back to the tower. Would the portal work in the opposite direction?

"Well, whatever the method, I need to get out there and figure out what's going on," he grumbled, carefully etching his first rune.

"Report," Maria said, coughing as the word came out.

"We struck the ship twice; it looked like we broke off one of those masts that stick out from the side with one of them. The first shot blew up one of those big rings at the rear, too. We almost brought it down," the young man informed, doffing his militia helmet and standing rather smartly at attention next to her bed. He must have served in a military back on Earth.

"Do you think they'll have to stop?" she asked, shifting uncomfortably. Dr. Gibraltar had given her meds for the pain and stopped her bleeding but wanted to wait until Dr. Cho could be found to attempt a true healing.

"We really don't know, ma'am. When she started to dive after we broke off that mast, the other rings all over her keel lit up brightly and lifted her up. Then she was out of range."

"Funny how people refer to ships as *she*. You weren't even a sailor back on Earth, were you?"

"No, ma'am. I have no idea why I did that. Must be from watching a lot of VRs." He grinned, a bit chagrined, perhaps, and continued, "We can't get any news from the tower. We've sent two more people to attempt entry, and they both passed out when they got close. We can't even get anyone close enough to pull them away—four people are now sleeping in the grass near those steps."

"All right. Clearly, those assholes didn't want Morgan getting involved. Hopefully, he can figure a way out. In the meantime, we need to get a force together and start marching. We have to hope that ship will need to set down for repairs. Any sign of Bronwyn?"

Of the First Landing council, five were captive on that ship, Morgan was trapped in his tower, Olivia was a thousand miles away, and Bronwyn was missing. Maria was all on her own, and she was bedridden.

"No sign, ma'am. We have reports of her leaving out the north gate a week ago. I'll get together our fastest, highest-leveled people and see if I can get a squad moving out ASAP." He saluted again, and Maria held out her hand.

"What's your name?"

"Corporal Tran, ma'am."

"Good, Corporal Tran. Good. You're doing damn good work. Keep me posted." Maria smiled, not easily because of the dark thoughts running through her mind, but she managed it.

"Thank you, ma'am. May I?" He gestured toward the door.

"Yes, good luck. If you see Alice . . . I forget her last name, the lady who owns that new restaurant, um, Purple Grass, will you tell her where I am? She's trying to get an idea of how many people we had taken tonight."

"Yes, ma'am. I'll see that everyone in town knows where you are before we leave."

He started toward the door, and Maria opened her mouth to speak, to ask him if he had to go with the rescue squad, but she stopped. It was nice having a reliable person in town, but he should go where the most people needed him. Hopefully, that Alice lady would show up soon.

# ॐ OLIVIA ॐ

Olivia held a little mirror behind her back, looking at Barnt's handiwork in his larger bathroom mirror. The big Vodkin had been surprisingly gentle and dexterous with his little Energy-driven needle. He'd sketched the tattoos on her flesh before applying the permanent ink to be sure she approved, and Olivia had been quite impressed by the exact, perfectly copied lines. The final tattoos were just as good—no, better than the sketches had promised.

Barnt's ink seemed alive, shimmering under her skin, and though the tattoos were just symbols and runes in an interlocking pattern, they were done with clever shading, and transitioned from black to pale blue in a way that gave them depth and vibrance. They were more than she'd bargained for. The one around her waist curved under her belly button and over her hip bones, almost like a fabric belt hanging on her flesh, and she thought it was beautiful.

The band around her throat was low, just above her collarbones, and not easily seen when she wore her robes. Olivia traced her fingers along it, amazed her skin wasn't stinging or raw in any way; Barnt had applied an ointment with a mild healing effect, speeding up a process that might normally take several days or even a week.

Olivia buttoned up her blouse, slipped into her robes, and walked back to where the gigantic ex-legionnaire waited. He'd acted absurdly nervous that she wouldn't like his work, despite Olivia practically falling over herself exclaiming how beautiful the ones she could see were. Barnt hadn't liked it when she'd had to pull up her robes, either, when it came time for the tattoo at her waist. Olivia had asked him if he'd act that way with one of his legion comrades, which had settled him down—he just imagined he was going to war with her.

"I love them, Barnt. Shall we see if they work?"

"Work?" he asked, his voice rising into a squeak.

"Oh, relax, they look right. If something goes wrong with the spell, it will be my fault."

"Spell?" Barnt backed up a foot.

"Watch," Olivia said, building the pattern for her new defensive spell in her pathways; she'd practiced it a hundred times while Barnt was doing his work. Once it pulsed in completion, she channeled a braid of her four elemental affinities into it. The finished spell rushed through her pathways and out through her new tattoos, causing them to flare with the Energy's passage.

As it flowed out, the Energy spread around Olivia's body, snapping into a shimmering bubble which seemed to reverberate and shake for a moment as it flickered through a rainbow of colors before it subsided, falling transparently to her flesh.

**\*\*\*Congratulations! You have learned the spell: Chromatic Personal Barrier—Advanced.\*\*\***

**\*\*\*Chromatic Personal Barrier—Advanced: Prerequisite: Four or more elemental affinities. You channel a barrier of elementally-attuned Energies which is maintained by a static runic structure and fueled by the Energies in your Core. This barrier will stop various types of damage, defined by the runic structure and dependent upon your Energy reserves. Energy cost: Varied. Passive maintenance: 5 Energy per second. Cooldown: Minimal.\*\*\***

"Five per second—" Olivia started, but Barnt cut her off.

"Wha' was tha'?" His eyes bulged out. "Did my tatts do that?"

"Well, you certainly got them right, but no, it's the design combined with my spell. Thank you so much, Barnt!"

Olivia offered the dazed man a handful of quad-attuned beads she'd made, usually in the hours before bed each night when she would normally have read to fall asleep. She found the process almost as relaxing and much more rewarding—her beads had a value among the populace that greatly exceeded the standard System Stone rate. "Will this cover it? They're quad-attuned."

"Oh?" Barnt held one of the beads up to the light and marveled at the interplay of the different elements for a moment. "Yes, ma'am, they'll be quite enough. I'd have done it for free if I knew I'd be part of such a work of amazing magic!"

"Oh, really?" Olivia pulled back her hand with the beads and giggled when he stammered for a response. "Just kidding! Here." She poured them into his big palm. "Listen, Barnt. I have a lot more to do, so I'm going to head back to the academy. I'll always remember how you dropped everything to help me."

"My pleasure, Miss. Thanks for the conversations we had. I feel like I got as much out of this as you did." Barnt moved to the door of his little apartment studio. He didn't have an official business, but it was clear he had clients on the academy grounds. Half his apartment was filled with objects having to do with his craft—a custom-built reclining wooden chair, a stool, a desk for his ink mixing, and even a little alchemy set. When Olivia had asked about the latter, he'd said he was dabbling with making his own inks.

"See you around, Barnt," Olivia said, smiling as she passed through his open door, ducking beneath his arm as he held it from closing.

She strode purposefully back toward the academy. It was early evening, and people were still about; she was sure she could go back to her dorm and find her cohort there, waiting and worrying and ready to read her the riot act for disappearing on her own all day.

They'd have to wait, though. Olivia felt like she was up against a clock, and there was more for her to learn. She felt better walking around with her new defense, but she needed more utility. Thinking of her spell, she thought back to the description—five Energy per second.

"So three hundred a minute." Olivia pulled up her attributes as she walked up the main road toward the academy.

| Energy Affinity: | 9.1, Fire 9.6, Earth 9.6, Water 9.6, Air 9.6 | Energy: | 10,322/11,070 |
|---|---|---|---|
| Strength: | 20 | Vitality: | 72 |
| Dexterity: | 50 | Agility: | 20 |
| Intelligence: | 206 | Will: | 192 |

"So with zero regeneration, I could keep this shield active for nearly forty minutes . . ." She mulled things over, looking at her Energy attribute several more times as she walked. It became clear that she was losing Energy much more slowly than three hundred a minute. Less than half that, it seemed. She figured she could keep the spell ready for nearly two hours if she didn't mind draining herself.

The more she thought about it, the more Olivia figured it would be a clever idea to create a mana battery of sorts which she could wear or carry attached to a weapon or staff to fuel her shield. "In fact, I could create a recharging mana battery!"

She smiled at the student who looked at her with wide eyes, perhaps not used to crown-wearing, tall, slightly shimmering humans striding around talking to themselves.

Olivia walked right past the stairs which would take her to her dorm, continuing on directly to the library. She had plans to dig through the stacks for some more spells before figuring out her next step. She hoped that, with a little luck, she might find a spell which would help her with that. More than anything, she hoped to figure out a way to set a trap for the killer.

Obviously, he had an interest in her—she just had to think of the best way to use that.

"Olivia!" Professor Oylla-dak called sharply, jerking Olivia out of her thoughts and startling her back to the present. She'd walked, without paying attention, into the library and had already begun to steer herself toward the rear stacks, nearly brushing past Oylla, Carlu, and another professor she didn't know.

"Oh! Oh, Professor, you startled me!" Olivia said, stopping and turning toward the trio.

"You shouldn't be startled! You should have been quietly resting in the library when I came to talk to you! I'm afraid that wasn't the case, though, was it? You've been gone for hours, and we've been scouring the campus looking for you!"

"I'm sorry, Professor, I had to get something done at the market—"

"I'm sorry, Olivia, but this simply illustrates that I can't deal with you on campus at the moment. It's too dangerous, and it's too difficult to treat you with dignity and still maintain control of all the variables!" Oylla shook her two hands around her head as though to illustrate how many things she had going on in there.

"What are you saying, Professor?" Olivia asked.

"I'm saying that you'll need to go home for a while . . . until this killer is apprehended."

"I'd like to be a part of your investigations, not sent packing!" Olivia exclaimed, her lackadaisical demeanor suddenly stripped away as her anger and frustration surged forth out of the corner where she'd pressed those feelings down.

"Yes, but this world doesn't revolve around you, Olivia. We have others here at risk. We have others here whose job is to keep students safe and deal with situations like this. It's not fair to them to keep you around. Nor is it fair or safe for you to be involved in the investigation anymore. It's become far too personal, Olivia!"

Olivia opened her mouth to argue, wanting to scream that she deserved to be there. She deserved to help punish the awful, psychotic creep that had hurt Adaida and defiled and slaughtered sweet, kind Alyss. She knew it wasn't rational, though. She knew that, even on Earth, among the law enforcement professions, people so connected to a case wouldn't be allowed to work on it. Surprising everyone, including herself, she said, "If you're sure, professor."

Olivia's mind raced in a panic. One minute she'd been planning to figure out how to capture the killer, and now she was giving up. Was she letting the killer win? Olivia was sure she cared, sure she wanted to get justice, but when Oylla had spoken to her, bluntly telling her to leave, it had triggered deeply buried feelings, and at that moment, the only thing she could think of was Alyss's head, eyes staring, mouth held in its default expression of determined kindness.

Olivia could only see that image in her mind and realize she'd never hear her professor's voice again. She'd never be able to ask her for advice. She'd never hear her tell her how proud she was that Olivia had done something remarkable.

Whatever dam had been holding back Olivia's grief burst then, tears pouring from her eyes as she fell into Oylla's quickly open arms, sobbing out her endless, immeasurable grief.

"I can't believe she's dead! I can't believe this fucking guy is killing all these people! Why couldn't I stop him before he did that to Alyss? Why would anyone hurt a person like Alyss?"

"Hush, Olivia," Oylla said, pulling her in as her body sagged more and more. "We don't know why, but don't you waste another minute thinking about that. Alyss doesn't care why. She's with her ancestors, and she'll either stick around to meddle with us for a while, or she'll be moving on to a new life. We'll stop this killer, and that's all Alyss would care about. I promise you: we'll get him. I also promise I'll come to you if there's any way you can help."

Olivia stayed like that for several minutes, soaking in the warmth of Oylla's embrace. It felt like a hug from her mother, and she knew how ridiculous it was to want to hug your mother at her age, but she couldn't help how she felt. It felt like a failure to go home, but something in her wanted to go, to let the professionals handle things. That guilt, that feeling in the pit of her stomach, kept her huddled in Oylla's arms longer than was probably comfortable for the professor. Still, she handled it with aplomb, holding onto Olivia and quietly saying, "Shhh, shhh."

"Can I take some books to study?" Olivia asked, finally. She straightened and sniffed, brushing the wrinkles out of her robes. "Sorry about that," she apologized, looking down.

"Don't be! Thank you for showing me your feelings, Olivia. I was beginning to worry about you!" Oylla smiled and reached out to smooth the collar of Olivia's robes. "Yes, you may choose some books from the library. Gather them up, and then say your goodbyes to your cohort. I'll have Professor Voyle-dak, here, escort you. He'll walk with you to the Travel Pavilion. We'll give that portal a test, hmm?"

"All right." Olivia nodded, then glanced back toward the rear of the library. "Even the spell books?" She cursed herself as she said the words. Why couldn't she have just taken them and asked for forgiveness later?

"Hmm." Oylla frowned and massaged her temple. "You may take three of the spell tomes. Only three! If they hear of this, I'll be skewered at the next board meeting, so you better bring them back with you!" she hissed, grimacing at the prospect.

"I will! I promise, Oylla." Olivia glanced at Carlu and the other professor, who must be Voyle-dak, now lurking a dozen feet away, ostensibly talking about a book. "I mean, Professor."

"Don't worry about them," Oylla dismissed. "They were only here in case you didn't return. Carlu was helping me organize the search. You really had us worried!"

"Thank you, Professor, for everything."

"Hush, Olivia. We'll get this sorted quickly and bring you back so you can get on with some real learning. What a trial this has been for you! I'm so glad you've listened to reason."

Olivia nodded, squeezed Oylla's hand again, and hurried off to the rear stacks. She had no idea what books she'd take, but she didn't care. When Olivia got there, she performed the same strange ritual she had the first time: closed her eyes and walked along the stacks with her hand trailing over the spines of the books until she felt something. A tickle or a hunch, she didn't know. Still, Olivia acted on it, taking the book under her fingers. She did this three times, slipping each tome into her storage ring.

"Got what you needed?" Carlu's voice startled her. She hadn't realized the little inspector had stuck around, nor that he'd come so close. She looked up to see him leaning against a nearby stack, watching her through his spectacles.

"Yes. Um, where's Professor Voyle-dak?" Olivia asked, looking past Carlu and not seeing any sign of Oylla or the other professor.

"He had a class, so I offered to be your escort. I was hoping to interview you a bit on the way. Will that be all right? We can head straight to the Travel Pavilion—I've sent word for your cohort to meet you there. Oylla-dak thought maybe one or more of them would like to go home with you. Would you like that? Some company while you're gone?"

"I'd like for this killer to be caught so we can get on with our lives," Olivia said, frowning at the slight Shadeni in his perfectly pressed suit.

"Of course, Ms. Bennet, I'm working on it! Please, let's walk. I have a feeling some of your answers to my questions might very well point me in the right direction."

"I'm not sure how, but that's fine with me. Let's go."

Olivia brushed past the inspector, taking the lead, and he hurried to catch up, pulling out his notepad and clearing his throat.

# OLIVIA

"No, for the tenth time, Carlu, I don't have any idea what the poem means. I think the killer was trying to get under my skin or perhaps send pursuit off on a red herring. I mean, look at the time you've been wasting today. How thoroughly have you managed to go through the killer's belongings that we found? Have you at all, or was your inspection interrupted by Alyss's murder? I hope you've got guards on all that stuff—" Olivia would have kept ranting, but the inspector stopped her by grabbing her elbow.

"Wait! Ms. Bennet, we should walk out to the pavilion through the rear gardens. It's a slightly longer route, but we'll be less likely to run into any trouble."

Olivia stopped at the door she'd been about to go through and jerked her arm away from the slender, dapper man, not pleased with how his fingers dug into her flesh.

"If you think so," she replied, pausing to let him lead the way. She knew how to get to the rear gardens, but she was irritated enough by the way he'd grabbed her arm that she didn't want him lingering behind her while they walked.

"Thank you," Carlu said, starting up the hallway to their left. "I'm not a slouch when it comes to personal combat, but I'd rather not have to face the killer on his terms. Let's get you safely to the Travel Pavilion, then I can focus on tracking him down, hmm?"

"Yes, but I'm telling you, focus less on Alyss and that poem and more on the objects we found in the killer's lair!" Olivia followed the inspector past another large hallway which led toward the cafeteria and up a side passage which she knew would open into the gardens, or at least the cobbled path leading to the gardens.

"I'll take your advice to heart, Ms. Bennet, but I'm not one to let such a set of clues go so easily. Never fear, however—I have the ability to multitask, and I'll be sure to continue my investigation into the killer's belongings. You're quite right on one account: I'm sure those effects will eventually lead me to him. I'm treating the dear professor's murder as a way to speed the process, hopefully."

Olivia didn't answer him. She was tired of thinking and talking, especially about the killer. She just wanted to hug Adaida and slip through the portal back to Morgan's tower, where she could relax and forget about all of this. Thinking of her friends waiting to say goodbye to her, Olivia had a momentary panic about leaving them all here to the killer's mercy, and she determined they'd all be coming back to First Landing with her, even if she had to drag them through the portal.

They'd made it up the cobbled walkway to the flower garden Carlu wanted to cut through when he paused, flipping the lenses on his goggles and staring at the air around him. He held up a hand when Olivia started to ask what he was doing, then he stepped forward and stared at the stones in front of the gate for several long heartbeats. Finally, he turned to her, his mouth slightly open and his eyes huge through his lenses. "Olivia! Would you mind casting that tracking spell again? The one we devised to hunt the killer's Energy?"

"You see something?" she asked, already building the pattern in her pathways.

"Yes, I do! Please hurry!"

He wrung his hands agitatedly, staring at her.

Olivia didn't answer, finishing the spell and watching as her magenta tracking winds swirled around the gateway and then rushed off into the garden. "They have the scent!" Olivia said, pushing past Carlu.

"Wait! Shouldn't we get help?" he asked, grabbing onto her robe.

"Let go, Carlu! You can get help if you want, but I'm not going to lose this trail!" Olivia jerked free of his grasp for the second time that day and hurried down the path. She heard him coming after her and felt a little guilty about putting him in danger, but wasn't this his job?

"No, I won't leave you alone. I'm with you, Ms. Bennet," Carlu said, confirming her thoughts.

"Thank you, Carlu," Olivia replied while she hurried after her breezes, following their twisting path through the garden, moving deeper and further to the left than their path would have taken them if they'd gone straight to the Travel Pavilion. One of her breezes would always wait at a turn, ensuring she caught up before rushing after the others. Olivia glanced over her shoulder several times, ensuring Carlu was still with her and that no one was sneaking up on them; she had visions of a black-robed murderer lurking down one of the side paths.

She could see a bit into the rows nearest her, as most of the flowering shrubs had gone dormant for the winter. Still, it seemed those who had designed the garden had managed to plant a large variety of species which appeared to produce leaves and flowers even this late in the year. Olivia caught herself thinking about what sorts of plants would be able to grow with such chilly nighttime temperatures and shook her head.

"Need to stay focused," she growled, turning around another corner where one of her magenta breezes had been circling.

She stumbled to a halt when she found the ground had been dug up in a little alcove of planters; a trapdoor had been left open, exposing an ancient-looking wooden ladder that descended into the darkness. Her breeze dove into the dark opening as she took in the red, sticky splashes and puddles surrounding the hole.

"Oh God! Did he kill someone here?"

"Hmm, I'm not sure, Ms. Bennet. There's not as much blood as at the other murder sites. Perhaps he's injured someone and taken them down? Or perhaps he, himself, is injured."

"C'mon, Carlu!" Olivia urged, summoning an orb of plasma and letting it sink into the opening. The crackling, hissing orb of brilliant blue-white Energy revealed nothing more than a few feet of the narrow, dirt-lined shaft, so Olivia began climbing the ladder down, looking past her feet as her orb descended ahead of her. She'd made it down about six feet when her orb winked out, plunging her into darkness. Olivia had been in the midst of taking a step, and when the ladder suddenly shifted under her hands—changing from dry, ancient wood to something slick and flowing—she cried out as her foot met nothing but air and she fell.

She plunged downward, her first instinct being to cast Elemental Form and taking on her air aspect. As she pushed the Energy into her pathways and cast the spell, however, nothing happened other than the Energy being sucked out of her. And not just the Energy for the spell—all of her air-attuned Energy was drawn from her Core. Olivia panicked, instantly aware of what had happened. She was falling into a space with wards like those in the detention cells.

Just as she connected the dots, her back slammed into something solid, like stone. If it weren't for her robes, she was sure it would have hurt. Nevertheless, her magical clothes did their job and absorbed most of the impact, and she rolled to her knees to stand up, staring into the darkness, her breaths coming quick and shallow. The only light was the square of sky up the shaft she'd come down. She glanced up at it, but her hope dissolved as it winked out. Someone had closed the trapdoor.

Olivia reached into her storage ring and pulled out an object she hadn't needed in a very long time: a glow lamp she'd carried with her since she'd been a tier-zero nobody who'd gone to face a Yovashi with her friends. The soft, pale light lit up the space she stood in, and Olivia saw that she was in an oval stone chamber. The shaft leading up from the ceiling was nearly ten feet over her head.

At her feet, atop the stone, was a blue, metal latticework of runes arranged in a circle, and she knew it was the source of the Energy-sapping wards.

The metal circle was about eight feet in diameter, and it met the walls neatly around the chamber, though one end of the space was open, a dark stone corridor leading away. Olivia strode toward the tunnel, hope blooming in her chest, but when she came to the edge of the rune-covered metal frame, her foot simply couldn't step over it. It was like being in a perfectly clear glass cage, one that ate the Energy from any spell she tried to cast.

"Dammit," Olivia cursed, kneeling to get a better look at the lattice. She hoped that maybe she could damage or deface it somehow. When she touched the cold metal with her fingers, she froze, ice sliding down her spine. It felt exactly like the Energy signature she'd been chasing ever since the killer had attacked her and Adaida in the Alchemy Gardens. It was cold and slippery and left a dirty feeling on her fingers. Olivia took a sharp knife from her storage ring and began to scrape and carve at one of the metal runes.

She grunted in frustration as her efforts were unrewarded; the metal was tougher than steel, as far as she could tell. In further frustration, she tried—again—to summon a plasma orb, only to have her air and fire-attuned Energies drained from her Core. There hadn't been much air, but with it gone and her fire Energy gone with it, she felt cold and lethargic, and frustration threatened to fill her eyes with tears or bring a screech of rage from her throat. She took several deep breaths to calm down and think, and that's when Carlu spoke up.

"You won't find a way out of there, Ms. Bennet."

Olivia saw he'd approached her from the stone corridor and was leaning against the wall, watching her over the tops of his strange gogglelike glasses.

"Carlu! Help me out! Get help if you must!" Olivia exclaimed, standing up, but when she saw his expression, she finally connected the dots. "Oh. You're not going to help me."

"Bravo!" Carlu said, slowly clapping his hands. Olivia had time to wonder if he'd really said *bravo* or if the System had translated some other Shadeni colloquialism for her before he continued, "Finally, the genius, the prodigy, the powerhouse who needs no help has managed to compute some simple arithmetic!"

"But why? Are you angry that I was interfering in your investigation?" Olivia, despite Carlu's sarcasm, still hadn't put everything together. She couldn't fathom that he and the killer were one and the same; hadn't the killing started before he arrived at campus?

She cleared her throat and said, "Carlu, the killer made this trap! I can feel the Energy. I know you're angry with me, but you need to get me out of here. He could be nearby!"

"I thought you were smarter than that, Olivia. You're right; the killer made that ward circle, tailored quite specifically to block your abilities, I might add. I, however, made this trap. Imagine the arrogance! To think you could solve these murders while a Vesneya-trained investigator was on the premise. What a fool you are. What fools the staff here are!" Carlu broke into a laugh then, clearly savoring the moment. "I could have scried out or tracked the killer from the first day I was here. In fact, I found it more challenging to drag out the investigation without arousing suspicion!"

"But why, Carlu? Are you friends with the killer? You're protecting someone?"

"You dolt. Why does anyone do anything in this world? Power, my dear. Power. I'll be greatly rewarded by the one who hired me. Now, be a good girl and don't hurt yourself in there. My employer will be here before long, and I'm sure he'd prefer to have you whole and hale for whatever purpose he had in mind." Carlu doffed his bowler-style hat, sketched a mocking bow, then turned and walked up the hallway, ignoring Olivia's cries for him to stop and listen to reason.

# ⚭ BRONWYN ⚭

Bronwyn crouched low, keeping to the shadows of the big, twisting tunnel as she stalked behind the lumbering swamp troll, easily masking the sound of her passage with its shambling gait. The troll was probably eight feet tall and covered with shaggy mosslike growths which seemed to weigh it down in such a way that it stooped, shuffled, and frequently stopped to groan and breathe heavily.

She'd come to realize that the older these trolls got, the more overburdened with those growths they became, and so, ones like this weren't very common. Bronwyn figured the harsh environment and the trolls' natural enemies made it hard for them to survive as they grew large and slow.

She'd spent the last few hours working her way into the depths of the Hollows. She'd had to kill a few trolls, but they weren't challenging, especially when she took them one by one. They were much weaker than the Rehavash she, Olivia, and Morgan had fought in the dungeon on Unu. Though her memory might be skewed, they seemed easier to kill than the forest troll she'd fought when she'd been on Thun's trail, too. Of course, she hadn't had her hatchets back then. Bronwyn grinned as she brandished the two crescent-bladed weapons; when she charged them with solar Energy, they made short work of the trolls' mossy armor and hide.

Her idea was to work her way as deep as she could, hoping to find the troll matriarch and put an end to this problem as soon as possible. She knew she had a day but didn't know when the timer had started. Had it been as soon as she'd gotten out of the Umbrilak tunnel? Had it begun when she'd killed her first troll? She feared it was the former, which meant she was already six hours into her free day. If she didn't finish this troll problem in the next eighteen hours, then the Winter Court would move against Olivia.

"That's how I understood things, anyway," she said under her breath.

Bronwyn was about to follow the old troll around another corner when she noticed a darker spot in the wide tunnel floor, just behind a pile of jumbled stones. She glided over to investigate and found a steep mossy tunnel that led down at a perilous angle. "Well, I wanted to get deeper faster, didn't I?" Bronwyn stepped into the narrow passage and, leaning back to keep from toppling down the incline, started inching her way down into the depths of the Hollows.

As she descended, Bronwyn recalled her conversation with Whitestar. She'd run back to the Urghat encampment as soon as she'd gotten clear of the Umbrilak, and nearly tripping over her words in her haste, she'd told Whitestar that she needed to get the Urghat ready for an assault. She'd told her to move as close as possible without getting surrounded by trolls and to watch them. "Hope I was right," Bronwyn hissed as she recalled telling Whitestar they'd know when she'd succeeded; that the trolls would react when the matriarch was slain. "I really fucking hope I was right," she repeated.

The tunnel grew even steeper, and Bronwyn was forced to sit and slide down, using her axes to break her speed every time it started to get out of hand. She began to worry she was descending so far that she'd be out of the Hollows by the time it ended and she'd have to find another way back toward the trolls, wasting more of her precious hours, when she fell clear of the passage, soaring from a high hole in a cavern wall to squelch into a bed of slimy fungi. She knew then she was on the right track: outside the fungi pit, two enormous moss-covered trolls sat chewing on the carcass of an Urghat.

Bronwyn saw bones, fur, and other remnants which helped her conclude she'd descended through a feeding chute of sorts. These trolls were too slow and covered with moss to move much at all—the others were feeding them in a twisted show of respect to their elders, she supposed. Not wanting to raise a cacophony by fighting these two old, hillock-size trolls, Bronwyn edged her way through the slippery, smelly offal pit filled with fungus and the remnants of animals and people, and holding her breath, slipped onto the solid ground far to the side of the ancient, feeding monsters.

The cavern was enormous, and she didn't have a hard time finding shadows to lurk in, as the only light came from bygone orange Energy crystals which hung in rusted brackets—remnants from a time when the Urghat lived in these depths. Bronwyn had seen these crystals in every part of the warrens she'd been through, and she silently thanked them for not forcing her to carry a light, which allowed her to avoid many, many battles.

As she slithered through the long shadows cast by boulders and stalagmites, one of the enormous old trolls started to sniff the air, turning great, white, rheumy orbs in her direction and then back at the pit. It snorted something in a guttural tongue to its companion, and they both returned to their munching, crunching down on the bones of the dead Urghat. Bronwyn figured the creatures must be used to dead or incapacitated meals coming down the chute; they didn't seem up for a chase. Bronwyn hurried from the cavern, turning down the first tunnel she came to.

The tunnels were wide down here, and the stone was very clean—no rubble littered the ground, and no moss clung to the walls. A warm, dry breeze seemed to be coming from deeper still, and Bronwyn found herself following it around corners and past dark chambers where she heard the sounds of grunting and dragging flesh and claws. She knew an army of enemies was at her back, and if she was wrong about killing the matriarch, she might end up dead down there. Her pulse was quick with adrenaline as she slipped by yet another enormous cavern which echoed with the grunts of trolls, and she wondered if they were fighting, eating, or fucking.

"Gross," she hissed at herself.

The tunnel sloped down, and then she saw what she'd been hoping for; an ancient metal door signaled something important, but more than that, the two young trolls standing outside it, brandishing sharpened sticks like spears, told her she'd reached some sort of inner sanctum, perhaps the lair of the matriarch.

Bronwyn contemplated her options, considered the urgency in her heart, and decided to go with her gut and act with haste and decisiveness. She cast Mirage Double, and when her twin materialized next to her, she grinned and nodded to it, a little weirded out when it did the same. Bronwyn cast Solar Arms and Solar Shell before she charged down the tunnel, blazing like a torch made of sunlight. She fell upon the troll on the left while her double, following her silent commands, charged the troll on the right.

Bronwyn's flaming hatchets carved burning hunks off the troll, taking off limbs and opening its torso in a series of sizzling chops. The creature was dead before it could really react, and then Bronwyn launched herself at the flank of the screaming troll being distracted by her double. In two hacks, she'd severed its spine and split its skull. Suddenly, silence resounded around her, but a distant racket told her that her murders hadn't gone unnoticed. She'd have company soon.

Bronwyn turned to the doors, held her hatchets in one hand, and yanked on the right side. It protested with a squeal of rust, but it moved.

She pulled until it was just wide enough to slip through and glided between the doors with her hatchets still ablaze. As she stepped inside, pain erupted in her head when massive jaws bit down, scraping along her scalp and up along her neck. Rows of jagged, dirty teeth ripped away part of her scalp and her right ear, and Bronwyn screamed, pulling away, leaving her flesh flapping in the tall, lanky matriarch's mouth.

In a red haze of pain, Bronwyn reactivated Solar Shell, adrenaline helping her sprint away from the monster while she dug around in her storage necklace for one of Thun's potions. She wrapped her hand around one just as the troll smashed a long, razor-clawed arm into her shoulders, sending Bronwyn sprawling and singing its own flesh. As she slid over the stone ground,

Bronwyn tipped the potion to her lips, and she suddenly understood how Morgan had felt when she'd poured one in his mouth.

The blood stopped sheeting out of her torn scalp, and she felt scabs form and the pain subside. More than that, though, her heart started to thunder and race, and she felt like she had to move or her vessels would burst. She launched herself into a roll and turned to face her attacker, pacing sideways with her hatchets blazing and ready.

The troll matriarch was not as massive as the older, shambling trolls, but she was taller, with long, grasping arms and a lean, naked torso, sporting six thick, greenish-gray breasts. Overall, she looked greener than the other trolls, and her skin was smoother, absent of the moss and fungus which seemed to sprout over her kinfolk's hides. She had a narrow face more than half occupied by her wide, tooth-filled jaws, and perhaps the most troubling, she had long black hair hanging from her head and between her legs.

One of the matriarch's hands was smoking; she turned her bulging yellow eyes on Bronwyn and screamed. Bronwyn didn't react to her right away. Instead, she turned to the door and saw that it still stood slightly open and that a heavy bolt could be thrown to lock it. She raced that way, ignoring the matriarch's long-limbed charge, and slammed her shoulder into the door, closing it. Just as the matriarch was about to slash her again, Bronwyn ducked to her left and drove the bolt home. Then, she turned to face the creature that had bitten her ear off.

"All right, bitch. Let's dance!"

The troll was fast and vicious, and Bronwyn knew that if she hadn't had solar Energy blazing from her hatchets, the creature would have healed from her cuts before she could pile up enough damage to hamper her. As it was, Bronwyn ducked under her long-clawed slashes and slowly hacked the giant troll apart. The creature screamed in rage and agony as Bronwyn's solar Energy burned through her flesh, and though she managed to claw Bronwyn a few times, the cuts weren't terribly deep, thanks to her quick reflexes and to her Solar Shell causing as much—if not more—damage to the furious troll's claws.

As the potion began to wear off and Bronwyn felt fatigue start to set in, she backed away from the hobbled matriarch and cast Wrath of Summer, not wanting to risk failure by stubbornly trying to win with just her hatchets.

A blinding light erupted from the ceiling of the enormous cavern, illuminating the entire space for the first time. Bronwyn gasped when she saw what lurked in the shadows outside the light of her blazing hatchets: hundreds of piled, glistening eggs like mounds of giant caviar. She was so taken by the sight that she missed her spell's destruction of the matriarch; when the bright light faded and she looked back, the troll was nothing more than a pile of ash.

Bronwyn stood there, chest heaving, scalp stinging, and ears ringing, and watched as a hundred large, purple-gold Energy orbs coalesced over the ashes and streamed into her.

**\*\*\*Congratulations! You have achieved level 26 Summer Banneret and have 28 attribute points to distribute.\*\*\***

The pain in her scalp faded entirely with the euphoria of the Energy infusion, but when she reached up a hand to feel at her ear and the spot where her flesh and hair had been ripped away, she found only smooth skin. Realizing her ear was gone, she hissed in anger and frustration and flipped her hair over that side of her head.

"That sucks," she groused, walking deeper into the cavern and recasting Solar Arms so her hatchets would light up the space again. "Time to crack some eggs!"

# MORGAN

Three days had passed since Morgan's tower had been locked down. Three days during which he'd scribed thousands of runes on more than a hundred rods and other internal parts for Tiladia's new body. He'd seen Issa create some truly awesome marvels, from a pulsing metallic heart to a round crystal orb filled with shimmering gemstones and a silvery liquid that Issa said would allow Tiladia to keep learning and growing—an artificial brain.

The brain had been impressive, but when he'd seen how Issa had shaped the calepsii horn into an orb, surrounded it with a platinum casing, and inscribed thousands of tiny runes in a spiral pattern from its top to its bottom, Morgan's jaw had dropped. The Energy pouring out of it was palpable, and the fine detail and clever design of the rune pattern simply stunned him; it looked like an ancient artifact left by some great old master, not something his sweet wife-to-be would craft in their home.

Issa held it in the palm of her hand on the third day of their confinement and announced, "I'm ready. I can start to assemble her now. Morgan, you need to figure out how to release her from the tower's binding." As she spoke, the orb containing Tiladia's Core pulsed and flexed, thousands of tiny seams in the platinum casing expanding to reveal the yellow glow of the Energy-infused horn. *No*, Morgan corrected himself; it wasn't a horn any longer: it was a Core.

"All right, I will. Am I allowed to watch you? I want to see the process, and I still have no idea what she's going to look like."

"Ask her," Issa said, gesturing to the floating, misty form of Tiladia as she drifted into the room, perhaps having listened to them and aware that her time was nigh. She'd been on duty at the front door, watching to see if the colonists figured out a way to get close enough to the tower to speak with them.

The poor colonists had tried several solutions, from a breathing apparatus to protect them from invisible gases to using magical boots which allowed them to sprint twice as fast as without. Nothing had allowed them to reach even the base of the metal stairs. The only small blessing was that they'd begun to tie a rope to the test subjects, pulling them away from the tower when they collapsed. It looked as though they woke up immediately upon leaving the warded area.

Thinking of the town, Morgan reflexively used his Guardian's Senses ability to check on Arthur Ballard; he was both glad and troubled to see he was still off to the east, about half as far from First Landing as Tarn's Crossing was.

"So something like fifty miles," Morgan sighed, then cleared his throat and exclaimed, "Tiladia! Are you excited? I am! Issa's almost ready, and the body she's making you will be so much better than anything Vormendion made for his guardians."

"Yes, Morgan! I am very excited, and I knew that already; we've discussed the quality of Lady Issa's work many times in the past few days."

"I know, I know. You see, I'd really like to watch her finish her work; I want to see the magic, as it were. I know you want your body to be a surprise, but would you allow me to stay?"

"Morgan! Do you truly ask me for permission? I cannot stop you!" Tiladia whooshed past him and stopped to hover in front of his face. He imagined she had come close to look at him, verifying his honesty.

"No, but I'd respect your wishes." Morgan gently reached out a hand toward her misty form, and she curled around it, cool, moist air brushing the hairs on the backs of his knuckles in a featherlight touch.

"This is why I wouldn't choose to leave, even if free, Morgan. I thank you for your kind regard, and I would be honored to have you watch me be born, once more, into the physical world."

"Thank you, Tiladia. While Issa gets things set up, would you help me figure out how to unbind you from the tower?"

"In the basement, Morgan. If you walk past the prison cells, you'll come to a blank wall. Simply rest your hand upon it, and a chamber will open. Within that chamber, you'll find a warded cage which contains a small fragment of me. Release it, and my spirit will be made whole so Issa can work her magic."

"That easy, huh?" Morgan looked to where Issa was starting to lay out the components she'd so carefully prepared over the last week and nodded. "All right. Issa, I'll be right back." She briefly waved to him without looking up, and Morgan hurried out of the workshop. He felt Tiladia following him and asked, "Are you coming with me?"

"Yes. This is a big moment for me," Tiladia said. Morgan, for the millionth time, wished he could better read her emotions in that strange, tinkling voice of hers.

"All right. Together, then."

Morgan motioned her up next to him, and they descended the stairs, passed through the dining room and kitchen, and descended into the cellar level of the tower. Morgan walked past Tkron's cell and caught himself avoiding looking within.

"Nah, you need to face things you aren't proud of, too," he murmured, taking a step back to activate the viewing portal.

Tkron squatted in the far corner of the cell, his gray face expressionless as usual, but Morgan was surprised to see he had some sort of wooden device with various strings and sliding beads and washers on thin dowels. "What the . . ."

Morgan activated the speak-through feature and said, "Tkron, where'd you get that?"

"You startle me, human," Tkron replied, looking anything but surprised in his stoic countenance. "The human counselor, Geert Hagen, gave it to me. He said it would be good for my stress. I find the puzzle rather stimulating, I must admit."

"Right, I'd forgotten he came to see you."

"He was supposed to return yesterday, but I've had no contact," Tkron said. Morgan thought he detected a note of disappointment, but it was hard to tell with the Yovashi's grinding voice.

"Sorry, Tkron. There's been a bit of a crisis, so nothing is going to plan right now. I'm sure he'll be back soon, though. Good luck with your puzzle."

Morgan killed the view panel and speaker and continued down the hallway, shaking his head. If the psychologists from First Landing could figure out a way to help Tkron, that would be great, but he wasn't going to hold his breath. He passed the last cell and stopped before the blank, bronze wall at the end of the hall.

"This it, Tiladia?"

"It is!" She managed to stretch her amorphous form into a kind of pointer, and Morgan followed her direction, placing his hand on the wall where she'd indicated. A yellow seam of Energy flowed out from where his hand met the metal and traced the shape of a doorway in the wall. A moment later, it hissed and slid upward, seemingly into the ceiling. Morgan stepped forward into the secret chamber and found that it was oval, nearly twenty paces across, and with a ceiling a good fifteen feet overhead. The walls of the room were absolutely covered in golden, glowing runes.

In the center of the chamber was a round pedestal, and resting atop it were nine gleaming cages arrayed in a $V$ shape, one at the center and four down each side. Morgan stepped closer and saw all the cages were empty save the center one, which held a faintly shimmering, almost imperceptibly vibrating shard of crystal.

"That's it." Morgan wasn't asking—he could see how the fragment was similar to the ones that tinkled and chimed within Tiladia's misty form.

"Yes! I'm happy to see the guardians' captive shards are gone. Vormendion was less duplicitous than I feared."

"Oh," Morgan said, looking at the empty cages again. "I get it now. Do you think these cages are made of something valuable? Maybe I should bring them to Issa; I can't see myself filling and using them the way Vormendion did."

"They're made from Sun Silver, and yes, quite valuable," Tiladia replied, quickly adding, "Please release my shard before you store them!"

"Yeah, of course. Don't worry, Til." Morgan smiled and reached out to touch the cage holding Tiladia's shard.

"Til?" Tiladia said before his fingers made contact.

"Yeah. Human's like shortening speech. It's called a nickname."

"I'm aware of the concept, Morgan. I just hadn't been called that before. I like it, but you should know: Tiladia is already a nickname. You'll see when you touch that cage."

"Oh? All right, let's see!" Morgan rested his fingertips on the warm metal, and suddenly, a menu opened up in his vision:

***Pain Stimulus*** ☐***
***Summon Entity*** ☐***
***Prime Containment*** ☐***
***Destroy Shard*** ☐***
***Open Containment*** ☐***

"What the hell? *Pain stimulus*?" Morgan frowned, wishing he could get his hands on Vormendion.

"Yes. Please don't activate that, Morgan." Tiladia floated very close, brushing her mists along his arm as if to remind him she was there.

"I won't. Which do I push? I'm guessing not *Summon* or *Destroy*. What about *Prime Containment*?"

"No, Morgan, that's needed to place a new shard within. Simply open the cage."

"Right." Morgan touched the button next to Open Containment, and another notification appeared in his vision:

***Warning! This is the shard of Til'danishea, the Steward Spirit for this tower. Releasing the steward will result in the loss of some automated features, such as admitting and banishing guests, note-taking and reminders, and general dwelling information systems. Are you sure? Y/N***

Morgan suddenly understood what Tiladia had meant about her nickname. He wondered if she liked being called Tiladia or if that was how Vormendion had instructed her to style herself because it was simpler to say. "Was he really this much of an asshole?"

Morgan snorted and pushed the yes option. The cage clicked open, and the shard within shimmered and disappeared from his vision, apparently moving in a way that he couldn't detect to join with Tiladia's whole. It must have worked because she launched into a circular race around the room, and all of her tinkling crystal bits broke out into a ringing crescendo that echoed in the round, metal chamber while she whirled around, faster almost than Morgan could track with his eyes.

"Thank you!" Tiladia's ringing, chiming voice said over and over, and Morgan's cheeks started to hurt from smiling as he watched her celebrate.

After a few moments, however, he laughed and called out, "Tiladia! Come on! Let's go see if Issa can finish the process! You need a body!"

"Yesssss! Morgan!" She streaked out of the chamber and away, clearly not intending to match his slower pace through the tower.

"Heh." Morgan shrugged and scooped the soul fragment cages into his storage ring. That done, he locked up the secret control center of the tower and made his way back to the workshop. He found Issa setting up all the parts of Tiladia's new body on one of the longer workbenches near the rear, and he immediately saw why the dragon spirit had wanted to keep her new body a secret. The unmistakably humanoid arms, legs, feet, and hands gave away the secret: Tiladia wanted to look like the people she lived with. Well, at least him and Issa, Morgan corrected himself, not seeing any long spider legs.

"These are beautiful," Morgan breathed as he drew nearer, seeing the shimmering, silvery metal of the body parts etched with tiny, perfect lines of runes, though only in certain areas; Morgan had no idea what had determined their placement.

"I'm going to look like a human, Morgan!" Tiladia chimed, swooping out of the air where she'd been continuing her celebration of the wholeness of her soul.

"Really, Tiladia? Is that what you want, or is that what you think I want?" Morgan asked before he could think better of it.

"Of course that's what she wants!" Issa snapped. "Do you think we didn't have many long conversations about this?" She scowled at him, trying to make eye contact, and Morgan realized his reaction to Tiladia's announcement hadn't been ideal. The little cloud of mist and ethereal crystal was now slowly moving around the table, and Morgan couldn't help seeing that much of the excitement had left her.

"Tiladia," he said, clearing his throat. "I couldn't imagine a better compliment to humankind. You're such a wonderful spirit, such a wonderful *person*! I'm so honored that you'd like to take the shape of my people."

"Oh, thank you, Morgan!" she exclaimed, swooping close again. "I love all the humans I've met. I love little Ykleedra, too, but I like your form better. It's not very unlike one which I used to take when I was a dragon!"

"Really?"

"Yes! I would take the form of a fae from time to time to make travel and trade easier when I visited their realm."

"You . . . visited the Fae Realm when you were a dragon?" Morgan, once again, berated himself for not knowing enough about Tiladia.

"I visited many places, Morgan, and having my spirit whole again has helped me to remember many things I'd let fade. Thank you again for my freedom!"

"This is lovely," Issa said, "but we have a town to save or something, and I can't concentrate while you two chat."

She grunted softly, and Morgan saw she was carefully slotting rods into one of the silvery legs, her slightly protruding belly bumping against the workbench.

"Can I help?" Morgan asked.

"No. Please just sit on that shop stool and watch. If all goes well, everything will be done in a few hours, and then you'll really see the magic of this new alloy!" Issa had a gleam in her eyes and a smile on her face, and Morgan felt very glad that she'd agreed to take the inheritance and that he hadn't frivolously used the skills to keep them out of someone else's hands. He pulled up a stool and settled in, watching Issa put her legendary-ranked Artificer class to work.

# MORGAN

Issa gently lifted the globe of sparkling, gem-filled liquid and nestled it among the thousands of curled, hairlike copper, gold, and silver wires in Tiladia's new head. A shimmer of Energy passed through the nest of wires before fading. Morgan watched, with rapt attention, as Issa carefully placed the top of the silvery skull over the dome, gently running a finger along the seam to seal it with a pulse of Energy.

"Wow. Issa, that looked incredibly complicated. Where'd you get the materials for that . . . um, crystal brain?"

"I purchased all the raw precious metals I needed, but many of the more esoteric items, like the memory gems, came from Vormendion's stockpile. I should have talked to you about this, but I knew you'd say it was all right."

"Yeah, of course—"

"Well, I should mention that some of these objects would fund a household in Tarn's Crossing for years . . ." Issa said more softly, sort of trailing off, glancing nervously at Morgan while she worked.

"Huh. Well, it's only money, right? This is worth it."

Issa didn't reply, but Morgan could see the smile on her face while she worked. Tiladia's silvery body was nearly complete. As Issa had finished the interior of each limb, each digit, she'd been slowly, steadily assembling the body. Once she placed the head atop the neck, carefully closing the seam where the artificial vertebrae touched the base of the skull, Morgan could see a complete, silvery woman lying on the bench.

"She looks like an early Noah Unit," he commented, forgetting for the moment that neither Tiladia nor Issa had any idea what that was.

"Noah Unit?" Issa asked, only half paying attention to him.

"They were, uh, artificial people that we developed to help manage our spaceships. The early ones had metallic bodies like this."

"I'm not artificial," Tiladia noted, hovering behind Issa and watching her progress.

"No, that was the wrong sort of comparison to make. I'm sorry," he apologized.

"She won't look metallic for long. When I finish and she bonds with the new body, it will take on an aspect from her mind. I'm so excited to see how it looks; this alloy made it possible!"

"Really? This is incredible, Issa."

"It's all made possible by many lucky circumstances, really. I can't take credit for everything. My class is part of it, but Vormendion worked for decades to acquire the skill and spell I learned. Put that aside and look at the fortune of materials we had access to." She glanced at Tiladia's amorphous form and added, "And a very special spirit willing to go along with my design!"

"I'm eager to be part of this, Lady Issa. I couldn't possibly thank you enough." Tiladia curled gently around Issa and then floated back, giving her room to work.

"Everything is assembled," Issa said, surprising Morgan as she straightened and gestured at the silvery body. "Two more steps are needed: Tiladia, you need to bond with the body, but it will remain inert until someone primes the Core with a surge of pure Energy. Morgan, I'm not sure I have enough, but if you hold hands with me and push some of your pure Energy toward me," she paused and spoke very clearly, "*Not* your void Energy, Morgan." He nodded, and she continued, "Then I will be able to draw on it as I activate the body."

"I'm ready," Tiladia declared, her crystal voice speaking so quickly that the independent notes ran together, making it hard for Morgan to understand.

"You'll feel strange, Tiladia, maybe even lose consciousness while we prime your Core. Don't be worried; I promise it won't last long."

"God, I feel like we should have some sort of ceremony or something. This all feels so . . ." Morgan grasped for the right word and finally settled on, "momentous. We don't have time to mess around, though. Til, when you're ready."

Morgan stood up and moved beside Issa, holding out his hand. Issa took it, resting her other hand on the silver body's stomach, right above the carefully sculpted navel.

"Tiladia, just settle down over the body. You'll feel the pathways meant for a spirit. Flow into them, and I'll cast Vormendion's spell, binding you to the vessel." Morgan heard Issa inhale and knew she was holding her breath while they watched Tiladia gently settle down.

The spirit rested above the body—an amorphous, glittering, tinkling cloud—for just a moment, and then she seemed to flow into the chest, right between the two small breasts Issa had crafted. She was gone in the space of two of Morgan's breaths, and he thought he detected a brighter shimmer emanating from the body's silvery skin.

Issa concentrated for a moment, Morgan feeling Energy surge from her, and then the body pulsed with a brilliant silver-turquoise light. Morgan squinted against the glare until it faded, and soon, the body returned to its usual luster. "Ready? Morgan? Push a thread of Energy into my hand, please."

Morgan had spaced out, watching the light show coming from Tiladia's new body, and it wasn't until Issa said his name that he registered her voice. "Right, here it comes."

He teased a thread of Energy from the maelstrom circling his Core, pulling the pure Energy out along his pathways and pushing it toward Issa. He felt her take hold, and his instinct was to resist, but he tamped down on his will, letting it flow. Soon, a steady ribbon of Energy was pouring out of him and into Issa.

She began to radiate with the Energy, and when he looked at her hand touching Tiladia's new belly, he saw the bright silver-turquoise Energy signature again. As it grew in brightness, he became aware of an almost subsonic hum coming from Issa. Looking at her, he saw her partially open mouth and thousand-yard stare, and began to worry.

Had she taken on something that was too much for her? Should she have to use his Energy to jumpstart her creation? Was she hurting herself?

He needn't have worried, however. Almost as soon as his thoughts began to spiral, he felt the tug on his Core lessen, and then the stream of Energy flowing out to Issa tapered off. The pulsing Energy around her hand subsided, and Issa inhaled deeply through her nose before smiling, looking up at Morgan. "It's done."

Morgan looked at the inert but softly shimmering body. "She's not moving or anything."

"I can see that, Morgan." Issa tsked and gently brushed Tiladia's brow. Even with her shimmering skin, Morgan could see Issa had put a lot of love and attention to detail into crafting Tiladia's face. It was faintly heart-shaped with a pert nose, full lips on a small mouth, a gentle indentation above her upper lip, and a graceful jawline stretching up to her finely detailed, elegant ears.

"Will she have hair?" Morgan asked, noting the utter lack of it.

"That's the plan. I think right now she's settling in. As her soul meshes with the body, it will start to read her intent, and then she'll take on her new aspect. I'm not sure how long it will take . . ." Issa trailed off, gently resting her hand on Tiladia's belly again. "It's working, though. I can feel the Core pulsing and feeding Energy into her pathways."

"Will she be able to shape-shift?" Morgan asked, imagining the body shifting to look different based on Tiladia's intent.

"No, silly. Her intent is subconscious, and this is a one-time process. Look!" Issa pointed to a circle on Tiladia's chest where the shimmering surface had grown cloudy, resolving into a patch of pale pigment. Morgan watched as the color spread, dulling the reflective, metallic surface and gradually shifting to look like actual skin. "Morgan, hold your arm up here." Issa took his fingers, too impatient for him to register what she meant, and pressed his hand on Tiladia's stomach. Their skin tones were a perfect match.

"She's copied my skin." Morgan laughed. "God, it feels real. It doesn't feel like metal at all!" Morgan quickly pulled his hand away, aware that he'd been resting it on Tiladia's naked stomach. As his eyes drifted upward, he jerked his head away—Tiladia's breasts had taken on a fleshy aspect as well. "Give her a blanket or something!" he sputtered.

Issa laughed, pulling her magical cloak from her ring and draping it over Tiladia's torso. As she did so, Morgan saw little hairs start to sprout from Tiladia's scalp. He pointed, watching them lengthen into a lustrous mane of wavy, shimmering, silver-colored hair.

"Oh, it's beautiful, and I don't think this is a remnant of the alloy. Tiladia told me her dragon scales were silver!" Issa clapped her hands together.

"Damn, it looks amazing," Morgan said, noting that Tiladia's eyebrows had also sprouted thick, silver hairs. A moment later, the reborn dragon spirit shuddered, opened her mouth to reveal sharp, white teeth, and inhaled. Then her eyes shot open, and gleaming silver irises regarded Morgan and Issa.

"Am I alive?" she asked, her voice clear, wholly unique, and beautiful. It rang with clarity and had a lilting tone, very different from her old incarnation's false chiming voice.

"You are!" Issa said, taking up one of Tiladia's perfect, delicate hands. "How do you feel?"

"I feel . . . I feel . . . I *feel*!" Tiladia exclaimed, her voice rising in excitement with each repetition. "Lady Issa! I can see you more clearly now! I can feel you! Oh, Gods, you're warm!" Tiladia sat up, Issa's cloak sliding down and revealing her pale chest, but she didn't care. She reached out and grabbed Morgan's hand, pulling it close. "Morgan! I've wanted to hug you, to touch you. Oh, Elder Gods! Thank you! Thank you both!" Tears formed in her perfect, bright eyes and began to stream down her cheeks, and Issa was suddenly sobbing, pulling Tiladia into an embrace.

"I'm so happy for you, Til. I'm going to give you a minute to get dressed. I'm sure Issa has something for you." Morgan turned away, but Tiladia laughed, pulling back from Issa.

"I'll get dressed, but don't worry, Morgan. I spent much of my old life without clothes. This doesn't bother me."

"Right," Morgan said with a chuckle. "You're not a dragon anymore, though."

"Well, the System still thinks I am, at least partially! My race says Dragonkind." Her lilting voice was so clear and her humor so evident that Morgan couldn't believe it was the same Tiladia whose emotions he'd struggled to read for so long. She smiled as she shrugged into the silky black shirt Issa handed her, and before he could turn away, she stood up to pull on a pair of matching leggings.

"God," Morgan blurted, looking away quickly.

"So the System recognized you right away?" Issa asked, cutting him off.

"Yes! I'm only Base Zero, so no class or levels, but my Core is Improved Five! I can't wait to start leveling again, Issa. You did a perfect job!"

"That's fantastic! And your race?"

"Base Seven! Don't you think that since the System ranked it, I can continue to improve it?"

"Yes, that makes sense!" Issa agreed, picking up her cloak and slipping it back into storage.

"This is all wonderful," Morgan said, watching as Tiladia tried out her legs. She was slender and nearly the same size as Issa, and she had a natural grace to her movements which spoke volumes, either about Issa's ability to integrate her into a new body or her existing knowledge of bipedal locomotion. "But do you mind seeing if you can go outside? I need to get out there as soon as possible."

"Of course! The townsfolk! They must be counting on us," Tiladia exclaimed, hurrying past Morgan for the stairs. She started down once she got to them, and Morgan and Issa followed. In a few steps, he walked into the entry hall with Issa, but Tiladia was nowhere to be seen.

"What the—" he started, but Issa laughed.

"She doesn't have permission for the stairs, Morgan. Can you grant it?"

"Oh shit," Morgan said. Staring into space, he reached out to feel the tower. He concentrated on the spot where he felt Tiladia, her Core blazing brightly with pure golden Energy, and with a tweak of his will, he granted her permission to the staircase and, while he was at it, permission to enter and exit the tower. Seconds later, Tiladia came stumbling down.

"That took a lot longer than I thought it would!" she said, her laugh ringing happily around the chamber.

"I forgot to—"

"I know, I know, Morgan. I forgot also! Let's see about these wards!" Tiladia strode toward the door, still hanging open.

"Tiladia!" Issa called, "be careful to hug close to the tower. If you get outside a certain radius, the secondary effect will hit you, and you'll be rendered unconscious."

"Right! Never fear, Lady Issa," Tiladia called, and then she was outside the tower.

"It worked," Morgan breathed, realizing that part of him had never believed she'd be able to walk through the barrier.

"Of course it did. I told you how the wards were working, didn't I?" Issa asked, raising an eyebrow. Morgan smiled at her as he started slapping his gleaming armor on, happy for its automated nature and the lack of straps.

He was pulling down his visor when Issa spoke.

"She should only need to break or remove one of the wards. I hope they're not too deep or heavy or indestructible . . ." She stopped speaking as a red haze shimmered over the doorway before bursting into a hundred thousand little sparks, sizzling as they flew through the air.

Morgan didn't wait, didn't hug Issa, didn't say another word. He stepped toward the door and cast Void Step, placing himself fifty yards outside the tower. He drew Bloodfang, cracked his wings wide, and shouted toward the militia members stirring on the grass nearby, "What the hell is going on out here?"

# OLIVIA

Olivia sat in her trap and seethed. Had she really been so stupid, so naive? Thinking back to Carlu's charming banter when they'd first met, she still couldn't believe he'd been helping to kill innocent students—kind, sweet Alyss—this whole time. An angry sob surged up from her chest when she thought of Alyss and the idea of that evil little shit pretending to investigate her murder.

"Was that the plan?" she hissed. "To keep me emotionally involved and stupid?" Olivia rapped her knuckles against the blue metal pattern beneath her. "Wonder who made you," she said, though she knew she'd find out soon enough. She looked at her Core for the hundredth time and saw that her fire and air affinities were slowly recharging despite the cage.

She'd avoided casting more spells, not wanting to drain herself again. Still, a certain part of her, perhaps the raging primal elemental within her, wanted to unleash everything she had, channeling all of her Energies into a singular, massive Elemental Bomb and using the Crown of Nightmarch to amplify it. Could the trap stop that? Was it possible she might overwhelm it?

One thing kept her from acting, however: Carlu had seen her use the crown. He had an idea of what she was capable of doing. Would he so confidently walk away if there was a chance she could overpower his trap? He probably wanted her to do so, to empty herself and make it easier to beat her and drag her somewhere else. Growling with frustration, Olivia looked through her storage ring for anything which might allow her to escape, and she spied the three books she'd taken from the library.

Sitting in the dim glow of her lamp, Olivia pulled the books out of her ring and read the titles aloud, her voice in the dark, deep pit bringing her some comfort. "*Teneshel's Theories on Agricultural Workings*. Oh, brother." Olivia slipped the book back into her storage ring. "*Borlim-dak's Better Baking*. God, I'm an idiot." Olivia angrily stored it away, then—with very little hope—picked up the final text.

The book was thin but heavy, and it made her fingers itch as strange Energy crawled over her skin. It was the first book she'd picked, and that feeling was why she'd stopped and taken it in the first place. "*The Book of Tveklis.*" She looked carefully at it, noting the thick layer of dust on the top—this text hadn't been pulled from the shelves in a very long time. It was bound in leather, stained black. Upon closer inspection, she saw the title had been added after the binding, written on paler leather and stitched with red thread to the original.

"So you didn't use to have a title, hmm?" Olivia opened the cover, saw a blank page, turned it, and stared at the incomprehensible text on the next page.

"Goddammit!" she cursed. "*Of course* you're written in a non-System language!" Something about the symbols was familiar, however, and Olivia hissed in sudden recognition, slamming the book shut. To be sure, she pulled the tapestry Bronwyn had given her what seemed like a hundred years ago from the Yovashi lair. Sure enough, the runes were similar, and some of them were definitely repeated in the text.

"Of course. Tveklis. It's a Yovashi name. A Yovashi spell book at Fainhallow?"

Olivia frowned and put the tapestry away before she picked up the book and opened it on her lap. Something about the itchy, tingling feeling it gave her was intriguing, and though she couldn't understand it, she stared at the runes and symbols, wondering if there was some way she could make sense of them. Nothing happened, however, and she closed the book, looking at its cover where the title had been stitched.

She absently plucked at the red thread holding the title in place, and she felt the tingling sensation intensify. Curious, she held the palm of her hand over the stitched-on title, feeling it again. "Interesting . . ." she breathed, pulling a knife from her ring and carefully prying the thread out of its holes. As she began to free the square of leather from the book, she caught glimpses of blue and green stitchwork. She hurried, cutting away the rest of the thread and pulling off the pale leather.

Beneath the stitched-on square was the original title of the book. The strange Yovashi symbols were made with green and blue metallic thread, and even if Olivia couldn't understand them, she could feel the Energy emanating from them. It was unlike anything she'd felt before; no attunement she'd been exposed to matched the weird, tingling pressure emanating from those threads. There were seven stitched runes, and though Olivia was frustrated at her inability to read them, she felt her eyes drawn to the perfect symmetry of their design and how they each seemed to flow into the next.

Olivia felt the pressure of knowing the killer could show up at any moment, but something about the book had captured her attention, pushing such concerns into a small corner at the back of her mind. "What are you . . ." she breathed, tracing the runes with her fingertip. She felt another surge of the strange Energy, and she pulled her finger away. As she watched, the runes seemed to lift from the book, flowing into each other and toward her. Olivia panicked and flipped the book over, clamping her eyes shut.

She realized the book wasn't meant to be read by normal means. It was like the self-learning spell scrolls and tomes people could craft and that the System tended to utilize for rewards. The triggering runes had been in the title, and whoever had covered them had either known that and done so as a precaution or had inadvertently done it because they took a while to start working. "Well, I'm assuming a lot," Olivia said, opening her eyes to look at the blank back of the book.

Was she desperate enough to let an unknown spell tome, likely crafted by a Yovashi, fill her brain with information? Would more spells help in her situation? Carlu had said the ward circle had been tailored to block her abilities. The only way they could be sure of that was if it had been made to contain all of her affinities. Olivia knew it worked to absorb plasma, so it was a thorough job, blocking even her meta-elements. What if the book gave her another option? What about the pure Energy at the center of her Core?

Olivia pointed a palm at the circle and built the pattern for Fiery Burst in her channel, feeding it pure Energy instead. Once she felt the spell was ready, she pushed it forth. The Energy surged out of her palm and was instantly absorbed by the circle, along with all of her pure Energy. As a System message appeared in her view, she sagged forward, weak and nauseous from the sudden drain:

\*\*\***Congratulations! You have learned the spell: Energy Burst—Basic.**\*\*\*

\*\*\***Energy Burst—Basic: You conjure forth a destructive beam of pure Energy. Energy cost: 100. Cooldown: Minimal.**\*\*\*

As she read the message, a scatter of Energy motes coalesced in the small chamber and rushed into her, partially replenishing what the ward circle had drained. "Ugh, so it blocks all of my affinities, including pure Energy. I suppose that would be obvious."

At first, Olivia wondered how they'd learned about all her affinities, but then she laughed, remembering her display in the auditorium, her practice sessions in class, and even her conversations with other students with elemental affinities. No, it wouldn't be hard for any sort of investigator to learn about them. Besides, who knew what Carlu learned when he studied her with those lenses of his?

Again, Olivia contemplated the back of the Yovashi book. Was she out of options? Was this her only hope? Should she just wait and see what the killer wanted? Maybe she'd find an opportunity to escape if he moved her.

"Or he might come in here, overpower my magicless ass, and do God-knows-what to me." Olivia was good at many things, but coping with feeling helpless wasn't one of them. She picked up the book, flipped it over, and stared at the strange metallic runes, waiting for them to do their thing.

When the runes failed to start shifting around and flowing toward her, Olivia had a moment of panic. Had she wasted the magic? She almost threw the book in frustration after five minutes of staring, but then remembered how she'd traced the runes with her finger, and she quickly did it again, being sure to mimic the way she'd done it before, concentrating on the strange Energy signature and how it made her flesh tingle. Sure enough, as she finished tracing the last symbol, they seemed to shimmer and flow into each other, lifting into the air. Olivia reasoned they weren't actually lifting into the air, just their image, but it was all the same to her eyes.

As the runes floated toward her, Olivia forced her eyes to stay open. Once the strange symbols were all she could see, she felt that tingling, almost itchy Energy pass into her, and everything went dark. At first, Olivia wondered if she'd passed out, but a strange, echoing, harsh voice sounded in her mind, so loud that any other thought was banished.

*MIND COMPATIBILITY: NINETY-TWO PERCENT.*

Olivia tried to say something, but she couldn't feel her mouth nor hear herself. The strange tingling spread throughout her pathways, and it seemed like she was being examined. Again, the booming voice rang out in her mind.

*SUPERIOR AFFINITY AND ABOVE AVERAGE CORE. NO MIND ATTUNEMENT OR AFFINITY. SELECT AN AFFINITY TO REPLACE: FIRE, WATER, AIR, EARTH, NONATTUNED.*

"Um," Olivia could hear herself this time, though it seemed she was speaking in her head, not physically. "I don't wish to replace an affinity."

*SELECT AN AFFINITY TO REPLACE: FIRE, WATER, AIR, EARTH, NONATTUNED.*

It almost felt like she was speaking to a computer program. Was it capable of nuance? Could she cancel this process?

"Help," she tried.

*SELECT AN AFFINITY TO REPLACE: FIRE, WATER, AIR, EARTH, NONATTUNED.*

"Commands."

*SELECT AN AFFINITY TO REPLACE: FIRE, WATER, AIR, EARTH, NONATTUNED.*

"Cancel!" Olivia shouted into the blackness of her mind, deciding she'd rather deal with the killer than this strange Yovashi relic.

*SELECT AN AFFINITY TO REPLACE: FIRE, WATER, AIR, EARTH, NONATTUNED.*

"Oh, dammit!"

*SELECT AN AFFINITY TO REPLACE: FIRE, WATER, AIR, EARTH, NONATTUNED.*

Olivia started to fear that she'd doomed herself somehow. Would she be stuck in this loop forever unless she let this Yovashi book mess with her affinities? Was she sitting helplessly in her cage right now? Would the killer just slit her throat or worse? She wanted to talk to herself, to admonish herself for getting into this mess, but she knew that anything she said would trigger that horribly loud voice to tell her to select an affinity.

One hasty decision after another had led her into this mess, and now she'd done something which could change or damage her in ways she didn't think there were fixes for.

"I guess I have to make a sacrifice . . ."

*SELECT AN AFFINITY TO REPLACE: FIRE, WATER, AIR, EARTH, NONATTUNED.*

Mentally groaning, Olivia thought about her spells and her class and decided that if she had to give up an attunement, she'd rather it wasn't one of her elements. "Nonattuned."

*IMPARTING.*

Olivia felt a terrible coldness at the pit of her being, and she knew what was happening: the Yovashi book or cursed relic or whatever it was was taking away the center of her Core, her pure Energy. As despair settled in—and Olivia knew she'd be crying if she could feel her body enough to do so—a spark ignited where that cold void had grown, and she felt a warm, tingling glow begin to build where her Core sat.

Again, the booming voice rang out. *IMPARTING.*

Suddenly, the glowing tingle grew, and warmth filled her as her Core was mended, though it felt different, and Olivia knew she had a new affinity, something she'd never felt before.

*ATTUNEMENT AND AFFINITY COMPATIBLE. IMPARTING KNOWLEDGE.*

The blackness surrounding Olivia's consciousness abruptly burst with a rainbow of colors as Yovashi runes streamed around her and then into her. As the flood filled her brain with a pleasant warmth, understanding began to replace Olivia's confusion, and she became aware that she could read the symbols. As new waves of knowledge filled her mind, the booming voice announced the things it was teaching her:

*IMPARTING: YOVASHI PRIME DIALECT.*
*IMPARTING: CULTIVATION ROUTINE.*
*IMPARTING: SUGGESTION.*
*IMPARTING: THOUGHT SPIKE.*
*FURTHER IMPARTMENT NOT POSSIBLE AT THIS ENERGY LEVEL.*

Suddenly, the runes stopped swirling around her, the darkness faded, and Olivia realized she was looking through her eyes again. She still sat in her cage, the book closed and inert on her lap. Blinking rapidly to clear her vision, she noticed several System messages were waiting for her attention, but she also heard the sound of bootheels clicking on stone, distant but drawing nearer.

# OLIVIA

Olivia took several breaths to steady herself. What she'd just gone through shouldn't have been possible, not according to everything she'd learned in her Spellcrafting or Artificing classes. A Yovashi text had just interfaced with her . . . brain? No, more than that: with her Core as well. And not only that; it had altered some fundamental aspects of her nature.

As the clicking on stone drew nearer, she steeled herself and looked at the System messages:

\*\*\*Warning! Non-System interface detected!\*\*\*

\*\*\*Warning! Non-System Core alteration detected!\*\*\*

\*\*\*Warning! You have lost your affinity with nonattuned Energy!\*\*\*

\*\*\*Warning! You have lost the spell: Energy Burst—Basic.\*\*\*

\*\*\*Warning! Non-System Core alteration detected!\*\*\*

\*\*\*Congratulations! You have gained an affinity with mind-attuned Energy!\*\*\*

\*\*\*Warning! Non-System knowledge impartment detected!\*\*\*

\*\*\*Congratulations! You have gained familiarity with @#%@#!\*\*\*

\*\*\*Warning! Non-System knowledge impartment detected!\*\*\*

\*\*\*Congratulations! You have learned the spell: Suggestion—Improved.\*\*\*

\*\*\*Suggestion—Improved: Prerequisite: Mind Affinity. Using your mind-attuned Energy and the force of your will, you are able to plant suggestions in the minds of those with whom you speak. Success is determined by the strength of your will versus theirs. The more complex the suggestion, the more Energy intensive the spell, and the easier it will be for others to resist. Energy cost: Varied. Cooldown: Short.

\*\*\*Warning! Non-System knowledge impartment detected!\*\*\*

\*\*\*Congratulations! You have learned the spell: Thought Spike—Improved.\*\*\*

\*\*\*Thought Spike—Improved: Prerequisite: Mind Affinity. Using your mind-attuned Energy and the force of your will, you manifest a physical attack in the mind of your target. Though your spell will not physically harm your target(s), if they do not resist your will, they will believe they've been harmed and suffer as though the attack were real. Energy cost: Varied. Cooldown: Short.***

"What the . . ." Olivia hissed, quickly pulling up her status screen:

| Status | | | |
|---|---|---|---|
| Name: | Olivia Bennet | | |
| Race: | Human - Improved 8 | | |
| Class: | Elemental Paragon - Legendary | | |
| Level: | 25 | | |
| Core: | Mental Prisma Class - Improved 2 | | |
| Energy Affinity: | Mind 9.2, Fire 9.6, Earth 9.6, Water 9.6, Air 9.6 | Energy: | 11,070/11,070 |
| Strength: | 20 | Vitality: | 74 |
| Dexterity: | 50 | Agility: | 20 |
| Intelligence: | 206 | Will: | 192 |
| Points Available: | 0 | | |
| Titles & Feats: | Elemental Heritage, First Elemental Archon | | |
| Skills: | System Language Integration - Not Upgradeable<br>Animal Taming - Basic<br>Stealthy Maneuvers - Basic<br>Prisma Core Cultivation Drill - Basic<br>Mind Cultivation Drill - Improved | | |
| Spells - Basic: | Icy Shards<br>Stunning Ice Shards<br>Fiery Burst<br>Wind Gust<br>Frost Blast<br>Arcfrost Cascade<br>Pyrosteam Drill | | |

|  | Magma Ray<br>Surveying Breeze<br>Hunt Energy |
|---|---|
| Spells<br>- Improved: | Elemental Bomb<br>Suggestion<br>Thought Spike |
| Spells<br>- Advanced: | Elemental Form<br>Chromatic Personal Barrier<br>Plasma Wave |
| Spells - Epic: | Orb Manipulation |

"God," she breathed, reading over the information as quickly as possible. When she'd finished, she turned her mind's eye inward. There, as always, pulsed her beautiful, prismatic Core, her four thick bands of elemental Energy swirling around it. However, where her Core's center had been the brilliant yellow-gold of pure Energy before, now it pulsed with a pink-white glow. The Yovashi tome had altered it, just as her status sheet indicated. She no longer had a pure Energy affinity, but she'd gained this strange mind affinity.

"Have you given up? Staring into space, hoping for some sort of reprieve? Begging one of your human gods for a rescue, perhaps?"

Olivia's eyes snapped open at the sound of the voice, and her lips curled down in a frown. "Of course it's you," she said. "And you know about human gods? More familiar with Earth than you let on, hmm?"

"Ahh, yes. A necessary subterfuge. As you've no doubt guessed, I'm not bound by the truth as my purer brethren are," Professor Somhairle replied, squatting at the edge of the ward ring on which Olivia knelt.

"So you aren't a pure fae? That much was true?"

"No, several generations separate me from my fae grandmother, but that's not why I'm here, Olivia." As he spoke, she became aware of more footsteps approaching. She allowed hope to blossom for a moment, thinking it might be someone coming to look for her, but then she brought herself down to earth, realizing it was probably just Carlu.

"Well? What's the point of all this?" Olivia asked. "Did you really need to go to these lengths? Did so many have to die so you could contain me?"

"Oh no. I'm sure I could have thought of a different scheme, but this one was so delicious, and I've always been a fan of serial murders. I did need to get you into a certain emotional state, and this seemed to work just fine, don't you think?" He paused, and when Olivia opened her mouth to answer or cuss or something, he held up his hand and continued, "Tut, let's not get into a debate, shall we? Your wish for divine intervention may have been answered."

"What do you mean?" Olivia asked, watching Carlu saunter into view and lean against the wall, grinning lazily at her.

"Well, some silly fae-human has managed to make a deal. My betters are offering me a bit of a promotion to let things be here on Fanwath, including you."

"What?" Carlu and Olivia spoke at the same time.

"Oh, yes." Somhairle looked over at Carlu, his smile becoming even more predatory. "Sorry, partner of mine. It looks like I'll need to pull up stakes, and I'll need to take this ward circle with me. Duchess Rime would be angered if I left it behind."

"You can't! What about my reward? You promised me you'd deal with her!" Carlu nodded toward Olivia, who couldn't help the smile spreading on her face.

"Oh, I'm sorry, but part of my orders was to harm her no further." He paused and looked at Olivia kneeling in his ward circle, gently stroking his chin with his thumb. "Well, how would anyone know how much she tried to cast spells in there? I'm sure no one would mind if I activated the wards once before I collected the circle. It'll be best for everyone's safety, in fact."

"Yes! Why, if you hobble her, I can deal with her myself, and then it will be trivial to pin your murders on her. You'll be able to return freely!"

"Don't ingratiate yourself further, Inspector." Somhairle laughed. "I'll not be back in your lifetime, if ever."

"You killed them all?" Olivia asked, mind spinning while trying to think of a way to keep Somhairle from leaving. Before he could answer, she added, "What do you mean a fae-human made a deal?"

"Oh? Are you intrigued? It seems the Summer Court is willing to part with much in order to keep my hands off you. Something to do with your little lover, perhaps? The one you were sobbing about in the garden?" He chuckled, and it was a cold, cruel sound. "Was it confusing, dear Olivia?"

"What?"

"The poem. Did it keep your mind whirling? Did you wonder who the *obedient love* was? I found it rather clever, and to think I came up with it at the spur of the moment! I hadn't even meant to write a poem when I toyed with young Alyss."

"You fucking asshole!" Olivia snarled, her despair, self-loathing, and regrets all channeled into anger at the man before her.

"Well, that's enough of that." He chuckled that cold, brittle laugh then leaned down and touched a finger to the edge of the ward circle, appearing to concentrate for a moment. Olivia started to stand, but she was brought to her knees as the runes burst into bright blue light. She felt her Core being drained, all of her elementally attuned Energy being sucked from her and into the ward circle.

"Oh, lovely," Carlu commented, watching Olivia writhe on her hands and knees.

"Yes, that should do it," Somhairle said as the runes began to fade and Olivia was left gasping on all fours. "Now, I'll just tap this here," he continued, holding a small egg-shaped black stone out to the ward. As the stone clicked against the metal three times, the circle grew warm and then burst into blue smoke, flowing into the stone egg.

Olivia, still on her hands and knees, eyes on the stone between her hands, took a deep breath and, with a crooked smile, stood up, glaring at the two men. "Thank you," she declared, her voice perfectly clear and strong.

"What?" Carlu said. "Professor, did your ward fail?"

"That's your concern, Inspector," Somhairle dismissed, turning his back to Olivia and holding out another small object. Olivia felt a surge of cold, slippery Energy, and a swirling blue portal began to open.

"Wait!" Olivia commanded, casting Suggestion for the first time. Somhairle had drained her elemental Energies, but the heart of her Core still pulsed with the pink-white glow of her mind Energy, and though she was unfamiliar with it, she could feel its power as she drove her will into the simple command.

Somhairle paused midstride, holding his foot in the air as he seemed to battle with himself. Finally, he set his foot down and turned to regard Olivia, the swirling blue portal casting strange shadows on his face and on the cowering Carlu. "What's this, then?" he asked, clearly at a loss.

"I had been hoping for a deus ex machina like you suggested, Somhairle, and I regret to inform you that it arrived just before you did. Now look me in the eyes and tell me you committed all those murders." As she spoke, Olivia opened her connection to the Crown of Nightmarch, which began to glow limned in white, ghostly flames.

"I did. I enjoyed it, fool child. Now, I promised to leave you intact, but if you're going to use some artifact to hinder me, then I'm going to have to teach you a lesson."

Olivia felt his cold, slippery Energy begin to gather, but she simply looked at him and, using the crown, cast Thought Spike.

Carlu saw Olivia's crown flare with rose-colored flames, saw them reflected in Olivia's eyes, and then he saw Somhairle clap his hands to the sides of his head. As he swayed, writhing in apparent agony, Somhairle's eyes turned red, and he began to cry tears of blood. His face turned pink, then red, then purple, and then he collapsed, rivulets of blood pouring from his ears. He twitched thrice before lying still.

The swirling blue portal seemed to pause, strangely reversing its motion before it snapped shut with an audible *pop*.

"What have you done?" Carlu asked the sorceress, backing away.

"Stop!" Olivia ordered, and he felt his legs turn to wood, rooted to the stone.

"W-What . . ." Carlu stammered. "Ensorcellment? You'll be staked out and burned for this!"

Olivia walked toward him, cold fury in her eyes. "How strong is your will, Carlu? Do you want to live? Do you think Alyss wanted to live? I can't suffer you to exist in the same world as I. *Stop Breathing!*"

The sorceress was on fire now, blue and white flames licking her shoulders and surrounding her crown. Her eyes blazed like blue magma, and when Carlu heard her command, he wanted nothing more than to obey. He clamped his mouth shut and gave in to her will.

Who was he to challenge a goddess?

Olivia watched as Carlu finally stopped jerking and writhing, his body unhappy about his mind's decision to stop taking in air. When he was finally still, she knelt and took the rings from his fingers, feeling around his belt and inside his vest for hidden storage devices but only finding a few odds and ends—a pipe, glasses, a pocket watch, a handkerchief, and even a snuffbox.

"You were a pretentious little creep," she said, still not feeling an ounce of remorse for what she'd done.

She gave Somhairle the same treatment, quickly stowing the black egg and his rings into a pocket of her robes. She searched for whatever he'd used to open the blue portal but found nothing; either he'd used it up making the portal or the fae were good at keeping those sorts of things out of the hands of the non-fae. Olivia looked at Somhairle's face, his flesh purple and his expression twisted, and she frowned.

"You deserved worse, you fucking monster. You deserved to suffer for years."

Olivia stood and started down the passage. She'd let Oylla know about Somhairle and Carlu, but then she wanted to get back to First Landing. She had to talk to Bronwyn, had to stop her from going through with whatever deal she'd made with the fae.

# MORGAN

"I can still feel them, though," Morgan told Maria. "They're only around fifty miles to the east from here. I'm going."

The militia had shown him to the clinic and into Maria's room, where she lay bedridden, unable to move her legs. The colony's best healers had been taken on the airship, and the ones still in town weren't capable of mending her spine. She had high hopes for a full recovery, however, if Dr. Kerns or Dr. Cho survived whatever Captain Gella and his people were doing to them.

"Wait, Morgan," Maria said, holding out a hand. "Don't you think you should get help? Olivia or Bronwyn or the militia? We have a squadron already out. They're on foot, but they can't be far if the airship stopped so close!"

Morgan glanced at Issa, who'd followed him to the clinic. "No. No, I'm sorry, but no one can keep up with me. Not even Olivia can fly . . . yet. Those bastards locked me in my tower for a reason—they fear me, and I'm about to show them why." Morgan leaned over to kiss Issa, and she simply nodded, her face resolute.

"We'll be ready when you return, and if you need to retreat, we'll have cannons on the wall primed and ready. Lead them to us, and we'll show them what a few millennia of human warfare have taught us," Maria growled, slapping a fist into her palm.

"Right. Yeah, keep the militia on the wall. I hope I'm back soon." He paused, reconsidering a few things, and said to Issa, "Please keep the tower secure. Watch out for Olivia or any other sort of surprise. I think we're outside their plan now, having knocked them out of the sky, but I still think we should be wary of any further subterfuge."

"I will, Morgan. Tiladia and I will keep the tower ready. We can also take refugees in if it comes to that." She turned to Maria as she said the last then stepped closer to Morgan, tilting her head so she spoke toward his ear in a low voice. "Watch out for Tanna, Morgan. She's far cleverer and more deceptive than the others. I wish I could go with you."

"I'll be careful, and honestly, I'm glad you won't be there to see what I might have to do," Morgan growled.

He kissed Issa one more time and marched out of the room. He slid his visor down as he strode through the clinic, and as soon as he was outside the front awning, he cracked his wings and launched himself into the sky.

Morgan had been flying a lot since his return to First Landing, but only short flights around the community. He didn't know how long it would take him to cover fifty miles. He didn't even know if he could fly that far. His wings had never felt tired during the short flights he'd made, so he had no idea what to expect when it came to their endurance. He figured step one was to gain as much altitude as he felt he could handle and then try to figure out how to glide.

He pumped his wings, holding his feet and legs out straight, following some sort of instinct which must have been awoken with his bloodline, and briefly wondering what kind of magic allowed him to fly like a bird when his only feathers were on his wings; he had no tail feathers, and he was undoubtedly denser than a typical bird. Perhaps it was simply that—magic. Perhaps it had to do with his Energy levels and how his body now interacted with the natural environment. Not much of his current existence would be explainable using Earth's science.

He continued to push against the air, climbing ever higher as he soared toward the east, and soon, the forest surrounding First Landing was just a blue-green carpet below him, the trees too small to distinguish easily. As he cleared the first foothills beyond the woods and saw the low, craggy peaks ahead, he realized he was already high enough to soar through a gap in the first range, so Morgan stopped pumping his wings and tried to glide, allowing the air to buffet and push against their bottom.

He felt the strain in his back, not exactly in his wings, but it wasn't painful, and he knew he had a lot of endurance left. As the wind buffeted him, knocking him side to side, he began to get a knack for tilting the angle of his glide to cut the gusts and keep himself on track. He even managed to catch updrafts and avoid losing much altitude.

Within an hour of leaving First Landing, Morgan had already passed through the first gap in the mountainous territory to the east, and he saw a small line of moving figures on the rough landscape below. Morgan dove toward them, noting they marched eastward. When he activated his Void Vision, he grew fairly certain that he was looking at the militia from First Landing.

Morgan worked his way down, slowly spiraling toward the body of soldiers. As he drew nearer, he saw they were in a sorry state; they were struggling to climb a rocky slope, loose, crumbling stones slipping beneath their feet. They all carried the new Energy rifles, and most were using them as walking sticks to keep from sliding backward. They looked ragged and tired, and many had ripped clothing and bloody bandages on their limbs.

When Morgan touched down, sending up a shower of dust, they leveled their rifles at him. Two soldiers fell, sliding on the loose scree from the sudden movement.

"Hold your fire!" Morgan cried.

"Morgan?" a lean man with short black hair and a clean, unscratched rifle asked. His uniform had officer stripes, and he looked less winded than the others; he clearly hadn't fallen or needed to use his weapon as a crutch.

"Hey. Yeah, it's me. I finally got out of my tower. Are you guys all right?"

"We're fine, just making shit time and worried we'll never catch up to that damn airship. We were hoping it had crashed in these hills."

"You're doing a pretty fantastic job of heading in the right direction," Morgan said, nodding up the hill to the east. "You're on the right track, but more mountains are in your way. I'll catch those bastards; you all should head back to town. I think it'll take you another four or five days to get there."

"Fuck," one of the soldiers let out, spitting through dusty lips.

"Yeah, it's not fair, I know," Morgan commiserated, pulling his wings in. "I can cross all this rough terrain easily. Let me deal with this, all right? If I fail, you all might as well go to Tarn's Crossing and take a boat toward Ridonne 'cause, no offense, but if they kill me, they'll kill you twelve, too."

"Fucking balls on this guy," one of the other soldiers grumbled.

"I'm not trying to sound full of myself, guys," Morgan said, scowling at the burly, bearded soldier. "I'm just saying I'm tier four and wearing some damn good gear. There's a lot you all haven't seen, trust me."

"Lock it down," the lean officer ordered. He glared at the militia members, and none of them held his gaze. When the muttering had stopped, he looked at Morgan and held out a hand. "All right. Thanks for the head's up. We'll keep moving, though. Do us a favor and let us know if you win, okay? I'll turn around when I know the townsfolk are free or when I see that ship in the air confirming we can't catch it."

"Fair enough," Morgan agreed. He had to admire the man's dedication. Morgan could see the disgruntled looks most of the soldiers affected when they heard his words, and he knew he hadn't made things easier for the man. "If you don't hear from me in a day or so, keep your guard up—I'm probably dead. Good luck!"

With that, Morgan snapped his wings and launched himself into the air. As he cleared the ground, he stared straight up and cast Void Step, instantly gaining a hundred meters of altitude.

Guardian's Senses told him he'd closed the distance to Arthur Ballard by more than half, so Morgan kept his Void Vision active, appreciating how it had made the Energy signatures of the militia members flare and reasoning it might give him a chance to avoid an ambush. He saw many weak, small signatures, and he figured they were animals down among the scrub and sporadic trees. Occasionally, he saw other birds in the air nearby, but they angled away from him and passed so quickly he rarely caught more than a glimpse.

As he glided past the second row of peaks, enjoying the thrill of the flight so much that he had to remind himself to stay vigilant, Morgan saw a bright Energy signature launch into the air from behind a nearby boulder. He turned his head that way, trying not to give away the fact that he'd seen it. The aura approaching him was bright, and it trailed glittering motes of Energy. Even without his Void Vision showing him the hateful intention pulsing out from him, Morgan would have recognized Baron Finneal.

Morgan banked, angling downward to pick up speed while acting like he hadn't noticed the Ghelli flanking him. He felt a surge of Energy, knew an attack was coming, and turned back toward the baron. Just as a claw of dark, shadowy Energy began manifesting in the air near him, Morgan cast Void Step and placed himself behind Finneal.

Void Step was a curious spell when cast at high rates of momentum. Though he placed himself behind Finneal, effectively reversing his course, Morgan still surged forward at the same rate as before. He had little sympathy or patience for the Ghelli after what he'd heard from Maria, and Morgan didn't hesitate to place Bloodfang squarely between Finneal's shoulders, activating Backstab for the first time in a long while.

His sword carved through Finneal's red-enameled dress armor, completely punching through his torso and out the front. The blade didn't even slow down as it hit the armor, and Finneal screamed in agony as the heavy sword split his spine and sheared away part of his heart. The Ghelli instantly stopped flying, becoming a dead weight on the end of his sword. Morgan kicked his body away, sliding Bloodfang free and flapping his wings heavily to regain his upward momentum.

He watched as Finneal fell, spiraling in a tumble to the rocks below, crashing and bouncing with an audibly wet crunch down the side of a scree-covered slope. Finneal might have been able to fly more nimbly than Morgan—he supposed he'd never know—but there was no way he stood a chance when it came to mobility. Void Step trumped wings. Morgan scanned the surrounding peaks and rocky valleys but saw no other aggressors moving toward him.

He reached out with Guardian's Senses once more and felt Arthur Ballard just a few miles further, likely past the next row of low, rocky ridges. Whipping some of the blood off Bloodfang's edge, Morgan cracked his wings and dove eastward, wondering if the others would force him to fight or if they'd capitulate.

* * *

"We're almost ready to lift off again," Gella said, smiling at Tanna while he puffed on his pipe, trying to get the stubborn, damp yiil weed to burn. "Do you mind calling in Finneal and the other sentries?"

"What's he doing?" Tanna asked, ignoring Gella and pointing to Hakudak, who seemed to be making his way to the port boarding gangway. Gella saw why Tanna had asked; the lumbering axe warrior was wearing his travel cloak and was leading a large, warded roladii.

"Why would he leave now? We'll be soaring over his head in an hour's time." Gella cursed, spitting angrily over the rail and stuffing his pipe into his captain's coat. "Come with me, please!"

He thought he heard Tanna grunt in assent, but he didn't wait, clambering down to the mid deck and striding toward the port passage behind Haku. His boots and heavy strides made his approach evident, and Haku paused to consider him over his shoulder.

"What?" the big warrior asked.

"Where are you going?"

"I'll make my own way," he said, shrugging his boulderlike shoulders and continuing to lead his mount down the sloping wooden passageway.

"What the old bones do you mean, you'll make your own way? We're about to set sail again!" Gella exclaimed, speaking with more vehemence than he usually dared when facing one of ap'Gravin's champions.

"What's going on, Haku?" Tanna asked, her voice a crystal clarion that cut through Gella's sputtering.

"Have you spoken to your sentry lately?" Haku inquired, not slowing his movement.

"Finneal?" Tanna scoffed. "He rarely checks in."

"Well, I paid one of the scouts and gave him a page from my Far Scribe book. He wrote that he saw a fight in the air, and Finneal fell like a sack of meat." Haku's boot crunched onto gravel as he exited the gangway and led his roladii clear, pulling himself into the saddle. "Good luck, Tanna. I'll report your bravery to ap'Gravin when I describe this doomed venture. If I don't dally, I figure I should reach Gelica in a month."

"You're running because some jittery scout sent you a message about Finneal? What was it? Morgan? If he won free of my wards, then we can face him together, Haku."

"We've had this talk. Many times." He shrugged. "Good luck," he repeated, kicking his heels into the roladii's flanks. The animal reared, and then he was going, rushing along the smooth ground near the downed airship before charging up a rocky slope.

"He really just left?" Gella said, trying to wrap his mind around what had happened.

"He did, and I've half a mind to follow. I just don't know if Morgan is the kind to let people escape unscathed after what we did. Why did Finneal have to kill some of them?"

Tanna closed her eyes, and her lips moved as she seemed to recite something to herself.

"What?" Gella asked, wondering if she'd said something he should have heard.

"Quiet," she said, then continued muttering under her breath, eyes closed. After a moment, she opened them, staring with bright green eyes into Gella's. "Get some of the prisoners and bring them onto the deck."

# MORGAN

Morgan circled the downed ship, watching the flurry of activity on the deck from hundreds of meters above. He could see the bright blue and red Energy aura of Tanna ap'Cilla, overshadowing the much dimmer auras of the rest of the crew and the captives they held before them. He counted thirty visible crew members, each with a human, collared and on their knees before them. Tanna stood at the center of the congregation, bright eyes tracking his movement in the sky above.

"Want to play dirty, then?" Morgan growled, replaying sudden memories of hostage situations he'd seen back on Earth during the chaos that had unfolded as the great nations started to crumble and devolve into sparring factions. Morgan whipped Bloodfang, still crusty with Finneal's blood, and dove toward the center of the grouping.

He aimed to put himself directly in front of Tanna and he did so, landing with a thunderous crack of his wings and a tremendous thud as his armored boots smashed onto the wooden deck. His face was visored, so all he presented to Tanna was a smooth, mirror-polished silvery countenance. He held Bloodfang high and said, "Threatening these people is the wrong move to make with me."

"We're only ensuring we don't end up slaughtered like Finneal, Morgan. This crew isn't a match for you. Do you want to murder weaklings? Is that the kind of man you are?"

"How many people have you hurt or killed?" he asked, looking at the despairing, bruised faces of the people closest. He saw Arthur Ballard held at Gella's feet, and though the captain didn't have his saber to the older man's throat, he held it by his side in a white-knuckled grip. Morgan glared at the man, trying to see the eyes beneath his pretentiously high captain's hat, but Gella refused to look directly at Morgan's shiny visor.

"None! The only fool who laid a fatal hand upon a human has already been punished—Finneal."

"Convenient that he's not here to speak for himself. So, how do you see this playing out, Tanna? Was it you who bound me in the tower? Should I let bygones be bygones?"

"No, Morgan. I've thought this through, and I have a solution in mind. A way for me to make amends and for your people to benefit as a result of our transgression." Tanna looked at his visor, her green eyes steady and open, and Morgan didn't feel any Energy being gathered by the woman. He studied her with his Void Vision, and the only emotion he could read from her was fear, which surprised him. She'd always seemed so confident and self-assured. Was he so intimidating?

"I'm listening." Morgan glared around the deck, studying the auras and emotions coming out of the gathered crew. He predominantly read fear and a flickering white flare of hope from many.

"Take this ship. Take it as payment for our crime. Turn this crew loose and let them find their way through this mountainous wilderness back to Gelica. I'll stay with you and your people, Morgan. I'll help you fly this thing back to your town, and then I'll go with you to Tharcray. I'll help you petition the empire for member status and put an end to the schemes of men like ap'Gravin."

"Just like that?" Morgan asked. "You'd turn on your master?"

"You use the term as an insult, but you're right. I live as a slave to ap'Gravin. He holds leverage over me, and when I betray him by helping you, he'll put a price on my head and cash in his leverage. I'll lose everything. I'm being transparent, Morgan. I'm offering my service to you so you won't kill me but also because I think your people are worth helping, and I tire of having a yoke on my neck. Do you believe me?"

Morgan scrutinized Tanna while she spoke, studying her aura and emotions. He only read desperation, a glimmer of hope, and honesty; he didn't think she was lying. "All right, show me you mean it. Remove those collars and have your crew put their weapons away."

Tanna looked at his implacable visor for several long moments, her eyes darting to Bloodfang's soiled blade and Morgan's broad, dark wings before she nodded. "Do it!"

"But, Tanna . . ." Gella began, and she hissed at him.

"Quiet, *Captain*." She gestured to Arthur Ballard. "Are you willing to slaughter a helpless man to try to keep ap'Gravin happy?"

"No. No, I suppose I'm not. Do as he says!"

Gella led by example, sheathing his saber and touching Arthur's collar, pulling it away with a series of clicks. The rest of the crew followed suit, and the humans stood, some angrily, some with tears in their eyes. One large man started shoving the crew member who'd been holding him, and Morgan spread his wings, holding Bloodfang up.

"I know you're angry! You should be! But let's not turn this into a bloodbath. Gella, get your people together on the port side of the deck. First Landing citizens! Come stand behind me."

"They have more of us below decks, Morgan!" Arthur said, hurrying over to his side of the deck.

"Yeah, I figured. Tanna? Get our people free and out here, and then we can discuss your terms."

He saw she was about to speak, but then her eyes went wide, and Morgan felt lancing, ripping pain from his right wing. He cried out and stumbled sideways, blood and feathers bursting into the air as he tried to roll his shoulders toward the source of his pain.

"Thought that I would die so easily, fool?" Finneal boomed, and Morgan was startled by his appearance. He'd grown huge, easily topping seven feet, and though his physical body could be seen through them, he was cloaked in roiling shadows. His long, shadow-clad arm had ten-inch claws extending from each finger which dripped Morgan's blood on the deck as he strode forward. Each of his steps thudded and vibrated the wooden planks, and he laughed, yellow-red eyes gazing out of the shadows under his hooded cloak.

"Finneal, stop!" Tanna cried, holding out her hands. "I've brokered a deal!"

"Your Ancestors can lick my balls, Tanna. Take your deal and shove it into that icy ass of yours!" Finneal's voice was guttural, harsh, and clearly mad. He surprised Morgan—and Tanna—by leaping at the woman, drawing his two massively clawed hands down her front, raking her flesh, shredding her pale blue robe, and spraying the deck with blood. She screamed and fell back, rolling on the deck in agony.

"Have you gone mad?" Captain Gella shouted what everyone was wondering, and Finneal whirled on him, moving at the speed of thought. Before Morgan could think to intervene, Finneal had speared the captain through his belly and lifted him from the ship's deck, blood showering the planks to the tune of the captain's mortified screams of agony.

Morgan's mind finally had a chance to catch up to what had happened: Finneal was alive and devastatingly strong, and he'd nearly torn Morgan's wing off.

"Motherfucker," he hissed between pain-clenched teeth, and then he cast Void Missile, holding out his open left palm toward Finneal's back. Morgan couldn't fathom how the man still had his back turned to him, but there it was. He seemed busy with his disembowelment of Captain Gella.

Morgan felt his Core provide the void-attuned Energy to the spell, saw a ball of nothing displace the light and space outside his palm, and watched it streak outward faster almost than Morgan could track, blasting into the huge shadow man's center-left back.

Finneal howled in agony, yanking his claws apart and nearly bisecting the captain as he spun around. Morgan's missile had done its work, boring through one of Finneal's shadow-decked wings and halfway through his torso, leaving a gaping hole of writhing shadows and glistening wet tissue.

"You!" Finneal barked, solidifying in Morgan's mind the idea that he had lost his sanity. Had he forgotten Morgan was there?

"You're killing the wrong people, dummy," he said, Bloodfang held ready to drop into the Crane Defends the Nest, unsure what more Finneal might throw at him.

"Strike me in the back! Is that all you ever do?"

Finneal gathered himself to leap, clearly projecting the move, and Morgan cast Energy Drain, reaching out and tugging at the shadowy Energy coating the other man. It came away easily enough, yanked into Morgan's pathways and into his Core, and as he pulled from the prodigious pool, Morgan directed it out to his injured wing where he felt the flesh stitch and new feathers sprout forth.

Finneal ignored Morgan's drain and pounced, leaping into the air and bringing his claws down in a mad, double-handed rake, just like he'd hit Tanna with. Morgan thought the man must have lost his wits. How could he believe he would stand still for it?

He cast Void Step, and as he came out of it a dozen paces behind Finneal, he fired a Vortex Lance at the huge man and renewed his Energy Drain.

Finneal landed, swiping at empty air while Morgan's lance tore into his lower back, blasting a hole the size of a fist entirely through him. Shadows flew out with the impact, accompanying Finneal's ruptured flesh and blood. Morgan continued to siphon Energy, and all the while, the Ghelli screamed and raged, practically cartwheeling in his hurry to turn toward Morgan and charge forward again, claws swiping.

Morgan saw that most of the First Landing citizens and crew members of the *Skybreaker* had cleared the center of the ship, but one young man, someone Morgan had seen a time or two at Green's Tavern, wasn't fast enough, and Finneal caught him with a stray swipe, slicing his leg off at the thigh. Morgan saw Energy flow out of the fallen man, bolstering the shadows around Finneal.

"Feeding off the damage you do?" he asked, realizing it was a similar ability to his Energy Drain, though it seemed to strengthen Finneal, not heal him.

Finneal didn't answer, just screamed in inarticulate rage and leapt toward him again. Morgan used his parry form to block the massive swipes coming his way, and as Finneal struggled to land a blow, he cast Void Wave. The destructive Energy ripped away the light and sound around him, dissolving the wood under his feet and engulfing Finneal. The two of them fell into a wide hallway that traversed the second-level deck, Finneal screaming and clawing at the Energy that was eating away his shadows and flesh.

Morgan landed lightly, backing away and firing another Void Missile at the struggling, screaming madman. The bolt tore into one of his thrashing arms, severing his shadowy, clawed hand at the wrist. The screams rose an octave as his struggle against the Void Wave lost ground.

When the air cleared, Morgan looked upon the man: smaller, gaunt, barely wreathed in any shadow, and badly damaged. His wings were nothing but blackened nubs sticking up over his shoulders, and his fancy suit had been reduced to patches of cloth hanging by threads.

"Bastard," Finneal hissed, drawing his thick broadsword with his good hand and charging, fury and hate seething forth from him in Morgan's Void Vision. Morgan met the blow with Bloodfang and watched as his sword bit into and notched the other man's weapon. The Ghelli was back to his old size, so Morgan leaned into his hack, lifting a foot to kick the man in the waist, sending him sprawling.

"Yield," he said, looming over the smaller man.

"I think not," he said, and Morgan saw he'd dropped his sword and was holding a vial thick with shadows and sparkling with red rage in his enhanced vision. Morgan didn't wait, stepping forward to hack the man's other hand off at the elbow as he tried to quaff the draught.

"Ancestors balls! Damn you, freak!" Finneal barked. Staring at Morgan, his eyes went black, much like Morgan's, but swirling with shadows. Morgan felt a tremendous gathering of Energy and knew one thing: he needed to get the fool away from the other people on the ship. He'd never tried casting Void Step while holding someone before, afraid it might harm one of his friends, but he figured now was the time to try.

Moving almost on instinct, Morgan rushed forward, lifted Finneal under his armpits, and hugging him close, he looked up through the hole in the deck and cast Void Step, sending himself and Finneal fifty yards above the ship into the blue sky. As soon as they appeared in the air, he cracked his wings, pulling them both higher still just as Finneal exploded.

Standing with the other huddled, recently freed captives, Arthur saw Morgan and the insane Ghelli burst into existence above the ship, their appearance accompanied by that uncomfortable crackling sound Morgan's magic tended to make. He saw that Morgan had the madman held close, flapping his wings to bring them higher into the air, and Arthur wondered if he meant to drop his enemy to his doom. He'd just pointed to the two when suddenly, with a *whoosh* like a tremendous fire sparking to life, they burst apart in an explosion of cutting shadows.

Of the Ghelli, the mad shadow-wielding enemy, Arthur couldn't see any sign—he appeared to have burst into microscopic pieces.

Morgan, though, Morgan was sent flipping backward, his wings, the only part of him not shielded by his silvery armor, broken and shredded by the blast. Morgan's body tumbled back and down to crash onto the ship's top rear deck, bouncing like a rag doll until it smashed through the railing and fell out of view.

"Here!" a high, clear voice shouted. Arthur turned to see Tanna, still bloodied and wan, lying on the deck but holding up a glimmering, cream-colored vial. "Help me up; we have to get this to him. Pour it down his throat if we must. Hurry!"

# ⊛ MORGAN ⊛

"Can't get this thing open. Careful with his back!" Morgan heard the voice sort of like it was echoing down to him from the top of a well while he lay at the bottom. He blinked his eyes rapidly, and looking through his magical helmet's visor, he saw dirt and jagged little rocks—he was clearly facedown. Morgan tried to speak but could barely manage to inhale enough to keep himself conscious. He thought he could hear his heartbeat in his ears, but he felt very little beyond that.

"Wait!" said a familiar voice. Who was it again? He strained his mind, trying to remember how he'd gotten into this situation, when the voice spoke again. "Give the System a minute to send the Energy from Finneal. Considering the fool blew himself up, it might take a few minutes."

*Finneal!* Morgan suddenly remembered the crazed, shadow-formed Ghelli. How'd he come back, anyway? Some sort of artifact? A healing spell or potion he'd managed to quaff before he died? Morgan tried to grunt, tried to lift a hand to slide down his visor, but nothing in his body wanted to do what he asked.

"I see Energy motes gathering out there. Look!" another voice exclaimed. Was it Arthur?

"Yes, Finneal blew himself into a billion parts. Give it a minute. I'm sure the System will credit Morgan," the clear, ringing woman's voice said. Was that Tanna? Hadn't Finneal shredded her? Maybe she'd had a potion or two. Morgan would have shrugged if he could move, would have dug out a healing potion of his own.

"Here it comes!" Arthur pointed out, voice high with excitement. He'd probably never seen Energy gather from a vanquished foe.

. . . no, that couldn't be right—he'd been at the Urghat battle.

Suddenly, Morgan felt heat and vibrant Energy surge into his pathways, and with it, his nerves suddenly roared to life. He almost lost his grip on consciousness from the wave of agony that rolled throughout his body, feeling an uncomfortable grinding twitch in his neck before warmth flooded there and much of the pain subsided.

"Ungh!" he grunted.

"He's alive," Arthur breathed.

"Yes, but that Energy wasn't enough to fix him. Well, he's moving now, at least." Tanna's voice was closer now, and Morgan thought she was probably leaning over him. "Can you open your visor, Morgan? I have a healing draught here." He felt hands gently turn him onto his side, and then he could see Tanna. She was still drenched in blood, her pale blue robes hanging in shreds as she knelt before him, holding a shimmering off-white potion that radiated with Energy.

"Ungh," he grunted again, and with a monumental effort, he jerked a hand up to his visor and flicked it up with the two fingers that were listening to his mental commands. The world brightened, sounds became harsher, and he squinted his eyes against the glare.

"Here." She pressed the little vial to his lips, and Morgan, with only a tiny misgiving, drank the liquid. It was cool and dissolved to vapors on his tongue, flowing down his throat and into his lungs, seeping through the flesh of his mouth and throat. As the wave of healing Energy flooded through him, Morgan finally inhaled a full breath.

"Jesus. Did I break my neck?" he asked, still reeling from the residual pain and the rush of healing Energy.

"And then some, Morgan!" Arthur said, leaning into his field of view. "You looked like a pretzel when we found you down here. I thought you were dead!"

Morgan shifted into a sitting position, groaning from the effort and the pain that still tingled in his hips. He felt the potion still working, pushing throughout his body, and when it started to spread into his wings, he stifled an inarticulate cry of pain. As the magic seeped into his feathered appendages, he felt them popping and clicking as the dozens of broken little bones straightened. He grimaced, gritting his teeth and squeezing his eyes shut while he waited for the process to run its course.

"The potion is potent, but it won't be enough. Your wings are straightened, the breaks repaired, and the flesh healed, but you lost a lot of feathers," Tanna said.

"Hang on," Morgan said and pulled out one of the two miracle elixirs he'd looted so long ago. He figured it might be overkill—maybe his wings would recover with cheaper healing draughts or with just the passage of time—but he didn't want to seem weak in front of Tanna and the airship crew.

Before he could analyze that thought and question his motives, he popped the cork, breaking the orange wax seal, and chugged the little vial. This potion was hot and flooded him with warmth as the strangely vanilla-flavored liquid coursed down his throat and into his stomach. Morgan stood up with the surge of vibrant Energy it provided, extending his wings and watching as the wave of warmth spread throughout them and black, perfect feathers populated the bare, scarred flesh. In just a minute, he was whole and feeling fantastic to boot. He spread his wings, gave them a flap, and smiled at Arthur.

"Feeling better, Arthur. I take it Finneal is no more?"

"The madman destroyed himself in an attempt to take everyone with him. You saved us all, Morgan," Tanna replied.

Morgan looked at her for a long moment, taking in her bloody but uninjured appearance. He nodded to her and said, "You could have betrayed our agreement. You could have finished me and retaken Arthur and the others."

"It doesn't make me a good person, if that's what you're getting at. I chose your side consciously, and I still think it's the winning side in the long run. I'm throwing my lot in with you because I know you won't treat me like a slave and make me do things that turn my stomach. Ap'Gravin has power now, but I think First Landing will soon eclipse the strength of even the grand old cities. This is me being honest, Morgan."

"Fair enough." He looked around at the gathered crowd for the first time. He saw crew members and many of their former captives. They stood on opposite sides of a semicircle around him, some talking in low voices, others watching him raptly. "You're all, no doubt, wondering what comes next. First, tell me, did Captain Gella live?"

"He's dead," one of the crewmen said, a large Vodkin with a messy, too-tight uniform.

"You all have fifteen minutes to get your belongings and enough food for two weeks. Tanna, you're in charge of ensuring they only take what they need and don't damage the ship further. I know many of you have nothing to do with ap'Gravin, but I don't know which ones of you might. That said, you all need to go. Time starts now. Get going!" Morgan drew Bloodfang in emphasis and watched as the crew scurried up the rocky slope toward the boarding ramp.

"I understand where you're coming from, but I think, if you want to take this ship, you should keep a few of them. Five of the engineers and one helmsman should be enough to get you back to First Landing, then you can send them packing," Tanna suggested. Morgan thought about it and nodded, and she turned to follow the crew as they scurried up the slope.

"You heard him! Move faster!" she yelled, her voice cold and brooking no dissent. Morgan heard some of the crew members turning to plead with her to stay, but she curtly refused them. Morgan knew he couldn't fully trust her, but he felt he could manage to keep an eye on her and maybe a handful of the crew; he couldn't say the same for the dozens of others.

No, it was best they went on their way.

"Will they die out here?" Arthur asked.

"I doubt it. They're all Energy users. They should be able to manage a trek through the wilderness, especially if they stick together." Morgan turned to the other humans nearby and said, "Come on, let's go make sure everyone's out of their holding cells and collars. When Tanna's done chasing most of the crew away, we'll get this ship in the air."

"Right. I'm glad you're okay, Morgan. I'm glad you beat that madman. We'd be flying toward slavery right now if you hadn't come," a friendly voice spoke, and Morgan turned to see that Alec Green was there, holding out a hand.

"Shit," Morgan let out, shaking his friend's hand. "I didn't realize you were here. How many were captured, anyway?"

"Hundreds," Arthur answered. "We're not exactly sure either. Let's go, people; we've got friends who need releasing!" He clapped his hands, and the gathered humans finally snapped out of it and started moving quickly up the slope to board the ship.

Morgan nodded and said, "Meet you there," then looked up toward the ship railing and cast Void Step. He appeared a few feet above the deck and glided down, striding toward the boarding ramp and listening to see what Tanna might be saying to the crew as they marched aboard.

". . . not open for debate. Be glad he isn't executing us all. How do you think Finneal would have responded if we'd done this to his hometown? Even Haku-dak would probably cut our heads off, but at least he wouldn't torture us." Morgan heard a grumbled, deep-voiced curse, and then, "Enough, Reeja! You'll not be staying. I need one helmsman, and that will be Teeg."

Morgan stepped back to the side as the crew members started filing onto the ship. When they saw him lurking near the gangway, most of them flinched and hurried their steps. Once Tanna came out and saw him, she nodded and cleared her throat.

"I'm glad the wings still work. That was a nasty explosion."

"He was tricky. Not sure how he survived our first encounter." Morgan glanced to the west, where he'd sparred with Finneal in the air.

"We had scouts out there. Probably one of them gave him a healing draught, and then he drained them dry. His shadow only grows like that after he's made some kills. His affinities were a mixed bag of shadow and rage—a Hybrid Spirit Core. He'd clearly gone mad with it by the time he arrived here. I'm glad you were able to defeat him so handily. If not for his suicidal explosion, I think he'd have hardly been a challenge."

"Maybe," Morgan said, narrowing his eyes. "We still have a long way to go before I'm not feeling like binding you and locking you away, Tanna. Let's get this crew moving, hmm?"

"Right." She nodded and berated a nearby group of crew members who hadn't hurried below to get their belongings. Morgan watched and waited as nearly a hundred people gathered their things and departed the ship, hiking over the stone ground toward the east. Tanna picked out a handful of engineers and the one helmswoman she'd had in mind, and they all waited on the deck, sitting against a railing while the human captives were gathered from below decks and given their freedom.

Morgan nearly had to fight with a few former captives who wanted to string up the *Skybreaker*'s crew. They railed at him, cursing in fury as he forced them to stand back and watch their kidnappers hike away into the hills.

One woman, a tall blonde lady Morgan was sure he'd seen around town a few times, said, "How can you let them go? They killed Thomas and Yolanda. I'm pretty sure they killed Maria, too!"

"They're criminals, for sure," Morgan replied, speaking loudly so all the gathered humans could hear. "They deserve to be punished, and you can believe they're in for a hell of a lousy time hiking from here to civilization. They'll have to answer to their employer, and that's the person who really deserves our justice. Most of those people owe him a debt of one kind or another, and that's why they've done this.

"Even Tanna, here, was operating under duress. Don't get me wrong—she's got a lot of amends to make. In any case, their captain is dead, and Finneal, the one personally responsible for the deaths, is also dead. And I don't have the stomach for mass executions. I'm not going to slaughter those people. We're taking their ship, and I'm going to make sure this sort of thing never happens again. You can count on that."

He'd spoken more than he usually would to such a crowd, and he cleared his throat, gazing over their faces, looking for dissent, disagreement, or questions. He could hear some muttering, could see some angry faces, but no one spoke up. He tried another angle.

"Do you people trust me? Did you see me fighting with everything I had to help you? Do you believe I care about First Landing?"

"Yes!" one young woman shouted. Morgan knew her—she was Greta, one of Alec's cooks. Other affirmative sounds broke out, and then someone else called out, "Thank you, Morgan!"

"You're welcome, but that's not what I'm getting at!" he shouted, raising his voice to be heard over the noise, letting it boom out from the depths of his chest. The crowd grew quiet again, and he said, "Just keep trusting me, okay? That's all I ask. Give me a chance to seek justice against Lord ap'Gravin and to secure protection for First Landing. I'll do it. Whether it takes words or money or blood, I'll do it."

The crowd cheered, and Morgan smiled, watching their faces and seeing their belief in him. His gaze fell on Tanna's green eyes and her blood-smeared face, and he saw she was looking at him with an expression he couldn't place at first, but then it clicked, and he realized she was admiring him. She was impressed by him, and he could tell she was pleased with herself, thinking she'd made the right decision.

# ❦ BRONWYN ❧

Bronwyn watched as the Urghat filed into the enormous cavern housing the Well of Ancestors. She wasn't sure why they called it a well—the pool at the center was filled with something, but it wasn't water; more like a viscous gel which seemed to absorb Energy from anyone who touched it.

Whitestar and her "elders"—the older, more respected Urghat who'd joined her clan—stood arrayed, wearing ceremonial sashes or headdresses, whatever their families had crafted over the generations. Each piece of ceremonial garb was covered with beads, gems, bones, and feathers, and when Bronwyn passed nearby, she could feel the Energy pulsing within them.

Whitestar and Soft-fur had asked her to be part of the ceremony, and though she'd protested that she was almost out of time, they'd finally convinced her, promising to perform the ritual immediately. They needed to, anyway—Soft-fur was on her last legs. The Urghat stood gathered in a loose circle around the central dais where Whitestar and the elders waited, watching the tunnel entrance where Bronwyn stood, in turn, waiting.

More than four hundred Urghat had joined the raid. Whitestar had gathered all of her forces, all of her hunting and scouting parties, in her temporary base of operations, and they'd lingered just outside the Hollows, watching for the sign that Bronwyn had promised they'd see. She'd been right, miraculously. After the troll matron had died, many of the trolls which had been lying patiently in ambush had begun to amble out of their hiding spots, wandering in twos and threes into the wooded valley where Whitestar's people awaited.

The Urghat had overwhelmed the monsters, killing them in small groups, whittling down their numbers, and then pushing their way into the Hollows. It was as if the trolls had lost their ability to plan or cooperate without their matron, and the horde of Urghat had managed to drive them out or slaughter them in just a handful of hours.

Bronwyn, for her part, had destroyed all of the matron's eggs. By the time she'd finished and worked her way up from the depths of that stinking, damp cave, she found herself walking through tunnels occupied by Urghat. That's when she'd found Whitestar and been strong-armed into helping with this ceremony.

Some of the Urghat began to beat on large, hide drums, and Bronwyn blinked her eyes, bringing herself back to the moment.

The drums were her cue; she was supposed to help Soft-fur walk to the Well. Bronwyn turned to face the dark, sloping tunnel, and she saw why the drummers had started. Soft-fur was being led—no, more like carried—toward the Well chamber by two large, burly Urghat, one of whom was very familiar to Bronwyn: Ironhide.

"Underclaw," Ironhide said by way of greeting as he and the other big Urghat carried Soft-fur, their arms under her armpits dragging her along, with her feet barely touching the ground.

"How is she?" Bronwyn asked, stooping to lift the embroidered black cowl hanging over the young Urghat's face. She was conscious, her eyes glazed and red-streaked but open, and Bronwyn thought she saw her black lips begin to spread into a smile beneath her muzzle's soft, gray-white fur. "Poor thing," Bronwyn said, bending to scoop an arm behind the girl's knees and putting the other behind her back. "I'll take it from here, fellas." She straightened as the two Urghat released Soft-fur, lifting her cradled in front of her.

"Your new scars are impressive, Underclaw," Ironhide grunted.

"Yar," the other one added.

"Thanks, boys," she replied, flicking her head so her long, copper-red hair fell to her scarred side. She then turned and, still accompanied by the drumbeat, began walking between the gathered Urghat toward the dais. As she made her way down the central stone walkway between the mass of hairy, leather-clad Urghat, she was stunned by how quiet they were. The only sound in the enormous cavern was the repeated *da-dum* of the drums.

As she drew near the dais and the Well, Bronwyn felt Soft-fur begin to stir, and so did the enormous wave of Energy waiting within the girl. Bronwyn stopped and stood before Whitestar, resplendent in her high, imposing headdress.

"Praise to Soft-fur! Praise to Underclaw Bronwyn! The magic of our people will persist for seven more generations!" Whitestar bellowed, and the Urghat in the cavern stomped their feet and clapped their hands, mimicking the rhythm of the drums but magnifying it a hundredfold.

Whitestar stepped back and to the side, clearing the path to the steps leading into the Well and gesturing with one hand for Bronwyn to proceed. Bronwyn nodded and carried Soft-fur down the stone stairway, her feet sinking into the thick liquid after just three steps. She continued, the fluid climbing to her knees, her thighs, and though she felt her Energy begin to bleed into the Well, it was slow; she knew she could be out long before she noticed the loss.

Soft-fur stirred, writhing weakly in her arms, and then she spoke. "I feel it, Underclaw. I feel the Energy trying to leave. Please, lower me in."

"I'll be right here. You've got this," Bronwyn said. Gently lowering the girl into the pool, she felt the thick, cold liquid come alive. As streaks of pearlescent Energy poured out of Soft-fur into the Well, the fluid instantly warmed and began to flow as though a sluggish current had come alive. Bronwyn gently held Soft-fur in her arms, allowing her to float at the top of the Well's water. As Soft-fur's massive store of Energy continued to bleed away, the current increased, and Bronwyn felt the tug as it swirled around the stone edge, creating a gentle whirlpool.

"Ancestors be good!" Soft-fur let out, her voice suddenly vibrant. "Such sweet relief, Underclaw! Thank you!" She gripped Bronwyn's arms, her bright eyes clear and her brow unfurrowed for the first time since Bronwyn had found Whitestar's camp. "It's out; we can leave the waters now."

"Right." She helped Soft-fur stand on the step before the two of them carefully climbed up and out of the Well. The Urghat were cheering, stomping, and roaring raucously, and Bronwyn found Whitestar waiting atop the steps to grab her and Soft-fur up in a rather literal bear hug.

"Our people's traditions are safe, and so is our prophetess. Thank you, Bronwyn. If you hadn't helped us retake the Hollows, what progress we've made would be lost, and we'd fracture, becoming more savage and lawless. Now we can focus on building on our traditions, making strides to create peace with our neighbors. With luck, by the time the Well needs replenishing again, it will be a matter of course, and the city I dream of will be here, atop the Hollows, and our elders will know what to do. Soft-fur will be the last to suffer as she did."

"Will you stay for the celebration, Underclaw?" Soft-fur asked, her warm, strong fingers wrapping around her wrist.

"No, Soft-fur. I'm sorry, but my time is limited, and I need to see someone I care about before it's too late. I have to leave this world for a while."

"Is there something we can help with?" Whitestar offered, her lips frowning down around her long canines.

"No. Thanks, though. In fact, I really need to get going. Congratulations, Whitestar and Soft-fur." Bronwyn paused and looked Whitestar in the eyes, saying, "Be sure you go get Cal for your celebration—he's going to want to know things worked out. I'm trusting you to get him back to First Landing safely, all right? I have to haul ass and won't be able to talk to him." The Urghat had insisted on leaving Cal back at their forward camp, not wanting to bring him along on the invasion and also not wanting an outsider to view their ceremony. Bronwyn was, apparently, an exception because of her Underclaw status.

"Of course," Whitestar growled. "I'll get him now. Goodbye, Underclaw Bronwyn."

"Goodbye, Underclaw Whitestar," Bronwyn said with a grin, offering her forearm to the tall, lanky Urghat. She gripped it, her long, steel-band fingers wrapping around her wrist, and they smiled at each other, though Whitestar's smile could have been described as a snarl. Then they let go, and Bronwyn hurried out of the hall, shouldering past the milling Urghat and lengthening her strides until she was practically jogging up the long, sloping tunnel toward the upper reaches of the Hollows and the exits to the outside world.

It took her a solid twenty minutes to climb free of the warren of tunnels and step into the afternoon sun. As she started jogging through the twisted woods of the valley, pushing herself into a run and letting her Blessing of the Herd do its thing, she breathed deeply, no small amount of pride tinging the bittersweet feeling that she'd be leaving soon, and though she was soon to see Olivia, it would be to say goodbye.

Bronwyn wasn't sure how she'd get to Olivia before the end of the next day when she was due to leave this world, but she trusted the Summer Queen and knew she'd find a way. In the meantime, she intended to run toward First Landing until she heard otherwise.

Bronwyn had just burst free of the woods and was practically sprinting toward the trail that would lead her out of the valley when a bird swooped in front of her, its warbling, piercing cry catching her by surprise as its long tail feathers nearly slapped her in the face.

She slid to a halt, watching the crazy bird as it arced around in a wide circle and made another pass toward her. This time, it landed in the grass in front of her, and Bronwyn saw, just as before when she'd been sitting with Olivia, that it had a message clutched in one of its talons. This bird was similar to the long-tailed birds that swooped around the pond in First Landing, but it was larger, around the size of a big duck or a goose. The feathers along its back were glossy and black, but underneath, along its chest and down to its tail feathers, they shone white with a silvery iridescence.

"You're pretty, aren't you?" Bronwyn said softly, squatting and holding her hands out, palms up. "Got something for me?" The bird walked closer, its long tail swaying with its steps, and Bronwyn admired its bright orange beak and gleaming, gold-flecked blue eyes. "God, really pretty!" Bronwyn had to assume this bird was coming directly from the Fae Realms because she'd never seen its like on Fanwath. "You're too smart and lovely to be a normal bird, isn't that right?"

The bird didn't answer her, though she might not have been surprised if it had. It bobbed its head and held up its clenched talon. Bronwyn held out her hand, and it released the rolled parchment, squawked, and then turned, trotting away and flapping its wings until it had built enough momentum to get airborne.

"All right," Bronwyn said, unrolling the paper. "Let's see how this is going to play out."

*Daughter of Summer,*

*Congratulations on your victory! I'll be brief: bond with this note, and it will disperse into a cloud of Energy motes which will guide you to a Way Tree. The tree will take you to the forest near your home, to which your friend Olivia travels as we speak. Bronwyn, she will have news which may trouble you. Please remain steadfast in your determination to complete your end of the bargain. I cannot foresee all the consequences should you not.*

*With a warm heart,*
*Queen Aestasia*

"News which may trouble me? What else is fucking new?" Bronwyn groused, holding the note up and trickling some of her solar-attuned Energy into it. As promised, the paper exploded into a million little motes of light which streaked away between some trees. They left a long trail and were bright in the fading sun, so Bronwyn had no trouble following them through the valley, up a steep rise, and into a copse of ancient, wide-trunked trees. Before long, the motes flew straight into the hollow of a lightning-blasted tree and disappeared.

"Here we go." Bronwyn walked up to the tree, noting its gnarled bark, stunted branches, and feathery, gray leaves. "You aren't dead, are you? Did the queen send the lightning which made you a Way Tree, or did it happen naturally? Are you being used, just like me? If so, I'm sorry, and I hope it doesn't hurt when you do your magic. Thank you, old tree."

Bronwyn laid her palm on the rough bark next to the black hollow in the trunk and tried to imagine she could hear the tree breathing. After a long moment, she took her own deep breath and stepped inside, ready to face whatever the queen had been trying to warn her about.

## OLIVIA

By the time Olivia had made her way through the tunnels, up a damp, stone stairway, and out through a cluttered gardener's shed, her fury had cooled substantially. She was still reeling, if she was being honest, about all that had occurred. It wasn't just the fact she'd killed two people, but that something had been changed within her, something central to the kind of person she was.

She couldn't help but wonder about and fear the effects of the Yovashi book on her. What had changed which she couldn't detect? Had it only given her knowledge and changed one of her affinities, or had it also altered her mind, her personality?

"No," she said through clenched teeth as she walked through the gardens back toward the academy building. "No. I would have killed them with or without it. The book only gave me knowledge; understanding of the Yovashi language and this new affinity."

She hoped she was right.

The light outside was gray and the air chilly; it seemed she'd spent the entire night held in Carlu's trap. As she stepped out of the garden and crossed the lawn toward the main academy commons, Olivia wasn't surprised when she didn't see anyone out and about.

With her breath pluming forth, she hurried over the grass, her boots crunching the thin layer of frost. She didn't feel the chill—the air felt comfortable to her, and she knew it was because of her First Elemental Archon feat. When she pulled on the brass handle of the double doors leading into the academy, she felt the tingle of Energy, and they clicked open in response to her Copper cohort ring. She rarely had cause to go out this early, but she knew it was normal for the doors to be locked outside regular school hours.

Olivia didn't know where Oylla-dak's personal quarters were, but she figured she could just wait for the professor at her office. She walked through silent, dim hallways and up an echoing staircase before making her way through the administrative offices to the back hallway and Oylla's office door.

The door was open, and a dim light shone from within. Olivia stepped inside, looking immediately to her right where Oylla's desk sat. There, working under the amber-colored desk lamp, was her mentor, carefully scratching out some missive or another on a piece of parchment with a long, elegant quill.

"Professor." Olivia's voice was small, and she realized her emotions were catching up to her again. The relief that flooded through her at the sight of Oylla had caught her by surprise, and it dawned on her that she'd been girding herself for yet another horror, afraid the murderous duo had done something terrible before they'd come to deal with her.

"Olivia?" Oylla looked up from her work, squinting into the dim light outside the glow of her lamp, her starfield eyes glittering as they found her. "Are you back already? We haven't made any progress with the murderer."

"No, Professor." Olivia stepped closer, taking a seat in front of Oylla's desk. She sighed heavily and continued, "I never left. Carlu tricked me, led me to a trap."

"What? That little—"

"Wait"—Olivia held up a hand—"let me continue. He trapped me in a secret tunnel under the flower gardens. He'd been working with the killer, Somhairle." Oylla tried to interject again, standing up from her chair explosively, but Olivia kept doggedly speaking, "Somhairle was working more closely with the fae than he'd let on, an agent of the Winter Court. Anyway, I managed to surprise him, and they're both dead. He admitted, gloating, to committing all the murders before he died. You can test me for the truth if you want."

"Can this be true? Ancestors, Olivia! I'd thought you were safely away and that Carlu was making himself scarce because of his utter ineptitude. He'd been working with Somhairle all along?"

"Yes, Professor, and all those people died so they could screw with my head. I don't get it; I really don't! How can anyone be that cruel? That evil?" Olivia felt her eyes begin to well with tears, and she angrily shook her head, channeling some fire-attuned Energy into her pathways. Letting her eyes flare with her elemental nature, she reduced the nascent tears to steam.

"Olivia," Oylla started softly, coming around the desk with her hands out like she was trying to soothe an angry terrier, more than a little worried it would bite her. Olivia knew where this was going, and she didn't want comforting right then. She didn't want Oylla's sympathy or guilt. She didn't want to listen to placating nonsense about how this shouldn't have happened to her, nor did she want to have to explain how she'd killed the vile men who'd held her captive.

Olivia stood up, pushing her chair back and holding out a hand, almost like a barrier between herself and the professor.

"I can explain more, but not now. You'll find a trapdoor in one of the gardener shacks in the back flower garden. It leads down to the tunnel where they held me and where I killed them. I'm sorry, Professor, but I have to go home now."

"Olivia, you need to take a breath; let's talk this through," Oylla said, her tone soothing in a way that grated away Olivia's patience.

"You have access to the portal. You know how to get a hold of me. I promise I'll return, but for now, I have to go speak to my friend. Somhairle told me she'd gotten mixed up with this trouble; it has something to do with the fae."

Oylla stepped back, regarding her appraisingly before speaking. "All right. I believe you, and I appreciate you coming to me with this news. You know how things work around here. There will be an investigation, and Headmaster Jaxin-dak will want to speak to you about what happened. I'll tell him you needed time to sort yourself out but that you'll return within the week. Does that sound fair?"

"Yes. Thank you, Professor." Olivia turned then, and marched out of the office. She moved like a gray ghost, her tall figure and black crown casting eerie shadows in the dim lighting as she swept through the hallways and outside.

Olivia cut through the very garden where Carlu had deceived her, taking the shortcut he'd suggested, and though it was only a day ago, it felt like a distant memory, an experience had by someone else. In moments, she came out of the garden onto the manicured lawn with its marble planters outside the Travel Pavilion. She strode through one of the big, open breezeways and made her way to the portal leading to Morgan's tower.

The black iron archway was gone, replaced by a bronze one, and Olivia looked around in puzzlement. Had she remembered the location wrong?

"No, this is identical, just different metal," she noted softly, reaching out to touch it and activate it with a touch of her Energy.

**\*\*\*Morgan Hall's Tower Portal #1\*\*\***
**Open Portal**
**Lock Portal**
**Assign Permissions**

"Oh? Morgan's tower now, hmm? Good for you, Morgan," Olivia said as she selected option one. Almost instantly, magenta, blue, and purple bands of Energy sprang to life at the center of the arch, pulsating and spinning like a kaleidoscopic whirlpool. They spread from the center until they filled the gateway, and Olivia knew the portal was ready and open; she simply needed to step through. Still, she hesitated for a moment. Should she check on Adaida first? Was she prepared to face Bronwyn? What kind of bargain had she made? Should Olivia bring help?

"Quit hiding from your feelings," she breathed, stepping into the vortex of Energy.

Olivia stepped out of the portal into the familiar, round portal hub in Morgan's tower. The room was different than she remembered it, however. Much like the archway housing the portal, the parts of the wall visible to her were bronze, not dark iron. The lighting seemed brighter, and things seemed lighter overall—cheerier. As the portal snapped shut with an audible swooshing, popping sound, Olivia headed to the spiral staircase that ran up and down from the center of the room.

Once again, Olivia admired the bright metal of the railing and steps, glad the gloomy cast-iron look was gone. She stepped on the downward flight, thinking of the tower's entrance hall, and in just a few moments, she arrived onto its polished hardwoods. Glancing around, she was startled to see a beautiful young woman with long silver hair and stunning bright eyes watching her from near the foyer. She had pale skin and wore a lovely blue silk blouse over velvety, tight leggings.

"Those are Issa's clothes," Olivia noted, smiling.

"Miss Olivia!" the woman exclaimed, striding toward her. "It's wonderful to see you!"

She spread her arms as though she were going to hug her, and Olivia stepped back, again taken by surprise. Her voice was lovely, crystal clear, and lilting, and Olivia wanted to like her—almost let her hug her—but she was still on edge, and it felt bizarre for a stranger to be so familiar.

"Do I know you?" she asked, holding up a hand to keep the woman at bay.

"Oh! I'm so sorry, Miss Olivia! It's me! Tiladia! Lady Issa crafted me a new vessel. No, a new *body*!"

"Tiladia? Really?" Olivia's mind whirled.

"Yes! Morgan finished clearing the tower and found Vormendion's inheritance: powerful crafting knowledge which he passed on to Lady Issa."

"Have I been gone so long? It seems like I only just left, but I sure missed a lot . . ."

"May I hug you now? I love how people feel! Miss Olivia, I went for so long without feeling!" Tiladia stepped closer, and Olivia hesitantly lowered her arm.

"Sure, Tiladia." She'd barely said the words when the young-looking dragon-spirit woman wrapped her in a warm, soft embrace, nuzzling her head into her chest. Olivia didn't realize how badly she needed the affection—still didn't want to admit it—but she squeezed her back, and it felt very good. "That's nice. Thank you."

"Morgan and Lady Issa are in a council meeting. Did you hear about the airship? Were you coming to help?"

"What?" Olivia extricated herself from Tiladia's embrace, pushing her back. "I don't know what you're talking about, but before you explain, can you tell me if you have seen Bronwyn?"

"Lady Bronwyn hasn't been back since you left. She went north, that much we know, on some business with the Urghat."

"Damn it! I have to find her, Tiladia!"

"Morgan can help with that," she said, frowning and narrowing her eyes in concern. She must have felt Olivia's despair.

"Oh! You're right! He can sense her location. You said he's in the council chambers?"

"That's right! Should I tell you what's been happening?" Tiladia reached out a hand to gently take Olivia's arm above the elbow as she tried to walk past her. "A lot has occurred."

Olivia hesitated, then nodded. "I guess so. I don't suppose I should barge into the middle of a meeting and demand Morgan help me, anyway. How long has the meeting been going on?"

"Well, Morgan returned with the captured airship a few hours ago, and he and Lady Issa went to the council building around forty minutes ago—"

"Captured airship? I thought you were talking about the, uh . . . *Skybreaker*!"

"Oh, I am! They kidnapped hundreds of citizens, and then Morgan chased them down! He banished their crew and forced some of the others to fly the ship back to First Landing. That sorceress with black hair and green eyes helped him, or so he said. I don't trust her," Tiladia told her, saying the last in a conspiratorial whisper, leaning close.

Olivia couldn't believe the person in front of her wasn't a naturally born human. Everything about her seemed so real, from her touch to her breath to the moisture in her eyes.

"Tiladia, I'm feeling overwhelmed. I thought a lot had happened with me, but you keep adding more and more crazy on top of crazy. Let's start from the beginning . . ."

## OLIVIA

Olivia looked at Tiladia with increasing interest, studying the way her mouth moved and the expressions in her eyes as the beautiful dragon spirit told her about all that had transpired in First Landing. She couldn't believe the person before her had a body made of a magical alloy which Issa had created. She couldn't fathom how the saliva coating her teeth and the perfectly articulate tongue could once have been stiff, hard metal.

"I feel like you're examining me more than you're listening to me," Tiladia said.

"You're just so . . . amazing!" Olivia admitted, reaching out to squeeze the smaller woman's shoulder. "The metal just took on this aspect? Can you eat? Do you sleep?"

"Oh, Ancient Gods!" Tiladia huffed, blowing out a long breath. "Yes to all of the above. Issa sang her song of creation well. She willed me to have a body which was natural and alive, and the components she used in my creation were truly rare. I require rest, but not any more than someone else with an improved racial status. I can eat—what I consume is turned into Energy and used to nourish my body, much like the food you eat."

"Will you . . . die?" She hastily added, "I mean, eventually?"

"Much like a human who advances their race significantly—you and Morgan, for instance—age won't be much of an issue for me. I'm sure I could be killed; I have a heart, a Core, a brain. If my pathways were disrupted by trauma, I would suffer just as you would."

"I'm sorry for the personal questions, Tiladia. I'm just fascinated by all of this. But I should get going to the council, don't you think? I can't imagine they'll be meeting much longer, and I need Morgan to point me toward Bronwyn."

"Shall I come along?"

"Oh, that's right! You're no longer stuck here! What will you do now that you're free?" Olivia asked as she started heading toward the front door.

"I want to learn and grow. I want to try to recapture some of the glory of my old life. If I grow strong enough, I'll seek a return visit to my homeworld so I might gaze into the eyes of my kin once more. In the meantime, I'm happy here. I love Morgan and Issa, and I want to continue to spend time with them." Her voice sounded wistful at first but then turned with conviction, and Olivia gave her a second look; she really did love Morgan and Issa. How strange that she'd found such a connection in the weird limbo service life she'd been cursed with!

"They are good people, aren't they?"

"Indeed, and let's not forget about young Ykleedra. She'll need my help with her siblings, that's for certain!"

"Oh God! I can imagine! I'll try to give them a visit, but first, I have to figure out what's going on with Bronwyn." As she finished speaking, Olivia was startled to see the front door open, and the very subject of her words step into the foyer.

"Hey," Bronwyn greeted with complete nonchalance.

"Bron!" Olivia's voice squeaked in her surprise. She stepped forward and reached out to hug Bronwyn, saying, "I was just on my way to interrupt the council so Morgan could point me in your direction!"

"Well, a bird told me you were here, so no need for that." Bronwyn winked at her and pulled her into an embrace which felt very much like home. Bronwyn smelled like sweat and dust, with an undertone of woodsmoke, and Olivia breathed in the scent hungrily.

"A bird . . ." she murmured into Bronwyn's neck. She opened her eyes, leaning back a few inches to look at her, and that's when she noticed the scars peeking out around her jaw and the strange way her hair was lying over the right side of her head. "What happened?"

"Don't look at it," Bronwyn said, pushing Olivia back. "Damn it! I swear I didn't care about the scar until now. I guess I care that you still think I'm pretty." She took another step back, looked over Olivia's shoulder, and narrowed her eyes. "Who's this?"

"Uh—" Olivia started, but Tiladia cut her off, coming forward.

"Lady Bronwyn, it is I, Tiladia! Welcome home!"

"Til? Holy shit, you look great!"

"Thank you!" Tiladia replied, pulling off an actual blush and curtsying.

"Tiladia, you're blushing!" Olivia pointed out, turning her attention away from Bronwyn's scar but not forgetting about it—she'd get an explanation soon.

"Oh, wow . . ." Bronwyn teased, smiling at Tiladia and clearly enjoying her discomfort.

"I'll be stepping out now," Tiladia announced, curtsying again and quickly moving toward the door.

"Til, I was just teasing! Don't go!" Bronwyn said, reaching out.

"Don't go!" Olivia spoke at the same time.

"Don't worry, ladies." Tiladia turned with a grin, once again blowing Olivia's mind with her beauty and natural appearance. "I'm not embarrassed. Come now, I've lived a long time! Still, I will be heading out. You two can use some time alone, if I'm not wrong."

"We'll catch up later," Olivia called as the dragon-spirit woman walked out of the tower. She glanced back to Bronwyn, who had eyes only for her. "You don't understand how amazing she is," Olivia told her. "Issa crafted that body!"

"Oh?" Bronwyn asked, glancing toward the door, then back at Olivia. "That's cool, but I don't have much time, and I want you to get all of it. Come on, let's go to your room, and we can talk."

"Nobody's here, Bron. We could sit in the library or—"

Bronwyn hushed her by stepping forward and kissing her. She pressed hungrily at Olivia's mouth, breath hot and hands groping at her back and butt. Olivia kissed her back, and they stumbled together to the stairs and up to the fifth level. Laughing and holding hands, they ran down the hallway to Olivia's room—why Bronwyn picked her room, Olivia didn't know—and burst into it, slamming the door behind them.

Bronwyn started to guide Olivia toward the bed, and she went along at first, but then a wave of guilt rolled through her, originating in her gut, and she pulled back. "Wait, Bron. We need to talk. I need to tell you something . . ."

"Liv, don't stress about my scar. I got surprised by a huge troll, and she bit off a bunch of my scalp. I'm sure I'll heal more when I advance my race again—"

"It's not the scar, Bron. I mean, yeah, I'm sorry that happened to you, and yes, you idiot, you're still beautiful! It's . . . well, it's me. I did something . . . I don't . . ." Olivia choked up. Her carefully rehearsed lines and logical explanations fell away from her mind, and she began to panic. She clamped her mouth shut and paced in a small circle at the foot of her bed, stealing glances at Bronwyn's puzzled face from where she sat on the edge of the mattress.

"This is weird," Bronwyn finally said. "I thought I was the one who'd be hiding my face, stressing out about how I was going to explain what *I did*." True to form, Bronwyn grinned and managed a wry chuckle, despite Olivia's distress.

"What you did?" Olivia asked, finally making eye contact, her voice small and shaky.

"Yeah, Liv. You're going to hate me; I'm pretty sure."

"I couldn't, Bronwyn! I couldn't hate you! I love you! I really do!"

"Man! You really are worked up. What's the matter? Come on, spit it out. Come sit next to me. I promise nothing you say will be worse than my news. How could I be too upset with someone who loves me?"

"It's that bad? You go first, then," Olivia said, sitting down on the mattress next to Bronwyn.

"Oh no. You're not getting off that easily! You'll hear my news, and then you'll get all worked up and storm out, and then I'll never know what you were about to confess. Come on, tell me what it is."

"I . . . do you remember the girl I told you about from my cohort? Ad—"

"Adaida. Yeah, of course I do. What happened, Liv?" Bronwyn's voice had lost its joking tone, and she spoke softly, like she was trying to coax something out of her. Their faces were inches apart, and Bronwyn's big green-gold eyes were staring into hers. Olivia took a big, shaky breath, then nodded. She had to get this out.

"We kissed. She . . . I feel so fucking stupid and horny when she's around. I'm an idiot!"

"You kissed," Bronwyn repeated softly, her eyes going unfocused for a moment. Then, she leaned forward and kissed Olivia gently, sweetly. "Like this?"

"No," Olivia breathed, excitement and relief washing through her. She reached up and groped gently at Bronwyn's neck, pushing into her and pressing her curves into Bronwyn's. They fell back to the mattress, and Olivia kissed hungrily at Bronwyn's mouth, licking between her lips, tasting her, breathing hot, quick breaths, with soft little moans escaping her the whole time. "More like this," she sighed.

"Lucky girl," Bronwyn breathed, kissing her back, pulling at her robes, trying to get her hands up under them. "But you love me, right?"

"Yes, I love you," Olivia said, desire flaring brightly within her.

"As long as you keep loving me, Olivia, I'll just consider myself lucky, too."

After that, there wasn't much to say, and Olivia and Bronwyn fell into a furious bout of lovemaking. They couldn't pull each other's clothes off fast enough, and everything Olivia touched on Bronwyn's long, freckled body seemed somehow new and familiar to her. She explored every nook and cranny, every tan line, lingering on the scars that marred the right side of her head, caressing them with her fingers, kissing them, and moving on to parts she'd traversed dozens of times, tracing Bronwyn's lines and curves, exploring better-known territory.

Bronwyn seemed desperate and hungry, and it wasn't lost on Olivia—the pleasure she felt from Bronwyn's ravenous kisses, licks, and caresses was tempered by the knowledge that she had something to confess, something she'd said was worse than anything Olivia could say. Still, she pushed those fears and doubts to the back of her mind, embracing the sex, and it was a long while before they lay still, spent and exhausted, their clothes scattered around the bed, their bodies slick with sweat.

Olivia took Bronwyn's long fingers in hers, holding them up so she could admire the contrast of her pale hand with Bronwyn's more tanned, scarred fingers. She rubbed her thumb along one particularly long, white mark under the bottom knuckle of Bronwyn's ring finger. "What's this one from?"

"Morgan! That prick hit me with his sword when we were sparring." Bronwyn laughed. "I'm going to miss him."

"What?" Olivia scooted to her side, propping her head up on an elbow so she could look into the other woman's face. "Out with it, Bron."

"Liv, I have to leave. I have to go away from Fanwath for a while."

"Away from Fanwath? Off this world? Why? For how long?" Olivia's mind raced, and so did her heart, literally beginning to beat rapidly. She recognized a true panic attack coming on, the likes of which she hadn't felt since she was working on her PhD.

"Chill, Liv. Take a breath. Come on, look in my eyes. You know I love you, right? Nothing can change that." Bronwyn took her hand and pressed Olivia's palm flat to her bare chest, taking a deep, slow breath. "Copy me. Come on, breathe like me, then I'll tell you the rest."

"Don't patronize—" Olivia started, but when she saw the honest concern in Bronwyn's eyes, she stopped herself. Staring into those big eyes, she breathed, slowly and deeply. The whole while, her own eyes started to fill with tears, and she felt the knowledge creeping into her mind that this might be the last time she'd be with Bronwyn.

"That's it, love. Listen, I had to bargain with the fae so I could do two things at once: save a sweet little Urghat girl and keep the Winter Court from messing with you."

"A bargain?" Olivia's voice was small, her mind racing. This was what Somhairle had meant. He'd said he had to leave, that he couldn't go through with the plans he'd made with Carlu. "But I . . ." She started to say that she'd beaten him, that she'd killed Somhairle, and that Bronwyn hadn't needed to make a bargain. She almost did, but then she thought about Bronwyn, about how she'd made a sacrifice for her, and she didn't want to tell her it hadn't been necessary. She bit her tongue and said instead, "What did it cost you?"

"The Winter Court wants me *off the board* for ten years. I'll have to go somewhere else. The Summer Queen has an idea where; I'm not sure. But I'll be back, Liv. I'm not saying you have to wait for me, but—"

"Of course I will!"

"Liv, ten years is a long time. Let's see what happens, all right? No expectations other than this: I promise I'll keep loving you, no matter what. Will you promise me the same? That's enough, isn't it? We can see where we are in our lives when I get back."

"I promise, Bron. I promise, but are you sure you have to go? What if you broke your bargain?"

"Come on, silly. You know better than that. What are ten years, anyway? We're going to live longer than the elves in *Lord of the Rings*. You want to start a feud with the fae over ten years?" Bronwyn smiled and rubbed her calloused thumb under Olivia's eye, brushing away the tears.

"Yeah. I guess that's a valid point. Ten years, then."

"Ten years. Promise me one more thing, Liv?"

"What?" Olivia asked, barely breathing the word, leaning her head close to Bronwyn's so their foreheads touched.

"Every time you kiss that girl, you think of me, all right?" Bronwyn giggled, watching Olivia's eyes shoot wide open in surprise.

"You bitch!"

# MORGAN, BRONWYN, OLIVIA, TIL

Morgan watched the lights moving around the deck of the downed airship, still listing sideways on the grassy field north of the colony's wall. Engineers from First Landing had been combing over it for days now, studying the mechanisms that made it work, planning their iterations and improvements. He didn't doubt First Landing would have their own, better ships flying within a year.

He felt a mixture of shame and pride when he recalled Boris suggesting mounting their new Energy cannons to the ship almost immediately. If there was one thing humans were good at, it was waging war. He felt Issa's cool fingers lace with his and turned to see she'd come out to the balcony with him. She held a glass of wine up to him, and he took it. "None for you?"

"I probably would be fine, considering my advancements, but I think I'll keep the drinking to a minimum." She pressed his hand against her stomach, and Morgan smiled, savoring the soft warmth. He hadn't felt the twins move yet, and Issa assured him it was too early. Still, he sometimes imagined he felt a little hand or foot pressing into his fingers. He took a sip of the wine, sighing almost wistfully. It was a rich, smooth vintage made from a very dark grape that grew southwest of Tarn's Crossing.

"I hope the council doesn't get antsy and jump the gun with this ship or any new ones they make. I hope they give me time to make things happen with diplomacy."

"They promised. You've got plenty of time, don't you think? You better not be gone more than a few months!" She squeezed his hand, her tone edging toward scolding.

"Yeah. No, you're right. I'll be here for their birth, don't worry," Morgan reassured her, lifting his arm over her shoulders to pull her tight to his side.

"I wish you weren't bringing that woman with you," Issa said softly, and Morgan sighed again, this time far from wistfully. This was a topic they'd beaten to death.

"I know, love. I know. I promise to keep her at arm's length; I mean it. I don't trust her at all, other than as far as I believe that she believes she can benefit from helping us. As long as she sees some gain in it, I think she'll be a valuable asset where I'm going. I don't even know how to get to the capital, let alone whom to speak with or how to arrange an audience, all of that stuff."

"I know. I wouldn't have thought of going to the academy through the gateway and traveling from there. That was a good idea, I'll admit."

"Well, we might have thought of it. Heck, Olivia might have suggested it. But yeah, it was a good idea. We'll travel from the academy to Persi Gables and try to book passage toward the capital. Shouldn't take too long. You know I'm bringing a portal stone, so the trip back will be very quick!" He kissed the top of her head in punctuation.

"Arthur wasn't happy that you wouldn't bring him or other council members along." As she spoke, Morgan sighed again. Was she trying to remind him of all the arguments he'd had over the last couple of days? Was this a review of the problems with his thinking before he left?

"Yes, but you know very well why that is. The same reason you agreed not to come along. If Tanna does double-cross me, or if I'm met with hostility at the capital, I don't want to have to worry about another person. I want to be able to teleport or fly or fight without holding anything back. You know it's the best move."

"I do. I do. I'm sorry I'm rehashing all this. I think I'm trying to convince myself that I'm doing the right thing by staying home. I feel guilty, Morgan. I feel like I should insist, that I should argue with you, even though I want to stay. Isn't that dumb?"

"God, no! The last thing you are is dumb, Issa. I'm glad you're going to be safe here, and I'm glad I'll know it. While I'm out there, dealing with who-knows-what kind of bullshit, I'll be able to take comfort in that. I'll think of you and Ykleedra and Til, and nothing else will matter. And let's not forget about the Far Scribe books we bought!"

"You better write me an update every night!" Issa smiled and reached for his glass, stealing a sip of his wine. The Far Scribe books were going to be a huge benefit, Morgan mused. Being able to keep in touch with the colony, report on his activities, and get input from the council would make his task a lot easier. The books were pretty neat, too—whatever he wrote in his copy showed up in Issa's copy and vice versa.

"You think you're close to level forty-one?" Issa asked, moving to lean against the balcony so she could look directly at him.

"Yeah, I think so. Finneal was no pushover. My status sheet is getting ridiculous. The way my intelligence is compounded by my will to create my Energy pool—it feels like cheating."

Issa leaned forward and squeezed his hand between the two of hers. "Tell me about your attributes; read me your status page. I want to know how much trouble those old monsters in the capital are in for."

"All right," Morgan said, and he obliged:

| Status | | | |
|---|---|---|---|
| Name: | Morgan Hall | | |
| Race: | Human (Anemoi Bloodline) - Advanced 2 | | |
| Class: | Void Master - Legendary | | |
| Level: | 40 | | |
| Core: | Vortex Class - Improved 3 | | |
| Energy Affinity: | 9.2, Void 9.2 | Energy: | 14,443/14,443 |
| Strength: | 100 | Vitality: | 121 |
| Dexterity: | 92 | Agility: | 140 |
| Intelligence: | 248 | Will: | 217 |
| Points Available: | 0 | | |
| Titles & Feats: | Human Champion, First Hollow Guard, Ardeni Friend, Mark of Loyalty, Yovashi Bane, Legacy of the Azure Paladin, First Vortex Duelist, First Void Adept, First Void Master | | |
| Skills: | System Language Integration - Not Upgradeable<br>Animal Taming - Basic<br>Stealthy Maneuvers - Basic<br>Melee Weapon Mastery - Basic<br>Fighting Crane Style - Advanced<br>Sword Mastery - Advanced<br>Vortex Core Cultivation Drill - Improved | Backstab - Basic<br>Energy Drain - Advanced<br>Circle of Combat - Improved<br>Guard Ally - Basic<br>Hollow Charge - Improved<br>Azure Burst - Basic<br>Azure Sight - Basic<br>Vortex Lance - Basic | |

|  |  | Void Wave |
|--|--|--|
|  |  | - Improved |
|  |  | Void Vision |
|  |  | - Improved |
|  |  | Void Step - Advanced |
|  |  | Void Window - Basic |
|  |  | Void Gateway |
|  |  | - Improved |
|  |  | Void Missile - Basic |

Bronwyn stepped out of the Way Tree into the gentle late afternoon light of the fae glade and inhaled deeply. Ever since she'd taken on the mark of Summer, she'd felt more at home, more relaxed, and more robust when she was in the fae queen's territory. Before she could take a walk to savor the atmosphere, however, the queen's voice came to her from the edge of the clearing.

"And so you've left Fanwath. Are you well, daughter?"

"I'm well but not wholly happy. It wasn't easy saying goodbye to Olivia, and you were right about the troubling news. Still, I want her to be happy, so I put on a brave face." Bronwyn wasn't lying. Acting nonchalant about the other girl at the academy had been very hard, but she'd seen how Olivia had been torturing herself with guilt, and the only thing she'd wanted to do was make her feel better.

If Bronwyn were honest, she'd admit she didn't know how she felt about Olivia spending time with Adaida. Would they grow closer? Would Bronwyn be forgotten or pushed out? Would it have helped things if she'd made Olivia swear to stay faithful and not so much as glance at another person in longing? In her experience, ultimatums and forced promises only made people resentful. No, she had to leave, but that didn't mean Olivia had to suffer. Let her find love and comfort where she could—Bronwyn intended to do the same.

"She told you about Somhairle, then?"

"Wait, what?" Bronwyn stepped over the springy grass toward the queen—beautiful, imposing, full of love. The queen was tall, though she didn't tower over Bronwyn anymore. Her features were impossibly perfect: full, bow-shaped lips, blemish-free skin, huge, liquid eyes in which depth's Bronwyn could get lost; although, after spending time with Olivia, she didn't seem so unbelievable anymore. Even so, Bronwyn, ever under the influence of the queen's aura, couldn't help the pleasure that thrilled through her at its touch.

"Somhairle. The agent of Winter. Olivia slew him. She didn't tell you . . ." For the first time in Bronwyn's experience, the queen looked surprised, maybe even confused.

"Are you talking about the agent who was supposed to leave her alone because of my bargain? She killed him?" Suddenly, the queen's aura lost some of its impact, and Bronwyn felt an icy knife of panic stab her in the gut.

"Yes, daughter! I thought it sure she would tell you, but . . . is it possible she didn't want to hurt your feelings? She wanted you to feel your sacrifice hadn't been in vain?"

"Goddammit!" Bronwyn hissed. "Well? What the fuck am I doing here? I shouldn't have to leave if their agent fucking failed before he could leave her alone!"

"Daughter, your bargain wasn't with me—it was with Faekind. Such things aren't undone without great costs, and Olivia's interference doesn't warrant an annulment. I'm sorry."

"So I'm screwed? I'm giving up ten years with her for nothing?"

"Not for nothing, dear Bronwyn. You've accomplished great things, and they are a shadow of what you will do; this I'm sure of. Olivia is safe; she bloodied Winter's nose, but your bargain holds—they'll not send others for retribution. Take heart in that."

"I guess that's something," Bronwyn sighed. She'd not held out much hope that things could be reversed, having resigned herself to her fate even before confronting the troll matriarch. "I'm just so frustrated. I'm so mad at myself. I feel like this is all happening because I let you talk me into working with the fae." Surprising herself, Bronwyn flopped down to the grass, sitting on her butt and folding her arms over her knees, refusing to look the queen in the face.

"Bronwyn. Daughter, I know the ways of the fae are frustrating for mortals. Well, you're more than a mortal now, but still, you won't understand our ways for another few hundred years. It takes time and experience dealing with us to start to grasp the nuance of the dance. I'm trying to be as transparent with you as I can. It's been long, as you know, since I've dealt with humans. I know you're angry with yourself and frustrated at your fate, but I wish you could try to focus on the opportunity before you."

"Opportunity?" Bronwyn scowled at the grass, reaching down with one hand to rip some blades free.

"Yes! Ten years isn't so long for you, and I think you know it. You have my favor, Bronwyn, and I intend to reward you. There are places where people and magic have existed for far longer than Fanwath, places like Earth used to be, though without the presence of humans. I have such a place in mind for you to visit, a place of wonder where you can hone your skills, learn new ones, and find treasures lost to the annals of history.

"I have companions in mind for you, people with similar spirits who will aid in your growth. Does that sound so terrible? When you return to Fanwath, you'll be stronger, more knowledgeable, and ready to aid humanity in its struggles, and I foresee many struggles ahead, daughter."

Bronwyn looked up from the grass at the beautiful Summer Queen of the fae, basking in the attention she was giving her. She stuck a blade of grass between her teeth and said, "I guess it's not that terrible. Olivia said she'd keep loving me, after all."

"That's the spirit, brave Summer child. Now, let's review your status—let me be sure I have the right companions in mind for you."

"All right." Bronwyn sighed heavily, and then pulled up her status sheet:

| Status | | | |
|---|---|---|---|
| Name: | Bronwyn Tallow | | |
| Race: | Human (Fae Bloodline) - Improved 2 | | |
| Class: | Summer Banneret - Epic | | |
| Level: | 26 | | |
| Core: | Summer Class - Base 7 | | |
| Energy Affinity: | 5.6, Solar - 7.6 | Energy: | 2430/2430 |
| Strength: | 102 | Vitality: | 80 |
| Dexterity: | 68 | Agility: | 120 |
| Intelligence: | 75 | Will: | 72 |
| Points Available: | 0 | | |
| Titles & Feats: | First Colonist, Underclaw 10, Agent of Summer, Blessing of the Swarm, Blessing of the Herd, Blessing of the Summer Storm | | |
| Skills: | System Language Integration - Not Upgradeable<br>Unarmed Mastery - Basic<br>Tracking - Basic<br>Cartography - Basic<br>Spear Mastery - Basic<br>Axe Mastery - Improved | Solar Shell - Basic<br>Wrath of Summer - Basic<br>Solar Arms - Basic<br>Mirage Double - Improved | |

Olivia smoothed down her robes, checked that her hair was the way she wanted it, stood up straight, and knocked on the office door. Her knuckles had just touched the wood when a familiar voice, loud if a bit shaky, called out, "Come in, Olivia." She wanted to be surprised, but she wasn't. Somehow, it made sense that Chol ap'Vun would know she was coming.

She pulled the door open and stepped into his very cluttered office.

Chol sat behind his desk, nearly obscured by the stacks of tomes, sheaves of paper, and scrolls piled in front of him. His bald, blue head with its bushy tufts of white hair was pointed down, and Olivia saw he was scribbling some tiny notations on a very densely written-upon page.

"Hello, Professor," she greeted, placing the tin of butter cookies she'd gone to great lengths to acquire on his desk.

"Sit," he said, not looking up. Olivia turned to the single wooden chair in front of his desk, saw it was piled with books and several dusty cloaks, and then shrugged and lifted the books, setting them on the floor next to the front-left leg of his desk—one of the few open areas on the dusty hardwoods. She sat in the chair, leaning back against the lumpy pile of cloaks.

Olivia watched him scribble for a while before she shifted, pushing the cloaks further to the side for comfort, and crossed her legs, determined not to be the first to speak. Several minutes passed, and Olivia began to daydream, thinking of her time with Bronwyn, of their farewell, of all the things she didn't tell her—Somhairle, her mind-Energy affinity, the people she'd killed, and . . .

"Lots on your mind, eh?" Ap'Vun had stopped writing and was regarding her through the multiple lenses on his steampunk-style glasses.

"Yes. It's been an eventful couple of weeks."

"Yet here you are, just as I said you'd be, hmm?" Olivia could see he was exceedingly pleased with himself. He reached for the tin but pulled his hand back, winking at her. "Better wait until after lunch!" He studied her face, smiling, then nodded. "Some changes, however, if I'm not wrong. Let's see here. A bit of an edge to you, eh? Had to kill a man or two?"

Olivia's mouth fell open at the bluntness of his question, and he chortled and continued. "No, no. I can't see that. I was present for the board meeting where we all learned about the criminal activities you put to an end. An auspicious start as my apprentice, don't you think?"

"I wasn't your—"

"A minor quibble. What about this other, though?" he asked, reaching up to lift one lens and drop another in front of his bright, yellow eye. "A new affinity? One not entirely sanctioned, if I'm not wrong. We'll have to approach that delicately. No, no!" he said as Olivia opened her mouth. "Don't explain it. Let's, as I said, be delicate. We can tickle that thorn loose when the time is right."

"As you say, Professor," Olivia agreed, happy enough not to talk about the Yovashi book for the time being.

"Well, you're here, hmm? Ready to take on your first case? A dangerous anomaly has been detected in a nearby city, Persi Gables. Relip Bol, one of my other assistants, is readying himself to investigate. You'll go along. Here." He pushed a large, black leather-bound book her way. "Some studying material for the flight."

"The flight?"

"Oh yes. You'll be taking my airship."

Til'danishea—Til, as her closest friends called her; Tiladia, as an evil mage had named her—walked through the grass, feet bare, savoring every sensation in the beautiful world of Fanwath. She gazed up at the bright blue sky, even smiling at the steel-gray clouds on the horizon. Was their first winter storm inbound? How exciting to feel and taste snow again!

The air was crisp, and it tasted good in her lungs; what a wonder that she had lungs! The light breeze played with her shoulder-length silver hair, and she loved the feeling and the glimmer of the impossibly fine, metallic strands; they reminded her of her old body's scales.

People she passed smiled and waved at her, and she returned the gestures. The men seemed especially eager to greet her, and Til'danishea wondered if Issa had made her too comely. Would their advances grow tedious?

"Not yet," she said, smiling at a stocky, red-haired man ambling by, grinning at her around a large barrel he carried. "Oh Gods, but it feels good to be alive!" she cried, turning her amble into a run, charging for Bronwyn's Hill and the Settlement Stone atop it.

Children laughed with her as she ran by, and people, old and young, watched her with pleasure in their eyes—here was a spirit of joy, someone who might brighten their day simply by passing near. As her bare feet slapped on the cobbled steps and walkway around the stone, Til'danishea slowed her pace. Huffing for breath, she placed a delicate pale hand upon the cool, dark surface.

Her eyes unfocused as Til traversed the System menus and, with just a bit of searching, found the option to officially join the rolls of First Landing as a citizen. The System congratulated her and then surprised her with another message:

**\*\*\*Congratulations, Til'danishea! You are being offered a quest as the first of your kind on Fanwath: Traverse the warren of caves in the mountains to the east, clear the way to the portal within, and enter the Crucible. Survive. Reward(s): Commensurate with achievements. Accept? Yes/No.\*\*\***

"Oh, how fortuitous," Til said, hovering her finger over the *Yes* selection.

# ABOUT THE AUTHOR

Plum Parrot is the pen name of author Miles Gallup, who grew up in Southern Arizona and spent much of his youth wandering around the Sonoran Desert, hunting imaginary monsters and building forts. He studied creative writing at the University of Arizona and, for a number of years, attempted to teach middle schoolers to love literature and write their own stories. If he's not out enjoying the beach, you can find Gallup writing, reading his favorite authors, or playing *D&D* with friends and family.

www.ingramcontent.com/pod-product-compliance
Ingram Content Group UK Ltd.
Pitfield, Milton Keynes, MK11 3LW, UK
UKHW041304180426
11947UKWH00009B/670